Father's D[ay]
From the B[o]

Texas Mutiny
Bullets, Ballots and Boss Rule

By
Sheila Allee

SAC Press
Austin, Texas

©2003 by Sheila Allee

Published by SAC Press
P.O. Box 10514
Austin, TX 78766

Printed in the United States of America

All rights reserved. No part of this publication may be reproduced, stored in a retrieval system, or transmitted in any form or by any means – electronic, mechanical, photocopy, recording or any other – without the prior written permission of the publisher. The only exception is brief quotations in printed reviews.

ISBN: 0-9720466-2-3

Dedication

For my parents, Mae and Doug Allee, who always told me I could do whatever I set my mind to.

Acknowledgements

Many individuals gave of their time and recollections to help make this book possible. My thanks go to Spurgeon Bell, Caro Brown, Dr. George Beto, Sam Burriss, Bub Carlisle, Jr., Kellis Dibrell, Homer Dean, Parker Ellzey, Rudy Garza, Archer Parr, Robert Patrick, Sam Reams, James Rowe, Bud Shivers, Donato Serna, Jimmy Holmgreen, Joyce and Charles Ondrusek, S.O. Woods, Jr., Mrs. Buster Kern, Viola Klevenhagen Dickey, Dorothy Price Miller, Edgar W. Henley, and Larry Warburton, Jr.

I want to express special thanks to Edith Jones Floyd, Bruce Patterson and Harry Patterson. Captain A.Y. Allee, who is a distant cousin of mine, also deserves thanks for the interviews he granted. It was the story of his life as a Texas Ranger that led me to this book.

I would also like to thank my parents, Mae and Doug Allee, for believing in me and encouraging me throughout the process of researching and writing this book.

I owe a great deal of gratitude to Denise Nowotny, my editor and guide throughout the entire process of publishing this book. Her professional expertise and overall good judgment have proven invaluable to me.

Most of all, I want to thank Edith Floyd Patterson Puddephatt. Her collaboration, support, and trust were essential to the completion of Texas Mutiny.

Prologue

For a while, after Bill Mason got shot dead in broad daylight, I thought it was open season on reporters. A lot of people who had ways of knowing—the FBI, the Border Patrol, the Texas Rangers—warned me to grow eyes in the back of my head. At the very least, they said, buy a gun and carry it. I gave them heed because if there's one thing I've learned in my 30-plus years as a journalist, when cops and reporters start getting killed, somebody threw the rule book away.

The killing didn't stop with Bill Mason. Before all was said and done, a cop had gone down and a real-live political assassination went haywire. But those are other stories that I will tell later. Right now, it is enough to say that the Wild West lived on in Duval and Jim Wells counties in the great state of Texas well into the 1960s.

Nobody paid much attention to that godforsaken patch of dust and caliche and mesquite for the longest time. My mother always said ignorance is bliss. Well, the rest of Texas stayed pretty ignorant of what was going on down there until 1948, and then the bliss came to an end.

That wasn't the year Mason got the bullet in his belly, though. That came the next year. No, 1948 was the year that Jim Wells County—you might say with the help of some folks from Duval County—elected a U.S. senator. And not just any U.S. Senator. Lyndon B. Johnson went on to be Senate Majority Leader and Vice President and, yes, ultimately, President of the United States.

It was, perhaps, the finest hour for George Parr, a giant in these parts even then, though little known outside South Texas. He and his father before him each carried the mantel of Duke of Duval," ruthlessly commanding thousands of votes throughout much of that broad expanse from the Gulf of Mexico west to the Rio Grande River. They call that stretch of land just south of San Antonio the Nueces Strip. It was George Parr's domain. Some folks said there was a "mesquite curtain" just south of San Antonio. Go through that curtain, and you'd step onto the stage of a world far removed from the rest of Texas.

It looked like Mexico, this land of George Parr's, only absent of mountains and trees and vegetation. In many respects, it was hard to distinguish most of the villages from their counterparts across the border. Each one had its plaza for local celebrations. Each had a whitewashed Catholic church that towered over the plaza. The streets were unpaved, lined with dirty gray shacks and roamed by barefoot children and starving dogs.

Some of the land surrounding these hamlets is rich and fertile, but for centuries it could not be cultivated for lack of water. Rainfall is sparse in Jim Wells and Duval Counties, but the Gulf winds keep the air damp. In the summer, the temperatures soar to near 100 degrees more days than not, so only the hardy need apply.

Ranching has always been the primary means of livelihood. Vast sheep herds roamed after the Civil War, but made way for beef and dairy cattle in the twentieth century. Plentiful oil and natural gas reserves were discovered in the Nueces Strip in the 1900s, but the newfound wealth went to the oil companies and the landed gentry. The *peones* stayed wretched and poor.

By far, the majority of the inhabitants of the Nueces Strip are of Mexican descent. They are brown-skinned; their hair is so dark it is Indian black; and they are brief in stature. Their eyes are the color of the black gold that flows from the land.

Long ago, the *peones* tied their fortunes to wealthy landowners and ranchers, falling in step with a feudal order that mirrored Old Mexico. Known as the *patrón* system, it was built around one powerful benefactor who possessed all land, all wealth and all political capital. The godfather of the *patrónes* was Richard King, the steamboat captain who settled south of Corpus Christi and staked out the vast and famous million-acre King Ranch. The *peones* worked his cattle, and he in turn fed, housed and clothed them. When it came time to vote, El Patrón told them how to mark their ballots.

By the 20th century, the Nueces Strip had a handful of *patrónes*. In Anglo parlance, they were bosses. George Parr was the most powerful of them, forming alliances with the lesser caesars to offer up blocks of votes. If the Texas populace knew little of him, Texas politicians knew George Parr well. Anyone who wanted to move up in Texas government knew he'd better have George Parr in his corner. If you were running for office in Duval and Jim Wells, George's nod was essential.

I got to know George well as I covered the theatrics in Duval and Jim Wells. I use the term theatrics because it describes so well the events there in the late 1940s, the 1950s and early '60s. What I saw behind the mesquite curtain was drama in its rawest, most human form; the classic struggle between good and evil. I saw violence, murder, hatred, greed, revenge, hope, courage, manipulation and tenacity on both sides of the struggle.

Like I hear they say up in the theater district of New York, it was the best show in town. Duval and Jim Wells counties together made up the best show in Texas, and I was lucky enough to record it all for the history books. I was in my mid-30s when the *San Antonio Enterprise* added the Nueces Strip to my beat. I became one of those roving reporters, covering South Texas right on down to the Rio Grande Valley. The *Enterprise* had readers in rural Texas clear to the border, and I served as their eyes and ears.

In those days, newspaper readers likely were in the minority, mostly because much of the population was uneducated. Like I said, folks were poor in that part of the world, and not every child went to school. The Mexican children especially gave up their schooling to help support their families. But still, newspapers were the way most folks got their news. A few were lucky enough to have radios.

As I look back on all the killing and vote stealing and corruption in Duval and Jim Wells, I can't say I'm surprised it went on so long unnoticed. San Diego, the county seat of Duval, and Alice, the county seat of Jim Wells, are smack in the middle of one of the most desolate stretches on the planet.

I'm pretty handy under the hood of a car, so I never worried much about breaking down on a lonely piece of road. But I always checked the fuel gauge when I was on one of my assignments. A man wouldn't want to get stranded out there in that brutal sun. Some one would come along eventually. Often it would be a pickup truck driven by a Mexican peon with his wife and a truck bed full of children. The man would smile and gesture as he spoke in rapid Spanish, offering a spot among the children in the back of the truck.

When I started roaming this area, I sought audience with the other bosses. Manuel Raymond held a tight hand on Laredo, and the Guerras had a stronghold in Starr County. They cooperated with George, especially when it came time for elections. Together they could deliver a voting block of 25,000 votes, enough to assure they got the attention of the big boys in Austin.

Folks were so used to political bosses running the courthouses and banks that they thought anybody who exerted some power deserved the name of boss. That's the title some people gave to a lawyer named Jake Floyd. But I never thought of Jake as a boss or a patron. He owned three dairies near Alice, where he practiced law. He was on the board of the Alice National Bank. And folks came to him with their problems, just like they would George Parr.

But Jake Floyd didn't deal in patronage. He might show a little favoritism to a friend seeking a loan at the bank, but he didn't pay debts for the locals or tell them how to vote. He was free with his political notions, but he didn't have the power—nor did he want it—to command a block of votes.

There were times I'm sure Jake Floyd was tempted to resort to George Parr's tactics. Especially in 1952, when the violence hit very close to home. I'm just as sure, for Jake Floyd told me himself, that he thought more than once of getting his shotgun and going over to San Diego and putting an end to the Duke of Duval.

But lord knows there were enough shootings and beatings and intimidations without the opposition trading in their white hats for black ones. I spent many an hour in Jake's office. He was a valuable source for me. I would have spent a like amount of time with George Parr if he had allowed it.

But like most small-town folks and people with something to hide, George was suspicious of outsiders. And he was especially distrustful of reporters. He had a particular dislike for one of my colleagues named James Rowe, a reporter for the *Corpus Christi Caller*. James Rowe, he claimed loudly and angrily, was trying to ruin him. He vented his wrath at me from time to time, claiming I had the same objective in mind every time I wrote a story. I always responded with the same answer—if he would give me his side of the story, I could present to the readers balanced reportage.

I'll admit I compared George Parr and South Texas to something akin to a horde of thirsty ticks on a scrawny head of beef cattle. But it was damned hard to totally dislike the guy. The man had a sense of humor. And if you could get him to drop all his pretensions and talk, really talk, you'd see that he saw himself as something of a philanthropist. Not to be sacrilegious, but George thought of himself as similar to a holy father who took care of his parishioners.

The sword of justice fell on George a few times through the years. He became acquainted with the U.S. Justice Department long before he helped that Democrat Lyndon Johnson win a place in the U.S. Senate in 1948. After that, when the Republicans were in the White House, George could count on an indictment of one sort or another. It was always on indiscretions like income tax evasion or mail fraud, charges the feds lodged when they couldn't get a man for anything else.

It was damn hard to convict someone like George. Nobody would testify against him. He went to prison once, in the '30s, for tax evasion. But he never went behind bars again.

Jake Floyd didn't waste his energy trying to put George there, either. It was easier to bring down his followers and, in the process, open the way for more honest souls to fill the vacuum.

The thing about Jake Floyd—he was smart enough to see beyond the obvious. He could see past the skinny children and the potholed streets. There were oil companies and natural gas companies and businesses galore that would flock to the area if not for El Patrón.

Jake Floyd was a man who could see potential, who was angry enough to struggle for change and who was financially independent enough to work behind the scenes to achieve his goals. George considered Jake his number one enemy—ranking him above Republicans, the feds and James Rowe.

It was the '48 election that caught my editor's attention and added Duval and Jim Wells to my beat. Over the next few years—16 to be exact—I spent more time there than anywhere else. I nearly lived at the courthouses, covering trials, talking to the sheriffs, chewing the fat with the clerks and the judges and anybody who cared to share information.

I went to political rallies and hung around polling places on election days. I frequented clandestine political meetings and spent a good deal of time tracking down folks on the telephone. A reporter is only as good as his sources, so I concentrated on cultivating a few. I worked both sides of the street, but had better luck with Jake Floyd's corner. Until the day I retired from the *Enterprise*, George Parr and his followers regarded me with that distant, suspicious look that small-town folks often adopt at the sight of a stranger.

After the opposition simmered past the boiling point in the early '50s, I decided it wasn't just the 1948 election that brought a revolution to George Parr's kingdom. It was the *peones* themselves. Some said it was the war that did it. The young Mexican boys went off to the Pacific or to France to war against tyrants. They came home to find one in their midst.

The story I am about to tell is the result of 16 years of newspaper reporting. The characters are presented as I saw them, and the action is as I witnessed it or as others described it to me. Reporters rarely are lucky enough to witness news in the making. They rely on others to re-create events for them and, always, they depend on the players to interpret what happened.

When I asked folks to explain to me why George Parr did what he did, I always heard them use his nickname, Tecuache. The Mexicans are fond of nicknames and carefully choose them. Tecuache is Spanish for *possum*. Possums are rodent-like creatures about the size of a large house cat. In South Texas, they live anonymously under foundations or in underbrush. They come out at night and will steal you blind, eating anything left within their path. They raid garbage cans, dog food bowls and compost piles and then slink off before morning's light. Mostly they'll run from a human, but if you get close enough to threaten them, they'll bare some fierce, sharp teeth and will attack. As everyone knows, possums are famous for pretending to be asleep or dead. It's a ruse so they can escape and plan the next raid. It was a deadly accurate description of George.

George relished his nickname. He spoke Spanish fluently and lived a curious mix of both Anglo and Mexican cultures. He gave nicknames to friends and enemies alike. To Jake Floyd, he attached the name Vibora Seca, the dry snake.

Snakes are plentiful along the Nueces Strip, and some are particularly deadly. I have seen eight-foot rattlers and brightly colored coral snakes smaller around than my thumb. It was generally good policy to kill such reptiles, for they were a menace to livestock and man alike. But I always gave them a wide path, rationalizing to myself that I am an observer of life, not a participant.

I am sure George Parr thought of Jake Floyd as a poisonous snake that had been milked of its venom. It was as if he were telling *"Mi gente,"* as he called his people, that Jake Floyd might look dangerous and act sly. But up against the possum, he was only a dry snake.

Section I
1948

Chapter 1

One second Jake Floyd was lying still as a corpse on the bed. The next he was sitting straight up, as if he'd been doused with ice water. Taking catnaps was part of his daily routine. He made time for them once or twice a day, after lunch and after work. With all that Jake had to do on any given day, naps were the way he kept his energy up.

He'd lie on the bed fully clothed, his starched, long-sleeved khaki shirt cuffed at the wrists, a string tie around his neck and pressed khakis belted around his thin waist. Even in the worst summer heat, he never loosened his stiff collar or rolled up his sleeves. He'd lie there 15 minutes, dead asleep, not breaking a sweat.

Raul could watch his wife cook up a dozen tortillas while Señor Floyd took his nap. She'd pull the twelfth tortilla off the griddle and he could hear the springs squeak on the bed in the guest room. It never failed. Raul sometimes wished he could be a fly on the wall in that little room when his boss took a nap. He could imagine him shooting off the mattress like one of those Roman candles he bought his kids on the Fourth of July.

On this 28th day of August in 1948, like every day that Jake visited his South Texas farm after work, he strode out of the guest bedroom with purpose in his step. He wore a straw Stetson on his head to protect his fair skin from the ruthless sun. On his feet were his hand-built cowboy boots with his initials JSF on the side.

As usual, Jake had a serious look on his long, slender face when he walked into Raul's kitchen. His blue eyes were intense, like he was worried about something. As a rule, Jake didn't smile much, and when he did, he pressed his narrow lips together to hide teeth stained from years of cigar smoking. But there were other reasons Jake didn't smile. It was primary runoff day back in town in Alice, and Jake was thinking about the shenanigans that were going on at the polls. He'd have to see about that later, he decided as he pulled a small hardcover ledger book from a kitchen drawer.

Sitting at the rough wooden table next to the stove, he and Raul went over the day's receipts for supplies. Fifteen cents for grease, 45 cents for a bucket, milk can $2.50, oil and gas $16.73. Every expenditure, no matter how small, Jake wanted it in the ledger book.

Raul was the kind of foreman Jake wanted. He wrote down every penny he spent, milked and fed the 100 or so cows, sold the milk and generally kept the place running real smooth. Raul worked "on the halves" with Jake. That meant he got the house rent-free and a small salary, equipment, supplies and cattle. At the end of the year, he usually got a bonus. There was one idiosyncrasy to the deal: Raul had to reserve a bedroom for Jake to take his *siestas*.

The kitchen was as hot as a blast furnace with the stove fired up for cooking the tortillas. Raul urged his boss out onto the porch, where they gulped cool water pumped from the well. He marveled at how Mr. Floyd never seemed to suffer from the heat, regardless of its intensity. Even after sitting next to the cook stove in the hot kitchen, his boss's cheeks were barely flushed. Raul, meanwhile, mopped his forehead with a soggy bandana, revealing sweaty rings under his armpits.

"Where's Cricket?" Jake asked, inquiring of the chihuahua that always went with him to the farm. Cricket liked to ride in the truck with the two men as they made the rounds. Raul nodded in the direction of the barn a couple hundred feet from the porch. There was Cricket, sniffing his way around the foundation of the clapboard barn.

Jake called his name, and the dog streaked to the pickup truck, leaping to the seat with the ease of a much larger dog. Cricket came to live with Jake and his family only two years before, and he was a regular at the farm.

He was the first dog Jake had owned in almost ten years. The last one had been a chihuahua, too, named Nicki. Jake was wild about that dog; he took him everywhere. When he was at home, Nicki was in his lap. When he went to the farms, Nicki went too. That little dog had a little bell on his collar so people wouldn't step on him. Jake would walk around the house, a jingling shadow at his feet.

Nicki wasn't allowed in the courthouse or at Jake's office. Some Sundays, when Jake went to the Baptist Church, Nicki would follow his trail the three blocks from the house to the sanctuary. The church doors would be wide open because it was always so warm and Nicki would trot in, his bell jingling, and hunt until he found his master. Jake usually let Nicki sit in his lap during the sermon.

Once, Nicki had followed Jake's car four blocks from the house to a hotel downtown where he was going to a Lions Club meeting. When Jake got out of the car, little Nicki raced across a street to greet him and was struck by a passing automobile. Jake never mentioned Nicki after that, but he stopped going to Lions Club meetings and it took his wife almost ten years to persuade him to get another dog.

In the passenger seat, Jake was quiet as the three bumped and tossed in the pickup truck through the sendera, a wide path that had been carved in the mesquite and huisache. Raul guided the truck around clusters of prickly pear cactus and stray mesquite saplings. Quail too lazy to take flight scurried out of the way.

The hot sun burned in the sky as a gentle breeze carried moist air in from the nearby Gulf of Mexico. This was unforgiving land—rocky, dry and yielding little to those who inhabited it. About the only way to making a living off it was to run some livestock or strike oil or natural gas.

Jake instructed his foreman to look into applying a strong dose of poison to the sendera. The mesquite could not be eradicated, but it was choking off the sendera, their only pathway to the pastures.

Cricket was enthusiastic, as usual, about riding in the truck. He did a canine dance on the seat between the two men, yipping and yapping in a frenzied greeting to the cows that grazed in the distance.

"Mr. Floyd," Raul decided to ask, "is something wrong?"

Jake sat unresponsive for a moment and moved his bony hand to his lips, probing for the cigar that wasn't there.

"It's the runoff," Jake said.

Raul had heard there was an election in town that day. Señor Floyd had told him about it—the Democratic primary runoff. The way the boss talked about it, Raul knew it was a really important election. Señor Floyd had told him of the fierce battle in the county Democratic Party for the chairmanship. Jake's man was Harry Lee Adams, who was running against the incumbent, Tom Donald. Donald was vice president and cashier at the Texas State Bank in Alice. The bank was owned by George Parr, the man folks called the Duke of Duval, the Boss, El Patrón. Señor Floyd called him a sonofagun.

For sure, Tom Donald was a Parr man. As county chairman, he had a nasty habit—to Jake's way of thinking. It was Tom's job to keep a copy of the tally sheets people signed when they cast ballots. Sometimes, he would lock up the ballot boxes and the tally sheets in the bank vault. With the numbered ballots and the signed tally lists, there was no such thing as a secret ballot in Duval and Jim Wells counties. It was as George Parr said to *mi gente*, "my people," as he called them: "Nothing goes unnoticed in heaven or on earth."

Another thing Señor Floyd had told Raul about the runoff. There was another race that was getting a lot of attention, not just in Duval and Jim Wells, but all over Texas. It was the race for the Democratic nomination for U.S. Senate. The incumbent, Pappy O'Daniel, had decided to forego a run for another term. And since Texas was a one-party state, the Democratic nominee would undoubtedly become the next Texas senator.

It had been a contentious campaign. Former Gov. Coke Stevenson, a rancher and a highly respected statesman, faced Lyndon Johnson, a schoolteacher and little-known congressman from the Texas Hill Country.

"Which race, boss?" Raul asked, knowing that these were the only two races Jake had expressed concern about.

"Both. There's trouble with the poll watchers."

Jake squinted into the sun as Raul pointed the truck west. The foreman wondered if the boss would provide any details. Sometimes he was so preoccupied he barely spoke on their afternoon excursions.

"They're getting arrested," Jake said, "or they're being forced to stay so far from the election judges they can't see what's going on. The *pistoleros* are crawling all over town—like a pack of coyotes—scaring the chickens away from the polls."

Jake opened the glove compartment and probed through its contents.

"Have I left any cigars in the truck?" he asked.

"No, Señor Floyd. Don't think so."

Jake fell silent again, thinking about the evening ahead. He and his daughter Edith Maude were going to the Nayer School across the tracks in Mexican town. That was where Box 13 was and where most of the Mexicans in Alice voted. Of all the boxes in Jim Wells County, it was the one George Parr had the best chance of controlling.

Edith Maude was grown and had gone to graduate school in Boston for a year. She was home for the summer, with plans to become a schoolteacher. Strong-headed and smart, she had been more of a son to Jake than his boy Buddy.

The two siblings were as different as Texas and California. Edith Maude was studious and musical and as interested in the law and politics as Jake. Buddy, three years younger than his sister, was mischievous and tenderhearted, the gleam in his mother's eye. For him, school was a place he could horse around with his friends. But he was a good kid, and Jake had hopes that someday he would join him in his law firm.

A few months before the runoff, Maude, as Jake called her, had sent letters to all the candidates in the local races asking them to sign affidavits requesting poll supervisors. That was how they got a couple of anti-Parr men inside the polling place at the Nayer School. They'd had to go to a judge to get a court order, but Jake and the opposition got their poll watchers.

Jake knew a mere presence while the votes were being cast and counted didn't guarantee an honest election. George Parr had been stuffing ballot boxes and scaring off any opposition for a long, long time. When it came to lubricating a political machine, El Patrón was a master mechanic.

Except for the white voting boxes, he controlled the vote in Jim Wells County. And in Duval County, where he was the Duke, he reigned over all of the polling places. As a result, he had complete control of the county courthouse in San Diego, county seat of Duval, and strong influence at the courthouse in Alice, county seat of Jim Wells. Jake was tired of Parr's patronage with county jobs and tired of his control of the district court. He was tired, too, of Parr's stranglehold on the local economy. The big oil companies wouldn't get close to Alice because of the Parr corruption.

Raul slowed as they approached the herd and stopped the truck at a shed that held sacks of feed. The boss would want to give the animals treats as he examined them. The two men eased out of the truck, careful not to startle the herd. Cricket protested loudly at being left behind in the truck.

Jake examined the animals one by one, checking their coats and their eyes. A glossy coat and clear, shiny eyes were sure indicators of a healthy cow. The herd, about 35 strong, knew the routine. After Jake conducted his inspection, the herd began stirring toward the feeding troughs. Jake and Raul hauled out sacks of feed pellets and tossed them into the steel containers. It was like giving biscuits to a dog. Jake had a name for each cow, and he called out to each one as he stroked its massive head. As the herd jockeyed for position in front of the troughs, Jake asked Raul about the day's milk production.

Jake wasn't the sort of man folks would guess was a dairyman. He looked more like a man with a desk job. It was his physique that gave him away. He had long, bony limbs and a narrow chest and shoulders. His thin hair was combed straight back except for an unruly strand that strayed onto his forehead. His features were small for a man of his stature—he had narrow lips and small eyes that focused intently behind wire-framed glasses. His nose was only slightly prominent, making his oversized ears his most noticeable feature.

Some folks wondered why Jake moonlighted on his dairy farms when he had a thriving law practice and so many other responsibilities. If anyone had come out and asked him, Jake would have had to think for a minute. Then he would have said he was born for lawyering. The law was something he had studied and was good at. But dairy farming—that had to do with the land. Land was precious; it was the source of life. If the Bible was true, he had come from dust, and to dust he would return. The land,

Jake would say, was worth all number of sacrifices. They weren't surprising words to hear from a man who had grown up on a dairy farm near the Texas coast not far from Alice.

Jake made swift work of the afternoon inspection. Satisfied that the herd was healthy, Jake instructed his foreman to ride the fences the next day to make sure the barbed wire was intact. He had noticed a few loose wires as he drove into the farm.

As Jake and Raul made the bumpy trip back to the frame house, Jake made a mental note to buy cigars on the way to Box 13. It was going to be a long night. Jake Floyd wasn't a superstitious man, but he couldn't shake the thought that 13 was a very unlucky number.

Chapter 2

George Berham Parr leaned back in his high-backed chair, puffed a cloud from his overstuffed cigar, and grinned at the brown-skinned man seated across the desk. The small-boned Mexican man, straw hat in hand and grimy work shirt across his torso, bore a hopeful look in his deep brown eyes. Lupe was his name. Lupe Calderon.

He pushed a shovel for a living, working for George's road construction company. It was a good job, Lupe thought, better than he ever hoped to have. His uncle had gotten him the job. Uncle Guillermo had a big position at the courthouse; Lupe wasn't sure what it was. But the uncle had gone to El Patrón and asked him to give Lupe a job.

There was plenty of steady construction work, and for that Lupe was very grateful. *Gracias, gracias,* he said to El Patrón a few score times, between chews on his thumbnail. Lucky for Lupe, George's Duval Construction Company won the bidding on every highway and road project that passed through the Duval County Commissioners Court. When there wasn't paving to be done, El Patrón had a project for the crews at his *hacienda* or his racetrack.

Lupe's wages were minimal, barely enough to buy food and pay the rent on the dirt-floor shack he shared with his wife Juanita and their four children. But Lupe expected no more from life. He was happy as long as there were a few dollars left to buy beer at the *cantina*.

Lupe had never been in El Patrón's office; in fact, he had never been in such luxury. He stroked the armrests of the leather wingback he was sitting in and soaked in the chilled air from the window air conditioner. He was awed by George's massive carved desk. It was solid wood and very dark, almost black. Lupe thought it might take five or more men to move it.

The man behind the desk intimidated Lupe, both physically and psychologically. He was a good four inches taller, but he still was not tall for an Anglo man. His pressed white shirt concealed a solid, powerful chest, a pair of muscular arms and a firm waist. His short legs were stocky and strong. If Lupe didn't know better, he would have thought El Patrón worked on a road crew. In truth, George possessed a naturally muscular build, which he kept in form by pounding a boxer's punching bag.

Even though Lupe had never met the Duke of Duval, his life had been intertwined with the boss for a long time. George Parr had paid for the midwife who presided at the birth of Lupe's children. His mother's funeral had been paid for by George Parr. And then there was Lupe's job. Anything good in Duval County, it came from George Parr.

That was why Lupe now sat in the big wingback. He looked down and fidgeted with his straw hat as he spoke softly to El Patrón. It was his little girl, Pepita, he said. She was feverish and her breathing was labored. Her lungs were tight with fluid, and she could not sleep for wheezing.

"My little Pepita, she is so sick." Lupe's voice sounded somber and small in the paneled office. He spoke in Spanish. "Please, *señor*, she must go to the doctor."

George shoved the cigar to the corner of his mouth and swung his feet off the big desk. In perfectly accented Spanish he told his friend he could help. Without hesitation, he pulled open a drawer and drew out a massive, bound check register. With many flourishes of a fountain pen, he produced a bank draft and peeled it out of the book.

"Have you voted, Lupe?" George Parr rose to his feet, the check still in his hand.

Lupe stood up quickly, but stared at the carpeted floor. "No, *señor*," he muttered. "I have been so worried. I have not had time..."

George skirted the desk and put his arm around the stoop-shouldered man. "Come, my friend. Voting is your duty, a God-given right. It will only take a minute, and then you can return to your family."

As they stepped from George's pleasant, air-conditioned office, they were assaulted by the weighty dampness of the South Texas heat. Three Mexican men lazing on wooden benches beside the door jumped to their feet and tipped their *sombreros* in George's direction. Each wore a pair of pointed-toe cowboy boots and a bullet-studded gun belt. Lupe knew almost everyone in San Diego, but he was not even a nodding acquaintance with these men. Like most residents, he preferred to give a wide berth to George's cadre of *pistoleros*.

George summoned one of the trio and grinned broadly. "Pablo," he said, "take this fine gentleman to the courthouse so he can vote. If necessary, take him to the front of the line. He's got a daughter who's plenty sick and he needs to go see her."

George handed the check to Lupe and shook the laborer's hand. Lupe nodded his head sharply, mumbled "*Gracias, gracias,*" and walked off with Pablo in the direction of the courthouse.

George rubbed his chest in satisfaction, gave a wave to the two remaining *pistoleros* and returned to his office. It was nice, George thought to himself, having a couple of pistol packers around. Not that he needed them. George could handle a gun, and physically, he was powerful enough to defend himself. It was just nice having a couple of the boys with him when he went to the Windmill Cafe for a soda or to the courthouse.

Mi gente, he thought with satisfaction, scattered like wild horses when the *pistoleros* were with him. But when it was just El Patrón, they ventured close, greeted him, and if he invited them, they drank beers as he gulped sodas at the cafe.

He parted his lips in a wide grin, revealing large, slightly uneven teeth. If nature had given George one more tooth, his gums might have overflowed. He had a fleshy face and a jaw so full that when he smiled he often looked like he was sneering. Folks said when he smiled that sneering smile, he looked like a cornered possum. El Tecuache, they called him.

George lit a cigar and flopped into his chair. He liked a good cigar now and then, especially when he was feeling good. But he didn't touch cigarettes and he had little taste for alcohol of any kind. George hated to think it was because of the preaching his mother used to do. She was dead against drinking. George's grandfather, she often reminded her six children, had died in a barroom fight.

"Don't you ever drink," she told them. "One member of the family getting killed is enough."

Her husband, Archie, didn't drink or smoke or swear, which was far beyond what George thought should be required of any man. Goddam, a little swearin' never hurt nobody. Might move some folks back in line.

Dad might have been a straight arrow about drinking and swearing, but he was also a master at politics. He was the original Duke of Duval, handing down his hard-won empire to George when he became too blind and too sick with diabetes to go on. George had been the Duke of Duval ten years and, damn, he was having a good time.

Helping folks like Lupe made a man feel good. It was almost like being a damn missionary in some desperately poor country. If there was a need, he could fill it. All you needed to do was ask. El Patrón wouldn't even make a fellow prove he was in trouble. He'd just help out; no questions asked.

George didn't like to think too much about church or missionaries. He gave a little shudder and sat down in his big chair again. Momma had taken him and his brothers and sisters to the Episcopal Church when he was a youngster, but Archie never went with them. They didn't do any praying at the dinner table or at bedtime. And they sure didn't read the Bible like some of his friends from school. George often wondered why his mother ever bothered with church.

All those church-going folks were no different from the heathen. They stole and lied and fornicated along with the rest of humanity, but said all they wanted in the end was to sit beside God in heaven. George snickered at that thought, and the big teeth glistened.

No, George thought. He'd much rather spend eternity down in hell with the devil. He'd be one of the top lieutenants, slinking around with a whip and a pitchfork. He'd act as a guard, keeping the anguished masses in line. No danger of being lonely in hell. All his friends would be there, too.

His thoughts turned to the runoff and to Coke Stevenson. The man had once been a state senator, then lieutenant governor and finally governor. He had once been a friend of the Parrs and, as such, he had been the recipient of large blocks of South Texas votes.

George could deliver those votes because he had forged solid political alliances with bosses throughout the area. There was Manuel Raymond, monarch of Laredo down on the border. Judge Manuel Bravo ruled Zapata County and Sheriff Chub Pool held La Salle County in an iron grip. In Jim Wells County just next door, Hubert Sain was in the saddle. In all, George could deliver about 15 counties in any given statewide race. With better than 25,000 votes at his command, George Parr entertained many vote-shopping candidates in his San Diego office. His voting block translated into clout in Austin and in Washington, a fact that was not lost on a smart lawyer like Coke Stevenson.

"Calculatin' Coke," as he was called, was a rancher from Junction, a good 200-plus miles northwest of San Diego. As a politician he had been beloved by Texans, winning office easily every time he had run for a statewide position. Not that he had needed it, but Coke had been the recipient of a 3,310-to-17 margin in Duval County in 1944, the year he ran for his last term as governor. George and his father had long been on friendly terms with Coke. When the elder Parr died, Coke had been a pallbearer at his funeral.

But the climate between George and Coke cooled considerably while Coke occupied the governor's mansion during World War II. The governor had refused George's request to appoint Jimmy Kazen, a cog in the wheels of Laredo politics, as district attorney in nearby Webb County. Kazen was a relative by marriage of Manuel Raymond. George remembered vividly the meeting he and Manuel had with Coke in a Laredo hotel room. The governor had been reluctant and evasive and when George left to drive back to San Diego, he was convinced he would not get his way.

He did not know at the time that Coke had also been visited in Laredo by the commanding general of the local Army Air Force base. The officer had pleaded with Stevenson to appoint an independent, a man who wouldn't hesitate to prosecute the prostitutes who were consorting with his soldiers and spreading diseases. To Coke's way of thinking, it was wartime, and he needed to do the patriotic thing. He appointed an independent, and George never forgave him.

George ran a hand through his auburn hair, which he wore combed straight back from a widow's peak. Despite his 47 years, there were but a few strands of gray. Adjusting flesh-toned glasses, the Duke of Duval leaned back in the chair and reflected on Coke's latest campaign. He was running for U.S. Senate. He had come out of a brief retirement at his treasured Hill Country ranch and was campaigning in his down-home style. He traveled the state in his Plymouth, gave stump speeches on courthouse lawns and walked the sidewalks, shaking hands with voters. Folks loved it, but it was a backbreaking campaign style that was easily outshone by his flashy opponent.

George chuckled, thinking about the time Lyndon Johnson campaigned in Alice. His appearance had quite literally stirred up some dust just 12 miles east of San Diego. The jug-eared, big-boned Johnson was campaigning in a helicopter, barnstorming Texas in a whirlybird he had nicknamed the Flying Windmill.

When he descended on Alice, he drew a crowd of curious Texans intrigued by the helicopter, a vehicle few had seen before. As the Flying Windmill settled into a vacant lot downtown, it whipped up so much dust that the crowd scurried away when Johnson alighted. Undaunted, Johnson waved his Stetson and wooed the crowd back with the help of a public address system that had been built into the helicopter.

George had talked with Lyndon several times by telephone during the campaign. He told him he liked the Flying Windmill. A damn clever idea and just what the campaign needed to liven it up. Frankly, he told Lyndon, kissing babies and stumping on the courthouse steps was boring.

Pappy O'Daniel had it all figured out in the '30s when he won the governor's mansion. He had toured the state in a red circus wagon with his Hillbilly Boys, singing country songs like "Beautiful, Beautiful Texas." Now that was campaigning, to George's way of thinking. A little cornpone, but to the mostly rural Texas electorate, it was powerful. Pappy demonstrated in a trademark style that he was just a plain ol' country boy.

George had never really stopped to analyze what it was about Pappy O'Daniel that was so appealing to Texans. It was as though both he and Pappy innately understood a universal political truth. George, without planning or scheming, was one of his own people. Unlike his father, who was gone on cattle drives or later serving as a senator in Austin, George had stayed pretty much in San Diego.

He didn't want to hold public office. It was little better than being an office boy, he said. And by growing up in San Diego, an advantage Archie did not have, George had Mexican children for playmates. He learned Spanish a little better than English; he even boasted he thought in Spanish. For damn sure he could cuss a man to ribbons in Spanish.

George knew little of the science of campaigning and had no cause to. His candidates always ran unopposed. But he knew an eye-catcher when he saw one, and Lyndon Johnson had one in the Flying Windmill. No doubt about it, Lyndon had learned a lot from Pappy O'Daniel, especially after the special election of 1941.

In that year, Lyndon ran against Pappy for a vacant U.S. Senate seat. Lyndon was a congressman from the Texas Hill Country. Pappy had been a popular Texas governor. George had helped Lyndon all he could, but Pappy skunked him. After all the boxes Lyndon controlled had reported, Pappy's boxes turned in their totals. The difference was enough for Pappy to win.

George wrote Lyndon a sympathetic letter after that bitter loss. "We all regret very much that you were beat out of the Senate seat—when you really won it. We will all be with you any time in the future that you decide to take another run at it."

In the intervening years, George and Lyndon forged a solid friendship. Lyndon remained a congressman representing the Hill Country, but on occasion, he would drive down to San Diego for some barbecued goat at the Parrs' *hacienda*.

When he was in Washington, Lyndon did what he could to win a pardon for George, who had been convicted in the '30s and served time at El Reno, Oklahoma, for federal income tax evasion. In 1946, the pardon came through, signed by President Harry

Truman. But it was not all Lyndon's doing. The congressman from George's district, John Emmett Lyle, Jr., helped it along, too.

Today, August 28, 1948, was payback day, the day George would make good on his promise to Lyndon when he lost to Pappy in 1941. George was unperturbed by predictions that Coke was certain to win. Why, he'd even heard that Coke had gone to Washington to look for a place to live, while Lyndon dive-bombed Texas in the Flying Windmill.

It was no wonder Coke had left the campaign trail, if only temporarily. He had a 70,000-vote lead from the initial primary vote, a comfortable margin in a race that drew about a million votes. There was no reason to doubt victory. Whoever won the nomination would go to the U.S. Senate. There would be no formidable Republican opposition in November; in Texas there never was.

George smiled as he slid the check register back into the desk drawer and reached for his hat. The thought of a close election gave him the same invigorating feeling he got when he watched his quarter horses skim around the racetrack. This is going to be an election to remember, he thought, as he stepped out the front door and motioned for the men in *sombreros* to follow.

***

As tin ballot boxes go, this one looked rather forlorn. Cylindrical and padlocked, it bore dents and bruises from elections past. But it wasn't made for looks. It was made to hold ballots, and it was doing just that as it rested on a portable table in the hallway at the Nayer School. In days to come, after the box had become infamous, Parr's followers would paint "Precinct 13" on its underside and pose for pictures with it. But on August 28, 1948, it was one of thousands of tin drums used as ballot boxes throughout Texas.

Luis Salas eyed the two poll watchers who had been assigned to the precinct by the Jim Wells reformers. They sat in folding chairs a good 50 feet from the portable table. Salas had put the chairs there himself and had informed Jimmy Holmgreen and Ike Poole that they were to move no closer. Salas towered over the two seated men as he issued the order, his massive, muscular frame adding emphasis to his warning. He didn't wear a gun, but every now and then a Parr *pistolero* would wander into the school cafeteria.

Salas told Holmgreen he hoped they wouldn't have a repeat performance of the trouble they had had in the first primary a month earlier. On that occasion, the poll watcher had been insistent about an over-the-shoulder view of the ballot counting. So Salas had called in Deputy Sheriff Stokes Micenheimer, a hulk of a *pistolero*, to pack Holmgreen off to jail. Jake Floyd had bailed him out after a few hours.

Salas, nicknamed "Indio" because of his swarthy complexion, was one of George Parr's most trusted lieutenants. An immigrant from Durango, Mexico, he was a Parr-commissioned deputy in three counties—Jim Wells, Duval and Nueces. He was a big man about town, buying everyone in the bar a drink and paying medical bills for the poor Mexicans.

He was George Parr's enforcer, driving the disloyal out of their businesses. He usually carried a large handgun on his belt, never hesitating to use it. Stories abounded of Indio's savage temper, including the time he had beaten an Alice restaurateur into submission and then used a barstool to dismantle the man's eating establishment.

Indio had been given clear instructions before runoff day. Deliver Box 13 for Lyndon Johnson. Indio didn't ask for a reason. He'd seen El Patrón with Mr. Johnson and some of his men on several occasions. He figured they were friends.

When Jake and Edith Maude arrived at the school, Salas' election-day tent was still functioning in a vacant lot across the street from the school. A trio of *pistoleros* were posted outside. But under the canvas, election workers drank bottled beers and propped their feet on the metal tables. If it had been earlier in the day, they would have been handing out poll taxes and "strings," pieces of twine knotted in strategic places. An illiterate voter could place one of the strings next to a ballot and refer to the knots as pointers to the appropriate candidate.

By Texas law, two election judges could assist illiterate voters with ballots. Asked who they wanted to vote for, the Mexicans usually said, "Señor Parr." It was the go-ahead for the judges to mark the ballot in favor of all of George's candidates.

A second tent for the Old Party, Jake Floyd's party, was set up about a hundred feet from George's New Party tent. Women were bringing in coffee and sandwiches in preparation for a long night. Jake fully expected Luis Salas to drag out the count. They would do lots of singing and shouting come about 4 A.M., trying to keep each other awake.

The polls had been closed less than a half hour when Jake and Edith Maude entered the hallway at the Nayer School, Jake's trusty chihuahua Cricket trailing them. Jimmy Holmgreen was already as nervous as Cricket was. During the first primary, he was convinced that Salas had given Johnson dozens of Stevenson's votes. He was certain, he told Jake, that the same thing was happening again.

From what Jake could tell, it looked like Holmgreen was right. Salas was sitting at the portable table, the tin box on the floor beside him. Three stacks of ballots lay on the table, and Salas, with the help of three other election clerks, was counting the votes. Jake heard Salas call out "Johnson" ten times to every one time he called out "Stevenson." It was easy to see who was going to win this precinct.

When Salas noticed Jake and Edith Maude, he abruptly halted the vote counting and marched across the cafeteria toward them, his cleated cowboy boots clicking on the linoleum. Out, he bellowed at them. Holmgreen and Poole could stay, but everybody else—outside.

Jake took his time leaving. He could hear Salas drone "Johnson, Johnson, Johnson," as the door slammed behind him. The partying had already begun in their tent. Half a dozen people were singing "The Eyes of Texas Are Upon You" as the Floyds stepped under the canvas. Before long, a *pistolero* pulled up a folding chair across the sidewalk from their tent. He had a carbine draped across his lap. He stayed there all night.

Chapter 3

A blast of air conditioning and a fog of cigarette smoke greeted Indio Salas as he shoved the heavy door open and entered George Parr's office. The whitewashed one-story building stood like a fortress. There were iron bars on the high windows and the two solid oak arched doors would have done proudly in a medieval castle. The office was cold as a dungeon. El Jefe must have the window unit turned down to 60 degrees.

George, in his customary station behind his oak desk, was the only one of the four men in the room not puffing on a cigarette. In chairs lined up in front of his desk sat Ed Lloyd, George's trusted attorney from Alice, Bruce Ainsworth, a San Diego city commissioner, and a tall, lanky man dressed in a fancy business suit. Indio had never seen this gringo, who was puffing just as furiously as Mr. Lloyd and Mr. Ainsworth.

The man couldn't be from San Diego or Alice. Indio would have recognized him. No, he must be from Austin or San Antonio. Nobody except El Jefe wore suits that looked that expensive.

Indio had some idea why he had been summoned. When El Jefe phoned him to come over from Alice he mentioned Lyndon and Box 13. Just get over here fast, he had said.

The stranger was definitely not Lyndon Johnson. Indio had seen the congressman before—at George's *hacienda* and right here in the office. He remembered Lyndon Johnson as a forceful presence, like a gamecock, aggressive and combative. This man was more reserved, more reflective. He spoke like a lawyer, his words carefully chosen. Indio did not get an introduction, but it was clear from the conversation that the man was an emissary from Austin.

It had been three days since the runoff, and it remained unclear who would win the nomination. It was a real scraper of a race. Stevenson had 494,396 votes. Johnson had 494,277. The former governor led by 119 votes in what was being described as the most exciting Senate race in Texas history. The vote totals changed daily, as the various counties double-checked their counts and reported errors to the state Election Bureau.

The mood was serious in the tiny office, a departure from the usual tone of meetings involving El Patrón. George liked to salt and pepper his conversations with a taste of verbal jousting. A good joke, he believed, made his guests feel welcome. But there was no friendly banter this morning. Indio stood just inside the door and waited for El Jefe to recognize him.

"Indio," George finally said, motioning for Bruce Ainsworth to pull up a seat for the new arrival.

The two conversed in Spanish for a moment, George inquiring of Indio's wife and children. The other three men sat smoking in silence, seemingly unaware of the exchange. Finally, George addressed the business at hand.

"The man says all they need is 200 votes," George said, still speaking in Spanish.

There were no more votes to be had in Duval, Indio told him. There had been a nearly 100 percent turnout of voters, or at least, all the poll tax receipts had been used up. It would be too risky to add any more names to the tally sheets, he advised. It looked suspicious enough that Lyndon had gotten 4,662 votes to Stevenson's 40.

George propped his elbows on the desk and chewed what was left of a fingernail.

"What about Jim Wells? Any room there?"

Indio looked at El Jefe, wondering why he had been asked such a question. El Jefe knew as well as anyone that Box 13 was the only precinct he had completely controlled three days earlier.

"Of course, El Patrón," Indio replied. "Box 13."

"Then add 200 names to the poll list and hold onto it. Wait until I tell you to report an amended return."

Indio went stiff. He felt his throat close off and he stuffed his hands in the pockets of his khakis. He could feel his insides tighten and his belly start to burn. It was the kind of fire in his belly he felt years earlier when he was a teen-ager, when he rode with Pancho Villa. It was an army of *compesinos* that Pancho Villa led, and they were nothing more than land pirates. Los Dorados, they were called, the golden ones, plundering Chihuahua and Durango of all that had value. They took all of his father's livestock and when they learned Indio could operate a telegraph wire, they kidnapped him.

Indio had felt the burn in his belly many times since Los Dorados released him. His mother told him once that it was a sign from God—a sign that trouble lay just ahead. History had proven her correct many times, and Indio had learned to pay heed.

Heretofore, whatever El Jefe wanted, Indio delivered. But this he could not do. The flames in his belly were telling him something. He had best not ignore them.

"El Patrón," he said, still speaking Spanish, "I will find someone to add the names." He did not look at El Jefe. "Then I will certify them. We will do it tonight, tomorrow, whenever."

George looked at him long and hard. The three other men tended to their cigarettes, waiting for a report from George in English. Indio was glad their conversation was private. He would not want El Jefe to be embarrassed.

"Bueno," George said after a long silence. "Meet me back here in two hours."

When Indio returned with deputies Willie Mancha and Ignacio Escobar, George was alone in his office. Save for the pile of cigarette butts in the ashtrays on George's desk, there was no trace of the morning's visitors.

Indio had the poll lists from Box 13 with him. He had driven to Alice and asked Tom Donald to retrieve three copies from the Texas State Bank vault. Box 13, according to the lists, had produced 765 votes for Johnson and 60 for Stevenson. Indio brought the poll tax list as well.

Willie and Ignacio sat opposite George and took turns adding names to the lists. George directed them to copy straight from the poll tax roster, and they began with last names beginning with A. Willie wrote about ten names and then Ignacio would take over.

"El Patrón," Indio protested, "not in alphabetical order. Mix them up …"

"Shut up," George said harshly. "No one will ever see it."

It was best not to argue. Indio was already in bad with The Boss for refusing to fully cooperate with this scheme.

When the deed was done, Indio drove the lists back to Alice. By law, one of the sheets was to be sealed in the ballot box, one was to be in the hands of the chairman of the county Democratic Party and one was to be in the custody of the precinct election judge. Salas made the necessary deliveries, finishing up with Tom Donald, who locked his copy in the vault at the Texas State Bank where he worked. Donald, who had been ousted by Harry Lee Adams as the new county Democratic party chairman, was the keeper of the votes until January 1.

His duties accomplished, Indio retired to his favorite bar, the Baile Española. Maybe if he bought everyone a round of beers, he would feel better. Maybe a few beers would put out the fire in his belly. He drank until the barkeep closed the *cantina* down, and then he shuffled home, his belly still burning.

Texas Mutiny: Bullets, Ballots and Boss Rule

***

Over the next two days, Indio waited for a phone call from The Boss, a phone call directing him to report an amended Box 13 return. But the call never came. Meanwhile, the election remained extremely close.

George had already delivered a bloc vote for Lyndon in the counties he controlled. Duval, Starr, La Salle, Jim Hogg, Zapata and Brooks turned in more than 10,000 votes for the congressman and a mere 1,300 for the former governor. The Parr-controlled precincts in Corpus Christi offered up another 3,000 votes for LBJ. The rest of the Rio Grande Valley provided a margin of 27,000 ballots.

Still, as the week after the runoff progressed, the race remained tight and undecided. Stevenson retained a slim lead. By Thursday, five days after the voting, the rancher from Junction held a margin of 351 votes. Newspapers throughout Texas were declaring him the victor. Stevenson, himself, told reporters he was certain he had won. But Friday, the Valley counties reported more amended returns. Johnson began chipping away at Stevenson's lead.

In Alice, the Jim Wells County Democratic Party Executive Committee met for a final canvassing of runoff returns. The men sat at a large oak table in a first-floor room at the county courthouse. One by one, they opened the ballot boxes and reviewed the polling lists.

Jake Floyd sat erect in a hardwood chair next to a whitewashed wall. It was his habit to attend these meetings, even though Tom Donald always protested loudly that they were closed to the public. I'm not the public, Jake would tell him. I'm a poll-tax-paying member of the Democratic Party. As a citizen of Jim Wells County, Jake would tell Tom Donald, he had a right to be there.

Besides, Jake thought to himself, Jimmy Holmgreen had seen Luis Salas stealing votes. And Coke Stevenson had asked him to be there. Jake and Coke had been friends for years. To the Alice lawyer's way of thinking, the former governor was the kind of man to represent Texas in the U.S. Senate. He loved the land with a religious fervor, and he loved the law just as much. Come the devil or high water, Jake thought, he was going to do what he could to help Coke Stevenson get elected.

Tom Donald bypassed his usual protest against Jake's presence and the canvassing began. Committeeman B.M. Brownlee pried open the tin boxes, pulled out the polling lists and double-checked the reported number of ballots. Everything checked out until Brownlee retrieved the tally sheet for Box 13.

The total is different for Box 13, Brownlee announced to the committee. On election night the precinct reported 765 for Lyndon Johnson. The total was now 965. Stevenson's total was 62.

"It looks like someone has marked over the 7 and turned it into a 9," Brownlee noted as he checked the signature sheet. Sure enough, the number of names on the sheet matched the number of votes cast.

Jake was on his feet and pacing around the table like an angry cat. He and Edith Maude had been at Nayer School almost two days while Luis Salas drug out the vote count. When they finally left Monday night, the total for Johnson had been 765. Stevenson had gotten 60 votes.

"Are you going to certify that this is the vote?" he demanded. "This is the most blatant tampering with a voting box I've ever seen. Surely an investigation..."

"Jake," Brownlee said sharply, "I don't need to remind you that you are an observer and not a participant."

"But I was there. The total for Johnson was 765; I heard Salas say it. Dear Lord, man, it took Salas two days to count the votes. He must have counted them sideways and backwards to take that long. It doesn't take a genius to figure out something is seriously wrong here."

Brownlee removed his glasses and wearily rubbed his eyes.

"Jake, we're going to adjourn here in a minute. And as soon as we do, I'm going to go into the clerk's office and call the Election Bureau. I'm going to tell them that the count for Jim Wells has gone up by 202 votes, with Lyndon Johnson getting 200 of those votes."

It was clear there was no use protesting any more. Tom Donald was firmly in control.

It was not until that night that Jake learned what Box 13 meant to the election. A friend at the Election Bureau in Austin called him and told him the news. Box 13 had given Lyndon Johnson the boost he needed. With all boxes reporting and the count 100 percent complete, the congressman had beaten the former governor by 87 votes. Out of nearly a million votes cast, Lyndon Johnson had won by less than one hundredth of one percent.

Jake was in his office when the phone call came. It was early evening, and everyone had gone home. In the quiet, Jake sat, pondering the week's events. He had been right about this election. He had been right about Box 13. And he was right about something else. The fight for the U.S. Senate seat had just begun.

Chapter 4

Jake Floyd strolled through the long central corridor that spanned the rear of the Alice Bank & Trust Co. It was 7:45 A.M., and he had already been at the bank an hour, going over the day's previous loan applications.

That was how every workday started for Jake, going over those loan papers. He would wake up by 6 A.M., don his shower cap and step into a hot shower. As he showered, he would sing loudly and off-key, a habit that embarrassed Edith Maude and Buddy when they were teen-agers. Edith, his wife, had gotten so used to it she barely noticed the racket from the upstairs bathroom. She had gotten so she didn't notice when her husband screamed at the end of his shower either. He would turn the hot water off and turn a blast of cold water on. It closed his pores, he claimed.

A meticulous dresser, Jake wore monogrammed white shirts special-ordered from a tailor in St. Louis. His arms were so long and his frame so spare that shirts off the rack engulfed him like a nightshirt. His closet held a half dozen high quality suits. He would wear one suit all week and then pull the next one off the closet rod the following Monday morning.

After a breakfast of homemade biscuits, bacon and eggs, Jake would head to the bank building. He had helped bring the bank back to stability after it failed during the Depression. At Jake's urging, some of his wealthier clients invested in the bank—

folks like Tom and Arthur East, whose family fortunes were rooted in the King Ranch empire; rancher and oil man A.C. Canales of Premont; and the Cuellar brothers, who also had oil and land holdings in Duval County. With deposits from Jake's clients, who also served on the Alice Bank & Trust board, the bank moved from mere solvency to a solid bottom line.

On this September day in 1948, like he always did, Jake climbed the stairs at the back of the bank to his second-floor office. The law offices of Perkins & Floyd occupied the bank's second floor; oddly enough, it was directly across Main Street from the Parr-controlled Texas State Bank.

Jake's office was sparsely furnished, almost austere. There was a wide mahogany desk and a couple of leather-backed chairs. The floor was bare linoleum, and one wall was lined with shelves of his law books. Jake's office reflected his own tastes and didn't intimidate the Mexicans who visited him daily. The ranchers and his clients from the oil companies—Magnolia and Humble—seemed comfortable enough in those leather chairs.

The other three walls were mostly bare. There was a painting of some rusted farm implements nestled in a sea of bluebonnets and stacked against a gray shed. And there was a photograph of Jake in a belted Army uniform. He wore jodhpurs and knee-high boots and stood in a valley in Turkey. The photo was a fond reminder of the years Jake had spent in Europe during World War I. The Army almost didn't take him, he was so skinny. He was 6-feet-1 and weighed only 113 pounds. But eventually he gained a little weight and volunteered, spending two years as an attaché to an Army general.

Jake's secretary, Betty Foster, was constantly emptying the heavy marble ashtray on his desk. Jake smoked several cigars a day, and his visitors added their own residue to the tray. It was one of Betty's pet peeves, that ashtray. Keeping it clean was essential to the professional atmosphere in Jake's office, she believed. The sweetly fragrant cigar smoke troubled her as well, so she often opened the windows for a good airing out.

Jake hired Betty shortly after he began practicing law and she had been with him long enough to know all his idiosyncrasies. She knew the whereabouts of hundreds of files and even more hundreds of books. Jake could ask her for anything from an affidavit to a paper clip and she would be at his desk with the requested paraphernalia within seconds.

On a particular afternoon just a few days after Lyndon Johnson had been declared the Democratic nominee, she appeared in Jake's doorway.

"Mr. Floyd, there are some gentlemen here to see you," she said tentatively.

As she stepped aside, Coke Stevenson strode in. Broad-shouldered and tall, Stevenson took in the entire room with a sweeping gaze. He looked Jake square in the eye, and the two lawyers shook hands.

Coke was not alone. With him were three men, one readily recognizable to Jake. He was a hulk of a man, and as if his height and 200-plus pound body weren't imposing enough, a gun belt was strapped around his thick waist. He wore cowboy boots and a Stetson, and Jake recognized him immediately as famed former Texas Ranger Frank Hamer.

Jake knew Coke and Frank Hamer had been allies for decades. Coke once told Jake that when he was county attorney back in Junction, he and the burly Texas Ranger hunted down cattle rustlers together in the brush country. Hamer went on to become as feared as he was famous. The most celebrated case of his career ended in the bloody gun battle deaths of the notorious bank robbers Bonnie Parker and Clyde Barrow.

Coke introduced the other two gentlemen with him. The slight man of medium height was Kellis Dibrell, and the youngish, big-boned man with balding hair, Jake learned, was James

Gardner. Both were lawyers from San Antonio, and both were former FBI agents. Jake had heard that Coke and his men were in town and that their mission was to get a firsthand look at the polling list for Box 13. Jake braced to hear if they had seen the list.

"It was doctored, Jake; no doubt about it," Coke said of the list, a dour look settling onto his thin lips. Then he recounted the events of the past hour. It sounded like a scene straight out of a western movie.

Coke and his three companions had walked from the Alice Hotel to Tom Donald's office at the Texas State Bank. The street, Coke said, was lined with Parr's *pistoleros* watching their every step. Main Street was dead silent save for the sound of their cowboy boots striking the pavement. Hamer, the only one of the four out-of-towners who was armed, kept his right hand poised over his holstered Colt .45. The gunmen and the curious seemed to melt into the sidewalks as Hamer approached.

Once they were inside the bank, Tom Donald grudgingly agreed to let the men look at the lists. But he refused to let Dibrell and Gardner write down any names. The lawyers memorized a few names and noticed that the last 200 or so on the list were written in the same blue ink. The handwriting looked the same, too.

"Dammit, Jake," Coke said, "we've got to get a court order so we can look at that tally sheet." His eyes had the steely look that had earned him the nickname Calculatin' Coke.

Jake wondered if Lyndon Johnson knew what he had taken on in a man like Coke Stevenson. Here was a man who was largely self-educated. He had had very little formal schooling and had taught himself the law, bookkeeping, architecture and government.

He had the kind of profile that Texans respected and identified with. He had grown up in poverty and went to work at the age of 10 to help his father support the family. By the time he was 21, he had dug ditches, built fences and herded cattle. No wonder his other nickname was "Mr. Texas."

"Did you come away with any names at all?" Jake asked.

Kellis Dibrell rifled through his briefcase and pulled out a small leather-bound notebook.

"Recognize any of these?" the one-time G-man asked, handing the notebook to Jake. There were about a dozen names scribbled on the pad.

"Might check the cemetery," Jake said, a rueful smile on his lips. "No, sir, I don't, and I know just about everybody in these parts. I do know this fellow, Eugenio Soliz. He's a construction worker ... does highway work. He's the only one."

"Time's not on our side," Coke said as he dipped a lighted match into the tobacco in his pipe. "Kellis and John are staying down here, and I'm sending in a team of men to check out every name we managed to get down on paper. But that's going to take more than the two days we have until the state convention."

The Democratic Party state convention was due to convene on Monday morning in Fort Worth. The party's nominee for U.S. Senate would be formally named at the convention.

"There's another option, Coke," Jake said, pressing his fingertips together. "Perhaps you haven't thought of this. The local party executive committee could reconvene and withdraw its certification of the votes."

Coke sat pensively for a moment, then drew the pipe from his lips.

"See if you can pursue that. If not, we can look at getting a court order."

"I tell you what, gentlemen," Jake said. "I'd like to help you out. You're welcome to use my office in any way you see fit. Use our law library for an office. There's a telephone in there, plenty of desk space. My secretary, Betty, will be glad to help you in any way."

After Jake showed Coke and his two lawyers the law library

and introduced them to Betty, the visitors left. Jake returned to his office and sat, lost in thought for a few moments.

It was astonishing how alike he and Coke Stevenson were. Both came up from impoverished childhoods; both had gone to work at young ages. Jake scanned his bookshelves until his eyes rested on the Texas Code of Laws. Then they fell on the painting of the farm implements. A prettier picture he couldn't imagine. This was the land that had helped him achieve his dreams.

The youngest of ten children, Jake had done what he could to save money for college. He milked cows as a youngster, and between semesters at Corpus Christi High School, he worked as a caretaker at a resort that catered to wealthy northerners who headed south in the winter.

Jake reached for a cigar, bit into its tip and spit into a trashcan. He paused to consider his young self in the photograph. During the war, he recalled, he was far removed from combat and saw much of Eastern Europe. He had been enrolled at the University of Texas when he volunteered, and when he returned from the war he had no money to pick up where he had left off.

Through friends, he heard about a job as a stenographer for Judge Perkins, Alice's most prominent lawyer. Jake was disheartened at the thought of taking another detour from his schooling, but the job with Judge Perkins proved to be more than clerical. He was really an apprentice lawyer. He got so much experience, he was able to take the state bar exam in 1920. He passed with a score in the high 90s.

Just as surely as Jake knew he was a born farmer, he knew he was a born lawyer. He believed in the law more surely than he believed in God and democracy. He was at his finest when he was cross-examining a witness or making final arguments. Folks admired the way he swung his arms like a windmill when he was making a point in the courtroom.

Like a small-town doctor who did everything from delivering babies to pronouncing people dead, Jake was a small-town lawyer who practiced nearly every form of law—oil and gas, tax, estate and criminal—and took just about any case that came his way. People from all over South Texas hired him. One of his grandest hours involved a woman who gunned down her husband as he knelt in prayer—his mistress at his side—in a Catholic church. Jake argued that she had been grievously wronged; the jury agreed and acquitted her of murder.

Despite their similarities, Jake and Coke had one glaring difference: Jake relished the political world, and Coke despised it. The irony was that Jake had never held public office, and Coke couldn't seem to stay out of public service. Jake knew the powerful, the wealthy, the influential in South Texas, and he had healthy connections in Austin. He preferred to work behind the scenes, however, raising money for candidates, recruiting poll watchers and challenging election results in the courtroom.

If Coke could have his way, he would spend his days working his ranch near Junction and practicing law. But his wife, Fay, when she was living, and the townsfolk in Junction had prevailed upon him more than once to run for one office or another. Coke was fascinated by the Constitution and by government itself. But he had no stomach for the backroom dealing and backslapping that made up the game of politics. Still, he had been county attorney, state senator, lieutenant governor and eventually governor. And until this year, he had never lost an election.

In the days following Stevenson's visit to Jake's office, the headlines thundered accusations from Stevenson and denials by Johnson. Kellis Dibrell and his companion took Jake up on his offer and could be seen coming in and out of the law office. They used the telephone for a few hours, then left, lugging heavy briefcases and a portable typewriter. The typewriter would go into use if they found any so-called Box 13 voter willing to sign an affidavit.

They did find one such voter, Eugenio Soliz. His name was

the last to appear on the voting list before the 201 additional suspicious names. He told the lawyers he had voted at about 6:40 P.M. When he left the Nayer School, no other voters were waiting to cast ballots. Dibrell and Gardner tracked down several other names from their memorized list. None of those people had voted, and three were dead.

As for the county executive committee meeting, it never happened. Lyndon's lawyers persuaded a judge in Austin to issue a restraining order barring the committee from meeting. The committee members, the lawyers said, were conspiring to throw out the votes from Box 13.

"Balderdash." That's what Coke Stevenson called Lyndon's claims when he talked to Jake that weekend.

Jake sympathized with Coke. And he was convinced that Coke wouldn't give up without a battle. After all, something had been stolen from him. Like any true Texan, Coke was going to bring the guilty bastards to justice.

So Coke had his lawyers persuade a federal judge from Fort Worth to impose a restraining order barring Lyndon's name from appearing on the ballot. Lyndon retaliated by appealing to Supreme Court Justice Hugo Black, who had administrative authority over the Fort Worth court. Black threw out the restraining order, and the full Supreme Court refused to consider the matter. Five weeks after the August runoff, the battle was done. Lyndon's name was placed on the November ballot, and he easily defeated the Republican candidate Jack Porter. Lyndon Johnson became a U.S. Senator, and forever was beholden to George Parr.

Section II
1949–1950

Chapter 5

It pleased Bill Mason no end that folks in Alice and San Diego called him a varmint. If people thought he was a nice guy, it meant he wasn't doing his job. Nice guys worked as grocers or machinists. A man couldn't be a nice guy and a journalist, not to Bill's way of thinking. He had to be a bit of a scoundrel to dredge up the really juicy news.

To be sure, Alice had never seen anyone like Bill Mason before he hit town in 1947. He learned the news business in the big leagues—the *New York Times* and the *San Francisco Examiner*. Like many journalists, he tried his hand at public relations, working for General Tire and Rubber Company for a time. One of his favorite positions was as an investigator for Earl Warren, the district attorney in Alameda County, California.

When Mason moved to Texas, it was to take a job as state editor at the *San Antonio Light*. After only a couple of years in San Antonio, he decided to move to Alice, where he could be a street reporter again. That was what he loved. His title at the *Alice Daily Echo* was managing editor, which meant he could write editorials.

It was Mason's own brand of journalism that sparked the trouble. He had a way of writing articles that were half opinion, half fact. They would appear on the front page of the *Echo*, not on the editorial page. The article that caused the biggest ruckus was about the Taxpayer League. Mason decided the group needed investigating after several members filed property tax protests with the county and the school board. Some of Alice's most prominent citizens were in the league. When Mason asked for a list of members, he was turned down. In no time, the president of the league paid a call on the editor of the *Echo*, V. D. Ringwald. Mason had no respect for Ringwald. He was a real milquetoast. The man had shown guts for a while, writing editorials every day on the evils of the Parr empire. But when a Parr deputy assaulted him in broad daylight on a street corner, Ringwald put away his fiery pen. There would be no more investigation of the Taxpayer League, Ringwald informed Mason. Well, no publisher was going to muzzle Bill Mason, not with all the corruption in Duval and Jim Wells.

So Mason turned in his resignation, marched down the street to KBKI-Radio, and bought some radio time. "Bill Mason Speaks" was a half-hour commentary that aired at noon every Monday through Friday. He made it sound like a news program, but it was really Bill Mason's opinions.

"Eat hearty, folks, this is Bill Mason with the news," people got used to hearing every day as they sat down to chicken-fried steak and black-eyed peas.

A lot of people didn't take Mason seriously. His bombastic tirades were viewed as nothing more than entertainment. No one got greater enjoyment out of the radio programs than Mason's favorite target, George Parr. George could have put a stop to it all if he had wanted to. After all, his lawyer Ed Lloyd co-owned KBKI-Radio.

But George would rather sit around with his cronies, drinking soda pop at the Windmill Cafe, and wisecrack about the broadcasts.

"Say, Meek," he would say to Walter Meek, Jr., "Hear about Mason's latest? He's camping out by the water tower every night—thinks he'll catch kids painting graffiti."

Mason was 52 by the time he started the radio broadcasts on KBKI. For all his worldly experience, he didn't look the part. He was wide-eyed, bewildered looking most of the time. Short and stocky, he had dark, wavy hair and a pronounced widow's peak. His lips curled downward, concealing a gap between his two front teeth.

Bill's causes were many. He talked about city sanitation, proper policing of the local meatpacking plants, care of vacant lots, city and county politics. Jim Wells County Sheriff Hubert Sain, he once told his audience, was making quite a tidy profit off a building he was renting to the county. The commissioners, Mason urged, ought to look into the matter.

Sain, who was a Parr man, didn't take kindly to the ribbing he got from that broadcast. One of Sain's deputies, Charles Brand, cornered Mason on a downtown street one morning, and an argument ensued. The two men scuffled; Mason's belt broke, and his pants fell to the sidewalk. In a gesture of defiance, Mason draped his pants on a lamppost.

When he went on the air later that day, Bill Mason was indignant:

"This morning, I was the target of a vicious attack by a man sworn to uphold the law. Deputy Sheriff Charles Brand accosted me and physically attacked me. This is an outrage—an obvious retaliation for a report earlier this week. In that exclusive story, I reported that Sheriff Sain is having questionable dealings with the county. If the Sheriff's hands are clean, why would one of his deputies attack me?

"I ask you, my faithful listeners, do we enjoy the protections of the Bill of Rights in Jim Wells—in Duval? No, ladies and gentlemen, we do not. It's clear to me we're becoming a police state. If our citizens cannot be safe from attack by our own law enforcement officers, then we had better vote these jackals out of town.

"One more thing before I sign off. This incident today will not halt the cause of truth. My faithful listeners, be assured that 'Bill Mason Speaks' will forge ahead. We will not be bullied.

Anyone who wants to see if I'm serious can meet me under the lamppost in front of the Alice Hotel."

No one took up Mason on the challenge.

Now it was late July 1949, and Mason had a new cause: Sam Smithwick. The Jim Wells County deputy sheriff was, according to Mason's investigation, the owner of a beer and dance hall on the San Diego highway just outside of town. The girls who worked at Rancho Allegro, Mason claimed, sold more than beers and dances.

Mason talked to his audience about Rancho Allegro as if he had made an archeological discovery. But the one-story beer hall offered nothing more than a long bar, some tables and a few booths. If "loose women plied their trade" there, as Mason claimed, they had to take their clients elsewhere.

Rancho Allegro was a nest egg of sorts for Sam Smithwick. He was 60 years old and had spent much of his life in law enforcement. He had been a constable in Duval County before moving to Alice and becoming a deputy sheriff under Sain.

Half Mexican, Smithwick could neither read nor write English, but he spoke the language rather courtly. In his younger days, he had been something of a legend. He was known as probably the best "brush popper" ever in South Texas, showing great skill in flushing wild steer out of dense underbrush.

Sam couldn't understand why that Mason fellow was after him. Even though he was a Parr man in Alice, Sam was also known as a gentle giant. He might be big enough to wrestle those wild steers he once chased, but he could be as gallant as he was tough. The ladies in Alice had long since lost their fear of his imposing figure. He greeted them softly when he passed them on the street. And when he met a lady in person, he would gently remove his *sombrero*, hold it to his ample chest, and bow from the waist.

Sam's father was Irish, and his mother was Mexican, which accounted for his fairer complexion and his Latin culture. He was married to a Mexican woman who spoke no English, but she could whip out the best homemade tortillas and chili con carne de puerco that Sam ever swallowed. They had seven children, most of them grown and raising their own families. Sam lost count of how many grandchildren he had—about 25, he estimated, when folks asked. Sam had a mistress, too. She lived on the south side of Alice not far from Rancho Allegro.

By the 30th of July, Mason was on another tirade. The roads in southern Jim Wells County were atrocious and needed attention from the commissioners court. He had put aside the Rancho Allegro story for the time being. No one ever figured out where Sam Smithwick got the idea that Bill Mason was going to mention one of his children in his broadcast that day.

That morning Mason sat at his desk, an Army-issue gray metal table, working on his remarks for the upcoming broadcast. The day before, he had been out to the Tex-Mex Depot to see Luis Salas. Among his many duties in Jim Wells, Salas was telegraph operator at the train depot. It was Salas who brought Mason's attention to the sorry shape of the roads across the tracks in Mexican town. They had traveled the potholed roads together, and Mason had visited Commissioner Dan Scruggs to talk about their shameful condition.

Mason was writing his script when the telephone interrupted. "Bill, honey," the female voice said. It was Vera, his wife. She was breathless.

"I just got a phone call from a woman. Wouldn't give her name. Said she'd overheard a conversation. She told me my husband's in danger, then hung up."

Mason cradled the telephone between his cheek and shoulder while he sharpened a pencil. After more than 25 years of marriage, he had hoped Vera would get used to the threats. But they still unnerved her.

"Now, Vera, we've been through this a thousand times," he

said. "Just hang up. Just hang up."

He rarely succeeded in soothing her. So he listened to her for a few minutes and rang off. He was going to say something about these threatening phone calls on the air. Vera never listened to the broadcasts, so he needn't worry about upsetting her further.

"To my opponents and critics," Mason said as a postscript to his show that day, "I want to say that hardly a day goes by that I don't get some kind of threat. This morning, my dear wife received a phone call threatening my life. Well, I'll thank you to leave my innocent wife out of this.

"Anyone wants to threaten me, call me here at KBKI. The number's 2144. If you want to threaten me, just call me up. But don't be a coward and call my wife."

That said, Mason signed off and left the station in his black sedan. He wanted to see if anything had been done about the roads in Mexican town. On his way, he picked up Avelino Saenz, who shared Luis Salas' discontent with the road situation. If anyone could get the roads fixed in Mexican town, Saenz believed it was Bill Mason.

Saenz, a tall, thirty-ish fellow, grew up in Alice and was a store clerk by day, a student by night. He wanted to get his high school diploma and had dreams of becoming a barber. It would be a long time before he could move his family to the nicer part of town. Getting the roads fixed on the south side would make the area easier to navigate at the very least.

The two men cruised down the San Diego Highway at a leisurely speed, and just as they entered the warehouse district, Mason noticed a cherry red pickup truck heading in their direction. An enormous man was behind the wheel, and he motioned out the window for Mason and Saenz to stop. Mason pulled off the highway and into the dirt-packed yard next to a warehouse. The truck stopped parallel, and Sam Smithwick emerged.

The deputy's belly swelled over his gun belt, and he yanked

his pants up as he walked to Mason's car. A .45 revolver was holstered on his hip, and he was walking fast.

"Are you Mr. Mason?" Smithwick asked, his voice trembling. Perspiration beaded on his forehead underneath his *sombrero*. Sweat rings stained the armpits of his khaki shirt. Mason was eye and nose level with the armpits as Smithwick cast a shadow over the driver's window.

"Sure am, Mister," Mason answered, leaning away from the window.

"Name's Smithwick," the hulk said, stooping down to look inside the vehicle. His right hand was on the .45.

"Mister," he said, addressing Saenz, "You better get out of the way."

Saenz didn't hesitate. In a flash, he was out the passenger door and stepping away from the car.

"Why you go and say all those things on the radio about me?" Smithwick whined to Mason. "You just some mean son-bitch or—"

"Just doing a job," Mason said. He slid over on the seat and held his hand up as if to deflect a punch. "Nothing personal, sir, just doing a job."

"Ain't no call for you t'go and do that. Ain't no call. Nice little business I got out there," Smithwick said, motioning to the west. "Ain't hurtin' nobody. It's all I got, and you gotta ruin it—"

The gun was out of the holster, and Smithwick was aiming it at Mason.

"Now, sir, let's talk," Mason said, leaning still farther away from the deputy. "Put it away . . . "

Smithwick fired once, and the bullet cut through Mason's chest. The impact knocked him backward onto the seat, but he sat right back up, amazed that all he felt was a jolt. He saw red ooze on his shirt just below the pocket. The gun was still pointed at him. He had to get out of the car, he thought.

Smithwick pulled the trigger again, but the .45 clicked dead. He squeezed the gun harder, but it did not fire. The delay gave Mason time to make his way out the passenger side and crawl underneath the car.

Saenz stood 20 feet away, witness to the whole thing. But he started running toward a tavern when Smithwick got the revolver firing again. A bullet zinged by his leg.

The deputy shot wildly at Mason, who dragged himself out from under the car and crawled underneath the red pickup truck. Five, six shots, Mason counted. He made a run for a low wire fence and climbed over it.

"Help!" he shouted at a man on the cement dock just ahead. "I'm Bill Mason. Help me, please!"

Smithwick reholstered the .45, lunged back into his truck and thundered off in a hurry, dust and gravel flying in the wake of his tires.

Mason collapsed on the dock, his white shirt turning crimson front and back. When Smithwick was out of firing range, Saenz ran for the dock, shouting at the man standing there.

"Help me get him in the car!" Avelino said.

"Mr. Mason? Mr. Mason?" He lifted the wounded man's head. Mason did not respond, but a vein still pulsed on his neck. Saenz hoisted Mason up and dragged him to the sedan; the worker on the dock was speechless, too stunned to do anything but open the car door.

Saenz drove wildly down the streets of Alice, arriving at the hospital within six minutes. He must have known it was no use.

"The bullet must have passed through an artery right by his heart," the doctor told him.

Word of the killing moved like a thunderstorm across town. Jake was at Dena's Cafe having coffee with Clarence Perkins, the judge's brother and his law partner, when the county clerk, Hap Holmgreen, came in with the news. It was all over the courthouse, Hap said. Sam had turned himself in to Sheriff Sain.

"He just walked into the jailhouse, picked up a key and locked himself in a cell," Hap said. "Beats everything."

"Can't say I'm surprised," Jake said, gnawing on a very long unlit cigar. "About the killing, I mean. Sam's not the smartest man. He probably thought Mason could actually do him harm."

"From what I've heard, Jake, the sheriff was getting pressure to shut that joint down," Hap said.

"Maybe," Jake said. "But there isn't much of a chance Smithwick will get indicted. Not with Judge Broeter running the courthouse."

Lorenz Broeter was a Parr man, had been for all 35 years he had been on the district court bench. Everyone knew that district judges control grand juries in Texas, and Judge Broeter's grand juries had never indicted a Parr man.

"Don't be so sure," Hap said. A lock of brown hair drifted onto his forehead. He was of medium height and slight and wore horn-rimmed glasses.

"Judge Broeter's been acting strange lately," he said, ordering coffee from the waitress. "You'd never know him, the way he whistles all the time. Why, he used to mope around that courthouse all day, not a word or a smile for anybody."

Jake snorted.

"Whistlin' proves nothing, Hap."

"It's not just that," Hap said, sitting up stiffly. "I hear tell he turned down a motion Frank Lloyd filed last week in some case. Now, that's never happened—not in my recollection."

Jake lit the cigar. Dena's was filling up with afternoon coffee drinkers. It was always crowded when there was big news in town to gossip about. He decided to drink up and head back to the office.

"Gotta go," he said, reaching for his hat on the seat beside him.

"If I was a betting man," Hap said, "I'd wager Smithwick goes down on this one. Why, they'll have to indict him, Jake. It happened in broad daylight. There were witnesses . . ."

"Maybe," Jake said. "Be seeing you, Hap. Clarence, see you, too."

***

Main Street in Alice was deserted by mid-afternoon that day. The shopkeepers closed up, and the businessmen went to Dena's. The housewives stayed home.

The men crowded around tables at Dena's, talking in hushed voices as if fearful that someone might hear them. The waitresses kept the coffeepots brewing and the cups filled. By 3 o'clock, they were out of pecan pie and chocolate cake.

At the Windmill Cafe in San Diego, business was jumping as well, but another atmosphere prevailed. The beer was flowing.

"Say, Hal," said one overall-clad fellow who had sipped a few brews, "suppose ol' Smithwick'd take care of a few o' my bill collectors?"

"Why, sure," was the response. "But be sure and tell him not to shoot 'em in broad daylight!"

"Whoa!" said another beer drinker. "You'll have to do your own killin'. Sam'll be too busy guardin' his henhouse!"

A beer-chased round of laughter roared across the table.

At George Parr's office next door, the Duke of Duval got the news from Walter Meek, Jr. "That stupid sonofa . . ." George said. "He can rot in jail for all I care. He thinks I'm gonna get him outa this—he'd better think again!"

George picked up a leaded glass paperweight, the one Lt. Gov. Allan Shivers had given him, and slammed it on his desk. It turned into a spider web of cracks but held together.

"What the hell's wrong with Hubert? Can't he keep his

deputies in line?" George asked, staring out the window.

Walter sat placidly in a wingback, dressed perfectly as usual in his pinstripes. He knew better than to try to talk sense to George right away. Let him cool down first. The two men had been friends all their lives, and they shared mutual respect that had weathered the years. Walter, who inherited his wealth, did not participate in George's regime. He didn't need to. But he regarded George as the best friend a man could have.

"Hubert's a fool sometimes, George," he said, his voice even. "But let him handle it."

George picked up the paperweight and shook his head. "No tellin' what he'll do. Why, that town'll go wild. Mason's a goddam martyr."

"Not to mention Smithwick's a laughingstock," Walter said in a monotone.

George had just gotten a toe-hold in Jim Wells County with Hubert Sain's election to sheriff. He didn't need one of Hubert's fool deputies lousing things up.

George ranted for a few more minutes, and Walter listened, his composure undisturbed.

"They'll be expecting you at the Windmill," Walter reminded George. George picked up his felt hat, and the two men walked next door.

When they walked into the cafe, George flashed a big grin and shook hands with the men in his path. He headed straight for the checkered-cloth-covered table reserved for him in the middle of the restaurant.

"The usual, Maisie," he called out to the waitress, who nodded and grabbed a coffee cup for Walter and a soda for George.

"We've got some celebrating to do!" George bellowed. "That varmint Mason is going six feet under!"

***

Sam Smithwick mopped up the last of the gravy with a slice of white bread and shoved it in his mouth. Food in the county jail's pretty good, he thought, setting the empty plate on the cell floor by the door. Nothing like roast mutton and mashed potatoes to satisfy a hungry man. The only thing better might be his wife's chili con carne and some of her fresh tortillas.

He rubbed his bulging belly as he sat back on the bare mattress, resting his head on the wall. He was wearing the same khaki pants and shirt he had worn when he checked into the jail. A few tiny drops of blood stained his shirt and tie. The sweat rings on his armpits had expanded. It was hot, no air moving in the jail cell.

It was Saturday night, the day after the killing. Smithwick thought George Parr would have sent a lawyer over to the jail, but nobody had come. Oh, well, still plenty of time for that. The first time he'd go before a judge would be Monday morning.

The food made him drowsy. He wished the other fellows in the neighboring cells would hold down the clatter. That was another thing about the jail. It was too noisy to get enough sleep.

"Say, Smithwick," a Mexican fellow in the next cell said in Spanish. "You sure caused a lot of trouble. The whole town's riled up. They're going to get you a gun to protect yourself!"

The other inmates laughed at the joke, but Smithwick sat expressionless on the bunk.

The main door to the cellblock opened, and Deputy Charlie Brand appeared with a ring of keys.

"C'mon, Sam," he said, "you're being transferred."

Charlie handcuffed his prisoner, and Smithwick trotted out of the jail like a well-fed puppy dog. Once he was in the patrol car with Charlie and Hubert, they headed down the highway toward Corpus Christi.

"Hate to tell you this, kid," Hubert said. Hubert called

everybody 'kid.' "But a carload of wild Indians drove by Rancho Allegro tonight and shot up the place."

Smithwick was silent.

"Nobody got hurt, but the front of the place has a slew of bullet holes," the sheriff went on. "Good thing it's made out of concrete blocks. Otherwise some folks on the inside might've gotten hurt."

Smithwick wanted to know if the "wild Indians," as Hubert called them, had been arrested.

"Nah," the sheriff said. He wasn't driving, so he waved his hand outside the open window. "They drove off before anybody knew what was happening. Didn't even get a plate number.

"The town's gone wild since yesterday, Sam. Folks are either locking themselves up in their houses or they're carrying guns everywhere. Called in a couple Rangers to help us out. We're short, kid, without you on the force.

"I been hearing rumors some vigilante group was planning a raid on the jail. That's why we're taking you to the jail in Corpus."

Smithwick sank low into the back seat. He couldn't think of a word to say. He wondered if the food in the Corpus jail was any good.

***

The funeral was Sunday. It was standing room only at First Presbyterian Church in Alice. Friends as well as the curious jammed into the sanctuary and wilted in the August heat. The ceiling fans stirred up a bit of air, and the mourners fanned their faces with hand-held fans supplied by the mortuary.

The folks who peered in the windows from the outside were a bit cooler. A Gulf breeze offered some relief from the relentless sun.

News that a reporter had been killed in the line of duty spread all over the country, luring dozens of journalists to Alice. Writers fought for seats in the church, and photographers hovered around the doorway outside.

The gleaming black casket was closed; an enormous spray of flowers rested upon it. The altar was buried in what looked like a field of fragrant flowers.

Frank Lloyd delivered the eulogy.

"As co-owner of KBKI radio, I must say the report of Bill Mason's death hit me like a ton of bricks," he said. "It is very, very unfortunate that this had to happen. I hardly know what to say at a time like this.

"I feel like he has gone down for the right to say what he thought was right. One of the principles on which this nation is founded is freedom of speech, that a man should be allowed that privilege without being shot for it."

The church's pastor, the Rev. Andrews Byers, had this to say:

"I speak as a man who respected Bill Mason's abilities and courage and did not like his weaknesses. He had his good points and his faults, as do we all. We know the things of his life that he set out to do and did do, and we know the failures. There remains little to be said in the way of an obituary.

"This should be a period of the calmest, quietest, most reflective thinking we have ever done. The light of the world has centered on our community. From this moment on, we should chart the way of the Lord."

Vera Mason asked Luis Salas to say a few words, too.

"We, the residents of the South Side, want to extend our heartfelt sympathy to Mrs. Mason and the family . . . Bill was born to be a great leader among us. He had many friends on the South Side." Luis recalled that Mason stayed on the air all night once during flooding that threatened the streets of the South Side.

"Not everybody has the courage to deal with this kind of

work, and believe me, Bill had what it takes. He never tired of hearing of our necessities and wants."

The funeral seemed to be a rite of passage for the citizens of Alice. Once it was over and Mason was buried, folks calmed down. Hubert decided to escort Sam Smithwick back from Corpus Christi. The sheriff there, Dan Harney, reported that Smithwick had been in a "very pleasant mood" during his stay and he "certainly had a fine appetite."

George Parr finally did send legal help for Smithwick. Nago Alaniz and Raeburn Norris, two lawyers from Alice, and Charles Lyman and Sam Pittman, both of Corpus Christi, represented him in the preliminary hearing. Smithwick pleaded innocent and was ordered held in the county jail until a grand jury could look at the case.

***

The polished, smooth boards on the corridor bench ground into Jake's knobby hip bones like saws. He longed for his favorite stuffed chair at home. He was in the Jim Wells County Courthouse, under subpoena to appear before a grand jury. The bailiff instructed him to wait just outside the deliberation room until he was called. That was 45 minutes ago, and Jake and his posterior were growing impatient.

Despite the bailiff's stern orders, Jake decided to take a brief stroll to the end of the hallway. Jake had always liked the Alice courthouse, despite its absence of architectural appeal. Twin turrets topped the north and south entrances, incongruous ornaments to what otherwise would have resembled an Ivy League classroom building.

A silver dome bearing a Texas flag crowned the two-story sandy brick structure, which housed the county clerk, the district court and the tax assessor. It was the atmosphere inside that Jake loved. Telephones sounded distantly, a murmur of soft voices drifted through the transoms of the various offices, and the whole place had a cool, clean feel. The smell of ammonia laced the air. The building had an air of efficiency and order, and Jake felt at home.

The lawyer nodded at Judge Martineau, who nodded in reply as he strode by. It would be improper for the two men to speak, although they knew each other well.

Paul Martineau, beak-nosed, large-eyed and lanky, had called the grand jury into session. Originally a lawyer from Corpus Christi, he stepped into the district judgeship at the request of Judge Lorenz Broeter after Broeter learned he had prostate cancer. His buddy George Parr had made several suggestions, but Lorenz had ignored them all. He appointed Judge Martineau, a Wisconsin native who had been in Corpus Christi 20 years. He had been a judge there for six. He and George were members of the same country club; other than that, they had no connection.

Jake knew Lorenz well; he had tried several cases under him. He had seen Parr's lawyer Ed Lloyd bully Lorenz to the point of tears in a crowded courtroom. It looked like Hap had been right. Judge Broeter had made a declaration of independence from George Parr.

Martineau, once he assumed the district bench in Alice, wasted no time naming a trio of grand jury commissioners. When the grand jury assembled, it was packed with reformers—Harry Lee Adams, Wash Storm, Jr., T. E. Breedlove and Coman Shear, W. A. Cobb of Premont, H. J. Baca of Orange Grove and W. L. Smith of Sandia. None felt allegiance to Parr.

Martineau gave them carte blanche that went beyond the Smithwick case. "Investigate the beer taverns operating in violation of the law and the houses of prostitution. If you do this, you will go a long way toward stopping the shootings in this county," he instructed.

In short order, the grand jury indicted Smithwick for murder. The panel said they wanted to continue working. They began calling witnesses, questioning them about Box 13. The jurors interviewed Frank Lloyd, Luis Salas, and Bruno Goldapp, vice president of Alice Bank & Trust. Then they summoned Jake.

"Howdy, Jake." Ike Poole sauntered down the hallway, extending a hand. Ike smiled a lot, but underneath, Jake usually sensed something sobering was on his mind. "Grand jury?" he said, nodding his head in the direction of the deliberation room.

"That's right," Jake said. "Box 13."

Jake plucked a cigar stub from his lips and tapped it on the rim of an ashtray, the kind that perched on a stand. "Never thought I'd live to see this day, Ike."

It had been almost a year since Box 13 made Alice famous. After the Supreme Court refused to intervene and Lyndon Johnson was named the Democratic nominee for U.S. Senate, Jake and Kellis Dibrell launched a legal campaign to get the courts to reopen the inquiry. They pored over thousands of cases and interviewed dozens of men and women, but it went for naught.

"You sound like you think something might come of this," Ike said, joining him on the bench.

"Let's just say I'm optimistic," the lawyer said, sitting down again. Too much time had gone by since Box 13. Tracks had been covered.

"Kellis was down here yesterday," Jake said, referring to Coke Stevenson's lawyer. "He got subpoenaed, but they never got around to talking to him. Went back to San Antonio last night."

"Guess you heard about the Smithwick indictment," Ike said. "Bet ol' George is scrambling to get that one thrown out."

"George is losing his grip, that's for certain," Jake said, "what with Lorenz off the bench. My guess is he never expected Sam to get indicted."

Jake stood up. His bones needed a rest from the bench.

"That Mason was a strange bird, wasn't he?"

Ike nodded. "Didn't do the cause much good," he said. "Seemed more ego than anything else."

"But nobody deserves to get gunned down like that." Jake was pacing. "Have you listened to the show since he died?"

Mason's son Burton had taken over the noontime slot, but he hadn't the verve of his father. And he hadn't the journalistic, ink-in-his-veins instincts of Bill Mason.

"Once or twice," Ike said.

The door to the grand jury room opened, and Hector Cerda stepped into the hallway. Dressed in pants and shirt too generous for his slender girth, Cerda glanced at Jake and Ike, hesitated a moment, and then turned and strode toward the courthouse exit.

Cerda's name appeared on the Box 13 polling list, but he had told Kellis Dibrell's investigators he did not vote in the 1948 election. He couldn't have. He was attending classes 30 miles away at Texas A&I College in Kingsville that day.

"Mr. Floyd." The door to the grand jury room was ajar and all Jake could see was the bailiff's blond head. "You can come in now, Mr. Floyd."

Jake shook Ike's hand and disappeared behind the opaque glass of the jury room door.

Chapter 6

George grinned as he looked out the rear window of his *hacienda*. A group of college students splashed around in his swimming pool. The young men were trim young bucks, just like he had been at that age. And the girls...well, the *Alice Daily Echo* couldn't print what George was thinking about those girls. The occasion was a party his nephew Archer Parr was throwing for some of his friends. Summer vacation was almost over, and Archer would be heading back to law school soon. An invitation to a party at George's was rarely turned down. George was a perfect host. The kitchen help laid out a spread to rival the White House. Beef and turkey and ham; homemade corn tortillas wrapped around beans and cheese; soft, chewy, kitchen-baked cookies; and tubs of iced down colas and root beers.

Sometimes when Archer had a party, George would bring the horses out and parade them in the corral. Other times, he would invite Archer's friends to the track to watch a couple of races. But today, George's nephew and friends seemed content to play water volleyball and toss each other in the pool.

To George, Archer was the son he never had. He was his sister Marie's boy, born of a young marriage that ended shortly after the baby's birth. Senator Archie had adopted the boy, his namesake, and that was how he came by the Parr name. Archer grew up at the senator's knee and had already been big-game hunting with his Uncle George. He was the only one of the grandchildren who showed a hint of interest in politics. Young Archer was already on the slow track to becoming the next Duke of Duval.

He was a good deal taller than George and didn't really favor his uncle in looks. His hair was dark, his face long and his prominent ears were like jug handles. He was smart, and all indications were that he would sail through law school and return to Duval to help run the regime.

As George scanned the swimmers, he frowned at the sight of Buddy Floyd. Talk about jug ears. That kid would have to wear a hat every day of his life to keep them from flapping in the wind. But take away those ears and he was a fair looking boy. Straight blond hair, blue eyes, fair skin—tall and gangly like his father. He even walked like Jake, swinging those long arms like he was in training to take over Perkins & Floyd.

From what George had heard, that was precisely the plan. Buddy was heading for law school at the University of Texas, where Archer was going. Word was that when he graduated, he would sign on at Perkins & Floyd. The possum grin crept across George's face. Jake Floyd would throw a rod if he knew where his son was at this moment.

Young Buddy was engaged in a vigorous splashing match with one of the girls. Ever since high school, when Buddy first came to the *hacienda*, he had reveled in water games. He was certainly not a chip off the old block. He was the class clown. Archer had told George some of the stories, about how Buddy and his friends stole a watermelon off a moving truck as they passed it on the highway to Corpus Christi. They got arrested for that prank.

Buddy ran around with Beb Lloyd, Frank Lloyd's son, Barbara Sain, Hubert's daughter, and Bobby Wright, Halsey's son. Those kids from Alice seemed oblivious to the politics going on right in front of them. Entertainment must be hard to come by in Alice, George thought, because these kids spent Friday nights standing on bridges and dropping watermelons on trains passing below. There were other stories about Buddy Floyd, about how he and his friends put a dead jackrabbit in their English teacher's desk. George had to hand it to the kid. He had it all over the old man when it came to having a good time.

But there was one thing about the kid George couldn't understand. It was his religion. From what Archer had said, Buddy was a bigger Baptist than his father. The old man was a deacon and a Sunday School teacher, but he didn't go around trying to save lost souls. It seemed Buddy was the evangelist of the family. He believed in God and Jesus Christ, and he said so. Archer said he wasn't obnoxious about it, but he could sure turn on that Baptist lingo if you asked him. George couldn't stand that kind of stuff.

The splashing match between Buddy and the girl was over, and the two climbed out of the pool together. They had come as a couple to the party. Archer said the girl's name was Elinor, and she was Buddy's girlfriend. She went to Baylor, where Buddy was going to undergraduate school.

Buddy draped a long, skinny arm around her small shoulders. She was a delicate thing, small-boned, with wavy dark hair. George could tell by the way she looked at Buddy that she was smitten. He tried to remember his own college days and wondered if he had been that love-struck.

He certainly had had a more mature physique in those days than the Floyd kid. He played football in high school, delaying graduation until he was 20 so he could have two more years of eligibility at Corpus Christi High. As hard as he had tried, he did not make the team at Southwestern University, the Methodist school in Georgetown, outside Austin, where his mother had attended college. At 5 foot 6, he was too short to make the roster.

As it turned out, college hadn't been for George. His tenure at Southwestern was short-lived. He slipped out of town one night after being accused of leaking team plays and strategies to a gridiron opponent. The opposing team won by 76 points. George had brief enrollments at the University of Texas and Texas A&M, but he never graduated. He did attend law school through the University of Texas, but never finished that either. He passed the state bar, but he never practiced law.

Hell, George thought, when he was Buddy and Archer's age, he was wasting time in Tampico. He had gone down with some buddies from San Diego who wanted to find jobs in the oil field. George went to have a good time. George thought about all those whores in that lusty seaport. Rumor was that there were 3,000 of them, and he had met as many as he could in the two months he was there.

As much as he liked watching the girls in the pool, George decided to head to the racetrack. He hadn't been able to interest the kids in a race, so he decided to take in a few himself. When he arrived at the track, the sun was burning hot in the sky. He grabbed a bottle of red soda pop and drained half of it in two swallows. Damn sure tasted good on a hot day like today. He made a note to himself to have the county crews build an awning over his box at the track. A little shade would make these blistering afternoons a little more tolerable.

He leaned forward on the bleacher, elbows on his knees, and admired the track. The boys had done a fine job putting the place together. They didn't know anything about quarter horses or racetracks—had never been around either. All they knew was general maintenance chores—scouring the roadsides for trash, scrubbing the courthouse and the like. But you couldn't tell by the looks of the track. George had given them a set of working drawings, and within a month they had laid out a smooth one-mile track, bleachers, a starting chute and judges' stand.

There was nothing like a fine quarter horse. Sleek and quick and powerful, quarter horses were sheer pleasure to watch. George could get lost in a race and forget about all the trouble over in

Alice. That sawed-off son of a bitch Broeter. The judge would find out real soon it didn't pay to double-cross George B. Parr.

George took advantage of a lull between races to mull over the news one of his *pistoleros* had brought him. Judge Martineau, that beak-nosed fellow from Corpus, had just turned the grand jury loose. Sent them home. They hadn't changed one vote of the 1948 primary count. So much for the Jake Floyds of this world. They could go to hell and rot with their pompous claims of fraud.

As for Sam Smithwick, he had gotten what he deserved, the old fool. The worst of it was that Martineau transferred the case to Belton upstate for trial. They had a reputation for a tough brand of justice up that way. George told the hulking deputy he would hire him a lawyer, but he had little hope Smithwick could get off or even draw a light sentence. He didn't expect those white farmers up there would look too kindly on a gun-toting Mexican who wasted a gringo in broad daylight.

The funny thing was, when Luis Salas found out that George would do no more than hire a lawyer for Smithwick, he was hotter than a case of chili powder. He came by George's office that morning and hell if he wasn't in a state. He said Smithwick had been a friend to the Parrs for more than 30 years. The Boss owed him more than just paying some damn lawyer's bill. Indio reminded George he had friends all over Texas, friends who owed him favors. Time to cash one of them in, he said.

George told him he could no more influence somebody up there around Waco—where those Baptists were running wild—than he could fly. The truth was, George could have found a way; he just didn't want to. And Indio knew it. It was hard for George to muster much sympathy for a man like Smithwick, who had let his Latin machismo run afoul of common sense.

So Indio left George's office angrier than when he had arrived. He'll get over it, George decided. He'll have to. Otherwise, there would be no more of those nocturnal deer hunting trips on the King Ranch—just the two of them. Indio was always eager to go whenever George called on him, even if it was midnight.

George would take a small machine-gun and sit on the passenger side while Indio drove. They always took one of George's older cars. He kept two vehicles, sometimes three, in the garage behind the *hacienda*. Bob Kleberg didn't keep the entire King Ranch fenced, so a hunter could sneak onto the property at night—easy—catch a few deer in the headlights and drop them at 15 feet.

Indio shared George's sense of glee at slipping onto Kleberg's famous ranch and cutting down a few deer. Indio had asked George one time why it was that he went hunting on Kleberg's ranch when he had three ranches of his own. George just smiled, and said he liked to bother his neighbor to the south. George's closer friends knew the real reason. Bob Kleberg had cost George's dad his seat in the Texas Legislature. Or at least that's the way George remembered it.

Years ago, back in the '30s, Senator Archie got into trouble with the voters when he didn't pay his taxes and the Internal Revenue Service caught him. When it came time to run for re-election, the senator's opponent was using the issue as ammunition and with great success.

Senator Archie decided if he could build a highway through the million acres that made up the King Ranch, he was sure to win re-election anyway. Folks were weary of driving 50 or a hundred miles out of their way just to go around the Kleberg empire. But Bob Kleberg wouldn't hear of it. Why, he was an absolute mule about it when Senator Archie and George paid a call on him to ask for the favor. As the Parrs left, George warned Bob Kleberg he was crucifying Archie Parr, the Duke of Duval. "I'll gut you for this if it's the last thing I do," George promised.

Even though Senator Archie paid the past-due taxes, the case proved his undoing. He lost his Senate seat and went home to the family ranch, Los Horcones, to live out his time on earth.

George wished Dad could be here to enjoy the racetrack. After the old man came back from Austin, he seemed to stop living. His eyesight failed, and a diabetic condition steadily weakened him. He died in 1942, still bitter over Kleberg's betrayal.

Ironically, Kleberg's brother Richard and a host of former governors—Coke Stevenson, James E. Ferguson, Pat Neff, Dan Moody and James Allred—were among the honorary pallbearers at Archie's funeral. George shook his head, lost in his thoughts. Yes, sir, Dad had been one powerful man in his day.

George shook his head again, hard this time, as if to toss his thoughts out onto the racetrack. A race was about to begin. There was nothing the Duke of Duval liked better—except for sweaty poker games or supple young females—than a quarter horse race. George had always loved horses. He raised a stable full of them behind his mansion. And every Sunday, he spent at San Diego Downs with his cronies. He usually went home with more cash than he had come with.

George leaned back in the wooden folding chair and took another gulp of the red soda. Perspiration beaded on his upper lip, and he rubbed it off with the back of his hand. The duke's own box was down close to the track, a few rows of bleachers behind it. Not many people at the track today, just the few George had invited. In the shade underneath the bleachers, concessions were offered free of charge to the betting clientele. It was the least George could do for his friends who wanted to play the horses with him.

As the Duke of Duval fanned himself with a newspaper, he marveled at the power in the horses as they streaked by. He recalled happily the days when he and brother Atlee used to charge across the polo field like a couple of marauding Cherokees. Their father supplied them with several cow ponies, and together with

Walter Meek, Jr. and a few other friends, they organized a polo team. George was the best of the San Diego players, for he was muscular and overly competitive. Walter said George could have been a professional if he had wanted.

George lured a world-renown polo coach to San Diego, but the fellow turned out to be a demanding bastard. He wanted the team to use proper flat polo saddles instead of their Western saddles. He suggested the San Diego team give up their cow ponies in favor of more appropriate polo steeds. To top it off, he wanted them to get proper riding clothes and discard their khakis and cowboy boots. The nerve of this guy—where did he think he was? Buckingham Palace? Within a few days of his arrival, the coach left Duval, disgusted with the San Diego polo crowd. George's polo madness left with him.

George's favorite horse flashed by the box. Viceroy was sleek and dark, swift and sure to win the upcoming race. George loved being around horses—everything about it. He was at home amidst the sweet fragrance of hay, the sounds of the horses snorting and swishing their tails. He was especially partial to Viceroy, the winner of many races and many wagers for him.

George had learned his respect for horses from Senator Archie, who had been a real cowboy. Archie had taken to the cattle trails when he was only twelve to help support his brother and widowed mother. Eventually, he put together his own spread near Benavides, just south of San Diego. He called it Los Horcones, ranch of the forked poles. Archie had been dead seven years, but George's mamma, Lizzie, still lived there. Atlee worked the spread. Speaking of Atlee, here he came, striding down the sidelines toward George's box.

Atlee was a freakish looking fellow. A childhood accident in which his nightgown caught fire left him badly scarred on his face and torso. The skin on his right jawbone looked as if it had melted; his right ear was mauled, the lobe completely burned off. Atlee tried to cover the scars with a beard, but his fair skin produced sparse cover.

The accident had marked Atlee for life. Ashamed of his appearance, he preferred the lonely life of a cowboy. And he lived it. It was a surprise to George to see his youngest sibling in so public a place as the racetrack. He motioned his brother into the box, and Atlee took a seat next to him.

"What brings you out here?" George asked, handing his brother a soda.

"Nothing special," Atlee said, taking a long swallow from the bottle.

George was pleased. Atlee came out of his shell now and then, and it was always pleasant when he did. He could be a right good conversationalist when he wanted to. George figured his brother must be lonely. He had never married and had slept alone nearly every night of his life in the corner bedroom of the ranch house at Los Horcones.

Atlee had left the ranch once, and his parents thought it was to go off to college. Even though he had told them since he was a teen-ager that he wanted to work the ranch, Senator Archie and Lizzie insisted that he go to Austin and enroll at the university. Lizzie packed all his clothes in two bags and put him on the train in Corpus Christi. A month later, she and the senator received a collect phone call from Atlee. He was in San Francisco, calling from a whorehouse. After that, Archie and Lizzie gave up their dreams for Atlee and allowed him to return to the ranch.

All's well that ends well, that's what Lizzie always said. And it was certainly true in the case of Atlee. With the senator gone to Austin to the capitol every other year, and then later too old and feeble to run the ranch, Atlee turned out to be a godsend for Los Horcones. He was a peace-loving man, Atlee was. He had little appetite for things political. George had inherited all the political genes in the Parr family.

"B," Atlee said, calling George by his middle initial as the Parr family had always done, "you remember Dad tellin' us the story about John Cleary?"

George glanced at the track as the jockeys warmed up the horses for the next race. Viceroy was looking fine, just fine.

"Sure do," George said, squinting into the bright afternoon sun at his prized steed.

John Cleary had once been Archie's biggest foe. A rancher and oilman, he was a staunch Republican. In Duval, they had descriptive names for the two parties. The Republicans were known as La Bota, the boot, the party of the upper class. Archie was a Democrat, or El Guarache, the sandal, the party of the people. The two men were bitter enemies, ideological and physical opposites. Cleary was tall and angular; Archie short and squat. Cleary represented the Anglos of San Diego; Archie was standard-bearer for the Mexicans of Benavides.

Both had served on the commissioner's court for a time around the turn of the century. Their respective political ambitions led them into physical battle before the election of 1902. They came to blows in the town plaza, with Archie knocking Cleary flat to the ground. Cleary recovered and clubbed his foe in the head with a pistol.

Eventually, Cleary moved up at the courthouse and became the county tax collector. It was an unwelcome development for Archie, who felt his adversary had been enough trouble on the commissioner's court. Now the blasted La Bota was in charge of collecting taxes and setting tax rates on Duval property. One thing about John Cleary, he was honest. With him watching the dollars and cents at the courthouse, Archie wouldn't be able to use the county treasury to help the poor Mexicans. And by God, it was his duty to help his less fortunate brethren.

When John Cleary found out Archie had instructed the folks in the county treasurer's office to write checks for specified amounts to unspecified parties, he hit the roof of the second floor of the courthouse. When he found out Archie was handing out jobs on the county payroll to any Mexican who wandered in his office, he decided to take action. He threatened to call in the state auditor if the check writing didn't stop.

"Haven't thought about John Cleary in years," George said, gnawing on a fingernail. "Why'd you bring him up?"

Atlee was quiet for a moment, as if deciding whether he should proceed.

"Well, you know, Dad told us all those stories about him. About how they fought on the commissioner's court. About how all the Anglos supported Cleary and how all the Mexicans supported Dad," he said, setting his empty bottle down. "Funny how history repeats itself."

George settled his blue eyes on his brother.

"Just what are you getting at?" George asked, cocking his head in the direction of his cowboy brother.

"You remember, don'cha George, what happened to John Cleary?"

George remembered all too well his father telling the story about how John Cleary met his Maker. He even had faint recollection of the time in 1907 when it happened. George had been just a small boy then, but Cleary's death had created such a stir in San Diego that he would never forget it.

It happened one rainy December evening, when Cleary and two business associates went to a Mexican restaurant in San Diego. The three sat at the counter, Cleary with his back to the entrance. Midway through their meal, a load of buckshot fired from the street hit Cleary in the back and severed his spinal cord. He crumpled from his stool and fell dead on the floor.

Local lawmen, who were engrossed in a fiesta celebration, failed to take quick action. They claimed that noise from the fireworks and the confusion surrounding the festivities drowned out the gunfire and allowed the gunman to flee.

The next day, two Texas Rangers from Alice, Sam McKenzie and J. D. Dunaway, arrived in San Diego to take over the investigation. There were rumors that the assassin lived in San Diego. Others said the killer had been imported from Monterrey, Mexico, and had gone back there after the murder. The *Corpus Christi Caller* reported that scores of people knew or were "morally sure of the identity of the men who fired the fatal shots." Some suspected Archie, but no one came forth with any evidence.

Four months later, in April 1908, Rangers McKenzie and Dunaway arrested three suspects: T. J. Lawson, a merchant; his son Jeff; and Candelario Saenz, a former deputy sheriff believed to have fired the fatal shot. The Lawsons, who were Republicans, drew suspicion after the officers learned they had been in a dispute with Cleary over control of the Piedras Pintas oil field. Cleary owned some valuable land in that field. When the case came before the grand jury, the Lawsons were cleared because the evidence against them was circumstantial only. Candelario Saenz alone was indicted, but he never came to trial. Charges against him were dropped after two witnesses died of heart attacks.

Regardless of who was responsible for John Cleary's murder, the impact of his death soon became clear. Archie Parr emerged as the political boss in Duval County. There was no one left in La Bota strong enough to challenge him. He instructed the new tax collector to refuse poll taxes from members of La Bota. In the elections that soon followed, illiterate voters were handed marked ballots, and armed guards kept the voters in line at the polls. Archie was on his way to becoming El Patrón. Duval County was about to get its first Duke.

"That was 50 years ago," George scoffed at Atlee. "Enemies come. Enemies go. But we still take care of the people, just like Dad did. That never changes, never will."

Atlee was not going to let it drop, even though George was

not in the mood for his opinions. Occasionally Atlee would turn on the faucet, and shutting him off was not easy.

"That's not what I'm talking about and you know it, B. We've all worked hard to get where we are—the ranches, the courthouse, the banks, the fellows in Corpus and in Austin. I won't go down the list. You'll throw it all away, B, if you go messing with snakes."

Atlee leaned forward onto the railing and studied the horses exercising just beyond the bleachers.

"There's more than one way to deal with a snake," he continued. "Now rattlers, I mainly shoot 'em when I see 'em. But there's other snakes I just leave alone—give 'em a wide path. Don't like snakes no more than the next man, but some snakes I just leave alone. Don't even hack their heads off with the hoe. Some snakes have been known to grow new heads, you know."

George stood up and fanned himself even harder with the newspaper. He slapped his brother on the back and flashed a big grin at him.

"Like I said, you worry too much," he said and signaled to a *pistolero* to bring two more sodas. "You're too serious. Loosen up, enjoy the race. I'll place a bet for you—but it has to be on Viceroy. How much?"

Atlee did not look at his brother. He was not finished.

"You remember the story about C. M. Robinson?"

George sighed. Of course he did. Dad would never let them forget it when they were kids.

"Yup," George said. C.M. Robinson was the snake that took John Cleary's place.

Archie had told his boys the story at least a hundred times, as much to brag to his "little dogies" as to show them the ways of politics. He would gather Atlee and Givens and George around him on the porch of the ranch house. He would pick pecans clean with his pocketknife, toss the nutmeats in his mouth and chew while he told them how he became the Duke of Duval. Marie, George's older sister, would listen sometimes, too, because she liked politics. But after a few renditions of the same story, she would excuse herself to help her mom in the kitchen. As the boys grew older, they envied their sister as she disappeared behind the kitchen door.

Archie always began the story by saying he and C. M. Robinson were once friends. They hunted deer together and played poker. But there was always a tension between them, and eventually it became clear to Archie that C. M. Robinson was more enemy than friend.

George spent most of these story-telling sessions tossing a ball down the long front porch; nevertheless, he took in every word. Archie spoke as if he were giving a political speech—with a loud voice and gestures. That was kind of funny, because Archie never fancied himself an orator. In fact, in his 20 years in the Texas Senate, he never gave a major speech. But he liked to perform for his boys, so he strutted on the porch like a tom turkey while he told his tales. He quickly gained the upper hand with C. M. Robinson, he told his sons, and in the process, he captured the undying respect and loyalty of the Mexican *peones*.

"Always be good to the people," Archie would tell Givens. He was the one Dad groomed to take over Duval. "If you do, they'll go with you to the last breath. If you don't, they'll run off like wild horses."

Givens never listened to the stories like George did. He'd read snatches from a book while Dad wasn't looking. Being the oldest didn't mean Givens automatically had the requisite cunning for a career in politics. Givens was a leader all right, and smart, too. After all, he went to Yale and was captain of his football team.

But he wanted to be a businessman more than anything. He served for a while as county judge, at his father's bidding. But he left to take a seat on the Dallas Cotton Exchange and later returned to run the Parr bank in Alice. So the mantle fell to George, Archie's fifth born. No one considered Atlee, not even Atlee himself.

But Atlee was proud of the way Archie protected the Mexicans and seized undisputed power in Duval. It had happened on May 18, 1912, when Archie orchestrated an election to incorporate San Diego. The opposition, including Las Botas and some rebel Guaraches, feared he would use the new city's coffers for more graft.

On election day, C. M. Robinson joined up with Dr. S. A. Roberts and C. K. Gravis and went to the courthouse early. They wanted poll watchers, they told a Parr election judge. When the judge rejected their demand and ordered them out of the courthouse, the trio emerged from the building ready for a fight. It was still early; the polls hadn't opened.

When the men arrived on the lawn outside the courthouse, they met Antonio Anguirro, a deputy sheriff; Pedro Esmal, a county clerk; and Candelario Saenz—the same Candelario Saenz who had been acquitted in the murder of John Cleary years earlier. Robinson and Esmal argued, and gunfire broke out. When the shooting was over, all three Mexicans were dead, each felled by two bullets.

The killings enraged the Mexicans of Duval. They clamored in an angry mob outside the courthouse after the three Anglos turned themselves in to Sheriff A.W. Tobin. Concerned for their safety, Tobin took his prisoners to a house near the courthouse before the Mexicans began congregating. Word of the shootout spread swiftly to Alice, where Sheriff W. A. Hinnant deputized twelve men and rushed to San Diego. Hinnant escorted Gravis and Roberts to Corpus Christi, where they were freed on bond. Robinson, who was unarmed at the time of the shootings, was not charged.

As for Archie Parr, he took the side of the Mexicans, urging them to hold their tempers and re-holster their guns. As a precaution, he put Lizzie and the kids on the train to Corpus Christi. Then he went to town to reason with the Mexicans. He had other plans for revenge, he told them; he would carve out a new county from Duval and make Benavides the seat of government, he promised. The Mexicans would have their own domain.

And with that, Archie sealed his position as El Patrón. In fact, he grabbed undisputed claim to the title of the Duke of Duval County. By the time Gravis and Roberts were tried for murder in Richmond, near Houston, and acquitted, Archie had the Mexicans well under control.

Atlee scratched his beard.

"Things ain't the way they used to be," he told his brother. "In case you haven't noticed, B, not every fellow in Duval is in your herd. And you sure as hell ain't loved in Jim Wells."

"Just what do you want?" George said. The Duke of Duval wanted to watch the races, not reminisce.

Atlee looked squarely at his brother's profile.

"Are you listenin'?" he said.

"Yeah, listening, listening," George said, his head moving from left to right as another race went by.

Atlee shrugged.

"It don't take no genius to see George Parr is a man who's headed for trouble," he said. "All these damn *pistoleros* runnin' loose and thinkin' they can shoot at anybody gets in their way. I told you a long time ago I'd stay outa your politics and I meant it. I guess you'll say I'm breakin' that promise today, but I don't see it that way.

"The way I see it, George, I wouldn't be a fit brother if I didn't say my piece. Sure, some head banging must go on. But you're gettin' way beyond that. The time's come for the head cowboy to do a little ropin' and herdin'. Otherwise, your herd's gonna get you in a heap a' trouble."

George was standing, still following the horses around the track.

"You're right," he said, his blue eyes still on the race. "You're breaking your promise. That was the deal. You run the ranch, Givens runs the bank, I run the politics. Dad wanted it that way.

"He used to say if it ain't broke don't fix it. It ain't broke, Atlee."

Again, George's head moved from left to right as he watched a quartet of horses whiz by. Atlee swallowed a few more sips of soda and stood up. George didn't notice as he stepped out of the box. Atlee was halfway down the sidelines before he heard George call out to him. The Duke of Duval was waving good-bye, his hat in his hand.

Chapter 7

Jake heard plenty of gossip about how Sam Reams got appointed district judge, and he figured most of it was true. He was pretty happy about the appointment; Sam was young and bright and honest. He had been friendly toward George Parr early on, but Jake had good reason to believe that Sam had limits he wouldn't compromise.

That was how it was with men who loved the land, and Sam was one of those. He'd grown up on a farm near Corpus Christi, just like Jake, and had gone on to law school and into practice in Falfurrias. He'd served as Brooks County attorney and state representative.

At first, Sam got along fine with George. World War II forced a lull in South Texas politics in the early 1940s, so the two enjoyed a peaceful coexistence for a while. Then in '48, Sam decided to run for district attorney. Frank Lloyd, the prosecutor for 12 years, decided to step aside and join his brother Ed Lloyd in his Alice law firm.

Being a smart fellow, Sam went to George before paying his filing fee and asked for his support. The Duke gave it, and Sam ran unopposed. From what Sam told Jake, he made no promises and George asked no favors. But all three knew it was just a matter of time before George called in the credit he had extended. It was part of the code of Duval—a favor given is a favor earned.

George must have sized Sam up and decided he wouldn't be

a menace to the regime. The fact was, George and Jake and everyone else who understood the Texas court system knew that district judges were some of the most powerful elected officials around. District judges controlled appointments to grand juries, and grand juries issued indictments. Since a Texan could be indicted only in his home county, it was essential to George that he have a cooperative district judge in place.

It was Hap who had told Jake about how Sam got the judge's job. As the district clerk, Hap heard all the gossip around the courthouse. He knew everybody in town, so when folks were in the courthouse for one reason or another, they would stop by and chat. The lawyers were the richest source of information about local politics. No sooner would he hear something than he would stroll over to Jake's office and pass along the news. The door to Jake's office was always open to Hap; he welcomed the pipeline.

"Seems like the governor thought he was doing George a favor when he put Sam on the bench," Hap said, crossing his legs as he sat in the wingback. Betty had opened the windows to air out the office, so the sound of cars on the street below drifted in and mingled with the conversation.

"How's that?" Jake said, his small blue eyes peering through his glasses.

"Now that's an interesting story," Hap said, rubbing his hands together as if he were about to attack a steak dinner.

"From what I hear, the whole thing started months ago when Shivers became governor." Allan Shivers had moved up to governor from lieutenant governor after Governor Beauford Jester was found dead of a heart attack.

"George and Ed went down to Mission to call on the new governor at his office down there," Hap said. "I'm sure they were mighty impressed with Shivers' spread down there. He's running that citrus and ranching operation of his father-in-law's, you know."

Jake nodded, his elbows on the desk, his fingertips pressed together.

"Anyway, seems Governor Jester promised George he'd appoint Harry Carroll, that district judge over in Corpus, to the Court of Appeals. Shivers told George and Ed the promise was still good. And they shook on it.

"But when it came time for the appointment, the deal hit barbed wire. George told the governor he wanted Luther Jones, Jr., to be Harry Carroll's replacement as district judge in Corpus. Well, the governor said he couldn't do it. Said his supporters in Corpus wouldn't stand for it. Some of them were his fraternity brothers at UT, you know.

"Anyway, George said it was Harry Carroll and Luther Jones, Jr., or nothing. The governor begged for an out, but George said forget it. A promise is a promise."

Jake issued a snort.

"I hear Harry Carroll got embarrassed and just bowed out," the lawyer said.

"Yep. And Lorenz came out of his surgery just fine. So the governor appointed him to the Court of Appeals, Sam Reams to the district court and Homer Dean to Sam's old district attorney job."

"I don't imagine George is too mad about Homer," Jake said. Homer Dean had been an associate in the Lloyd law firm.

"No, but I hear he's cussed a few blue streaks about Lorenz," Hap said.

"Sometimes I wonder about that George Parr," Jake said. "I've always thought he was mighty shrewd. Could judge a man within an inch of the truth. But the way he's been acting lately, it looks like he's bent for hell. The way he treated Sheriff Garcia last year and now the governor. Makes you wonder."

George had turned down Sheriff Dan U. Garcia's request that he be promoted to county judge after the incumbent, Dan

Tobin, Sr., had died. Garcia thought it a reasonable request, since Tobin had been sheriff before he was made county judge. To add salt to the wound, George had himself appointed county judge.

Jake had really puzzled over that episode. Next to the district judge, the sheriff was the most powerful, the most influential man in town. The Mexicans both feared the sheriff and looked up to him for protection. No doubt about it—George was going to need a friend in the sheriff's office.

"Well," Hap said, standing up, "I've got to get back to the courthouse."

"Thanks, Hap," Jake said. "If I know Allan Shivers and George Parr, this is just the beginning of a nasty feud between those two. The worst of it is, the rest of us will be along for the ride."

***

Even though George didn't have Sam Reams in his pocket, he decided to leave the judge be for the moment. He didn't put up a candidate against him in the primary in the summer of 1950, when Sam had to stand for election. He was too busy worrying about the sheriff's race in Alice.

Hubert Sain had quite a tussle going with Halsey Wright. Sheriff Sain had already beaten Wright once, on a write-in vote in 1946. But Wright, an independent like Sam Reams, ran again in 1950.

On primary night, July 22, Jake got a call to go to Noonan School, home of Box 15. The votes were being miscounted in favor of Hubert Sain, the caller told Jake. When he arrived at about 2 A.M., there was an angry crowd outside the school. Sheriff Sain and his deputies were patrolling the scene on foot. It had just been announced—there would be a runoff between Hubert Sain and Halsey Wright.

A weary-looking man stepped up to Jake as he entered the schoolyard.

"Hubert's girlfriend is in there counting votes. She's miscalling them, Jake."

The lawyer kept walking.

"We want a recount," was repeated to him over and over as he moved through the knot of people.

When Jake arrived in the school cafeteria, Ed Lloyd was there. Clarence Perkins, who had called Jake to the school, sat in a folding chair beside the three ballot drums. Harry Lee Adams, newly re-elected county Democratic Committee chairman, was too nervous to sit.

The election judge, Joe Sherbert, paced the cafeteria with a clipboard secured under his arm. Democratic executive committeeman B. M. Brownlee sat next to Clarence. "I told them we didn't need to call you," Brownlee said, addressing Jake and Ed.

"But that mob," Joe Sherbert said, gesturing in the direction of the door.

"We decided if the two bosses in town wanted a recount, there'd be a recount," Brownlee said.

The cigar between Jake's lips sagged.

"There are no 'bosses' here," the lawyer said. "And even if there were, there are laws that govern this kind of thing. Mr. Sherbert, you're the election judge. The law says you have some authority here."

"Well, Mr. Floyd," Sherbert said, "I reckon I don't feel right about doing a recount. I don't think the law says I can do that. Now, if the courts—"

"That's right," Ed Lloyd interjected. "The courts could order a recount, but I don't think Mr. Sherbert—"

"Well, then, let's get Hubert in here," Jake said. "Is Halsey around?"

Hubert and Halsey were summoned, and within ten minutes they were being briefed in the school cafeteria.

"We have one hope of busting up that crowd out there," Ed said, his voice much more imposing than his appearance. He was barely five feet tall. "And that is, if you two fellas will go out there and tell them there'll be no recount. Tell them it's been an honest election. Tell them it'll be honest again next month in the runoff."

"Tell me it's been honest," Halsey growled. "Tell me about the runoff."

Hubert could be quiet no longer.

"Listen, Halsey, while you're in here grousing about the vote count, there's a storm kicking up out there," the sheriff said. "Every man in the schoolyard has a gun. C'mon, man, let's get movin'."

There was no more discussion. Hubert and Halsey broke the news to the crowd, and Halsey did an admirable job of acting satisfied with the vote count. After awhile, the gathering began to disperse. The deputies broke up a few scuffles and made a couple of arrests, but by 4 A.M., the school was calm again and deserted.

The pot simmered over the next month. Jake developed a sense of dread about the runoff. The night before August 27, voting day, George Parr's loyalists staged a rally. They, too, were concerned about the balloting. For one thing, they believed too many absentee ballots had been cast. County Clerk Hap Holmgreen, they charged, was overzealous in handing out absentee ballots.

Both sides worked endlessly on runoff day, ferrying voters to the polls. More than 200 cars were used to transport voters. George Parr spent the day in Jim Wells County, hovering around Box 13. That afternoon, Jake got an excited phone call from Hap. The county clerk wanted Jake to meet him at the Nayer School.

When Jake arrived, school was out for the day. Voters were lined up outside the door into the foyer, where the booths were set up. George was sitting with another man in his sleek black sedan parked at the curb outside. Jake found Hap in a classroom with

Parker Ellzey, the Jim Wells county attorney. Parker was a nice enough fellow, a Parr man. He had a signed affidavit from a voter who swore Hap had improperly marked his ballot. The voter said Hap came to his house, marked the ballot for him because he could not read, and then would not let him see the ballot before it was deposited in the absentee box.

"Looks like I was caught red-handed," Hap said. His lips pressed together in a straight line. His blue eyes were aflame.

"Is that how you account for this?" Ellzey said, waving the pages of the affidavit.

"It's a stinking lie, and I'll prove it," Hap said, the veins on his forehead bulging. Hap summoned an election judge and asked him to pay a visit to the voter in question. When the judge returned, he reported to Hap, Jake and Parker that the voter now claimed his ballot was properly marked. Parker did not change his expression. He pulled another affidavit from his briefcase, this one from a voter who said Hap had voided his absentee ballot because of reports that the man was a Mexican citizen.

"Let's get one thing straight," Hap said. He was standing toe-to-toe with the county attorney now, shaking his finger. "I run an honest operation—no funny business. You're just shadowboxing, Ellzey."

"Now, gentlemen." Jake's baritone voice was even. "If there's any dispute about the voting, the courts will have to decide the matter. There's no point in battling it out here and now. Let's all go home and get a little rest. We've got a long night ahead of us."

Jake was eager to get home. Saturday nights were his favorite. He watched his favorite television program, *Perry Mason*, and then went to the Reyes Cafe for Mexican food with Edith and Buddy. According to the ritual, they would return in time for *Gunsmoke*, but tonight, Jake would have to miss that. He wanted to be at Box 13 when the polls closed at 7 o'clock.

Before he could switch on the television set Jake got a phone call from O. D. "Kirk" Kirkland, a member of his opposition party. He was calling from the city jail. Could Jake come and bail him out?

Jake sighed as he hung up the telephone. He should have known better than to plan on *Perry Mason* and Mexican food. He told Edith and Buddy to go on to the cafe without him.

When Jake arrived at the Alice police station, Kirkland was visibly agitated. A small man with large hands and feet, he was sitting on the iron bedstead of his bunk when Jake strode in. When Kirkland saw the lawyer, he sprang to his feet and grabbed the steel bars with his oversized hands.

"Boy, am I glad to see you, Jake," Kirkland said. "Damndest thing I've ever seen. That sonofabitch stole my car keys and . . ."

"Hold on. Wait just a minute," Jake said, holding up his hand. "Start at the beginning."

Kirkland stepped back from the bars and rubbed his jaw. "I've been punched and kicked, Jake. It's like the goddam communists have taken over, right here in Jim Wells County."

Jake motioned for an officer to open the cell door, and the three men walked to a small conference room outside the cellblock. With the officer standing guard outside the bare-walled room, Jake and Kirkland sat at a sturdy metal table.

"I was over at the Bonham school, you know, Box 6. Just standing around keeping an eye on things," Kirkland said. "And it was a good thing I was there. George had some of his *pistoleros* hanging around, a mean-looking bunch. One of them, a really big Mexican, seemed to be their leader. He was kind of a show-off. Wore his shirt sleeves rolled up to show off the muscles in his arms. A real mean-lookin' brute."

Kirkland leaned back on the rear legs of his chair and massaged his knee.

"That bum kicked me right here," he said, pointing at the knee. "The same leg I got wounded in the war. It's never been the same and he kicks me there."

"Maybe you should have a doctor look at it," Jake suggested.

Kirkland righted his chair on the floor and rested his elbows on the table. "Well, anyway, things were going all right at the school, in spite of this pack of bruisers hanging around. They were lying around in the back seat of some flashy new sedan. They had a tub full of iced-down beer back there and they were drinking steady.

"That big Mexican, well, he had a nickel-plated Luger tucked under his belt. The other guy—he never said nothing, just stared at you—he had a revolver in a holster. They put down their beers and got moving when a car with Halsey Wright placards all over it pulled into the parking lot. There were three men in it. I didn't know any of them.

"Two of the fellows in the Halsey Wright car got out and went into the school. The other guy, he just sat in the front seat, and after awhile, it looked like he was sort of dozing.

"Then that big Mexican walked up to the car. It looked like he was going to say something to the sleeping man when the two guys who went into the school returned to the car. The Mexican, real sarcastic like, asked who was the driver of the vehicle. By then, the fellow who had fallen asleep was awake and he had stepped outside the car.

"The driver of the car produced his papers, proving that the car was his. He even pulled his car keys from his trouser pocket. When he held them up, that damn Mexican grabbed them and told the three men to start walking. Well, you should have seen the look on the driver's face. For a minute, he was shocked, but the next instant he was furious. He lunged forward like he was going to punch that mangy Mexican, but his two friends grabbed him by the arms and urged him to do like the man said and start walking.

"I was standing by my car, not 50 feet from all this. The three men, kind of reluctant at first, started walking in my direction. When they got closer, I asked if they wanted a ride. Well, you would have thought I had insulted that Mexican's mother. He came charging over, cussing and hollering and waving his arms. I noticed his gun was still tucked under his belt, thank God."

Kirk was talking pretty fast, but he stopped suddenly. His voice became hushed.

"You know something, Jake. I wasn't afraid of that mongrel. I stared down a gun barrel too many times in the war to let a no-good like that give me the shivers.

"He got right up in my face and blew his beer breath all over me. His eyes were dull looking, like he'd been drinking all day. They were scary eyes, Jake. Like there was no soul behind them.

"He hollered at me to butt out and mind my own business. I asked him, in as civilized a voice as I could muster, who he was. He was really mad by now, but he seemed kind of proud when he pulled a little leather pouch from his pocket. It was one of those silver deputy badges George gets for all his bullies. Makes 'em feel important. He flipped it open with a twist of his wrist, and held it there long enough for me to see his name. It said 'Mario Sapet, Deputy Sheriff, Jim Wells County.'

"Well, deputy or no deputy, I wasn't going to let no bully run these fellows off for no good reason other than they were Halsey's supporters. So I told him to back off. He had no cause to keep me from giving those men a ride. The next thing I knew, I was on the ground and he was standing over me.

"When I got up, he had his gun out and he started clubbing me in the face and kicking me in the legs. The other three guys dared not jump in the fray because by now the other Mexican was on hand and he had his gun pulled, too.

"I don't know why, but the big Mexican, Sapet, only hit me a couple of times and then stopped. He called the silent one over and told him to take me to the police station. Before we left, he took my car keys. And that's how I got in this crummy place.

"I'm tellin' you, Jake, I feel like Hitler won the war. It's like we're in Nazi Germany."

Jake sat pensive for a moment, making a mental note to find out who this Mario Sapet was. He knew most of George's most unsavory characters, but this Sapet fellow must be a new recruit.

He stood up abruptly and motioned toward the door.

"Come on, Kirk, let's go see the judge and get you out of here."

It was a few hours before they could get an audience with the justice of the peace, but when they finally did, bond was set at $100. The charge was resisting arrest.

Later that night, Jake and Kirk and their Free and Independent Party had cause to celebrate. The sheriff's race was safely won by Halsey Wright, who bested Hubert by 900 votes. And W. R. "Buster" Perkins, Clarence's nephew, was the new Precinct 1 county commissioner, edging out Parr's man Dan Scruggs by a mere 72 votes. However, Woodrow Laughlin, another Parr man, was the new county judge.

It was Woodrow who showed up outside Jake's office well past midnight that night on a mission for his benefactor. Woodrow was rotund and sawed off and so stubborn he had earned the name "El Burro." Jake thought George probably had big plans for the new county judge.

Woodrow's pockets were jingling as he strode up to Jake.

"Got something for 'ya," Woodrow said, producing two handfuls of automobile keys.

"I trust you'll know how to get these to their owners."

Jake counted sets of keys for at least 20 cars, all of them stranded at various polling places. Mario Sapet had been pretty busy that day.

Texas Mutiny: Bullets, Ballots and Boss Rule

***

It looked to Jake like Parr's machine learned a few lessons from Coke Stevenson's crowd. The day after the runoff, the new District Attorney, Homer Dean, filed a motion seeking to impound all the election ballots. The motion spelled out that Homer wanted all ballots Hap had in his office and any he might have at his home.

Hap was livid over Homer's motion, but not half as livid as his wife. When she found out Homer suspected there might be ballots in her home, she tracked down her husband at the Alice Hotel. She demanded that the front desk clerk summon her husband to the phone from a Kiwanis Club luncheon.

"How dare he target our home!" she screamed.

Hap held the receiver a few inches from his ear.

"When it comes to a matter of the home, my Irish gets aroused," she continued. "You know that, Hap. My mother would never stand for something like this and she raised me the same way."

"I want you to call up the sheriff and send him over here right now," she said. "He can search this place from ceiling to floor if he likes. How dare they accuse you of something so low."

When Homer heard of Mrs. Holmgreen's outrage he telephoned Mrs. Holmgreen and apologized. All he had intended, he explained, was to make sure none of the ballots were destroyed. No search of the Holmgreen home was necessary, he assured her. Her word was all he needed. Mrs. Holmgreen responded that her husband's word should have sufficed.

The next thing Hap knew, Judge Reams had signed Homer's motion to impound the ballots. He couldn't believe it. He thought Sam was a friend, an ally. He tracked the judge down in Rio Grande City and asked him over the telephone if it was true.

"Yes, Hap, I signed it," the judge said.

"Did you read it? Did you see what they want to do?" Hap roared.

"Of course, I did, Hap." Reams was chuckling. "But that kind of language is laughable. You know and I know and everybody else in Alice knows that you run an honest shop. You can call someone a dirty name but that doesn't make him so. I'm sure everything is all right, Hap."

"You're damn right everything is all right." Hap returned the receiver roughly.

Even Jake was no help.

"You may not like it," the lawyer said, "but the judge has the authority and the duty to grant Homer's motion. And he's right about another thing, too, Hap. Even if they do decide to search your house, you have nothing to worry about."

The next day, George Parr and Ed Lloyd drove to Brooks County south of San Diego and called on Sam Reams at his home in Falfurrias. The three men sat on the front porch, sipped lemonades and made the requisite preliminary small talk.

After about 20 minutes, George broached the subject that had prompted their visit.

"Sam, I want you to remove Hap Holmgreen," he said.

Sam sat silent for a moment in his wooden rocker.

"Remove him—what for?" Sam said.

"Ol' Hap, he's a fine ol' boy," George said. "but he's gotten too footloose and fancy with the absentee ballots. He's gotta go, Sam."

George chewed on his thumb and eyed Sam closely.

"And just how do you propose that I accomplish this mission of yours?" the judge said.

"All you've got to do is get Homer to sign an affidavit. Ed will talk to him. It'll say that Hap strong-armed voters and stuffed the absentee box. All you'll have to do is read the affidavit and tell Hap to clean out his desk."

"George!" Sam stood up abruptly. "You're talking about getting somebody killed at the courthouse. Why, Hap will go gunning for Homer the minute he hears of an affidavit. You know he will."

"Oh, hell, no," George said. He had a way of drawling out the "hell" when he said it so that the sentence literally dropped off to nothing as he said the "no."

"Ol' Hap, he'll grumble and curse, but he'll go peaceable. I want you to appoint Raeburn Norris as his replacement."

Sam couldn't tolerate Raeburn Norris. He was the human equivalent of a salivating hyena.

"I can't do it, George," the judge said, still standing. He placed his lemonade glass on the porch railing. "No one's presented any convincing evidence to me that Hap has done what you say. Maybe you're right, but frankly, I doubt it. Hap may have a short fuse, but he's an honest man."

George looked at Ed, and the two men stood up.

"Well, I guess there's no point in having Homer draw up the papers," the Duke of Duval said. And with that, he and Ed excused themselves from Sam Reams' front porch.

***

The heady aroma of chili sauce hit Nago Alaniz in the nostrils as he walked into the Reyes Cafe. All he wanted was a few beers and a plate of enchiladas before he headed to Mexican town. There were a couple of *señoritas* waiting at a *cantina* for him.

As he scanned the tables, looking for an empty one, his gaze was interrupted by a wave from a man in the corner. Luther Jones, Jr., was drinking a bottle of Pearl beer. After the two lawyers shook hands, Nago straddled a chrome chair, his elbows resting on the back.

"Drowning your troubles, *hombre*?" Nago grinned. He was

still wearing the tailored dark suit he had worn to court that day. Nago was trim, dark and a sharp dresser. It was little wonder the *señoritas* found him irresistible.

"That sonofabitch Reams," Luther said, spooning some rank-smelling menudo into his mouth. "He wouldn't know a bogus vote if it up and bit him in the ass."

"Yeah," Nago agreed. "*No tiene huevos*. Damn shame, too. All that work down the chute. I must've interviewed 150 people." Nago motioned for the waitress to bring him a beer.

Nago and Luther and a team of other lawyers had subpoenaed 400 people and spent two weeks in court, only to have Judge Reams rule that no voter fraud had been proven. The election stood.

"Mr. Happy Holmgreen," Jones said, snarling. "He and Jake Floyd visiting voters after dark, taking absentee ballots. And all the judge can say is there did seem to be an effort to encourage absentee voting."

Jones brought his beer bottle down hard on the table.

"We appeal, don't we?" Nago said, taking a long swallow from his own beer.

"What do you think I am, Alaniz?" Luther's beer was mixing with his anger. "We start first thing tomorrow morning on the brief."

"If you ask me, we never should've wasted so much time proving Jake Floyd filed his response too late," Nago snorted.

"Listen, you little wetback," Luther said, pointing a finger at Alaniz and glaring at him with bloodshot eyes. "I never wanted you on the team anyway, but the Big Boss said let you have some work. That's why they call him El Papa, I guess, 'cause he tries to take care of everybody, even if he can't stand 'em.

"And he can't stand you, Meskin. After that shit you pulled in court against Frank Lloyd, the Boss said he'd run you outa town. But Ed wouldn't let him. I don't know why. Ed can't stand you, either.

"You're just a mangy dog, Alaniz, licking crumbs—"

Nago hurled a fist at Luther's mouth and nearly knocked him out of his chair. Luther scrambled to his feet as beer bottles crashed to the floor and chairs overturned. He lunged at his foe, and the two men were on the floor, writhing and punching.

Luther was getting the worst of it when the cafe manager pulled the two apart. People at tables nearby had scattered and were standing in a half circle, gawking.

"Get out of here, both of you!" the manager ordered the lawyers.

Out on the sidewalk, Luther rubbed his jaw and breathed heavily. Nago smoothed down his suit and adjusted his tie.

"You shouldn't of done that, Meskin," Luther said. "Shouldn't of done that."

Nago grabbed Luther by his tie and with a rough jolt pulled Luther's face close to his own.

"Don't ever—" he said, then stopped and loosened his grip. He stared Luther in the eyes for a long moment, then shoved him away. Luther staggered to his car and drove off, leaving Nago standing on the sidewalk.

The lawyer lit a cigarette and decided to walk over to Mexican town. There was a cool breeze blowing in from the Gulf, and he wanted to simmer down before getting to the *cantina*.

As he walked and smoked, Nago wondered if he had done the right thing moving to Alice. They didn't take kindly to outsiders here, and they sure as hell didn't in San Diego. What little work he had gotten from Mr. Parr was sure to dry up now.

He thought of his wife and two little girls. He'd boasted to his wife that one day, he'd be George Parr's number one attorney. At least they didn't live in Mexican town. At least he'd gotten enough work to rent a house on the good side of town.

But maybe they should pack up and move back to Beeville.

He'd told Jake Floyd a few weeks before that he was growing more and more concerned that Frank Lloyd might have him jailed on some pretext. The two had almost come to blows in a courtroom one day. Frank accused him of using shyster tactics. Shyster? What the hell did that mean?

"You ever need any help," Jake had said, "just call me. If you're doing your job and they try to put you in jail, Nago, you call me. I don't care what time of the day or night it is. I'll come get you."

Nago decided he might be able to trust El Vibora Seca. He'd been hearing that the older lawyer liked to coach the younger attorneys, sort of be their mentor. But he was, he reminded himself, the dry snake. Jake Floyd didn't offer help if it didn't suit his purposes.

Nago sucked the last draw from his cigarette and tossed it to the pavement. He quickened his pace. The *señoritas* were waiting.

***

George Parr never said anything about the election dispute. He let El Burro do the talking for him.

"It was a close point," Woodrow said. "Reams could have ruled either way. He should have ruled in favor of his friends. He owes everything he's got to George Parr."

It would be election day before Sam Reams found out what revenge was, á la George Parr. Allan Shivers got his come-uppance a little sooner, in the primary. He was much too popular a governor for George to turn out of office. In fact, Shivers won renomination by an 8-to-2 margin statewide. But he got an embarrassing 108 votes in Duval County. A little-known candidate, a Waco attorney named Caso March, received 4,239.

After the primary, Shivers's path crossed that of Jake Floyd, who was in Austin working on a case. The governor asked the lawyer what George Parr had against him. Jake assured him he did not know.

"I thought I was doing him a favor by appointing his judge to the Fourth Court," the governor said. "but, you know, Jake, George didn't invent good ol' boy politics. I can take care of my friends and cut my enemies' throats—right up there with the master himself."

As for Judge Reams, rumors were abundant that George was organizing a write-in campaign against him. According to some, State Rep. A. J. Vale of Rio Grande City was to be Parr's candidate. Jake suspected the rumor was true, but when he confronted Vale about it, the representative said he knew of no such effort in his home county of Starr.

Sure enough, on election night, there were no write-in votes for Vale in Starr County. But in Jim Wells and Brooks, Vale got 935. Sam drew 5,205 votes, not enough of a hedge against the number of votes Duval County could muster.

There was another "long count." Duval County didn't report for six days. When the ballots were canvassed by the commissioners' court, there were reporters on hand from all over Texas. The Associated Press, the *Houston Post,* the *Houston Chronicle,* the *Fort Worth Star-Telegram* and the *San Antonio Evening News* and *Express* and the *San Antonio Enterprise* all sent representatives.

For district judge, George announced, Duval County was reporting 4,739 write-in votes for Rep. A. J. Vale of Rio Grande City. Judge Reams received but 43 votes. It was enough to give Vale the victory.

"We were for him the first time, but against him the second time," George said, explaining the difference between the vote in the primary and the general election. He had that sly *tecuache* grin on his face.

"That's all there was to it."

Chapter 8

"Somebody should've warned George Parr not to fool with Allan Shivers," Jake said between bites of coconut cream pie. It was his favorite.

Dena's had the usual crew of mid-afternoon coffee drinkers. Jake sat at a table with Sam Reams and Donato Serna, a pharmacy owner from San Diego. Jake and Donato held mutual interest in a small oil company and a mutual disdain for George B. Parr.

"Well, are you going to tell us about it or do we have to watch you eat that entire piece of pie?" Sam asked, amazed that a man so thin could eat so much.

"Let the man eat," Donato said, grinning. He was short and spare and spoke English fluently, but with a heavy accent. He mastered the language while on the debate team at San Diego High School. "Can't you see the man is starved? We'll hear the story when he's through."

Jake forked the last of the custard in his mouth and chased it with a sip of black coffee.

"I never saw so many reporters," he said, "not since Box 13. And there were lawyers from all over this part of the state. I talked to some of them on the way back from Austin about what we're going to do next. But I'll tell you about that in a minute.

"Like I said, the governor's reception room was packed. It was dark in there with all that mahogany paneling. It was overcast outside, so they threw back the sashes and opened the windows—to let in more air and light."

"Don't paint a picture; tell us what happened," Sam said. His brown eyes were eager.

"God's in the details, Sam. Anyway, everybody was smiling and shaking hands. The governor had just gotten back from a duck-hunting trip, and he looked more relaxed than I've seen him."

"Let me ask you something, Mr. Floyd," Donato said. "The governor called you and invited you to come?"

"Didn't say a word about what was going to happen," Jake said, nodding. "But I'd already heard that John Ben had asked Price Daniel to research throwing out the votes."

As Secretary of State, John Ben Shepperd was the state's official canvasser of votes. He shared duties with Price Daniel, the attorney general, and Allan Shivers, who together made up the State Election Board. Every election year, right before Thanksgiving, the State Election Board canvassed votes from all over Texas. It was usually a routine affair. The fanfare Jake was describing was unheard of.

"Come to think of it, Price was the only man in the room who looked unhappy," said Jake. "He told me later that he had briefed the law and told John Ben all he could do was a rubber stamp.

"But John Ben stood there behind that polished table, a serious look on that baby face of his. Said Sam had won the primary with no opposition and that A. J. had decided to go back to his seat in the House.

"Under the circumstances, he said, he couldn't conscientiously count the Duval County votes in the district judge's race. Said he based his action on a strong feeling in his heart that it was the right one.

"The governor was standing right next to him and he piped

up. Said he wanted to commend John Ben for his decision. Said it was the only one good conscience would allow. Price was standing right there, too, but he didn't say a word. They said it was the first time in history something like this has happened."

Judge Reams lit a cigarette and smoke streamed through his nostrils. He extended a match for Jake's cigar.

"It couldn't have happened without you, Jake," the judge said.

Jake was veiled behind a cloud of cigar smoke. He swatted at the smoke as if to clear the air of both the fumes and the judge's remark.

"If you hadn't called the governor," Sam said. "If you hadn't organized all the lawyers…"

Jake had persuaded Sam to fight for the bench and recruited lawyers in South Texas to put pressure on Austin about the district judgeship. Jake had been a bit surprised that Sam needed prodding. For a politician, he didn't have much fight sometimes.

"The important thing is you're in, Sam," he said.

"I just hope Angelita calms down a bit," Sam said of his wife. "She's never been happy about me running for office and all. She can hardly stand it when I go down to Rio Grande City to hold court. Have to take a bodyguard with me and translators. Nobody speaks English down there."

"If it makes you feel any better," Jake said, "I think all we'd have to do is ask Shivers and he'd send the Rangers down here. My guess is he's thinking about it already."

Sam shifted uneasily in his chair.

"I'd rather not get caught in their cross fire," he said.

"Suit yourself. But keep it in mind."

Sam thought about what his father used to say about the dangers of public service. Robert Reams was a farmer who ran for the local school board and served a few terms. He was fond of a Machiavellian quotation: "Princes and governments are by far more dangerous than other elements within a society."

"Mr. Floyd," Donato said, "what did your son think?"

"Buddy? He had the time of his life. He's an outgoing kid, might make a good politician himself one of these days."

"Maybe we can get one Floyd to run for office," Sam said, smiling.

Jake smiled, too. Proud papa.

"I think he really liked meeting the governor. I was glad he could get out of school a little early for the holiday and go with me."

"How's he doing in school?" Donato asked.

"He's finally getting serious, making up for all that time he played around in high school. His friends call him the 'Briefcase Kid' because he carries his books wherever he goes. He's going to law school at UT next year."

"Following in the old man's steps," Sam said.

"Well, he's straightened up. We used to have some trouble, the two of us, when he wouldn't study."

"Think he'll take over the practice one day?" Sam asked.

"We've talked about it. It's up to him. You know I discouraged Edith Maude's husband from coming here. Just too much of a political mess."

Jake drained his coffee cup and grabbed his felt hat.

"Tell Sam about the letter-writing campaign," Donato said.

"Oh, yeah, Sam, George isn't going to take this like the possum he is. I figure it's just a matter of time before he files some kind of suit challenging your election."

"No doubt," Sam said.

"I talked about this with some of the other lawyers on the way back from Austin yesterday. John Ben's going to need help when George files his challenge. We thought about launching a letter-writing campaign—you know, write letters to hundreds of lawyers, maybe as many as a thousand. Set up a regular brain trust for John Ben.

"We'd be at his disposal to do research, depositions, whatever. And if nothing else, it would show solidarity. What do you think?"

Sam sat, expressionless for a moment, as if methodically processing what Jake had just said.

"Sounds good," he said. "When do we start?"

Jake told the judge he was getting a list of all lawyers in Texas from the State Bar. The lawyers who had agreed to help in the cause would write to other attorneys they knew in Texas. "It's already been in the papers," Donato said. "Read it in the *Corpus Christi Caller* this morning."

Sam remarked that George Parr must be stewing about now.

"Yes," Jake said, putting on his hat. "In his own sweat."

***

George Parr popped a vitamin between his lips and drank from a glass of water. He was sitting in his favorite chair, upholstered with extra stuffing, his feet propped on the matching ottoman. The chair was in his favorite room of the house—the great room. It was the most comfortable chair in the whole 14-room house he built for his wife, Thelma. The rest were couches and wooden-armed parlor chairs, each covered in cowhide. A bear-head trophy from a hunt in Alaska presided over the fireplace. The bust of a buffalo was mounted opposite.

The floors were terrazzo, the walls whitewashed. George had designed much of the house himself. He and Thelma divorced in the late 1930s but remarried a short time later. As a second wedding present, George told her to design a second story. The result was more bedrooms and servants quarters.

The house had that bachelor look—jackets and shoes strewn on the floor, a half dozen used glasses here and there. George and the former Thelma Duckworth had parted company for the final time the year before. "Duck," as he called her, moved back to Corpus Christi, where she grew up.

To the rear of the house was a garage that could hold four cars, accessible through archways that supported the second-floor servants quarters. A pool and stables were in the back, and the entire complex was encircled by a knee-high whitewashed concrete-block fence. It looked like the home of a Mexican aristocrat. Folks who didn't understand George wondered why he had built it on the poor side of San Diego.

There was a wet bar in the great room. Juan Barrera Canante had never before seen a wet bar, but he thought he could get used to such luxuries. He poured himself a tequila shot and sat down on a cowhide-covered couch. This was the first time he had been invited to El Patrón's mansion. He gazed up at the high ceiling, the whitewashed plaster bolstered by rough oak beams.

The rear wall was lined with hunting rifles. One case held a cache of particularly menacing-looking weapons. The carbine reminded Juan Barrera of the time George showed up at the courthouse, rifle in hand. He was on a manhunt for an enemy he never found. George always carried a gun—usually a .22 in a shoulder holster. But that day at the courthouse was the only time Juan ever saw El Patrón with a weapon in plain view. George didn't really need to do his own manhandling. He had a regiment of ruffians to do it for him. But sometimes his temper ruled his head.

Juan had arrived with Pete Saenz, chief deputy in the sheriff's office and one of El Patrón's most trusted men. Juan had been a Parr deputy for a few years. He was good with a gun, so he had moved rapidly up on the force. Folks around San Diego allowed Juan a wide path. It was his reputation with the gun that afforded him this kind of respect. His size would not have done the job. He was small-boned and wiry. What hair he was missing atop his head, he made up for with a neatly trimmed beard.

Until after the war, when the Rangers made a sweep through town, Juan frequented San Diego's red light district just outside of town. It was his domain. El Patrón gave it to him—even gave him his own little business. It was a busy place, El Ranchito, what with all the sailors from Beeville and Corpus and Kingsville swarming in on weekends. Juan's brother Raul ran the place and Juan provided security, which meant mainly that all of Parr's *pistoleros* were free to roam the place. They had to pay the whores, though.

Of late, El Patrón had given Juan greater responsibility. He was moving up in the organization. The narcotics business was booming—reefer and cocaine were being flown in from Mexico and sold all over South Texas and beyond. Juan's job was to keep the drugs flowing and to make sure the dealers didn't run afoul of local law enforcement.

El Patrón had yet to complain about Juan's work. And Juan had begun recruiting *pistoleros* for the force. He was especially proud that he brought Mario Sapet on board. A man could count on Mario. Give him a job, and he'd do it with little direction.

Juan's boss, Pete Saenz, had been in George's mansion many times, and before that, he had visited Los Horcones. He had grown up with El Papa and the first Duke of Duval. Pete's father was Candelario Saenz, one of the three Mexicans gunned down by the Anglos that historic day in front of the courthouse.

Pete sat in one of the parlor chairs looking a bit out of place in his denims, cowboy boots and gun belt. He was taller than Juan, and his face was pitted from a bad case of childhood chicken pox and adolescent pimples. His hair had turned prematurely gray, but he had a full head of it.

"Dammit," George erupted. It was the first of a string of fiery expletives in both English and Spanish.

"Should have gotten rid of the sonofabitch years ago," he bellowed in Spanish.

"We'll run the judge out of town in the next election," Juan offered.

"And what'll we do until then!" George screamed. "He's already cost us. Hubert. What's next?"

He popped another vitamin on his tongue and sucked it like a candy.

"I think it's a good idea to keep an eye on Jake Floyd, El Duque," Pete said.

"Yeah," George said. "Shivers might as well set up an embassy in Alice, in Jake Floyd's office. What's this about a letter-writing campaign?"

Pete said he had heard only a little about it and he would find out more.

"El Vibora Seca," George said, recalling the nickname he had given Jake Floyd. "He's a dry snake all right, crawling silent through the grass. Cold-blooded bastard."

"There's no way to get rid of somebody like that," Juan said. "Can't fix an election. He's just there, causing trouble. We could scare him. He got any daughters?"

"No," Pete said. "Not living around here anyway."

"Somebody ought to plant that bastard," George said. He stood up and walked over to one of the built-in gun racks on the wall. There were at least 30 weapons of varying calibers and size—a carbine, a small machine gun, several revolvers, an automatic pistol. He lifted the carbine from the rack and cradled it like an infant, stroking it as he would a crying baby.

Juan looked at Pete, who appeared to be uninspired by the last comment.

"I'll keep an eye on him," Juan volunteered. "I have to be over that way all the time anyway." He had contacts in Alice who could keep him informed.

"Find out about the letter writing," the duke ordered. "And find out where Reams is going to live. He can't stay in Brooks County—too damned inconvenient."

George walked out of the great room, and Juan and Pete could hear him talking in a distant room. Presumably, he was on the telephone, for they didn't hear another voice talking back. They decided to let themselves out the front door.

Section III
Early 1952

Chapter 9

It was only early June, but it might as well have been August. The summer heat had settled in like an overbearing relative come for a long visit. The sun bore down on the native buffalo grass, the air sizzling with grasshoppers and crickets singing a lament. All a man could do was make the best of it. Captain Allee of the Texas Rangers leaned his barrel-chested frame against a scrub oak underneath a small umbrella of branches. A damp, warm breeze trickled in from the east, but it did nothing to halt the steady stream of sweat that dripped from the captain's head.

A stub of a cigar protruded from a corner of his mouth, his face shaded by a cream-colored Stetson. His white unmarked sedan was parked a few feet away in the shade of a clump of huisache. The Freedom Party was staging a progressive rally. A caravan of cars had converged at the city park in San Diego and then proceeded to Freer. "Cap," as they called him, led the cavalcade, and Rangers Wiley Williamson and Tully Seay brought up the rear.

It had been a peaceable affair, despite the presence of the *pistoleros* who lurked like hungry buzzards. A trio of them stood near the flatbed truck that had been rigged as the speaker's platform. A few others sat on the hoods of their vehicles parked at the four corners of the gathering. They drank beer and watched, silent and sullen.

The captain guessed there must be 400 people in the open

field. Mexicans and Anglos alike settled on blankets and quilts, fanning themselves and drinking beer and sodas. Mothers shaded babies under wide-brimmed hats. Three or four men barbecued goat in a pit west of the conclave, the Gulf breeze carrying the smoke away from the crowd.

It's the only show in town, Cap thought to himself. That's why they're here. Free *cabrito* and soda pop draw a crowd any time. At least half the Mexicans had joined the caravan in San Diego. The rest were from Freer, where anti-Parr Anglos dominated both the population and city hall.

Cap and his men had been in Duval County going on a month on orders from Gov. Shivers, and so far there had been no trouble. They had rented a small apartment in San Diego, just across the county line in Jim Wells. The county line ran smack through the middle of the county seat, so that part of San Diego was in Duval and part was in Jim Wells. All the better, to Cap's way of thinking. The *pistoleros* respected that county line enough to leave the Rangers alone.

If anybody had asked, Cap would have admitted he was a bit disappointed that hostilities seemed to be corked for the moment. There was an uncertain peace, but Cap was ready for it to give way any time. He liked trouble. He'd admit it straight out. As long as he was enforcing the law, then he'd be as tough as he pleased. Folks in Texas were fond of saying the Rangers were just as mean as the criminals; the difference was that the Rangers drove company cars. Those folks must have been thinking about Cap Allee when they said such things.

Cap turned his attention to the flatbed truck, where Sam Reams was hollering into a microphone perched on a stand. He was keeping a close eye on the judge. There were rumors he might be assassinated at the rally. Reams was an exuberant speaker. He adjusted his tone and volume like he was giving a sermon at a Baptist church.

Sam started off talking about his 1950 race for judge.

"In a county where one man says what men get the votes and his man gets 4,000 votes and his opponent gets 40, that's not democracy, that's dictatorship," he said, pounding his fist into his palm.

"When a political boss can tell the sheriff to resign and tell the county commissioners to name him sheriff and they do so, that's not democracy. That's dictatorship." He pounded his fist again.

"When a political boss can tell a city official to move a bus station and they do it, that's not democracy, that's dictatorship." Donato Serna, the pharmacy owner, had lost his lucrative bus depot contract. The bus company had moved the bus stop down the highway to a gas station.

"The political boss of Duval County is scared," Judge Reams continued. "He's blabbering and jabbering. He has the grand jury jitters!"

The crowd laughed.

"The Freedom Party is now snowballing, and George is right to be scared because it's going to roll him right out of office!" Sam made a sweeping motion with his arm as he made the statement, then jumped off the truck bed to cheers.

A look of disdain crept across Cap's blue eyes. Tecuache was too kind a name for George Parr, thought the captain. "Rabid skunk" would be more fitting. Cap had sized up the Duke of Duval the first time he met him. It was in the hallway of the courthouse in San Diego. The Duke shook Cap's hand too hard and cracked too many jokes. That and those steely blue eyes gave him away.

From what Cap had been told, political rallies were a novelty in Duval. There was never any opposition in the local races, and statewide candidates rarely bothered with a county so sparsely populated as Duval. The only chance for any kind of countywide celebration were when El Patrón would throw barbecues after 4-H Club shows and everybody would come out for the free beef and sodas.

The next speaker on the flatbed was Donato Serna.

"Under George Parr's political domination of the past 10 years, while the rest of the state gained 23 percent in population, Duval County lost 23 percent of its residents. His political tactics make a mockery of democracy."

Dan Foster, Freedom Party candidate for Precinct 3 commissioner, was next.

"I've never sought political office before, because I thought a politician had to be halfway crooked. I believe what makes politicians rotten is staying in office too long."

Robert Leo, candidate for county superintendent of schools: "We don't have a single decent common school building in the city. The Copita school, for instance, is fit for pigs rather than children."

Manuel Sanchez, the grocer: "We want freedom in Duval County. A life without liberty is not worth living."

Manuel spoke at ground level, not bothering to haul his 400 pounds onto the truck bed. As Manuel handed the microphone to a man on the truck, Cap noticed two swarthy *pistoleros* striding confidently through the crowd. He knew the name of one of them. He was Raul Guerra, Juan Barrera Canante's brother. But the other one he had never seen.

The captain watched carefully the movements of the other fellow. He had a certain bravado about him. He was distinct from his *pistolero* brothers because he wore a Panama hat. The short sleeves on his white *guayabera* shirt revealed muscular arms and a blue tattoo—a snake coiled around a sword. He wore meticulously pressed, pleated trousers on a thick but trim frame.

The townspeople avoided this new *pistolero*'s eyes as he passed them. When he strutted past the captain, he focused his gaze straight ahead. Still, the captain could see from the man's profile that he had very dark eyes and smooth brown skin. It was the same man he had seen driving in a green Packard up and down the main street in San Diego every day that week. The Ranger asked Donato the man's name. Mario Sapet was the answer.

***

There were more Freedom Party rallies that summer, most of them at American Legion halls in San Diego or Benavides or Freer. By July, more than 2,000 folks were showing up for the beer and speeches. After one such affair, Mac McDonald paid a call on Jake Floyd to find out why he never came to any of the rallies.

Unofficially, Jake was the leader of the Freedom Party. He had called on friends all over Texas, soliciting donations for the fledgling party. And he was Sam Reams's campaign manager. Jake and the judge met daily, plotting strategy to assure that the 1952 election would be an honest one. If it took a court order, they would have honest poll watchers. And they'd raise enough money to rent a fleet of cars to ferry voters to the polls.

He didn't go to the rallies, Jake said, because he preferred to work behind the scene—keep a low profile. It was just his style.

"Well, Jake, I've got to eat some crow," Mac said after settling into a wingback at the lawyer's office. Jake had been telling Mac for months to steer clear of George. He was not a man to be trusted. But Mac was new in Duval and hungry for acceptance.

"It doesn't matter, Mac," Jake said. "I'm just glad Sam's making sure we've got honest grand juries. George is stepping lightly these days because of it."

The Freedom Party was beating George at his own game. With an anti-Parr grand jury, there was a better chance for honest elections. And at this point, that was the most the new party could hope for. George still held a firm grip on San Diego and had considerable influence in Alice and southward.

"I want to tell you something, Jake," Mac said, leaning on the lawyer's desk. "If you ever need anything—anything at all—you call me. I don't care if it's the middle of the night, I'll be there."

With that, Mac stood up, shook Jake's hand and left. Jake scratched his thinning hair. Oh, well, he thought. Mac usually took himself a bit too seriously—much more seriously than George was taking the Freedom Party.

***

At first, George had scoffed at the news of the emerging new party. "They're just a few straggling goats," he had told his friends. "They'll be lucky if they get 500 votes."

But as the summer wore on and the Freedom Party rallies began to draw thousands instead of hundreds, he modified his forecast. The Freedom Party, he said, wouldn't draw 1,000 votes. His final prediction: "They can't beat us."

George decided to fight fire with fire. He held his own rallies, offering not only free beer and barbecue but also live music and dancing. He always spoke at these fiestas, railing against the Freedom Party and extolling the accomplishments of his Old Party.

The election had evolved into a showdown over the district judge's seat. The Freedom Party was behind Judge Reams. George's Old Party was behind Woodrow Laughlin, the county judge.

Sam Reams, George screamed at his listeners at one rally, "is anti-Latin-American. If you vote for Sam Reams, it's a vote for sending your brothers to the penitentiary."

As for Jake, the campaign was consuming most of his days. Evenings and weekends he spent at the office, keeping his caseload up to date. The dairies were being neglected, and there was no time at all for Edith and Buddy.

But Buddy was fairly distracted that summer as well. Home from the University of Texas law school, he was spending a great deal of time with his girlfriend of the past two years, Elinor Lewis. Edith Maude's roommate had introduced them, and the two had been a couple ever since. The relationship had taken a serious turn and Jake would not be surprised if they became engaged soon. By the time Buddy joined Perkins & Floyd in a couple of years, it looked like he would be a married man.

Primary day 1952 dawned like every other July morning in San Diego. The sky was cloudless and the sun was already beaming relentlessly by 9 o'clock. The air was still and oppressive. The townsfolk began stirring early. There were even a few waiting in line at the Duval County Courthouse when the polls opened at 7 A.M.

Captain Allee brought in reinforcements for the day. A dozen Rangers were patrolling the polls in Jim Wells, Duval, Brooks and Starr counties by 6 A.M. Some folks said the Rangers just made a spectacle of the four counties. Others, mostly the Freedom Party members, said the Rangers were a welcome sight.

Using a converted bus, Captain Allee set up election day headquarters in San Diego just inside the Jim Wells County line. The mobile unit, parked in the shade of some weary mesquites, was outfitted with communications equipment, a coffee pot and a tiny refrigerator stocked with cold drinks.

Donato Serna and his Freedom Party *compadres* pitched a green funeral-like tent catty-corner from the courthouse. They had soft drinks and beer on ice, sandwiches and coffee, all free to anyone who would listen to their political talk. The rebel party even set up a loudspeaker, and Donato, Manuel Sanchez and several others took turns preaching the virtues of the Freedom Party and the evils of George Parr's Old Party.

Not to be outdone, George set up business in a warehouse east of the courthouse. He had window unit air conditioners installed in a dozen of the windows as an added attraction. He had *mariachis* and food and free drinks. It was a regular San Diego extravaganza.

Early in the day, Jake won a court order from a district judge in Corpus Christi to impound all of the Duval County ballots after the polls closed. The voting boxes were to be locked up in the district clerk's office in the Alice courthouse. If the order wasn't followed, the judge instructed the Rangers to seize the boxes.

The day progressed without major incident. Aside from the usual fights that result from too much drink and too much heat, primary day went smoothly. No one was barred from a polling booth, and the ballots were counted in what Captain Allee considered an orderly way. The paper ballots had to be hand counted, so the results weren't in and final until Sunday morning.

The Old Party made a clean sweep of the election. Woodrow Laughlin drew enough votes in Duval and Starr counties to outpoll Sam Reams. But the vote was surprisingly close. Out of 18,000 ballots cast, Laughlin won by only 700 votes. Duval County, while giving a majority to Laughlin, awarded Judge Reams an astonishing 1,000 votes.

It was a moral victory, the Freedom Party said.

"We have proved to the world that there are 1,000 free-thinking people in Duval County, people who can make up their own minds without asking George Parr," Manuel Sanchez told reporters. "We have just begun to fight."

Donato Serna, who lost the county judge race to Dan Tobin, Jr., publicly said he was satisfied. But privately, he was disheartened. He had hoped for at least one victory—to make a statement, to gain a toehold.

George Parr, who had run for Duval County Sheriff, was elected, and one of his lawyers, Raeburn Norris, edged out Mark

Heath to become district attorney. The ballots were impounded, as ordered, and the 1952 primary season drew to a close. George tried to convince himself he'd sent those straggling goats—including Jake Floyd—out to pasture. But something told him he was dead wrong about that.

Chapter 10
July

The body of Ed Wheeler lay stripped naked on the embalming table. He had been about 40 years old, of medium height and build, with dark features and a crop of thick dark hair. His lower arms, neck and upper chest had been bronzed by the harsh South Texas sun.

His was the second body to come in since midnight at Moyer Mortuary in Alice. When mortician Jimmy Holmgreen got the call from the funeral home in Mathis, it was about 1:30 A.M. and he had been busy embalming another body. He asked Hartwell Dobie of the Dobie Funeral Home to bring Wheeler's body the 30 miles from Mathis.

Like most of the folks he prepared for burial, the man on the table was someone Jimmy knew. Ed Wheeler was senior inspector at Alice for the U.S. Border Patrol. He spent his days and nights visiting farms and cheap taverns in search of illegals. Unlike the high-profile officers in the sheriff's office or the gun-brandishing *pistoleros* in Duval County, Wheeler kept downwind. His was the painstaking, detailed legwork that goes with policing a nation's border.

Wheeler was found dead in his patrol car after a highway accident. From the looks of his body, he could have just as easily perished from a heart attack. There were no obvious bruises or lacerations. Jimmy punctured the jugular vein to drain blood from the body, then opened the carotid artery to inject the embalming solution. His assisting mortician, Ray Bedgood, gave him an inquisitive look.

"Do we know anything about the accident?" Ray asked.

"All Hartwell said is it was a near head-on at the Nueces River Bridge," Jimmy said. "A carload of men from Orange Grove said Wheeler's car veered over into their lane. Wheeler's car ended up smashed into a guardrail."

"When did it happen?"

"About 10 o'clock last night."

Jimmy cradled the dead man's jaw in his hands. He noticed a touch of darkness around Wheeler's eyes and a trace of dried blood on his jawbone. The mortician stroked the jawbone with his finger, and it came up wet and bloody. The thick hair on the right temple was damp.

Jimmy parted the hair in several spots before finding a small puncture. Small amounts of blood were draining from the opening.

"Hand me that probe," he said to Ray, pointing to a stainless steel rod the thickness of two sewing needles. He inserted the probe into the wound and pushed it in as far as it would go. Ed Wheeler's head had been pierced almost from ear to ear.

"That's odd," Ray said. "I've never seen—you suppose some flying debris from the accident went clear through his head?"

"Possible, but I doubt it," Jimmy said. "It's rare, but sometimes bullet wounds don't bleed that much, especially if a small caliber weapon is used. There's a bullet in this man's head, I'd lay money on it."

Ray adjusted his glasses and glanced at a note pad on a counter a few feet from the embalming table.

"Says here the J.P. plans to sign the death certificate listing accidental death."

"Makes sense," Jimmy said. "Hartwell said they found him

on the front seat. He was the only person in the car. They probably thought he fell asleep at the wheel."

Jimmy began aspirating fluids and blood from the body's vital organs. He and Ray worked together like a well-lubricated machine. Jimmy had done the procedure so many times he could shift into automatic with his hands while his brain was miles away on another subject.

"I'm going to call Sheriff Halsey in the morning," Jimmy said after several minutes of silence.

The next morning he summoned both Halsey and Dr. Edwin Virgin, Ed Wheeler's personal physician, to the mortuary. After the two men examined the puncture in Wheeler's right temple, they agreed it could have been caused by a bullet. At Halsey's request, the border patrol agent's body was transported to the Alice hospital for a head X-ray. It revealed that a bullet had entered the right side of Wheeler's head, traveled the width of his skull and come to rest on the opposite side of the cranial cavity.

Halsey called the FBI mobile crime lab in Corpus Christi and asked them to do an autopsy. An FBI medical examiner found powder burns on Wheeler's right temple. The bullet he removed from the agent's head was from a small caliber weapon, probably of foreign origin. The bullet, he said, definitely had not been fired from Wheeler's .38 service revolver.

***

Captain Allee shuffled noisily, circling Ed Wheeler's champagne-colored sedan three times before stopping at the rear bumper. It was askew due to the impact of the collision, but still firmly attached to the vehicle. The Texas Ranger ran his hand underneath the chrome and came up with a handful of dried mud.

"Is the lab analyzing this?" he asked in his customary growl.

He addressed this question to John Holland, Ed Wheeler's

boss from San Antonio. Holland had asked Captain Allee to join him in combing through the car, which was impounded at the police station in Corpus Christi. Less than 18 hours had elapsed since Jimmy Holmgreen found the wound in Ed Wheeler's head. "Drop it in here," Holland said, holding up a large plastic evidence bag.

"Looks like the kind of mud you'd find on that riverbank," Captain Allee said. A soggy cigar dangled from a corner of his mouth as he studied the clump of dried dirt. The Ranger had spent the better part of the morning looking over the Nueces River Bridge where the accident occurred. His investigation had included the riverbank below.

"We've got reason to believe he was driving down there along the river that night," Holland said. "The local sheriff down there at Mathis has some men going over the area near the bridge right now. We'll have tire track molds before the day is out."

Holland's neatly pressed suit and smart tie belied his expertise at investigative work. He had been a Border Patrol agent for nearly 12 years before he was promoted to a desk job in San Antonio. He had known Captain Allee his entire career. Hell, everybody knew the Ranger captain from Carrizo Springs. He was one of the most trusted lawmen in South Texas. That's why Holland called him to help with the investigation.

He had a wide choice of officers to choose from. The FBI had entered the case, as they always do when a federal agent goes down. And of course, police in Mathis and Corpus Christi and several sheriff's offices had joined with U.S. Immigration investigators. But Holland preferred Cap.

"The last time anybody saw Ed alive was yesterday afternoon," he told the Ranger. "He paid a visit to his son's Boy Scout camp on the lake. Left about 4:30, and we haven't been able to find out much about what he did from there on out.

"A carload of kids saw this car turn off the same highway

earlier that night," Holland told the Ranger, nodding in the direction of Wheeler's sedan. "It was heading to Lake Corpus Christi State Park. We got a nearly positive ID on it because the kids remember it was the same color and the license plate had the prefix J."

"Tell me about the accident," Cap said. "How did this bumper get so cock-eyed?" "Pretty strange accident, Cap," Holland began. "The driver of the other car is a Milton Mareth of Orange Grove. He was driving south on Highway 59 when it happened. He had three other men in the car with him—some were relatives and one, I think, was just a friend.

"Anyway, as their car drove onto the Nueces River Bridge, another car approached from the opposite end. Mareth said the other car had its brights on, so he signaled several times with his foot-dimmer. Nothing happened. The brights stayed on.

"As the two cars approached each other on the bridge, Mareth noticed the other car was veering across into his lane. He slammed on his brakes, but the front left wheels locked for a second. Then the other car scraped the driver's side of Mareth's car. His elbow was crushed. He had it propped up in the open window.

"The other car just kept on going. The driver never hit the brakes. Mareth never heard tires or brakes squealing. Finally, it crashed into a guard rail a couple hundred feet from the point of first impact."

Cap withdrew the cigar from his mouth and spit a particle of tobacco.

"Where was Wheeler when they found him?"

"Well, Clarence Mareth, the brother of this guy who was doing the driving, he jumped out of the car and went to investigate. He found Wheeler slumped over in the front seat."

"Behind the steering wheel?"

"He was kind of leaning over to the right. These Mareths

swear they didn't touch the body. They seem like honest folks, so I'm inclined to believe them. When the local sheriff's office got there, he looked like he had been behind the wheel but had fallen over. His service revolver was on the right floorboard.

"Now that gun—that's another peculiar thing about this case, Cap. There had been two shots fired from it, or at least two, maybe three attempts to shoot it. The first shot apparently misfired because we found a slight firing pin depression on the cap.

"The second round in the cylinder skipped. The third round was fired."

Cap replugged the corner of his mouth with the cigar and spoke out of the other corner.

"Sounds like Wheeler had a goll-dang fight with somebody over that gun."

Cap ran his eyes quickly over the car.

"Any bullet holes anywhere?"

"Well, that's what I want us to look for. But earlier today some of the fellows looked it over pretty good and they found *nada*."

Cap circled the car once again.

"So it looks mighty certain that Wheeler wasn't killed in the car."

"Yep. And we're sure that he wasn't killed with his own gun. The bullet in his head was from a smaller caliber weapon."

Cap stood next to the driver's side and surveyed the car. The right front of the vehicle was smashed, and the left front corner looked as if someone had taken a sledgehammer to it.

"Ol' Wheeler was shot somewhere else, no doubt about that," Cap said. "Probably underneath that bridge. Whoever did it propped his body up behind that steering wheel and sent the car rolling down the highway and into that Mareth fella's car."

Holland was ready to call the vehicle inspection to a close. He invited the captain to go with him to the U.S. Immigration office in downtown Corpus Christi. He had some matters to discuss in private.

When they had settled into vinyl chairs, mugs of hot coffee in their hands, Holland brought up a case Wheeler had investigated nearly two years before.

"Remember the Flying Bootlegger?"

Cap nodded. How could he forget Orville Chambless, the Oklahoma Flying Bootlegger?

"Wheeler did some undercover work, trying to find out what he was up to."

The Ranger grunted.

"That goll-dang s.o.b. was running drugs in from Mexico and using the airport at Alice as his landing post," Cap growled. "Wheeler called me and asked me to keep an eye on him.

"Flashy guy, that Chambless. Liked to wear big ol' diamond rings and gold watches. Folks at the airport said whenever he bought gas he pulled out a big wad of bills—fifties and hundreds.

"I never liked the looks of that guy. He combed his hair like a hood, all greased back, long and thick. I used to see him hanging out with some of George's *pistoleros*. They'd be riding around in San Diego late at night. Stop off at the grocery and buy some of Parr's beer, then go off and park downtown and drink it all."

Cap didn't think much of beer drinking. He never touched alcohol and told the men in his company they better not have booze on their breath when they were on duty.

He swallowed some coffee and continued. Holland had heard these stories before, but his memory could stand refreshing.

"He played a little Texas two-step on me and I finally had to get tough. He was a fugitive, remember, from a manslaughter conviction in Oklahoma—"

"That's right. I knew there was an Oklahoma connection," said Holland.

"He kept getting arrested for this or that and kept getting turned loose," Cap continued. "I don't remember it all. It was goll-dang frustrating. Finally, the chief deputy over there in San Diego, Pete Saenz, he turned that ol' boy over to Nago Alaniz.

"Alaniz is one of ol' George's lawyers, you know. Gets table scraps mostly. Reminds me of one of those mangy, skinny dogs you see slinking down the streets in San Diego. He'd do anything if you throw him a bone, even if it's already picked clean.

"They'd trumped up some car theft charge against Chambless so he couldn't be returned to Oklahoma. I told Sheriff Garcia over there they'd better turn him over or I'd arrest him on sight.

"Well, ol' Homer Dean, the district attorney, he dropped the car theft charges and turned Chambless over to me. That sorry s.o.b. cried while I drove him over to Alice to meet some of the officers from Oklahoma. He said if he had to go back to the penitentiary at McAlester, some of his enemies would kill him for sure."

Holland loosened his tie and placed his coffee cup on a side table.

"As far as I know, he's escaped the wrath of his enemies," said Holland. "He's still up at McAlester, but I hear he may be paroled soon."

He swallowed some more coffee, then looked at Cap as if sizing him up for the first time.

"You're one of the few people who knew, Cap, that Ed was a narc. He posed as an airport employee one time to see if he could trace Chambless' plane. But Chambless was too clever. He refused to respond to their radio calls.

"That was one thing that always worried me about Ed. I warned him several times about it. He kept things too close. He didn't confide in me, not anyone. He kept no files, no records. We don't know who his informants were. Hell, we don't even know what he was working on the day he got killed.

"I guess his behavior's not all that surprising," Holland continued. "He got his early schooling in investigative work during the war. He was in the Army Counterintelligence Corps; cut his teeth in the India-Burma theater. That's one of the reasons we hired him. He was a trained investigator when he came to us. We would have been fools not to grab him.

"He'd been poking around Mathis for several months. We'd been getting a lot of reports of drug activity in the area."

"Well, that reminds me. There's something else I wanted to tell ya', " Cap interrupted. "I dang near forgot. I got a call this morning from that Rowe fella—you know, James Rowe. The reporter from the *Corpus Christi Caller*.

"Claims he saw Wheeler a few days ago and Wheeler said he was about to have a big story for Rowe. Wheeler said a bunch of important people were going down.

"Said Wheeler told him some strange story about a fella from Duval flying up to New York and trying to smuggle a gold bar through that airport up there—what's it called—some Italian name—"

"La Guardia," Holland prompted.

"Yup. That's it. Anyway, Rowe said Wheeler told him U.S. Customs picked this Duval fella up at the airport, but he hid the bar of gold in a bathroom. The dang thing was worth more than $13,000. I don't know, the whole thing doesn't make sense to me. I guess they let him go take a piss and he was out of sight for a minute or two.

"Anyway, they found the gold brick, or whatever you call the thing, but had no way of tying it to the Duval County guy. So they let him go."

"That's all Rowe told you?" Holland asked.

"*Es todo*," Cap said. Cap's conversations usually were sprinkled with Spanish phrases. He had grown up speaking the language.

Holland picked up the telephone and buzzed an agent in a nearby office on the intercom. He repeated the reporter's story to the agent, instructed him to check it out and hung up.

"Holland," Cap said, "remember last year when a bunch of us Rangers went in and did a vice raid at a place called El Ranchito?"

"Sure, Cap," Holland said. "Clint Peoples, that nice young Ranger from Austin, busted the place."

"Yup. We knew there was gambling and prostitution, but all the Rangers in my company were familiar faces in Duval. So we asked Clint to come down and check the place out.

"Well, by dang if they didn't have rooms for poker and dice back behind the beer hall. And behind the place, they had a little tourist court. Several of the girls tried to get Clint to go back there with them. It was only six bucks, and they were mighty pretty little Mexican *señoritas*—probably wetbacks.

"Well, George's ex-wife owned that place, and George did too before they got divorced. They let one of George's hoods, a sorry no-good named Raul Guerra, run it. It was a patronage job just as sure as working at the Duval County Courthouse. Raul has a brother, another sorry Mexican *hombre* named Juan Barrera Canante. This Canante fellow—he's one of George's nastiest characters. A knuckle man.

"Wheeler told me a couple of times he had an eye on this Canante. Said he'd seen Canante a few times around Mathis. And he was in El Ranchito every time Wheeler went over there to check for illegals.

"You know, we had good reason to believe ol' Canante was the boy who took a shot at that D.A. up in Belton. You know, the D.A. who was trying ol' Sam Smithwick back in '49. Evetts was his name. Jim Evetts. He was putting his car in his garage one night during the trial and somebody took a shot at him. Fired twice but missed both times. They never caught the guy.

"I went up there and took some mug shots of likely characters from Duval and Jim Wells. Found two men who said they'd seen Canante in a tavern up there a day or two before Evetts got shot at. We never found any other evidence, though. Never found the gun."

Holland lit a cigarette and motioned through one of the big plate-glass windows for a secretary to bring more coffee. Cap had worn his cigar down to nothing, so he tossed it in a trash can and pulled the cellophane off a fresh one.

"Whatever happened in that Smithwick case, Cap?" Holland asked when the secretary came in with the coffeepot.

"Well, ol' Smithwick. If he weren't so dang stupid he might have made a halfway decent deputy. He got a life sentence. Hell, they should've put him in the chair. Murder, in broad daylight, with witnesses. Well, anyway, he got life and they sent him up to Huntsville. He had a cell all to himself, away from the other prisoners. You know how they do when an officer goes to prison. Keep 'em away from the other inmates so they don't tangle with anybody they helped convict.

"Smithwick was probably in prison a little over a year when they found him hanged. He'd tied a towel around the upper bunk in his cell and put his head through a makeshift noose.

"The prison folks called me down there to look into it. I was suspicious at first. Sam knew plenty about George's machine down there in Duval. And George didn't get him off like he usually does. Sam could've sung like a bird down there at Huntsville—about all kinds of things.

"Then we got a call from Coke Stevenson. That made us even more suspicious. Said he'd gotten a letter from Smithwick a few days before they found him hanged. The letter said Smithwick knew where the ballots were for Box 13, you know, that box in Alice that George stuffed. Got Lyndon Johnson elected. Smithwick said the ballots were hidden somewhere and he knew how to find them.

"Coke was going to go down there and talk to him, but before he could make it, Smithwick was dead. If Smithwick was going to spill beans about what went on at Box 13, then goll-dang it, there'd be a few folks who'd want to kill him. But the letter didn't make much sense. We knew where the ballots were. They were in the boxes. It was the poll lists and tally sheets we needed. That's where the 200 names where added.

"Anyway, we decided there was no way anybody could get in his cell and hang somebody the size of Sam Smithwick. The coroner ruled it a suicide, and we never found proof it was anything else."

Holland lit another cigarette and sat back on the vinyl cushions, his head enveloped in a cloud of smoke.

"You were telling me about El Ranchito. Ed used to go there looking for illegals."

"Oh, yeah," said Cap. "Like I was saying. We did a vice raid down there and arrested about 20 people. Some young girls who didn't speak English and a few men who ran the bar and the poker tables. Neither Canante or his brother got picked up.

"I decided I didn't want to mess with that place any more. As soon as we let those girls out, they were going right back. We didn't have enough undercover officers to do vice work. So I asked Homer Dean, the district attorney over there, to get a court order and padlock the place.

"There was a hearing in Judge Reams's court and Wheeler testified. Said it was a whorehouse and they ran dice and poker. Reams said that was all he needed to hear and he shut the joint down. It's the only time anybody has been able to shut down one of George's operations.

"And I tell you, Holland, it's just about the best thing that's happened to me since I been coming to Duval and Jim Wells. Saved me a lot of headaches. I got enough to deal with.

"By gosh, I've been doing vice since I got to be a Ranger. That and chasing cattle rustlers. But hell, down in Duval, they got so much else going on that's twenty times worse. I don't put any stock in drinking and carousing. But when you start robbing—I'm talking about robbing folks of their votes. Robbing from the county and the school district. Robbing a place so bad that it's stripped to nothing. That's worse than bootlegging or gambling any day.

"I spend a good bit of time keeping an eye on ol' George. I once heard him tell a crowd of his Mexican *peones* that there's nothing under heaven or on earth that isn't found out. The message is—Papa's watching everything.

"I tell you, Holland, a man's gotta be armed—and with more than a big gun—down there in Duval. Hell, I carry a Thompson submachine gun with me. I carry it in a big heavy canvas bag on the front seat of the Ford. They don't look pretty but by gosh they sure do shoot. I haven't had to use it yet, but by gosh, if I see George Parr walking around town with a carbine again—

"But like I said, a man's gotta have more than a gun down there. Hell, there isn't a night goes by I don't read a Chapter in the Bible. If I was sick, maybe I wouldn't. But most nights, that's the last thing I do before I switch the lamp off.

"I been a lawman for more than 20 years, Holland. And goll-dang it, I've never seen anyone like that George Parr. Some days when I'm driving over to San Diego, I just say a little prayer—both for me and my men.

"I'm mighty sorry about Wheeler. You've lost a good man. Had a lot of respect for him. He was getting too close to something, that's for dang sure.

"You ever been close to a possum, Holland? Well, you wouldn't want to. They're mean as hell if you get right up next to 'em. And they smell bad. Suppose it's cause they eat garbage and hide in the same kind of dark places that roaches and rats do. Nasty varmints. I smell a possum, Holland. I smell *tecuache*."

Chapter 11
Labor Day Weekend

Mario Sapet perched on the barstool and draped himself over the counter, his short, thick arms encircling a mug of Coca-Cola mixed with beer. It was his favorite drink. His dark eyes level with the rim of the foamy mug, he stared absently at the mirrored wall across the bar. It was Labor Day weekend 1952, and this was his fifth mug of brew in the hour and a half that he had been in El Jardin Internacional. Mario didn't mind wasting the hours at El Jardin. It was a class joint, classier than the taverns he usually frequented. Besides, he had met George Parr at El Jardin, and that was a welcome memory. Mario liked quenching his thirst alongside thoroughbreds.

Like a lot of folks from San Diego and Alice and San Antonio, George came to Nuevo Laredo for the bullfights. And while he was in town, he always came to El Jardin. Mario detested bullfights—too much high drama. Give him something cool to drink in a nice bar, and he could be happy.

Mario glanced out the expansive windows alongside the bar. It was a bright hot day, and he was enjoying the air conditioning El Jardin's owners had just installed. Every seat in the bar was taken; folks were cooling down before heading to the bullfights.

Mario liked Nuevo Laredo. The town had been good to him. He had found as much success in the border town as he had in San Diego and San Antonio combined. It was here that Mario had opened the Blue Heaven, a hugely successful brothel on the edge of the factory district. He had borrowed the money from his foster mother to start the business. It was for an investment, he told her. She could share in the profits, he promised. And she did. Mario had brought her some cash every month when he was in San Antonio. She never asked where the money came from.

The Blue Heaven had been a success primarily because Mario had the good fortune to hire a once-beautiful hooker named Teresita to run it. Teresita had worked the streets of the factory district for years. She knew how to lure the young whores to the Blue Heaven, and she kept them fed and relatively free of disease. She also knew how to entice the factory workers to her doors. The tequila was cheap at the Blue Heaven; the entertainment, a bit pricier.

Few things had given Mario greater pleasure than striding through the front door of the Blue Heaven. It may have been a ramshackle converted hotel, but it had been a castle to Mario. And he had been king. The whores had regarded him with a distant respect. He never consorted with any of them; Teresita was against it. It wasn't good for business, she told him. She seemed to know her way around, so he believed her and took his pleasures only with Teresita.

Mario could trace the downfall of the Blue Heaven to the day that Teresita crumpled in a faint. After that, she never was herself again. She took to her bed and refused to see a doctor. She lingered for months, the pounds melting from her bones. By the time Teresita breathed her last, the Blue Heaven had closed down.

Mario took a long drink from the mug and surveyed the mob in El Jardin Internacional. He searched for a familiar face, but they were all out-of-towners. It was vexing to wait so long for a *compadre*. It was already half past one, and he and Alfredo were to be in San Diego by 3 o'clock.

Alfredo Cervantes had been a frequent a customer at the

Blue Heaven. He lived near Guadalajara, hundreds of miles south of Nuevo Laredo, but he came to the border often. His business was smuggling drugs and cars—drugs across the border to the rich gringos in America, and cars across the border of Texas so the poor Mexicans could have vehicles. Mario couldn't remember how they became friends other than they just started going to El Jardin together. One thing about Alfredo, he didn't drink. He had no taste for the stuff, not like he had for reefer. He'd just sit there at the bar with Mario and drink a Coca-Cola and smoke Lucky Strikes.

Alfredo had never met George, but he would soon. Mario would see to that. Mario recalled the day he first met George himself. The Duke of Duval had come into El Jardin with his customary entourage. There were three or four *pistoleros*; Mario admired their guns and their *sombreros*. And there were several attractive Mexican women, powdered and painted and showing off plenty of cleavage. George had his nephew Archer with him and some other rich-looking gringos. As usual, El Patrón bought drinks for everyone in El Jardin, making a big show of it when he called out to the bartender in Spanish.

Mario had been impressed. He had heard a lot about the Duke of Duval—how he was a millionaire, how he had a road construction company and an oil company. He had ranches, too—two or three of them—and a big *hacienda* in San Diego. He had about a hundred or two hundred *pistoleros*, all getting paychecks. Mario had been at loose ends then. The Blue Heaven had closed and he had a bar in San Antonio, but he was tired of it. It wasn't making much money—not like the Blue Heaven had. He needed something new, something that offered quick cash. Maybe this George Parr was just who he was looking for.

He wove his way through the Parr entourage and sidled up to a *pistolero*. He was bearded and small, not at all muscular, but he had a big automatic tucked underneath his belt. His name, he told Mario, was Juan Barrera Canante.

Juan talked endlessly about El Jefe. He'd do anything for the Mexican people. Just go knock on his door and he'd give you fifty—no questions. And the man knew how to give a party—always barbecued beef, never goat. George Parr was no gringo, Juan Barrera Canante said. No, sir, he spoke Spanish better than English. Why, if it weren't for El Jefe, half the Mexicans in Duval would be in jail and the other half would be starving.

Juan introduced Mario to George, who was distracted by a Mexican *señor*ita leaning on his shoulder and playing with his ear. Talking was not what George wanted at the moment. He would exchange a few sentences with Mario, then snicker because the girl had tickled him. Still, Mario was impressed. Here was class, power, money and sex in one package. Mario hit it off with Juan Barrera Canante so well that when he left El Jardin that day, he had signed on as a deputy sheriff in Duval County. It meant $400 a month in ready cash.

Mario lit a cigarette and sipped again from the mug. He still couldn't believe what a stroke of good luck it had been to become a Duval County deputy. For 400 bucks a month, all he had to do was spend a few days a week walking the streets of San Diego with a gun belted to his waist. He had few responsibilities—just do what Juan or Pete or sometimes El Patrón told him to do. Mostly, his job was to look menacing. "Mi gente," George had said of his people, "need to feel secure. That's your job. Make them feel safe."

Mario was beginning to feel weak. A mild diabetic condition made him a poor candidate for places like El Jardin. He ordered a plate of tamales and another drink. The food would clear his head. Mario never told El Patrón or anyone of his ailments, of which there were others. Since infancy, he had had infrequent and unpredictable epileptic seizures. No two were alike. He might suddenly feel cold and clammy, and his body would freeze, his eyes rolling back into his head. Or he would stop breathing and collapse.

As he grew older, the seizures came more often. He learned to read the warning signs. He would become excessively tired, and his head would throb like it was being trampled by stampeding horses.

The bartender had just set down the plate of tamales when Mario felt a tap on the shoulder. It was Inez Mendez and her husband, Encarnacion, proprietors of a bar in San Antonio. They were in Nuevo Laredo for the bullfights, she told Mario. He gave her his stool and stood at the counter to eat his tamales. Inez was petite and she walked on crutches, her leg crippled by polio. They called her La Trecha, the crooked one, but there was steel in her spine.

She had built her San Antonio bar into a profitable enterprise on her own. Inez's Place was in a four-story brick building on West Commerce. The second and third floors belonged to the prostitutes. Encarnacion, a quiet, self-effacing man who worked just as hard as Inez had married a smart businesswoman.

"I'm waiting for Alfredo," Mario said, stuffing a whole tamale in his mouth.

"That Alfredo," Inez said, "always late. Not very reliable. You going to the bullfights?"

"No. We're going to San Diego. Got a job to do."

"Oh?" Inez said, motioning to the bartender to bring her and her husband beers. "Is Alfredo a *pistolero* now?"

"No, no, no," Mario said, smiling. "You know El Tamburero. He makes an exception for me. But mostly, he stays as far away from the law as he can."

Those who knew Alfredo called him by the Spanish nickname, which meant "the drum." Mario supposed it was because Alfredo's big belly was round and solid like a drum. He would have to ask his friend one day where the name came from.

Folks called Mario "El Turco." His mother was Syrian, and he looked like a Turk. She had died when Mario was only 10, and his father had died when he was even younger. Mario had no recollection of him.

"El Tamburero, he likes coming to the States," Mario said. "He never wanted to leave in the first place."

Alfredo liked to reminisce about the war days, when he had worked an auto assembly line in Detroit. It was easy to get a green card then. All the able-bodied men were in the armed forces. He would have stayed except for the brutal winters, he told Mario. But his marijuana habit weakened his respiratory system, and a bout of pneumonia convinced him that he should return to his homeland.

Inez sipped her beer pensively.

"Hate to tell you this," she said. "but you'd be smart to pay a call on your place in San Antonio."

Mario's was on the West Side. It was just a *cantina*, not a real establishment like Inez's place. He had bought it when he was making money on the Blue Heaven. He had hired Pedro, El Ardillo, to run it. Pedro he knew from his days at the state prison in Huntsville.

"El Ardillo, what's he done now?" Mario said, popping a fourth tamale in his mouth. They didn't call Pedro the Squirrel for nothing. At Huntsville, where he and Mario both served time for murder, he earned the nickname because he was forever stashing contraband in his mattress. He always had cigarettes, girlie pictures, candy and a bottle of some sort of industrial strength spirit in his cache.

Mario had hired him to run his *cantina* for two reasons: Pedro needed a job, and he had the requisite street savvy to handle the clientele. He might steal cigarettes, but Mario knew he would keep his fingers out of the cash register.

"He's running cockfights out back of the place," Inez said. "The cops raided it last night."

The cops kept a vigilant eye on Mario's tavern. He might

have been able to run a quiet operation if he hadn't had a rap sheet longer than his arm. Mario knew the inside of the San Antonio police station well; he had been booked there too many times to count. The charges ranged from assault to gaming with dice to drunkenness and vagrancy.

"He in jail?" Mario asked, gulping his boilermaker.

"As far as I know," Inez said. "I went down this morning to see if I could bail him out, but he hadn't even been to see the judge. Heard they picked up six or seven other fellas, too."

Mario would have to tend to the San Antonio situation later. The Duke had a job for him and Alfredo, an important job.

El Turco felt a nudge in his ribs. Alfredo had finally arrived.

"Only two hours late," Mario said, wiping the foam from his moustache with his shirtsleeve. Alfredo shrugged and ordered a Coca-Cola. His dark eyes were dull and vacant.

"Alfredo, you come to my house in San Antonio. I make you menudo," Inez said. Alfredo loved her menudo.

He lifted his glass in salute to her and drank. Alfredo wasn't talking this afternoon, lost in a marijuana haze.

Mario drained his mug and motioned for Alfredo to follow him. He told Inez they would visit her and Encarnacion soon, maybe in the next week. And they were gone.

***

The emerald green Packard was Mario's prized possession. A V-8 engine, automatic, hi-fi radio, the works. The Duke helped him buy it. He drove it, brand new, off the lot in San Antonio that summer of 1952. He loved how the *peones* in San Diego turned their heads when he drove by.

The windows were rolled all the way down and the radio was blasting as he sped down the highway to San Diego. El Tamburero had yet to say a word. He sat mute in the passenger seat, not even looking at the scrub oak and mesquite as they whizzed by.

Alfredo was a big man, especially for a Mexican. He was only 5-feet-7, but he carried more than 210 pounds on his frame. He didn't smile often, but when he did, a shiny gold tooth shone between his lips. A large, puffy brown scar slashed across his left elbow, a souvenir of barroom fisticuffs. He wore his black hair cropped close to his ears and neck, but longer on top so that his head was crowned with wavy locks. His dark eyebrows were thick and bushy near his nose, tapering off to a thin line over his eyes.

Alfredo had told Mario something of his childhood—that he had grown up in a family of *peones*. His father and mother had worked the agave fields near Guadalajara, harvesting the succulents that provided the nectar for tequila. It seemed to Alfredo, he once mused, that his father had worked hard in the fields so there would be enough spirits in the *cantinas*. For when he wasn't harvesting, he was drinking his earnings. He gave Alfredo's mother a few pesos now and then to feed Alfredo and his four brothers and three sisters.

"You lucky bastard," he would say to Mario, envious that his friend had grown up an only child. "You don't know what it's like fighting for every bite of food." Alfredo seemed proud of the fact that he and his brothers had slapped their sisters around so they wouldn't try to eat. Their father would catch them shoving the girls around, and he'd pound the boys for it.

The car drove east into a damp, hot Gulf wind. It must be over 100 degrees, Mario thought, rubbing his sweaty forehead with his shirtsleeve.

"Tamburero," he said, shouting over the Spanish music that roared from the radio, "you nervous about meeting the Duke?"

Alfredo didn't move. He didn't say a word.

"No need to be, *amigo*," Mario continued. The tamales had settled the pounding in his head. But all the beer and cola were creating other physical symptoms.

"He's like a big *padre*. Some of the *peones* call him El Papa. Takes care of everybody. Look what he's done for me. He'll take care of you, too."

No response.

Alfredo got like this sometimes, usually when he'd been staying up day and night, smoking marijuana steady for days. Mario decided to pull over and take a piss.

The two men rolled into San Diego about 4:30. George's black Buick was still parked outside his office. Mario hoped Alfredo would snap out of the mute routine. It wouldn't look good for his first audience with the Duke.

Pete Saenz was in George's office when Mario and Alfredo entered. Pete introduced Alfredo to the Duke.

"He's going to be on the payroll for awhile," the deputy sheriff said.

"Fine, fine. Glad to have you aboard," George said, showing Alfredo to a wingback. He lit the Mexican's cigarette.

"Tell me about yourself," the Duke said. He looked genuinely interested.

To Mario's relief, Alfredo talked. Then he began to worry that he would never shut up. Uncork that bottle and the words flowed like a river.

Alfredo told George about his wife and seven children, about their ranch near Guadalajara, about his mother, Guadalupe. Mario noticed that every time Alfredo talked of his mother, his tone changed slightly. He spoke of her as if she were a nun.

"Nice to meet a man who respects his mother," George said. "My mother, she's still alive. Lives on the family ranch near Benavides. I see her often."

"Alfredo, he's handy with a gun," Pete said. "Can knock a tin can off a fence at a hundred paces."

Mario wished he could make the same boast. Because of his

seizures, he never concentrated on target practice.

George asked Alfredo to tell him the story of his nickname. The river kept flowing.

He had been at a dance hall one evening years ago, when he was in his twenties, Alfredo began. He was there with friends, a group he had grown up with. The band was playing polkas, and Alfredo had danced but little. He had preferred instead to beat the rhythm of the music on the table. He liked how the vibrations of his hand drumming sent the tequila glasses into a dance on the tabletop. Alfredo drummed on George's desk, in illustration.

Alfredo and his group had stayed late into the night, and the band continued to play. The girls long ago had given up on coaxing him to the dance floor. It was well past midnight when the band stopped abruptly. It wasn't that the dance hall was closing. It seemed the drummer had taken ill. The dance hall was full, and the bandleader considered playing on without a drummer. Alfredo's friends had been insistent that he must take to the drums. He had never played drums in his life and for a long time he refused. But they kept pestering him until he complied. Alfredo was amazed at how quickly he became even slightly proficient.

He knew all the songs the band had played, and so he knew all the rhythms. The band played until dawn, and by the final song, Alfredo had earned a nickname, The Big Drum. Mario glanced at Alfredo's stomach and chuckled to himself again about its resemblance to a drum.

George said he was heading to the Windmill for a plate of enchiladas. Would they like to join him?

Mario declined for himself and Alfredo. Pete said he was hungry. George instructed the sheriff to make sure Alfredo had what he needed. After an effusive farewell, Mario and his companion drove to Alice and checked into a tourist court.

They would start the job the next day.

Section IV
Late 1952

Chapter 12
September 5

The two-story house was spacious and fine by Alice's standards. It looked long and lean—like Jake Floyd. To Mario Sapet and Alfredo Cervantes, it looked like the home of a gringo lawyer. They must have circled the block around Fourth and Reynolds streets 20 or 30 times, studying the California-style house. Sometimes, they would even see Jake Floyd walking from the house to the garage, where his late-model Buick was parked. Alfredo studied closely how El Viejo moved, swinging his overly long arms in an easy rhythm. The lawyer walked slowly and deliberately, his feet striking the walkway with a clean, crisp sound. Alfredo could never get an unobstructed view of the gringo—his woman was always close to his side. They'd walk the 40 feet from the house to the two-car garage, or back to the house. Sometimes a cleaning woman would bring laundry to a little room attached to the garage.

Between the house and the garage was a smaller house, its roofline too low and doorway too small for anyone larger than a child to walk through. There was a flowering huisache tree and massive lazy mesquites whose limbs reached low to the ground. They were perfect for kids to climb on. But Mario and Alfredo saw no kids at Jake Floyd's house. It looked like El Viejo lived there with his woman and no one else.

As the two men rode past the front of the house in the green

Packard, Alfredo studied the structure. There was a small stoop of a front porch dead center of the house. It was appointed with a wrought-iron arbor, fancy and ornate, like the rich lawyers' houses in Guadalajara. The lower story of the house was whitewashed brick, the upper story, covered in whitewashed redwood siding.

To the rear of the house were two long porches; one ran the length of the upper floor, while the other, made of polished Mexican tiles, skirted the ground floor. The branches of a huge bougainvillea snaked over a trellis to the second story. There were wooden lawn chairs on the lower porch, and bushy plants in fancy planters.

After a week of cruising the neighborhood, Alfredo and Mario concluded that dusk was the perfect time to do the job. The gringos were in their houses eating supper. The streets were deserted, and the light was still good. El Viejo always seemed to show up about that time.

But as soon as they hit upon the plan, the rhythm of the neighborhood and of the Floyd household shifted. El Viejo didn't come home at dusk, and when they did see him, he was with the woman. And, too, they noticed an unfamiliar car in the driveway. It was a Henry J coupe, parked with its rear facing the garage. It looked like the gringo lawyer had a houseguest.

Alfredo looked sullen. He hadn't said much since the night before, when he smoked so much reefer he passed out on the bed. They were moving from one tourist court to another every day—spending one night in San Diego, the next in Alice. El Turco was like a warden—no whores, no *cantinas*, no nothing. After the job was done, he said, Alfredo could screw his brains out. For now, they had to keep their heads low.

When they finished scouting Jake Floyd's house, they stopped off at a *pistolero*'s house, and Mario went inside. He returned to the Packard carrying a bottle of whiskey and a bag of reefer. They found another motel room and repeated the routine of the night before.

The next day was the Friday after Labor Day. Mario left the motel early in the morning and didn't return until late in the afternoon. Alfredo was just beginning to show signs of life when El Turco turned the doorknob.

"We got a new plan, Tamburero," the Parr deputy said, turning up his nose. A haze of smoke hung in the room, and Mario swung at it with an open hand. Alfredo was sprawled on the bed in his shorts, his curly hair in knots.

"But no action until Monday. Monday night's the night. We got it all set up. A Parr man's going to set a trap for El Viejo, get him outa the house. You'll be there."

Alfredo rubbed his eyes and sat up slowly.

"And where will you be?"

"I'll tell you about it in the car. Get dressed. We're going to Corpus for the weekend."

Those were the most beautiful words Alfredo had heard in a week—at least since Mario told him he could get $3,000 for doing the job. Alfredo had wondered why Mario didn't do the job himself. When he asked him about it, Mario said he was too well known. They needed somebody who wasn't a local and, better yet, a man who could disappear in Mexico when El Viejo was taken care of. Mario had too good a deal going in Duval County to spend the rest of his life across the border.

But Alfredo suspected there was more to it than that. He doubted Mario was much of a marksman. He seemed shaky with a gun in his hand; he recalled the time Mario broke out in a sweat and then passed out cold. They were shooting at turkeys on one of George's ranches. Alfredo didn't know what to do except to drag Mario to the car and take him to a doctor. Mario revived before they got to town and refused to go to the hospital. There was something wrong with El Turco, but he would never admit it.

Alfredo dressed, and the two men were on their way to

Corpus Christi in less than 30 minutes. El Turco said he had a good friend who owned a bar in Corpus where they could hoist a few. It was dark and off to itself. They wouldn't be noticed. The drive to the port city was less than an hour, and Mario used the time to outline the new strategy in detail. Another Parr man was entering the plot, he said, a lawyer named Nago Alaniz.

Alfredo was still mulling over the new plan when they walked into Jesus Pompa's bar. It was about 4 o'clock, and the place was deserted, save for the bartender, who was toweling down the counter.

"Mario, *mi amigo*!" the bartender held his arms out as if he planned to hug El Turco. "How have you been?"

Mario stepped up to the bar and introduced Alfredo. Jesus and Mario commenced to talk in Spanish like two men who had known each other for years. Alfredo slouched onto a barstool, perched his elbows on the bar and said nothing as the two men caught each other up.

Mario ordered a beer, and Alfredo his usual Coca-Cola.

"So, how is business?" Mario asked his friend.

"Up and down," Jesus replied. "Labor Day weekend we couldn't keep them out of here. But it's been dead ever since."

Mario gave a knowing nod. "That's what I hate about this business. Too much up and down. Now, I got a deal going, Jesus, that might be just what you're looking for."

Mario went on to tell his friend about his job as a deputy in Duval County. Easy money, he said, and instant respect. Folks in San Diego stepped aside when Mario walked down the sidewalk. In fact, Mario said, grinning widely, he had a new gun he wanted Jesus to see. He was giving it to Alfredo, he said, glancing at his traveling companion.

"It's out in the car. In the glove compartment," Mario said, again looking at Alfredo. "Would you go get it so we can show it to my friend?" Mario slapped Alfredo on the back heartily and belched.

Alfredo shrugged his shoulders and left the tavern. He didn't take kindly to playing with guns, but he could tell about this mood Mario was in. There would be no peace until El Turco could show off the gun.

When Alfredo returned, he pulled a .38 Colt revolver from his trouser pocket and laid it on the bar counter. It was a compact weapon, no bigger than Mario's hand. It had a stag horn handle and a shiny snub-nosed barrel. The shank of the gun was a rough, grainy metal. It was dark and powerful, and Alfredo regarded it with his customary respect.

Jesus admired it with relish, picking it up and spinning the chambers, taking aim at imaginary people in the tavern booths and pulling the trigger. He laughed as he fired with abandon throughout the darkened room, and Mario joined in. Alfredo sighed and stretched out in a booth.

"Pow! Pow!" Jesus snickered as he pulled the trigger, pointing the Colt at the reclining Alfredo. El Tamburero bolted out of the booth like he had been poked with a spear.

"Give me that gun, you stupid. . ." Alfredo said, lunging over the bar and grabbing Jesus' neck with one hand, the Colt with the other. The bar keeper's eyes grew wide and his body went limp. Alfredo said nothing; he just stared into Jesus' bug-eyed face.

It seemed like five minutes they stood there that way. Finally, Jesus began choking under Alfredo's grip, and the Mexican let go. He stuffed the gun in his trousers and stalked out of the bar.

"He's nervous, Jesus," Mario explained. "Got a big job to do. Please—forgive him."

Jesus rubbed his neck with one hand and waved off Mario's apologies with the other. El Turco decided it was a good time to leave.

"*Mi amigo*, I will see you soon. Perhaps tomorrow," Mario said, reaching across the bar to shake Jesus' hand. "I promise you, my friend will show manners when we come back. So sorry."

Jesus waved Mario out the door and slumped into a chair. Frankly, he doubted Mario and his foul-tempered friend would be back at the bar any time soon. He wasn't sure he'd let them in if they did.

The next afternoon, late, Jesus was walking out the front door of the bar on his way to the post office and practically ran head-on into Mario.

Jesus halted and allowed Mario to put an arm around his shoulder. Alfredo was not in sight. The two men exchanged pleasantries. Mario always wanted to know how Jesus' wife was. As usual, he inquired of the tavern keeper's children. Then he asked Jesus where there was a good place to eat fish.

"I want the freshest seafood in town," Mario said expansively, breathing stale beer fumes onto the tavern keeper. "Only the best for me and my friend," he said, gesturing toward the green Packard parked on the street. Alfredo was slumped against the passenger side window, his hat at an angle on his forehead.

Jesus took a few steps down the sidewalk in the direction of the green vehicle, then pointed to a restaurant across the street. "Over there. The best in town." Then Jesus excused himself, saying he needed to reach the post office before it closed. Mario nodded and headed for the car.

***

By Saturday night, Alfredo had had enough of Mario. The rooster strutting, the bragging—he needed a break. He told his companion to take him to the bus station. He was going to San Antonio to see Inez Mendez, La Trecha. He'd be back in Alice by noon on Monday. Mario tried to talk him out of it, but without success.

It was almost midnight Sunday when Alfredo arrived at

Inez's Place. He had no trouble finding it ; he and Mario had been there dozens of times in the past year. It was in a warehouse district just west of El Mercado. Alfredo had come there many nights after getting off work at the market, where he sold fruits and vegetables. He had to have a job to keep his green card, and he needed the green card to stay in the States. So Mario had got him that crummy job in the market. It was the best he could do, he had said.

It was Sunday night, so Inez's Place wasn't very crowded. The whores tried to spark some interest from Alfredo, but he sulked at the bar, sipping on a Coca-Cola without interest until closing time. Inez and Encarnacion shut the place down at midnight, and Alfredo suggested they go get a plate of Mexican food. They were agreeable, but first, Inez said, she had to go to a wake.

They drove to the funeral parlor, a flat-roofed brick building, and Alfredo went in with Inez. Encarnacion stayed behind in his Cadillac and drank a beer. The maple casket was small—barely four feet in length—and it was open. The body of a boy of about seven years lay inside. The box was surrounded by candles, and a few folding chairs were scattered about the small room. Two heavyset women wearing black lace veils sat near the casket and wept loudly.

Alfredo stayed to the back of the small room as Inez, clutching a rosary, pulled a chair up to the casket and looked inside. She sat there, fingering the rosary, for at least an hour. By the time she pulled herself off the chair, steadying herself with her cane, the two weeping women had left. She was dry-eyed but unsteady on her twisted legs, so Alfredo took her arm and helped her to the Cadillac.

They drove to a place called Hector's, an all-night *cocina* specializing in *chile con carne de puerco*. Encarnacion stayed behind in the car, sipping beer again, as Alfredo and Inez went inside. Alfredo was ravenous, unable to remember if he had eaten the previous day. Over cigarettes and plates of spicy pork, Inez broke her silence.

"He was my nephew," she said of the boy in the casket. "Drowned in the Guadalupe. Went swimming with his brothers and sisters and went down. My sister is nearly insane with grief."

Inez puffed on her cigarette between bites of pork. Alfredo wasn't sure what he saw in her eyes, but they were ringed with dark bags. If nothing else, she was exhausted.

"So, my friend," Inez said, her tone a touch brighter. "What brings you back to San Antonio?"

"Had to get away," he said. "Mario—he was driving me loco."

Inez nodded. "He can do that. If you need to stay in town awhile, we've got a place we sublet. You could work at the market awhile."

"No, no," Alfredo shook his head. "I've got a job to do. If I do it, you'll never see me again. If I don't, I'll be back in a week." Inez studied her companion for a few moments, then continued to eat and smoke.

"You sound mysterious," she said, but Alfredo didn't respond. She offered him the sublet apartment for the night and he accepted. He slept but a few hours and was awake before dawn. At 10 o'clock, the Mendezes were back to pick him up. They were on the way to the nephew's funeral, and they dropped Alfredo off at the bus station.

When the bus rolled into the stop in Alice, Mario was waiting, his backside leaning against the Packard. He had the windows rolled down and the radio turned up loud, Mexican salsa music blaring on the speakers.

As they drove to San Diego, the music blasted Alfredo's eardrums and Mario sang just as loudly. But the open car windows let in a welcome breeze as they flew down the highway. It was sunny and hot, just like any other September 8 in South Texas.

Summer was a long way from being over.

Alfredo reached into the glove compartment and pulled out the Colt .38. He thought about that ridiculous bar keep in Corpus and the way Mario had bragged about the gun. He smiled weakly as he gazed at the weapon. He had to admit, it was a beauty. He retrieved a sooty rag from the glove compartment and began cleaning it.

It was almost 4 o'clock when they parked at the Windmill Cafe. Pete Saenz was waiting for them in a corner booth. Mario ordered tamales and french fries, and Alfredo asked the waitress for a cup of coffee. Their conversation was aimless for a few minutes; then Alfredo decided to get down to business.

"When do I get paid?" he blurted.

"Shut up, you idiot!" Pete Saenz said in a half-whisper. He glanced around the tiny cafe to see if anyone had heard.

"Are you thinking of backing down, Cervantes? 'Cause if you are. . ." Saenz's dark eyes were menacing.

Mario's cheeks were bulging with tamale, and he could not speak. Alfredo shrugged.

"Look," he said. "Tell me, or the deal's off."

Pete didn't say anything. He just swigged coffee and smoked.

"Let me put it to you real straight," Alfredo said. "I want my $3,000 before I cross the border."

Pete glared at Alfredo. "You'll get your money," he said through clenched teeth.

The door to the cafe burst open, as if it had exploded off the hinges, and George walked in. The atmosphere in the place changed in an instant, as if someone had drawn a curtain. George was his jolly self, shaking hands with everyone in his path on the way to the table, tipping his hat across the cafe at more distant admirers.

"Boys," he said in Spanish, pulling up a chair and straddling it backward. He winked at the Mexican girl who brought him a cup of coffee. The table conversation turned to horses. George was heading to the track outside of town for an early evening race. Two of his finest steeds were to run, and he was charged up about it.

"Nothing like a rousing horse race to get your blood going, make you glad to be alive," George bellowed, slapping Pete on the back. "Pete, when are you going to join me at the track? You've been swearing for months that you'll take in a race. Well, tonight's the night."

Pete shook his head, but George didn't notice. He insisted that Alfredo and Mario join them.

"El Jefe," Mario said in a plaintive tone. "Another night." He scraped the last of the chili sauce from the plate and spooned it into his mouth. "Tonight's no good."

"I won't take 'no' for an answer." George said, standing up to leave. His full cheeks were firm, but he had a big grin. "Well, then, let's go," Pete said, rising from his chair. He joined Mario and Alfredo in the Packard as George trailed in his black Cadillac. On the way to the track, the three men discussed the evening's itinerary. Mario needed to catch a bus in Corpus bound for San Antonio at 6:30. There was time to see one race, and then he and Alfredo would have to head east. Pete would stay behind at the track and placate El Jefe.

Alfredo wished he had never gotten mixed up with Mario Sapet, George Parr and his band of hoodlums. They were a bad lot. He had more loyal, more sensible friends back in Guadalajara. In a few hours he would be back with them and would never have to mess with this bunch of *tontos* again.

It was 5:30 before Alfredo and Mario could get away from the track. Alfredo wanted a smoke bad, but that would have to wait. He got behind the wheel of the green Packard and hit the gas hard. They arrived in the Corpus bus station with time to spare.

Alfredo didn't even wave at Mario when the bus pulled away from the platform. He was already on his way to the parked

Packard, his mind on his next destination—Alice, Texas.

***

Nago Alaniz hoisted the longneck to his lips and drank thirstily. He'd lost count of how many beers he'd had that day. It didn't matter. He'd rather not have a clear head, not with what he had to do.

The *cantina* was dark, even though it was midafternoon. Nago decided it was a good thing he couldn't see the place too well. Even in the shadowy light, he could tell the place needed a thorough scrubbing. He guessed the tavern keeper didn't worry about such things. In Rio Grande City, there weren't many other places to quench a thirst.

Next to Nago was a man with a black patch over one eye. Octavio Sanchez's visible eye was droopy and bloodshot, but the man was in a chatty mood. Alcohol made him talkative.

"Someday, my friend, you be a big man," he promised Nago, slurring his words. "El Papa, he go to you always and first. He like you best. You see. It will come. You see." He drained the rest of his beer from the bottle.

"It is not so easy," Nago said. "I am from the outside. El Patrón, he likes his own people. He doesn't know me so well."

"But he will," Octavio said, rubbing his good eye. "You do as the gringos say—pay dues. Pay dues, my friend. You get into the club."

Alcohol and pep talks notwithstanding, Nago still had his doubts. He'd been paying dues for 15 years, and he was still nothing more than a chore boy for El Patrón. The thing with Pete and Mario was a go-for-broke deal for Nago. If that didn't open the pipeline to George, he'd have to reassess, maybe even go back to Beeville.

"To tell you the truth," Nago said, "I'm beginning to wonder if I want in this club. You know how it can be, Octavio. You want something so long, after awhile, you don't care anymore."

"Ah, my friend, you care, you care." Octavio's beer-chased voice was soothing. "Take my word. You stay with El Patrón. You do what he says. You will win him over."

Nago hadn't shared with Octavio his latest assignment. All it required was a phone call, a simple phone call. But Nago didn't want to do it. It was dirty business, this phone call thing, dirty business.

He paid his bar tab and bid Octavio farewell. He had a few taverns to hit on the 90-mile trip back to Alice. He didn't want to get back too early. Nine o'clock was the appointed hour.

***

Buddy Floyd burst breathlessly through the loose-hinged screen door of his mother's kitchen with Elinor in tow, pulling on her hand as he dashed into the Floyd house. The kitchen smelled of stew and cornbread, a menu Buddy quickly verified by lifting the lid off the dutch oven. His mother was nowhere in sight. But his dad was sitting at the octagonal kitchen table, a few bites of stew in his bowl. He was dipping a long spoon into a glass of milk, generously sprinkled with chunks of cornbread. It was one of Jake's favorite desserts, cornbread drenched in sweet milk.

Buddy and Elinor looked flushed, evidence of an afternoon on the coast at Corpus Christi. Both were wearing swimsuits, but Elinor had slipped on a pair of pedal pushers over hers. Buddy was still in his trunks, barefoot and wearing an oversized cotton shirt. They were in a fine humor, laughing and shouting comments to their friends Frank Ingram and Frances Thompson, who had come in for a day of sun with Elinor and Buddy. In a moment Frank and Frances entered the kitchen. They, too, were sunburned.

"Dad," Buddy said, "we were thinking of going over to the Reyes for Mexican food. Could you float me a loan? Ten bucks should cover it."

Jake was savoring his dessert and did not want to waste a second of the taste by talking. So he nodded, pulled out his billfold and handed his son the requested $10. Frank and Buddy went upstairs to change clothes, and the girls went to the downstairs bedroom where Elinor was staying. She had been visiting the Floyds for several days. The fall term was about to begin, and she and Buddy wanted to be together as much as possible before they had to go to separate campuses for school.

They had been making some early plans for their wedding the following summer. They had spent hours looking at books full of sample invitations at the local print shop, finally choosing one with gold embossed lettering. And they had browsed through the local china shop, looking at dish and silver patterns.

Buddy was quite solicitous of his fiancée. Whatever she wanted was okay with him. A shopping trip, an afternoon at the coast, Mexican food at the Reyes Cafe—Buddy was agreeable. With any other girl, his dad might have been concerned. But Elinor seemed genuinely sweet, and Jake found it difficult to believe she would take advantage of Buddy's good nature.

Jake read the *Alice Daily Echo* as he spooned the crumbly wet cornbread into his mouth. Edith had gone to a Sunday School party with friends and wouldn't be home until later that evening. Jake decided to read the newspaper for a while, then head back to the office for a few hours of work. He and Clarence were preparing for a trial the next week, and that always meant hours of evening and weekend preparation.

The lawyer had retired to the living room and was reading the *Houston Press* by the time the kids returned to the Floyd house. It was about 8:45 P.M. After Frank and Frances said their farewells—they had to be back in Corpus Christi that night—

Buddy and Elinor went upstairs to listen to records.

By the time the telephone rang at 9 o'clock, Jake had just put on his suit coat and was preparing to walk to the office. It was Nago Alaniz, and from what Jake could tell, he was scared and upset.

"Jake, is that you?" he said in a nervous whisper.

"Yes. Nago?" Jake recognized the lawyer's voice.

"Yeah. Now, Jake, listen." Nago was in a hurry to get this over with.

"How are you, Nago?" Jake said. "Haven't seen you in a while. How's the family?"

Nago was in no mood for chitchat. "Jake, I've got to see you right away. "

"Sure, Nago. Come right over. I was just heading to the office, but that can wait."

"No, Jake. You've got to meet me. I'm at Jewel's Drive-In."

"Okay. A dish of ice cream would taste good."

"No, Jake, listen." Nago was still whispering. "Meet me behind Jewel's. I'm in my black sedan. I need to talk to you about something very important."

"Sure, Nago. I've always told you if you ever needed anything to call me. I'll see you in a few minutes."

Jake prepared to hang up the receiver when he heard Nago shouting into the telephone. "Jake, Jake!"

"Yes, I'm here. What is it?"

Nago was silent for a long time. Then he spoke again in a whisper. "Don't drive in your car. Call a cab. I don't want anyone to see us together."

Jake was puzzled, but he decided to play along. "Okay, Nago. I'm on my way now. See you in a few minutes."

When Jake hung up the telephone, he heard footsteps on the stairs. It was Buddy coming down to the living room.

"Who was that, Dad?" he asked as he arrived at the foot of

the staircase.

"Oh, it was a Parr man. He asked me to go meet him. I think he has some information."

Buddy thought for a moment as Jake lit the stub of his cigar, puffing a cloud of fragrant smoke into the living room.

"Are you going?"

"Yes. To Jewel's Drive-In. I'll be back directly."

"I'll go with you," the younger Floyd said.

Jake squinted through the cigar smoke. "No, son. You stay here with Elinor. I've got to go to the office afterwards."

"But, Dad…" Buddy protested.

"I'll call you when I get to the office," Jake said, a note of finality in his voice.

There was no use arguing with one of the town's best lawyers. Jake called the local cab company, ordered a taxi sent to the house and then put on his hat and headed for the front door.

"Just be careful, Dad," Buddy admonished as his father strode out to the sidewalk. The younger Floyd watched his father through the front door as the lawyer paced up and down the sidewalk, a glowing cigar stub in his mouth. A lone streetlight a block away cast a dim glow on the front yard.

After ten minutes a taxi rolled up to the curb and ferried Jake away. As soon as the car rounded the corner, Buddy galloped up the stairs, two at a time. Elinor was sitting on the floor, her back propped against a bed, and she was listening to a record.

"Elinor, I need to go out for a few minutes. Will you be all right?"

He was so earnest she felt concern.

"Is something wrong?" she asked. "Where are you going?"

"I just need to go out for a few minutes. It won't take long. I just wanted you to know I'd be out of the house."

He touched her bare arm and looked directly into her eyes. He kissed her lightly on the lips and headed down the stairway.

Elinor could hear the screen door in the kitchen bang shut as he headed for the Henry J parked in the driveway.

***

It took only five minutes for Jake's taxi to arrive at Jewel's. When the car pulled into the parking lot, a young woman emerged from the restaurant. She had on a black uniform and white apron. She approached the cab driver and told him to drive around behind the restaurant. A black Pontiac was parked in a darkened corner next to a wooden fence. Jake ordered the cab driver to halt about 50 feet from the Pontiac. Telling the driver to wait, he strode over to the parked vehicle. Nago was sitting in the driver's seat, motioning for Jake to go around and get in on the other side.

"I see you took my advice and came in a cab." Nago sounded relieved. The area they were in was so dark that Jake could see only his companion's shadowy profile.

"What's going on, Nago? Why the mysterious phone call and this cloak and dagger rendezvous?"

Nago took a draw on a freshly lit cigarette and exhaled a cloud of smoke.

"You're a dead man, Jake Floyd. They're going to kill you."

Jake sat, unimpressed, and withdrew the well-chewed cigar remnant from his lips.

"What are you talking about? Who's 'they?'" he replied.

"I can't tell you that, Jake. All I can tell you is that you are a marked man. You better get eyes in the back of your head or a bodyguard or something. I wouldn't kid about something like this. They're going to get you, Jake."

Jake sat calm, his elbow propped on the window frame as he flicked ashes from the cigar onto the pavement.

Nago continued, aware that Jake remained unconcerned.

"Jake, they've hired a professional killer from Mexico. They've been casing your house for days. At this very moment, that killer is waiting in your garage to gun you down."

"Why would anyone want to kill me? I haven't done anything."

Nago sighed. "Jake, believe me. You are going to be killed."

"Who's going to do it?"

"If I told you, they would kill me," Nago answered.

"Look, Nago, you're not making sense. If you can't give me more to go on, I can't put a lot of stock in what you're telling me."

Nago kept insisting, and Jake kept questioning. Finally, in exasperation, Nago told Jake that the New Party at Rio Grande City was behind the plot. Sam Reams was a marked for death, too.

"They're afraid you're going to put Judge Reams back in office in the November election. They're afraid you're going to organize a write-in vote."

Jake rubbed the stubble of his beard, his cigar parked between two fingers. "Why, Alaniz, there is no talk of a write-in vote. The election is over. They've won."

"You won't believe me, Jake, but let me tell you something. You know how close I am to George Parr. Do you remember two years ago when the county clerk's office was broken into? I did that. George made me. We bribed one of Hap's deputies."

He paused for a moment, almost out of breath. Jake was silent.

"Jake, you've got to do something. These people are going to kill you."

"Does George Parr have anything to do with this?"

"I don't know, but somebody's putting up the money. Jake, you've got to believe me."

The younger lawyer recounted how he had driven 90 miles an hour from Rio Grande City that evening to bring the news of the murder plot.

"I'm going to tell Sheriff Wright about this," Jake said.

"You can't do that. If they find out I talked with you tonight, they'll kill me. Tell Halsey someone from Rio Grande City told you." Nago paused for a moment, as if deciding something.
Then he spoke. "I'll tell you this. I'll give you a lead. Mario Sapet is the leader of the killers. He drives a green Packard. They've been watching your house."

Mario Sapet. The name struck a chord with Jake. Just a few days before, a Freedom Party friend had been in his office for a chat about politics. At the end of the conversation, the friend handed Jake a slip of paper with the name "Mario Sapet" on it. He was someone to keep an eye on, the visitor told Jake.

The elder lawyer reached into his suit coat pocket and felt for the scrap of paper. It was there. He pulled it out and looked at it in the dim light.

"If they were going to kill anyone, they wouldn't tell you or anyone else," he said.

Nago sounded annoyed. "All right, Jake. Here it is. I'm in on this. I'm a part of it. I've agreed to say the killer was with me when he killed you."

The two men sat in silence a few moments Before Jake reached for the door handle.

"I'm going to see Halsey," he said.

"Call him, Jake. Call him from right here at the drive-in. Sapet and his gunman are staying either at the Gunter Courts or the Auto Motel Courts."

But Jake got out of the car and headed back to the cab. He told the driver to take him to the county jail.

In the cab, he thought about what Nago had just told him. He just couldn't believe it, but Halsey should be told—especially since Sam Reams might be involved.

By the time he reached the jail, it appeared that everyone, including the prisoners, had retired for the night. The barred windows were darkened, and the front door to the sheriff's office was locked. Jake rang the buzzer several times before Edna Wright answered the door. She was sleepy-eyed, her brown hair arranged in pin curls.

Jake apologized for the intrusion and told her he was looking for Halsey.

"He's over at Orange Grove. Had to go over there and pick up a prisoner. Don't know when he'll be back, but I can reach him by radio if it's an emergency," she said.

Jake was apologetic. "No, it's nothing serious. I've been talking with a fellow who says Judge Reams's life may be in danger. But I think it's a wild tale. Nothing to bring Halsey back at this time of night. If he gets back before 10:30, have him call me at home. Otherwise, I'll talk to him tomorrow."

***

Buddy had been afraid for his father ever since the day he had gone to the vote canvassing at the state capitol—the day John Ben Shepperd had thrown out all those write-in votes and declared Sam Reams the district judge. Jake had been awfully happy that day, but Buddy had a sick feeling in his stomach.

Never mind that he'd been to a dozen or more parties at George Parr's *hacienda*. Never mind that he and Archer Parr sometimes ran in the same circles. Buddy knew his father was roping and hog-tying Mr. Parr on that judge thing. Nobody did that to Mr. Parr. It was dangerous business.

And now his dad was going to see a Parr man, at night, on the edge of town. Well, Buddy couldn't stand it. He decided to tail his father. Jake would never know the difference. Buddy would be back home and in bed before his dad got home from the office.

After kissing Elinor, Buddy was out of the house in a flash. He was walking so fast he nearly slipped on the tile porch. The night air was cool and damp, and he could smell the freshly mowed grass of a neighbor's yard.

The Henry J was parked as usual with its rear up against the garage, so the driver's side door faced the house. As Buddy reached to open the door, he heard a loud pop. The sound seemed to knock his hand free of the door handle.

Then there was a second pop. It was coming from the garage. A third. Buddy felt his head lurch involuntarily. Another loud pop, and he was on the driveway. The gravel dug into his back and legs, and his forehead felt wet. He couldn't open his eyes. He couldn't move. He couldn't breathe. He heard footsteps on the gravel, running to the alley, a crashing sound, then more footsteps. Someone was running, running, running…

Chapter 13

Elinor decided to go to bed after Buddy left the house. The bedroom windows were wide open, and a soft breeze drifted in, cooling the warm room. As she turned down the bed covers, she was startled by four loud cracking noises. The sounds were sharp and piercing, but Elinor could not decide exactly what she was hearing. It sounded like a burst of firecrackers, or maybe a car backfiring. The sounds came from the rear of the Floyd house, so she decided to go outside to investigate.

She went no farther than the kitchen screen door. The back porch light was on, but its beam illuminated only half of the backyard. There were no streetlights in the area, so the other portion of the yard, the driveway and garage were cloaked in darkness.

"Buddy?" she called out through the screen. No answer. Just the sound of a car. Perhaps it was in the alley behind the garage; she could not tell.

"Buddy?" she called again, a little louder. Still silence. Elinor stood for a few moments, puzzled.

"Mr. Floyd?" she shouted into the darkness. Except for the sound of a departing vehicle, there was no response.

She padded back to her bedroom and slipped into bed, all the while unable to shrug off a nagging concern that something was amiss. She decided to distract herself with a book. She had been reading for about ten minutes when the telephone rang.

"Is Mr. Floyd in?" It was a male voice. The caller did not volunteer his identity.

"No, sir. May I take a message?"

The caller paused for a few seconds then declined the offer and rang off.

Elinor, still feeling ill at ease, forced herself to concentrate on her novel. Buddy and Mr. Floyd would be home soon, she told herself.

***

Alfredo's foul mood did not improve on the drive back to Alice from Corpus Christi. He turned the radio up loud and rolled down the windows, as if the coastal winds and the Mexican music would air out his mind and soothe his nerves. It was still light outside, but the sun had slipped below the horizon when he passed the Alice city limits sign at 8:30. He cursed the heat as the green Packard moved down the streets of the deserted town. He was wildly hungry again, not having eaten since the meal with Inez the night before. But he dared not stop for even a Coca-Cola. He would have to hold off until Nuevo Laredo. It wouldn't be long, he told himself.

It was 8:35 P.M. when he pulled to a stop on Reynolds Street near its intersection with Fourth. He cut off the engine and sat in the car a few minutes, studying El Viejo's house. Lights were on in every room. Stupid gringos, he thought. Wasteful every day of their lives. Good, he thought. No lights on in the garage. The back porch light was on, but the two-car garage was cloaked in darkness. The garage door closest to the house was open, and El Viejo's Buick was parked inside. Parked in front of the other garage door was a maroon sports car.

The street was empty—no traffic, no kids, no old folks rocking on porches. The gringos must be draped over chairs, sucking in air from fans, Alfredo thought. He'd be in front of a fan, too, or in the air-conditioned Jardin if not for this lousy job.

Alfredo studied the house just across Reynolds Street from the Floyd house. The windows were open, and the Venetian blinds were adjusted so that a passerby could see inside. Those gringos must be rich. They had one of those new television boxes. Alfredo could see the lights from the set flickering. Good, he thought. With that box on, nobody will be watching anything else.

The house directly behind the Floyds', the one across the gravel alley, was dark. There were only two other houses on Reynolds Street in that block, and they both seemed closed down for the night.

After a few minutes Alfredo reached into the glove compartment and retrieved the .38. He slipped it under his belt and stepped out of the car, closing the door as quietly as possible. Within seconds, he had found a hiding place in the laundry room of the Floyd garage. The cubicle couldn't have been more than 8-by-5 feet, but there was enough room for the solid Mexican to wedge himself between the washer and dryer. The appliances backed up to a window that faced the house. He opened the window, leaving the door to the garage open as well. Perfect, he thought. He could see the house and the yard, and make a speedy departure. This might work after all, Alfredo told himself. All he had to do was wait for the signal. He stood there, breathing quietly in the dark. Waiting.

At 9 o'clock, right on the dot, he could hear the telephone ring inside the house. One ring, two rings. Then the third ring was cut short. Alfredo pulled the gun from his waistband and leveled it against the window screen, pointed at the back door of the house. The night was so calm he could hear voices inside the Floyd home. He could not make out what was being said, but mingled with the songs of the night crickets were muffled conversations. The talking was intermittent for ten minutes or so, and then he heard nothing. The house was maddeningly still.

Then more voices upstairs followed by a brief silence, maybe 30 seconds. Then a tall, skinny man burst through the back screen door. He dashed toward the driveway and was out of Alfredo's view in a couple of seconds. Alfredo lunged for the door just as his target reached the driveway and extended an arm to open the door of the car parked outside the garage. Alfredo emptied four chambers at the dark figure; the first shot hit the target's right arm. He jerked and jolted with the first and then the second bullet. The third and fourth bullets went astray, but no matter. The gringo collapsed onto the gravel. Alfredo could hear the man gasping for air as he darted past his crumpled figure. He dumped the weapon into an open garbage can in the alley and ran as fast as his stocky legs would allow to the green Packard.

The damn car wouldn't start. Alfredo turned the ignition key several times, and the engine didn't catch. The streets and sidewalks, the Floyd house were still quiet. Finally, the Packard fired up. Alfredo eased the car around the corner and drove past the front of El Viejo's house. He drove two blocks before picking up speed. He was on the San Diego highway in two minutes flat.

He slammed the accelerator to the floor, and the mesquite trees whizzed by. This baby could fly, he thought, and he was going to take her off the ground like she had wings. His mind raced, too. The gringo was dead, or a goner, one or the other. Got what he deserved, the lousy dude. Alfredo didn't even know the guy or why Mario wanted him planted. But judging from that fancy house and the big car, the gringo probably needed to be blown away.

The Packard could do only 95, but that was good enough to put Alfredo in San Diego in less than seven minutes. The town was even more asleep than Alice. A few streetlights beamed here and there, but mostly the houses were dark. Alfredo slowed as he hit the city limits. Pete had said he would meet him briefly. As he approached the Windmill Cafe, still lit up, he saw Pete's black sedan pull away from the curb. Alfredo pulled up alongside the deputy, leaned over and rolled down the passenger window.

"At least two bullets in the bastard," he said through the window.

Pete nodded. "He dead?"

"Breathing his last when I left. Where's the money?"

"Keep your shirt on. Mario will meet you at the Jardin at 2 o'clock tomorrow—if you did the job."

Pete waved him on. No use arguing, Alfredo told himself. One more day, and he would be rich. He floored the accelerator again and headed west toward Laredo. It was a clear, starry night. So clear and bright that Alfredo could have seen the line of the highway without his headlights. But he left them on. No use drawing attention.

It was just before 10 o'clock when the border guard in Laredo waved him across the international bridge. Alfredo didn't even look back when he cleared the Rio Grande.

***

It was at least 30 minutes after Buddy and Mr. Floyd had left that Elinor heard the screams. They were the screams of a woman, and they were coming from the rear of the house. It sounded like Mrs. Floyd.

Elinor burst through the kitchen door and found Mrs. Floyd crouched on the driveway sobbing, her form captured in the beams of the headlights of her car. The car motor was still running, and it had been parked at a crazy angle a few feet away.

"Somebody, help!" Mrs. Floyd screamed. "Somebody, help my boy."

When Elinor got closer, she could see Buddy's limp form on the driveway. He was lying on his back, his right arm outstretched and his left arm close to his side. His body was slightly twisted, facing the car, as if he had fallen while trying to open the door of the Henry J. He was not moving. In fact, he was very, very still.

Mrs. Floyd knelt over her son, immobilized and screaming for help. Elinor crouched next to Buddy and held his hand. Blood oozed from a wound in his upper right arm. A hideous hole about the size of a quarter gaped in his forehead. His face was covered with blood. Elinor felt his wrist for a pulse and thought she detected a faint one.

Mrs. Floyd's screams finally aroused the neighbors. First to arrive was Mary Helen Atkinson, the Floyds's next-door neighbor. She told Mrs. Floyd she was going to get Dr. Wyche, who lived just around the corner. Her own father, also a doctor, was not home. Quickly, other neighbors began to arrive. It seemed like an eternity before Dr. Wyche came.

"Somebody call an ambulance, immediately!" he ordered, opening his medical bag and kneeling down to minister to the bleeding man. By now, Mrs. Floyd was weeping uncontrollably. Elinor tried to comfort her, wrapping her arms around the woman.

When Jake arrived home again, the cab dropped him off at the front curb. Mary Helen Atkinson was standing in the front yard, smoking a cigarette.

"Jake," she said as he entered the house. "Something terrible has happened."

"What?"

"Somebody shot Buddy. He's on the driveway."

Jake could hear voices in the back as he ran through the house. An ambulance, its red lights flashing, was just arriving as the crowd moved away, Jake could see Buddy's body. Dr. Wyche was bent over him.

"What's happened?" Jake said, kneeling at Buddy's side.

"He's hurt bad, Jake," the doctor said, "shot in the head."

Jake grazed the back of his hand across his son's bloody

cheek as the ambulance attendants lifted Buddy onto a stretcher. After the ambulance sped away to the hospital, Jake found Edith. She alternately screamed and sobbed and would not let Jake hold her. Elinor stroked Edith's hair and tried to soothe her.

Jake asked Elinor to stay with his wife. Sheriff Wright had just arrived, and Jake had much to tell him.

Chapter 14

When Jake told Halsey Wright he was the target of an assassination plot, the sheriff didn't believe him.

"Call the Border Patrol in Laredo, now!" Jake said. "They might catch the assassin going across the check point. He's in a green Packard."

"Now, wait a minute, Jake," Halsey said slowly. He was a deliberate, quiet man, not given to rash action.

"I'm telling you, Halsey, a Mexican national was hired to kill me and he shot Buddy by mistake. He's heading for Mexico right now."

The two men were standing in Jake's driveway. The ambulance had just left, taking Buddy, Edith and Elinor to the hospital.

Halsey scratched his head with a huge hand. It was the first time he recalled Jake Floyd sounding irrational.

"Now, listen, Jake. You're upset. Try to calm down a little. Tell me how you know all this."

"There isn't time to tell everything, Halsey. All I know is one of George Parr's deputies—a Mexican named Mario Sapet—planned it. They've been casing the house.

"It's mistaken identity, Halsey. The gunman thought he was shooting at me. Now, please, call the border."

"Who told you this, Jake?"

"Make the call. I'll explain later."

Their conversation was interrupted by a highway patrolman shouting at Halsey from the alley.

"Come over here. Look at this!" The officer was Fred Pendergrass. He was holding a 38-caliber revolver in a handkerchief.

Halsey instructed one of his deputies to get the crowd away from the driveway and to call Captain Allee. Then he and Jake joined Jack Butler in the alley.

"It's still a little warm," Pendergrass said as he held the weapon out on his extended palm for inspection. "Found it in the trash can."

"It's gotta be wiped clean, but maybe there's at least one print on it," Halsey said. "Get a bag for it and have it sent up to Austin. Better drive it up there yourself after we get through here."

The state crime lab was in the capital city, about 200 miles north of Alice. Halsey sent all his ballistics work and some fingerprint analyses up there.

Jake looked at his watch. It was 10:08.

"Halsey. Call the border. There's no time to waste."

The sheriff looked at the lawyer with forlorn eyes.

"Who would I tell 'em we're looking for, Jake?" he asked.

"Like I told you. He's a Mexican national. He's in a green Packard. That's all they need to know."

"I'll call them in a minute," Halsey said and started to herd the growing crowd away from the back yard.

***

Sam Reams and his family were in high spirits when they got home from the drive-in movie. It was a Walt Disney picture, and his 12-year-old son, Gail, had especially liked it. He hadn't fallen asleep like he usually did. Even Nellie, his elderly mother-in-law who had lived with Sam and Angelita for years, enjoyed it.

Since it was a school night and the start of the workweek, everyone turned in early. Sam got into bed and, as was his nightly ritual, he started reading. Walter Prescott Webb's *The Texas Rangers* was so interesting it was keeping him up late every night.

Sam's house was on the eastern edge of Alice, within hearing distance of the highway to Corpus Christi. Sometimes the judge could hear faraway truck engines, but mostly there was just the lullaby of chirping crickets.

Sam had been reading about 30 minutes when Tippie, his collie, started barking furiously outside the bedroom window. Always an enthusiastic watchdog, Tippie warned of invading cats, dogs, possums, raccoons and other varmints that ventured in from the fields near the Reams house.

But this bark was a different one. It was the frantic kind, reserved for human intruders. Tippie's protests were so loud Sam couldn't hear anything else—no car driving up, no footsteps. He decided to investigate. He peered through the bedroom curtains and then through the back windows of the den. He saw nothing.

The telephone rang. It was Halsey Wright.

"Sam, you okay?"

"Of course, Halsey. What's up?"

"There's been a death threat against you. Just checking."

"I was about to go outside. Our dog's going wild out there, barking at someone or something."

"Stay put, Sam. Don't leave the house. I'm coming right over." Halsey hung up.

He was there in four minutes with one of his deputies. They scoured the yard with flashlights, provoking Tippie once again.

"Nobody here," Halsey said after Sam opened the front door. "When did the barking start?"

"Must have been about 10:30. I had just gotten in bed."

"Did you hear anything?"

"Nope. Just the dog barking."

"Sam, you've got to be real careful. Something bad's happened. Buddy Floyd's been shot."

"Shot?"

"That's why I was so worried about you. Don't have time to explain now."

Halsey walked off to his patrol car.

"Halsey, is he going to be okay?" Sam shouted from the doorway.

"He's at the hospital," Halsey answered. "I'll call you later."

***

Jake decided to walk the two blocks to the hospital. When he got there, Edith was on the telephone in a hallway. She was talking to her brother, a physician in Gatesville, 300 miles away. She covered the mouthpiece and looked at her husband, her face stained with tears.

"He knows a good surgeon in Corpus. They're coming tonight."

Jake put his arm around her shoulder and stood beside her as she talked. When she hung up, she led him to the end of the hallway to the swinging doors of the operating room. Through windows in the doors they could see Buddy's bare feet and legs on a gurney. He'd been stripped of his clothing and was draped in sheets. Dr. Wyche, surrounded by four nurses, was tending to the head wound.

A big hand squeezed Jake's shoulder.

"Jake." It was Clarence Perkins, Jake's law partner. He hugged Edith and told them he had just called Edith Maude in Houston. She was leaving immediately for Alice.

Jake wrapped his long arms around Edith as she sobbed into his chest. Friends and neighbors, discouraged from hovering around the Floyd house, began showing up at the hospital.

Already, they filled three empty hospital rooms adjacent to the operating room.

At 11 P.M., Dr. Wyche emerged from the room.

"I'm not going to lie to you." He looked solemnly at Jake and Edith. "He's been hurt badly. He has a bullet in his right wrist and another in the right lobe of his brain. We're waiting for a brain surgeon to come over from Corpus. As soon as he gets here, we're going to operate."

Dr. Wyche paused for a moment and looked at the anguished couple. "We're going to do everything we can to save your son."

Edith clutched Jake's hand.

"Will he live? Is there a chance?"

Dr. Wyche was a country doctor who believed in leveling with folks.

"I'll work all night if I have to and do everything I know how. But, Edith, I don't want to give you false hope. Buddy is gravely injured."

The Corpus Christi surgeon arrived about midnight and went to work immediately. Jake and Edith watched through the doors but couldn't see much—only Buddy's bare legs twitching on the gurney. A nurse told them he was having involuntary muscle movement—common during surgery.

Jake tried to get Edith to go into one of the hospital rooms and rest. But she insisted on joining her friends from the Baptist Church, who were on their knees praying next to a hospital bed. The preacher arrived and led the prayer vigil. So many friends came to the hospital that some had to wait downstairs in a waiting room.

Around 1 o'clock, Captain Allee and Halsey arrived and asked to see Jake alone. The Ranger wanted to hear the story about the Mexican national and Mario Sapet. He closed the door to the hospital room as the three men went inside.

"Where'd you get this information, Mr. Floyd?" the captain asked after Jake again related the information.

"Nago Alaniz. He called me last night and asked me to meet him at a drive-in on the edge of town. He gave me all the information about Mario Sapet and the green Packard."

Jake repeated the conversation he had the night before with Nago.

The captain grunted and chomped on his cigar.

"Obviously, you believe him."

"I do," Jake said.

"And you're convinced Parr had something to do with it?"

"Like my informer said. Somebody put up the money."

The Ranger paced beside the bed. Halsey sat next to Jake on the mattress, rubbing his forehead.

"If you'll press charges, Mr. Floyd, I'll go bring this Alaniz in."

"I'd rather not—not just yet, Captain. I'd rather give him the chance to come in on his own."

The Ranger continued pacing, his cowboy boots clicking a steady rhythm on the linoleum.

"Just don't understand it, Mr. Floyd," Allee said. "Your son in there on that operating table. . ."

"I suppose it doesn't make much sense," Jake said. "But it could cause another killing if we move too fast. I'm talking about Nago. A few hours won't make any difference. The killer's long gone."

Halsey looked up.

"I called the Laredo check point," the sheriff said. "A guard said he remembers a green Packard going through a little after 10 o'clock."

"So now do you believe me?" Jake asked.

Halsey didn't answer. The Captain stopped pacing and looked directly at Jake.

"You're so worried about Nago, Mr. Floyd. Start thinking about yourself. I don't want you leaving this hospital without an officer with you. I'll get Wiley to stick around."

"I'm not going anywhere—not till I see what happens with Buddy. Edith couldn't stand it—" Jake's eyes brimmed with tears, and the three men were silent.

Halsey put a hand on Jake's shoulder.

"Can't tell you how sorry…" the sheriff said.

Jake nodded and stood up.

"I need to talk to Clarence," he said. "If you need me…"

"I'll get Wiley over here right away," the Captain growled as he and Halsey left the hospital room.

Jake found Clarence in the hallway and asked him to step inside the same room where he had just met with the lawmen.

"I need you to do something," Jake said.

"Anything."

"Go over to the office and call Nago Alaniz. Tell him to call Halsey or Captain Allee. Tell him I'm asking him to do it."

Clarence studied his law partner's face. The two men were best friends—closer than brothers.

"He mixed up in this, Jake?"

"I'll explain later, Clarence. Please. Go now."

"There's a pay phone downstairs…"

"I don't want anyone to hear you. The office would be better. Or go to your house. Just so no one hears."

"All right, Jake. But what if I can't find him? You know how he is—stays out all night and boozes up. He may be chasing some woman."

"Just try to find him. That's all I ask."

Clarence left on his mission, and Jake went in search of Edith. She was outside the operating-room doors. Elinor was beside her, standing on tiptoe to see inside.

Edith Maude and her husband, Harry, arrived in the early

morning hours. Raul showed up sometime in the night, as did Jake's other dairy foreman. All Jake's political allies came as well—Sam Reams, Hap and Jimmy Holmgreen, Ike Poole and ten or more others. It seemed the entire congregation of First Baptist Church turned out as well.

At dawn, Edith's brother Kermit Jones arrived. Buddy was still alive, but his respiration was shallow. Dr. Jones inserted a respirator tube in Buddy's mouth, and the breathing steadied.

The news from the operating room was grim. The bullet that entered Buddy's head had split apart. The Corpus Christi surgeon was able to remove only a fragment of the bullet. Any attempt to remove the rest might cut off vital functions.

At about 7:30 A.M., Clarence returned to the hospital. His tie was loose around his neck, and he had a day's growth of beard. He and Jake went into a hospital room alone.

"Finally found him," Clarence said. "He wasn't home all night. His wife said she didn't know where he was. I checked some bars and drove around town a little bit. Even went over to his office. Finally, about 6:30, I went back by his house and his car was there."

"What did he say?"

"Nothing. I gave him the message and he just looked at me. Not a word. We stood on the front porch while I told him. He just turned around and walked into the house."

"Thanks, Clarence."

Jake decided to give Alaniz a few more hours.

At 3:45 that afternoon Buddy stopped breathing. The doctors could not revive him.

Wiley Williamson drove Jake and Edith back to the house. He hung around on the back porch smoking cigarettes while they went inside. The house was full of people.

When Jake got upstairs to his bedroom, he pulled off the suit coat he had worn for nearly two days and folded it neatly on the bed. He crouched under the box springs and pulled a long white box from under the bed. A hunting rifle and a .38 automatic were inside.

He checked the chambers of the handgun. Empty. He sat on the edge of the bed for a long time holding the gun. Then he took a box of bullets from the white box and loaded every chamber. When he heard Edith coming up the stairs, he returned the gun to the box and slid it back under the bed. It was ready if he ever needed it.

Chapter 15

By the time Mario stepped off the bus in downtown San Antonio, it was 10 o'clock. Lampposts and neon signs drenched the streets of San Antonio's west side in light. The greasy odor of refried beans drifted from the windows and doors of the eateries as Mario headed on foot down the grimy city sidewalk, the taps on his loafers clicking to the beat of the *mariachis* performing in El Mercado. He had spent many an evening in the marketplace, drinking beers and dancing with the beautiful *señoritas*. He would have done the same this night, if not for a bit of pressing business.

The streets of San Antonio were busy for a Monday night. Couples walked hand in hand in the direction of the *mariachi* music; families window-shopped and wandered into restaurants. Mario was hungry again, but he would have to wait until he got to Mama's.

It was a hot, damp night, with not a breath of a breeze to be found. By the time Mario reached the police station, he was breathing heavily and sweat was beading on his forehead. The police station was a squared-off concrete building. It stood directly beside the Bexar County Courthouse, a red granite structure that towered over the city's main plaza.

It had been months since Mario had been to the police station, and it was the first time in his life he had entered the building on his own. As usual, the lobby was a noisy, busy place. Dozens of *peon* women waited on benches, watching their broods of children. Mario had seen the scene many times. They were probably waiting for sons or husbands or boyfriends who had been arrested. A few were probably crime victims.

Mario wanted to avoid the crowd, so he took the stairway two steps at a time up to the second floor. There he was met by an open room with several rows of Army-metal gray desks. Uniformed officers occupied about a quarter of the desks—talking on telephones, interviewing suspects, rifling through sheaves of papers. The room was about as noisy and bustling as the lobby.

Mario resisted an urge to turn and get out of the place. There were no pleasant memories in the room for him. And besides, he thought, it might look more suspicious than anything else for him to show up unsolicited.

He steadied himself against a polished wood railing that bordered the massive room and scanned the scene for a familiar face. Mario knew many police officers in San Antonio. Surely at least one of them was on duty that night.

"Can I help you, mister?" It was a female voice coming from behind him. Mario turned to find a small, brown-haired woman, about 30ish, looking up at him. She had on street clothing, but was obviously an employee, probably a night secretary.

"I am looking for Melrose, Melrose Olsen," Mario said, taking off his hat.

"He's off duty tonight. Can someone else help you?" The woman appeared preoccupied and intent on getting Mario out of the way.

"Mario." It was a male voice this time, and it was coming from a desk in the corner by the windows. Mario looked across the room to see the familiar face of a tall Anglo, spare of build and in his late 40s. He was somber-faced as he strode across the room to greet El Turco.

"Fred," Mario said, extending his hand. "Haven't seen you in—how long? How you been?"

"Fine, *hombre*. Sure has been awhile. I see you've been keeping out of trouble."

Fred Sorensen had been the investigator on several occasions when Mario had been picked up by San Antonio cops. The two had spent many hours in interrogation rooms, going over evidence. Fred asked the questions, Mario answered when he felt like it. The two went way back, but they had few fond memories from those days.

"I've had business down in Nuevo Laredo and in San Diego," Mario said, "Haven't been in town that much."

"But I see you've still got your bar," Fred replied.

"Yeah, but haven't spent much time there lately. I imagine I will now, though. I have plans for that place. How's the wife and the boys?" Mario knew Fred well enough to know that the officer had two sons.

"She's fat and sassy, and the boys, well, they're grown. Tom is at A&M and Gerald is going through training at the police academy. Following in his old man's footsteps." For the first time, Fred smiled.

"What brings you by this hot night?" Fred had warmed to Mario's presence slightly. The secretary had disappeared, so it was just the two men, chatting at the top of the stairs.

"I was looking for Melrose," Mario responded. Fred recalled that Melrose, in his days as a patrol officer, had befriended Mario during a burglary case "He's off tonight. Not sure when he'll be back on duty, but I can check," Fred offered.

Mario shook his head. "That's all right, my friend. Just tell him I came by to say 'hello.' I'll be back one of these days."

Mario extended his hand but avoided eye contact with the investigator. The two men said so long, and Mario descended the stairs feeling like he could go home and sleep easy that night. Fred Sorensen watched as Mario left and wondered what a professional hoodlum was doing hanging around a police station. He shrugged his shoulders and went back to his desk. He figured he would find out soon enough.

***

Once Alfredo passed the final checkpoint at the international bridge, he slowed the Packard. No sense in attracting attention by racing through the streets. Besides, he was safe now, across the border and safe. He decided to drive around for a while. There was no need to hurry. He wanted to listen to the radio in the Packard—find out if news of the shooting had gotten out.

He flipped the radio tuner up and down the dial. The airwaves were jammed with Spanish music. Occasionally, there was an English-speaking station from across the border. He could pick up WOAI in San Antonio. It had incredible range, especially at night. For a half hour, some gringo droned on about home repairs. Then a woman came on the air and talked about gardening. It was 11:30 before there was any news.

"THIS JUST IN FROM ALICE, TEXAS" The male announcer sounded excited. "YOUNG BUDDY FLOYD, SON OF PROMINENT ALICE ATTORNEY JAKE FLOYD, HAS BEEN SHOT. YOUNG FLOYD WAS GUNNED DOWN OUTSIDE HIS HOME AT ABOUT 9 O'CLOCK THIS EVENING. HE IS IN CRITICAL CONDITION AT AN ALICE HOSPITAL. POLICE HAVE NO ONE IN CUSTODY AT THE MOMENT. BUT THEY ARE SAYING THE SHOOTING WAS POLITICALLY MOTIVATED. WE WILL KEEP YOU INFORMED OF DETAILS ABOUT THIS STORY AS THEY DEVELOP…"

Alfredo stomped on the brake pedal and halted the Packard in the middle of a street. He put the car in neutral, jerked on the hand break and jumped out. He lay his head on the roof of the car and pounded the vehicle with his fists. The streets were empty and silent except for Alfredo.

Eventually, a dented and noisy pickup truck rounded the corner a few dozen yards away and rolled to a stop behind Alfredo. The driver honked his horn a few times, and then gave a long blast. Alfredo got back into the car, put it in gear and drove off.

He drove around aimlessly in the neighborhood of El Jardin Internacional. About a block from the bar, he noticed a familiar figure walking down the street. It was Caspar Guzman Davila. A small man and very thin, Caspar was walking toward his house. Alfredo slowed the Packard.

"Hello, Guzman," Alfredo said through the car window.

"Hello, Cervantes. Where is Mario?"

Alfredo stopped the car and leaned out the window.

"Shut-up. If Mario knows I am here, he will kill me."

Caspar laughed. Alfredo was always the melodramatic one.

"Sure, *amigo*. Which whorehouse did you leave him in this time?"

Alfredo cut the engine off and jumped out of the car. Caspar, still laughing on the sidewalk, was stunned when his friend lunged at him and grabbed him by his loose shirt.

"Shut-up! You stupid bastard! Shut-up! Now tell me, have you heard from Mario? Is he looking for me?"

Caspar gaped at Alfredo and shook his head. No, he said. He had not talked to Mario in at least a week.

"What are you doing then? Where are you going?" Alfredo was still holding him roughly.

"I was going home. I just closed up the Jardin and I was going home to bed."

Alfredo motioned with a nod of his head toward the car.

"I'll drive you."

It was no time to argue, so Caspar got into the car. The two rode silently through the streets to Caspar's house. Half a block before Alfredo arrived at the tiny bungalow, he shut off the headlights and rolled quietly to a stop at the curb.

"Don't tell anyone you saw me," Alfredo warned. "You do and I'll slice your head off."

Caspar got out of the car and scurried into the house.

Alfredo did not leave. Instead, he sat in the idling Packard and looked straight ahead for the longest time. He could see Caspar peeking at him through the curtains. Finally, he drove off.

Will I ever do anything right, Alfredo asked himself. He had botched this job, and now he could never go back to the States. That didn't matter because Mario would kill him as soon as he found him. He wondered where Mario was now—if he knew. He probably had gone home to his mother's and had a plate of something, washed it down with a few beers and passed out. He would find out soon enough.

Alfredo stomped on the floorboard and cursed himself. He needed that money. There was nothing for him back in Jalisco—just cockfights and reefer.

He had just a few dollars and some pesos in his pocket. If he was not going to sleep in the Packard that night, and he had decided that was a bad idea, he would have to go to Gumescindo Montez Gonzales' house. He had stayed there with Mario before. When he arrived, Gumescindo was asleep. No, he said, he had not talked to Mario. Alfredo made a bed for himself on the couch and slept restlessly until light began filtering through the cracked shades.

The first thing to do, he decided, was to ditch the Packard. Without waking Gumescindo, he left the house, fired up the Packard and drove toward town. He flipped on WOAI and drove around long enough to hear the news.

"A SHOCKING CASE IN ALICE, TEXAS, LAST NIGHT. BUDDY FLOYD, SON OF PROMINENT ALICE ATTORNEY JAKE FLOYD, WAS SHOT AND SERIOUSLY WOUNDED OUTSIDE HIS HOME. THE YOUNGER

FLOYD, A LAW STUDENT AT THE UNIVERSITY OF TEXAS, IS IN CRITICAL CONDITION AT AN ALICE HOSPITAL. POLICE SAY THEY BELIEVE THEY HAVE FOUND THE MURDER WEAPON, A SMALL HANDGUN FOUND IN A GARBAGE CAN NEAR THE FLOYD HOUSE. BUT THEY HAVE MADE NO ARRESTS. JAKE FLOYD HAS BEEN ACTIVE IN LOCAL AND STATE POLITICS FOR YEARS. HE HAS OPENLY OPPOSED THE BOSS RULE OF GEORGE PARR OF DUVAL COUNTY. AUTHORITIES SAY THEY BELIEVE THE SHOOTING WAS POLITICALLY MOTIVATED. THE TARGET, THEY SAY, WAS PROBABLY JAKE FLOYD HIMSELF AND YOUNG FLOYD WAS SHOT BY MISTAKE."

Alfredo wanted to pound his aching head on a wall. How could he have been so stupid? He drove the Packard to the parking lot of a restaurant near a popular downtown hotel. Leaving the Packard there, he strode to the hotel and hopped into a taxicab. He arrived back at Gumescindo's just as he was getting up.

Alfredo gathered up a few belongings he had at the house—a radio, a couple pairs of pants and a shirt—stuffed them into a paper sack, and bid Gumescindo goodbye.

Gumescindo watched through the front window as Alfredo walked briskly toward downtown. He suspected his friend was in trouble. He also suspected he would never see him again.

***

When Mario awoke that morning, it was to the sound of someone pounding on the front door of his mother's bungalow. He had lain awake much of the night, twisting and turning on the bed, perspiring despite the breeze from the floor fan. He could not silence the questions running through his brain. What had happened with Alfredo? Had the job been done? Was he in Mexico?

Mario would find out soon enough. If all went as planned, they would meet at the Jardin later that day. Mario would take the money, and then Alfredo would leave for Guadalajara. Alfredo would be happy—he would have his money. And Mario would be happy—he would be one of El Patrón's top men.

It was around 9 when the pounding on the door woke him up. Mario went to the door in the wrinkled pants he had slept in. When he saw who was making the racket, he groaned. It was Zeno Smith, a Texas Ranger. Mario and Zeno had met several times before.

"Mario Sapet." The Ranger was formal and matter-of-fact, like he didn't recognize El Turco.

"That's me," Mario nodded and pushed open the screen door.

The Ranger introduced himself and told him he was to report to the police station six blocks away. Mario asked the reason.

"It's some shooting. Nothing bad, just some shooting in Alice." Zeno was gruff, nonchalant. Mario invited the Ranger in while he put on a shirt and some shoes.

"I'll just follow you if you don't mind," the officer said, removing his white Stetson as he entered the small living room.

Mario hastily buttoned up a *guayabera* and slipped on some moccasins. He put his billfold in his pocket and left the house in the Ranger's white patrol car.

When they arrived at police headquarters, Zeno introduced him to a deputy from Jim Wells County, a muscular fellow named Bob Miller. A none too friendly guy, Miller grabbed Mario roughly by the arm and informed him he was under arrest. Mario shot a questioning look at Zeno.

"Do you have a warrant for my arrest, Mr. Zeno?"

"Mario, there's nothing to it. You'll find out. Just go with the man."

Zeno Smith and Deputy Miller drove Mario about halfway to Alice, meeting Captain Allee in George West. When they arrived at the sheriff's office in Alice, the captain, Halsey and Miller took him into a bare-walled interrogation room.

Mario admitted owning a green Packard, but he told the lawmen he hadn't seen it since the afternoon before. He had loaned it to Alfredo Cervantes, a Mexican national. He had an appointment to meet Cervantes in Laredo that afternoon to retrieve the car.

Mario said he had been on a bus to San Antonio at 9:15 the night before. It was a little after ten o'clock, he said, when he paid a call at the San Antonio police station.

That was about all he would say. Captain Allee slapped him around a little and even threatened to shove his hand down Mario's throat and turn him inside out. But Mario kept his mouth shut.

***

That night, Jake paid a call on Sam Reams. The judge told him about what had happened with the barking dog the previous evening. In turn, Jake related everything that had occurred from his perspective in the past 24 hours.

"I shouldn't say this since you're a judge," Jake said, "But you're also my friend. There's no doubt in my mind who is responsible for this. I've been turning it over in my mind all day. I've been on the verge of getting my gun every moment since I saw Buddy on the driveway last night.

"I even got it out this afternoon. Keep it under the bed. I've always kept it there in a white box, a box that came with a pair of work boots. I've never used the thing, Sam. Never even put bullets in it. But this afternoon, I loaded it. It's still loaded—in that box underneath our bed."

Sam was sitting in his favorite wingback, puffing on a cigarette. Angelita had brought the two men coffee, and now Sam took a sip.

"What does Halsey say? And Captain Allee? Are they going to question George?"

"I understand that they are," Jake answered. "But you know as well as I do that there will be no way to trace this to George. He always has folks to do his dirty work, and they know better than to point any fingers."

"Then how do you explain Nago Alaniz?" Sam wondered.

"Nago… I don't know about Nago. Before yesterday, I never thought he had much in the way of guts. But he took a huge risk by telling me all he did last night. Still I think he was part of it all. His original plan was to get me out of the house so that the killer could get me.

"But something—maybe a brief flash of decency—stopped him. And if Buddy hadn't tried to follow me…" Jake held a large and bony hand to his forehead. His eyes were dry; his thin lips were pressed tightly together.

There was a long silence and finally Jake looked up.

"I am enormously proud of that boy," he said, looking Sam in the eye.

"I would be, too, Jake." The two men sat quietly for a few minutes.

"Captain Allee arrested Nago this afternoon," Jake said.

"I heard," Sam said. "By the way, Mac McDonald came by the courtroom in Falfurrias this afternoon. He sends his regards and deepest regrets," the judge said, looking soberly at Jake.

"He told me a man—he wouldn't say who—came by his house the other night and warned that he and several other men were marked for death. Mac offered to come over to my house and stand guard outside for a while.

"You know how dramatic he can be. I told him not to worry.

But I couldn't pass off what he told me. I told Halsey about it this evening after I got back into town. Just thought you'd want to know."

When Jake stood up and excused himself, he shook the judge's hand.

"Be careful, Sam," Jake said. "The killing may not be over yet."

Sheila Allee

Jake Floyd

Texas Mutiny: Bullets, Ballots and Boss Rule

George Parr

Corpus Christi Caller-Times

Sheila Allee

Buddy and Jake Floyd

Texas Mutiny: Bullets, Ballots and Boss Rule

Buddy Floyd and Elinor Lewis standing in the driveway of the Floyd home on Edith Maude Floyd's wedding day, July 21, 1951. Buddy is standing on the spot where he was shot.

Sheila Allee

Nago Alaniz

Texas Mutiny: Bullets, Ballots and Boss Rule

A mugshot of Alfredo Cervantes

Chapter 16

Two days after Buddy died, the *Alice Daily Echo* quoted Jake Floyd as saying, "I know in my heart who is responsible for the death of my boy. The perpetrator intended to kill me and killed my son instead. And I promise that I won't rest until the people responsible for my son's murder are brought to justice."

The next day, George Parr had his brother-in-law, B. G. Moffett, deliver to the *Corpus Christi Caller-Times* a letter typed in red ink on dove-gray stationery. His words, too, were printed in the newspaper:

"It was with shock and deepest regret that I heard of the killing of Jake (Buddy) Floyd, Jr. My sympathy goes out to the parents of this young man, and I sincerely hope that the perpetrators of this atrocity will be brought to speedy justice. Despite rumors current at the present time, my conscience is absolutely clear and I can only say to Jake and Mrs. Jake Floyd, Sr. that in this, their hour of sorrow and trial, they have my heartfelt sympathy and compassion."

The Floyds were inundated with sympathy cards and telegrams. So many flower arrangements were ordered for the funeral that the florist gave the Floyds credit for 100 bouquets. More than 140 memorial contributions were made to the church on Buddy's behalf. When Jake and Edith arrived at the church for the funeral, the sanctuary was overflowing with mourners, the altar ablaze with flowers. The bronze casket bore a cascade of red roses. The congregation sang "The Old Rugged Cross"—it was one of Buddy's favorites.

"Almighty God," the pastor prayed, "who hast created man in thine own image, grant us grace to fearlessly contend against evil and to make no peace with oppression. May we reverently use our freedom, and help us to employ it in the maintenance of justice among men and nations, to the glory of thy holy name, through Jesus Christ, our Lord, Amen."

Edith cried during the entire service. Jake was stoic.

They buried Buddy at the Masonic cemetery between two live oak trees. The inscription on his headstone quoted Matthew 6:21—"Where your treasure is, there will your heart be also."

***

It was later that same day that Captain Allee drove the green Packard back to Alice. Police in Nuevo Laredo found the vehicle abandoned in a restaurant parking lot. A thorough search turned up one bit of interesting evidence. There was a white slip of paper tucked under the visor on the driver's side. "Jake Floyd, Sam Reams" were written in black ink.

The fingerprint man said there were latent prints all over the car and it would take a few days to match them to any prints on file. A check of the registration showed the vehicle belonged to Mario Sapet. The sheriff's office summoned a number of Floyd neighbors, and several identified the Packard as the vehicle they had seen in the vicinity of Fourth and Reynolds the week before Buddy was killed. No one, however, could positively say they had seen it in the neighborhood that night.

Meanwhile, Sapet hired a prominent attorney from San Antonio named Louis Schlesinger. Since Alaniz and the newly nominated district attorney, Raeburn Norris, were law partners, Jake appealed to Gov. Shivers to appoint a special prosecutor.

Shivers obliged and named Houston attorney Spurgeon Bell, his friend from law school at the University of Texas.

In announcing the appointment of the special prosecutor, the governor issued a statement. In it, he said Buddy's murder "carries the most serious implications, and every person who had any connection with it should be punished immediately. I will do anything possible to see that this is done."

Bell, a bookish fellow with a reputation for tenacity in the courtroom, readily agreed to take on the job. But he attached one condition—he wanted a bodyguard. Shivers agreed, and Bell handpicked Johnny Klevenhagen, a lanky Texas Ranger who was tough, tall and anything but talkative.

Sapet held a news conference and claimed he was being manhandled at the jail. He hired a second attorney, Fred Semaan, who complained about his client's treatment in telegrams to Shivers, FBI Director J. Edgar Hoover and Ranger Chief Homer Garrison. Captain Allee snorted to reporters that Sapet and his lawyers were "just a bunch of lying s.o.b.s."

"Nobody's been beaten or tortured by any Texas Ranger," Allee told them. "Put that ol' boy to the test, and he won't be able to show you any bruises anywhere."

After the news conference, Sapet's picture appeared in newspapers all over Texas and several other states. In Oklahoma, the FBI got a call from a family in a small rural town. Their son had seen Sapet's picture in the *Daily Oklahoman* and recognized him. He said he had seen Sapet hanging around his Boy Scout camp near Mathis, Texas, a few weeks before. The sighting coincided with the murder of Ed Wheeler. The FBI sent an investigator to question Sapet, but he got less than Captain Allee and Halsey Wright.

At Alaniz's preliminary hearing, 600 spectators showed up in a courtroom built for 250. The justice of the peace let some stand in the back. The rest had to wait outside. The newspapers all said

Nago looked "dapper" in his pinstriped gray suit. His straight black hair was combed back with pomade.

Dr. Wyche was the first witness called. He said he heard three or four rapid popping sounds the night Buddy was shot. It sounded like firecrackers, he said, but he told his wife he wondered if it was gunfire. About a half hour later, he said, his telephone rang. A woman in the vicinity of the Floyd house was screaming, he was told.

"I told my son, Jimmy, to go ahead while I dressed and got my bag," he said.

"I ran over to the Floyd home and found Jake Floyd, Jr., lying in a pool of blood in the driveway of the garage at the rear of their home. He had been shot in the forehead and through the right wrist," the doctor said.

The next witness, highway patrolman Fred Pendergrass, testified he was one of the first officers to search the murder scene. He had arrived at the Floyd home about 10:40 P.M. In a trash barrel about 30 feet from the Floyd garage, he found a .38-caliber nickel-plated handgun. He had showed it to Captain Allee, he said, and later had taken it to be fingerprinted.

Alaniz's attorney Charles Lyman cross-examined Pendergrass at length. How many murder investigations had he been involved in, the attorney wanted to know. Only one, the officer said. Did he look for tire tracks at the murder scene? Yes, but he had found none. How about footprints? Pendergrass responded that too many people had been on the scene by the time he arrived to locate any footprints linked to the crime.

"You don't know where this gun came from?" Lyman asked.
"No."
"You don't know who put it in the barrel?"
"No."
"These 25 to 30 people meandering around there—?"
"Most of them were on the lawn."

"This pail had no lid?"

"No."

"Was the garbage pail across the alley from the garage?"

"Yes."

"Can a car travel there?"

"Yes."

Jake was called to the stand after the lunch break. Dressed in a tan suit and brown tie, he sat erect in the witness chair as he recounted the events of the evening Buddy was shot, his meeting with Nago Alaniz and his convictions about who was responsible for the crime. It was a bungled assassination plot, he said; it was politically motivated.

Jake said Nago had admitted he was a part of the assassination conspiracy and that a man named Mario Sapet was the leader of the killers. Sapet, he had said, drove a green Packard. Alaniz claimed his role was to give Sapet an alibi.

During cross-examination, Lyman asked Jake if Nago Alaniz's actions on the night of the murder indicated a concern for Mr. Floyd's safety."

"It indicated a concern for himself," Jake said flatly. Lyman hammered the point, and finally Jake amended the statement. "It indicated a concern for me and a concern for himself."

Lyman asked Jake if he had ever had trouble with Buddy.

"My son?" Jake said. "None whatever."

"Was your son in any way addicted to gambling that you know of?" Lyman asked.

"No, sir," Jake said emphatically.

The defense lawyer asked Jake why he broke his promise to keep Alaniz's name secret.

"When I saw my son in a pool of blood, I felt like any obligation I had to Alaniz was null. My son was murdered, Mr. Lyman."

Elinor was the next witness called. She was composed, and

her voice was soft as she answered questions.

It was, she said, "a matter of seconds" after Buddy left the Floyd house that she heard "four loud cracking noises—just as rapid as someone could pull a trigger."

"I had been frightened since I heard Mr. Floyd tell Buddy 'some Parr man called me, and I'm going to meet him,'" she said.

Aside from Jake, the sensation of the day was Jewel Gutschke, owner of Jewel's Drive Inn. Wearing tight-fitting pants and shirt and a billed cap, she had a yellow silk kerchief tied smartly around her neck. She smacked gum on one side of her mouth. The night of the murder, Jewel said, she went to work about 9 o'clock.

"It wasn't long after I got there that I saw him, Nago, sitting in a car outside my place," she recalled. "He was just sittin' there, lookin' straight ahead through the windshield like he was in a daze or something.

"I went out to talk to him. I'd known Nago for several years, and we was friends. When I got to the car, I saw he had an empty beer bottle on the seat, and he handed it to me. He smelled pretty boozed up, but didn't talk like he was drunk."

Later that evening, she said, "one of the carhops told me a cab was coming by soon. That's pretty unusual for a place like mine. Most folks just come in their cars, stop by for a soda pop or a burger. Nobody comes in a cab. Sure enough, a cab drove up in a few minutes. I didn't see who was in it. One of the carhops said she told the taxi driver to go around back."

After the taxi left, Jewel testified, Nago stayed around. "Every time I looked out there, he was there. Finally, at closing around midnight, I told him we was shuttin' down for the night. He didn't say much. Just cranked his engine and drove off."

At the end of the hearing, Lyman pleaded for "protection of the rights of American citizens to make bond."

Homer Dean asked that no bond be granted.

"I plead for freedom from assassination," he said.

The judge bound Alaniz over to the grand jury and denied bond.

The next day, Sapet's examining trial began. Among the witnesses called was Justo Tijerina, a ginner from San Diego. Tijerina, a Freedom Party member, testified that he saw Sapet driving his green Packard, accompanied by Pete Saenz, on the day of the shooting.

"George Parr was driving along behind them, about half a block back," Tijerina said.

Jesus Pompa testified about events at his bar the weekend before the murder. Sapet had done a lot of bragging, he said. He claimed he made "in the neighborhood of $400 a month" as a deputy for Sheriff George Parr.

Mrs. W. B. Nance, a neighbor of the Floyds, said she had seen the green Packard several times in their neighborhood prior to the shooting. Her husband testified he had heard gunfire the night of September 8 and that he had gone outside on his porch. He said he had seen a car drive off from the curb near the Floyd house. Jake then repeated his testimony from the previous day. At the close of the hearing, the judge denied bond and ordered Sapet bound over to the grand jury.

Buddy's murder provoked more unwanted notoriety for Alice, reminiscent of Box 13. Reporter Caro Brown of the *Alice Daily Echo* expressed the town's shame in her weekly column, "Street Scene."

"Enough time has elapsed since the slaying of young Buddy Floyd for Alice people to get an idea of the far-reaching effects of the crime. Letters from relatives of Aliceans who live in far-away states have told of the big play the story got in the press and radio and some even sent copies of papers showing the large headlines the story received."

One such episode, she reported, involved an Alice man who

was planning a hunting trip in Wyoming. He phoned ahead to get a hunting license for a friend who would go on the trip, and the official said, "Oh, wait just a minute. I just don't know whether we want to give a license to carry a gun in our state to somebody from Alice or not!"

The column continued: "And a headline on an editorial in an out-of-state newspaper says, 'Alice Again in Limelight.'"

Mrs. Brown asked her readers to consider what little chance Alice had of persuading people to establish their businesses and bring their families to a town that gets this sort of publicity—"the truth of which we can't deny."

She continued by citing the *Shreveport Journal*, which in an editorial dated September 20, wrote: "If the Alice area expects to get rid of the smear it has been receiving because of political evils and other unwholesome things, it must have something done about getting rid of the criminals and the crooks. The State of Texas also has a responsibility which it cannot afford to let go unmet.

"In the old days of the West, characters such as those having part in major crimes, including assassinations, would have been dealt with promptly, without the benefit of courts. Those committing crimes nowadays should be handled with proper punishment according to the laws, but there should be certain punishment."

Caro Brown concluded: "That's our town they're speaking of, folks. Aren't we proud of it?"

Section V
1953

Chapter 17
January 1

Bub Carlisle, the Jim Wells County District Clerk, had just gulped down a plate of fresh black-eyed peas and a wedge of cornbread when he heard a knock at the kitchen door. He wasn't expecting a visitor. Long-legged and slender, Bub wore khakis and a short-sleeved shirt. It was warm in Alice on the first day of January.

His visitor was Woodrow Laughlin, the newly elected district judge. He was not his usual smiling self, standing there on the porch, a sheaf of papers tucked under his stubby arm. Bub didn't even give him a hello.

"What's wrong, Woodrow?" he asked, opening the door.

"I just need to file these with you." The stocky lawyer tossed the papers on the kitchen table and dropped in a chair as if exhausted.

"What's wrong?" Bub asked again. "You look terrible."

"Been driving all night. The wife and I've been in West Texas for the holidays. Just got back."

"Well, what's so gosh-awful important that you've got to drive all night and come over here on New Year's Day? We'll open the clerk's office tomorrow morning, 8 o'clock sharp."

Woodrow opened a file folder and scanned a paper inside. His thick, black-rimmed glasses perched loosely on a triangular nose. His face was puffy and red, as if he had run all the way from

West Texas instead of driving.

"This here's my oath bond," he said, handing Bub a sheet of embossed paper.

"You've already been sworn in?" Bub said.

"My father-in-law did it last night," Laughlin said, peering over his glasses at the district clerk.

Bub studied the document, which explained that Woodrow had been duly sworn in as Judge of the 79th Judicial District.

"Your father-in-law?" he said.

"Yep. And this here's an order to discharge the grand jury," Woodrow said, handing Bub a second bundle of papers.

"Wait, wait, wait a minute," Bub said. "Slow down. You're already sworn in as judge?"

"That's right."

"Now let me get this straight. It's 1:30 in the afternoon on New Year's Day. New Year's Day is the first day you can take office. You been driving all night from West Texas and you say you took the oath last night. I don't figure it, Woodrow."

Woodrow sighed and drooped in his chair.

"If you'll let me have a cup of coffee—I need it strong and black—I'll explain everything."

Bub poured the requested coffee and studied his barrel-chested visitor. He'd known Woodrow almost 15 years—ever since he had been elected county attorney back in '38. He had been county judge for the past few years, slowly moving his way up in county government. He had always been a Parr man, and a hard-headed one at that. No wonder the Mexicans called him El Burro.

"My father-in-law's a notary public," Woodrow said, clutching the coffee cup with a single paw. "He's out in Alpine. That's where we were. We spent New Year's Eve out there with the in-laws. Just after midnight, he administered the oath and signed this bond."

"Looks like you couldn't wait to take office," Bub grinned.

"As my first action," Woodrow said, "I'm ordering the grand jury disbanded."

Bub thought that's what the judge had said the first time, but he couldn't believe it.

"Woodrow—"

"I want you to write each of the grand jury members a personal letter thanking them for their service and telling them they are discharged from duty."

"I suppose you know what you're doing—"

"I know what I'm doing."

"But I think you should know the grand jury indicted you last week. Did you know that?"

"Heard it on the radio. The wife and I drove out to Carlsbad for a few days and, would you believe it? We could hear WOAI in San Antonio real good on the car radio—way out there in New Mexico.

"The wife was pretty upset, started crying. And that started my little girl crying. She went with us. We left our son with the in-laws. The poor wife. She's been under so much strain ever since we got that death threat against the boy."

In the three months since Buddy had been murdered, Woodrow received two anonymous letters threatening the life of his boy.

"She hasn't let him out of her sight," Woodrow said. "I didn't think I'd ever persuade her to leave him with her parents so we could get some rest.

"I told her it was nothing, this indictment. It was just politics. Jake Floyd and his gang been after me for months, ever since I kicked Sam Reams' ass off the bench. Now, I hear Sam's leaving town, tail between his legs. Got himself a job with Humble Oil in Houston."

"I take it back," Bub said. "You don't know what you're doing. You disband that grand jury, and it'll be like dropping an atom bomb on this town.

"Think about it, Woodrow. This is the grand jury that investigated Buddy Floyd's murder. They still haven't caught the man that pulled the trigger. That case is still open and they could issue more indictments.

"And that's not to mention the fact that they just indicted you. Have you thought about how it's going to look when you kick them out of the courthouse?"

"I've thought about it. And I know what I'm going to do. I'm going to return the money the county paid me for my law library and I'm going to take the books back. That should be about all the district attorney needs to drop the charges."

Bub was nonplused.

"I still say you're firing the first shot in what promises to be a humdinger of a war. The whole town knows the grand jury considered charging your brother with something. What was it?"

"They seem to think that since he's on the commissioner's court, he can't make a living. They're all in a huff because he sold the county some caliche for a road project."

"Now how's that gonna look, Woodrow," Bub said, "you kicking out the grand jury when it might indict your brother?"

"They won't. They already said they won't in that report they put out about a month ago."

"Well, that's not what I've been hearing. I hear they've put together about a dozen indictments against him. I also heard they were going to arrest you as soon as the indictment came down. I even heard they were going to slap some kind of injunction on you to keep you from getting sworn in.

"Look, Woodrow, the town's all worked up about the murder and the elections. Take it easy. The grand jury's gone home for at least a month. That should give you a few weeks to lay low and figure out what you're gonna do."

Woodrow gave him a weary look and stood up to leave.

"I'd appreciate it if you'd file these in your office first thing tomorrow morning. I'm going home and sleep for about 18 hours."

Bub stood up, too.

"Before you go, just thought you'd like to know, your brother's arranged for your bond. Personal recognizance."

"I know. He called me last night. I'll see you at the courthouse tomorrow, Bub."

***

Bub Carlisle was right. Woodrow might as well have dropped a bomb on Jim Wells County. If George Parr thought Jake Floyd was a threat before, he hadn't seen anything.

When news hit of Woodrow's actions, Jake wasted no time recruiting a number of Alice area lawyers to help plot several courses of action. First, they would take their grievance to the State Bar of Texas.

As for the grand jury members, they refused to be disbanded. They announced they would ask the Supreme Court to order Woodrow to rescind his order. In an unprecedented response, Gov. Shivers invited the grand jury to Austin to meet with him. They spent an hour in the governor's private office, and when they emerged with Shivers, the governor told a band of waiting reporters that he and Secretary of State John Ben Shepperd would help the grand jury in whatever way possible.

Grand jury foreman Dean Allen was not placated by the governor's promise. He was not satisfied, he said, with the work the grand jury had done on the Buddy Floyd slaying. "There was more to it than we were ever able to bring to the surface," he told a reporter. "If Alfredo Cervantes is ever found, we'll all have a lot more to write about."

Just a few days into his term, Woodrow did something that

made matters worse. He ordered Bub Carlisle to turn over to Archer Parr the ballot boxes and voting stubs for the November election. Archer had become Duval County Sheriff a few months earlier after George abruptly resigned. It looked as if George was making good on his threat that "There are no secrets between heaven and earth that we can't find out about, and we will find out how you voted."

While waiting for the State Bar to take action, Jake recruited State Senator William Shireman of Corpus Christi to initiate removal proceedings against Woodrow in the Texas Legislature. Unable to muster the required number of votes for such a proceeding, the effort died when the legislature adjourned.

But that wasn't the end of it. Ed Lloyd, George Parr's attorney, came to Woodrow's office one day and said the word was that Jake was piling pressure on the State Bar to do something. Failing that, he would go to the Supreme Court.

"Well, the eggs are scrambled and they are just going to stay scrambled," Woodrow said, pushing his glasses back into position on his fat nose.

"Well, make an omelet out of it," Ed said, sighing. "Face it, Woodrow. You're in a box. If you don't call that grand jury back, they're going to run you out of town. Mr. Floyd's so mad he might do it single-handedly."

"The damn thing leaks like a sieve," the judge said.

"What?"

"The grand jury. Dean Allen calls Bruno Goldapp every morning and tells him what happened the day before. Then Goldapp runs over to Floyd's office and blabs."

Ed chuckled, and Woodrow gave him a questioning look.

"You heard what Bruno Goldapp said, didn't you?" Ed said.

"What?"

"He told Jake a bunch of them ought to go over to San Diego, take their high-powered rifles, and stand across the street from George's office and fire when he walks out. That way they'd never know who killed George."

"Very funny."

"True story."

"If I bring back the grand jury, Jake Floyd's going to know everything that goes on. He's already practically running the damn thing."

"Let him," Ed said. "There are other ways of getting what you want, Woodrow."

"Any suggestions?"

"You'll figure it out."

On January 30, Woodrow rescinded his order disbanding the grand jury, and two weeks later the grand jury reconvened, intent on interviewing more witnesses in the slaying of Buddy Floyd. Spurgeon Bell could not attend, so he summoned Bill Allcorn, district attorney in Brownwood, where the Alaniz and Sapet cases were to be tried.

When Jake arrived in the grand jury room about 10 o'clock that morning, the place was already tense.

"What's Raeburn doing here?" Jake asked the grand jury foreman, Dean Allen.

Raeburn Norris, the newly elected district attorney, and his assistant O. P. Carrillo stood off by themselves in a corner. Raeburn puffed on a Pall Mall and peered out at the group through half-open eyelids. He looked like he had been drinking hard all night, but Jake couldn't be sure. Raeburn always looked like that.

"I imagine he thinks he's going to present cases to us," Dean responded.

The district attorney walked up to Jake and Dean and asked when the grand jury was getting started.

"When you and your goon get out of here," Dean said.

"It's my job—" Raeburn said.

"It's your job not to get in the way. And that's what you'll do if you insist on staying in here while we work," Dean said. "Mr. Allcorn can handle the prosecutor's duties."

"As I was saying," Raeburn said, an indignant look on his face, "it's my job to present cases to the grand jury. That's what the voters elected me to do and it's what I intend to do."

"Did the voters elect you to spy for defendants?" Dean asked, his bushy eyebrows twitching as they always did when he was angry. He gnawed slowly on a plug of tobacco tucked in his cheek. "Does the word ethics mean anything to you, Raeburn? Didn't you learn something about that in law school?"

"Gentlemen," Jake interjected. His voice was calm and even. "May I suggest—if there's a dispute, why don't you go into the courtroom and discuss it with the judge?"

"Good idea, Mr. Floyd," Raeburn said, momentarily entranced by the twitching eyebrows. "I think they're just doing jury selection for a civil case right now. He ought to be able to talk to us."

Dean made the announcement to the eleven other men, and they obediently filed into the courtroom behind him and sat in the jury box. About 25 men sat in the gallery of the courtroom, and two attorneys were questioning them. Woodrow ignored the grand jury; he didn't even nod his head at Raeburn or Jake Floyd as they took seats.

Jake thought surely Woodrow would ask someone what was up, but they might as well have been invisible. No one paid them a bit of attention. Woodrow cleaned his fingernails with a pocketknife as the attorneys droned on, interviewing potential jurors. As the minutes ticked away, Jake noticed Dean Allen's eyebrows doing their dance again. After 30 minutes, the grand jury foreman had had enough.

"Judge Laughlin," he said, standing up. "We have something to discuss with you."

The two lawyers stopped their droning and waited for the judge's response.

"As you can see, Mr. Allen," Woodrow said, aiming his eyes through his thick glasses, "I'm busy at the moment. You will have to come back."

"As far as I can tell, Judge, you're not doing anything but giving yourself a manicure. We have something of importance to discuss with you and we'd appreciate a moment of your time."

Woodrow banged his gavel threateningly.

"Like I said, Mr. Allen, I have a case here. I'm going to be tied up until 5 o'clock this afternoon. I'll meet with you then in my chambers."

Jake caught Dean's eye and with a nod of his head, motioned for the foreman to make an exit. Dean didn't say anything. He just walked out of the courtroom. The grand jurors, Jake, Raeburn, O. P. Carrillo, Bill Allcorn and Sammy Burris, the county attorney, brought up the rear.

Back in the grand jury room, Ike Poole, who was on the grand jury, approached Raeburn with a conciliatory smile.

"Can't you see the spot we're in, Raeburn?" he said. "How about having the good grace to step aside and let us do our work?"

"I'm not leaving with Jake Floyd and Sam Burris still in here."

"Well, of course, we understand you not wanting Mr. Floyd in here. And I don't think he intends to stay. But there is no conflict with Sammy. He's the county attorney, for crying out loud."

Raeburn didn't say anything. He just went to a chair in a corner and sat down.

"I've got an idea," Ike said, addressing the grand jury. "If we can't have privacy in here, maybe we can on the courthouse lawn. Let's go."

The men debated the idea for a moment, then decided to do it. As they left the grand jury room, Jake noticed a heavyset

Mexican man with a black patch over one eye standing outside the door as if he were guarding it. It was a few moments before Jake could place the face. The man was Octavio Sanchez, who, according to reports, was drinking with Nago Alaniz the afternoon of Buddy's murder. Sanchez was to give Alaniz an alibi if he was ever questioned.

Jake wondered where Alaniz was at the moment. He'd finally been released on bond and then had disappeared. His wife and kids were still in town, but Nago was invisible. His trial was in March in Brownwood, as was Mario Sapet's. El Turco, who never made bond, had already been transferred up there to the Brown County Jail.

When the grand jury got outside, they milled around under the sprawling live oaks. It was a balmy day, perfect for working outdoors. Jake took Dean Allen aside and handed him a typewritten list of names.

"These are some people I think you should subpoena. One of them is Octavio Sanchez. I just saw him in the courthouse—"

Ike nudged Jake in the ribs.

"Look. Woodrow is up there at that window wondering what the hell we're doing."

Jake glanced up, pursed his lips, and continued.

"I just saw Octavio outside the grand jury room. I'm going to find out what he's doing hanging around there. Anyway, the other person I think you should call is Santiago Barrera. This guy lives on a ranch near the beer joint where Nago was drinking that night. He raises racehorses, and he and George are very close.

"I have information from sources in Duval County that Santiago is the alibi man. He'll say Sapet, Nago and Cervantes were with him at his ranch that night. Of course, he probably won't disclose anything, but if his testimony is taken under oath by a reporter, he can't change his statement down the road."

Jake was interrupted by Halsey Wright, who was marching

toward them.

"Dean," he said. "Dean, the judge wants ya'll to meet him in the grand jury room."

"I thought he was too busy," Dean said, spitting a stream of tobacco juice on the lawn.

When they got back to the grand jury room, Octavio Sanchez was still stationed outside. Captain Allee and fellow Ranger Wiley Williamson joined them inside the room.

Woodrow listened to Raeburn and Bill Allcorn make their respective speeches, then he asked them to reduce their requests to writing. He was inclined, he said, to exclude Raeburn, O. P. Carrillo and Sammy Burris, the young man who had just taken over as county attorney for Jim Wells, from the grand jury room.

He would approve out-of-county subpoenas, he said, but he didn't want the Rangers delivering them.

"The Rangers are our bailiffs," Dean said. "Judge Reams appointed them."

"They're not your bailiffs anymore," Woodrow said. "I have appointed Octavio Sanchez to take over."

"Now just a minute," Jake said. "This man is a material witness to this case."

"What you got against the Rangers?" Captain Allee asked the judge.

"Not a thing, Captain. I just think we've imposed on you long enough. You've got a lot of other counties to take care of and I think we need to let you tend to your other business."

"Our business is right here in Jim Wells County," the Captain growled as he pulled a half-soggy cigar from his lips. "Homer Garrison has assigned Company D to this area until further notice. I take my orders from him."

Ike Poole piped in.

"Woodrow, you realize that those Rangers are our bailiffs and we can use them whether you want us to use them or not."

"If you do, you won't get any more subpoenas approved by me."

"May I suggest a compromise?" Bill Allcorn said. "Any out-of-county subpoenas can be served by Captain Allee or Mr. Williamson along with the local sheriff."

"That'll never work," Ike said. "The minute Archer Parr finds out we want to talk to somebody, he'll have 'em on the road to Mexico."

"I think it's the best we can do," Dean said. "I'll vote for that."

"That's fine," Woodrow said. "I just have one other matter to discuss with the grand jury. Things around this courthouse are mighty tense right now. And they're tense out there on the street, too. I want you to do your job as grand jurors, but I don't want any indictments issued out of spite or to give people bad publicity. I think we'll all agree we've had enough bad publicity around here the past few months—enough to last a long time.

"For that matter," the judge said, "I'd like to keep this whole matter today to ourselves. I'd appreciate it if all of you would say as little as you can to those reporters hanging around outside."

It was about lunchtime, so the grand jury recessed while Jake, Bill Allcorn and Sammy Burris dictated their request to Burris's secretary. Woodrow spent the afternoon in the courtroom and didn't sign the order until 6:30 P.M. It was 8:30 before the Rangers were able to return to the courthouse with any witnesses from San Diego.

The grand jury worked late that night and all the next day. When they were through, Bill Allcorn called Jake.

"We didn't get anywhere," the district attorney said. "We managed to round up three witnesses from Duval County. One of them went to Mexico, just like Captain Allee said."

"Santiago Barrera," Jake said.

"Right. His wife says he goes down there all the time. He

trains racehorses or something."

"He's hooked in with George somehow. What else?"

"Well, there was one witness from Duval County I was sure knew something."

"Who was it?"

"I'll say this much. He lied. I'm sure of it. He knows something but isn't talking. I'm driving back to Brownwood tonight, Mr. Floyd. I'm sorry we couldn't do any better."

The grand jury was finished with the Floyd murder investigation, but Jake wasn't through with Woodrow Laughlin. He prodded the State Bar to take action, and after months of silence, the Bar spoke. They called Woodrow's behavior "reprehensible in every respect," but declined to impose any sanctions against him.

***

Two weeks later, Jake Floyd was sitting at his desk when the telephone rang. It was Sammy Burris.

"Just called to tell you we've dropped the charges against Woodrow," Sammy said.

"What happened?"

"He came to commissioner's court this morning with his lawyer, that Luther Jones fella from Corpus. Said he didn't know selling his law books to the county would cause so much trouble."

"He's a lawyer and a district judge, and he doesn't know it's against the law for a public official to have a contract of any kind with the county?"

"That's right. He didn't seem very sorry. Woodrow was doing a lot of smiling as he handed the commissioners a check for two thousand and something. The commissioners gave him his books back, and everybody seemed happy.

"I thought, what the hell are we doing prosecuting this thing if he is going to nullify the contract? I wish you could have seen

Judge Salinas's face when I moved to drop the charges. His mouth actually fell open. I know what he was expecting. He was expecting me to move that he be disqualified.

"I told him I was going to move for his recusal on Saturday, when they tried to have Woodrow's trial the first time. But he said it wouldn't do me any good. He was going to throw out my motion and go ahead and have the trial."

"Where do Woodrow and his lawyer get off thinking they can call up the judge of their choice and set up a trial?" Jake asked, rhetorically.

"Well, they dredged the bottom of the barrel when they picked Ezekiel Salinas. All of 'em—Woodrow, Luther and Raeburn—all of 'em swear they hardly even heard of the guy. Never mind that he's one of two judges in Laredo. Hell, no, they never heard of him.

"Luther said that under the constitution he and the prosecutor can agree on a judge and call him up and invite him over. I understand Woodrow called him and they did what they call exchanging benches.

"They didn't want a judge from Corpus. Luther hates the *Corpus Christi Caller-Times* and James Rowe, and he ranted on and on about how he didn't want a judge that was influenced by the *Caller-Times*."

"Well, it doesn't make any difference—about the indictments I mean," Jake said. "Woodrow hasn't cleaned his nose, yet. He's got Dean Allen so mad he's talking about going up to Austin and asking the governor to step in and do something so the grand jury can come back."

"He and Ike and several other men on the grand jury were over at my office just the other day," Sammy said. "They asked me to write up a *mandamus* for the Supreme Court. I think I'll take the wife and we'll drive it up to Austin on Wednesday or Thursday."

"One more thing before you hang up, Sam. I got an anonymous phone call this morning. It was a Mexican man. Said he lived in San Diego. Said he'd been arrested for not paying his child support. Said when he was in the courthouse, while they were booking him, they took him through a room that was full of what looked like ballot boxes.

"They were open, and there were rolls of what looked like used ballots, some tied tight with string, like we did those ballots after the election, and some that were just open, lying there on a table. There were two or three men in there going through the boxes and looking at the rolls of paper. "

"Duval County was a lot safer place when those ballots were over here, locked up in Bub Carlisle's vault. Just another Christmas gift to thank Woodrow for."

The two lawyers hung up, with Sammy promising to keep Jake informed on the latest courthouse news. There would not be a lengthy lull.

The following Saturday morning, Sammy was in his office interviewing a witness in a case he had coming up. It was a sunny winter morning, so bright in his first-floor courthouse office that he didn't need an overhead light on. Sammy liked working Saturday mornings, when it was quiet. He could usually get a lot done that had gone wanting during the week because of telephone calls and trials.

The peace of the morning came to an abrupt halt about 10:15 A.M., when Deputy Sheriff Jack Butler barged into Sammy's office.

"Sammy, what's going on upstairs?" the deputy asked breathlessly.

"Nothing that I know of. Why?"

"I ran all the way down here." Butler grabbed a few gulps of air and continued. "Nago Alaniz is in the courtroom upstairs. He's up there with Archer Parr and Percy Foreman. And Judge Salinas is back."

"What the—"

"They're up there holding some kind of court."

Sammy went up the stairs two at a time.

"Good morning, Mr. Burris," Judge Salinas said cheerfully when Sammy entered the courtroom. "We are glad to see the state represented here."

Sammy glanced around the room. No Raeburn Norris. He saw Nago, dressed as usual in one of his natty suits. He was sitting behind the defense table and was handcuffed to Archer Parr, who was grinning as if he were being entertained. Percy Foreman, the famous Houston lawyer, was at the defense table next to Nago, and he was reading aloud from a stack of documents. He stopped talking when Sammy barged in.

"What's going on, Judge?" Sammy said, standing directly in front of the bench.

"Well, we are having us a little hearing here this morning."

"Where's the district attorney?"

"I don't know where he is."

"Well, where is Mr. Bell—Spurgeon Bell?"

"Well, I don't know that either."

"Is there anybody representing the state here?"

"You are, Mr. Burris."

The judge motioned for Sammy to take a seat in the jury box. Then he continued.

"I don't want any mystery made out of this proceeding. Yesterday, I was called by Judge Laughlin, who asked for my help. He said that he wanted a *habeas corpus* hearing in the Alaniz case. I am now sitting in this court by authority of the constitution.

"I have told Mr. Foreman that I do not wish this matter to be discussed in chambers. I told him that in this particular matter, I wanted everything to be said in open court. It is not necessary for representatives of the state to be present. However, I am glad to see the county attorney," he said, nodding at Sammy.

A bailiff handed the judge a note.

"Mr. Burris, I have here a note from Mr. Bell asking to speak with me. Would you call him and explain that I am refusing to hear these matters in chambers or discuss it with attorneys for either side?"

"Your Honor," Sammy said, "I feel certain that Mr. Bell wouldn't tell me the things he wants to talk to you about."

The judge instructed Bub Carlisle to telephone the special prosecutor. When Bub reported back, he said Bell had complained he had not been told of the hearing.

"He'll be heard before I make any kind of final order," the judge said.

Foreman droned on, reading fast so he could get all the motions into the record.

"How come the regular judge of the district court isn't sitting on the bench?" Sammy interrupted.

"You don't have to be given a reason," Salinas said. "I don't know. I didn't ask him. He might have wanted to go fishing or he might not have felt good. I just didn't ask."

"I understood that Judge Klein was to hear all matters relating to this case."

"The court can't explain why this is done," Salinas said. He sounded like the Wizard of Oz. "I'm just sitting here. I don't want any innuendoes or insinuations. I get my authority from the constitution."

Foreman had a stack of motions at least three inches thick. It took him three hours to read them into the record. Sammy objected to every one.

When the hearing was over, Archer Parr escorted Nago out of the courtroom, an overcoat thrown over their handcuffed wrists. A news photographer asked to see the manacles for a picture, and Nago obliged, removing the overcoat and holding up his cuffed arm. He and Archer grinned for the camera like they were brothers at a family reunion.

Chapter 18

A medley of odors hung suspended over the *palenque*. The sweet and alcoholic scent of beer mixed with a warm and acrid smell of blood. Every once in awhile, Alfredo caught a whiff of urine. He cursed the stench and breathed deeply when the breeze flushed it from his senses.

It was a cool night in Tepatitlan, Mexico. A light shower had washed the village in late afternoon and gently cooled the surrounding Sierras. This is the way it always is during fall in the mountains that roll through western Mexico. The Pacific Ocean is not far to the southwest and that, combined with the high elevations, assures that the people of Tepatitlan and nearby Guadalajara spend much of their time outdoors.

Indeed, they practically live outdoors. Their mean brick houses, hardened mortar oozing out between adobe bricks like melted ice cream sandwiches, have no screens and no doors. The shops are open wide to the streets, and the merchants stack their wares on the sidewalks or even in the cobblestone roads. During the day and each night until about 10 o'clock, the town is electric with activity. In the evenings the streets are filled with couples walking arm in arm, bent old ladies clutching the arms of married daughters and excited children dancing ahead of their mothers. The men sit on the iron benches in the plaza or walk in twos and threes toward the nearest *cantina*.

Perhaps a hundred of the men of Tepatitlan were in the

palenque this night. It was a particularly rowdy evening, and despite his nasty mood, Alfredo was making a nice sum. There was always ready money at the cockfights, although Alfredo could never understand why. It was nothing better than a poor man's bullfight; a bloody battle that made a smelly mess in the 10-foot ring that formed the *palenque*. Alfredo saw no sport in it, and he could never get caught up in the pandemonium that always erupted.

Nevertheless, he was a master cockfight bookie. Since his youth he had frequented the weekly events and he knew all the handlers around Guadalajara. He knew the good ones, the compact, dark *mestizos* who bred their stock on the chicken ranches outside of town. The birds, their plumage flaming and bold, their large heads crowned with trimmed fire-red combs, were hatched and raised to fight. God had equipped their scaly legs with sharp and threatening spurs. Always angry and aggressive, the birds would scuffle for supremacy, slashing with their spurs and pecking with their menacing beaks.

Knowing the best handlers was not enough to be a skillful bookie. Alfredo was also able to judge the nuances of a fight. Cockfights could take sudden and unpredictable turns. But to a practiced eye like Alfredo's, the outcomes were often predictable. As a bookie, his job was to provide a loud and numerical color commentary on the fights. As the duel drew more blood, his odds changed and he shouted them to the drunken onlookers.

If Alfredo had possessed a greater imagination, he might have pretended he was a trader on the New York Stock Exchange. For such was the clamor that he directed at cockfights. A cluster of *compesinos* hovered around him, first watching at the battle inside the ring, then screaming their bets. Littered around the ring were dozens of dusty men, every one of them sucking on a bottle of beer and bellowing at the raging birds. A few prostitutes hung on the shoulders of the onlookers, laughing and joining in the revelry.

The fights were unfolding in an alleyway squeezed behind a

rowdy *cantina*. Light shone through the undraped windows of the noisy bar, the only illumination for the combat in the *palenque*. Off in the darkened corners, handlers crouched with their roosters tucked between their thighs, bouncing them gently up and down. For Alfredo, the fights had lost their allure. There was a time when he had relished the blood and the fury. Watching the birds as they stalked and slashed one another, he had felt masterful and strong. But now, as he observed the dance in the ring, he felt stripped, powerless.

Perhaps if things had gone differently in Texas. In fact, Alfredo had promised himself he would never set foot in a *palenque* after Texas. With the three grand for the job, he would be too rich to consort with the lowlifes at a cockfight. He would have money to waste for a change. He was weary of running fights and smuggling drugs. At 41 years of age, it was time he settled back and took it easy for a while.

He would be taking it easy if not for that sorry *fullano*—that Sapet. Dammit, the money belonged to him. He had done the job. It wasn't his fault the kid got wasted. It wasn't his fault the kid looked like El Viejo. He had put his neck on the line by hiding in that garage, driving faster than lightning to the border. He had put up with Sapet's braggadocio and had listened to all his stories a dozen times. That in itself was worth something. He had been double-crossed. Everyone had bailed out on him when the going got rough.

Life would have been sweet with the three thousand. He and Norma could have left this squalor and headed for the coast. They could have wasted the days smoking grass and lying intertwined between fresh sheets at a fancy hotel. Alfredo could have had it as good as the gamecocks. Norma would have fed him pomegranate seeds and run her slender fingers through his hair. And when he tired of her, he could have found a serious game of five-card stud at a *cantina*. He would have had money to spare and could have played with confidence.

Alfredo knew it was a fantasy that would have been short-lived, and eventually he would have left his mistress and come back to Irma, his wife. Not because he loved her, but because she was his wife. If he were really honest, Alfredo would have said he would come back mostly because his mother lived with him and his wife. His father had left long ago and his mother, Guadalupe, had been with them since. His father had been a sorry waste of an existence, but his mother, his mother was the one person Alfredo truly cared about. She was not an ideal woman, by any means. She annoyed him more than anything else. But his loyalty to her never wavered.

And then there were the children—so many that Alfredo sometimes lost count. There were five girls and three boys, grimy, tattered little ones who scampered around the ranch most of the time. Alfredo had no use for any of them. They were Irma's responsibility. Alfredo had been back to the ranch only once since his return from Texas. The whole affair in Alice had unnerved him, although he would never admit it to himself or anyone else. He had heard El Viejo was looking for him, a sobering thought given what he knew about the man he was supposed to have killed. Alfredo planned to melt imperceptibly into the lush green landscape of the state of Jalisco. And while he was at it, he would gather a few pesos off the lascivious appetites of the men of Tepatitlan.

For a while, the crowd lost interest in the fight, and the lag gave Alfredo the chance to survey the onlookers. Many of the *compesinos* he had known all his life. Their families lived on ranches near his own, wresting a meager existence from the soil. They grew corn and raised chickens mostly, and ran a few cattle.

Alfredo caught the eye of Ruben Gutierrez, known as El Diente, "the Tooth." Ruben's eyes were as dark as a black man's, but he was *mestizo*. When he smiled, his large teeth flashed in the light, brilliant with the gleam of tiny encrusted diamonds. A round stone, smaller than the lead of a pencil, shone on one of his two big front teeth—the right one. Lesser flecks, almost like dust, beamed from the other upper teeth. The result of Ruben's adornment was that people always looked at him square in the face during conversation. He was a show-stopping sight.

Ruben was a big man in Tepatitlan and in Jalisco for that matter. Scores of prostitutes called him their *padre*. He commanded dozens of couriers who hauled in drugs on the coast and ferried them in by car and train. If you needed a car, Ruben could get one for you—clean and nice—and he'd even pull off the Texas plates and get Jalisco ones. If you needed guns, Ruben had them. If you needed help from the security police, Ruben could arrange it.

El Diente ran his operation out of a spread that was once a *hacienda* north of Tepatitlan. Surrounding himself with a flock of heavily armed *guaruras*, Ruben rarely left his compound. That was why Alfredo was a bit surprised to see him at the cockfight.

There was no question about it, Ruben was staring at him. He flashed that brilliant smile and locked eyes with Alfredo. Ruben nodded his head in the direction of the *cantina*, summoning him there.

"After the fight, El Diente," Alfredo waved.

Within 30 minutes, there was one gamecock dead, another seriously wounded. After settling with the bettors, Alfredo had to admit it wasn't bad for an evening's entertainment. His pockets jingled with pesos as he walked into the *cantina* and he saw Ruben seated at a table.

"Tamburero."

"Ruben!" Alfredo was effusive in his greeting. They sat at a raw, rough wood table in the *cantina*. Ruben's guards hung back by the door, but Alfredo was on edge. He and Ruben had respected each other's territories; their enterprises had not commingled. Alfredo suspected that the man with the diamond teeth had something to say to him regarding Texas.

Ruben leaned back in the crude wooden chair and called to the bartender to bring dos *cervezas*. He was more Indian than many Mexicans. Black, shiny straight hair and dark, dark skin that accentuated the brightness of his shiny smile. He was taller, too, than most, and had the kind of square jaw line that the women went for. He waited until the barkeep delivered the beers, then drained a few inches of the brew.

"Alfredo, *mi amigo*," he said, leaning back in the chair again, "you run a tight fight. You should let your bettors win more!" He smiled in delight.

Alfredo was expressionless. "But they are only *compesinos*, glad to win anything." He was not in the mood for chitchat. It was obvious Ruben was.

"Ah, *compadre*, it is a beautiful night, is it not?" Ruben's electric teeth shone like white neon. A soft breeze drifted through the window by the crude table. There were at least a dozen men leaning against the bar, each with a bottle of *cerveza* in his paw. All seemed oblivious to the acrid smell of urine emanating from a pail parked at the corner of the bar. Every once in awhile, a *campesino* would shuffle to the corner pail and make a deposit. Just as unceremoniously, he would return to his position at the bar. The procedure drew as little attention as the *mariachi* strumming a guitar in the corner.

"Life is good, Alfredo," Ruben said, hoisting his beer bottle in salute. " Every morning, one of my *señoritas* washes my hair. Another cooks up huevos rancheros and the most succulent tortillas a man could hope for. I sit in *la cocina* while they cook and tend to my grooming, and I drink coffee."

Alfredo was feeling sick to his stomach. He would much rather be back at the cockfight than listen to such a disgusting rendition of Ruben's good fortune.

"They are not servants, Alfredo," Ruben said, hoisting his

brew again. "They do it because they love me. If I asked them all to swim the Pacific for me, they would head for the coast without a question from their lovely lips. The same goes for my men. I could not ask for more loyalty. Perhaps it is because I am so good to them.

"There is always lots of food at the *hacienda*. The *señoritas* cook feasts of *cabrito* and stuffed chicken, stewed fruits and vats of spicy rice. I can work up an appetite just thinking about it. And there is always plenty of tequila." A satisfied look settled across Ruben's face and he took a draw from his bottle.

Alfredo drooped over his beer. Because of his longstanding habit of smoking the weed, he was able to tune out whenever he chose. This seemed like the perfect time.

"I have told them all the *hacienda* '*es su casa.*' But they know who the *jefe* is. And they know what the boundaries are. More than one of my people has found out the price of getting too free with my bounty."

Ruben paused. He was studying his companion.

"It works well, Alfredo. We are like a family. We go through the hard times and the good times together."

Alfredo was listening again. Funny, he thought. He talks like a proud *padre*, but he doesn't look like one.

"Now the police, Alfredo, they are like my family, too. Sometimes the officers, they come to my table wearing their guns and their floppy *sombreros*. The *jefetura*, he is one of my best friends. We have known each other since we were boys. I can ask anything of him. He will do it."

Ruben was silent. He swallowed some beer and seemed finished with his discourse.

Alfredo knew the *jefetura*, the chief of police in Tepatitlan. Pablo Escobar was his name, a fat, mustachioed man who rarely ventured from his office in the city hall on the town plaza. Alfredo had spent some time in his jail and had gone to some difficulty in the past few years to stay out of it.

"He is a good friend for any man to have, Alfredo." Ruben motioned to the bartender for more beer.

Alfredo stared at his bottle and pondered Ruben's monologue. He and El Diente had never worked together. Ruben was not the kind of man you could become partners with. He ran his own operation, and any attempt to buddy up to him would be interpreted and dealt with as a threat.

Likewise, Alfredo ran his own deals. Had his own women. He was a maverick, working alone or with his brother Miguel. *El hermano* had three or four *pistoleros* on call. Lived in Zapopan just northwest of Guadalajara. Together, they had put together a respectable operation. But nothing like that of Ruben. He was truly the *jefe* around this part of Jalisco.

That rankled Alfredo. He had always had big plans for himself. Someday, he had promised, he would command a household of foot soldiers and have women waiting at the door to do his bidding. Now, that prospect looked pretty dim.

"It is not good for a man to keep looking over his shoulder." Ruben tapped a finger on his temple. "It eats at a man. Can make him loco. He is like a coyote, his tail between his legs, afraid that the man with the gun will shoot him down for killing his chickens.

"The poor coyote. He is just trying to live. If the ranchero is going to leave his chickens defenseless, what else can he expect?"

Ruben took a final draw from the bottle and slammed it on the table. His guaruras snapped to attention as if in a military force. This was their cue that El Jefe was about to depart.

"Tomorrow I am coming into town again," he said. "I have business with El Jefetura. I will talk to him. I will fix it so the coyote can stop looking over his shoulder. So he can live in peace."

Alfredo looked at his companion and felt churning in his stomach again. Ruben's statement was issued as a fact. It wasn't a gesture, nor was it posed as a question. The coyote could have all the protection he needed. Alfredo just wondered what price the hunted dog would have to pay for such a favor.

"Tomorrow evening," Ruben continued, "I am serving stuffed poblanos and rivers of tequila. I feel like having guests to share my bounty. Alfredo, could you join me and my little family?"

The announcement of the payback apparently would have to wait until then. Alfredo said he would be there and Ruben offered farewells.

When Ruben had gone, Alfredo lingered at the table. Waves of nausea rumbled through his body. He writhed in his chair, his arms across his swollen belly. Twisting to the side, he belched some bile onto the floor. He wiped his mouth on his sleeve, stood and stumbled out the door.

***

The inside of Ruben's house was furnished with massive pieces. An ornately carved mahogany bar occupied one wall in the main room. It must have been 25 feet in length, its mirrored backdrop stacked with shimmery crystal glassware and rows of tequila bottles. Alfredo had heard that Ruben distilled his own tequila. He had seen a field of agave on the way to the house, so the rumor must be true.

What seemed like dozens of people bustled through the house. Ruben was at the main kitchen table, a long, rough wooden affair, with benches to either side. He greeted Alfredo effusively and poured him a tall tequila.

The conversation meandered, as they always do in Mexico.

The two men talked aimlessly for what seemed like hours before they sat on the benches in the kitchen and attacked stuffed *poblanos* and roasted goat. After stuffing themselves, Ruben and Alfredo retired to the front veranda. It was a clear night and the moon shone full and bright.

By now, Alfredo was so mellow from his smokes he would have agreed to just about anything. Finally, Ruben began to unveil his plans for Alfredo.

"The narcotics—the opium, the marijuana—they are becoming more popular across the border," Ruben mused, the moon glancing beams off his sparkling teeth. "Lucky for me, I have fields of both. Acres and acres. Did you see them? I will have to show you. Quite impressive."

Alfredo knew that Ruben housed scores of *compesinos* in bunkhouses a few miles away. His operation was very sophisticated, from planting to harvest and beyond.

"It's like a well-oiled machine." Ruben was becoming obnoxious. Alfredo was becoming uncomfortable.

"There is one part of the machine, however, that needs attention," Ruben said, a cigarette glowing between his lips. "Did you know Arturo, Arturo Silva? He was one of my most faithful and trusted men. He was in charge of transportation. He worked with the boys who bring in the cars from the states and get the stuff across the border. He was a master at it; only lost one shipment to the Rangers.

"I lost him a few weeks ago. He got into a fight at a *cantina* and lost. Stabbed 14 times. We are all still in great sorrow."

Ruben gazed up at the moon and flicked ashes from his cigarette.

"I need a good man to take his place. Someone who knows that end of the business. Someone I know will not betray me. I have always heard the coyote is extremely loyal. If a man takes a coyote in, the coyote will never betray him. The coyote knows that the man offers food and liquid and safety."

There it was. Alfredo expected as much. The coyote had been backed into a corner, and Ruben was offering the only safe way out. It was just like Ruben to add a barb to the deal. He knew full well that Alfredo had a drug business of his own. Not nearly as sophisticated as El Diente's, but it kept a steady flow of pesos in Alfredo's pockets.

Alfredo knew his options. He could fight and run, or take over El Diente's motor pool. In reality there was no choice. He emptied his tequila glass and took a long pull on his hot cigarette. The night took on a hazy glow, and the conversation ebbed. One thing about this place, Alfredo mused, it had all the reefer he could ever hope to smoke.

Chapter 19

The Brown County Jail looked like a medieval castle, its granite turrets reminiscent of battle stations in an ancient war. It was an elegant building, though, pink and incongruent with the gray and unadorned streets of Brownwood, Texas. It was a plain town, in a plain, flat open part of West Texas.

The history books said the jail was built in 1902. The Brownwood newspaper reported when the jail was finished that it was constructed to "contain a strong and excellent cage, one that will be file and saw proof and will be so constructed that it will baffle the ablest efforts of the most experienced criminal."

That it was escape-proof was something Mario Sapet could verify. He calculated that it would take two or three years to scrape even a tiny hole in the thick limestone wall. The three narrow windows in his cell were impassable. Even if he were thin enough to squeeze through them, he would have to saw through a set of iron bars mounted to the outside. The ceiling offered no options, since it was the floor to the third story and the architecture afforded no crawl space.

The cell, which Mario owned all to himself, was stone blocks on all sides. A heavy metal door opened into another cell-block. But to get to the other cells, Sapet had to step across the trap doors of the jail's gallows. Sapet hated that. What if they gave way? He would crash to the first floor, landing on the jailer's desk; he imagined impaling himself on a message spike.

If Mario was unhappy about his accommodations, he was equally unhappy about his lawyers. Fred Semaan and Louis Schlesinger were supposedly two fancy lawyers from San Antonio. So far, they hadn't done Mario much good. They hadn't been able to get him out on bail. Hell no. But Alaniz was free. Alaniz had that swaggering hotshot from Houston, Percy Foreman. With Percy Foreman, the sky was the limit. With Mario's lawyers, the Brown County Jail was the limit.

This was day number 75 in the Brown County Jail. Sheriff Wright and Ranger Klevenhagen had driven him up the day after Christmas after the case was moved to Brown County. They had said they wanted him out of Alice. Things were getting too tense. His trial was set to begin March 16—the next day. Semaan promised he would be in sometime for a pretrial conference.

Mario didn't have a chance. Who was it who had said Brownwood was full of a bunch of Ku Klux Baptist Anglos? A Mexican, a Catholic Mexican, hadn't a prayer in this godforsaken place. Why fight it? He'd been to the joint before. And this time, he would have somebody to keep him in dough and cigarettes and to give him all the protection he would need in Huntsville.

The whole thing had been a big waste of time, anyway. Sam Reams had gotten only 5,000 write-in votes compared to Woodrow Laughlin's 10,000. Raeburn Norris was the new district attorney and Archer Parr was reelected sheriff of Duval County. So why were the big boys so insistent that Jake Floyd and Sam Reams be planted? It made no sense. None of it made sense.

Like why was Alaniz getting special treatment—that big shot Houston lawyer and making bail? The sleaze had blown the whole deal by telling Jake Floyd to take a cab to the cafe. In the long weeks since Mario had taken up residence in the Brown County Jail, there had been plenty of time to plot evil against Nago Alaniz. If they were ever in Huntsville together…

He had other plans for Alfredo, should their paths ever cross again. Mario had planned everything perfectly. It would have run like machinery if everyone had stuck to the plan. Instead, Alaniz balks on the telephone and Alfredo kills the wrong guy.

Mario's thoughts were interrupted by a knock on the cell door. The jailer, a rodent of a man, peered through the opening and told the prisoner his lawyers had come calling. The door opened and Semaan strode in, followed by a tall, graying, rather distinguished looking man in a suit—Louis Schlesinger.

Semaan was a squatty fellow, not much hair on his dome. He wore glasses and expensive suits.

"How are you feeling, Mario?" Semaan asked. "Are you ready for tomorrow?"

"How do I get ready to be the scapegoat in this whole deal?" He hadn't meant to head down that road, but there he was, putting up a fight.

"Mario," Semaan was trying to calm him. "Relax. We're taking care of everything."

That was what Mario was afraid of. For all he could see, Semaan and his buddies weren't doing anything. No plans to call any witnesses, nothing. Mario had no interest in being served up as a sideshow for a bunch of West Texas law-and-order types.

"What's my defense, Semaan? You going to tell them I was in San Antonio when the Floyd kid was murdered? You going to tell them I'm a deputy sheriff in Duval County—a lawman. You going to tell them I have a business in San Antonio? Or are you just going send me down the river to Huntsville?"

Semaan raised both hands as if to hush a squalling child.

"Now, listen. There's no cause for this. You have very fine legal representation. We have a strategy, one that has been effectively used before. So calm down. You're expecting the worst," Semaan said, before Mario interrupted.

"Damn right. I halfway expect that jailer to put my neck in a noose. I can feel it. He's itching to oil those trap doors and pull the lever."

Schlesinger could be silent no longer.

"Mario, you know, the folks in Duval have asked us to do everything we can. They take care of their own down there, and God knows you've been loyal. We want you a free man as much as you do."

"And don't worry about the jailer," Semaan said. "Nothing's going to happen to you. You'll get three squares and a roof over your head—that ain't so bad, is it?"

***

The first person Mario saw when he set foot inside the Brown County Courthouse across the street from the jail was Captain Allee. What a sonofabitch. He was as mean as any killer at Huntsville. The Captain glared at Mario as the jailer and a bailiff escorted him, handcuffed, into the second floor courtroom.

Reporters were everywhere. They swarmed around Mario and asked him for a quote.

"You got anything to say, Mr. Sapet?"

"Is George Parr behind the murder?"

Stupid questions. Mario focused his dead brown eyes straight ahead and didn't look at any of them.

The courtroom pulsed with a noisy mob. Allee and one of his lieutenants bulldozed a path for Mario and his escorts, and he was shown to a slat-backed wooden chair. Semaan had gotten Mario a suit. It was dark brown and looked pretty good on him. He wore his black hair slicked back; his mustache was freshly trimmed.

The prisoner caught sight of Percy Foreman in the corner. It was hard to miss him. He must have been 6-feet-5 and weighed over 300 pounds. He had distracted the gang of reporters away from Mario. Towering above almost everyone in the room,

Foreman seemed to bask in the media spotlight. It was clear he was in his element. Mario couldn't hear what he was saying, but he could see the reporters were copying down every word in their notebooks.

Jake Floyd sat ramrod straight in a chair just to the rear of the prosecutors. His suit was perfectly pressed, his bony legs crossed.

Vibora Seca, Mario thought. The dry snake. George had given him the perfect name.

The courtroom was so crowded it reminded Mario of the Jardin Internacional on a busy night. A body could hardly move in the knot of people. Even the balcony was jammed. Here he was—star of the best show in town. He straightened his shoulders and pushed his chin out.

It was at least 30 minutes before proceedings commenced. The judge ordered the Rangers and the local deputies to clear the courtroom of anyone who didn't have a seat. A few folks were allowed to stand in the side and back aisles, but about 60 people were relegated to the hallway.

Before Judge A. O. Newman gaveled the court to order, Percy Foreman took his place at the defense table. Alaniz sat at his side.

"Your honor," Foreman boomed when the judge had taken the bench, "I move to sever the case of the State of Texas versus Nago Alaniz from the case of the State of Texas versus Mario Sapet."

"Mr. Bell, any objection?" the judge asked lead prosecutor Spurgeon Bell.

"None, your honor."

"Motion granted."

In 60 seconds, Foreman had packed up his briefcase and he and Alaniz had made an exit. Bet that's the quickest he's ever ducked out of the spotlight, Mario thought.

Jury selection took two days, the result being a panel of 12 men. There was a real estate salesman, a bottling works employee, a dry cleaner, a city water works employee, and a farmer among them. To Mario, they looked like a bunch of Ku Klux Baptist Anglos.

Jake Floyd was the first witness summoned. The lawyer was somber and matter-of-fact as he described the events of the night of September 8, 1952. He repeated the story he told at the preliminary hearings.

Semaan objected when Floyd started to relate his conversation with Alaniz at Jewel's Cafe. It was hearsay, Semaan argued. But Judge Newman would have none of it. The jury would hear the conversation. The judge, however, did refuse to allow the jury to hear Floyd's testimony about the 1950 district judge's race when John Ben Shepperd threw out the Duval write-in votes. Prosecutors had wanted the evidence to show a motive for targeting Floyd for assassination.

"Mr. Floyd," Prosecutor Bell said, "you say that you did not believe Nago Alaniz at first?"

"That's right. But he insisted. 'Jake,' he said, 'I want you to know that I am a part of this. I have agreed to testify that the man who killed you was with me and I am to be the alibi for the killer.' I told Nago that I wanted to go and tell all of it to Sheriff Wright."

"And how did Nago Alaniz respond to that suggestion?"

"He said I couldn't do it. That if I did, they would kill him."

"And how did you respond to that statement, Mr. Floyd?"

"I asked him what I could do. I said, 'You won't tell me who the people are. What can I do about it?' Nago said I could tell Halsey that somebody from Rio Grande City told me about the plot. I asked him to give me a name, a name of someone involved in the conspiracy."

Spurgeon prompted, "And did he give you such a name?"

"Yes, he did. He said Mario Sapet, also known as the Turk,

was the leader of the killers. He said Sapet was driving a green Packard and had been staying at some tourist courts around Alice."

"Did you recognize that name?"

"Yes, I did. I knew Sapet was a deputy sheriff in Duval County. And someone had given me his name on a slip of paper a few days before my son was killed."

"Did you have any further conversation?"

"Yes, we did. He said he was leaving Alice and Duval County. He said, 'When they start killing people, I am leaving.' He also said they had hired professional killers to kill me and Judge Reams and that they had been casing my house for two weeks."

"Did Nago Alaniz give you any further information?"

"Yes, he said he knew I didn't believe what he was telling me. But then he said, 'Jake, you know how close I am to George,' and of course, I knew by that he was talking—"

Semaan was on his feet. "Now, just a minute Mr. Floyd, you are an attorney and you know better than that."

"Mr. Floyd," Judge Newman interjected, "you will refrain from any conjecture. Now proceed."

Jake continued with a description of his movements following his conversation with Alaniz. By the time he finished, it was nearly noon, and Judge Newman recessed for lunch. When they returned to the courtroom, it was Semaan's turn to cross-examine.

"Mr. Floyd," Semaan said, lifting his stocky frame from his chair, "isn't it true that you are the leader of the anti-Parr party?"

"Some people have called me that, but I do not consider myself such," Floyd said, crossing his legs and folding his arms.

"You would like to see the Parr Party destroyed and wiped out?" Semaan asked.

"I certainly would, and I would be glad to give you my reasons if you want them."

"Mr. Floyd, in your desire to destroy George Parr and the Parr Party, is it a fact that if an innocent man or two has to go to the penitentiary, that is all right with you?"

"No, sir, it is not." Jake shifted stiffly in his chair.

"Now, Mr. Floyd, you have given the same testimony in a preliminary hearing in this case, have you not?"

"That's correct."

"Isn't it true that last night you went over that same testimony with Mr. Bell and Ranger Klevenhagen?"

"We looked at it, yes."

"Now, Mr. Floyd, if we could go back to the night that your son was shot. Where exactly were you standing while you were waiting for the cab to arrive?"

"I was right in front of the house."

"What could you see? Could you see in the backyard?"

"No, sir."

"Could you see the garage?"

"No, sir, I could not."

"Did you see a green Packard parked on Reynolds Street?"

"I didn't at first. But then I noticed it. It was parked about 350 feet from the hospital."

"And where is the hospital?"

"It is in the next block over, behind the house."

"Mr. Floyd, you mentioned that someone gave you a slip of paper with the name 'Mario Sapet' on it a few days before September 8. Who gave you that slip of paper?"

"My law partner, Clarence Perkins."

"And what did you do with that slip of paper?"

"I put it in my pocket. "

"Now, Mr. Floyd, did you ever give a written statement about the events of the night of September 8?"

"Yes, sir, I did."

"And when did you make that statement?"

"I don't recall, exactly. It was probably the next weekend."

"And who took the statement?"

"My secretary."

"So you gave a statement on Sunday morning after September 8. Is that correct?"

"I don't think it was Sunday morning."

"But you said it was Sunday morning." Semaan's voice was elevating.

"Well, I don't think I did say Sunday morning."

"All right," Semaan said, his voice moderating slightly. "I won't argue with you."

"Well, I know, but you shouldn't." Jake said. "If the court please, I want to ask that this lawyer not be treating me like he is. He is just taking every technicality and exception and he is just acting ugly about it."

Judge Newman was unruffled. "Just a minute, Mr. Floyd."

Semaan interrupted. "Your Honor, I am going to take an exception to that and ask the court to declare a mistrial."

"No, sir," Judge Newman said, shaking his head. "Next question."

Semaan was finished with Jake.

When Edith Floyd took the stand, she was composed and serious. She wore a dark blue silk dress belted at the waist and a single rhinestone ornament on her lapel. The hysteria she had exhibited the night of the murder had given way to a calm and deliberate demeanor. Methodically, she described the events of the night of September 8. The Sunday School party, her return to 4th and Reynolds, her discovery of Buddy's wounded form on the driveway, the summoning of Dr. Wyche.

She told the court she had only seen her son alive one more time. That was in the hospital. He was lying in a hospital bed, his head covered in bandages.

"Mrs. Floyd," Bell said gently, "how far would you say it is from the terrace behind your house to the garage—in feet."

"I would guess about 40 feet," she said.

"Mrs. Floyd, did you and Sheriff Wright conduct an experiment following the night of September 8?"

"Yes, we did."

"Could you describe that experiment?"

"Yes. Sheriff Wright asked me to wait in the service room in the garage with the window raised while he went next door to the Atkinsons' and called our house. When the telephone rang in the kitchen, and by the stairway, I could hear it. I could hear the ring both with the window open and the window closed."

"Thank you, Mrs. Floyd. Your witness."

The defense attorney approached the grieving mother slowly. In a gentle, almost soothing voice, he asked if she had seen anyone around the garage or in the back yard, or any suspicious persons in the area that night.

"No, I did not," She said softly.

"Did you hear anything, like a car leaving the scene, someone leaving on foot?"

"No, sir."

Semaan knew he had little to gain with the jury by cross-examining the mother of the victim. He returned to his seat and passed the witness.

***

Dr. George Goodwyn Wyche had been a physician and surgeon for 35 years. For 20 of those years, he had practiced in Alice. And for nearly all of that time, he had lived on the opposite corner of the same block as the Floyd family. It was a perfect location for a doctor. It was just across the street from the hospital.

He testified he heard three to five gunshots the night of September 8. He wasn't certain of the number, but he was certain they were gunshots. He didn't go outside to investigate; he was already in bed.

When he was summoned to the scene, he found Buddy with a gunshot wound at the hairline and another in the right wrist.

"X-rays showed he had a bullet in his head, part of which lay on the outside of the skull and part penetrated," Dr. Wyche said. "We rolled him into surgery as soon as we could get a specialist from Corpus Christi. We removed the part of the bullet that was outside the brain, but the other fragment could not be extracted. We removed some brain tissues that had been exuded."

"Did he ever regain consciousness?" the prosecutor asked.

"No, sir. He died the next day about 4 P.M."

"And what would you say was the cause of death?"

"The bullet—it looked like a .32 or .38 caliber—that lodged in his head destroyed his respiratory center."

"Now, Dr. Wyche, other than in the newspapers, have you ever seen Mario Sapet before?"

"Yes, I have. I identified him after Buddy's murder as a man I had seen driving around the Floyd house...."

"Your honor," Semaan said, on his stubby feet. "I'll object to that."

"Sustained."

"I have nothing further."

Semaan's cross-examination was not illuminating. And he refused to question Elinor Lewis after she described the slaying from her perspective inside the Floyd house. A beautiful young victim—there was no way he could score with the jury at her expense.

Ballistics expert Fred Rymer of the Department of Public Safety lab in Austin testified the fatal bullet was fired from the Colt .38 found in the garbage can in the alley behind the Floyd garage.

When Captain Allee took the stand, his job was to relate

how he traveled to Nuevo Laredo to pick up the green Packard. He described it as a late model, four-door, emerald green Packard, which he delivered to Bowman Chevrolet in Alice. Sheriff Wright had asked him to deliver it to the dealership, where it could be combed for evidence in the garage. The police department had no investigative depot for such a large piece of physical evidence.

Before the day was finished, the Captain was recalled to the stand so he could correct his testimony that the Packard was a four-door model. The proper description, he said, was a two-door vehicle.

"It was just a slip of the tongue," he testified, explaining the discrepancy.

During a recess, Werner Gohmert, an Alice attorney who was working on Sapet's defense, stopped the Captain in the hallway outside the courtroom.

"Did you deliberately lie on the witness stand?" he asked, grinning impishly at the Ranger.

The next instant, the lawyer was on the floor, propelled by the thrust of Captain Allee's fist. Gohmert rubbed his jaw and limped away, swearing he had just been kidding. But Captain Allee was unimpressed. No one, especially not some smart aleck lawyer, was going to call him a liar and get away with it.

The next witness, a Floyd neighbor, W. B. Nance, said he saw the green Packard parked along Third Street a few days before Buddy was shot.

"There was a man in it. I saw it again the night of September 8. And later that evening, about 9 o'clock, I was sitting in my kitchen reading when I heard what sounded like pistol shots. They were coming from northeast of the house.

"I got up from the kitchen table, walked out on the front porch and the Packard was parked across the street, almost nearly in front of the house. I saw a man get in it and drive off. It didn't start right off. Seemed like it took awhile to get it started. But when it did start, the driver took off pretty fast. When he got to Reynolds, he turned south toward town."

Robert Kocurek testified he remembered exactly when he had heard gunshots the night of September 8. It was two minutes past 9 o'clock. His grandmother had just gone to bed, as she always did, punctually at 9 o'clock.

"When I heard the shots, I ran to the front porch and saw a man running. He got into a car parked across from the house."

"Did you get a good look at him?" Spurgeon asked.

"I saw him well enough to see he was a Mexican. He had on a dark jacket, dark trousers, a light shirt and a felt hat sitting straight on his head and pulled down over his forehead. I got a real good look at him when he opened the car door and the inside light came on. It must have taken him 20 seconds to start the car and then he drove off real fast.

"I went in the house and got a flashlight and decided to go checking around. I knew something was wrong. Before I went out the door, I asked my wife to call the police."

Prosecutors called a string of law enforcement officers and neighbors. Semaan and Schlesinger made spirited attempts to dismantle their testimonies under cross-examination, but made only a few dents.

Semaan decided to try a technical maneuver to save his client. He asked for a bill of exception—a claim that Sapet's rights were violated when he was not properly arraigned after his arrest. But after hearing Sapet testify and looking at pretrial records, the Judge was satisfied that the defendant was properly arraigned. Petition denied.

The prosecution resumed calling witnesses. Edith Floyd Patterson told the jury how her father and Buddy looked and walked alike. She showed the jury a photograph of Buddy and her father, taken the summer before Buddy's death.

Inez Mendez and her husband, Encarnacion, testified about

how they saw Cervantes and Sapet together in the days before the shooting.

Spurgeon Bell called accountant O. D. Kirkland to the witness stand and asked him if he had ever seen Mario Sapet. Yes, he had, on August 22, 1950. It was during a runoff election in the Democratic primary. Sapet, he said, was active in the Parr faction at that time.

Bell decided to call Jake Floyd once more to the stand, this time to testify about the 1950 election. He had worked hard that year, he said, to make sure Sam Reams was re-elected district judge. He had called friends and urged their vote, raised money for the candidate and helped Sam organize a campaign committee. They had spent hundreds of dollars renting cars to ferry voters to the polls.

Bell rested the state's case and Schlesinger moved for a mistrial, this time because he claimed the prosecution had made an insufficient case. Newman wasn't biting this time either.

By Saturday, the testimony in the case was concluded and it was time for final arguments. Semaan was particularly eloquent in his summation, urging the jury not to confuse the issues.

"Don't take a hand in washing their dirty linen down there in the 79th Judicial District," he pleaded. "Don't by your verdict set up Jake Floyd or George Parr as a leader down there. Let me remind you, gentlemen of the jury, it is Mario Sapet on trial, not George Parr. Mario Sapet, the man sitting in the brown suit right there.

"This gentleman was nowhere near the home of Jake Floyd the night Buddy Floyd was murdered. He was on a bus from Corpus Christi to San Antonio. He was even seen in the San Antonio police station that night, less than an hour after Buddy Floyd was shot."

When Bell gave his summation, he reminded the jury that Sapet had shown the murder weapon to Jesus Pompa only days before the shooting. He had introduced Alfredo Cervantes to Pompa. His green Packard had been seen outside the Floyd residence for days before the killing and witnesses had seen a man speed away from the area about the time of Buddy's shooting.

Furthermore, Bell reminded the jury, Sapet could be clearly linked to George Parr and his followers, all of whom had clear motives for wanting Jake Floyd removed from the scene.

"Gentlemen of the jury, this is your opportunity to make a clear statement," Bell admonished. "A clear statement that political assassinations are unacceptable in the state of Texas. That murder of any kind is unacceptable in the state of Texas. A clear statement that people who participate in such killings will pay for their crimes."

Judge Newman told the jury they could find Sapet guilty only if they decided he had aided and abetted Cervantes. The next night, Sunday, the jury returned a guilty verdict on a charge of murder with malice. Sapet was sentenced to 99 years in prison.

Chapter 20
December

Johnny Klevenhagen galloped up the marble steps in Mexico City's municipal building two at a time. The building was a heavy, ornate limestone structure possessing the architectural details of the centuries old city's colonial era. The Ranger noticed that for the first time since he had left Texas two days before, he was not mopping his forehead. Mexico City is nestled in a valley surrounded by mountains, and the December air was cool and inviting.

As he scaled the broad stairway, he held an envelope tightly in his hand. In it was a letter from the governor of Texas—a letter he was to use as an introduction to officials of the Mexican police.

"This letter will introduce Mr. J. J. (Johnny) Klevenhagen who is an agent of the State of Texas," the letter said. It was on fancy paper, an embossed seal at the bottom. Gov. Shivers had signed it personally.

"Ranger Klevenhagen is in Mexico on a special assignment through special orders from my office. I would sincerely appreciate your assistance and cooperation as he seeks to complete his mission."

The letter contained a paragraph about Alfredo Cervantes, and more fancy talk about how much the governor appreciated all the help he hoped Johnny would get. It was the last of three letters Johnny had brought to Mexico from the governor's office. He had delivered two of them the day before—one to Bob Melberg, an attache at the U.S. Embassy. Bob had grown up in South Texas and was a longtime friend of Captain Allee.

Johnny had also delivered a letter to the Presidential Palace. He couldn't help but be impressed by those high-sounding letters. He just wished he could have shaken hands with the President of Mexico. The letter said the President's name was the Honorable Adolpho Ruiz Cortines.

It didn't take Johnny long to reach the top of the stairs. He was about as knobby and wiry as a sure-footed mountain goat. And with his crease-topped Stetson and yoked khaki shirt, he stood out in the crowd that milled through the open-air building.

But nobody paid him any attention. Folks in Mexico City were accustomed to seeing Americans, especially lanky Texans with big hats. If he weren't so tall—he stood a full head above the natives—Johnny might have gone virtually unnoticed. His skin was pocked and brown, his hair dark and curly. His eyes were brown and sultry so that his wife sometimes teased that he resembled Humphrey Bogart.

When he reached the second floor, he turned to see if Rudy was close behind. Rudy Garza, a deputy sheriff from San Antonio, did not enjoy the benefit of long legs. He was still climbing, one step at a time. He waved the Ranger on.

Johnny could do a passable job of reading Spanish, so he looked for El Direccion Federal de Seguridad—the office of the Mexican Federal Security Police. He decided to wait for Rudy. After all, that was why he had brought the deputy along—to be a translator and because he needed another hand.

Rudy caught up with him and pointed a stubby finger to a corner office on the mezzanine. Rudy's hair was black and straight, trimmed at the collar and tucked underneath a wide-brimmed cowboy hat. A brassy sheriff's shield clung to the breast of his shirt.

They hadn't been in the Mexican Federal Security Police Office 60 seconds before they were shown to an empty office and offered chairs.

"That was quick," Johnny said to Rudy once they had been left alone.

"Don't get excited," Rudy said. He had warned the Ranger that Mexicans lived on *mañana* time. They had gotten a taste of it the day before when they had waited an hour and a half to deposit the governor's letter with the proper official at the Presidential Palace.

Johnny pulled out a pack of Lucky Strikes and offered Rudy one. It was a rare moment when the Ranger didn't have a cigarette in his hand. He was a three-pack-a-day man.

They didn't have to wait long for their host. Johnny had just lit his second cigarette when Jorge Lavin de Leon walked in. The Ranger took one look at Lavin and knew he was no ordinary Mexican police officer.

He was nearly as tall as Johnny and outweighed him a good 20 pounds. He was all muscle, his body the obvious product of intense physical activity. His hair was trimmed short, and he wore a grey-green military uniform. His jaw was square and firm, his cheekbones high and refined like a born aristocrat's. Johnny guessed him to be in his early 40s, same as himself.

There were the preliminary pleasantries that always tested Johnny's patience. It was part of the mañana mentality, Rudy had told him. In Mexico, getting to the point was downright rude. Johnny uncrossed his legs, leaned back in his metal folding chair and listened as Rudy chatted in Spanish with Lavin. He would have to wait for the wheels of protocol to turn.

"Mr. Ranger," Lavin finally said, his words laden with a Spanish overtone. "I speak little English, so please forgive me if I talk through Señor Garza."

"It's okay," Johnny said, groping for the right Spanish

phrase. "*Muy bueno.* Ask him if he got my letter about Cervantes," Johnny directed Rudy.

The conversation moved tediously, but gradually, Johnny learned that Lavin knew of Alfredo Cervantes. In fact, he had known of him for several years. Cervantes was one of those characters who crossed paths with police enough that his mug shot was updated in the files every few years.

"He says he can get us mugs and prints," Rudy said, adding that they were on file at the Mexican Federal Security Police headquarters a few blocks away.

"What about the police in Guadalajara?" Johnny asked. "What do they know?"

"They're protecting him. Lavin says no use even contacting them. They'll just tip him off when we're around. Says the most reliable information they've got is that our man is staying at a *hacienda* near Guadalajara. The *hacienda* is known as El Coyote.

"He says it's a *hacienda* owned by a big-time gangster named Ruben Gutierrez. He's got a regular cottage industry going, this Gutierrez. He's got an agave plantation there at El Coyote and he runs several smuggling operations out of the *hacienda*. He says Gutierrez is protecting Cervantes, giving him a place to stay.

"He says he'll give us eight men, some pack mules and ammunition, but he has to be reimbursed."

"Pack mules?" Johnny said, abruptly standing up.

"There's no roads out there, Johnny," Rudy said. "We'd have to drive over open land, and that would do away with any surprise ambush. We'll have to walk at least four or five hours from the nearest town. I hope you're in good shape. It won't be no hike around the Alamo, I'll tell you that."

Johnny sucked hard on his Lucky Strike, as if it imparted nutrients.

"Tell him our man in Texas is good for the money. All he's got to do is let me know." Johnny had already sized up this Lavin fellow. For a Mexican police officer, he appeared to be trustworthy. In fact, he looked tough enough to be a Texas Ranger, and that was more than a passing grade in Johnny's book.

"He wants to know do we want him any way we can get him?" Rudy asked.

"Dead or alive? Hell, he's no good to us in a box. Tell him the main thing is we want to put that bastard on the stand and find out who paid him."

Rudy and Lavin conversed awhile, then Rudy reported.

"He says they have informants, people who talk to Cervantes. They say he's claiming he knew he was shooting at the boy. He got spooked when the kid ran out the back door. He's been moaning he only got paid 30 bucks for the job."

"He's bound to be moving around a lot, on the run," Johnny said. "Ask him when we can leave."

"I already did. He says there's a flight tonight. The men are ready to go. The *federales* in Guadalajara will provide the mules and ammo. We'll need to hike out to the *hacienda* tonight. The more delay, the more risk he'll be tipped off."

"He coming with us?" Johnny asked.

"Don't think so, Johnny," Rudy said, grinning.

"Ask him where I can get a good chicken-fried steak," Johnny said, grinning back. "I'm starved."

***

Six hours later, they were on the outskirts of Tepatitlan in the company of a band of men who looked more like soldiers than police officers. Johnny had seen men like these piled in the back of large trucks that careened through the streets of Mexico City. They wore the same kind of military uniform Lavin had worn, and each carried a carbine and an ammunition belt.

The rendezvous point was a ranch owned by a Colonel

Fernandez. Lavin had two plainclothes men meet the two Texans at the airport and drive them to Fernandez's ranch. It was not as palatial as Johnny had expected; in fact it looked just like a working ranch.

The concrete block bunkhouse, a few hundred yards from the main house, was where they met Colonel Fernandez. He was a thick-chested man with a mustache and a habit of clearing his throat every minute or two.

A couple of burros were stationed near the bunkhouse, grazing. It was a clear night, and the moon was bright. Johnny was glad the stars would help them navigate, but cursed that they would be so visible. He and Rudy still had on their khaki shirts and trousers. He wished he had brought his blue jeans and denim shirt. At least he had a dark jacket. He'd need it in the mountain air.

Colonel Fernandez eyed Johnny suspiciously, then spoke to Rudy in Spanish.

"He says he's heard of the Texas Rangers—heard their plenty mean," Rudy said. "Wants to know if it's true."

Johnny looked the colonel square in the eye. He'd been to Mexico enough to know the natives mean something when they make eye contact. Johnny didn't like what he saw in the colonel's eyes.

"Says he's heard the Rangers beat up Mexicans," Rudy continued. "Says he's got a brother and two sisters living in Texas."

What a sorehead, Johnny thought. Rudy continued speaking in Spanish to the colonel. Johnny understood a word here and there, but had no idea what the deputy was saying.

"I told him you're plenty mean, all right, but you save your meanness for criminals. I told him about the time you found that escaped convict, what's his name—"

"Who? Oh—Joe McCamey," Johnny said, still looking at the colonel.

"Yeah, McCamey. Told him how you spotted him in a crowd of folks getting off a bus in Houston. How the crowd was almost all Mexicans. How you waited until those folks got out of the way before you shot him loose from his pistol."

The story did nothing to warm the coldness in the colonel's eyes.

"Ask him if he wants to stay behind," Johnny asked.

Rudy pulled the Ranger a few feet away and spoke softly.

"Not a wise move, Johnny," Rudy said. "You don't want to insult the man."

"Maybe I do."

"He's not our biggest enemy here. Our biggest enemy is time. If Cervantes is where we think he is, he'll get tipped off. It's just a question of whether we can get there before he does."

Johnny was silent for a moment; his cigarette glowed in the dark. He wanted to cuss a streak. He wanted to tell the colonel that, yes, he liked to beat up Mexicans. Would he like to step up to the mat?

"Seems to me this guy could be our biggest enemy," Johnny said. "Hell, it wouldn't surprise me a bit if he's hooked in with the Guadalajara police."

"Johnny—"

"Lavin's gonna hear about this. I got enough on my hands without some mangy Mexican spittin' in my eye."

"Johnny, the man does speak some English," Rudy said.

"Then let him talk to me instead of hiding behind you," the Ranger said.

The colonel remained silent for a long time. Then he looked at his troops and reeled off some orders. Johnny understood one word—"*andale*."

Johnny took a final drag on his cigarette and tossed it on the rocky dirt at his feet. He smothered the glowing butt with the heel of his boot, picked up his rifle and slung the long strap of a canteen around his shoulder.

"Tell the colonel I've studied the map and it looks like we head due north," Johnny told Rudy.

Rudy had a brief exchange with Colonel Fernandez, then said, "Just follow the North Star."

The colonel took the lead, a folded map wedged under his belt at the small of his back. He walked deliberately, as if he were certain of their destination. In all, there were 11 men in the party, and they walked silently through the night. The only sounds were their feet striking the sandy, rock-infested soil and the occasional distant calls of unseen coyotes.

There were a few wire fences to slip through and a couple of rock fences to scale. The further north they traveled, the more it became evident they were climbing. Johnny could tell because he was breathing harder and his leg muscles ached. He paced himself on the cigarettes; they didn't help his breathing.

They passed a couple of houses and saw a few head of cattle, but other than that, all Johnny could see was a big moon, bright sky and rolling hills up ahead. Johnny had been on many a manhunt in his 20-plus years in law enforcement. It was the kind of thing he had dreamed of when he was a kid growing up in Comal County just north of San Antonio.

He and Cap Allee had reminisced together many times about their childhood fantasies. Cap was a third-generation Ranger and had grown up listening to Ranger stories around campfires. Johnny had never enjoyed that luxury, but still he always knew he wanted to be a Ranger. When he wasn't even 18, he lied about his age in a failed attempt to get on the San Antonio police force. He finally got a job as a deputy constable, then worked as a sheriff's deputy before becoming a Ranger. When he got the call from Austin that he had become one of the elite force, he was told it meant a cut in pay. But Johnny didn't care. He picked up his Stetson, shouted to his boss that he was quitting and hit the highway for Austin.

He'd spent most of his career in Houston. Johnny and the sheriff there, Buster Kern, had teamed up on many a case. But just as often, Johnny would take on an assignment outside of Harris County. When Spurgeon Bell called him and asked if he would hunt down Cervantes, the prospect of adventure in Mexico was too good to pass up.

Besides, he'd do anything to nail that s.o.b. George Parr. The bastard couldn't be guiltier of killing Buddy Floyd if he'd pulled the trigger himself. Yep, it was going to be mighty satisfying when he could slap a pair of cuffs on that Cervantes. He'd told Mr. Floyd that he'd be glad to just kidnap that heap of maggot shit and haul him across the border to Alice. Mr. Floyd hadn't been against the idea. He knew extradition was going to be next to impossible, what with relations between the U.S. and Mexico not the best.

And there was the matter of executions. Johnny could never figure it. Mexico was as uncivilized a place as he'd ever been, but there was no death penalty. A Mexican citizen could burn, rape, murder, mutilate and torture, and never face execution. Instead, he'd rot in one of their dungeons for 30 years. Johnny guessed that might be worse than getting it over with at the end of a rope.

Because the Mexican government was so screwy about the death penalty, it made extradition of criminals all the harder. Unless Bell could cut a deal with Cervantes, he'd be facing execution back in Texas. And that prospect was sure to sour any extradition efforts.

That's why Johnny thought the best thing was to just cuff the guy, slap some leg irons on him and drive him back across the border. If they got lucky on this trip, that's what he'd do. He'd call Lavin and arrange for a car later. He hoped he wouldn't have any trouble from that fathead colonel. He was a regular fly on the varnish.

It was about daybreak when the colonel stopped the party

just under the lip of a small rise. He drank thirstily from his canteen and then summoned Rudy.

"He says the *hacienda* is just over that rise," Rudy said after a brief conversation in Spanish. "He says the men are going to spread out. Some are going north, some south. Try to surround the place as best they can.

"There'll be a bunch of out buildings and people may be up already. We'll have to get past those before we get to the main house."

"What does he suggest we do if we run into anybody?" Johnny said.

"We're gonna have to knock 'em out or tie 'em up, gag 'em. We've gotta move fast if we're gonna surprise the big house. That's where Cervantes is supposed to be staying."

A few clouds had rolled in from the southwest, obscuring the moon. But the advantage wouldn't last long. The sun was already climbing the horizon.

Johnny and Rudy and a half dozen of the men headed south; the colonel and the others took the north route. The Ranger and his party walked at least ten minutes before they rounded the edge of the rise and were able to survey the spread below.

Acres of agave sprawled as far as the eye could see. In such a vast, open space, it was hard to gauge how far they were from the *hacienda*, but Johnny guessed they were at least a mile and a half. And there was nothing to hide their approach. The agave plants would barely come to his knees.

The few trees that were on the property were to the east, as were various outbuildings. A long, low building, probably a chicken house, lay to the northeast, a good mile from the big house. Even though it was so far away, he could hear the din of thousands of chattering chickens.

There were no people in sight. The big house was dark and quiet, and not even a wisp of smoke escaped from either of the two chimneys. Johnny hated to even think it, but the place looked deserted.

"Let's move!" Johnny said, waving to the men with a sweep of his arm.

They scampered a few hundred feet and stopped short, like cats on a hunt. Johnny could see one or two of the colonel's men on the far side of the house. They approached some of the outbuildings and ducked low so they couldn't be seen as they passed by the windows.

The agave gave way to acres of a leafy green sweetly fragrant plant. Johnny kicked through the foliage and looked west. The marijuana extended to the end of the mesa. Back in the States, he thought, this field would get a man 30 years at Huntsville. The Mexican *federales* followed in the trail he trampled, unperturbed by the discovery.

The *hacienda* remained disturbingly quiet. Johnny didn't even hear livestock stirring in the sheds. Then the screaming started—piercing, jarring screaming. There was more than one shriek, from more than one voice, and it was coming from the north side of the *hacienda*.

Johnny tightened his grip on his rifle and broke into a run. Rudy and the *federales* followed suit. They could see the other party of invaders charging toward the screams. Johnny ran with abandon, his long legs carrying him well ahead of the others.

He halted at the corner of the house and peered around it. At first he saw nothing except an open feed hut, the kind used for hogs. It was enclosed on three sides. There were more screams. Johnny thought they sounded slightly inhuman. They were coming from the feed hut.

He motioned to stay next to the house, and then strode to the hut. Another shriek and then an explosion of feathers. A huge, brightly plumed bird jetted into Johnny's face. More flying feathers and beating wings. Two more big peacocks took flight in

Johnny's direction. One of the startled *federales* fired and dropped a bird at Johnny's feet.

Johnny stood in a stupor. He felt as if he had been punched in the forehead. His eyes were swimming in blood. The peacock had pecked him hard, just above his right eye. Mopping his wound with a bandana, he motioned with his rifle for Rudy and the others to head for cover.

But before they could scatter, the *hacienda* doors flew open and gun barrels appeared. Johnny could hear furniture scraping the floor inside. More gun barrels in the windows. The Ranger had his rifle aimed and a finger on the trigger. The other officers, scattered around the north end of the house, stood ready to fire as well.

There was a long silence, save for the screaming of the peacocks.

"*Abajo* El Rinche," said a deep, commanding voice. It came from a first-floor window.

Still mopping his wound, Johnny shot a glance at the colonel and caught him smirking. Goddamn that Fernandez. He'd been right about him. It was all a sorry waste.

Rudy started talking to the voice inside. He used the word *hombre* several times. That was the only word Johnny recognized. The voice inside responded, and Rudy and the others threw down their weapons.

"Drop it, Johnny," Rudy shouted.

As soon as he did, *pistoleros* strode out onto the porches, front and back. There must have been 15 of them. They moved slowly around until they had Johnny and his men surrounded. They stood there, silent for what seemed like three or four minutes. Then the deep, commanding voice again.

"Welcome to my humble dwelling," the voice said in fairly good English. Now it had a face and a body. There were long legs clothed in dungarees and a bare, hairless torso. The face was bearded, smiling—an odd sort of smile. "Please, come inside."

The man in dungarees disappeared inside the house, and the *pistoleros* motioned for the captured officers to follow. Rudy shrugged at Johnny.

"I told him we were looking for a man—a murderer," the deputy said. "He said nobody's here but him and his men."

"Is he that Gutierrez dude?" Johnny said.

Rudy didn't answer.

Once they were inside, Johnny couldn't get over the animals in the cages. The badger was what really got his attention. What kind of man would have a caged badger in his house, he wondered.

The big man led them into the kitchen, where some sleepy-eyed women were boiling coffee and scurrying around. They did not look at the visitors.

"Please—sit," the man said, motioning to the big table with the benches. Johnny wondered if there had been a breakfast invitation somewhere in the man's conversation with Rudy.

The visitors sat around the table, while the *pistoleros* trained their guns on them.

"Señor Ranger," the man said, grinning. Johnny could see the diamonds in his teeth. "How is Tejas?"

"Texas is fine," Johnny said testily. "Look, mister, I'm looking for somebody. That's all. Don't mean you no harm. I'm awful sorry we scared you out there, but we're not looking to hurt anybody. We just want to find our man and go home."

The man pulled a chair up next to a bench. He propped his bare feet on the table and smiled up at a *señorita*, who handed him a cup of coffee.

"*Cafe por todos*," he told her. "Señor Ranger, no harm done here. But please, don't be hurried. Let me tell you something. Let me tell you my name.

"I am Ruben Gutierrez. And this is my family. We were

sleeping peacefully just a few minutes ago. We heard a gun shoot."

"The peacocks," Johnny said. "Sorry."

"I see one of them sliced you. They are bad boys sometimes." Ruben motioned for one of the *señoritas* to tend to Johnny's gashed forehead. The badger paced more frantically.

As the men sipped coffee and a young woman applied a compress to Johnny's forehead, Ruben talked. The weather had been nice, a little on the cool side but nice. He had never been to Texas, he said, but always wanted to go. Maybe the Ranger could take him.

"Who is this man—the one you are looking for?" Ruben asked finally.

"His name is Alfredo Cervantes," Johnny said, glad to be through with the preliminaries once again. "He's from Tepatitlan. We had information he was staying here at your ranch. Have you seen him?"

Ruben glanced quickly at the colonel, then shook his head.

"Can you tell me what he looks like—this Cervantes, you say?"

"Cervantes," Johnny nodded. He sighed.

"He's a big man, not tall but big. Got a scar on his left ear. I have a picture—"

Johnny reached in his pocket, and the nose of a gun barrel nudged his temple. Ruben waved the *pistolero* away, then looked at the mug shot. He shook his head again.

"You say he's a murderer?" Ruben said.

"Yep. Look, are we under house arrest or something?"

Ruben looked astonished.

"Why, no, Señor Ranger."

"Then we'd like to go. We've got a long hike ahead of us."

Johnny stood up.

"But Señor Ranger, your men are tired. They are hungry. Can't you see? Have beans and tortillas—that is all I can offer so early."

Johnny agreed and sat down again. He was glad for the food and the coffee. He ate hungrily, along with his companions. Ruben stayed in his chair, feet on the table between their plates, and chattered.

When they were finished, he walked with them to the door.

"I must ask you," he said to Johnny, "to leave your guns. You understand, my friend?"

He stood close to Johnny, his eyes slivers of ebony.

This man is George Parr south of the border, Johnny thought. He nodded and turned to leave right behind the colonel. Then stopped short.

"Señor Gutierrez," he said to the ebony eyes. "Just one thing. How did you know I was a Texas Ranger?"

The diamond teeth sparkled in the morning sun.

"The peacock told me!"

Chapter 21

Donato Serna sat on a barstool and nervously sipped a soda at his brother's drive-in restaurant. There were only about five cars getting curb service outside the Rio Drive-In, and no one except Donato sat at the soda fountain inside. It was a far cry from what business used to be. Used to be Joe Serna couldn't keep enough waitresses and short-order cooks to feed the customers.

"If it gets much worse, Donato," Joe said, drying a glass with a cup towel, "I'm going to have to move out of San Diego."

"Maybe they'll let up," Donato said. "George hasn't circled his wagons for at least a month."

"They're not going to let up," Joe said. "Just like the Freedom Party isn't going to let up. The way Tecuache shows his teeth these days, you'd think he was a mamma possum guarding her young'uns."

Donato showed his brother his profile. He could hear Joe speak just fine out of his right ear. The hearing wasn't so good in the left ear, the result of a grenade explosion in the Philippines during the war. He'd won a Purple Heart for that.

"I talked to Lupe Calderon this morning," Donato said. "You know him? He works on one of the county road crews. He says Pete Saenz told him if he ever comes over here for a hamburger again, he'd lose his job."

"Let's add him to the list," Joe said.

"It scared him, bad. You'll never see him again."

"You going to be able to make it, Donato?"

"Sure. Losing the bus depot hurt us a lot. But the pharmacy and the soda fountain and the rest of the store will survive. I don't think George is stupid enough to run the only pharmacy out of San Diego. He wanted to bust my jaw, not knock me cold."

"The street's too narrow where they put the new depot," Joe said, curling his upper lip in disgust. "You'd think they could come up with something better than that."

"Well, it was Pete Saenz and his bunch who petitioned the bus company. None of them has much in the IQ column."

"I talked to Manuel Sanchez yesterday," Joe said. "He said the vice president of the bank told him he had to close his account and pay off the loan he's got with them. He's got to borrow money from the Alice bank to pay off the loan."

"I've heard the same thing from several of the fellows. I figured that was coming. I moved my account to Alice Bank & Trust last summer."

Joe picked up a big soda glass and began drying it slowly. He was trim and wiry like his brother, a white cook's apron wrapped around his small frame.

"You got any regrets, Donato?"

"No, sir," Donato said, draining the last of his soda from the glass. "I didn't get my ear blown off in the war to come back to this. I'm in it for the duration."

"What you mean by "the duration"? George'll never give up, and he may never die. Even if he does, some other gringo with ambition and no principles will step in to take his place."

Donato had to admit, things were getting out of hand. Not only had he lost the depot, but Archer Parr had shown up at the pharmacy one night demanding to search the place. He was looking for illegal narcotics, he said.

Archer had five deputies with him that night, and they had searched the stock room, his file drawers and his safe. They had left empty-handed, intending to leave a trail of intimidation. Donato had noticed when they drove off that George Parr and Raul Barrera were sitting in a car parked down the street. Nago Alaniz had been in a car parked behind the Duke of Duval.

Joe stopped drying dishes and stared out the window. A black sedan had just rolled to a stop in one of the parking slots outside. George Parr got out and crossed the street, meeting a man who emerged from another parked car. It looked like one of the constables.

Two other cars with Duval deputies pulled into the drive-in, and he could see three sheriff's office vehicles lined up on the street.

"I'm getting my camera," Donato said, slipping off the barstool.

He had a new 35-millimeter camera that Celia had bought him for his birthday. It was lying, loaded with film, on the back seat of his car parked just outside Joe's Rio Drive-In.

Donato aimed the camera in the direction of George and the constable and snapped three frames. Then he turned to the other vehicles that had just arrived and snapped another dozen shots.

When George saw what Donato was doing, he ran back across the street, reached inside his car and retrieved a pistol. Then he dashed toward Donato, shouting obscenities in Spanish. Donato couldn't make out every word, but he did catch "*excremento*" and "*bastardo*" before the pistol grip smashed into his skull.

George planted several blows on Donato's head before Joe arrived. Like Donato, Joe was no physical match for George, and he suffered numerous strikes to the head, too. Donato cradled the camera under his right arm and debated whether he should fight dirty and go for the crotch.

But just then, a deputy approached with his gun drawn.

"You are now under arrest," he told Donato. George cocked

his arm for another blow with the pistol.

"If I am under arrest, don't hit me," Donato said. His voice was clear and strong.

"Then get in that car," George said, motioning with the bloody pistol for Donato to get into the deputy's vehicle.

The jail was but two blocks away, and Donato dabbed his wounded forehead with a handkerchief during the whole trip. When they arrived, the Mexican deputy relieved Donato of his camera and set it on a table in the jailer's room. When George arrived, the bloodied pistol was stuffed under his belt and he was carrying a large five-cell flashlight. It was big and menacing, about the size of a sledgehammer.

George spit out more obscenities in Spanish and cracked Donato over the head with the flashlight. The blow knocked the slight Mexican into a chair and he sat there for a moment, stunned.

"Now, George," he said, breathless, holding his right arm over his face, "don't hit me any more. You got me under arrest. Don't hit me."

George saw the camera on the table and he cursed again. He slammed the head of the flashlight on the camera, shattering the lens. Pieces of the camera flew across the room, along with glass and broken pieces of the flashlight casing. Film spilled out of the camera and George grabbed it, exposing every frame.

"Get the hell out of here!" he screamed.

Donato stood up, holding his skull with his right hand and staggered out of the courthouse.

Chapter 22

On September 1, 1953, Johnny Klevenhagen received the following letter from Bob Melberg, attaché with the U.S. embassy in Mexico City.

Johnny:

Received yours of the 17th and have delayed answering while I contacted various people and collected the attached items. The attachments consist of the following:
1. Complete set of fingerprints of Alfredo Cervantes obtained from the files of the Jefetura here in Mexico City.
2. Picture of the subject from the file mentioned above.
3. Criminal record of subject from the above file in Spanish.
4. Record of the subject from the files of the Guadalajara Police Department, including attached photograph.
5. A separate photograph of the subject reproduced from the record of the Guadalajara Police Department.

You will note there are no fingerprints of Cervantes from the files of the Guadalajara Police Department. I do not know why they were not provided along with the record of the subject.

Items Nos. 1, 2, and 3 above were provided by Lavin. Items Nos. 1, 2, and 4 above also were provided by Colonel Fernandez, although the prints were a different set than those I am enclosing and not nearly so good, both originally and from the photographic repro-

duction standpoint.

It is still possible that we may receive the fingerprints of Cervantes from Guadalajara, since Galindo is still supposedly working on the matter. Lavin was able to produce the picture and prints from the Jefetura here in Mexico City within 48 hours of my request. He stated he had talked with Colonel Fernandez, who had shown him a copy of the same picture and fingerprints and stated that it was impossible for anyone else to get this information. Lavin agreed with him, at the same time having in his pocket the same data.

Concerning the actual apprehension of Cervantes, the situation is as confused as usual.

The possibility of sending Lavin and his partner Julio to Guadalajara to apprehend Cervantes was discussed with Lavin and he stated that it would be a waste of money for the two of them to take the trip for this purpose since the chances of finding the subject were practically nil. He further stated that, in his opinion, the only approach to the problem that would have any chance of success was to go to Guadalajara, make contact with certain individuals, and offer them thirty or forty thousand pesos ($4,000 or $5,000) to deliver Cervantes to the Mexican side of the Rio Grande, no questions asked.

This he said he would be willing to do if you were interested. He stated that this would be the only means by which Cervantes would ever be brought to Texas and would be only a gamble at best. It is his opinion that the moment Cervantes is openly apprehended it will be absolutely impossible to ever get him out of Mexico.

Colonel Fernandez stated that, in his opinion, it was still possible to apprehend Cervantes but that it would take time and, for the moment, he is doing nothing, since he feels that there are so many different people trying to do the same thing that they are getting in each other's way and defeating the whole investigation with none of them being able to do a good job. He said that if Galindo is going to continue to work on the case, he would prefer to drop out. He is therefore awaiting your reply to find out whether he or Galindo will continue *with the case.*

This just about brings you up-to-date on the situation, and in conclusion I will just say that it cost Lavin $180 (pesos) to get the fingerprints and picture from the Jefetura. I paid him this amount, so if you will just send me a check in the amount of $20.93 (dollars), it will take care of the matter.

As other information comes in, I will ship it on to you.

Sally and I expect to be leaving Mexico City on our way to Texas on the 16th of September and may or may not get over in your part of the country. We will undoubtedly see Capt. Allee in Carrizo.

Regards to your family.

As ever,
Bob
P.S.: According to the papers this morning (Sept. 1) our boy Lavin was in a shooting scrape last night and got scratched up a little. The other party got the worst of it, namely he died. Pictures all over the front page of the paper. Never a dull moment.

Another letter from Bob Melberg, dated October 14, 1953:

Dear Johnny:

Just a short note to let you know we arrived safely back in Mexico after beating ourselves to pieces driving.

Sorry we weren't able to make it over to Houston, but it seemed we got further and further behind schedule all the way along the line until we were doing good to get back at all.

I did not receive the letter you said you were mailing me concerning the authorization to Lavin to make a deal and I did not find a letter upon returning to Mexico, so am wondering if it might have gotten lost in the shuffle somewhere or just what.

At any rate, Lavin is willing to go ahead with the deal upon receipt of written authorization if you still want him to do so.

He is still in the hospital, not so much for his health as to let things quiet down, and he hopes to be out in a couple of weeks or so. He still has one of the bullets since it lodged next to his spine and the doctors are afraid to mess with it. He came close to being paralyzed but actually has only a slight limp to show for it at present.

No other word from your other people down here, so guess the next move is up to you.

As ever,
Bob

In response, Bob Melberg received the following, dated October 16, 1953.

Dear Bob:

I received your letter of October 14 this morning. The reason I had not answered your letter of September 1 sooner was because we expected you and Mrs. Melberg to visit Houston while you were on your vacation.

I am sorry to hear that Lavin is still in the hospital, but from your letter stating that the bullets were near his spine, he surely was lucky.

Bob, I discussed with the parties concerned over here, and as I stated to you over long distance, Lavin's idea of attempting to work out his angle is perfectly all right, and all the financial arrangements have been made to carry out the obligation on this side. I certainly hope he recovers soon and gets out of the hospital and can get his ideas to working.

I believe I told you on the phone how the fingerprints of Cervantes matched. They made a positive rap on the gun and also on the car that was abandoned in Nuevo Laredo, Mexico.

This just about covers everything at this time. I have not received any information from anyone from Mexico City since I

talked to you the last time, but I still have hopes that some way, some how, this deal may still work out.
As ever,
Johnny

***

Alfredo Cervantes dragged on his hand-wrapped weed and observed the two police officers approaching him. There was no need to elude them. They were friends. He had known Hector and Eusebio since he had returned from Detroit. Alfredo slapped his hands on his pants pockets to see how many pesos he was carrying. For as long as he could remember knowing the two policemen, he had given them pesos at every encounter.

Alfredo was somewhat surprised to see the officers at the cockfights. Usually, he ran into them at a *cantina* or simply on the streets of Guadalajara. Vaguely, in his marijuana haze, Alfredo thought they must have come looking for him.

It was well past midnight and the alleyway was a throng of *compesinos*, rowdy from hours of drinking and inhaling the weed. Alfredo had come for lack of anything better to do. As far as taking bets, he was off duty. This was not his cockfight.

Hector motioned with a jerk of his head for Alfredo to follow them to the other end of the alley, away from the pandemonium. The officer had buckteeth, a mustache, and an egg-shaped body. He stuck his hand out, waiting.

Alfredo placed a wad of bills and a few coins in Hector's palm. The policeman bypassed the traditional small talk.

"The *federales* are looking for you," he said, lisping through his protruding teeth. "They been over to the police station all day."

Eusebio grabbed Alfredo roughly by the arm.

"Word got around we know you," he said. Alfredo didn't

like Eusebio. He was skinny and wore a gold stud in his right earlobe.

Hector leaned up against Alfredo's ear and breathed beer fumes on him.

"We said we hadn't seen you in months, that you ran off to Oaxaca."

"Yeah," Eusebio said, "you killed your brother and ran off to Oaxaca."

"Why would I kill Miguel?" Alfredo asked, arching his back to escape Hector's breath. If he had a match, he was sure he could set the officer's breath on fire.

"He tipped off the police about where you were." Hector breathed gas again. "A good story, huh? It just came to me as we were talking to them. I thought about it because I saw Miguel the other day. I was over in Zapopan and he was just coming out of your uncle's house. He looked not very happy."

"He stays stoned most of the time," Alfredo said.

"We're supposed to bring you in if we find you," Eusebio said, grinning.

"Seb," Alfredo said, "you see that mob over there? I got friends in there. You try to haul me in and I'll scream loud enough for them to come running. You'll be outnumbered, guns or no."

Eusebio tightened his grip on Alfredo's arm.

"Relax, *hombre*. We're just passing along the news. You'd better get outa this town tonight."

"And if you don't leave," Hector said, "stay outa sight. You got no business hanging around a cockfight with the *federales* swarming all over the place.

"There's a reward out for you—40,000 pesos—enough to get those bastardos off their asses."

Eusebio let go of Alfredo's arm.

"There's an officer at the Jefetura. We know he's been in contact with the *federales*. Word is, if he needs cash, he'll sell them whatever he knows. And he knows plenty. He's got eyes all over this town."

"We'll see you again," Hector said. "We're going to be real thirsty. We'll want real money so we can buy plenty of *cerveza*. Maybe buy a round for the whole house. So, do yourself a favor and stay outa our sight. You do that, and the *federales* will never find you. Now, get outa here."

Alfredo walked off into the dark alley away from the cockfight. He thought for a moment, then decided where he would go. Hector and Eusebio were right. It was time to get out of Guadalajara for a while.

Section VI
1954

Chapter 23
January

Manuel Marroquin peered out the side window of the Hacienda Drive-Inn. It was a clear night on the outskirts of San Diego, and although there were no lights on outside the restaurant, the stars and the moon were bright enough that he could see his tortilla factory 100 yards to the south. It was a little whitewashed building, smaller than the factory he used to have in San Diego. But it was big enough to produce tortillas to satisfy demand in Benavides.

Manuel had to start selling in Benavides after he lost the San Diego market. George Parr had warned him he would. Manuel had asked him, point blank, if he was ordering people in San Diego to stop buying his tortillas. Yes, George had said, he had, and it would continue until Manuel proved he was on the Old Party's side again.

That will never happen, Manuel thought, scratching his mustache with a stubby finger. He sat in a metal folding chair, his Stetson propped on his belly, rounded from a steady diet of his own tortillas. He was glad he owned this land inside Jim Wells County, glad he owned the Hacienda and, despite all the trouble, still glad he was in the Freedom Party.

The Hacienda had proved a handy place for the Freedom Party to hold meetings. It was inside Jim Wells County but close to San Diego, outside the jurisdiction of George Parr and his *pis-*

tolero goons. At least once a week, usually on a Monday night, Manuel would close the place and invite the boys out. They talked about plans for the next primary in the summer of 1954, and they talked about George Parr's latest backlash against their political independence.

Manuel decided to tell the crowd of about 60 men crammed inside the tiny drive-inn about an experience he had at the barbershop in San Diego.

"I went in to get my hair cut, just like I always do on Wednesdays," Manuel said. "Incarnacion Pena has cut my hair every Wednesday for 10 years. I'd go over from the factory at lunchtime and he'd take care of me.

"I walk into the place last week and he looks at me funny. Doesn't say he's glad to see me like he always does. He just looks at me funny. He's got somebody in his chair, so I go to sit down, but he follows me and says I should step outside the shop.

"Then he tells me not to ever come back to his barber shop. I ask him why. He says because he doesn't want me killed in his barbershop. He says I'm a red light now that I'm in the Freedom Party. And he's in the Old Party. He says he doesn't want trouble."

Donato Serna spoke up. Manuel would know that voice anywhere. It was precise and clear, just like a man would expect Donato to speak. Manuel could make out Donato's face in the dim light. He was at a small table in the far corner of the darkened restaurant.

"He doesn't want trouble. There won't be anything but trouble around here for a long time. George and his papa didn't build Rome in a day. I imagine it'll take us a few years to bring down the empire.

"I guess you all noticed that Joe's closed his drive-inn. Moved to Alice. No customers any more. George ran them all off. But Joe's still with us. He's just busy tonight, working on setting up his new restaurant."

The discussion continued thus for several minutes and then the insurgents decided to call it a night. At the next meeting, they said, they would put the finishing touches on a slate of candidates for the upcoming primaries. The men wandered in a leisurely manner out to their cars, parked haphazardly in the expansive gravel parking lot. Manuel remarked to his companion, Manny Corrales, that he didn't miss the bright headlights and searches that used to go along with leaving a Freedom Party meeting.

"No doubt George knows every time we meet and that we're meeting at the Hacienda," he said. "It must really get his goat that he can't do anything about it."

As the two men got into the car, Manuel noticed a black sedan parked about 50 feet away, next to a mound of caliche. It was off to itself, and Manuel could see four men sitting inside. He'd had the rocky soil brought in for some grading work outside the factory. A car belonging to one of the Hacienda's customers had gotten mired in the caliche a few days before.

"Manny, look," he said. "You think that car's stuck?"

"Maybe they've got a flat tire," Manny said.

"I'm going to look."

The parking lot was nearly empty as Manuel approached the black sedan. He was about 15 feet from the car when both front doors flew open, and George Parr and Juan Barrera Canante stepped out. Both were carrying pistols. Manuel stopped in his tracks.

"Are you in trouble?" he asked. "Can I help you?" Stupid question, he thought, but he couldn't think of anything better.

George raged at him, calling him every obscenity in his vocabulary.

"If you don't stop holding these meetings, I'm going to kill you and every one of those bastards."

"Señor Parr, do not shoot. Please, do not shoot." Manuel was walking in reverse, his hands in the air like he was being held up by robbers.

"Get the hell out of here," George said, waving the gun. As Juan started advancing toward him, Manuel made a beeline for his car.

"Roll up the windows," he yelled at Manny as he got inside. The two men locked the doors, Manuel fired up the engine, and they blasted off, hurling a trail of gravel dust in George's face.

***

That night, Manuel went over to the sheriff's office in Alice and filed a complaint. The next morning, Captain Allee arrested Juan Barrera Canante at the Windmill Cafe. Cap couldn't find George that day. Archer said he was at his ranch and he promised to take his uncle into custody on Monday morning.

At the appointed time on Monday, Cap waited at the Alice courthouse while Joe Bridge and Walter Russell went over to Archer's office for the arrest. When they got there, Archer hadn't picked up his uncle. He promised to do so immediately and said he would bring George back to the sheriff's office. The two Rangers waited over an hour and finally a Duval deputy told them that George had gone straight to the courthouse in Alice.

Joe Bridge put the gas pedal to the floorboard on the way back to Alice. He had a few choice words for the Parrs.

When he and Walter arrived outside the sheriff's office in the corridor of the courthouse, Bridge saw Cap talking to George. Archer Parr stood a few feet away, on the other side of the hallway, and Alice *Echo* reporter Caro Brown was lurking nearby, as reporters so often do.

"I don't appreciate a damn bit the run-around I got," Bridge said heatedly as he walked up to Archer.

"Well, I know of some things you've done unbecoming..."

Archer didn't finish his sentence before his mouth connected with Bridge's fist. The blow knocked Archer's wire-rimmed glasses off his face, and they skidded across the tile floor like a hockey puck on ice. Archer lurched backward, momentarily stunned, and Bridge yanked the sheriff's service revolver from its holster.

George, interrupted in his conversation with Cap by the fracas, jumped into the fray, as if to shield his nephew. But Cap was close at his heels. The Ranger pounded George in the ear with his fist and drew his automatic.

"I've had all I'm going to take off you and the way you've been handling things," Cap hollered, the barrel of his gun poking George's chest. "I'm not going to put up with any more whipping with pistols or Winchesters in Duval County."

With his free hand, Cap grabbed George by his suit vest and yanked him forward. The two men were nose to nose. Cap was about to give another speech when he felt a small hand press softly on his back. It felt like someone had set fire to his jacket.

"Cap, don't! Please don't!" Caro Brown pleaded. She kept her hand on his back and just stood there. Her plea seemed to jolt the captain from his rage and he shoved George into a nearby courtroom.

Bridge collared Archer, and the two joined the others in the courtroom.

"We're going to finish this!" the Captain ordered, still pointing his gun at the two Parrs. George was rubbing his ear as blood oozed from the lobe. Archer, who had retrieved his glasses, was rubbing the lenses with a handkerchief. Remarkably, they hadn't broken.

"I'm tired of the way you're pistol-whipping people and carrying guns over there in Duval County," Cap said. "I want it stopped. Those people have a right to have political meetings without being molested."

"It'll stop, Captain, I promise you," George said.

"I'll come over there and personally blow your head off if it doesn't," Cap said. "Now, get the hell out of here."

The two Parrs slunk out of the courtroom, and Caro Brown pounced on them as soon as they emerged.

"Just a little misunderstanding," Archer said, brushing her aside.

Bridge grabbed George by the arm and escorted him to the courtroom upstairs, where Juan Barrera Canante was waiting. The judge set bond at $1,500 each on the Manuel Marroquin charge. They posted it and left the courthouse with Archer.

When Caro Brown got back to the Alice *Echo* that afternoon, she repeated the whole story to the editor, V. D. Ringwald.

"I'm awfully glad there was no gunfire," she told him. "All I could think about was how those bullets would ricochet off that marble wainscoting. No telling how many people would have gotten killed."

***

"This is serious business, George," said Gerald Weatherly as he inspected the Duke of Duval's impressive gun collection. The Falfurrias attorney had come calling, concerned about the splash of news coverage after the courthouse scuffle.

"You don't handle this right, you lose face," he said, turning from the gun case to study his host. Gerald was round-faced, bespectacled and paunchy around the middle, his tie pulled loose around his neck. Like Luther Jones and Ed Lloyd, he was a member of George's stable of attorneys.

George sat in his favorite chair, silently sipping coffee. .

"I've been thinking on that," George said. "Been thinkin' on it."

"You've got to deny everything," Gerald said. "Go to the papers and deny everything. Get Raeburn to file charges and push it with the grand jury. Make it look like that Ranger captain is trying to kill you. Get some sympathy going."

"No one's ever slapped me in public," George said evenly, his eyes glazed over. In a moment he popped free of his trance and the rage returned. "He's going to pay," George said, slamming a fist on the coffee table. "I'll kill the goddam *rinche* with my bare hands." He pounded the table again.

"Come on, George, talk some sense," Gerald said. "I've got an idea. It'll solve your problems with your people and it may even get the Rangers off your neck. This is a stroke of genius. Listen to this. You file a civil rights suit in federal court—"

"Civil rights suit?," George echoed.

"That's right. You'll say the Rangers are violating your civil rights and endangering your life. You'll ask the court to issue a restraining order to keep the Rangers away from you. Presto! You've saved face and gotten rid of the Rangers, all in one deft move. It's brilliant!

"And it gets better, George. I'll ask my old colleague Arthur Garfield Hays to represent you."

"Arthur Garfield Hayes," George said. "That's the guy who defended that fellow in the Scopes monkey trial. Pretty famous."

"He's getting up in years," Gerald said. "I think he must be past 70 now, but he's still going strong. I used to work in his law firm in New York. He's been general counsel for years for the American Civil Liberties Union. He knows the civil rights part of the Constitution like you know your gun collection."

"I don't know, Gerald. Ain't he Jewish? And a Yankee? How's that going to play?"

"Well, I'll be switched. George Parr, the champion of the people, a prejudiced man."

"Give me a break. I may hate niggers. But Mexicans and Jews, they're just like the rest of us. I'm just wondering how it's gonna look, bringing in some big hired gun from New York City."

"It's gonna look like you've got clout in high places," Gerald said. "Arthur is a respected lawyer, one of the best in the country. Defender of the downtrodden. I can see it now. He flies in to the Corpus airport; there's photographers and reporters all over the place. It'll be all over the papers. That's what you need, George, especially with John Ben Shepperd crying foul every day in the papers.

"You need an outsider, a big mouth to swoop in and defend you. I tell you, he's the man to do it."

"What makes you so sure he'll take the case?"

"I'm certain of it. I was his fair-haired boy when I was with his firm years ago. We've kept in touch. All it'll take is a phone call. Where's your phone?"

George motioned to a room behind the gun case. He stayed in the great room, while Gerald made the call. He could hear his lawyer talking loudly in the other room. In a few minutes, Gerald returned, a big grin on his face.

"He said he'd do it," the lawyer said.

***

Over the next few days, George got plenty of ink in all of the papers.

"He was trying to kill me," the *Alice Daily Echo* quoted George as saying of Captain Allee. "The reason he didn't was that Mrs. Caro Brown, the reporter from the Alice *Echo*, kept calling 'Alfred, Alfred.'

"You know, Alfred isn't as strong as he used to be. I am pretty weak, but I was able to hold him."

George told the newspaper it wasn't Captain Allee who drew blood from his ear. It was Carl Putnam, a Department of Public Safety employee who got caught in the fracas, who scratched him with a fingernail. Nobody knew what he was talking about.

Putnam was nowhere around when the fight occurred.

The Duke of Duval also denied carrying a gun at the Hacienda Drive-Inn that night. What Manuel Marroquin saw, George claimed, was not a pistol but a pair of binoculars.

When the Jim Wells County grand jury indicted Allee and Bridge for assault with intent to murder, George said publicly he didn't have anything to do with it. He had nothing, he said, against either Ranger.

Captain Allee said he wasn't surprised at the indictments either. In fact, he said in a jovial manner, he had been expecting them. However, he couldn't understand a grand jury indicting a lawman for enforcing the law.

"I came down here to do a job and I'm going to do it the best I can, regardless of that little fracas in the courthouse," he said told Caro Brown. "I've tried to by gosh enforce the law without any prejudice to anyone, regardless of their political affiliation."

Arthur Garfield Hayes filed a civil rights suit and Captain Allee and Ranger Bridge hired Jake Floyd as their attorney. A three-judge federal panel in Houston was assigned to hear the case. But before it could make it to court, Captain Allee had another skirmish with another member of the Parr regime.

The afternoon started out calmly enough, despite the fact that an informant had just told Cap he was the target of a death plot.

"Who was it, Cap?" asked Joe Bridge.

"I'd rather not say," Cap answered, stirring his coffee. He was at Dena's with Joe, Wiley Williamson and Walter Russell. "But he's reliable. He told me Raul Barrera and one of his sidekicks, a fellow named Jose Rodriguez, were hiring two killers from Mexico to put the bang on me. It was supposed to happen last night, but the killers broke down at Benavides and didn't make it."

"Hell, Cap, we better get you outta town," Joe said. "Either that or make sure you don't do a lot of lone ranger work."

"I got a better idea," Cap said. "Let's head over to San Diego. I want to tell George I know about his scheme; call him on this assassination thing. Pound a little sense into that thick head of his."

They drove straight to the Windmill Cafe. Odds were good that George was either there or at his office next door. When they arrived, there were at least a half dozen *pistoleros* guzzling from beer bottles outside the cafe. They leaned on car hoods and trunks until they saw the Rangers drive up, then discarded their bottles and stood almost at attention, their hands on their holstered guns.

It was dead quiet on that street as the Rangers marched down the sidewalk with Captain Allee in the lead. The only sounds came from the four Rangers' cowboy boots as they struck the concrete. Just as they got to the Windmill's door, Raeburn Norris sauntered out of the cafe.

"Well, Captain Allee," he said in a falsetto voice. He had a smirk on his face.

In an instant, Cap had the district attorney by his shirt, slamming him against the wall of the cafe.

"Don't ever speak to me again, you goddam low-life sonofabitch," Cap hollered into his face. "You ain't ever said nothing to me until I got indicted," Cap screamed. "And now you think you can sneer at me whenever you please. I don't like the way you've been doing things and I want it stopped."

Cap loosened his grip on Raeburn's shirt and kicked the district attorney in the shins with his cowboy boots. Then he grabbed the lawyer's jaw and kicked him in the legs again. He delivered a few more kicks before Joe Bridge jumped in and said, "Calm down, Cap, calm down."

Raeburn was a disheveled mess when Cap was through with him. He limped off as Cap opened the front door of the cafe and looked inside. George was not there.

He motioned for his men to follow him down the street to

George's office. The Duke of Duval was standing outside his front door, his arms folded. He had seen the whole incident. Cap marched up to him and shoved his face into George's.

"You can't assassinate me or any of my boys. Don't even try. I know about your plot to have me killed and I know for a fact you were behind the killing of Jake Floyd's boy. I'm putting you on notice right now. If anything happens to me or my men, I'm holding you directly responsible."

George just stood there, arms folded and his feet planted two feet apart. His eyes were cold and expressionless.

"One more thing, Parr," Cap said. "If I ever make up my mind to kill you, there's nothing to keep me from it."

George was silent for a long moment, his blue eyes locked on Cap's eyes.

"You have my word, Captain Allee," he said evenly. "Nothing will happen to you or your men."

***

Arthur Garfield Hayes walked with a cane, he wore heavy horn-rimmed glasses, and his hair was iron gray. But when he entered the Houston courtroom to argue George's civil rights claim against Captain Allee, it was with the calm self-assurance of a seasoned, successful lawyer. He may have been 73 years old, but his age was his ally, his badge of experience.

The courtroom in the Houston federal building was overflowing. Spectators fought for seats, and at least 20 reporters monopolized the first two rows of the gallery. John Ben Shepperd, now the Texas Attorney General, was there. He saved a seat for his old friend, former South Carolina governor Strom Thurmond, who happened to be in Houston. Before the hearing, Shepperd had sent a telegram to the American Civil Liberties Union in New York protesting its defense of "a political dictator against an oppressed and outraged people." Hayes countered that he didn't come to Houston as an agent of the ACLU. He was taking the case on his own.

Donato Serna, Manuel Marroquin, Manuel Sanchez and Cristobal Ybanez drove in from San Diego and asked to be interveners in the case. They all said George Parr had kicked them around and they needed the Rangers to stay in Duval County to protect them. The judges rejected their attempt to intervene.

The first witness Hayes called was Raeburn Norris, who described in colorful detail the time he was kicked and roughed up by Captain Allee. Jake Floyd asked the three judges to strike the testimony because it had nothing to do with threats against George Parr. The judges rejected the idea, and Jake went to work cross-examining the district attorney.

"Aren't you indebted to George Parr's banks?" he asked, his deep voice booming across the courtroom.

"Well, I do owe some money to some banks."

"Don't you owe money to the Texas State Bank in Alice and the San Diego State Bank?"

"I have loans at those two banks."

"And those banks are owned and operated by George Parr, are they not?"

"I don't know who owns them."

"You don't know who owns them?"

"That's right."

"How long have you lived in Alice, Mr. Norris?"

"Since 1946."

"Since 1946. You've lived in Alice eight years, and you don't know who owns one of the two banks there?"

"No, sir, I don't."

"You are acquainted with George Parr, are you not?"

"I am."

"He supported you when you ran for district attorney, did

he not?"

"He made campaign speeches for me."

Jake then turned the questioning to Norris' part in Parr's campaign of harassment and intimidation against the Freedom Party.

"Mr. Norris, do you remember last February 16? You and your assistant Mr. Carrillo, and the Brownwood prosecutor Mr. Allcorn and I and Sam Burris were in the grand jury room at the Jim Wells County courthouse?"

"I remember. Yes."

"And what was the grand jury considering on that day?"

"Well, that was a year ago, Mr. Floyd."

"Would it be correct to say the grand jury was considering the murder of Buddy Floyd?"

"That sounds right."

"And didn't you insist on staying in the grand jury room while that case was being investigated?"

"No. I only insisted that I or a representative from my office be there."

"As a matter of fact, didn't it require a court order to get you out of the grand jury room and keep you out?"

"Well, yes."

When George took the witness stand, he testified for an hour, retelling the stories of the night at the Hacienda Drive-Inn, the slapping incident at the courthouse and Cap's scuffle with Raeburn Norris. He said he was carrying binoculars, not a gun, at the Hacienda.

"First thing I knew of a pistol-carrying charge was next day when my nephew served me with a warrant," he said, his face flushed red.

During the fracas with Cap and Joe Bridge at the Alice courthouse, George said, he "grabbed Allee by the arms. I found out I was stronger than him and could control him." Laughter rippled across the courtroom at that remark, and one of the judges ordered silence.

George said Cap shoved him into a courtroom, and he asked the Ranger, "Alfred, what have I done to you?"

The Ranger replied, "I'm fed up with you. If you want to get rough, we'll get rough." George said he told him nobody wants to get rough and he repeated Allee's threat to kill him.

Cap testified for several hours, explaining that when he first arrived in Duval County in 1952, he paid a call on George.

"I told George Parr I had complaints against him and several of his men regarding the organizing of the Freedom Party, that there had been efforts made to break up the meetings. I asked him for cooperation. He said he was glad we were there and he would give us cooperation and that he didn't want any trouble."

The Ranger captain talked about his investigation of Buddy Floyd's murder, saying he first saw Mario Sapet at a Freedom Party rally. Attorney Hayes objected to the reference, saying, "They are trying to show guilt by association." The objection was overruled.

Cap remained soft-spoken and calm as he admitted he lost his temper with Raeburn Norris outside the Windmill Cafe. "But by golly," he said, "I'm not sorry."

When asked about threats to George Parr, Cap admitted he cuffed him, but he had no intention of killing the Duke of Duval. "But if anything happened to me or my Rangers, I would hold him responsible, because he would be responsible. I think George Parr would do anything under the sun. I just personally don't like him or anything he stands for."

Hayes had exacted a damaging admission from the captain.

"I would use force against George Parr as a dangerous man quicker than I would against an ordinary citizen if I thought it necessary."

When the Ranger stepped down from the witness stand, Hayes rose from his seat and told the judges, "I want now to pay my respects to Captain Allee. He is an honest man."

In his closing arguments, Hayes again called Cap an honest man.

"But some of the most dangerous men in history have been honest. Allee is the kind who makes a good soldier but not a good administrator.

"I am surprised at the meekness of my client. I am surprised at the meekness of District Attorney Norris, who took a beating because someone said he smirked. I am surprised that no one came to the defense of Norris. It seems that everybody down there is intimidated by the Rangers. All the meekness is on one side.

"If the injunction isn't granted," he told the judges, "you would be permitting an electrified atmosphere that at any time could result in bloodshed. You would be bringing about force and bloodshed."

Jake Floyd was emotionless, his voice powerful in his closing statement.

"It is most unfortunate that a distinguished attorney from New York should be here in the guise of protecting the civil rights of the man who has violated more civil rights than any other man in Texas. George Parr's political machine has run roughshod over the people of Duval County for too long. It is his own hostile actions that have provoked the tense situation in that troubled county."

Frank Knapp, Jake's co-counsel in the case, told the judges it would be monstrous to grant an injunction against the Rangers.

"To do so would make this court an abettor of iniquity," he said. "George Parr seeks extraordinary treatment from this court when he comes in here himself with filthy hands."

The hearing ended after two days with the three judges giving no indication when they would rule. A week later, they denied the injunction.

Eventually, George was convicted by an Alice jury of pistol

packing at the Hacienda Drive-Inn. He was ordered to pay a $150 fine.

Assault charges were dropped against Joe Bridge, but the case against Captain Allee was moved to Brownsville. After a day of jury selection, George stood up in court and said he had no desire to press charges any further against the Ranger captain. In truth, George needed to get back to Duval County. His kingdom was under siege from every direction.

Chapter 24
February

J. L. "Mac" McDonald strode into Jake's office, one hand clasping his Stetson and the other resting on the shoulder of a short, round Mexican man. Jake couldn't make out who he was. The fellow had his jacket collar zipped up over his mouth and he was looking at the floor, a hat covering the dome of his head.

The mystery man kept his head down as the two visitors took seats. Mac had called in advance and said he had something important to tell Jake.

"Diego, it's all right," Mac said, adjusting his shoulder holster. His Magnum nestled between his elbow and his broad chest. "You're safe here."

"I need a cigarette," Diego said, and Mac handed him one. The collar came unzipped, but the hat stayed on. Jake could smell the odor of stale beer.

"This is Diego Heras, Jake," Mac said, lighting the man's smoke.

"Pleased to meet you, Mr. Heras," Jake said. He gave Mac a questioning look.

"He's got something to say."

Diego Heras didn't move and didn't say a word. He smoked rapidly, the cigarette wobbly in his trembling hand.

"You sure nobody saw us?" he said. "I'm a dead man if they did."

"It's okay, man, I'm telling you straight," Mac said. "Relax."

Jake spoke up. "Mr. Heras, if it proves necessary, we can arrange for protection for you. But I can't help you if I don't know what's on your mind."

For the first time, Diego looked up at Jake. He had a chubby face, and his brown eyes were wild with fear. He took another nervous puff on the cigarette and exhaled heavily.

"Tell the man who you are," Mac prompted.

"I used to be secretary of the school district at Benavides," Diego said, stamping out his cigarette in the ashtray. He motioned for another. "I was damn good at it, too. Did a good job for 11 years. Even took a correspondence course so I could do the books.

"About a year ago, George got mad at me. I never knew why. He said I was boozing on the job. But that don't make sense. Everybody at the school office takes a nip now and then. He's come in, and we've had the bottles on the table. He never said anything before.

"Like I said, I got busted. He said I couldn't be secretary. I had to be deputy tax assessor. I said fine. No skin off me. I was still getting a paycheck.

"Then, last week, they fired me. Said get your things and get. No reason. No thanks. Nothing. Just get out of here."

Diego took a long drag and spit a bit of tobacco off his tongue.

"Show him the checks," Mac said.

Diego reached inside his jacket and pulled a fistful of checks from his shirt pocket.

"Before I left the office for the last time, I grabbed these," he said, placing them on Jake's desk. The attorney studied the pile of wrinkled checks as Diego continued.

"Mr. Parr used to come in the office two, maybe three times a month. Sometimes he'd have a list already made up. Sometimes he'd write it out after he got there. He'd hand me this sheet of paper with a list of names on it.

"Beside the names would be an amount of money and then beside that would be some service or something. Like this one," he said, pointing to a check. It was for $40,000, dated November 9, 1949, and drawn on the school district account.

"George gave me a piece of paper and said write that check, made out to no one. It was for the new school stadium, he said. And I did it. But I wondered what was costing so much money over at the stadium. It was finished in 1946, Mr. Floyd.

"Take a look at this one," he said, pointing to a check for $636.50. It was made out to Cosme Leal for electrical work.

"I know Cosme Leal," Diego said. "He's a ranch hand. Can't read or write and doesn't know a thing about electrical work. I figure the most he knows is how to flip a light switch. If you ask him, I'd wager he never got this $636.50.

"This check was kind of unusual. Usually, he had me type them up in even amounts, mainly for three thousand or twenty-five hundred. He countersigned them and I would endorse them.

"Then I'd go over to the Texas State Bank in Alice, where the school district keeps its money, and I'd cash the checks. Mr. Donald would take the checks and give me cash in an envelope. Sometimes I'd take the money to Mr. Parr, and sometimes he'd be there with me and just take it himself."

Jake leafed through the checks and noted the Parr signature.

"To my knowledge, George has no official position on the Benavides School District," the lawyer said.

"That's right," Diego said. "But he acted like our supervisor. He always wanted to know what was going on with the books. I hear since I left, he's had the books moved over to his office in San Diego."

Mac offered Diego a third cigarette. "Tell him about the tax bills."

Diego issued a burst of smoke and continued.

"The oil companies pay the taxes. We got almost $25 million in property on the rolls. When I was deputy assessor, I'd make up tax bills and send them out. If they were George's friends, I wouldn't send them out, I'd just stamp "paid" on them and put them in the drawer."

"Can you prove that?" Jake asked.

Diego nodded.

"I got a house and six lots on the tax rolls. I never paid a dime on any of them, just stamped them "paid." I got the receipts."

Jake removed a cigar from his lips and deposited it on the edge of the ashtray. He pursed his thin lips and studied the Mexican man.

"Mr. Heras, that's quite a story you've got," he said, his voice calm. "I have some ideas of what we might do with it. I was wondering about your ideas."

"Ideas? About what?"

"About what to do with these checks—your story about what happened over there."

"I don't know, Mr. Floyd. I was just hoping maybe I could tell you and then go on with my business. I mean, find a job somewhere so I can support my family."

"Well, perhaps we can help you there, Mr. Heras. But before we talk about that, I need to know how far you're willing to go."

"How far?"

"Mr. Heras, to build a case against someone like George Parr, we need hard evidence. And these checks are hard evidence. And we need witnesses. You would be a witness. You'd have to testify before the grand jury and possibly in court."

Diego exhaled a stream of smoke through his nostrils and looked down.

"They'll kill me, Mr. Floyd."

"Like I told you earlier, Mr. Heras. We can get protection for you. That will be no problem. I just need your word you'll stay with us, that you'll testify if we need you."

Diego's nose was turning red and his upper lip curled up. A tear trickled off his chubby cheek. Mac shifted uncomfortably and Diego grabbed the arms of his chair, gripping them as if he were holding on for a roller coaster ride. He bit his upper lip and took a deep breath.

"The way I see it," Jake said. "You don't have a choice. George isn't going to help you any more, so you won't be able to get a job. I suppose you could run off and start new somewhere, but you'd always be looking over you shoulder and wondering.

"If you stay here, you'll get a bodyguard or two and probably a job. Doesn't seem like much of a choice, does it?"

Diego rubbed his nose with the back of his hand. He did not look up.

"Okay, Mr. Floyd. Okay," he said softly.

Mac lit another cigarette for Diego, and then lit one for himself. He had a few things to add.

"That Mrs. Wilkins over in Freer, she's already been up to Austin to look at the state education records. She's made photocopies of bogus payments made by the school district. She's even found out they used the mails to send some of the checks. She brought back documentation of everything. I was planning on turning it over to the attorney general."

"Good," Jake said. "I don't know how we're going to get any indictments, not with Woodrow on the bench. But at the rate he's going, he may have hanged himself by the time we're ready for a grand jury."

"It just makes my blood boil to think about the way they're raiding the schools like that. That's my money they're fooling with—my money," Mac said, his voice getting louder.

Jake asked Diego to stay in the office for a moment while he and Mac talked in the library next door.

"Mac," Jake said, "Just wanted you to know I heard from Donato this morning. He says Archer and some of his deputies are looking for you. He says he's heard by the underground that they are going to try to cause some trouble for you."

"What kind of trouble?"

"Don't know exactly. He says the word is that they may try to provoke you into a fight and try to kill you."

"Send 'em on!" Mac. said, puffing his chest out.

"I've talked to Captain Allee, and he's willing to assign a Ranger to you until things cool down."

"Nothing doing. I can take care of myself."

"Listen, Mac, there's a time for bravery and there's a time for common sense. Think of your wife; what about her safety when you're gone? I wish you'd give it some serious thought. They know you're digging around, and I'm sure they know you've been talking to Diego."

"Archer Parr sets one foot on my property, I'll blow his head off from my front porch!"

Mac would not be persuaded, and Jake didn't have time to argue. He had an appointment with an Internal Revenue Service agent, and he didn't want Mac to see the man. The word would get around soon enough that the IRS was snooping around Duval County.

***

Bill Ninedorf was a few minutes late for his appointment with Jake Floyd and he apologized. He hadn't gotten away from Corpus Christi as soon as he had hoped. He and his partner Edgar Henley were staying at a motel in Corpus and driving over to Duval every day. It was safer that way and aroused less suspicion, although there was no way a stranger could so much as buy a tank of gas in San Diego without being noticed.

Ninedorf had been to Jake's office many times before. In fact, it was one of his first stops when he hit South Texas for the Parr investigation back before Buddy was murdered. Jake had suggested some folks to talk to and had given him free use of his law library to interview people.

"Jake, I need your help again," Ninedorf said after accepting a cigar from the lawyer. He was not quite as tall as Jake and not as lanky. His prematurely graying hair was cropped close to his head, as if he were in the military.

"You understand I can't give you much detail. Confidentiality and all that. But you've been a big boost to us and we've made considerable headway. We have every reason to believe there is a significant case here for the Internal Revenue Service."

Ninedorf's face changed expression. He looked like he was in physical pain.

"I've already written quite a lengthy report. It's been filed in every office from here to kingdom come, documenting what we're doing and what we've found. I'm screaming, literally screaming for more help, but getting nowhere.

"We've been promised as many as six more men. Mr. Crawford, the head of the intelligence office in Austin, was really enthusiastic about my report. He told Ed and I we could have as many men as we needed.

"Then the district chief, the head of the IRS in Austin, throws an axe in the middle of the whole thing. He tells me two weeks ago he's not going to put any more men on the Parr case. Says we're wasting our time down here.

"Well, the teeth nearly fall out of my mouth when he says that. Last spring, he's 100 percent behind us. Now, he's 100 percent against us.

"This doesn't add up, see, so I decided to do a little investigating on my own. This district chief, his name is Bob Phinney, and he came to us under some pretty strange circumstances last year. He was postmaster in Austin, and all of a sudden he's head of the IRS district. No experience in the Treasury Department. Nothing like that at all. Still, presto, he's my big boss.

"Well, I did some poking around and found out his brother, a guy named Carl Phinney, he was Lyndon Johnson's campaign manager in '48. As his reward, this Carl Phinney got to be postmaster in Dallas and his brother got to be the big post office cheese in Austin. And now, through some strange twist of fate, he's the big cheese in my office.

"I don't know, Jake. I just thought you might have connections, a pipeline into somebody who could break this thing open. Because it's going to take an outside influence, somebody doing some heavy hitting to get this train on the track again. I'm talking somebody big, Jake, like the U.S. attorney general, somebody like that.

"Me, I can't do it. It'll look like I'm some kind of whistleblower, a malcontent who doesn't like what the boss says. But you, Jake, you could make it happen."

Jake looked intently at the agent, his elbows propped on his desk and fingertips pressed together. Over the past several months, he and Ninedorf had corresponded often and met several times. Jake had reported pertinent information when he came across it.

"I'll have to think on this, Bill. The governor has been rock solid with us through all this, and I expect we can call on him. I don't know if you know, but he and George used to be on the same side. They had a falling out several years ago and since then, the governor has done everything he can to bring George down."

Ninedorf nodded.

"Mr. Shivers seems to have a mind of his own when it comes to politics," the agent said. "I think he's pretty shrewd at figuring out which way the wind is blowing. He'd have to be to do what he did last year with the Texas Democrats. Leading a bolt from the party to support Eisenhower."

"And he's been a hundred percent behind John Ben Shepperd and his investigation," Jake said of Shepperd, who had become Texas Attorney General. "Like I said, Bill, let me think on it. I'm sure the governor will be with us and I'll be thinking of other ways of pursuing this. Before you go, I'd like to mention something I heard the other day from a very reliable source.

"George owns several ranches in Duval, and one of them is called the Dobie Ranch. It's 50,000 acres at least and it's on some of the nicest land around here. It has a lot of wild game—whitetail deer and turkeys—and it's one of the best cattle ranching spots in South Texas, right on the Nueces River.

"What I've been hearing is that George acquired that ranch in the '40s with the help of the Duval County treasury."

"What do you mean?" Ninedorf said.

"Well, I mean the county essentially bought the ranch for George. At least, that's what I'm hearing."

"Ye gods. The man has the run of the whole place. No door is closed to him. No bank account is sacred. I'll say one thing for him. He's got one set of balls."

Jake pulled Diego's Benavides school checks and vouchers out of his desk and handed them to Ninedorf.

"We can have photostatic copies of these made so you and John Ben can each have a set. There's plenty of grist there for the both of you."

"Where did you get these?"

"The fellow was just in here. His name is Diego Heras, and he used to be the secretary of the Benavides schools. He got fired, and he's plenty mad about it. He took these checks with him when he left, and now he's decided to go to the other side. He's terrified of getting killed, and I promised him we'd get some protection for him."

"I don't blame him," Ninedorf said. "John Ben's having to interview witnesses out in the middle of nowhere. They go to abandoned ranch houses or barns in the middle of the night. Those poor people are so scared they park a mile away and hide their cars in some mesquite and then go on foot to the place where they meet Shepperd's men. He's got to where he calls 'em brush crawlers. You think this Heras would talk to me?"

"I think so. He told me he would before he left here this morning. I just think we'll have to keep a close watch on him and make sure he can earn a living. He's not doing this so much because it's the right and decent thing to do. No, I think he's doing it more because he's always played ball on the other team. He's just switching teams. It's the only way he knows to live.

"I think things are about to blow open, Bill. This thing with Captain Allee hitting George Parr. That's a powder keg that's going to keep going off.

"I talked to John Ben yesterday and he's ready to go public with his investigation. The timing is good. The Supreme Court will decide soon about Woodrow, and we're almost certain he's going to be removed. Then we can get an honest judge and an honest grand jury and start cleaning this place up."

***

A few days later, John Ben Shepperd announced that his investigators had been in Duval County for a year, looking into use of public funds by local officials. It wasn't news to the people of Duval, but it was big news throughout Texas. Reporters from all of the major newspapers in the state began to call Jake. He decided they were just as good a venue as any to put out the word that more IRS agents were needed.

The *Dallas Morning News* quoted Jake as saying, "Knowing the situation in Duval County and of the extent of certain matters concerning a school district, as well as other subdivisions in the county government, I question whether or not two men would be sufficient to conduct such an investigation."

Jake had already talked to John Ben Shepperd about the IRS situation, and the attorney general agreed to alert the governor. Within a month, four new IRS agents were combing through records at the courthouse, the school office in Benavides and George's two banks.

Ninedorf put aside his resentment of Bob Phinney and turned his attention to the Duval County auditor's office. He spent one Friday afternoon sorting canceled checks written on the county's account at the Texas State Bank. He set aside two piles of checks—one with about 800, the other with about 200. He told the county auditor, C. T. Stansell, Jr., to hold them until Monday morning; he wanted to take a closer look at them then.

When Ninedorf returned Monday, the checks were gone. Stansell said he didn't know what happened. He hadn't touched them. A few days later, Stansell was called into court to explain the disappearance. He asked the judge for 10 minutes to think about a response and left the courtroom. In a few minutes, he scurried back in and said he had nothing to say.

The presiding judge, Judge Arthur Klein of Brownsville, bore no allegiance to George Parr. He ordered all of the county and school district records impounded. By 5 o'clock, the Rangers had hauled a small mountain of ledger books and boxes into the courtroom.

That night, John Ben Shepperd called Jake.

"I've got even more good news for you," he said. "That Judge Klein granted immunity for Diego. And after he did that, Diego was so overjoyed that he signed an affidavit with some pretty damaging stuff in it."

"Like what?" Jake said.

"Like George's brother-in-law, B. G. Moffett, the lawyer from Corpus Christi, has been on the school payroll for years. He's been getting $500 a month for legal work, and Diego says he's never done a thing.

"This thing also says that Diego knows of at least 100 checks written to people who don't exist. It says George countersigned most of the school district checks even though he has no official connection with the schools."

"That's wonderful, John Ben," Jake said. "How's Diego holding up?"

"Looked fine the last time I saw him. One of the Rangers is sticking with him, and he doesn't look so wild-eyed anymore."

A few days later, Ninedorf was on the telephone calling for Jake. He sounded agitated.

He said he thought Jake would want to know as soon as possible that one of the new agents, Bill Dimler, was having the same trouble with missing records. Dimler was looking through files of the Texas State Bank, the depository for the Benavides school district, and discovered that entire years of records were missing. Another agent in Duval said he found the same thing at the San Diego State Bank.

In response, Judge Klein issued another injunction barring removal of the records. Captain Allee assigned two Rangers to stand guard at each of the banks.

Within a few weeks, the opposition got another break. On March 17, 1954, the Texas Supreme Court ordered Woodrow Laughlin to step down as district judge. Woodrow was cited for a dozen misdeeds, but the high court said the first charge was all they needed to remove him. The justices said Woodrow should never have dismissed the grand jury like he did.

A jubilant Jake Floyd and the ten other attorneys who started the removal effort drove to Austin the next day to meet with Shivers. Each offered their services as a replacement judge. Shivers, who had the power to make the appointment, said it was unlikely any of them would be named. Senatorial courtesy rules required the governor to run any potential appointee past the senator who represents the affected counties.

In this case, the senator was Abraham Kazen of Laredo. He was son-in-law to Manuel Raymond, the attorney for the Benavides school district and close friend of George Parr. Kazen had already told Gov. Shivers he would block Senate confirmation of any of the 11 attorneys.

The Supreme Court ultimately helped Shivers out of this politically delicate situation. The chief justice appointed a little known retired judge from East Texas, A. S. Broadfoot, to assume the 79th District Court bench. Broadfoot was ordered to serve until a replacement was named either by Shivers or by the voters.

Barely a month passed before Woodrow announced he would run again for his old seat on the bench. A few days later, George Parr said he would run, too, promising that if elected, he wouldn't be dominated by any political machine controlled by Jake Floyd or anyone else.

"My opponents said I control the district judge," George said. "Why not let me be the district judge? Then no one will control the district judge but me."

***

Johnny Klevenhagen took his gun and holster off before going into the warden's office at the state penitentiary in Huntsville, Texas. It was standard procedure when interrogating prisoners. He had come to talk with a Mexican prisoner named Andres Cardanes, a man so dark that Mexicans called him Blackie. It was a breezy fall day, and the tall pines rippled gently around the prison yard. Johnny could see through the windows hundreds of men milling about, smoking and talking, some playing cards on the packed dirt.

"You been here before?" Johnny asked Blackie.

Blackie shook his head, his eyes trained on his feet. His mouth was sullen, his narrow mustache drooped.

"Harlem Farm. They always put the Mexicans at Harlem Farm."

"I guess you'll be going back there."

Blackie didn't say anything. He just sighed heavily.

"How were you supposed to kill Sapet if he's here and you're at Harlem?"

"Alaniz had it figured this way. He said I was to get real sick and they'd bring me to the place here and I could do the job."

"You mean the infirmary?"

Blackie nodded.

The door to the office opened and two uniformed guards stepped aside. They were followed by the warden, Mario Sapet and a third guard. Mario had put on a few pounds eating prison gruel. His hair and mustache had flecks of gray. He had just turned 50 years old.

After everyone had taken seats, with Johnny between the two prisoners, the Ranger introduced Blackie and Mario. He offered them cigarettes.

"Long time, no see," he said to Mario. No response.

"Last time I was up here," Johnny said, "I told you to grow eyes in the back of your head. Right, Mario?"

"Yeah." Mario was more interested in his Marlboro than in the conversation.

"You didn't believe me, did you?"

Mario shrugged.

"My friend Blackie here has a story for you. Go ahead, Blackie," Johnny said. "Start at the beginning, back in '52."

Blackie put out his cigarette, and Johnny lit him another.

"I was in jail in Alice," Blackie said, his voice dragging as if he were stoned. Johnny figured he'd done so much of the weed his speech was in perpetual slow motion.

"Had me in there for burglary or something. I don't remember. One day, this lawyer comes through, stops at my cell. He gives me his card and says if I ever need a lawyer, to call him. I can't read or nothing, so one of the boys tells me the man's name is Nago Alaniz.

"It was a few weeks later and I found some hacksaw blades. I busted out and went straight over to that lawyer's house. One of the boys told me where it was."

Johnny interrupted. "Why'd you go over there?"

"I don't know. I just liked him. Seemed like he'd try to help me if I needed it."

"But he's an officer of the court, Blackie. Didn't you think he'd turn you in?"

"Oh, no. Some of the boys, they told me he was okay. So I went over there and he was real nice to me. So was his wife. They gave me food. I don't remember what it was. All I know is it tasted better than the slop at the jail.

"The lawyer and I, we drank beers for awhile. Then I left. I went to Natalia. That's where my old lady is."

"What'd you do while you were there?"

"Not much. Worked a little construction. My old lady, she had a steady job so I could lay low."

"Did you ever see Nago Alaniz again?"

"Yeah. He came to see me many times. Said he had a proposition for me. Said it was just a matter of time and I'd get picked up. Nothing he could do about it. Nothing I could do. It was just a matter of time.

"That didn't make me too happy. I thought I was doing good staying out of sight. But he said they were looking for me and I'd get caught. He said not to worry. He had a plan.

"Said when I got back to the prison, if I'd kill Mario Sapet, he'd help me get out. Said he'd give me five thousand cash and a new car."

Mario still looked bored.

"Did he say why he wanted Mario Sapet dead?" Johnny asked.

Blackie shook his head.

"Just said it wasn't him that wanted the killing. It was another man. Never said who it was.

"I wasn't pumped up about it or anything. Didn't know how I was going to get next to Mario Sapet even if they brought me back here. But Nago said I could find a way. Get sick and go to the hospital. That's what he said. That way I could be close to this man.

"I still didn't care. But then, Nago started pulling out hundred dollar bills. He gave me three of them and told me to call this lawyer in San Antonio. Said he was real good and he could fix things for me.

"He told me not to tell anybody about talking to me. Said when I got caught again, he'd talk to a judge in Alice, Judge Laughlin, and ask him to help me out.

"I never called that lawyer in San Antonio. Things started going good for me. I got a job doing construction and it paid decent. The boss liked me. It was steady work for a few weeks. And then the sheriff showed up. Took me back to the jail in Alice.

"I had to go in front of Judge Laughlin and he asks me where was my attorney. I say I don't know. He says who is your attorney? I say Nago Alaniz. He says go call him.

"So I call Alaniz and tell him what's happened. He says did I say his name in the court. I say yes. He says did anybody besides the judge hear me. I say I don't think so. He tells me again not to talk about the proposition. He says he will come see me at Huntsville."

Johnny interrupted.

"You think this Nago Alaniz turned you in?"

Blackie shrugged.

"Maybe. Can't say. But this Nago, he comes to court with me. The judge says I have to go back to prison. So Nago says he will come see me at Harlem Farm. I say no go. I am trying it straight. I tell him I got a good job and the foreman says I can come back when I get out. I am going straight, I tell him.

"He gets mad and says where's the $300. I tell him I don't have it, but I'll pay him back. He says he may find somebody to kill me at Harlem Farm."

Mario sat slumped in his chair, an elbow propped on the armrest, his chin in his hand.

"Look. You two want to talk in Spanish? Go ahead. I don't care." Johnny understood enough of the language to decipher what was being said.

The two prisoners conversed for 15 or more minutes. Nothing was said that the Ranger hadn't already heard from Blackie. When they finished, Johnny asked Mario what he thought.

"Don't know. Probably true. All of it." Mario said.

"Look, Mario, Blackie is no threat to you. I don't have to tell you that. He says he's going straight, and I think I believe him. But even if he's telling us a big one, we're going to be watching him like a hawk. There's no way he'll ever get close to you.

"But you know as well as I do, Mario, that there'll be others. Plenty of prisoners who'll put you away in return for a lot less than a one-way ticket out of here. We're watching you like a hawk, too, Mario. But someday, somebody might get to you. And then what's it all for?

"You've been the good little soldier and protected your people. But what's it all for? They ain't going to get you out of here, Mario. You're gonna rot behind these bars. Oh, they may send you a little cash every month so you don't have to roll your own cigarettes. You can go down to the canteen and buy your ready-made smokes and a candy bar, but so what? It's not the same as those boilermakers you used to drink, is it?"

Mario had heard this speech before, from Johnny and from Sammy Burris. But it was the first time either man had brought a would-be killer along.

"I need to think," he said. "Just let me think awhile."

"You do that, Mario," Johnny said. "You think about your friends out there living it up and you in here, locked away behind bars. It isn't fair, Mario. They ought to be in here with you. They're making you take the rap and putting contracts out on you. Is that what you bargained for?"

Mario uncrossed his legs and gripped the armrests.

"I will think about it. Now, can I go?" he said, looking at the warden.

The warden nodded, and the guards took both prisoners out of the office.

"I don't think you moved him one iota off center," said the warden. He wore a suit and had Woodrow Wilson eyeglasses.

"Probably not. We're just going to have to work on him awhile. The way I look at it, we're planting seeds. One of these days, we're going to have a whole goddamn garden."

"How'd you know he buys his cigarettes at the canteen?"

"Just guessed."

"You're right on target. Smokes tailor-made Camels. Turns his nose up at the two sacks of Bull Durham we hand out every week. It's a sure sign somebody's funding him."

"When did he come to the Walls Unit?"

"About three months ago. He's got a bad case of diabetes, and he has seizures now and then. Thought it would be best to move him to the medical unit.

"It's pretty laid back there. The guards tell me he keeps to himself. Doesn't talk much to anybody, even when they're out in the yard. They've never caught him preying on other prisoners, and there's never been any report he's a troublemaker. Yes, sir,

Mario Sapet is marking off his time, day by day."

"What kind of work detail is he on?"

"At first, we had him in the steward's department. Easy work, cleaning up the yard, sweeping, that kind of thing. Now, he's a gardener. They keep a vegetable garden over there and have some flowers. You know, brighten up the place a little.

"I wouldn't say he likes it here, Mr. Klevenhagen, but I don't think you're going to get anything from him. Not unless we hold him down and give him a truth serum or something."

Johnny stood, his Stetson in his hand.

"I don't think you understand, warden. I'm just as mean and stubborn as he is. And I'm damn good at waiting, just like he is. I'll be back."

***

A few months after the IRS sent additional agents to investigate in Duval County, Jake Floyd received this letter from Bill Ninedorf:

Dear Mr. Floyd:

You might like to know that there were never, at any time, more than two of us working on the George Parr case. The other men you met were working on collateral cases and were told not to help us on the Parr investigation. I received written instructions to the effect that I could not use any of these men. You may also like to know that the F.B.I. recently sent at least seven men into Duval County to investigate the missing records at the two banks. Henley and I spent a lot of time doing that. With all of the ramifications of an income tax case, the Internal Revenue Service could send in no more than two men on the case.

Last November, I was selected for a job as a group supervisor. I was then considered the most experienced for the job and the most capable in the entire district. I was to take over those duties upon getting off the Parr case. I stuck to that case until we came up with something worthwhile, much to the apparent disgust or displeasure of my superiors. Several weeks before I returned to my office in Houston, I was told the job had been abolished. That sounds like Duval County tactics. I have been told by my supervisor that I will not be promoted by reason of the fact that the inspectors were still holding an axe over my head as a result of what took place in Duval County.

I was told by certain officials that they could not spare the extra men to work on the Parr case, yet they did not hesitate to send two men down from Washington to see what Henley and I were doing. They were more interested in investigating the investigators than they were in investigating George Parr. It looks like they would like to take action against us more than they would against George Parr.

I have 25 years in government service and in five more years I could retire with a pension. I would not like to have an axe poised over my head that long. Upon returning home after my sojourn in and around Duval County, I found I had high blood pressure. I am under the care of two doctors at the present time. I have got to get the help from someone well known in Washington. I have in mind someone, but he is not a congressman. What would you suggest?

With highest regards,
W. H. Ninedorf

A few days later, Jake received a second, more desperate letter from the IRS agent:

Dear Mr. Floyd:

While in Austin last Thursday on other matters, I asked Mr. R. L. Phinney, the district director of the internal revenue, outright whether or not I was still under threat of some sort of disciplinary action. Mr. Phinney told me that I was still under threat but that he did not know what action would be taken against me.

My superiors have just about stripped me of everything in connection with my job, except the job itself. I expect to lose that within the next 30 to 60 days. Mr. Phinney proposed and urged me to apply for retirement on physical disability as soon as I returned to Houston. I told him I would think it over. However, I have no intention of applying for retirement because I was feeling good physically. I told the doctor about it and he laughed. He checked my blood pressure and found it within the normal range. There is nothing wrong with my physically, except that I had hypertension, which the doctor agreed was caused by emotional strain. That emotional strain was the result of being under threat of reprisal for not having made an effort to "whitewash" George Parr. By telling myself that right will eventually prevail, I have been able to control my emotions to a great extent.

I do not know what their next move will be, since I do not intend to retire. However, they are building up a case against me in the meanwhile. I am being harassed by several people who have been assigned the task of trying to "get something on me." I intend to fight their efforts, just as vigorously as I pursued the Parr investigation. I might add that I had far less trouble with George Parr, Manuel J. Raymond and all of Parr's henchmen than I had with my superiors. I wish I could have told you all these things when they occurred, but Henley and I were "gagged" so to speak.

Since I have nothing to lose now, I am going to use every means at my command to get the threat removed from over my head. You have my unconditional permission to discuss this matter with the governor, John Ben Shepperd or anyone else who might have connections in Washington who might intercede in the matter.

After the word gets to Washington, I intend to talk to Jack Donahue of the Houston Press and Dawson Duncan of the Dallas Morning News about the matter. I am going to propose that they call Phinney in Austin and B. Frank White, the regional commissioner in Dallas, and have the reporters tell those two officials that a rumor per-

sists around Houston that W. H. Ninedorf is being "railroaded" out of the Internal Revenue Service for having been too persistent in making an all out investigation of George Parr and his henchmen.

Their replies, if any, should make a good story. The reporters could say that I neither confirmed nor denied the rumor. When questioned by inspectors, I would simply tell them that since this was a personal matter and that I was the central figure, I had every right to tell my friends about it. The newspapers would get those facts as well. I am thoroughly convinced this would result in renewed public interest in the Parr cases. This would bring out into open a deplorable condition that exists in the Internal Revenue Service. And the honest taxpayers are footing the bill.

Sincerely yours,
W. H. Ninedorf

Two days later, Jake dispatched the following letter to John Osorio in Governor Shivers' office:

Dear John:

I am enclosing you herewith two letters from W. H. Ninedorf, the Internal Revenue Agent who investigated George B. Parr. It seems there should be some way to prevent this man from being crucified for doing his duty. It occurs to the writer that this is provoked, among other reasons, as a result of the fact that strong Democrats who are influential in Washington have been tipped off that Governor Shivers has taken an active interest in this prosecution. It is hard to believe that these people would be moved to take such drastic action, completely for the unwholesome purpose of protecting a racketeer who has voted for them in the past.

I believe it is imperative that you digest these two letters and get the matter to the Governor immediately with the hope that he will be able to communicate with Attorney General Brownell or someone else

who will be able to stop this persecution.
  With kindest personal regards, I am

Very truly yours,
Jacob S. Floyd

The harassment of agent Ninedorf notwithstanding, he and Edgar Henley had gathered enough information to warrant a grand jury investigation. In November 1954, after a month of deliberations and 30 witnesses, a federal grand jury in Houston indicted George for tax evasion. For the second time, he was accused of not paying income taxes, this time in the amount of $85,000.

Chapter 25
June

"The woman's nothing but trouble," Captain Allee had told Jake. "You're wasting your time."

He's probably right, Jake thought as he entered the county courthouse in Pensacola, Florida. Betty Bushey had been nothing but trouble so far, but she sure seemed to know something about Buddy's murder. Jake decided she was worth an airplane ticket and a couple of days away from Perkins & Floyd.

A bright hot sun burned in the June sky, making Jake wish he could withdraw under the brim of his hat. The jail cell would be ten times worse. Maybe they'd have a few fans. The lawyer thought of Mrs. Bushey and smiled. No doubt she'd have one or two of the jailers charmed; most likely, she had her own personal electric fan.

Jake thought of the first time he had encountered Betty Bushey. It was at Captain Allee's trial in Houston. She'd shown up out of nowhere—tall and redheaded, attractive in an unkempt way. She had on expensive clothing, but it looked like she'd worn the life out of her dress.

She told Judge Klein she had been George Parr's girlfriend for a time, that she had been present at poker games and horse races the Duke frequented. It was at one of those poker games, she had told the judge, that she overheard a plot to kill Captain Allee. She said she'd be willing to testify about what she knew at the

Captain's trial.

Jake had interviewed her, and he had been impressed with her answers. She named the killers—two hoodlums from Mexico—and said they were going to ambush the captain outside the apartment he rented just across the Duval County line. The plot was scuttled, she said, when "things got too hot."

Jake decided he believed her. She knew too many names and too many details. He said he would call her to the witness stand the following day, but she never showed up and the marshals couldn't find her.

Three months later, she surfaced in Pensacola, jailed for writing hot checks. A county constable by the name of Billy Kelson called Jake long distance and told him she was singing like a caged canary about Buddy's murder and Duval County in general.

Inside the Pensacola courthouse, it wasn't hard to find Constable Kelson's office. "For awhile there," Kelson said, after he and Jake had settled into varnished wood chairs, "she was saying she wouldn't talk to you or anybody from Texas until she talked to a lawyer by the name of Percy Foreman."

Jake nodded.

"She wrote me the same thing a few days ago. Has Foreman ever called?"

"No, sir. She's called his office a couple of times and wrote him a letter or two. But he doesn't seem interested in her."

"Well, she claims she wants to come back to Texas so she can get medical care," Jake said. "I don't know why she thinks she can't get it here."

"Wait till you see her, Mr. Floyd," the constable smiled. "All her talk about having TB is malarkey. The woman eats like she's a stray who ain't sure when the next meal is coming. I bet she's put on ten pounds in the two weeks she's been here—and we got lousy food.

"The gal has an angle," the constable continued. "I'm not

sure yet what it is. But she's got her eye on Texas and seems dead set on getting there. You got a reward out?"

"I do," Jake said. "$10,000 for the person who helps us capture the killer. He's a Mexican national, hiding out down there right now. He was a paid killer, Mr. Kelson, and I want him to swear under oath who paid him."

The constable studied his visitor. The lawyer was wearing a custom suit and a starched shirt monogrammed at the cuffs. His small blue eyes and the grim set of his mouth offered no emotion save for an unmistakable determination.

"Mr. Floyd," the constable said, "can I give you a bit of friendly advice? With money like that, it's like dangling a carrot in front of a rabbit. You're gonna hear from a lot of characters and most of 'em ain't gonna know squat. Oh, they'll know some little detail that'll grab you and suck you in.

"But all they want is cash. I've seen it happen a thousand times. They'll try to bleed you dry asking for expense money.

"Now, you take this chick Bushey. I can tell—she's a babe, or used to be. She's a pro at attaching herself to men who have money or power, but she'd rather have both. I tell you, she's a regular leech."

"All the same," Jake said, "I'd like to talk to her. She's convinced me she knows something. If nothing else, she could come in handy at a trial we've got coming up on this case."

The constable led Jake to Mrs. Bushey's cell. She was sitting on her bare mattress, reading a book. Sure enough, she had a small floor fan trained on her face.

Jake hardly recognized her. Her hair was blonde, dyed almost white and dark at the roots. She had on a straight white prison shift that hung loose. The constable was right; she had put on weight.

"Mr. Floyd!" she shouted, jumping to her feet. She was wearing jail-issue slide sandals.

Jake insisted on standing. The only place to sit was on her mattress.

"Mr. Floyd, I am so, so glad to see you," she said, smiling. Her teeth were crooked, but she had a good smile. Her bosom was full, larger than most women's. Jake could see why George Parr had taken up with her.

"Mrs. Bushey," Jake began.

"Please, call me Betty," she said, making a show of crossing her bare legs.

"Mrs. Bushey," Jake tried again. "I understand that you know something about my son's murder."

"Now, Mr. Floyd, please call me Betty. I just hate being formal. I'd like for us to be friends. It's more fun that way. Maybe someday you'll even let me call you Jake."

This wasn't going to be easy, Jake thought. He stuffed his hands in his trouser pockets and looked her square in her blue eyes.

"Mrs. Bushey, I'd appreciate it if you'd just tell me what you know."

"All right," she said, propping herself on an elbow on the mattress. "If that's the way you want it. When was it your son got killed? Oh, I was awful sorry about that, Mr. Floyd. Terrible, just terrible."

"It was September—almost two years ago."

"Oh, yeah. Well, we was at George's that night. He and the boys was playing poker. We was in that big trophy room he has. I guess you never seen it, but it's something. Big deer trophies all over the wall, and there's a buffalo head and a bear in there, too.

"George just loves to hunt. I'm not sure how good he is with guns. He brags a lot about what a good shot he is, but I went to target practice with him a few times. He's not so special."

She stopped talking for a moment and looked at Jake, as if sizing him up.

"Who was there that night? Who was at the poker table?"

"Well, let's see. There was George, of course. He loves to play poker, you know. And Juan Canante and his brother Raul. And there were some boys from Benavides. I don't remember their names.

"They was having a big time. I kept their drinks full. Everybody was drinking tequila that night, everybody but George. I never could get that man to take a drink. I finally decided he just didn't like the stuff. Kind of like I can't stand the taste of tomato juice. George couldn't stand the taste of booze. You know what I mean, Mr. Floyd?"

"So what happened? They were playing poker. You were playing bartender. What happened?"

"Well, the phone rang. I guess it was about 10:30. I answered it, and it was Pete."

"Pete Saenz?"

"Yep. He was all excited. Sounded like he'd been running or something 'cause he was all out of breath. He wanted to talk to George, but George wouldn't come to the phone. You know, Mr. Floyd, when George gets wrapped up in a poker game, you could parade a line of naked women past him and he wouldn't even look up. I never seen anything like it.

"Pete said it was really important and to get George on the phone. So I went in there and told him again. I told him it was Pete, and when George heard that name, he put down his cards and got right up.

"I could hear him talking on the phone. He wasn't too far from where I was sitting. He didn't say much, nothing that would help you out, Mr. Floyd. But when he got off the phone and went back to the poker table, he said something like 'the job's done.'"

"The job's done?" Jake said.

"Yes, sir. And Juan asked him where somebody was. I think he said the name was Cervantes. Yeah, that's it. He said 'where's

Cervantes?' And George said he was already at Nuevo Laredo. And then Juan asked him where Sapet was. And George said he went to San Antonio.

"That was all they said. They went back to playing poker just like nothin' had happened. I didn't know until the next day that your son had been killed. I read the newspapers and saw those names, Cervantes and Sapet, but I knew better than to ask George any questions. He didn't like me nosing in his business.

"A couple days later, Juan gave me an envelope with some papers inside it. Asked me to put it in a safety box at the Frost Bank in San Antonio. So I drove up there. That was one of my jobs – to run errands for George and his men. So, like I say, I took the envelope up to San Antonio. But before I put it in the safety box, I looked at those papers. One of the pieces of paper was a map—looked like the map of a house.

"There was a kitchen and a living room, and then it showed a back porch and a garage away from the house."

"Where was the garage?"

"You mean—it was at the back. I'm pretty sure it was your house, Mr. Floyd. I mean, your garage is away from the house, at the back? I know because that's what I read in the papers. I never been to your house, Mr. Floyd. Honest. I just put two and two together and figured it was a map of your house."

"What name is that safe deposit box under?" Jake said.

"Now, Mr. Floyd," she said, smiling coyly. "I can't tell you that. How am I going to get outta here if I tell you everything I know?"

"Mrs. Bushey, I didn't come all the way out here to play little games with you. If you don't tell me everything you know, you don't have a prayer of getting out of jail. You'll just stay in here and suffer with your tuberculosis, or whatever ails you, until they decide to let you out."

The woman stood up and primped her hair in front of a

small mirror bolted to the wall behind bars.

"What else do you want to know, Mr. Floyd?"

"What else can you tell me?"

"Let's see. What else." She sat silent for a moment, as if reviewing from beginning to end her two-plus years in Duval County.

"You said you ran errands. What do you mean?"

"Messages mostly. Sometimes I carried money. George would let me drive one of his cars. Oh, that man had nice cars. My favorite was the black Cadillac. He only let me drive that one once, but man, it was a smooth rider.

"You got a smoke, Mr. Floyd? They only let you have five cigarettes a day in this joint. I tried to tell 'em five cigarettes don't even get you breathing good in the mornin', but they don't care."

Jake was prepared for such a request. He pulled out from his breast pocket a pack of filtered cigarettes. He wondered about her supposed lung difficulties, but decided to stick to the subject.

"Who'd you make deliveries to?" he said, striking a match to light her cigarette.

"I'd go to Corpus, Kingsville, Alice, Houston. I don't remember names. There were some lawyers, a couple of road contractors; I'd go put money in the bank or put papers in safe boxes. I'd always take a peak at whatever I was delivering. A few times, there was bags of money—cash. Several thousand dollars.

"I was afraid to count it; didn't want to tempt myself. I knew if I pulled anything on George, he'd be after me faster than I could blink an eye. I never liked making George mad. He got mean when he was mad—hitting and punching and giving me all kinds of misery.

"So I just left it in the bag and smelled it. I just love the smell of cash, Mr. Floyd. Sweetest smell I know of. It's just plain inspirational."

She sat on the bunk again and arranged her dress so that her knees still showed, then cast a movie starlet glance at Jake.

"Do you remember any names at all?" he said. "Did you ever deliver cash to a man named Moffett in Corpus Christi?"

"I just don't recall."

Jake decided on another approach.

"Mrs. Bushey, do you think your memory would improve if you were back in Texas?"

She visibly brightened.

"Now, Mrs. Bushey, if we were to get you back to Texas, what guarantee would I have that your memory would improve?"

"Just call me the Yellow Rose of Texas, Mr. Floyd. When I get there, I'm gonna blossom," she smiled, and her crooked teeth glistened.

"I'd like to put you on the witness stand in a trial we've got coming up in Waco," Jake said. "It's Nago Alaniz's trial. Do you think you could handle that?"

"Oh, yes, sir."

"Did you know him?"

"I never saw him at George's house or at his office. But he hung around with Pete Saenz and Juan quite a bit. I never saw or heard anything about him being mixed up in your son's killin', though."

"You can just talk about that night at the poker game. "Now, let me ask you something else. I hear you know something about missing microfilm from George's banks in Alice and San Diego."

"George told me to do whatever the guys at the bank said. Sometimes they'd give me boxes of stuff to take and deliver to some safe box. I guess it was microfilm. Just looked like film negatives to me. I never asked questions, just did what they said."

"Have you ever testified before a grand jury, Mrs. Bushey?"

"Nope. George warned me once about grand juries. He said there were some mean ones and to watch it if I ever got called.

Said he didn't want to hear anything about me singing to a grand jury or to the cops. I told him all he had to do was treat me decent, like a lady, we wouldn't have any problems."

"Why'd you leave Duval County, Mrs. Bushey?"

"It was time to move on. George gave me a pink slip, you might say. I had a good time with Juan and his brother for a while, but pretty soon I could see the handwriting. San Diego was no place for a woman as ambitious as I am."

Jake wondered if she was serious.

"So I headed east. But since I been gone, I've done some thinking. I had some laughs there and found a few friends. A wanderer like me, I don't make a lot of friends. I need to hold onto the few I find. Should never have left Texas. It's where I belong."

"What's this about you think you can get better medical care back in Texas?"

"Oh, the doctors here are fine. It's just the air there. I'm not joshing you, Mr. Floyd. You know, I only got one lung. Had one removed because I had tuberculosis a few years back. I don't know how to say it; the air just goes down easier in Texas. It's clean, like mountain air."

"Mr. Kelson may have told you that a grand jury in Fort Worth is considering indictments against you for bad checks?"

"He sure did. I suppose that means I could go back to Fort Worth."

"It's possible. We'd send the Rangers to pick you up and bring you back."

"Oh, the Rangers. I sure do like that Mr. Williamson. Yes, sir, Mr. Floyd. I'd like driving all the way back to Texas with a tall one like that cowboy."

Jake signaled for the guard to let him out.

"I'll be in touch in a few days. If you hear anything from Duval County, I'd appreciate it if you'd let me know. Here's my card with my address. Just write me a letter. I suspect you'll be back in Texas within the month."

Jake handed the woman the pack of cigarettes.

"I can make life a lot easier for you, Mrs. Bushey. But this is no one-way street. I need information that we can back up with evidence. If you've got a map to my house, I need to put my hands on it. If you stowed microfilm records, I need to know exactly where to find them.

"We can get you as far as Fort Worth, but things can stop dead right there if you don't give us something solid."

Jake nodded at Betty Bushey and stepped out the cell door as the guard held it open.

"I'll see you in Texas," he said, and walked off.

Chapter 26

Nago Alaniz's trial was to be in July in Waco, but Alaniz got appendicitis and it was delayed again, for what seemed to Jake like the tenth time. That was what lawyers like Percy Foreman did—they delayed and delayed and delayed. Jake wondered if the appendicitis was real, but doctors assured the judge the defendant was seriously ill.

Finally, in October 1954, two years after the murder, Nago went on trial. He was 39 years old, and age was beginning to show on him. A few gray hairs appeared at the temples, and his jaw line sagged a bit. But he was still the dashing attorney from San Diego. He wore a cream-colored suit his first day in the courtroom. His wife and two daughters, Betty, who was 6, and Deborah, who was 3, sat behind him in the gallery.

Jake was grateful it was a small courtroom. He didn't want a big crowd like they had at Brownwood. It would be easier on Edith, who had begun showing the strain of the past months. She had spent two weeks in the hospital that summer with an impacted colon. The doctor said it was stress. Jake tried to get her to stay in Alice until she was called to testify, but she insisted on sitting through Nago's trial.

It proved to be a tedious event, and Jake wondered on the first day if the trial was doomed to another delay. Foreman showed up in court with a cart full of briefcases stuffed as fat as he was. He and his two local lawyers assembled their portable files next to the defense table and began filing a sheaf of motions.

Jake had seen Percy Foreman on several occasions, but he didn't recall him being so large. Knowing Percy, though, it was a good bet he kept the weight on so he could be all the more intimidating. His expensive suit was oversized, as if he had already dropped some weight. And he wore his thick black hair combed straight back, an errant strand always straying onto his forehead.

The indictment should be thrown out, Foreman boomed at Judge Bartlett, because Jake Floyd was present when it was drawn up by the grand jury. It was drawn up either in Spurgeon Bell's Houston law office, Foreman charged, or in the grand jury room at the Jim Wells County courthouse. Either way, he said, Jake Floyd was there.

Jake told the judge he didn't know where or exactly when the indictment was reduced to writing, and that seemed to settle the matter. But Foreman was armed with more motions aimed at delaying jury selection. Judge Bartlett told him to file the motions with the clerk and get on with *voir dire*. He wanted the trial over in a week.

The lead prosecutor was Tom Moore, Jr., the district attorney in Waco. Bill Allcorn of Brownwood assisted, as did Sammy Burris. By the third day of the trial, 12 men—a group of salesmen, clerks and industrial workers—had been selected for the jury.

Jake was the first witness called by the state, and he recounted in detail the events of the night of September 8, 1952. He also recalled a conversation he had with Nago five or six years before that, in which he promised to come to the young lawyer's aid, if necessary.

"He was very closely associated with George Parr," Jake said. "He came to me in great distress and said that he had had a verbal encounter with an influential member of the Parr party. He said he was fearful of the situation of practicing law in Duval County and was afraid that something might be done to him sometime because he was doing his duty in defending some case.

"I told him, 'Nago, if they ever put you in jail, you call me and I will come and get you out.'"

Foreman's defense strategy was immediately apparent.

"Mr. Floyd," he asked, "tell us whether you remember recommending that Governor Coke Stevenson appoint Nago Alaniz as a special Duval County judge to hear a certain estate case?"

"That is not true," Jake said.

"I told you to tell us whether you remember recommending that Governor Coke Stevenson appoint Nago Alaniz as a special Duval County judge?"

"That didn't happen."

"Tell us if you remember."

"I don't remember that happening."

"Tell us if you remember telegraphing Nago Alaniz $25 when he asked for a $10 loan in 1943 while Nago Alaniz was in the Army in Battle Creek, Michigan."

"Another falsehood."

"Tell us if you remember."

"I have no such recollection."

"Tell the Court if you remember throwing Nago Alaniz, who was a struggling young Alice lawyer, whom you promised to help, tell us if you remember throwing him a lot of work."

"I did no such thing."

"Isn't it a fact that Nago Alaniz warned you of a plot against your life because you had been his friend, counselor and guide?"

"No!" Jake said angrily.

Gumescindo Montez Gonzalez, a Mexican national and a waiter at the Jardin Internacional, testified that he had lived in Sapet's house in Nuevo Laredo during the summer of 1952. He said that Alfredo Cervantes had stayed at the house, too, and had told him he was going to Texas to kill a man.

When Foreman cross-examined Gonzalez, the exchange was

handled through an interpreter. Gonzalez spoke no English.
Q: How did you happen to come to Texas a year ago?
A: With a permit.
Q: Who got you the permit?
A: Ranger Captain.
Q: Which Ranger Captain?
A: Johnny.
Q: Captain Johnny Klevenhagen?
A: The Immigration gave me the permit.
Q: I asked him who got him the permit from the Immigration Department.
A: One of the Rangers. His name is Johnny.
Q: Will Ranger John Klevenhagen stand up, please, if he is in the courtroom?
Is this the man?
A: Yes, sir.
Q: All right. Now, how long were you in Nuevo Laredo before Captain Johnny got you this permit?
A: Eight months.
Q: And during that time, what, if any, work did you do, or if none, how did you live?
A: My profession is a baker.
Q: I did not ask you what your profession is. I asked you what you did, if anything, to earn a living?
A: I was working as a baker and also as a waiter.
Q: Where?
A: In the Cantina Jardin Internacional, and the Pana de Reia El Galo.
Q: Isn't it true that you are what is known in this country as a professional pool shark?
A: No, sir, I can prove that I worked.
Q: Can you also prove that you have made your living gambling on your pool-playing ability?

A: I play billiards.

Q: Excuse me, I should have said professional billiard gambler. Do you know an individual in Nuevo Laredo named Francisco Benevides?

A: Yes, sir.

Q: State whether or not, for the last several weeks before you left Nuevo Laredo, Francisco Benevides gave you money to support you?

A: Yes, he loaned me money by the accommodation of my uncle.

Q: Regardless of as an accommodation to whomever he accommodated, how much money, over how long a period of time, did this Francisco Benevides support you in Mexico before you came to Texas?

A: I think 140 dollars in Mexican money, pesos, in partial loans.

Q: Do you know whether that money came from and through one Jacob S. Floyd, Sr.?

A: No, sir.

Q: Isn't it a fact that the amount of money that you received was approximately ten times what you have stated you received from Francisco Benevides?

A: No, sir, I can prove it.

Q: Are you now working? If so, where?

A: I was working and I quit about two weeks ago.

Q: Where?

A: At the Beles Bakery in San Antonio, Texas.

Q: How long did you work there?

A: About three months.

Q: Then for the other nine months that you were here, before you went to work at Beles Bakery, what, if any, work did you do?

A: I worked at other bakeries.

Q: Where and for how long?

A: Nila's Cake Shop.

Q: Do you know one Rudy Garza?

A: Yes, sir.
Q: Where does he live?
A: I do not know.
Q: You don't know what city he lives in?
A: Yes, sir.
Q: Where?
A: San Antonio.
Q: What is his occupation?
A: He is a policeman.
Q: Are you telling us that you have not been paid money through Rudy Garza by any other agency or person?
A: I have not received any money from Rudy. I received from another person.
Q: Okay, then. What other person?
A: I do not know his name.
Q: Well, what office, if any, does he hold?
A: He loaned me $30.
Q: What office, if any, does the person hold from whom you received money? When not working?
A: Constable.
Q: How much money over the 12-month period did you receive from this person?
A: $30 one time.
Q: You claim that is all the money that you have received from any person when you were not working since you have been in the United States?
A: Yes, sir.
Q: You have not received any money from the Texas Rangers?
A: No, sir.
Q: You have not received any money from Jacob S. Floyd, Sr., either directly or indirectly?
A: I do not know the gentleman.
Q: Do you know whether or not any money was represented to

you as coming from him?

A: No, sir.

Q: Have you offered to sell your testimony in this case to either side that would pay the most money for it?

A: No, sir.

Bill Allcorn, on redirect examination, picked up the Floyd thread.

Q: Do you know Jacob S. Floyd?

A: No, sir.

Q: Do you know whether or not you have ever seen Jacob S. Floyd?

A: I saw him today.

Q: Where did you see him?

A: At the hotel.

Q: And has Jacob S. Floyd ever paid, or offered to pay, you money to testify in this case?

Foreman objected.

"Your Honor, I have not and do not intend to suggest that Jacob S. Floyd paid him any money for his testimony. I simply attempted to infer and do infer from my question that Mr. Floyd has contributed money, or at least someone has, to support the man for approximately nine months, but not for payment of testimony, which would be a reflection on Mr. Floyd, and I don't want to be doing that."

"In light of that statement, I will withdraw my question," said Allcorn.

Foreman got another shot at Gonzales later in the trial.

Q: Did you tell the Texas Rangers in Nuevo Laredo in September of 1952 that Alfredo Cervantes had told you, about two weeks before September 8, 1952, that he was going to Texas to kill a man?

A: No, sir, I didn't tell them. I didn't want to be mixed with it.

Q: Did you tell them that you did not know anything about it?

A: They were investigating me. I didn't say very much because I was afraid to talk.

Q: And how long did you continue to tell the Rangers, Mr. Gumescindo Montez Gonzales, that you knew nothing about Alfredo Cervantes' connection, if any, with the Floyd death?

A: I don't remember for sure.

Q: What is your best recollection as to when you started telling a different story about Alfredo Cervantes and the Floyd death, than you first told them in those days, meaning September 1952?

A: Whenever I got my immigration permit or papers, whatever it is, then I commenced to talk.

Foreman called but a handful of witness, among them H. Q. Heras, justice of the peace in Benavides. Heras said he was to meet with Nago the night of the murder but that the defendant had cut their meeting short. "I have to leave," Heras quoted Alaniz as saying, "I may save a man's life tonight."

Perhaps the most compelling witness Foreman called was Nago's wife, Anna. She said that in the early evening of September 8, 1952, she received a telephone call from a Spanish-speaking man who did not give his name. The caller said to tell Nago "the matter in Alice is true and it will be tonight." She gave her husband the message and he rushed out of the house, saying "it might mean saving a man's life."

The prosecution ended up not calling Betty Bushey, even though Fort Worth authorities went to the trouble to bring her back to Texas. Captain Allee had been right. She had little more than trouble to offer.

The case went to the jury Saturday afternoon and deliberations continued until 3:45 A.M. before the panel retired for the night. They reconvened Sunday morning and within an hour, they returned a verdict of innocent.

Jake returned to Alice more dejected than he had been since Buddy was killed. "My stock has been very low since the Waco trial," he wrote John Ben Shepperd.

He had great hopes that Alaniz would be convicted, and that facing a possible death sentence, Alaniz might start singing. Sammy Burris promised to make trips to Huntsville at least annually to see if Sapet would weaken. Other than that, Jake's final hope was that Cervantes could be caught and that he would point the finger at George Parr.

There was a glimmer of hope that Parr would get his comeuppance in some way. John Ben Shepperd told Jake he had evidence that Percy Foreman had been paid with checks drawn on the Benavides Independent School District account. His legal fee: $20,000.

Section VII
1955–1963

Chapter 27
Spring 1955

Bob Melberg decided to call Johnny Klevenhagen rather than write him, as was his custom. The news he had to report was big enough to warrant the phone call to Houston. The two men had become good friends in the two years they had been searching for Alfredo Cervantes.

Melberg, from his office at the U.S. Embassy in Mexico City, had kept in touch with the Mexican police officer Lavin, who had remained under house arrest, so to speak, since he was shot. Lavin's "shooting scrape" had involved some pretty tough drug dealers, the Henriquistas, who had put a contract out on his life.

"Johnny," Melberg said when the connection was made, "Lavin's out."

"It's about time," Johnny said. "When did it happen?"

"Two days ago. I just found out. He called to invite me to a celebration—a welcome-home party next week."

"I guess the *federales* are sure there's no risk?"

"Looks that way. But, cripes, the man's been either locked up in the hospital or in prison for 18 months. They have a different idea of what protective custody is in this country."

"He still ailing from the gunshot wound?"

"Well, last time I saw him—went out to Lecumberri prison with his wife a couple of weeks ago—last time I saw him, he was fine. The limp was gone, even though they never removed the bullet near his spine. He's got a permanent souvenir from the Henriquistas. But he's strong as ever. They had some barbells and weights for him, and he's kept in shape.

"The prison was much safer than the hospital, and cleaner. These Mexican hospitals, ye gods. Course, they had to keep him in a restricted area. There were plenty of Henriquistas in there who would like to do away with him. Damn dope smugglers."

"What's the plan for going to Guadalajara?" Johnny asked. He had been waiting for news of Lavin's release for months. After working with a number of Mexican police officers, Johnny found that he completely trusted only one—Lavin. And Lavin was certain that Cervantes was in the Guadalajara area.

"He needs a couple of days to line out some business. But he says the first thing to do is to go to Guadalajara and look for our man. There's a police official there he's going to see. He says if this fellow needs money and Cervantes happens to be in town, we might get lucky."

"Well, I still would like to do an exchange at the river," Johnny said. "But we'll do it the hard way if we have to. Did you get the extradition papers I sent?"

"I gave them to Lavin the last time I was out at the prison. We'll just keep our fingers crossed."

The two men rang off. It was about lunchtime, so Melberg decided to take a stroll down the street. The air was cool and damp, adding frizz to Melberg's already curly brown hair. He was a trim, compact man. He liked to keep in shape with noonday walks.

About a block from the embassy, he noticed that a young Mexican man was approaching him from across the street. He had an aimless gait and a questioning look. Melberg braced himself to be asked for a handout.

"Mr. Melberg?" The man extended a hand.

"Francisco Senna. I understand you are from Texas." He spoke in mixed Spanish-English.

"How do you know me?"

"You and me, we have a friend. Here, let me show you."

The man who called himself Senna pulled a thick sheaf of papers from his shirt and handed Melberg a document. It was some kind of commendation signed by the sheriff in San Antonio.

"I'm afraid I don't know Sheriff Kilday."

Senna shook his head. "Alfredo Cervantes. You know him?"

Melberg looked at the man, really looked at him. He was a typical Mexican-Indian in appearance, with straight black hair. His brown eyes were almost beady and his nose was smashed, as if his face had been rearranged a few times.

He looked to be in his late twenties or early thirties. There were knife scars all over his forearms, and from what Melberg could see of his upper arms, they were quite muscular.

"How about if I buy you a *cerveza*?" Melberg said.

When they got to a neighborhood *cocina* and sat down with their beers, Melberg asked Senna where he was from.

He had come from Washington, D.C., a couple of weeks before, he said. Left his wife back there. He came to box but was having trouble getting into competition because he was an American. Melberg doubted seriously this man was an American. More likely he was a Mexican citizen trying to get into the United States.

"How do you know Alfredo Cervantes?" Melberg asked.

"Nuevo Laredo. Saw him at the Jardin Internacional all the time. Him and Mario Sapet. Saw both of them before that murder in Texas.

"I didn't know about it. Tamburero said he had a job to do in Texas. He and Mario drove off together and never came back. I heard about that murder, Señor Melberg. All over Nuevo Laredo—Tamburero killed the wrong man, shot him down outside his own house."

"You have any idea where Cervantes is now?"

"That's why I talk to you. I see an old friend the other night. A boxing friend. His name is Raul Badillo, but they call him 'Guero.' I am at the Regis Hotel, and I see him at the bar. I am not drinking—I'm a fighter and I can't drink. I have Coca-Cola and I'm happy. My friends, they can't understand no beer. It's like beans and tortillas. How can I live without it? But I am fine. I want to stay in the ring. I am fine with Coca-Cola."

"You were telling me about this Mr. Guero," Melberg said, wondering about the beer Senna was drinking at the moment.

"Oh, yeah. We were sitting at the bar, me with my Coca-Cola and him with his beer, and we talk about boxing in Nuevo Laredo. I forgot. Guero used to hang out at Jardin Internacional, too, him and me. Sapet. Cervantes.

"Anyway, we talk about Sapet. How he's in prison for that killing. And then Guero tells me he's seen Cervantes. Says he's living at a place just outside Mexico City. I can't remember the name. Tenampa maybe. 40 kilometers."

Melberg thought for a moment. There was a village nearby with a similar name.

"Do you mean Tlanepantla?"

"Si, Señor. That is it."

"What else can you tell me?"

"Not much more. Guero had bodyguards. They kept jumping between us. And he had *putas*. They were all over him. I didn't stay long.

"Guero, he gives me the shakes. He's got notches on his gun. I can't count them, they are so many. Killing people, it is sport to him. Sometimes he gets paid to kill people."

"He doesn't box anymore?"

"Gave it up."

The two men sat silent for a few moments, sipping their

beers. Melberg thought about Lavin and his certainty that Cervantes was in the Guadalajara area. But this is Mexico, he reminded himself, and he was involved in a criminal investigation. Reality could be hard to pin down in these circumstances.

"Señor Melberg, there is a reward?"

"Forty thousand pesos."

"What would I have to do—to get it?"

"A hell of a lot more than tell me he might be 40 kilometers from here."

Senna thought for a moment, then drained his beer bottle.

"You must have a plane. A plane to get him out. It is the only way. And an airstrip, far away from the city—

"Maybe so, but we don't even have him in custody."

"I been thinking, Señor Melberg. Guero said he could take me to see Cervantes. He knows where he is and could take me. I don't know where Guero lives, but I could go to the Regis Hotel and hang around. Maybe I see him again."

"You do that, Senna. And get back to me."

After two years of wild goose chases, Melberg was not about to get too excited about some broken-nosed boxer who knew a few pertinent facts. But he had to admit, this fellow had struck a few genuine chords in their brief conversation.

"I'm in Mexico City for ten days. I tell you, let you know if I find anything," Senna said. "That reward money. I could use it. I been living off my wife for too long. I think she's tired of it. She hasn't sent me any money in awhile. She's got this job making hats for rich ladies in Washington.

"I guess she's been busy because no check in a month. Truth, Señor Melberg, I'm flat broke. I live cheap. Don't eat too much, but enough to keep my weight on to fight. Don't drink either. I'm just having this beer because I don't have another fight for a week."

"How much would it take to tide you over?"

"Just a little. A few hundred pesos?"

Melberg reached in his pocket and pulled out some bills. It was the equivalent of 16 American dollars.

"I'll pay you back, Señor Melberg. My wife—she send money any day."

"If you see this Guero, check out something, will you? I know you say Cervantes is at Tlanepantla but we've had reports that Cervantes is dead, that his body was found on a highway near Durango. There was a newspaper article about it in the Monterrey paper. We've been checking it out but nothing so far."

Senna agreed and Melberg handed him his card with his embassy phone number on it.

"What do they call you, Mr. Senna, when you're in the ring?"

Senna grinned and looked down.

"The Cisco Kid."

The next day, The Cisco Kid called Melberg at his embassy office.

"I got lucky last night, Señor Melberg. Guero, he is at the hotel Regis and we drink together for a while. I ask him about Cervantes. Is he dead. He said, hell no, he not dead. Said he talked with him the night before and he's in Tlanepantla."

"Good. Is he going to take you to him?"

"I asked him to tell Cervantes young Senna wants to see him. Guero said he would pass the word along but he didn't know. Cervantes is a big man around here, and he didn't know if he'd see me or not. I told him we were old friends. We used to be in jail up there around Laredo together. He will see me, I told Guero.

"He said he'd work on it. We're supposed to meet at a dive tonight about 11:30. It's on Agua Dulce, number 341."

"Senna, can you get me a photograph of this Guero?"

"Photograph? Maybe."

"It would sure help."

"I try, Señor Melberg."

That afternoon, Senna paid a call on Melberg at his embassy office. He didn't bring the requested photo of Guero. He had other business on his mind.

"The photograph, Señor Melberg, I have not found one. It is not an easy thing. But I try."

Senna just sat in his chair across Melberg's desk. He didn't say anything.

"What is it, Senna?"

"I paid for food last night, food for Guero and me and some of his *compadres*. We go to a *cocina* and have *chile con carne* and *muchas cervezas*. I pay for it. Please, Señor, do not be mad. I scratch Guero's back, maybe he scratches mine. Yes?"

"How much?"

"320 pesos."

Melberg reached in his trouser pocket and pulled out some bills. He would write Johnny and ask that Mr. Floyd reimburse him.

"So sorry, Señor. But it costs money to deal with Guero."

"This is it, Senna. Our man in Texas is no rich man. Even if he were, you'd have to start producing something, right quick."

"I promise, Señor. Not another peso. My wife, she is sending me 150 American dollars any day now. I will wait for the reward money. No more until then. We will find him, I promise, Señor Melberg. Guero, he knows. We will find him."

Senna paused for a moment.

"Do you talk to Señor Floyd?"

"Through an intermediary."

"Inter—"

"It's like you and Guero. You talk to Guero for me."

"Oh. Can you find out—I mean exactly—find out how much the reward is?"

"I told you."

"Will he pay in American dollars or pesos? Deposit in a bank or in an envelope? I just want to know."

"All you need to know, Senna, is the man's good for the money. You lead us to Cervantes, you get the 40,000 pesos. That's it."

Senna squirmed in his chair and stared at the floor.

"Señor Melberg, I didn't want to tell you this. I wanted to have it all knocked out before I speak. But I see Cervantes. Guero took me there last night."

Melberg sat up straight in his chair.

"Cut the crap, Senna. You haven't seen him and you know it. You want that reward money so bad you'd make up anything. I don't want to talk to you again until you have something solid. Now beat it."

The boxer never raised his eyes from the floor. He muttered an *adios* and shuffled out the door.

But he came back three days later, wanting to talk about the reward again. Melberg sent him away for an hour, telling him he was busy. Then he called Lavin and asked him to come by the embassy. He wanted him to meet the Cisco Kid, maybe talk some sense into him. From what Melberg had heard, Lavin had a way with his fists. He ought to be a good match for the Cisco Kid.

One thing about Cisco, he was always on time, probably because he could smell currency. Anyway, Cisco came back in exactly an hour, and Lavin was waiting for him. The police officer escorted the Kid to his own office at the municipal building.

"Now, what's this about seeing Cervantes?" Lavin said in Spanish, once they were alone in a room with no windows. Lavin was bigger than Cisco, who undoubtedly was in the lightweight class, if he actually was a boxer. Lavin had his doubts. More likely, he was just a thug who did more street brawling than anything else.

"I see him. Five nights ago."

"Where?"

"A house. West of the city. It takes an hour by car."

"What town?"

"I told Señor Melberg. It is hard for me to say. Starts with a 't.' Only he's not in the town. The house, it is outside the town."

"What does he look like?"

"Cervantes? He is as tall as me, but weighs more. Brown eyes, black hair. I don't know. I am not good at these things."

"Any scars or distinguishing marks?"

"I am not sure. I never looked at him too good."

Lavin jerked the Cisco Kid out of his chair, grabbing him by the front of his shirt and slamming his back against a concrete block wall. The chair crashed on its side.

"Look, Cisco. This is the way it is. You haven't seen Cervantes. You know something, but you haven't seen Cervantes. All I want to hear is what you know. Not anything you think. Just what you know."

The policeman loosened his grip and took a step back, then drew his service revolver. Cisco crumbled to a heap on the floor.

"You're not going to talk to Señor Melberg any more. You're going to talk to me. No more talk about the reward money. Not a word. I'll personally work you over if you try it again. I don't care if you bring us Cervantes on a sterling-silver platter, I don't want to hear another word out of your mouth about the reward. You got it?"

Cisco sniffed and struggled to his feet. He stared at the floor.

"Yes, *señor*. It is as you say. No more about the reward. But you must believe me. I have seen this man."

"Then take me there."

"Señor, there is no way."

Lavin heaved a punch at Cisco's jaw, and the boxer collapsed on the overturned chair. The policeman grabbed him by the shoulders, shoved him against the wall and punched him in his belly. It was hard with muscle. Maybe he really was a boxer.

Cisco doubled over and moaned.

"No more, *señor*," he said. "No more."

"Then talk. And quit the bullshit."

Cisco righted the chair and fell heavily into it. He rubbed his jaw and grimaced.

"Please, *señor*. I am a boxer. I cannot go into the ring already beaten up."

"You see this gun, Kid? You're going to feel some cold steel on that skull of yours if you don't start talking sense."

"Okay, *señor*. The truth. I tell only the truth and nothing else. I have not seen him. It is a lie. But that is the one lie I tell. The rest is true. About Guero, about Cervantes being in that town with a `t.' It is true. I swear on the Virgin. It is true."

Lavin sat down, his revolver still in his hand. He spoke in Spanish.

"Now, look, Kid. I can't even wipe my ass with that piece of information. It isn't worth the price of a beer. You get what I mean? You want money? Well, earn it. You make yourself stick to this Guero like a leech. Like a blood-sucking leech. You suck everything out of him you can.

"You go to Tlanepantla and you drift around. Sniff all over the place. And you call me every day. You got it? Every day. You don't do that, Kid, I don't ever want to see your ugly face again."

The Kid rubbed his belly, his face pinched up in pain.

"It is as you say, Señor Lavin. I will help. That is what I will do. I will go to Guero, and we'll drink beers. I'll go to the town, and I'll ask questions. It will be as you say."

"And you're going to pay the money back to Señor Melberg. All of it. The gravy train is off the tracks."

"My wife, she'll send me money any day. I'll pay back."

"You don't, Kid, and I'll hunt you down and put a bullet in that thick head of yours."

Chapter 28
1956

Alfredo Cervantes parked the Chevrolet on a strip of grass beside the gas station in Guadalajara. All the place had was a little hut, tin siding and roof, open at the front, and a single pump. A customer could drive up on the patch of weeds beside the pump and fill up a tank.

Alfredo didn't need gas. He had other things on his mind. He got out of the red sedan and closed the door gently. It was a brand new model, just in from Texas. Alfredo liked to take the new cars for himself, drive them awhile, then put them on the market. Sometimes he could get American dollars for the nicest ones. That was why he treated them like uncooked eggs—nice and gentle.

He'd been running Ruben's motor pool for four years. Still hated it. Still wanted his own operation. But El Viejo was still on his trail and Ruben had done what he had said. The cops left Alfredo alone. The only time he heard from the Guadalajara officers was when the heat was getting too hot. Then Alfredo would head to the border to take care of a job.

Sometimes he went to Mexico City, to a horse farm just outside of town at Tlanepantla. They raised quarter horses there, the general and his men. The general's name was Manuel; that's all Alfredo knew. But he called him general. The other *hombres* there were in the military, too, big *honchos* strutting around the place like roosters. Alfredo didn't like any of them, but he put up with them because Guero told him there was no way in hell anyone could find him there.

Alfredo had been hitting the weed all morning and he wanted more. He was out of cash. He'd have to sell the red Chevrolet unless he could come by some pesos. Before he could walk up to the hut, the proprietor strode out to greet him.

"Alfredo! Amigo," said the proprietor. His name was Martin Del Campo, and he had once been a regular at Alfredo's cockfights. Martin hadn't seen Alfredo in a couple of years and was glad of it. He'd heard his one-time *compadre* was running from the law. Besides, Martin owed him 200 pesos from the last cockfight Alfredo officiated.

Martin studied Alfredo suspiciously. His visitor was wearing a gun around his waist. Alfredo didn't used to wear a gun.

"You need gas?" he asked, looking at the pump.

"Forget gas," Alfredo barked. "Look at that car. You think a man who drives a car like that buys gas at a dump like this?"

He spoke slowly and his voice was deeper than Martin remembered. Years of smoking that stuff had changed Alfredo. The gas station owner took a step back and looked down. Alfredo advanced on Martin, his hand on the gun handle.

"I come to collect," he said. "Four hundred pesos. Bills. In my hand. Now."

"I only got 300 in the cash drawer," Martin said.

Alfredo pulled out the gun and pointed it at Martin's head. "Show me."

Martin had a cigar box under a cloth on a shelf at the back of the shed. He gave all 300 pesos to Alfredo.

"This'll do for now. I'll be back for the rest."

"But I only owe 200 pesos. Isn't that enough?"

"I'll be back."

Alfredo pocketed the cash, reholstered his gun and drove off in the Chevrolet, heading toward Zapopan. There was a place up there he liked to go, Casa Gato. He would hire two or three *putas* to spend the night with him. La Casa would supply the reefer. Alfredo was too stoned to go looking for his own.

***

The narrow street in Guadalajara where the vendors set up the daily market was jammed with people—mostly peasant women buying food. As the tall American passed by, they stopped haggling over prices and stared. Mac McDonald didn't even notice he was the center of attention. He was agog at the food that had been laid out for sale.

There was barbecued chicken, huge hunks of it, piled up in display boxes. Flies hovered around the meat, but the vendors ignored them. There was pan-cooked cactus and uncooked cactus—Mac had heard it was quite good. Tasted like green beans. He made a mental note to try it sometime.

He decided to stick with fresh fruit. He bought a bunch of bananas, two grapefruits and a bottle of hot soda pop. He had crackers and jerky back at the tourist court. That should hold him for a couple of days. His wife would be happy if he lost a few pounds. She'd been after him to lose that paunch of his.

There wasn't a cloud to be seen as the noonday sun warmed the city. For early March, the weather was cool and dry, a welcome change from the damp cold of Duval County. Mac stayed close to the buildings that lined the passageways they called streets. They were too narrow for cars, and it was just as well. The people were too poor for cars.

There were cars, however, at the tourist court. Mac's was parked just outside his two-bedroom unit. It had taken him two days of hard driving to make it to Guadalajara from Benavides. For most men in their mid-60s, it would have been grueling. But

Mac was on a mission. And when he was on a mission, his energy had no boundaries.

Jake had asked him to make the trip after Johnny started having problems with his heart. No more trips to Mexico, the doctors had told the Ranger. It was just as well. Johnny had just been made captain of Company A, and that meant more paperwork. Still, Mac thought, for a man of 44, Johnny seemed too young to be slowing down.

Mac had already met with the former chief of police in Guadalajara. The fellow was a friend of Lavin's, and Lavin had sworn he was honest.

The ex-chief had told Mac that he knew Cervantes personally and that he was a dangerous man. Cervantes always carried a gun and would shoot with the slightest provocation. Some officers on his force were protecting Cervantes—the ex-chief was sure of it—but he was powerless to do anything about it. It was the ex-chief's belief that Cervantes' stock with the Guadalajara police was now pretty low.

When Mac returned to his room at the California Courts, he spread his lunch on the tiny table next to the bed. He had just popped the cap on the soda bottle when there was a knock at the door. It was the ex-chief and another man Mac had never seen.

The other man, a former officer named Antonio, spoke better English than the ex-chief. Mac understood some Spanish, so they hopscotched their way through a conversation.

Antonio said he knew Cervantes and knew people all over Guadalajara. He was certain he could track the killer and haul him to the border. He'd be glad to collar Cervantes, Antonio said, because he had killed one of his friends. He'd need only 600 pesos a month to do the job.

Mac said he needed to ponder the offer and he would have to call the man in Texas to get an okay. He offered the two men crackers and jerky, but they declined and left him to his lunch.

The Texan gnawed on some dried meat and started a letter to Jake. Antonio seemed worth the risk; in fact, he seemed like he was mad enough he might just go ahead and look for Cervantes, pesos or no.

***

The pounding on the door came at 2 A.M. Mac grabbed his revolver from the night table and peaked through the curtains and saw two men.

"Señor McDonald." Mac recognized the voice as Antonio's, and he opened the door. The ex-chief was with him.

"El Tamburero, we have found him," the former officer said. "He is in a whorehouse, in Zapopan."

Mac climbed into his pants, buttoned a shirt, grabbed his revolver and left in his car with the two men.

"How'd you find him?" he asked.

"An informant. He deals in drugs. Made a delivery to a whorehouse in Zapopan. He recognized Tamburero there. Said he's sold to him before."

"When was this?"

"Around midnight. But our man said it looked like Tamburero was too stoned to go anywhere for awhile."

"When we get there, let's take it slow. I don't want to get anybody suspicious. Don't even say his name."

It was 3 A.M. before they got to Casa Gato, a whitewashed two-story building with ornate iron bars around a second-floor balcony. The place was obviously open for business; all the lights were on inside.

Mac motioned for the ex-chief to take the rear. He holstered his revolver and walked through the front door with Antonio. Three drunken *compesinos* were lounging on couches and a half dozen *putas* in various stages of undress were milling about. A record player blasted a Mexican tune, and a pair of dancers careened haphazardly across the floor. Two *señoritas* approached the visitors. One gave Antonio a nod of recognition and gave Mac the once-over. She smiled and brushed up against Antonio, coiling her naked arms around his left arm.

"Who is the tall American?" she asked in Spanish.

"He is looking for a pretty *señor*ita," Antonio said. "A certain one. He saw her on the street this afternoon."

"We have lots of pretty *señoritas*. How about this one?" The woman nodded at the *puta* standing right behind her.

"No," Antonio said. "It must be the pretty one he saw today. No one else."

"Look around," she said to Mac. "Maybe you will see her."

The woman smiled coyly at Antonio and drew him aside. The ex-officer gave a go-ahead to Mac and the Texan embarked on his search. The kitchen was to the rear of the front room, but there was no one in there. He opened the back door, and the ex-chief jumped up from a crouch, tossing a glowing cigarette to the ground. No one had come out the back door, he reported. A search of the upstairs rooms turned up nothing. They were empty.

"*Nada*," Mac said as he returned to the front room to find Antonio drinking a beer. The Texan went back out to his car and waited. It was 10 or 15 minutes before Antonio came out with the ex-chief.

"He was here," Antonio said after he got into the car. "He left about an hour ago."

"Somebody tip him off?"

"Couldn't tell, Señor. I didn't want to ask too much. But she said he was there. He paid for two *putas* and stayed three or four hours. He bought a bag of marijuana from my friend, the informant, before he left."

"Anything else?"

"Just that he's heading north. He has a job to do on the border, and he's heading north."

Mac dropped the two men off at their respective houses, then went to an all-night *cocina* for some good strong Mexican coffee. No use trying to sleep, he reasoned. Sleep would elude him until he figured out what to do next.

***

Alfredo swallowed the last of the mango juice and threw the empty bottle on the floorboard of the red Chevrolet. It was a clear night, and he could see the Pacific gleaming in the moonlight off to the left. He had always liked driving up the coast at night.

It would take him more than a day to make it to the border. Ruben had said to get the job done by week's end. He figured he'd get there by Wednesday morning, sleep all day and start the search by nightfall. There were only a few places in Piedras Negras to look—a few *cantinas* and a couple of whorehouses. The *hombre* would be in one of them because he wouldn't know Alfredo was after him. The *hombre* thought he was getting away with stealing El Diente blind. But Ruben still had perfect vision, and what he saw was the *hombre* dead on the floor. Don't shoot him, he told Alfredo. Stab him through the heart.

Alfredo turned east at Mazatlan. He was taking the long way on purpose so that he could drive across the Sierras as fast as he could. Get the mountain driving over with. If he'd gone as the crow flies, he would have snaked through the mountains for hundreds of miles.

El Salto was halfway between Mazatlan and Durango, and Alfredo knew a *cantina* there, just a piece off the main road. It was about noon when he walked into the place and asked the bartender for a beer. He'd been able to keep the stuff down lately, and he was glad of it. The alcohol eased the way back from the marijuana haze.

The *cantina* was crowded for so early in the day. The piss pail at the corner of the bar already had a sizable deposit in it. Alfredo propped his elbows on the bar and held his head in his hands, his eyes closed.

He was nearly asleep, his head about to drop out of his hands, when he heard a commotion outside. He glanced out the open door of the *cantina* but couldn't see anything. There was some yelling and laughing going on, but Alfredo decided to go back to his nap.

"Señor." The bartender tapped his arm. "Is that your red car out there?"

Alfredo hopped off the stool and wobbled outside. Two *compesinos* were standing on the hood of the red sedan, whooping and hoisting bottles of beer in the air. A third man was in the driver's seat, the door ajar.

Alfredo shook his head violently and staggered backward. He yanked his gun free of the holster and started firing wildly at the *compesinos*. They hopped off the hood and fled around the corner of the *cantina*. The man inside the car dropped to the floorboard. Alfredo didn't notice that he was wearing a uniform when he wedged himself in the door and fired again.

Alfredo emptied the revolver and the man didn't move. He reached inside the car and poked the guy. There was a bullet wound in his temple, and blood covered his jaw. Alfredo dragged him by the feet out of the car, cursing at the blood that smeared the cream-colored upholstery. He'd think about that later. Right now, he had to get out of town.

The bartender was leaning on the doorframe of the *cantina*, looking bored.

"You better hit the road, fast, *hombre*. You just killed the chief of police."

The dead man was lying face down on the rock road, his arms above his head. A pool of blood was forming under his temple as Alfredo stepped over the body and into the driver's seat. The Chevrolet wouldn't start. Shades of Alice, Texas. On the third try, it cranked up. Alfredo didn't stop again, except for gas, until he got to Piedras Negras.

***

A week later, Alfredo was back at El Coyote, the job in Piedras Negras behind him. He'd had to steal a knife from a pawnshop because he had forgotten to take one. Otherwise, everything went down easy. The Chevrolet was parked outside, and two of El Diente's men were working on the bloodstains.

Ruben had not been his usual smiling self since Alfredo arrived. In fact, he didn't say anything when Tamburero walked in the front door. Almost every time he came to El Coyote, Ruben would have the girls in the kitchen make him some food. But not this time. Since El Diente was not in a talkative mood, Alfredo decided to go outside and check on the cleanup job.

The men were scrubbing with wire brushes and a foamy soap. They looked at Alfredo, a distance in their eyes, then returned to their work. They said nothing to him. If their scrubbing didn't work, Alfredo thought, they'd have to yank some seats out of another car.

"Alfredo." Ruben was at the front door, motioning for him to come inside.

They sat at the kitchen benches, and Ruben ordered the cooks to leave. A caldron of stew bubbled on the stove as he talked.

"The *jefetura* came to see me," Ruben said. "It's getting too hot around here, Alfredo."

Alfredo lazily rearranged his body in an erect position.

"I need the car," he said.

"The car is ruined," El Diente said. "It will take my men

days to make it right."

"Then I need another one."

"Someone will drive you to Zapopan."

It was the last time Alfredo saw El Diente.

***

Mac stood beside his car and shook hands with Antonio. It was dawn, two days after the nighttime raid on the whorehouse.

"The apartment is rented for a month," the Texan said. "It's yours and the chief's, if you need it. And you'll get the check for your expenses soon. The man in Texas said he'd mail it today."

Antonio looked up at Mac.

"I need your word on something," Antonio said.

"What?"

"That the man will not be electrocuted. We will be killed. His brothers and friends will find us, and they will kill us."

"Put it out of your head, Antonio. All we want is for the man to talk. Just talk. He won't go to the chair."

"Señor McDonald, I know you are big man in Texas. But can you give me your word?"

"Look, Antonio. You find Cervantes. Bring him back to this motel room, and I'll come get him. No harm will come to him. You have my word."

Mac looked down at the slender officer and shook his hand once more.

"Call me every day," he said. He got into his black Oldsmobile and headed north.

Chapter 29

Eventually, John Ben Shepperd got his way, and Judge Broadfoot fired that "whitewashing" Duval County grand jury. The twelve-man panel, in its final report to the judge, said it didn't care what Diego Heras said, there was no reason to indict any Duval County officials for embezzling money from the school district.

George was scornful of Shepperd's success.

"He doesn't know what he's doing," he said. "I went to law school, got a license to practice, although I never have. He said he's operating under common law authority. We don't have any common law in Texas. We got a Constitution and statutes. If we're a bunch of crooks and if there is any basis for this, the suit should be filed in Travis County. That's where the attorney general has jurisdiction."

Then George went on the radio to deny that he controlled votes or owned a "political empire in Duval County."

"The only empire in this county is an empire of friendship where friends help each other," he said, adding that the new grand jury is "composed entirely of Freedom Party members and appears stacked."

Shepperd retorted that the new grand jury "represents law and order in Duval County for the first time in several decades."

"I have volunteered all of our evidence and all of the facilities of my office for its use in its investigation," he declared.

The new grand jury determined that "Judge Colt is no longer the law in the political empire that George Parr and his father built." They refused to work with Raeburn Norris and began cranking out indictments.

Among the first was an assault charge against George, this time for attacking a San Diego man with a carbine. The victim was Cristobal Ybanez, who said he was sitting on a curb one day, laughing and joking with friends. Ybanez, a member of the Freedom Party, said George drove by, stopped his car and attacked him with the weapon.

Remembering the fiasco that followed the Manuel Marroquin incident, George decided to meet this indictment head-on. He went to the district clerk's office to await the arrest warrant. His friends and followers streamed in and out of the office, pumping his arm and asking how he was doing.

"I'm having a hell of a time getting arrested," he said, that big possum grin on his face.

George's indictment was just the beginning. The grand jury turned out more: R. L. Adame, the county school superintendent, for stealing money from the school districts; D. C. Chapa, the former tax assessor-collector of Benavides schools, for robbing the school treasury; C. T. Stansell, Jr., the former Duval County auditor, for forgery.

Under John Ben Shepperd's guidance, more than 400 indictments were returned, charging George and his associates with falsifying bank records, conspiracy, removing bank records, misappropriating county and school funds, promoting perjury and a legion of other crimes. The grand jury was a regular "sausage mill," said Percy Foreman, whom George eventually hired as a defender.

The indictments resulted in scores of convictions, but no one ever went to jail. R. L. Adame was found guilty of stealing school funds, but the Court of Criminal Appeals overturned it.

The appeals court action not only cleared Adame, it also voided 104 indictments, including one against George for theft of $1,000 from the Benavides School District.

But things didn't stop there. When it became apparent that Judge Broadfoot might appoint Donato Serna to the Duval County auditor's office, the commissioners abolished the office. Broadfoot went ahead and appointed Serna, and the drug store owner spent a year battling in the courts to take the office.

When he did, he found the budget in the red, the road and bridge fund nearly out of money, and the county payroll in disarray. He refused to authorize paychecks to dozens of Parr patriots, saying their positions were either unauthorized or improperly classified in the payroll records.

Maneuvering to gain control of the district judgeship continued. After Woodrow was removed by the Supreme Court, he ran for judge again. It looked like he might get voted back in, so Jake asked the state bar to revoke Woodrow's legal credentials based on the same 12 infractions he had used in the ouster proceedings. In addition, the Freedom Party recruited Mark Heath of Falfurrias, a former law partner of Sam Reams, to run against Woodrow in the primary.

Despite the stigma of being removed from office, Woodrow won the nomination by 443 votes. Jake's campaign to have Woodrow disbarred unnerved George sufficiently that he decided not to back Woodrow in the general election. If Woodrow were cut down again, Shivers would have power to appoint another district judge.

So George recruited A. J. Vale of Starr County to run once again as a write-in candidate. Woodrow denounced Vale and urged the voters to elect him instead so he could be vindicated. The voters obliged, electing Woodrow by more than 2,000 votes.

Afterwards, George's use of A. J. Vale would cost him more dearly than he counted on. Woodrow, viewing Vale's candidacy as an outright betrayal by George, made peace with Jake and his allies. As proof of his new allegiance, Woodrow reappointed Donato as the county auditor.

Then he did what Jake and the Freedom Party had been battling to have done all along. He appointed an independent grand jury commission, which in turn appointed grand juries that weren't aligned with George. The indictments against George and his friends continued, and Woodrow transferred the cases to other counties for trial.

If the loss of the district judgeship were not bad enough, George suffered another serious setback when he was forced to dispose of his two banks. The Federal Deposit Insurance Corporation took a dim view of the disappearance of records at the Texas State Bank and the San Diego State Bank during IRS agent Ninedorf's investigation. The FDIC told George it would no longer insure deposits at the banks so long as he owned them. So in July 1954, he sold both institutions.

The case of the disappearing bank records was to prove one of the most costly of all events for George. Because microfilm for the years 1949, 1950, 1951 and 1952 were lost, the Internal Revenue agents turned their attention to bank records from earlier years. For the year 1945, they uncovered evidence that George had bought the 55,000-acre Dobie Ranch with the help of Duval County tax revenues.

With the approval of the county commissioners, George had helped himself to $500,000 from the Duval road construction fund. With the half million dollars, he purchased the Dobie Ranch. Two years later, he "borrowed" $172,000 from Duval County to pay his income taxes.

Over the next few years, George spent a great deal of time at the Dobie Ranch. He held extravagant hunting parties for well-known politicians and local officials, and spent more time there than he did at his *hacienda* in San Diego.

By the time IRS agents discovered the transactions, Sammy Burris had taken over Raeburn Norris's job as district attorney. He teamed up with an assistant attorney general, Sydney Chandler, and filed suit to recover the Dobie Ranch property. The two prosecutors also sought back rent and all revenues off the ranch land since 1945.

When Dan Tobin, Jr., the Duval County judge, broke with George, it signaled the end of the Duke of Duval's control of the county commissioners. In a last-ditch effort, George offered the commissioners title to the ranch in exchange for release from all claims for rents and revenues off the property. He also asked the court to forgive the $172,000 loan.

After more than a year of legal fisticuffs, George was ordered by District Judge H. D. Barrow to turn over the ranch deed and to pay the county more than $300,000 for rent and oil royalties and $172,000 for the loan to pay his taxes. His ex-wife Thelma Duckworth Parr was ordered to pay her share as well, since she was half owner of the ranch when she and George were married.

The final humiliation of the Dobie Ranch debacle came after George was elected Duval County sheriff in November 1956. His nephew Archer had quit the job to go to law school. It was Jake Floyd who pointed out to Sydney Chandler that since George owed the county money, he could not hold public office.

The county commissioners refused to certify George as the new sheriff. George went to court at least a dozen times over the next three years in a bid to take office, but the most satisfaction he ever got was a Texas Supreme Court ruling saying he was entitled to a hearing. Eventually, George gave up his effort to take office.

In early 1957, George filed for bankruptcy, claiming the various back tax claims against him had given him no other choice. He owed more than $600,000 in income taxes and $32,000 in property taxes and was in debt by nearly $400,000 to various business firms and attorneys. In his bankruptcy petition filed in

Corpus Christi, he listed total debts at $2.1 million and assets of $790,000. He still claimed to own half of the Dobie Ranch.

As a result of the bankruptcy action, George's assets were auctioned off. Sold were the 3,700-acre Hoffman Ranch, George's interest in the Parr-Delaney Oil Co. and his oil and gas leases, which were co-owned with his former wife.

The plunge into bankruptcy was never fully explained, since in 1952, George had listed his net worth at more than $2.5 million. Both his friends and his enemies claimed the Duke of Duval was never actually broke, but had always had cash stashed in several safety deposit boxes.

Bankruptcy was not George's final setback by any means. A few months after he was indicted for tax evasion, a Houston federal grand jury indicted him for mail fraud. Also indicted were D. C. Chapa, the former tax collector of the Benavides school district; Tom Donald, cashier of the liquidated Texas State Bank in Alice; Jesus Garza, Santiago Garcia, Octavio Saenz, Jesus Oliveira, O. P. Carrillo and Oscar Carrillo, Sr., all trustees or officers of the school district.

The mail fraud case, presented by the postal inspectors, involved people who lived outside of Duval County and who were mailed tax notices on property they owned in the Benavides school district. Federal prosecutors offered many examples of what happened.

A major oil company paid $85,000 in taxes by check. The check was canceled and a receipt issued the company. This tax revenue was never shown in the district's annual report to the Texas Education Agency. The money was never deposited into the school district bank account. Apparently, it was divided up among several people. Hundreds of thousands of dollars annually disappeared in this fashion.

George's attorney, Percy Foreman, as his opening act of the trial, diverted the jury's attention to Johnny Benny Shepperd, as he called him. The state attorney general, Foreman shouted belligerently, wasn't interested in a trial. He was interested in "political persecution."

Shepperd's investigators, Foreman said, had made their headquarters in Jake Floyd's office and Jake was nothing more than the George Parr of the Freedom Party. In the heat of his tirade, Foreman turned to U.S. Attorney Malcolm Wilkey and charged, "Jake Floyd's offices have been headquarters for this prosecution."

Prosecutors called Diego Heras to testify, and he told the court everything he had told Jake Floyd in their first meeting years earlier. Foreman seized every opportunity to discredit Heras.

He called a former school district secretary, who said she caught Heras escaping through a window at the district office when she went there one night to investigate a light. The next day, a book containing school board minutes was missing.

The former secretary said Heras was a known drinker, both on and off the job. She had found empty liquor bottles in filing cabinets and wastebaskets. One week he would be broke and the next week loaded, she said.

"Loaded?" Foreman asked.

"Both ways," she said. "Sometimes with money, sometimes with whiskey."

After 21 days of testimony, the jury went behind closed doors to deliberate. Six days later, they emerged and said they were deadlocked on 161 counts. As it turned out, one juror had stood in the way of conviction for George and his friends.

There was another trial and a second hung jury. A third attempt ended in a mistrial when it was discovered that one of the jurors lived outside the Southern District of Texas.

In the fourth trial, Foreman attempted again to divert attention from the charges. He called U.S. Attorney Wilkey as a witness.

"Did you discuss this case with Mr. Brownell?" Foreman asked, referring to the U.S. Attorney General.

"Yes, I did."

"Did Mr. Brownell tell you that this was a good way to get even with Lyndon Johnson because Mr. Parr helped elect him?"

"Mr. Johnson's name was never mentioned."

"Didn't this prosecution originate with Allan Shivers through Herbert Brownell—Shivers to Brownell to you?"

"This investigation originated under my predecessor, the honorable Brian S. Odem, who was appointed by Harry Truman," Wilkey said. "I've never met Governor Shivers but one time, having been introduced to him while I was in Austin last New Year's Day to see Will Wilson sworn in as attorney general (of Texas)."

On July 17, 1957, the jury returned guilty verdicts against George Parr and all the other defendants, and the following sentences were set:

George Parr: 10 years and a $20,000 fine. George was convicted on 19 counts of mail fraud and one count of conspiracy.

D.C. Chapa: 5 years.

Tom Donald: 4 years.

Oscar Carrillo: 4 years.

Octavio Saenz: 3 years, suspended.

Jesus Oliveira, 2 years, suspended, $7,000 fine.

O.P. Carrillo: 2 years, suspended.

The defendants appealed, remaining free during the process. Three years later, the U.S. Supreme Court reversed the convictions of George and the others. The court said they were guilty of "bad and brazen" behavior, but that they had to use the mails to conduct business. And such usage, the court said, could not be construed as an unlawful conspiracy.

In March 1963, Sammy Burris dismissed the last six state charges against George. The same day, U.S. Attorney General Robert Kennedy dismissed the income tax evasion indictments against the Duke of Duval. Later that same year, George's bankruptcy case was settled, with the government settling its tax claims for 10 cents on the dollar.

***

Alfredo Cervantes slumped in a pile on the concrete floor of a cell at El Castillo Negro, the Black Castle of Mexico City. The sour smell reminded him of the *palenque*s. What he wouldn't give to be at a cockfight now instead of in this dungeon. If he ever got out of this place, Alfredo thought, he would go back to the fights. He was tired. Too much traveling. He wanted a nice little place in Tepatitlan and his own *palenque*. It would be like the good old days, before he went to Texas.

There were a half dozen other men in the tiny space with him. The cell housed but two bunks and a single pail to piss in. Alfredo wished the guard would empty it. It stank bad.

This was his second day at Castillo Negro, his fourth day under arrest. The federal police who surrounded the house at Tepatitlan roughed him up only a little. His shoulder was sore, and so were his ribs. It could have been worse. They told him he should never have killed that officer in El Salto. They didn't even mention El Viejo.

He thought he was going to jail in Guadalajara. But without explanation, the police escorted him on a train and brought him to Mexico City. The two uniformed men who escorted him said they'd been looking for him for at least three years, ever since the American diplomats came to the Mexican government. There was a man in Texas, they said, who wanted him brought back alive.

"They say you were a hired killer," one of the officers said.

"I got hired, but I didn't get paid," Alfredo said.

"They want you back in Texas," the officer said.

"No way I'm going. They got that chair in Texas. The electric one. No way I'm going."

"They say he just wants you to talk. Then he'll send you back."

"I'm not going."

"You forget, you're a prisoner. You go to Texas if we say so."

Alfredo didn't say anything. He'd been around policemen enough to know when to shut up.

As he sprawled on the cold, damp floor, he reflected on the past few years. Things had not been so good for Alfredo since he had shot that policeman in El Salto. El Diente had been good for his word, and then the protection dried up. Things weren't so good after that.

He'd heard El Duque was having trouble of his own. Alfredo couldn't say he was surprised at all at the way things had turned out. He should have known it when Mario told him about the job. He never liked Mario.

***

Jake Floyd wasn't smiling, though he had cause to celebrate. He'd just telephoned Edith and told her the news. Alfredo Cervantes was behind bars.

Edith was excited—as excited as she ever got these days. The doctor had explained to Jake that the shock treatments affected different people in different ways. Some folks, he said, lose all or part of their memory. Thankfully, Edith had lost the part of her memory that had tortured her for years.

She had that lingering picture in her mind of Buddy, her only son, lying there in his own blood. She'd tried to save him; screamed for Dr. Wyche to come and send Buddy's wounded body to the hospital. But she hadn't saved him. Buddy had died right there in front of her. The memories drove her into a depression so severe that drastic action was called for. Electroconvulsive therapy, the doctor called it.

Her improvement was gradual, and by June of 1960, Edith was almost her former self. For a time, when things were really bad, Jake feared he would lose her. It was a surprise to him, because he had always thought of her as being strong as he was. She had that potent Baptist blood flowing in her veins.

As it turned out, her Baptist faith, boosted by the shock treatments, revived her inner steel and Jake returned his attention to getting Cervantes back to Texas. He was prepared for another long battle. Mexico didn't usually extradite its citizens to the United States for trial, especially those who could face the electric chair for their crime.

The door to Jake's office opened, and Clarence Perkins walked in. A couple of reporters were here and they wanted to see him, Clarence said.

James Rowe from the Corpus Christi newspaper, a reporter from the *Houston Press* and a fellow representing the *San Antonio Enterprise* came in and took seats. They had heard about Cervantes' capture, and they wanted details.

"The information I have is that Cervantes was staying with friends in a little village near Guadalajara. The Mexican police surrounded the house where he was staying and arrested him. He is being sent to Mexico City and we hope to extradite him from there.

"My hope is that they will extradite him on the basis of our new, more friendly relationship with Mexico, as reflected in the visits between President Eisenhower and Senator Lyndon Johnson with the President of Mexico.

"All I desire is to bring this man back to justice and to punish the people responsible for his act. There are others involved.

"The silence of some of these people and their refusal to cooperate makes me feel very strongly that I know who they are."

Jake told the reporters he had spent more than $10,000 in

his search for Cervantes, paying for expeditions by more than one Texas Ranger into the mountains of Jalisco. It was his understanding, he said, that Cervantes had been paid only $30 for killing his son.

The San Antonio reporter took down every word, and then studied the lawyer behind the desk. He saw no expression of satisfaction, no exuberance in Jake's eyes. Instead, he saw weariness, an exhaustion that 12 years of crusading will do to a man. But the reporter also saw an iron determination. He'd seen that look before; it seemed a permanent fixture in Jake Floyd's countenance.

As the reporters left the office, the San Antonio fellow lagged behind.

"Mr. Floyd, can I ask you something off the record?"

The lawyer nodded. He stood at the door of the office, the reporter a pace away.

"Why didn't you just hire somebody to kill Cervantes?"

Jake betrayed a faint smile and looked at the reporter square in the eye. He spoke slowly.

"I thought about it many times. It would have been much easier than what we've done the past eight years. And I could have done it cheap. Hired killers in Mexico don't make much money.

"But if I'd hired Cervantes killed, where do I stop? If I hire a man killed, what's the difference between me and the man who hired my son killed?"

The reporter thanked Jake for the interview, shook his hand and left. Jake went back to his desk and noticed it was only 4 o'clock. He decided to knock off early and get out to the farm before Raul's wife started making those wonderful tortillas. Maybe, just once, she'd let them take a few in the truck on their way out to the pasture.

He didn't feel like taking a nap today, he thought as he put on his hat and left the office. No, some fresh tortillas, a cool drink of water and a ride through the pasture would be a perfect end to a long-awaited day. He got behind the wheel of his car and pointed it south toward the farm. The sun was still bright, high in the sky, as he drove the narrow farm-to-market road. He could taste the warm goodness of the tortillas already.

Epilogue

I saw Jake Floyd many times in the years after Alfredo Cervantes was captured. I saw George Parr, too. Things hadn't gone too well for either of them. You could tell just by looking at their faces. I rarely saw that possum grin on George's lips; the events of the 1950s had left him battle-scarred and worn. As for Jake, he never lost that grim countenance.

From the day in June 1960 when Alfredo Cervantes was captured, Jake never ceased his campaign to link George to Buddy's murder. He massaged the diplomatic channels relentlessly in an attempt to extradite Cervantes for trial in Texas. The State Department badgered Mexican authorities for the release, but on December 7, 1961, Mexico formally denied extradition.

Undaunted, Jake sought to have his son's killer returned to Texas for questioning or to arrange a trade of a prisoner Mexico wanted. But Mexico would not budge. There was little historical precedent for extradition, and Cervantes faced the death penalty in Texas. In Mexico, there is no death penalty, but there is no parole, either. Once sentenced to a prison term, a convict serves it to completion in the dungeons of the Mexican prison system.

Around the time Cervantes was arrested, Lyndon Johnson was nominated for the vice presidency of the United States. He had tried for the presidential nomination but was defeated at the Democratic National Convention by John F. Kennedy.

When Johnson became vice president, Sammy Burris paid a

call on one of his top aides in Washington. Burris told Johnson's man it would behoove the vice president politically—especially in Texas—to put his weight behind the extradition effort. Burris left Washington with assurances that something would be done. Despite the promises, Johnson's office never cooperated in the extradition campaign.

Cervantes' trial began in October 1961 in Mexico City. Proceedings, unlike those in courts in the United States, were not held on a daily basis. The case dragged on intermittently for three years. Before it came to its dramatic conclusion, before Jake was summoned to Mexico City to testify, he became gravely ill. The diagnosis: colon cancer.

He lingered with the illness for more than a year, although he never admitted to anyone, not even Edith, that he had a terminal condition. By the time President Kennedy was assassinated in Dallas in November 1963, he had been in and out of a Houston hospital. If Kennedy's murder turned the world upside down, it also created a tantalizing, mysterious twist to the Floyd case.

Six days after Lee Harvey Oswald was arrested for the assassination of the president, the manager of radio station KOPY in Alice called the FBI with a bizarre tale. He claimed that Oswald had visited the station in search of a job on October 4, 1963. Federal investigators had traced Oswald's steps in the weeks preceding the assassination and knew he had spent the latter part of September and early October in Mexico City. He had driven from there to Dallas, and it was conceivable his journey had taken him through Alice, Texas.

The radio station manager, Sonny Stewart, said Oswald had been wearing blue jeans and a pullover shirt. "He was a little guy. He looked like a college kid," Stewart said. He said Oswald had told him he was interested in getting into radio, but he had no experience. When Stewart told him there were no opportunities at KOPY, Oswald asked about possibilities in stations in Pleasanton.

This last bit of information was of particular interest to investigators, because President Kennedy had made a brief appearance in Pleasanton, near San Antonio, the day before he was killed in Dallas.

Stewart said Oswald was traveling with a woman and a child, but they had stayed in the car. When Stewart asked Oswald to bring them inside, he declined, saying she spoke no English. In investigating Stewart's story, the FBI further learned that Oswald had purchased clothing in a store in Laredo a few days before he appeared in Alice.

After this odd piece of information was reported in the press, the U.S. Justice Department took a sudden and renewed interest in the Alfredo Cervantes extradition case. I was never able to trace a link between the two events, but I am convinced they were related. How else would you explain the fact that a few weeks after Sonny Stewart's story was printed in the papers, Bobby Kennedy sent an assistant United States Attorney General to the hospital in Houston to talk to Jake?

Until that day, Jake had been able to get only perfunctory recognition and assistance from the federal government. He had almost become accustomed to it. By the time the Assistant Attorney Aeneral arrived at the hospital in February 1964, Jake was in a coma. He never regained consciousness. On February 26, 1964, Jake Floyd died in that Houston hospital. He was buried in the Masonic cemetery in Alice, next to Buddy.

The Justice Department's sudden interest in the extradition case failed to bring about any results. Cervantes' trial kicked into full and final gear the summer after Jake's death. Edith flew with Sammy Burris to Mexico City to testify. Sammy brought the Colt .38 murder weapon and took along a ballistics expert and fingerprint expert from the Texas Department of Public Safety.

Unlike trials in the American judicial system, Mexican trials do not allow for cross-examination of witnesses. Edith's testimony was brief. Her memory of the night of September 8, 1952, had been dimmed by the shock treatments. Cervantes listened, expressionless, as the interpreter translated her testimony.

The most exciting thing that happened during the trial was that Nago Alaniz was spotted in the hotel where Edith and Sammy were staying.

"He was there the whole time, spying on us," she told me when she returned.

Finally, on November 28, 1964, six months after testimony concluded, Mexican federal judge Eduardo Langle found Cervantes guilty of Buddy Floyd's murder. The sentence was 30 years in a Mexican prison. In this case as in all others in Mexico, there would be no parole. Cervantes was 52 years old.

I never learned what happened to Alfredo Cervantes. I tried to track him down once, but finding a prisoner in the Mexican penal system proved as difficult as tracking him down in the mountains of Jalisco. Mexican prisons are not known for championing prisoner civil rights or providing good living conditions. And I can only presume that after a lifetime of abusing drugs, Cervantes died before his sentence ran out.

As for George, like I said, things didn't go well for him, either. There were a few flickers of hope for his regime in the resuming few years. The Freedom Party, which controlled Duval County in the late 1950s, went down in final defeat in 1960 when Parr's candidates swept county elections. Donato Serna gave up politics and returned to his drugstore.

The 1960s were peaceful in Duval. George reassumed his throne as El Patrón, and he stayed there unchallenged until 1974. That's when all hell broke loose again. In March of that year, George was convicted for the second time of failing to pay taxes on $381,428.32 in income. The sentence was five years in prison and $14,000 in fines.

His nephew Archer was convicted the same year of lying to

a grand jury about a $121,500 legal fee he claimed to have collected from the Duval Conservation and Reclamation District. His sentence was 10 years in prison at Ft. Leavenworth, a $60,000 fine and court costs. During his trial, testimony showed that the Internal Revenue Service investigation against Archer had been initiated by executive order of President Richard Nixon.

By this time, George was 73, clearly no longer the virile man he once had been. Balding and aging badly, he was in poor health, a fact that was not lost on D. C. Chapa and his sons, O. P. and Oscar Carrillo. Longtime allies of El Patrón, they sensed a power vacuum in the making and they primed themselves to fill the void. Rancher and oilman Clinton Manges, who owned vast land holdings in Duval County, was their covert backer.

Things got tense at the Duval County courthouse again, and occasionally, George and his men showed up with guns and the Carrillos turned out with an arsenal of their own. George might have mentioned that there were some people who needed killing, like O. P. Carrillo and Clinton Manges, but there was never any shooting.

The threats and the gun-carrying got back to the judge in George's income tax case. He called a hearing for March 31, 1975, in Corpus Christi. It looked as though George's appeal bond was about to be revoked. Nago Alaniz finally hit the big time. He represented George in that hearing, but George didn't show up.

"This is so unlike Mr. Parr," Nago told the judge. "The only reason he would not show up is because he is dead. That's how strongly I feel about it."

Nago was right. George's body was found the next day in a pasture at Los Horcones. He was slumped behind the wheel of his Chrysler, the engine still running, a bullet in his head and a .45 Colt revolver in his hand.

It was April Fools Day, and George Parr had gotten the last laugh.

CREATIVE DESTRUCTION:
transformation in the music industry

Copyright © 2004 by Gary Graham, Glenn Hardaker, Gerard Lewis, Mark Lewis
All rights reserved

No part of this book may be reproduced, in any form, without written permission from the publisher.

Published in the United Kingdom by BeyondLabels,
2004-08-02
Distributed by Lightening Source Ltd, United Kingdom.

Creative Destruction

edited by: Gary Graham

Includes Bibliographical references.

ISBN 1-905031-00-9

The BeyondLabels Press was established in 2004 as a not-for-profit alternative to the large, commercial publishing houses currently dominating the book publishing industry. The BeyondLabels Press operates in the public interest rather than for private gain, and is committed to publishing, in innovative ways, works of educational, cultural, and community value that are often deemed insufficiently profitable.

Professor Glenn Hardaker BeyondLabels Press
Learning & Teaching Innovation Unit (LTIU), University of Huddersfield, Queensgate, Huddersfield, HD1 3DH. info@beyondlabels.org, www.beyondlabels.org

Printed in the United Kingdom

Cover Design: Rob Chiu
Photography (inside pages): Andreas Johnson
Design (inside pages): Jane Gaffikin

In framing an ideal we may assume what we wish but should avoid impossibilities

ARISTOTLE

Dedicated to Diane Louise Armstrong
1973 - 2003
Love and Respect

FORWARD

The title of the book, "Creative Destruction", is of course a play on the views of the Austrian economist Joseph Schumpeter who argued that a healthy economy is one which is constantly being disrupted by technological innovation. In a similar vein, I share this view that a healthy music industry, for artists, record companies and consumers alike, will emerge from the current technological disruption it is currently experiencing. It reflects the revolutionary pace of change being experienced by the music industry as it struggles to get to grips with digitalisation. Its specific focus is with the electronic music sub-genre, which is really at the forefront of technology/music intersection. Creative Destruction takes you on a journey that starts with house in Chicago and techno in Detroit in the early 1980s and is completed with pan-European trance at the beginning of the twenty first century. The electronic music sub-genre as the book emphasises is a unique style with global appeal, and its high level of imagination, innovation and creativity is treated sensitively. This book really does prepare one for the electronic ocean of music in the twenty-first century. As the world becomes increasingly an information ocean, then music has become immersive with listeners floating in that ocean and musicians becoming very much like virtual travellers. The message is clear from Creative Destruction, that the aesthetic rather than the commodity will drive music in the digital age, and that for every majority there will always be a minority offering an alternative.

FORWARD
NIGEL MURLIS, DREAM TEMPLE RECORDS, LONDON, 2004

PREFACE

Creative Destruction resulted out of our need to make some kind of sense of the music industry and its relationship with technology. The title reflects our view that the relationship between music and technology is very much reciprocal – that technological progress can lead to a destroying of the creative but out of that destruction can arise creation. All sound – acoustic or electronic, can be manipulated in the digital domain. An information network is permeating our daily life environment and for the music industry the panic is on; immersion is one of the key words of the twenty-first century. Music can no longer be packaged and marketed by the record companies as a linear concept with artificial barriers, neatly separating the different sub-genres – rock, pop, disco etc, now that the artists are creating non-linear forms that know no boundaries. Digital technologies offer unprecedented opportunities for consumers to listen to their music. Wired and electronically connected – both producer and consumer are pushing music away from the commodity back to the aesthetic.

This book grew out of EU funded research exploring the impact of the Internet on the supply and consumption of music throughout Europe. In order to see the full force of this wave of digital change we focussed particularly on electronic music, a sector renowned for being at the forefront of the digital technological/music intersection, and characterised by being the most innovative and creative sector of music over the past twenty years (Toop, 1995, Prendegast, 2002). The project was part of the Leonardo da Vinci programme supporting research that explored the impact that the Internet was having on the rise of "creative", or sometimes termed "cultural industries" - throughout Europe, cultural in terms of both production and consumption. The music industry is deemed by the Leonardo programme to be very much at the cultural, economic and social heart of European civilisation. Research was undertaken at all levels in the music industry – from producer (the artist) to end consumer in four European countries – the UK, Germany, Denmark and Finland. A number of general issues pertaining to the music industry per se were researched and are presented in the book, but specific reference is also made to the electronic music sector throughout Creative Destruction.

In terms of structure Chapter 2 provides a discussion of the evolution of electronic music and the man-machine interaction, and the chapter is organised along the following threads: a retrospective, historical or allegorical thread with musique concrete as the main example, and a futuristic thread epitomised by Karlheinz Stockhausen. The themes merge with the advent of Kraftwerk, in the late 1970s and are traced through to current electronic music, in its plethora of guises. In Chapter 3 a number of style maps are presented to trace the evolution of electronic music from original house and techno blueprints through their fragmentation back to the hybrid – trance. A number of case studies are presented to illustrate some of the main issues and points raised by the authors. Chapter 4 explores the authenticity of electronic music and provides detailed coverage of its role in developing youth cultures and brand building. The focus of Chapter 5 is on the disruptive impact of the Internet on the production and distribution of music from an artist's perspective. Chapter 6 takes the analysis a stage further up the supply chain by considering the impact of the Internet on intermediaries (labels, retailers, wholesalers, distributors and the like). Then attention is turned to the consumer side. The chapter presents the results of research on the legal and illegal consumption of music, both digitally and in the physical sense— in four countries – Finland Germany, the UK and Denmark. Over 1,000 questionnaires were filled out and returned. Chapter 7 presents the main conclusions arising from the work and proposes a business model for the industry.

We owe a special debt of gratitude to Nigel Mirlees at DMT Records for generally sharing his passion for the book. We would also like to thank Dave Murphy at UMIST, for his vision in taking it on further and showing us how to do so; Janet Langer for making the introductions and Judy Jones for her painstaking and sensitive comments that have added a touch of class; and those, too many to mention, who have contributed to the book in many ways – both large and small. We gratefully acknowledge the assistance of the Leonardo office at the EU, for all their support and for allowing us to make this happen. Lastly our thanks go to all our friends and family for helping us follow this path. We hope that in Creative Destruction, you find an interesting and thought provoking work; **that still in the underground one doesn't find class, barriers, categories, stereotypes just heart and soul!** (NB meaning of the last phrase unclear: does the underground refer to the cultural phenomenon – as in alternative culture - or the underlying meanings in the book??)

PREFACE
GLENN HARDAKER

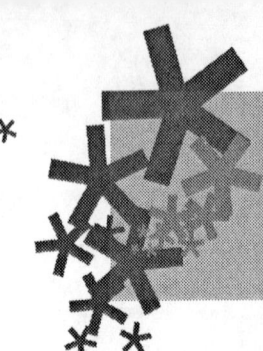

CONTENTS

Forward 5
Preface 6
Contents 8

Chapters

1 Music and Technology 10

2 History and Origins of Electronic Music 30

3 Electronic Music: Styles and Maps 54

4 Brands and Brand Building in the Music Industry .. 74

5 The Internet and Artists 90

6 Disrupting Supply Chain Intermediaries 116

7 Disrupting Supply Chain Consumers 144

8 Windows into the Future 164

Endnotes 172
References 176

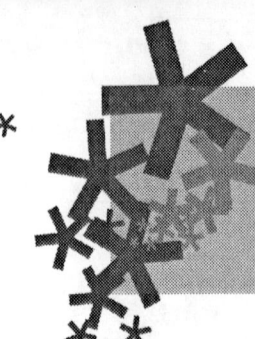

MUSIC AND TECHNOLOGY

The music sector is undergoing a revolutionary change through the incorporation of the Internet into the supply chain. Music plays an important and sometimes overlooked part in the transformation of communication and distribution channels. With a global market volume exceeding £25 billion, music is one of the primary entertainment goods in its own right (Kretschmer et.al., 2001). Since music is easily personalised and transmitted, it also permeates many other services across cultural borders, anticipating social and economic trends. This book presents one of the first detailed empirical studies on the impact of Internet technologies on a specific sector of the music industry – electronic music. Drawing on more than 500 interviews conducted between 2001 and 2003 with multinational and independent music companies in 10 markets, it identifies and evaluates the strategies of the major players, current business models, future scenarios and regulatory responses to the online distribution of music files.

Technologies for producing and reproducing sounds and images have heavily influenced the way in which music has been composed, communicated and consumed right from the twentieth into the twenty-first century, and this has been central to the development of a global music industry. The aim of this chapter is not to assess the impact that technology is having on music, given that technology is an external phenomenon exerting an influence on some pure and abstract form of expression known as music; but to suggest that musical meanings and practices at any one time cannot be separated from their realisation in and through particular technologies, and the way in which specific groups and individuals have struggled to exert control over the use and definition of these technologies. This chapter is, therefore, a deliberate attempt to avoid the sharp division which has polarised recent discussions between pessimistic "techno-phobes" who condemn technology for contaminating the authentic character of human expression and corrupting music skills, and optimistic "techno-philes" who have celebrated the "appropriation" of technology in the act of consuming commodities.

CREATIVE DESTRUCTION:
transformation in the music industry

Music Industry in a Spin

Five big record companies have dominated the music industry over the last decade. These are Universal Music ($5.97bn sales revenue, 10,800 employees), Sony ($5.303bn, 9,000), Warner Music ($4.3bn, 5,000), EMI ($3.83bn, 9,270) and BMG ($3.29bn, 4,600). The implications of online distribution, increased piracy and a more demanding and discerning customer base are quite evident. EMI has cut its workforce by 1,900 staff in the period 2001 to 2003. Warner Music is about to cut its workforce by 1,000 (Reece, 2004). Meanwhile, according to Reece, Universal is in the process of cutting its staff numbers down by 20% to 10,800 worldwide. Furthermore, the planned merger between Sony and Bertelsman Music Group will bring further job losses in the industry.

Figure 1.1 shows the tremendous pressure that declining global sales is placing on the music industry to restructure itself. From 1998 to 2003 global sales have fallen from 37$bn (peaking in 1999 at 39$bn) to 30$bn in 2003.

$bn (variable)

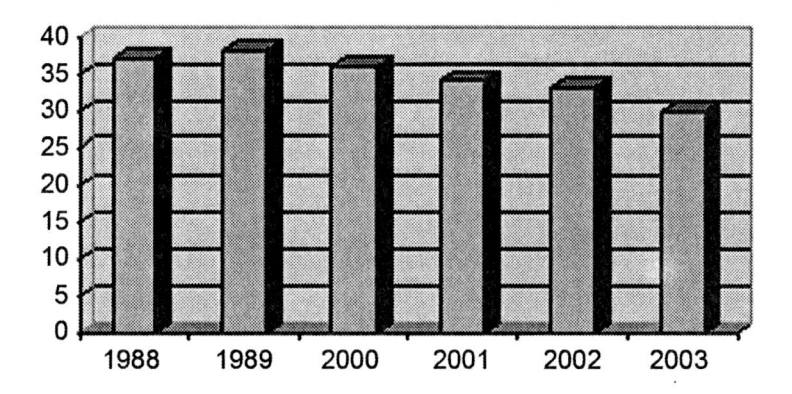

Figure 1.1 Global music sales
(Source: IFPI, 2004)[1].

MUSIC AND TECHNOLOGY

The UK industry has displayed a similar trend to that of global sales in recent years (shown in figure 1.2), reflecting, in part, the problem of piracy. But Sarah Simon, a media analyst at Morgan Stanley, recently said:

"We calculate that nearly half the decline in the global music market is related to the problems other than downloading and physical piracy. While physical and online piracy clearly account for a large percentage of the decline in the global music sales, we also see a fundamental decline with consumers less prepared to spend money on music".

(2004, p. 40)[2].

£m

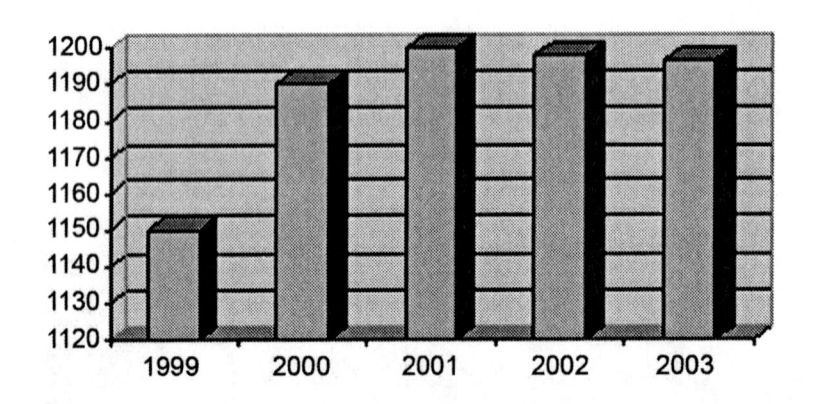

Figure 1.2 UK Music sales
(Source BPI, 2004, p. 40)[3].

The International Federation of the Phonographic Industry (IFPI) announced in March 2004 its intention to follow the example of the US and prosecute individuals in Europe and Canada involved in the illegal downloading of digital music files over the Internet. But analysts such as Morgan Stanley (Reece, 2004, p. 40) believe that piracy is not the real threat to the way that the music industry does business, it is more the way that companies are organised internally and the business models they adopt.

Legitimate online distribution and the portable gadget does offer an opportunity (Arthur, 2004, p. 39). But although the initial popularity of the Apple iPod[4] and

CREATIVE DESTRUCTION:
transformation in the music industry

Microsoft's plans for a Portable Media Centre[5] gadget (to be launched Christmas, 2004) provide a niche area of growth for the record companies, their revenues in relation to the total of the big five music companies' revenues is tiny.

Reece notes:

"... even though iTunes is spreading fast, the industry believes that the later adopters of the platform will download less tracks than early adopters".

(2004, p. 40).

Gadgets and legal online distribution seems to be only picking at the problem. Research for the Creative Destruction, which will be presented in subsequent chapters, seems to indicate that to fully exploit this opportunity the record industry will need to sort out bloated management structures and learn how to compete more effectively in a digital world. The findings also indicate that the future lay in shunning the short-term chart toppers for a longer-term approach to developing artistic talent with a longer shelf life. For Reece this will generate sales from new albums issued by artists with genuine long-term fans, and will help to create future revenue streams from their back catalogue. In Chapter 6 we present a much leaner and more agile organising framework for a hypothetical music company than that which currently exists and offer a new business model for the 21st century.

The next section introduces the electronic music sector. This sector is deemed by numerous writers to be at the heart of Creative Destruction and the technology-music intersection (Bogdanov et al., 2001).

Electronic Music

There are numerous definitions of electronic music and these are summarised quite succinctly in the preface of Bogdanov's (2001) comprehensive guide to electronic music. The notion of electronic music that we used throughout this work makes reference to it as the creation of particular styles of music, grounded in electronics for creation and distribution. In this context we feel that electronic music can be defined as: "any type of music produced using electronic devices and/or software", whereas e-distribution is "the supply of music to the customer using fixed and mobile Internet applications".

Electronic music has evolved from small centres around the world to become a global subculture. Kraftwerk from Düsseldorf, so the story goes, pioneered the techno sound and vision with their freeze-dried synthesizer sounds, which for some reason echoed strongest in the American motor-city, Detroit.[6] Meanwhile, in cities like New York and Chicago, hip hop, electro and house music was shaped. This all happened during the late 70's and 80's. And when the different styles were sent (back) to Europe via the 'white island' of Ibiza, it catalysed Balearic in Britain – a collection of offbeat styles and sounds, of contemporary as well as older music.

The rest is, as they say, history. Electronic music has evolved from a musical genre to become a way of life – a perfect match for the Internet generation; the generation who has – allegedly – been causing quite a few headaches at executives offices in the record business around the globe for the past decade. First it was home copying that killed the music business. Then it was Internet downloads. Recent research from Morgan Stanley[7] (2004) indicates however, that home copying and downloads should not be blamed for plummeting CD sales. The general economical weakening and competition from other types of media are more crucial factors, according to Morgan Stanley. Basically, consumers are less likely to spend their money on music. But the Internet does without question hold a great potential for the distribution of music, as various so-called peer-to-peer (P2P) services have shown, Napster being the obvious example.

Electronic Music Styles

The term "electronic music" has evolved into an umbrella covering a multitude of styles. These are treated in detail in Chapter 3. Here there is presented a condensed review of them. Its ancestors can be tracked to the early house, techno and electro movement (in Chicago, Detroit, and New York in the early 80's), and from these to the more abstract "funk" [8], the Düsseldorf four in Kraftwerk, and further back to the electronic / concrete split (Karlheinz Stockhausen / Pierre Schaeffer). Below follows a description of the main sub-genre categories.[9]

Breakbeat

Breakbeat covers basically all music based on sampled drum-loops. The breakbeat was introduced in New York City's Bronx by Jamaican born DJ Kool Herc who

CREATIVE DESTRUCTION:
transformation in the music industry

isolated and prolonged the music's "breaks" by mixing two identical records. Rap, breakdance and grafitti are other forms of this culture. Sub-genres include 2 Step (house), drum'n'bass (jungle), hip hop (the original breakbeat music, rap), jazzfunk (nu-jazz), jungle (this), nu-jazz (this), broken beats (nu-jazz), trip hop (English version of hip hop, more atmospheric, cinematic).

Dub / Roots / Reggae

Roots is the original reggae and dub was originally an instrumental remix. Dub is now no longer just a musical style originating in the old, tape driven echo machines in Jamaica, where people like Lee Perry and King Tubby found a means of expression. Dub has slipped into music as an effect and a means of expression in it's own right. Sub-genres include Ska (fast and with many horns, from before reggae became slow), dancehall (dancehall, jungle and contemporary dub are the latest developments in reggae), ragga (hip hop reggae).

Electronica

As information technology was brought out to the man on the street, he began to experiment with the computer's possibilities in creating synthetic sound by means of mathematical algorithms and slick software: micro noise and electron collisions organized into a listening- and process-oriented, hyper synthetic cut'n'paste funk, or music's answer to chess.

House

Essentially, house is disco music but with more beats and more percussion. The roots are placed in the black American club environment in Chicago, where house music cut its teeth at The Warehouse. There is only a small step from "Warehouse" to "house", and it was to be this last part of the name that stuck. House music dominates the Copenhagen clubs with the characteristic sound of heavy kick drum, booming away in 4/4s and in a tempo around 120-130 BPM, and with a crunchy hi-hat to enlighten it all.

Sub-genres include 2 Step (drum'n'bass plus house with vocals), acid house (house where the main ingredient is the sound of Roland's hysteric bass synthesizer, TB 303), broken beats (nu-jazz), Chicago house (simple bass lines, energetic percussion and synth textures), club house (the more accessible, commercial department), deep house (deep bass and soft bottom, ca. 120 BPM, simmering and floating energy, lots of percussion, Fender Rhodes and vocal samples), Detroit house (somewhat different in sound and a little faster than Chicago house), filter house (does not stem from Paris but from the American DJ Sneak who began to filter different frequency areas in the music and thus introduced the music's dynamic into the operational parameters, ca. 123-130 BPM), garage (New York's version of deep house but with real vocals; named after the legendary club the Paradise Garage), ghetto house (hi-speed cartoon house with laughing gas vocals), progressive house (as techno with trance elements but in house rhythms), tech-house (cf. techno), UK house (a mix of the styles found in Chicago- and New York clubs, lingering on the border to techno).

Jungle / Drum'n'Bass

This originated in London in the 90's from where it has spread to the rest of the world. It consists of a bouncy bottom of sampled hi-speed breakbeats (ca. 160 BPM) without the metronomical 4/4 kick and with massive bass booming from reggae on top at half speed, with and without vocals (MC).

Sub-genres include Dark (jungle as horror movie), hardstep/techstep (minimal jungle with melody cut down and cleaner breakbeats), jazzfunk (cf. nu-jazz), jump-up (hip hop elements), liquid funk (fat bass, lush keyboard washes, oversexy horns and moaning women).

Nu-jazz / Jazzfunk / Broken Beats

While jazzfunk can be dated to the 70's and before, both nu-jazz and broken beats are more recent efforts in genre dividing. Nu-jazz typically describes the latin-seduced and jazz-influenced electronic music. Broken beats arose in West London around Ladbroke Grove. The 4/4s are here substituted by a more hewing house vibe, based on breakbeats but with a stopping or 'breaking' effect; tempo as deep house.

Soul / Rare Grooves / R'n'B

"Black music": funk. Soul is the foundation of modern dance music. House without soul tends towards progressive house and trance. House with soul, on the other hand, becomes garage or deep house. Soul was spread all over America via the same routes that brought black rural workers to the industrialized cities up north. As these blues people went north, their music met the urban jazz and became rhythm & blues.

Techno

The electronic sound textures from the Düsseldorf quartet Kraftwerk slipped almost effortlessly into playlists alongside soul, funk and rare grooves at radio stations in Detroit in the 70's. It was here that the freeze-dried European synthpop was injected a shot of vitalizing funk by visionary black producers, who –via the holiday island Ibiza- sent the new music back to Europe: futuristic and synthetic sound.

Sub-genres include Electro (electronic hip hop with and without vocals), ghetto-tech (a technofying of Miami bass), Miami bass (lots of bass, ultra rapid electro rhythms and dirty rap), Tech-house (house with 125-127 BPM but with hard edges).

Trance

This began in the late 80's influenced especially by acid house, Detroit techno and the 70's psychedelic rock music. The sound is characterized by a stable 4/4 groove and spluttering synthesizers, faster than house, slower than drum'n'bass. Sub-genres include Goa-trance (many tones, many themes, more melody, and often with corny sci-fi samples), psychedelic trance (similar to Goa-), progressive trance (the bass is off-beat), deep trance (elements from psychedelic trance, with house bass and house percussion; slower and less hysterical than Goa-trance), minimal trance (few themes, few sounds, close to house).[10]

MUSIC AND TECHNOLOGY

These styles highlight that electronic music fully incorporates the use of technology in the creative process. No single viewpoint can ever present a true picture of electronic music in all of its bewildering, fascinating diversity. Many people believe that there is an "electronic style" of music and that this style is duplicated invariably from piece to piece. Having convinced themselves of this, they also assume the existence of a special breed of composers who concern themselves exclusively with electronics and whose works sound quite similar. Various catch-phrases are heard in attempts to describe whatever this allegedly singular quality evokes — "science fiction", "freakishness", "dehumanisation" — all of them indicating that the music is, in one way or another, puzzling. Perhaps it is — to be more specific, perhaps one particular composition you've just recently heard is, but, to be sure, there's no guarantee that the next piece won't be entirely comprehensible, or at least puzzling in an altogether different way.

Mention the phrase "electronic music", or equivalent words such as "computer", and "synthesiser", and the image appears: a bare stage devoid of human performers, but with the record spinning efficiently and cold-bloodedly on a music deck with an assortment of "non-musical" sounds (hisses, pings, thuds, and swoops) emerging from loud-speakers. When we speak of electronic music then bear in mind that (as with the clarinet or piano) we are concentrating upon a collective "instrument" — one instrument among many. A sizeable body of music literature has come into being within the last half-century, using electronic techniques for the creation and/or manipulation of sounds, either processed onto recording tape for future "performance" or played on the spot by live performers in concert. Electronic techniques for the recording and transmission of sounds are also crucial to this process. Electronic music offers the composer not only a new "instrument" — that is, an extension of performing resources — but a new technique for composing, enabling him to work directly with sound material in a way previously unforeseen.

The Supply of Music: Concurrent and Interrelated Technological Changes

Thomas Edison, after experimenting with telegraphy, telephones and electro-magnetism, first demonstrated his cylindrical phonograph in December 1877. However, frustrated with its shortcomings, he became more interested in the electric light and dismissed the phonograph as "a mere toy with no commercial value". However, when Bell Laboratories introduced an improved version of his machine, the cylindrical gramophone in 1886, Edison returned to his invention and began developing it as an office dictation device. Shortly afterwards a number of regional phonograph companies were formed in the United States, and began using the phonograph to produce recorded entertainment for penny arcades and amusement centres. Most notable was the 'nickel-in-the-slot' machine introduced by Louis Glass, a development which began pushing the phonograph in the direction of musical recording and entertainment rather than towards the other possibilities identified by Edison.

Hence, there was no inevitable logic to the way in which the recorded sound industry developed, as some writers have implied (Struthers, 1987). The initial technology introduced by Edison produced a range of possibilities, but its subsequent development, at least initially, was shaped by the competition between entrepreneurs, inventors and speculators, and the way in which the public responded to the machine.

The emergence of radio and the application of sound in the cinema were two further technological developments which changed the way in which music was experienced, and contributed to a further reorganisation of the recording industry. Companies initially structuring around the electrical connections of sound technologies now began to re-organise to become an integral part of the wider entertainment industry.

At the time of its introduction in 1952, the microgroove long player was the leading form of recorded sound with over 273 million LP's sold, compared to 125 million pre-recorded cassette tapes. The proportion of LP's compared to cassette tapes, however then began to decline, as the shift towards the tape as the preferred format of pre-recorded sound began. By 1986, the cassette tape had taken the lead position in terms of total sales, with the compact disc slowly entering the marketplace. The demand for the vinyl LP was slowly being transferred over to cassette tapes and the compact disc. Between 1986 and 1988, the process rapidly accelerated and the result was that the compact disc for the first time outsold vinyl LP's. The market for vinyl however, did not totally disappear, and as late as 1991, one could still find approximately 60 million turntables remaining in American homes (Blesser and Pilkington, 2000).

Today, according to Blesser and Pilkington (2000) the life-cycle of the vinyl LP is a clear example of a technology which has progressed through all the sequences of a "single thread" lifecycle and is now in death - although the antique value and nostalgia may prolong the obsolescence of the technology. Blesser documented the music industry in terms of global paradigm shifts and reported that all audio technology will progress through this 'thread' lifecycle.

Figure 1.3 illustrates the "threads" of technology for vinyl, cassette tape and digital technologies. Vinyl technologies have progressed through the life cycle paradigm and as Millard (2001) identified, it is evident that the market has practically disappeared. The cassette tape technology is now estimated to be in the adulthood stage of the life cycle with all the major record

Units Sold

[Graph showing units sold from 1930 to 2000 for LP Records, Microphones, Cassette tape, and Digital technology]

---- LP Records   —— Microphones   ▫▫ ▫▫ Cassette tape   ▪▪▪▪▪▪ Digital technolo

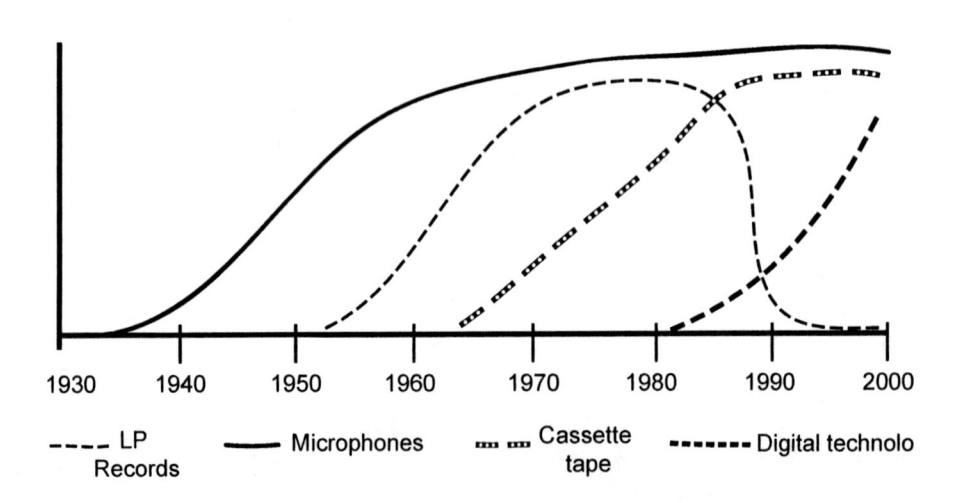

figure 1.3 Concurrent technological innovation in the music sector

companies continuing to supply all material on either a tape or compact disc format. One should note that the digital technologies as a thread are relatively young in the life cycle paradigm. New digital formats - such as the minidisc - ensure that the digital era is one that is constantly evolving. One thread of technology that has defied the traditional pattern of the paradigm and has sustained an extended life cycle and currently remains in adulthood is the microphone.

Blesser and Pilkington (2000) infer that technologies such as digital audio tend to have their beginnings in the early 1980's. At any given period of time, there is a

CREATIVE DESTRUCTION:
transformation in the music industry

multiplicity of 'threads' of technology all at different stages within the life cycle, as the diagram above illustrates. However this view is not universal. As one technology is introduced, it will progressively replace the previous dominant technology. For example, the magnetic wire recorder 'thread' started in 1939, but it died after spawning the magnetic tape.

The technology of the audio industry can be compared to a fabric with many strands of thread that are weaving together with all their interdependencies (Blesser and Pilkington, 2000). As the industry experiences a technical change, it is characterised by many threads that are ending whilst new threads are only just beginning. This analogy suggests that the technology of the audio industry is constantly evolving with many threads ending whilst others are being developed and in turn replacing those that have come before. This evolutionary transition tends to be an expansion of current technology, for example, the transition from 78-rpm records to the LP. In such a case, developments were made on previous experience and investment. The revolutionary transition does not experience the same customer continuum. The technology is radical with little, if virtually any detailed experience or knowledge of the new innovation.

No major companies during the LP record technology period were successful in the transition to the compact cassette, because the two technologies shared no commonality to support the development and introduction of such a technology, and for many companies during this period, it was not financially viable to fund cassette development. Throughout the 100 years of audio reproduction, the music industry has tended to depend heavily upon threads of technology from other industries. This trend seems to be repeating itself in the early stages of the 'digital' era (Hardaker and Graham, 2001). As Blesser and Pilkington (2000) recognised, it is simply a case of the audio industry being too small to invent everything for itself. The first Edison phonograph was developed primarily due to the telegraph technology of that time.

The concern so far has been with the "analogue" or "audio" innovations that have spurred change within the supply of music. We now consider the exciting, and very recent developments in "digital" technology, which are viewed as realising unprecedented changes in an already volatile industry. The mid-1990s onwards have been characterised by the second phase of the digital revolution, that of "streaming" technologies and peer-to-peer (P2P) sites based on the Internet. The availability of software able to compress sound and store it in fairly small files and the spread of standard digital communication instruments like the Internet are radically altering the strategy of recording companies, and considerably affecting the relationships between final consumers, distributors and artists as well as the recording companies themselves.

The compression of music into the MP3 format (M-peg layer 3), eliminating from files the range of sounds the human ear cannot detect, creates files that are much faster to download or play. One minute of standard quality sound from a CD occupies about 10 MB of space on a disk whereas the same minute compressed in the Mp3 file format occupies about one twelfth of the hard disk space. The widespread use of this new technological paradigm raises questions about the competitive positions and strategies of the recording companies, the role of new digital operators, and the emergence of P2P models of consumption, which allows the users to share and swap music files with clearly serious implications from the legal point of view. Napster is the most striking example of this phenomenon. Given the radical changes under way, the recording industry may act as a good field for analysing the different user orientations towards the consumption of cultural goods through digital platforms and showing the strategic role of the knowledge of consumer behaviour. In particular for the managers of record companies, reaching the audience whose consumption has shifted to the digital platform is becoming one of the main objectives for the immediate future. The recent downturn of CD sales in the recording industry, together with the rapid diffusion of file sharing, are forcing record companies to change their approach to music downloading.

Music, Cultural Spaces and Technologies

The music industry is the setting in which music (and money) is made, but songs and stars are not just cans of beans. The continuing need for "new" product, the irrationality of aesthetic tastes, and the central place of romanticism (its language of art and genius) in rock ideology means that the creative process itself – the set of social relations, rules, and practices within which the musical product is made is exceedingly complex (Frith, 1987). Music technologies have been and will continue to play a major role in the creative process. The development of electronic musical instruments has been of major importance, while from the late 1980s onwards, computer technology has made a major impact.

The modern era of electronic music began in the 1960's. Although the technical developments of the 1950s had made composition with tape a reality, composer interest in electronic music (to say nothing of general audience awareness) was a relatively isolated phenomenon. An explosive surge of activity in the field took place in the 1960's and has continued into the present. The 1960s's witnessed the marketing of the first units designed exclusively for the composition and performance of electronic music. The names of Moog and Buchla dominated the electronic music scene during this period. The Moog and Buchla synthesisers[11] were named, respectively, after their inventors: Robert Moog, working in Trumansberg, New York (a small town near Ithaca), and Donald Buchla, of the San Francisco bay area.

It's worth noting that, although Moog and Buchla and subsequent synthesiser-builders were "technicians" rather than "musicians", their products were designed with specifically musical ends in mind, often in collaboration with composers. This marked a significant milestone in the history of electronic music, because all equipment before this time had been originally intended to serve other purposes; that is, the classic studio was an assemblage of broadcast and hi-fi testing units, and the RCA synthesiser had been developed by the telephone industry to attempt speech synthesis.

Throughout the 1970s and 1980s synthesising technologies were being incorporated into dance music. Kraftwerk were one of the more prominent danceable electronic music outfits, whose recordings Autobahn and Trans Europe Express heralded the beginning of electronic trance dance music. The Italian Giorgio Moroder produced electronic studio based dance music with a similar cyclical groove, but added the

MUSIC AND TECHNOLOGY

voice of Donna Summer to his music, like the 17 minute "Love to Love You Baby" which may be described as the predecessor of electronic pop dance outfits (Toop, 1992). Most of the older synthesisers had no pre-programmed or sampled sounds, making them "inaccessible" to many composing artists. The late 1980s and early 1990s saw attempts to integrate pre-sampled sounds including: the programmable synthesising module and the populist pre-programmed sound module which often contains sampled sounds. Although its price put it out of reach for most people when it appeared on the market in 1979, the Fairlight Computer Musical Instrument was the first commercially available sampling device, followed by the cheaper Emulator, Synclavier, Ensoniq Mirage and Akai[12]. Samplers are a digital recording device which can manipulate the sound textures which have been recorded with it[13].

The 1990s saw the increased usage of computerised sequencers. The sequencer is able to record, memorise and replay a sequence of notes in the way that a word processor works with written text[14]. When programmed it can trigger sound generating modules such as synthesisers, drum machines and samplers, in a similar manner to a word processing application which triggers a printer. The sequenced sound pattern is communicated via a cable network called MIDI or the Musical Instrument Digital Interface. Through the use of an SMPTE[15] code, the sequencer can be synchronised with a multi-track tape recorder, so that non-digital music recording as well as sequenced overdubs[16] are possible (Braut, 1994).

As has been the case with all other (re) productive musical technologies, although exclusive at first, sequencers, samplers and digital audiotape (DAT) machines can now be afforded by the person 'on the street' at a grassroots level. A composition could be created at home without being dependent on large investments by the major music industry players and therefore without their interference (O'Shaughernessy, 1992). The home production of CDs straight from one's PC (personal computer) became a possibility in the mid-1990s. A consequence of the possibility of independent home recording is that the production of recorded music has been democratised; a less censored form of music could theoretically appear on the market.

As with other DIY musical genres, the multitude of home produced underground one-off electronic music track projects has brought with it a relative anonymity of the producers as well as a relatively short life span for most tracks. The anonymity of the recording artists is enhanced by the fact that their work is often represented by a DJ as part of a continuous sound track, rather than as a unique live performance or a representation of such. Rather than the artist, within circles of underground dance,

CREATIVE DESTRUCTION:
transformation in the music industry

to use Roland Barthes' terminology (Barthes, 1973), it is often the myth of record companies which sells records. Within electronic consumer circles it is customary to speak of a 'label', in order to indicate the company name as denotation of its connoted public image and reputation. Customers in electronic music shops in Europe often request products from a particular label and the specialist press write about these organisations as being genuine creative forces.

To producers and remixers the sampler is a useful creative tool which enables the reconstruction of a song. Parts of a song which are repeated in its structure such as the chorus only have to be recorded once. Often the most successful parts of the recording are sampled and inserted where they are needed as well. Remixers use a similar method of creating a new track, using only a few key elements of the original recordings. Existing songs and tracks can be cut up and parts such as hook lines can be recorded on the sampler, after which the samples could be triggered in a new order by the sequencer. In this manner, a new version can be obtained with the addition of a "fresh" drum-machine track and a certain number of synthesisers. When this type of 'remix' has not been commissioned by the original songwriter, performer or by other representatives which own part of the copyright of a song or its recording, its commercial release may be stigmatised as an act of theft and the product will be regarded as a bootleg.

One common use of samplers is and was to mimic the stuttering effect of "scratching" – a technique initially developed by DJs using record turntables. Another instance is the use of samplers to dub in segments of speeches, effects, or music – a technique those art-punk bands of an earlier era achieved by splicing tape with a low-tech razor blade.

It is this combination of sampling and sequencing (as evidenced in drum machines and digital music computers) that has eroded the divisions, not just between originals and copies, but also between human- and machine-performed music. In each area, that of originality and of "feel", the new music technologies place authenticity and creativity in crisis, not just because of the issue of theft, but through the increasingly automated nature of their mechanisms.

The focus of this introductory chapter so far has been on the creative potential of technology for creating and supplying music, with particular reference made to the electronic music, giving this work a particular uniqueness among contemporary works in this area. The remainder of this chapter will provide an overview of the more destructive aspects of technology; as it relates to copyright issues. First attention will be given to copyright, in terms of the supply of music with the rise of Internet-based streaming technologies such as MP3 and the rise of peer-to-peer (P2P) file swapping and secondly, some consideration will be given to copyright in terms of the creation of music using technologies such as digital samplers and computer sequencers.

Disrupting an Industry: the Rise of MP3

The proliferation of digital audio technologies reached new heights with the emergence of MP3, Real Audio, Microsoft Mediaplayer and Liquid Audio, which enable the compression of music files to a size in which they can be transferred over the Internet. The combination of both digital and audio technologies and increased bandwidth, with modem connections have resulted in a four minute song on a CD being compressed into forty megabytes of space utilising MP3 format. Motion Picture Expert group layer three (MP3) has become the de facto digital audio compression standard for music distribution over the Internet, very popular amongst Internet based music lovers and audio software developers. The MP3 format, however praised by the user community of digital distribution does not have the provision for a digital signature to identify and stop illegal music distribution.

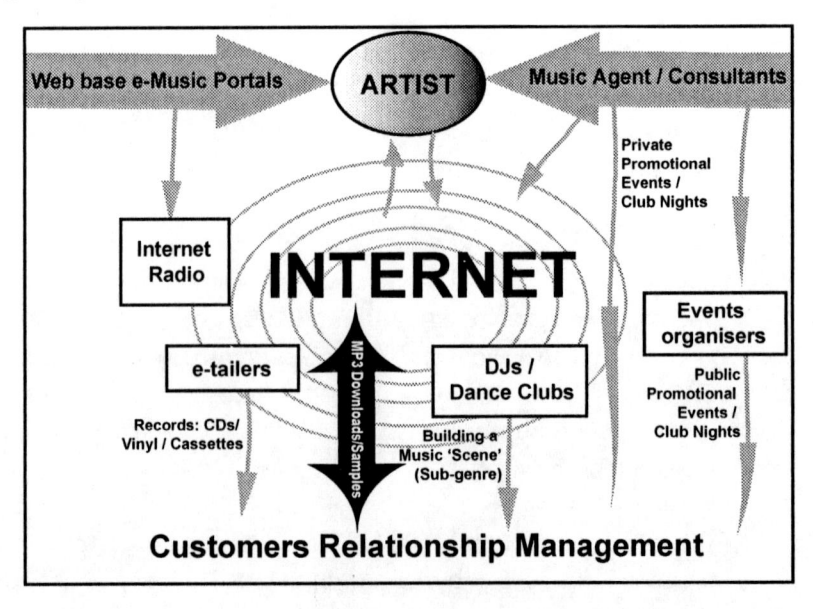

Figure 1.4 The Internet's Role in Music Piracy

CREATIVE DESTRUCTION:
transformation in the music industry

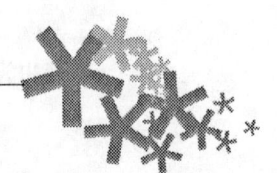

Figure 1.4 shows that whilst representing the music industry infrastructure with the impact of the Internet it fails to acknowledge the emerging peer-to-peer technologies. The music industry as represented in the diagram above differs from the previous industry structure. The industry structure above assumes that the major record labels no longer play an imperative role in the production, management and distribution of musical content. "My.mp3.com[17]", made it easier to distribute music over the Internet. Digital distribution of musical content over the Internet will have a profound effect upon components of the music industry supply/value chain. Physical operations of manufacturing and distribution in the supply chain account for a large percentage of the costs of a CD.

Digital distribution of musical content through the Internet therefore significantly changes the industry value chain, in particular the economics of the industry, as the total delivery cost of a compact disc composed of two thirds from activities that are directly threatened by digital distribution over the Internet. (McKinsey Quarterly, 2001) Distributors and physical retailers will therefore become marginalised as the new method of distribution in 'bits and bytes' do not require CD and audiocassette format. (Parikh, 1999). Figure 1.4 above illustrates that the traditional role of the label within the old music industry supply chain will disappear and their role will either change to conform to the new structure of the industry or will substantially reduce. The artist component of the supply chain will become more centralised within the supply chain, gaining more control over the marketing and distribution. Having profited enormously from the advent of compact discs in the early 1980s, large companies and small labels alike have struggled to come to term with the new digital formats. The impact of Napster was to thrust the music industry into the eye of a storm (Alderman, 2001).

The Politics of Sampling

There is a wide range of DJs, musicians, and engineers, who have made an aesthetic out of sampling. The most notorious are M/A/R/R/S, Cold Cut, Steinski and Mantronix. For this school of sampling, "stealing" segments from other records is a part of the meaning of the "new" text. The criminal offence of theft is defined as the use of a sample of a part of a song as the basis for a 'new' piece of work, whilst adapting the title and the lyrics for one's own purposes (Rietveld, 1998). In Britain, it is the Copyright Designs and Patents Act of 1988 section 107 that is often used to tackle piracy and put sampling under criminal proceedings, though no precedent has been set to date, since most cases have been settled out of court[18].

Running counter to the above view is the fact that sampling recuperates music history rather than denying it. This thread of interpretation is evident in the numerous instances in which digital montagists and scratchers claim to be educating their audience about its history. As Tim Simenon suggests:

"Take James Brown, all of his records are being reissued. Kids of 18, 19 wouldn't have heard of him if it wasn't for hip-hop".

(New Musical Express, 1988[19]).

Arguments about authenticity, authorship, and the aura in contemporary music are clearly very complex and no claim is being made here that the whole truth has been sampled. But it is clear that the view of sampling as stealing is clearly a very simplistic one as espoused in the past (Bradwell, 1988) by the British Musicians Union (MU). Beadle suggests that the technology of sampling:

" .. shifted the balance of power from singers, songwriters and instrumentalists to producers (…). Producers could emerge as artists in their own right".

(Beadle, 1993).

These producers can also be described as contemporary songwriting musicians. Kraftwerk called themselves "Musik Arbeiter", or "Music Labourers", who don't "make music" but who practice "sound chemistry" (Carvalho, 1992[20]). A landscape that revels in the fusion of originals and copies, and in which we cannot distinguish humans from machines, seems like unlikely territory for authors and auras[21]. Yet despite the apparently postmodern nature of so much contemporary music, the question of creativity and originality remains central. However in 2003 the notion of "creativity" has shifted far away from its 1970s progressive rock heyday (when musicians tried to invent new, unique musical forms, as well as original music). Music might be consuming itself, but the old ideologies and aesthetics are still on the menu. The most striking point in the analysis of music production is the fact that music made by machines, or to sound like machines, has not taken music's trajectory into electronic music, but has instead become the chief source of its dance music. Synthesisers, sequencers and digital samplers are identified less with modern composers (like Brian Eno) than with dance genres like hip hop, house, garage and trance. Musicians and audiences have grown increasingly accustomed to making an association between synthetic/automated music and the communal (dance floor)

CREATIVE DESTRUCTION:
transformation in the music industry

connection to nature (via the body). We have grown used to connecting machines and funkiness.

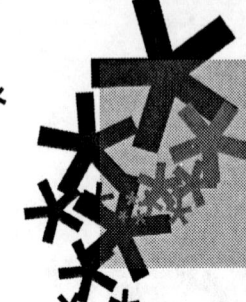

HISTORY AND ORIGINS OF ELECTRONIC MUSIC

*Introduction

"Techno is music that sounds like machines, not machines that sound like music". Those are the words of Techno godfather Juan Atkins, usually credited as one of the three pioneers of techno music (the other two being Kevin Saunderson and Derrick May). Though Techno alone doesn't make up the entire spectrum of electronic music, Atkins' defining motto makes sense as an overall characterization of the electronic genre as a whole.

This chapter assumes a basic concept for electronic music as an oscillation between the synthetic and the authentic; between the inorganic or computer-made, and the 'real' – sounds that are 'found' rather than synthesized. In the myriad genres and sub-genres of today's electronic music, these two 'pillars' – that of the 'machine-made' and that of the 'hand-made' – can be identified as performing an interplay, or making a tension, like the two poles of a battery supplying energy. This chapter explores the origins and developments of these two tendencies in electronic music. In order to do that we shall follow an historical path which begins at the end of the 19th century when Edison's phonograph was developed in 1877, later followed by the technique for magnetic tape recording, first presented by the Dane Valdemar Poulsen whose Telegraffon won the prize for scientific invention at the Paris Exhibition in 1900. As we will see, the techniques for recording of sounds play a major role in the development of electronic music throughout the 20th century. The recording of sounds is in our perspective representative of the 'real'. In contrast, the in-organic or machine-made tendency in electronic music began with tone-generators – an apparatus capable of producing sine-wave tones.

We shall follow this path through three major periods in time: the first period is The Early Years around 1950 where the French driven 'Musique Concrète' and The German-led 'Elektronische Musik' broke new ground for music. The second period spans the late 1960's through to around 1980, dominated by the Düsseldorf based quartet Kraftwerk whose elegant, hyper-synthetic pop tunes and freeze-dried percussion sounds spearheaded the Techno revolution in Detroit. This is covered

CREATIVE DESTRUCTION:
transformation in the music industry

by the third period: The development of Techno in Detroit vis-à-vis the electronic mutation of Hip Hop into Electro (in New York), and Soul and Disco into House music (in Chicago).

The Early Years

The breaking down of classic harmony and the opening of music towards all sounds founded by Arnold Schönberg's twelve-tone music and Luigi Russolo's Noise Music in the beginning of the 20th Century, was later taken up by the French composer Edgard Varèse and the American John Cage. Varèse, who moved to the USA in 1915, formulated in 1917 the natural consequences of Schönberg's and Russolo's visions:

> "I dream of instruments that obey my thoughts and which, with their contribution to a whole new world of unknown sounds, will be in the service of my inner rhythm".
>
> (Peyser, 1971, p. 141).

But the technological development did not catch up with Varèse's fantasy, and 20 years later, in 1937, John Cage predicted in a famous lecture that the "use of noise to make music will continue and increase until we reach a music produced through the aid of electrical instruments." (Cage, 1937, pp. 54-55) Cage and Varèse both dreamt of a musical instrument that would be capable of producing the total sound spectrum instead of merely re-producing a little bit of it, dependent on the instrument. This could be achieved only through the technological enhancement of the musical instrument. Already Thaddeus Cahill's Telharmonium apparatus shows the prospect for such a technological enhancement. Cahil patented in 1897 the so called "Art of and Apparatus for Generating and Distributing Music Electronically" and constructed a device which by means of little generators and complex switch mechanisms was able to combine sine wave tones, and distributed the music produced from these to hotels, restaurants and private homes via telephone cables for a short while from 1906 to 1908. (Chadabe, 1997, p. 3ff).

Electronic and Concrete Music

Edgard Varèse found that the characteristics for his time were speed and synthesizing, and expressed the need for instruments in the 20th century to help artists realize these in music (Russcol, 1972, p. xxviii). The instrument he was dreaming of wasn't produced until shortly after World War 2, and was pioneered by Pierre Schaeffer and Karlheinz Stockhausen. Both Schaeffer and Stockhausen were working to realize a musical form which, in Schaeffer's phrasing, is found "outside DoReMi" (Hodgkinson, 1987). In 1948 with his Étude aux Chemins des Fer, Pierre Schaeffer introduced what he called musique concrète, concrete music. Schaeffer's concrete music was based on the sounds of everyday life (e.g. trains and railways), manipulated into 'sound objects' and re-worked to form compositions beyond traditional tonality and instrumentation. There are many similarities between concrete music and the German 'electronische musik' that sprung out of the NWDR-studio (later WDR) where Stockhausen was amongst the most notable composers. This early, purely electronic music also liberated itself from traditional instruments and investigated new tonality and harmony. But in spite of this apparent similarity there are great differences between (pure) electronic and concrete music – both technically and aesthetically. The composer and music theorist Tim Hodgkinson has explained the fundamental difference as a question of a human vs. a technical activity:

> "For Musique Concrète, the essential character of music as a human activity is such that the listening experience and the 'ear' are crucial things. For Electronic Music, the priority is the idea, the system, the perfection of control, of precise rationalization... to become scientific."
>
> (Hodgkinson, 1987, p. 3).

Musique Concrète, Pierre Schaeffer

'The primacy of the ear' is for Schaeffer the first of three fundamental postulates for musique concrète. The remaining two are concerned with the preference for acoustic sources from everyday life and the communication between human beings by means of a musical language (Schaeffer, 1967, pp. 29-30). The fundamentals of musique concrète are in other words founded in the human world. Musique concrète is concerned with the natural, everyday sounds and their mediation; hence also the focus on the actual montage of the sound objects into the final composition. Musique concrète is preoccupied with the transformation and distortion of recorded sound, and finds its final form in the continuous experimentation with the expression.

Schaeffer named the music 'concrete' to distinguish it from traditional, classical music. Musique concrète begins with the empirical, with concrete sounds, recorded and re-arranged on magnetic tape. The sound object is not an absolute, but rather a consideration of the material and hence is also in opposition to the musical a priori found in serialism, continued at the time by Alban Berg and Anton Webern.

Electronic Music: Karlheinz Stockhausen

In contrast to musique concrete, the purely electronic music developed at the Nordwestdeutscher Rundfunk studio at the same time as Schaeffer began experimenting with tape and real sounds at Radiodiffusione Francaise, rests on a purely electronic production of clangs. Electronic music is not interested in recorded natural sounds; its focus lies elsewhere, namely with the fabrication of sounds to be induced directly on magnetic tape. Stockhausen did not want to use any found material – either objects or musical styles. He could spend months analyzing sound, dissect its frequencies and on the basis of these observations produce the required sound using electronic oscillators.

With his two full-blooded electronic compositions – Studie 1 and Studie 2, produced in the Cologne studio in 1953-54, Stockhausen demonstrated how virtually any sound could in principle be reached by means of technology. The sine wave tones of the oscillators are un-natural, 'pure' tones without overtones, but by grouping the sine wave tones in tone groups, Stockhausen could produce the exact sound he wanted. Both Studie compositions are made entirely from artificial, synthetic sound, and their structure is based on the serial composition technique, founded by the twelve-tone and atonal music by Arnold Schönberg and further developed by his two pupils, Alban Berg and Anton Webern. Stockhausen believed that all music should begin with Webern; that there was no other choice (Peyser, 1971, p. 74). Schaeffer, on the contrary, hated twelve-tone music (Hodgkinson, 1987).

Instead of following a redundant form as with classical harmony and tonality, the tones in serial music form part of a regularity not known before. Serial music does still follow a general and superior principle, but it is now its own, inner logic that organizes the sound image, not a tonic force. The electronic tone generators made it possible to bring in all aspects of composing in a serial logic; not only the tones, but also their strength, clang, attack and any other parameter could be drawn from the series and hence create a total structure in which every element was organized.

(Chadabe, 1997, p. 37). With his two Studie compositions, Stockhausen had created a 'complete logical, 'unnatural' material, as Jonathan Harvey puts it (Harvey, 1975, pp. 25-28).

Two-Faced Technology

The two positions described above make up the platform for electronic music as we know it. On the one hand a concrete sound, consisting of sound objects, liberated from their original context by means of technology and put into play in another. On the other hand an abstract, produced sound with a clang that precisely fits a logical-mathematical composition developed from the twelve-tone music of Arnold Schönberg. This is a fundamental difference which can be described in terms of 'open' and 'local' (Schaeffer) as opposed to 'predetermined' and 'global' (Stockhausen). Pierre Schaeffer's primacy of the ear points towards a phenomenological dimension – focus is on a human activity, and the reworking of the sound material describes an effort to reach a level of unconditionality, to make the material open for questioning. On the contrary, Stockhausen's compositions are conceptualized on the basis of a predetermined, logical-mathematical system. His serial compositions in the first years after Studie 1 and Studie 2 are highly complex manifestations of order and proportionality within different parameters.

The early electronic music is – unlike concrete music – radically 'new'. The musical material is thoroughly synthesized; it is logical and unnatural, both in materiality (sine waves) and in composition (logical-mathematical). Stockhausen's electronic works construct a new world, whereas Schaeffer suggests a world based on the existing, but reorganized or modified. Hence, concrete and electronic music represent two opposite relations to history. For Schaeffer it is a matter of one actual reorganization of the recorded among countless possible, whereas for Stockhausen it is a matter of a new ideality, drawn from the tone series.

For Pierre Schaeffer there are two possible relationships between art and technology: either technology helps the art (this Schaeffer saw as his own position), or technology becomes the art. For Schaeffer, technology is alien to art, a mere assistant or tool for the creative man. That meant that the tape recorder could offer a possibility to advance music in the form of collage, or montage of sound objects, referring to a real world phenomenon. Stockhausen's serial works, on the other hand, take on scientific or technological ideas as the organizing principle for music; first with the abstract-logical series, later with variable form which Stockhausen took up in the mid 1950's, e.g. with Klavierstück XI in 1956, where an element of chance is evident in the composition. The variable form is in effect the collage/montage form used as a generative complexity, and by using that, Stockhausen achieves a degree of liberation from the static work of art. Instead, it becomes a technological form, actualized dynamically, during performance.

Fundamentally, Schaeffer operates with 'the human'. It is the human conscience or perception that is recorded and reconfigured using technology. But this happens in a sort of reflecting naturalism, inspired by a melancholy or elegiac impulse. Schaeffer's collage technique does represent the technological in art, but as a model for the allegory. Like the fragments of collage, the allegory carries two contents in one and the same form – a contemporary and a past. Stockhausen articulates another possibility. When technology becomes art itself, this leads firstly to an electronic reservoir of precise and objective musical values (Hodgkinson, 1987), liberated from reality. Secondly, with Stockhausen's experiments with chance and other forms of indeterminacy a few years after John Cage, the technologicalization of art results in an open, fluctuating form, created real time.

HISTORY AND ORIGINS OF ELECTRONIC MUSIC

The Human and The Technological

For Pierre Schaeffer, technology is instrumental. It is a tool by which Man as the central organizing principle can radicalize his experiments. For Stockhausen, in a way, Man is also central, but Man and technology are two sides of the same thing — "a machine, a computer, is a quite natural extension of the brain," Stockhausen has explained. "It's like producing a baby". This idea was to become the core issue for a group of German producers/musicians in the next generation: Kraftwerk.

Kraftwerk: From Techno Pop To Post-Human

In 1968, Ralf Hütter and Florian Schneider-Esleben formed the quintet Organisation from a mutual interest in improvised avant-garde music, and the influence of British/American pop- and rock music that dominated Germany in the 1960's. With groups like Tangerine Dream, Can, Amon Düül, Faust, Neu! and Cluster, Organisation was among the driving forces in a German movement wanting to form a new musical expression based on classical avant-garde, pop, rock and the psychedelic music Stockhausen had brought back with him from a trip to California, where people like Grateful Dead's Jerry Garcia and Phil Lesh of Jefferson Airplane had been among the audience at his seminars. Outside Germany this new German music was called 'Krautrock', while at home it became the more grandiose 'Kosmische Musik'.

From the beginning, Hütter and Schneider were interested in the technological development of instruments, and they looked towards "a more technologically motivated future," as their biographer Pascal Bussy remarks (Bussy, 1993, p.15). In 1970 the first Kraftwerk album was released, and four years later they invested in a Moog synthesizer - a Mini-Moog, which at the time cost the same as a Volkswagen and – as Hütter put it, gave the same freedom of movement (Sinker, 1991, p. 96). To fully understand the radical range of the synthesizer's capabilities, one needs merely to realize that it took Stockhausen at least eight oscillators in a precisely calculated set-up to create a square curve. When the synthesizer was commoditized in the early 1970's it was possible to shift between as many as six different curve shapes by pressing a single button. The synthesizer made it possible to create any sound, including 'real' sounds that could be re-made by a combination of frequencies from the total sound spectrum, just like Edgard Varèse had dreamt of.

This was to become very important for Kraftwerk. "If you walk down the street you can hear a symphony if you are open enough to listen to it," Hütter told Triad

CREATIVE DESTRUCTION:
transformation in the music industry

36

Magazine in 1975. Hutter inferred that electronic music was created out of white noise, so you can take whatever frequencies you like, or you want, for your particular concept of music. In his words: "Like a painter, you can choose whatever colors of the spectrum you like for that projection of your painting". And Schneider added:

> That's what you learn from working with electronics. You go to the source of the sound and your ears are trained to analyze any sound. We hear a plane passing overhead and I know all of the phenomenon that go into the make-up of the sound, the phasings, the echoes. All these things that happen in nature."
> (Quoted in Smaizys, 1975, p.11).

The first outcome of Kraftwerk's new investment was Autobahn, a landmark album of historical dimensions. It was the first album made by the set-up that the world, throughout the 1970's and 1980's came to know as Kraftwerk, with the two 'electronic percussionists' Wolfgang Flur and Karl Bartos as the rhythm section of the now four-piece

Movement, Stasis/Process

The American Billboard Magazine called Autobahn's more than 22 minutes title track "a fantasy on the sensations of a drive along Germany's freeway system," (Billboard, March 22 1975, p 33). The sound material on the album is a composite of synthetic and concrete music. It opens with the recordings of the car setting in motion, and moves hereafter into a totally synthesized landscape. We take off on the (track) 'Autobahn' and arrive at (the track) 'Morgenspaziergang' in a synthetic landscape, albeit created in a realistic tradition, imitating the sounds of reality. By recording real sounds and using the tape material as both elements in the music and (to a higher degree) as templates for their synthesized car-sounds, Doppler effects etc., Kraftwerk balance right on the borderline between concrete and electronic sound, as Stockhausen had done before them with e.g. his Gesang der Jünglinge.

The English music writer Andy Hamilton calls it "romantic realism" (Hamilton, 1997, p. 77) - hypnotic, minimalist rhythms, inspired by American composers like Terry Riley, Steve Reich, Phillip Glass and LaMonte Young, mixed with the representing tradition found on albums like Autobahn and later Trans Europa Express in the use of speed sound and sound of movement, both imitated and as real sound. The registered (recorded) or virtual (imitated) movement on these albums is in stark contrast to the minimalist repetition. Minimalist music is characterized by stasis, and a tendency towards stagnation, both harmonically and dynamically.,(Strickland, 1993, p. 123) In essence it is non-allusive, and tends towards decontextualization and impersonality in its tone.(Strickland, 1993, p. 7)

With Kraftwerk, on the contrary, the real sound is used as a template for the perfectly simulated effects of dynamics, and the reference or imitation that lies implicitly herein, makes a connection precisely to that which minimalism seeks to avoid: the figurative, the realistic, and consequently the human. Compared to Pierre Schaeffer, who cuts through reality with the collage/montage apparatus and dissolves it in a non-linear matrix, Kraftwerk re-creates reality synthetically. Schneider calls the music "tone film" and describes it as "sound-images of real environments" (quoted in Hamilton, 1997, p. 77), while Hütter speaks of 'recreating realism'. Kraftwerk's sound images are in other words based on reality.

The simulated real sound is one of Kraftwerk's basic components. Another is the minimalist repetition. According to Strickland it was LaMonte Young's 'Trio For Strings' (1958) that heralded minimalism in music. This composition, entirely consisting of drones and pauses, Terry Riley associated with 'waiting for lunch at a space station' (Strickland, 1993, p. 121) and Strickland refers to it as an 'unearthly landscape'. Accordingly, he calls Reich's Pendulum Music (1968) for a "musical demonstration of entropy". Both the drone and the modular repetition is about the enhancement of a rudimentary material, but entropy, the sonic continuum, the absolute stasis, this ultimate element of periodicity explored by minimalism, does not exist. It is a pure abstraction that is non-human. Minimalist art thus erases the connection to Man and reveals only an abstract geometry, and minimalism hence marks a ground zero, which according to Strickland destructs the analogue relationship between Man and nature in a "phenomenological rejection" (Strickland, 1993, p. 292).

Thus, Kraftwerk represent on the one hand a space, not only empty and desolate, but also rejecting in a phenomenological sense any connection with the human. This takes place in the music's minimalist elements: repeating pieces of melodic movement, self-repeating rhythms whose synthetic texture and foreboding of entropy emphasizes its alien state. On the other hand, Kraftwerk also – and paradoxically – represent an incorporated human presence. But this human presence has its origin in the synthesizer, which imitates 'real environments'. On these early albums the group is constantly oscillating between conjuring up a world emptied of human beings, and

CREATIVE DESTRUCTION:
transformation in the music industry

placing a subject in it. But it is a subject that due to its synthetic origin both is and is not present.

Historical Displacement

The same double mode also works on a conceptual level. The album cover for Autobahn, designed by Emil Schult – the master mind behind the groups visual appearance, artwork, design and lightning in those years – was emphasized by the footage used for the live shows, consisting of "grainy monochrome films of a golden dawn of motorway driving when roads were clear and happy nuclear families made picnics on the grass verge to break their journeys," as composer and music writer David Toop has put it (Toop, 1995, 203). Florian Schneider recalls with a bit of nostalgia the group's highway image, which seems to attempt a recollection of an era long gone: "Even in the '70s our image of the autobahn was a bit idealized" (Bussy, 1993, p. 52).

Nostalgia and idealization are central to the Kraftwerk expression. Autobahn sets the scene for the modern world where the industrial epoch can be dramatized. But the media, the synthesized sound, already belongs to a different world: the immaterial and information based world of post-industrialization. Radio-Activität (1975), the cover of which shows a bakelite radio from 1930's Germany, accordingly splits the radio wave into epochs: one a pre-TV age in which the radio is the primary means of communication, symbolized by the antenna and iron pylon on the inner-sleeve; the other the (then) contemporary atomic energy. Kraftwerk let the novelty of the music accompany some sort of romantic longing with images and design from times past. Hence, they draw the listener in two different directions (Bussy, 1993, p. 69).

The same combination of new and old is found in almost all the visual material used by the group. The highway footage has been mentioned already, and the same retrospective gaze is found in the music video for 'The Model', Kraftwerk's biggest hit. Here footage from the 1950's and 1960's fashion shows by Pierre Balmain and Yves Saint-Laurent is shown (Bussy, 1993, p. 116). And on the cover for Trans Europa Express, Kraftwerk looks like a distinguished string quartet in an atmospheric, stylized Bavarian alp-scene from an earlier epoch. The video for the title track builds on these images, and shows the group making a train journey with Pacific 231, a futuristic looking train praised by Arthur Honegger in a 1923 poem (Bussy, 1993, p. 87). The train passes through a universe both historical and futuristic that could easily have been modeled on the film Metropolis, made by Fritz Lang in 1926, and through European cities like Paris (capital of modernity) and Düsseldorf (Kraftwerk's home city). The journey ends in a long tunnel, apparently leading to the heart of the Metropolis-city.

Metropolis re-appears in the title line for one of the tracks on the album The Man-Machine, the cover of which is made in 'classical' constructivist design, and even dedicated to the constructivist El Lissitzky for its inspiration. Like the group's use of fascist/communist symbol inventory, this reference also points backwards towards a not so distant past. Kraftwerk's uniform appearance both on stage and in the media began early, but The Man-Machine was the first to integrate the robot-figure directly in the group's expression. The exterior of the dolls is antiquated compared to contemporary hi-tech robots which by the late 1970's had long been rid of anthropomorphism. The music video for 'The Robots' showed the mechanical functions of the robots in which every movement is made with extreme slow precision. The Kraftwerk-doll is therefore, due to its physical-mechanical appearance, connected to the 1920's or 1930's (Platt, 1995, pp. 146-147), or even further back, to the automata of the 18th and 19th Century (Thau, 1993, pp. 47- 50).

Autobahn, Radio-Activität, Trans Europa Express, The Man-Machine and the single 'Tour De France' all illustrate an "antique modernity", as Hamilton calls it: "Old, nostalgically recalled visions of the future, polished and shiny with the awed glow of conviction, before the notion of modernism began to rust" (Hamilton, 1997, 78). By placing themselves, or rather the image of themselves in antique modernity, Kraftwerk blow up chronometrical time. The time is both 'then' and 'now', but due to Kraftwerk's presence in both of them, they are equalized, they implode. Time is both recollective and contemporary, it equalizes itself.

Science Fiction

Kraftwerk use a double exposure, a temporal composite that is historically insisting. The group's utopian scenario is of a future which due to the striking in the documentary material has become part of our own past (Jameson, (1982, p. 244). Kraftwerk inscribe themselves in the future of the past, which is no longer future or past, but forever part of the common historic past. This is an artifice widely used by literary science fiction. As noted by Frederic Jameson, the apparent realism in science fiction covers a complex temporal structure. When reality:

CREATIVE DESTRUCTION:
transformation in the music industry

> "...as we know it' appears in science fiction, it does not provide us with images of the future, but rather operates by restructuring the experience we have of our present. In this reconstruction of the present, to a version less known ... a process whose primary aim is to transform our present to "the determinate past of something yet to come"
>
> (Jameson, 1982, p. 245).

Science fiction is thus an endeavour to embrace the contemporary with a historic gaze, a possibility to write the present in the great book of History, to fictionalize or narrate the present, which otherwise cannot be embraced in a totalizing gaze. Science fiction becomes a possibility to write contemporary history in a time without history.

The Italian futurists could 'create' themselves by eliminating the past, destroy the museums, or, like Marinetti, jump up from the ditch after a traffic incident and praise the accident (Krauss, 1995, p. 18). But Kraftwerk is not just futurism. The group is also bound to a historic past and can only redeem the futuristic potential by a modification of this past and thus make a breach in time, make a break-in of something radically new which can form a temporal curve or an alternative historical course.

The Future Is Already Now

Kraftwerk play upon this alternative history that reaches correctively back and forth in time. By letting time absorb itself like the two cars in opposed directions on the cover of Autobahn, they reset the chronometrical time, bypass the linear perception of time and fabricate an expression that conveys both a step out of the contemporary and a (alternative) fulfillment of the past. This 'place', this conjured up future, taking place as a conglomerate of past and present, also becomes a place where History with a capital H is possible again, but as a synthetic history or construct. By means of technology, Kraftwerk can stage the historical time as dynamic collage or montage with endless possible referential combinations.

With the continuous play of realistic elements and the futurism of the sound, Kraftwerk stage a world with the characteristics of technology, a vision of an electronic, non-linear era, where the constructivist modular principles are applied on the real and to a certain extent 'tangible' world. The reductive effort, showing itself in the geometrical and sonic basic forms of constructivism and serialism, and reaching its climax in the repetitive grid structure of minimalism, is the natural form for such a project. This matrix-like structure, making up for a zone of possibilities, marks according to Rosalind Krauss the birth into a space of "aesthetic purity and liberty" (Krauss, 1995, p.19). Its basic form is the minimalist square, which is without any determinable origin, i.e. in a certain sense archaic, and hence possible only to re-invent. This game between archaic tradition and innovation, between repetition and anti-referentiality, between History and hostility towards narrative, which with Kraftwerk is expressed by means of the minimalist sound and the synthetic melodies in a historical jiggery-pokery, illustrates the complex relationship between the allegorical and utopian gaze of modernism.

Man-Machine

The album The Man-Machine from 1978 is especially interesting because it honors the android tendencies that Kraftwerk had carried with them from early on, and which from now on was inextricably linked to the identification of the group. Kraftwerk no longer conveyed a spirituality in the machine, but now demonstrated a quite different direct relationship between man and machine.

Robot – Automaton

Kraftwerk create a neutral zone between man and machine where the two work out together, symbolized by the oversized cable which, at a time when it was technically possible to use cordless transferal of signals, connected the large mainframe console with the small portable terminals used for instance to involve the audience when performing 'Pocket Calculator'. The group's heavy use of vocoder effect, merging the human voice with the synthesizer, also points to the exact spot where man meets machine. (Toop, 1999, p. 21). Were Kraftwerk the robots? Or were the robots Kraftwerk? "Sometimes we play the music, sometimes the music plays us, sometimes… it plays", Ralf Hütter told Sounds in 1975 (Quoted in Bussy, 1993, p. 63). In 1991 he elaborated this point of view when he said to journalist Sylvain Gire:

"We are playing the machines, the machines play us; it is really the exchange and the friendship we have with the musical machines which make us build a new music"

(Quoted in Bussy, 1993 p. 96).

Kraftwerk had become an indivisible unit, a composite of man and machinery. But such a composite does not belong to the domain of the robot or the android; Kraftwerk are not a mechanical construction, but a binding between man and machine, a cyborg.

Cyborg – Man-Machine

The doubling and exchange that can be seen between Kraftwerk's four members and the four robots hints at a mirroring between original and copy. The axis of this mirroring lies precisely in the technological ('we play the machines, but they also play us'). This points to a cybernetic field of information in which technology is no longer subject to man as means, tool or instrument. On the contrary: "The machines should not do only slave work, we try to treat them as colleagues so they exchange energies with us" (Hütter, after Hamilton (1997), p.80). The machine is man's equal and has become so by man stepping out of subjectivity. Subjectivity retires and lets the body become machine. "We are not artists nor musicians. First of all we are workers," Hütter explained (quoted in Bussy, 1993, p. 68) and thereby attaches the Kraftwerk phantasmagoria to Russian constructivism and the worker subject of the modern age. The worker exchanges his individuality with the idea of a collective subject, just as the feedback phenomenon that appears between man and technology in continuation of information theory and cybernetics, opens for an electronic collectivization of the human body (Thomas, 1995, p. 34).

With the cyborg, technology moves over to the domain of the human, and together they pass the dichotomies of modernity. It is no longer a question of man or machine, organic vs. mechanic, but instead of both. The concepts are confused instead of being divided in pairs. The cyborg is "a machine of simulation" (Goldberg, 1995, p. 237), writes Jonathan Goldberg; a man "produced through and succeeding as simulation" (Goldberg, 1995, p. 244) that bypasses deadlocks such as 'gender' and 'race', 'life' and 'death' by a total combination creating a composite of the necessary dichotomy of the organic (then/now, life/death) with the technological whose essence is 'non-linearity' (collage) and 'infinity'. The cyborg crosses man and machine, past and present, and is created in the real, i.e. in the collective consciousness. Through technology man can – as a cyborg – surmount the modernist denial of imitation, its division in conceptual pairs, and put instead a quivering "internuncial pool," as Norbert Wiener wrote, that can activate any meaning, any image or expression by a constructivist/syntactical manoeuvre (Wiener, 1954, p. 80). In this simulating/simulated, post-modern conception of time, the linear, chronometrical time has vanished. Kraftwerk can make a timeless imaginary/historical train journey in 1923, robots can appear in totalitarian and androgynous brilliance. By recreating themselves as robots, Kraftwerk make possible an industrial reproduction that deletes the causal relation between copy and original. "Only the obliteration of the original reference allows for the generalized law of equivalence, that is to say the very possibility of production," writes the French philosopher Jean Baudrillard (Baudrillard, 1983, p. 97). The eight equalized robots become an image of industrial production, just like the name 'Kraftwerk' expresses a technological process. By duplicating, Kraftwerk demonstrate at one and the same time the death of the original and the end of representation, and refers instead to a mutual exchange between equal models (Baudrillard, 1983, pp. 136-137), a multiplied quasi subject, synthetically manufactured from a total spectrum of memories, images, events.

Simulation

With Kraftwerk the relation between man and technology is expressed as a theme where – just as with the science fiction author Phillip K. Dick – it is the memory that constitutes the human being. Kraftwerk show, that if it is indeed the memory that gives us our identity, then this unique identity is lost in the era of the "post-human" where the organic can be separated from its subjectivity and they both can be modified as an object through technology. It is the inscription in a chronological stream and hence the memory, that creates time in man and shapes the subjectivity. The memory ties us to our bodies in time, but as a product of technology the man-machine becomes absolutely mobile and moves in an electronic field or 'sampler field', where time is plastic. The binding between man and technology creates an emblem or symbol of time travel, a dream of being able to move freely through the historical material (Goldberg, 1995, p. 244). Man is subject to time, to exist means to have the ability to remember. Hütter and Schneider are insistent about being without recollections from 'before', and this is the reset command by which they format themselves and become Kraftwerk, program themselves into a tabula rasa, a blank form, that is manifest in the doubled robots. Only Lester Bangs, in 1975 managed to wrench from them answers of a more personal character, for instance of their musical influences – which include both The Ramones and The Beach Boys (Bussy, 1993, p. 64). Later answers to questions of this kind have been "nothing… Silence". (Hütter, quoted in Bussy, 1993, p. 16).

By their constructed memories Kraftwerk become a model of a model, a construct or simulacrum, which transgresses the barrier between fiction and reality, between man and machine. When Kraftwerk, in the video clips 'Trans Europa Express', 'The Model' and 'Tour de France', are present in historic ("documentary") material, i.e. in a past occurrence, it is the same kind of manufacturing of memory and hence subjectivity, as we see as a theme in films like Bladerunner (1982) and Total Recall (1990), both of them built on original stories by Phillip K. Dick. When the models on the catwalk at the fashion show in 'The Model' step down from the podium they become available in the crowd as bodies, subjects. Kraftwerk never step down from the podium, they have left their subjectivity, body and memories in order to assemble in a technological form as Kraftwerk, the man-machine.

Cyberspace

Like Darth Vader, Kraftwerk have turned towards "the dark side", the dehumanization of technology, and have doubled themselves. The spirit has spread in a mutually controlled information-cybernetic system. Kraftwerk, the man-machine, is connected to the physical world through a system of prostheses: dolls, statements, vocoder, synthetic history, through sound and through bodies; synthesizer sound, one liners, repeating rhythms, man/doll doubling, electronic percussion. Through repetition and doubling Kraftwerk move from representing that industrial process the name Kraftwerkencapsulates, to become the very same. Kraftwerk develop from using a material of simulated, real objects (Doppler effects, railway sounds) to a formal language of a more complete abstraction. This development culminates with the tight electronic minimalism on the album Computerworld (1981), but has already moved past the real sounds at the time of The Man-Machine. This constant movement away from the real is to be taken literally. Kraftwerk phases out reality on these albums in favor of an autonomous system of perfect abstraction. The robots are reduced to sepia toned photographs on the cover of Computerworld, virtualized as the raw data of the computer image on Electric Café (1986), to appear revitalized in front of a blue screen on the cover of The Mix (1991) and the accompanying video 'The Robots'.

It is the principle of production, celebrating the possibility to part mind and body by a duplication through a technological system. By becoming the dolls' equals, their exact copy, Kraftwerk slide out of the domain of art to exist in that of reality as an autonomous, cybernetic organism with (de-)constructed subjectivity. Hütter-Schneider-Bartos-Flur did not give up their physical existence, but their own unique history in exchange for becoming a product. The simulated world is represented as a 'real' world by these cybernetic agents, but in BEING this world, that is produced, the question of representation is punctured.

When simulation seriously becomes virtual reality, the foundation will be laid for a world in which nothing needs to be the way we know it, and hence also can create sensations that are genuinely innovative. This virtual reality is a "consensual hallucination" as William Gibson calls it (Gibson, 1986, p. 12), but as a genuine physical and tactile construction. An imaginary world made flesh, a reality machine. As we have got used to the separation from nature, we are now also getting used to the post-human condition. The first signs of simulation in the physical-real are found in popular culture. Pop carries the first evidence of the post-modern, writes Andreas Hyussen (Hyussen, 1986 p. 188). Kraftwerk unite the avant-garde with mass culture by joining concrete and electronic music with the form language of minimalism in a template which is fundamentally pop.

By reproducing it technologically, pop art injures the unique object of modernism. Man recreates himself in the image of the machine to obtain another consciousness, untouched by charged discourse and personal history. Implants in the human body, plastic surgery and the Council of Ethics testify to this, but the last step towards the post-human is taken with a distribution of the self-consciousness and its transformation into image in popular culture. Cyberspace as this denaturalization is not an immaterial, vector based, graphical space, but alive and kicking and modified. Pop stars getting smaller noses and bigger breasts can now also sing in tune aided by pitch control.

Cyberspace has long ago made its appearance in the economy and society, where corporations like Pepsi, Nike, Tommy Hilfiger, FUBU and Givenchy are morphing themselves with real people that exist both inside and out of the public space, i.e. people with a history in both places. This is also the difference between the model of earlier times, and the supermodel, which is a model of the model. Kraftwerk are a prototype of this doubling, which Baudrillard calls hyper real, "the generation by models of a real without origin or reality" (Baurdrillard, 1983, p. 2). Cyberspace is

CREATIVE DESTRUCTION:
transformation in the music industry

far from being merely a vaguely formulated, far away place in cables and in the air surrounding the planet. Cyberspace is the public space, popular culture, populated by cyborgs in an information-cybernetic world.

May The Funk Be With You

Throughout the 20th Century man's relation to and understanding of technology has been under constant change – like technology itself. Pierre Schaeffer's grouping of technology under man and the dictum of the primacy of the ear, Stockhausen's omni-electrical universe, and Kraftwerk's consideration for technology as a Siamese twin, testify to a development of technical and of technological competence, that have brought man and technology closer and closer to one another. The historical development of electronic music, as shown above, beginning with man's control of technology as an instrument or tool, shows a tendency towards greater and greater integration of the human and the technical, to be rendered by Kraftwerk as a technical/human composite of technical character. The original incompatibility between Schaeffer and Stockhausen, which can be construed as a dichotomy between system and material, machine and man, found a balance with Stockhausen, but without the ability to integrate man himself. For Stockhausen, the organizing principle resides with the technical, first based on mathematics, later on arbitrariness.

Techno

Electronic music develops from Stockhausen's serial homeostat-like compositions to Kraftwerk's man-machine, in leading the music genre. In the history of cybernetics, as N. Katherine Hayles has shown, cybernetics moves from being a concept of closed systems to a concept of open systems that can accommodate the human actor-user as a phenomenological dimension in the system (Hayles, 1996). Likewise, a phenomenological position in electronic music is marked by the use of Kraftwerk in the early 1980s by people like Afrika Bambaataa in New York and Juan Atkins (aka Cybotron, Model 500 a.o.) in Detroit.

In 1982 Bambaataa released the single 'Don't Stop...Planet Rock', built around a sampling of Kraftwerk's 'Trans Europa Express', but integrated in a totally new context. Atkins on the other hand, wanted to create the same kind of music as the Düsseldorf four piece and had the year before (in 1981, the same year as Kraftwerk's Computerworld came out) released the single 'Alleys of Your Mind' with Rick Davis on the duo's own label Deep Space, using their Cybotron moniker. ('Alleys of Your Mind' is usually considered the world's second techno release, the first being 'Sharevari' by A Number of Names, released shortly before.)

The two genres more or less founded by Atkins and Bambaataa, techno and electro ("electronic funk"), is in a way repeating the 1950s incompatibility and opposition between pure electronic music and concrete music as a difference between produced and recorded music. Essentially, electro is hip hop, an innovative musical genre originating from the black ghettos of New York around 1970 and culminating in 1979 with the release of the Sugarhill Gang single 'Rapper's Delight' which spread the word around the globe, selling 14 million copies. Hip hop and electro use sound material from existing records, mixed and manipulated by a DJ. The first DJs worked with two identical copies of the same record to isolate the musical groove and prolong it into infinity. A DJ doesn't produce, but arranges, coordinates, performs. Like Pierre Schaeffer the DJ re-produces the existing, but dynamically: the crosscut- or montage-technique is directly operational in real time. Hip hop transforms music to a sampler field, and renders its history freely available. Techno, on the contrary, is a pure electronic music which like in the 1950s is produced using machines: synthesizers and drum machines.

Hip hop and electro are facing the existing, the history, as material that is broken up and reintegrated, but unlike the early electronic music, techno does not turn its back on history. In spite of their differences, both techno and electro strive towards a

CREATIVE DESTRUCTION:
transformation in the music industry

technological or electronic motivated futurism in the shape of Kraftwerk, but anchored in originality. In New York, electro was based on hip hop's use of original material on vinyl, but Bambaataa insisted that the music should also have funk: "I was always into Kraftwerk, Yellow Magic Orchestra, Gary Numan. I said there is no black group out here that plays strictly electronics. Herbie Hancock and all of them did that, but I'm talking about a strict funk type of groove." (Quoted in Toop, 1999, p. 23). The point of departure for Juan Atkins on the other hand, was synthetic music itself, but this should also be further developed to include an element of funk: "My concept was that Kraftwerk, Telex and Devo were good – but they weren't funky," Atkins has explained (quoted in Trask, 1996, p. 44). "I felt that if I could do that type of music and add a funky element to it then it would be a smash".

The word "funk" can be traced back to the roots of black culture and Congo in the 17th Century where it was an expression for the scent of the body. "Funk is earth, sex, rawness, nature, power, seduction," writes the German music writer Ulf Poschardt. (Poschardt, 1998, p. 417). Funk can be regarded as a metaphor for a black cultural essence, a kind of watermark of authenticity, set at play by the black people of America across the Atlantic between a lost originality and a new world. Funk is, in other words, that piece of information that sanctions any creation coming out of the black culture as a mark of authenticity. The basis for both techno and electro is thus a complex of originality and technological futurism, a binding between man and machine, but on man's conditions.

HISTORY AND ORIGINS OF ELECTRONIC MUSIC

Past-future

Tentatively, the decisive difference between techno and electro can be said to be that of temporal orientation: both techno and electro is directed towards the future, techno with a synthetic tone material, electro by reworking the existing. With funk as an immaterial originality it becomes possible to inscribe a space-time structure in the music that is bound to the human body. Both Afrika Bambaataa and Juan Atkins incorporated Kraftwerk's incorporeal music in this structure of bodily originality as a complex of past (originality) and future. The concept for techno can thus be described as a composite of retrospection and futurism, of man and machine, but on equal terms. With the words of Detroit producer Jeff Mills, the basic idea of techno is to create something one cannot imagine:

> "If you hear something that you'd never expect to hear — that's techno.[...] You have to be able to dream. You have to be able to leave everything that you know and everything you have learned. You have to create something completely new..."
>
> (Quoted in Kempster, 1986, p. 17).

Techno signifies a quantum leap into the future, whereas electro rather creates an alternative present with an unbiased and futuristic look at the contemporary world.

By sampling Kraftwerk, Afrika Bambaataa punctured the group's timelessness and established it in a social context of dancing bodies. Kraftwerk could bypass the space-time difference between themselves and the apparatus, and thus equalize the difference between the human being and the construction. Techno re-inscribes this lost dimension by insisting on the body (funk). It is not as with Kraftwerk subjectivity that is being technologically modified, in techno the machine assists man as a tool that can dissolve chronology and in other ways operate crosswise without dissolving subjectivity, just as the language can be broken down into smaller units, and be combined to mutated hybrid-words such as "cybotron" (cyborg+electron) – the electronic cyborg, and "metroplex" (metropolitan complex), the name of Atkins' own record label, founded in 1985. Techno can operate in temporality by e.g. using older technology. A synthesizer comes with a string of presets – fixed combinations of sounds and effects – used by most people, which date the apparatus to a certain epoch. By taking the detour across the machinery of the past, techno can create an alternative historic path, a futurism that can redeem the potential of the past. That was what Derrick May did, when he released 'Strings of Life' using the moniker

CREATIVE DESTRUCTION:
transformation in the music industry

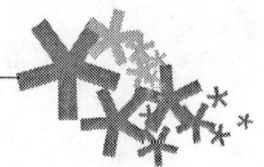

Rythim is Rythim in 1987. Derrick May, with schoolmates Juan Atkins and Kevin Saunderson are usually credited as the originators of techno music, used the older and slightly primitive Ensoniq Mirage instead of one of the popular synthesizers of the time, such as Roland JD-800 or Yamaha DX7. In doing so, he created a track which by its coupling of present and past led into the future. May broke the chronometric linearity, folded time and shaped the future through the past.

Likewise, a dated bass synthesizer became central for a whole sub-genre within house music. Acid house was based on Roland's TB303 Bass Line, introduced in 1983 as a bass synthesizer targeted towards popular music as a "band in a box" with the TB808 drum machine. It was irksome to program, expensive, didn't even sound at all like a bass, and was a failure. Until DJ Pierre of the Chicago group Phuture began to mess around with the filter-, resonance-, and modulation-buttons while the machine was playing a sequence. The result was a completely unknown destabilization of the tone material in real time, the characteristic acid sound, which emerged by chance and first was released on a record when Phuture put out the single 'Acid Trax' in 1987. Techno marks a development that in relation to Kraftwerk is only partly tied to technology; techno maintains the chronological history, inscribed as body.

HISTORY AND ORIGINS OF ELECTRONIC MUSIC

Summary

Electronic music has been investigated through the last half of the 20th Century. It has been described from the first experiments with advanced electronic machinery by Pierre Schaeffer and Karlheinz Stockhausen, Kraftwerk's reintegration of man in the machine, and finally the revitalization of the body in techno music.

As we have seen, electronic music does not only seek to convey an artistic message that can be interpreted through the sentiments established though the tone material in the listener. Electronic music is constantly reflecting the relation between man (the producer) and the instrument (the machine). The two schools of the 1950s, concrete and pure electronic music, marked the basic discrepancy in electronic music as a difference between man and the machine that is used in producing the music. The one prioritized the ear and the material, the other the complexity or the system. This discrepancy or fundamental difference culminated with Kraftwerk who quite explicitly inscribed the human in technology as a technological replication by staging the dissolving of subjectivity as a play or game with man's physical constraint expressed through historical chronology and robot dolls. Kraftwerk could freely combine – and hence produce – historical incidents in an electronic cycle where the metaphor is that of a non-linear, three-dimensional grid structure rather than a chronological, linear lapse of time. In this autonomous and closed cycle between man and machine, man is subordinate to technology. As Kraftwerk clearly demonstrate, it is possible for man to step into the auspicious simultaneous time solely if he renounces his physical existence, tied to the human body.

Techno, emerging as a mixed black/white musical form or genre in the beginning of the 1980s, adopts Kraftwerk's vision of technology as a futuristic principle. In techno the aim is also the future as an alternative historical path, a redemption of a potential, but contrary to Kraftwerk and the early purely electronic music, techno has a phenomenological dimension based in the human body.

HISTORY AND ORIGINS OF ELECTRONIC MUSIC

ELECTRONIC MUSIC: STYLES AND MAPS

The electronic dance music which emerged in the 1980s and 1990s directly benefited from developments already set forth decades before – from fringe audio-scientists who spent hours assembling cut and paste symphonies to the disco and hip-hop DJs who provided seamless dance mixes using two turntables, a mixer and a crate of vinyl (Bogdanov et al., 2001). In 1983/4 dance music was, indeed essentially disco, although hybrids such as electro, go go and rare groove also existed (Larkin, 1998). Mainstream America's dislike of disco meant that the major labels at the time wanted nothing to do with it (Prendegast, 2000, p. 372), though house music emerged during the early 1980s as a low –cost continuation of the disco aesthetic (Rietveld, 1998). Although initially the DJs were the undisputed king of the dance underground, house producers finally arrived. From the initial blueprint of house and techno music, electronic dance music diversified to include dozens of styles: trance, drum 'n' bass, electro, breakbeat, downbeat and intelligent electronica. This chapter will discuss the major styles[22] emanating from the original blueprint – house and techno, drawing upon the work of Bogdanov et al., (2001) to map the patterns of music development.

CREATIVE DESTRUCTION:
transformation in the music industry

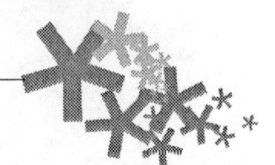

House Music

House music was built on the innovations of disco but with less of the '"flash" and even less of a reliance on lyrics (Larkin, 1998, p. 155). The music styles that influenced house music (electro, funk and disco) and the electronic hybrids it led to are presented in Figure 3.1. Although New York was the birthplace of house, it was in Chicago that the music grew up. Chicago House got its name from the electronic soul mixes of Frankie Knuckle's Warehouse parties, which played from 1977 to the early 1980s. Knuckles had moved from New York and inaugurated the original Warehouse club, and much of his DJ-ing was for gay audiences who preferred psychedelia to alcohol. Hence the flavour of early Chicago House was insistent bass figures, looping drums, and a strong erotic content delivered by a male drag figure (Prendegast, 2000, p. 368).

The music remained largely confined to the gay clubs until, led by local labels Trax and DJ International, house music exploded around the city, reaching an early peak for the style around 1986 with producers like Larry Heard ("Can you Feel It"), Marshall Jefferson ("Move Your Body – The House Music Anthem"), Farley Jackmaster Funk ("Love Can't Turn Around") and Steve "Silk" Hurley ("Jack Your Body") leading the way (Bogdanov et al., 2002). Their style, which favoured expressive vocalists and the organic piano-and-string runs of classic disco singles, made radio airplay quite viable – both Farley and Hurley hit the charts in Britain in 1986 (Rietveld, 1998).

As time passed and musicians like Larry Heard made the music both more instrumental and stimulating, labels like Trax were willing to invest more in innovation. Trax's owner, Larry Sherman encouraged his producer, Marshall Jefferson, to seek out new sounds and new artists. After they heard the work of Phuture, who used a squelchy Roland drum box in their music, Acid House was born. For Prendegast (2000) they had made an interesting connection between the 1960s Psychedelia Ultra-Minimalist and the simplistic, squirting, repetitive noises of Phuture's "Acid Tracks".

With America still a bit resistant to the new spin on an old sound, Europeans began taking up the slack, courtesy of worldwide house pop hits by M/A/R/R/S, S'Express, Bomb the Bass, Coldcut, Technotronic, and the KLF (Bogdanov et al., 2001). In just a few years emerged the most important youth-culture phenomenon the country had seen since the heady days of punk of the '70s. What had been a small but intensely fraternal scene during the mid-'80s exploded during 1988 – Britain's very own "Summer of Love" (Prendegast, 2000 Rietveld, 1995).

By the end of 1990, massive outdoor raves were being attended by tens of thousands of youths. While Detroit techno figured to a large extent in the sound of rave, it was Chicago and New York house music that defined the sound (Bogdanov et al., 2001). Even when Britain's first completely indigenous electronic dance style, jungle or drum 'n' bass, emerged in the mid-'90s, house music still retained its hold on the biggest clubs, the most tuned-in radio shows and the biggest-selling albums (Fleming, 1995; Kempster, 1996; Bidder, 1999).

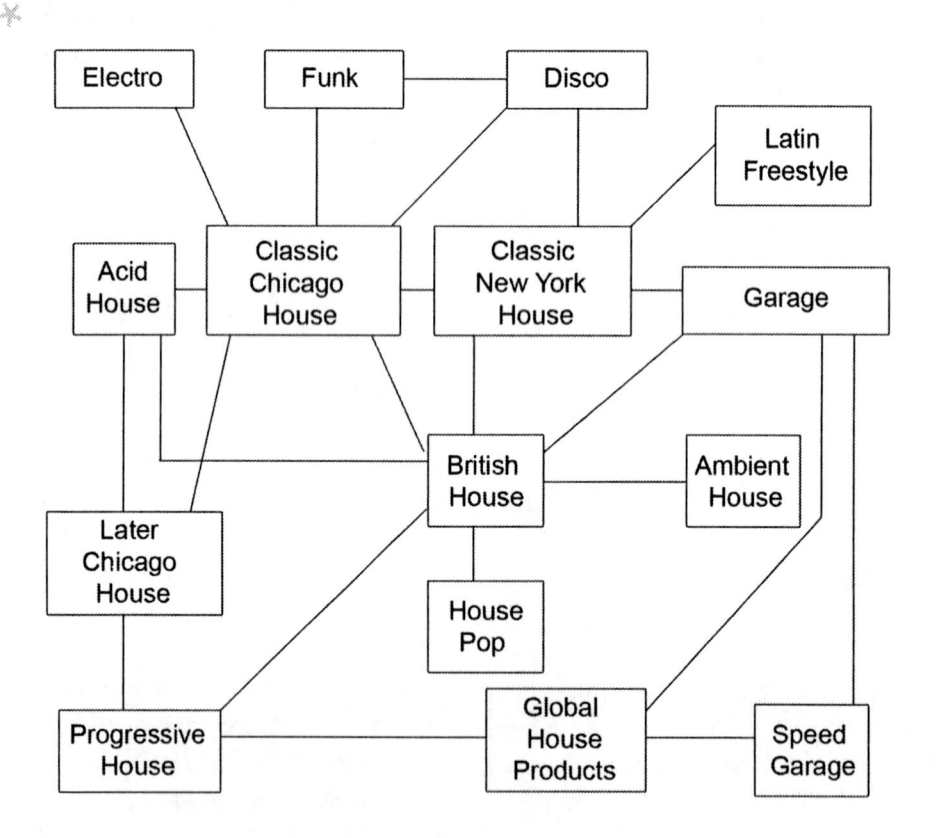

Figure 3.1 A style map of the house sub-genre
(Source: Adapted from Bogdanov et al., 2001, p. 630).

Techno

According to Larkin (1998, p. 335) techno made its way into the technicolour world of pop consciousness – officially at least - in May 1988 courtesy of an article by Stuart

CREATIVE DESTRUCTION:
transformation in the music industry

Cosgrove in that month's issue of The Face and the release of the Virgin compilation "Techno! The New Dance Sound of Detroit". It was used to describe the work of Saunderson (particularly "Big Fun"), Derrick May (who recorded the anthem, "Strings of Life" and Juan Atkins ("No UFOs"). The birth of Techno can be traced to the early 1980s and the emaciated inner-city of Detroit, where figures such as Juan Atkins, Derrick May, and Kevin Saunderson, among others, fused the quirky machine music of Kraftwerk and Yellow Magic Orchestra with the space-race electric funk of George Clinton, the optimistic futurism of Alvin Toffler's "Third Wave" (Barr, 2000). Juan Atkins declared:

> "The Detroit underground has been experimenting with technology, stretching it rather than simply using it. As the price of sequencers and synthesisers has dropped, so the experimentation has become more intense. Basically, we're tired of hearing about being in love or falling out, tired of the R & B system, so a new progressive term has emerged. We call it Techno".
>
> (Quoted in Barr, 2000, p. vii)

Having grown up with the latter-day effects of Fordism, the Detroit techno musicians (Atkins, Derek May, Vietnam veteran Rick Davies who called himself 3070, his dog tag number according to legend) found that Toffler's sound-bite predictions for change – "blip culture", " the intelligent environment", "the infosphere", "de-massification of the media de-massifies our minds", "the techno rebels", "appropriate technologies" – accorded with some, though not all, of their own institutions (Toop, 1995, p. 215). Techno also reflected the city's (Detroit) decline, as well as the advent of technology, and this tension was crucial to the dynamics of the sound. As Kevin Saunderson recounts:

> "When we first started doing the music we were ahead. But Detroit is still a very behind city when it comes to anything cultural".
>
> (Quoted in Larkin, 1998, p. 335).

Thereby a definition of techno would be as Juan Atkins put it:

> "You gotta look at it like techno is technological. It's an attitude to making music that is futuristic: something that hasn't been done before."
>
> (Quoted in Savage, 1996, p. 19).

ELECTRONIC MUSIC: STYLES AND MAPS

Derrick May once describe techno's man-machine fusion as "George Clinton and Kraftwerk caught in an elevator with only a sequencer to keep them company," (Quoted in Shapiro, 2000, p. 111). Early techno tracks (on such labels as Metroplex, Transmat, and KMS) were generally produced for limited-run 12" release, and although the global popularity of the music in the present day has ensured that many of them have remained in print, techno remained a local phenomenon until the records started showing up on European shores (Bogdanov, 2002). This largely reflected Detroit's post-apocalyptic mystique that is crucial to the mythology of Detroit techno. It's a unique contradiction of musicians creating an imaginary future while being surrounded by industrialisation" and "ghost town" emptiness (Shapiro, 2000, p. 115).

Techno exploded onto London's emerging acid house scene in the mid- to late-80s (itself a quixotic mix of Chicago and New York house) with labels such as Warp, GPR, Infonet, and Rephelx, and artists such as LFO, Richard H.. Kirk, Richard James/Aphex Twin, Reload/Link, Germ B12, and the Black Dog taking the spare electronic experiments of the early Detroit innovators to the next level of abstraction (Bogdanov, 2000). According to Saunderson (quoted in Larkin, 1998, p. 333) the difference between the Detroit techno and its re-interpretation "kind of lay in it lacking the spirituality of the original".

Though techno has been divided between those keeping to the original Detroit sound (Tresor, Force Inc, D-Jax Up Beats, R & S), primarily located in continental Europe[23] and the generation of UK producers emerging in the mid-1990s whose innovations in rhythm programming and edit experimentation swept aside the astral melancholy of techno – L.T.J. Bukem, Goldie, Foul Play, 4 Hero, Omni Trio, Roni Size, DJ Crystal (Toop, 1995).

A style map summarising the progression of techno from its Detroit origins to many different and interesting areas such as Jungle/Drum'n'bass, trance (these emerging areas will be discussed in more depth later in the chapter) is presented in Figure 3.2.

Its interesting to note in contrast to Saunderson's view that techno is in the US a marginal, underground music that has been slow to evolve in its birthplace (Bogadnov et al., (2001). Ironically it is the European reinterpretation of the techno – trip hop, jungle, intelligent electronic music - where much of the creativity and innovation is taking place (e.g. Aurtchre, Aphex Twin).

CREATIVE DESTRUCTION:
transformation in the music industry

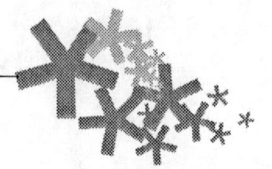

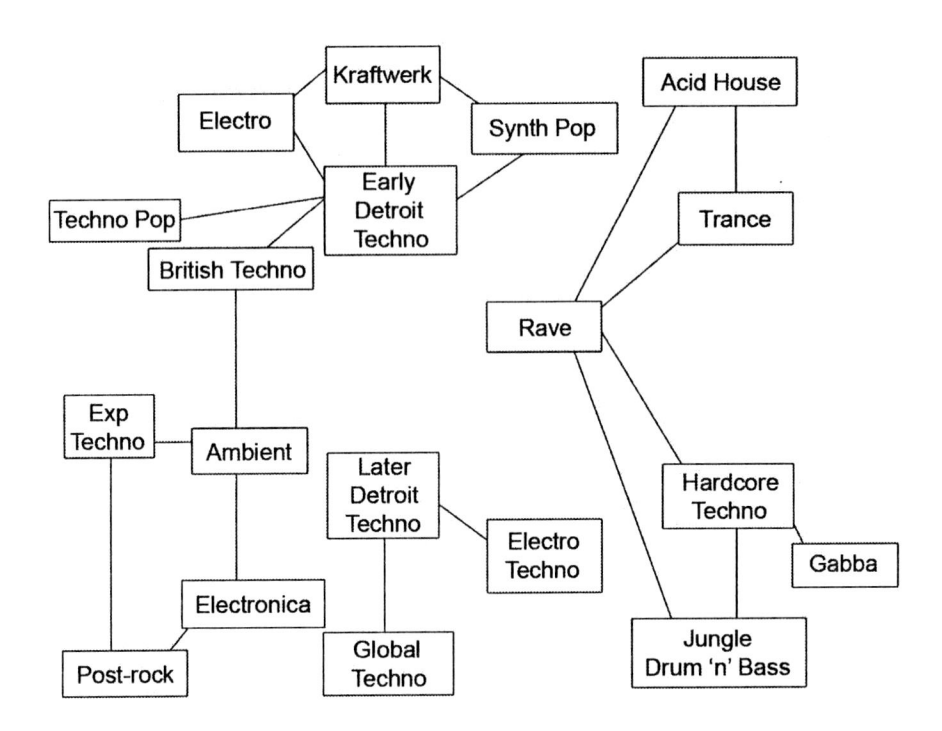

Figure 3.2 A style map of the techno music sub-genre
(Source: Adapted from Bogdanov et al., 2001, pp. 632 – 633).

Trance

The diversification of electronic dance music culture in the 1990s did not signal the end of the original techno and house, that came back with great popularity at the end of the twentieth century with trance (Prendegast, 2000, p. 372). Trance is a super fast offshoot of techno that uses sparse, repetitive structures, dense melodic textures, and high BPMs to induce a sort of mesmerised state (Bogdanov, 2001, p. 373). The new sound complemented a younger generation socialised in mobile phones, the Internet, gadgets such as personal digital assistants (PDAs) and MP3 players. Popular for its psychedelic themes and often used in combination with hallucinogens to enhance the psychotropic effects, the style has been the most popular in Germany where it originated during the early 1990s with the likes of Hardfloor, DJ Criss, Pete Namlook and Sven Vath. An increasingly ethnic-infused strain became popular in Goa, in the south of India during the mid-1990s, which became known as Goa trance, which plays up the spacey, psychedelic side with movie samples and heavy basslines. Paul

Oakenfold, is the re-mixer and producer who made a huge contribution to breaking house music in the UK during the late 1980s (Larkin, 1998). Oakenfold championed trance the world over and this would make him by the end of the century, one of the worlds most popular DJs (Prendegast, 2000). Hardcore techno artists such as Joey Beltram and Dave Clarke also helped to blur the line between trance and harder styles of techno, utilising highly repetitive rhythms layered with slight, slowly morphing electronics.

Ambient pioneer and prolific dance music re-mixer, William Orbit was thrust into the mainstream with his trance infusion into Madonna's 1998 Ray of Light album which he helped to co-write. By 1998, most of Europe's best known DJ's – Oakenfold and Sasha + Digweed plus Pete Tong, Danny Rampling – were playing trance in Britain's superclubs such as Gatecrasher and in the leading Ibiza venue – Space. America turned on to the sound (eventually) through leading DJs including: Christopher Lawrence, Sandra Collins and Kimball Collins. According to Prendegast (2000), trance reached its peak in 1999, with ATB selling a million copies and hitting the number-one position in the UK singles chart with the addictive repeated guitar sample of "9PM Till I come".

Drum 'N' Bass/jungle

The evolution of jungle is hard to pin down, though the music's mutation of elements from not only hardcore, but reggae, raga, hip-hop, jazz, and dub, as well as its origins in social and economic factors such as racist and class-based oppression, have a distinctly British mix. The roots of jungle are depicted in Figure 3.3. Born largely in the working class suburbs of London's East End and the island's Eastern seaboard and now popular throughout England, as well as Europe and North America, jungle has coalesced since its birth into one of the most exciting and distinctive British musical movements since the '60s rock explosion. (Bogdanov, 2002). Musically jungle rides on a combination of breakbeats and samples with staccato rhythms and subsonic bass (Larkin, 1998, p. 176).

The sound was pioneered in clubs by DJ Ron, Randal, Bob Konders and on radio by Jumping Jack Frost (on Kiss FM) and pirates such as Kool Fm, Transmission One and Don FM. Although, like most origin mythologies, jungle was fraught with intriguing stories of its birth and etymology (even extending to a street gang in Kingston, Jamaica known as the Junglists), most agree that somewhere down the line "jungle"

took on a racist connotation stemming from its popularity among England's inner-city black population (although, to a far larger extent than in America, England's inner-cities are of mixed race and are stratified more by class (Prendegast, 2000)).

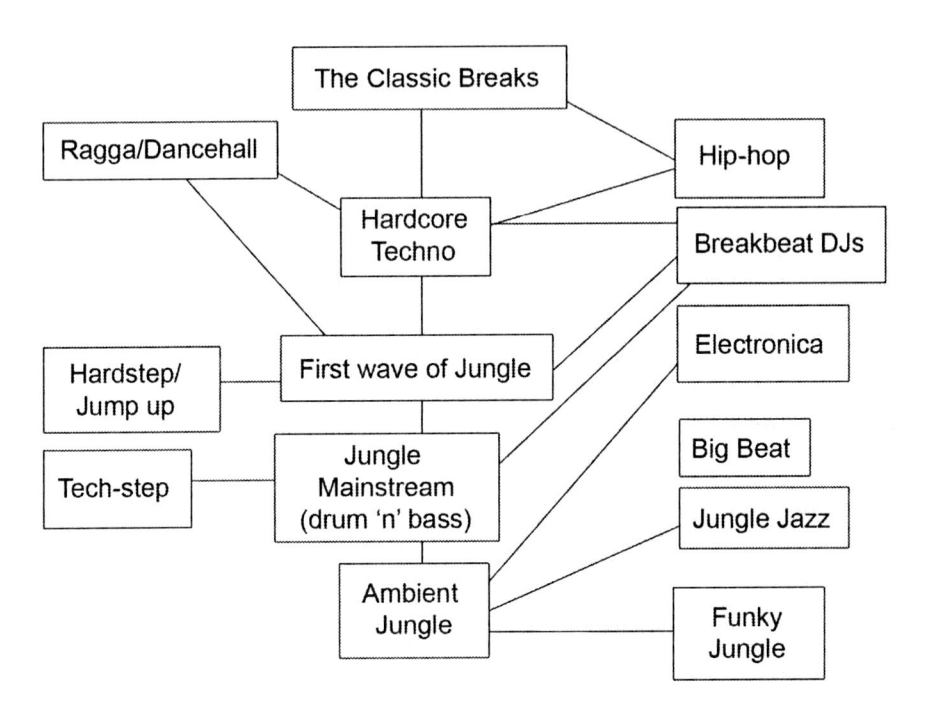

Figure 3.3 A style map for the Jungle/Drum 'n' bass sub genre
(Source: Adapted from Bogdanov et al., 2001, p. 637).

The evolution of jungle into drum 'n' bass is presented in Figure 3.3. Jungle was closely associated with ecstasy culture, as its fragmented drum-loop driven music was a perfect complement, its style post-house and primarily urban black. Increasingly though with the arrival of a new wave of artists such as Goldie, LTJ Bukem and 4 Hero who dug deeper into the world of computer-morphed drum sounds, the term "drum n bass" began to replace jungle and entered into the music mainstream. Goldie's fascination with contrasting fast and slow elements, orchestration and 3D sound-space was fully explored on Timeless (1995), which is largely deemed to be a genre-defining "drum n bass" masterpiece (Prendegast, 2000, p. 372).

Electro

Started by Afrika Bambaataa's "Planet Rock", electro music was first heard in the USA in the early 1980s and harnessed the video game craze and insatiable appetite for electronica and the computerised beat (Larkin, 1998, p. 108). Figure 3.4 shows that electro fused together 1970s funk (Kool and the Gang, Issaac hayes), disco (Donna Summer, Chic, Giorgio Moroder) and techno sound of Kraftwerk, and the synthetic pop of Gary Numan and Japan's Yellow Magic Orchestra). Electro's proper heyday was the period 1982-88, following the explosion of early hip-hop culture in a number of American inner cities (Bogdanov et al., 2001). Almost immediately electro began to evolve into various other styles – old style rap (through LL Cool J, Schooly D, and Ice-T, among many others), techno (Atkins', Cybotron and Model 500 projects), Miami bass and freestyle (Maggotron, Freestyle, Dynamix II, and Trinere), industrial (Front 242, Ministry).

The mid-1980s saw the arrival of Run DMC with their more robust, hard-hitting approach than the electro inspired old-school rap. The DMC style became the musical form of choice among inner-city (and suburban) youth. Electro soon began dying out, and up until the late 1990s remained the interest of historians and collectors. Interestingly, towards the end of the century, there started to be a renewed interest in updating electro's past. Bogdanov writes:

"Artists as diverse as the Jedi knights, Aphex Twin, Phil Klein...Autechre have built on electro's legacy in their own contexts, taking the hitting machine breaks of the music's early years and combining it with a digital aesthetic and increasing musicality that have re-fired its relevance"

(2001, p. 645).

CREATIVE DESTRUCTION:
transformation in the music industry

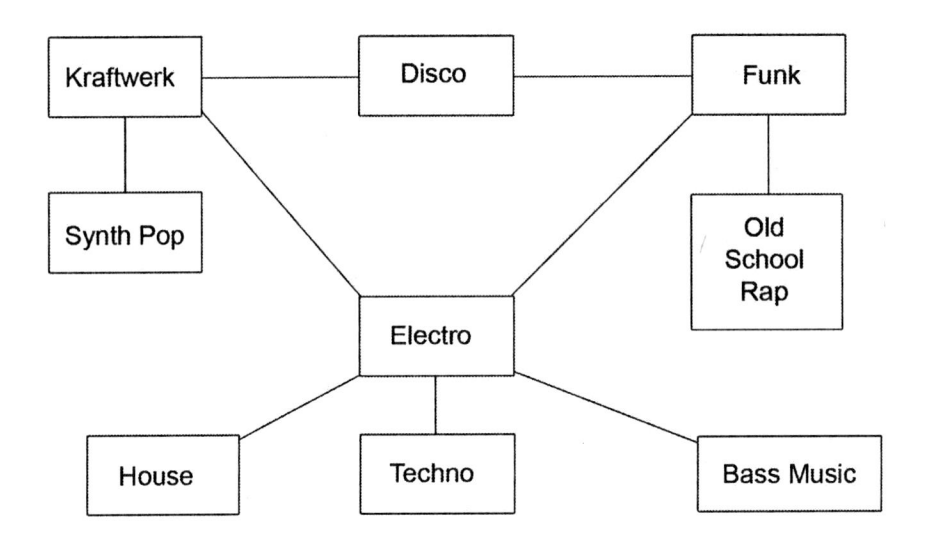

```
    Kraftwerk ──── Disco ──── Funk
        │                      │
    Synth Pop              Old School Rap
         \                   /
          \                 /
           \    Electro    /
          / |     |     | \
         /  |     |     |  \
      House   Techno   Bass Music
```

Figure 3.4 A style map of the electro sub genre
(Source: adapted from Bogdanov et al., 2001, p. 644).

The US also saw a movement in techno and hip hop (most noticeably 2Pac and the Bass Kittens) towards electro roots (Larkin, 1998). Both the European and American artists are taking electro's style into new innovative and creative directions: mixing it with techno, hip hop, house, Latin rhythms, the lyrical potential of rap, female vocals and simple melodies. The remainder of this chapter presents a series of small case studies of artists who have played a key role in the evolution of electronic music to where it is today.

Case 1   Wicked innovators: Basement Jaxx

House music has always been about combination; about putting two pieces together the right way. In the 1970's USA those legendary disc jockeys' disco music created a value vacuum in which the spellbound and hedonistic dancing audience could invest a corresponding emancipation in some sort of sublime ecstasy. And through the 1970's and 1980's, where disco first became a dance movie with John Travolta and later moved from New York to Chicago and became (ware-) house, deep house and garage, the four-to-the-floor dance music has been a post modern beauty, always keen to borrow, steal and rob from any source that was able to contribute anything.

Via the white island Ibiza, Europe was hit by the American dance fever as the 1980's came to a close, and especially in the UK dance culture broke lose. Manchester became Madchester, fronted by bands like Happy Mondays and 808 State who provided the soundtrack to the island people's drug-enhanced "2nd Summer of Love". Looking historically at it, it is probably here – in the similarity between the E-fuelled brain and hi-end technology – that one finds the roots of the development of house music in the 1990's. Both drugs and technology make possible the perfect changeover, the perfect transition between two samples, between a female vocal and a scratch, between instruments, styles, personalities.

In the 1990's, when samplers became ubiquitous and post modernity finally petrified and was deconstructed at the sight of its own ugly face in the mirror, a way was simultaneously paved for a new generation of producers who found the way back to house music's nerve and soul through the assembly of machinery's power cords and the electronic bits in the computer.

As the decade enters its final half, two of them – Felix Buxton and Simon Ratcliffe – throw a series of parties at a lurid Mexican restaurant in London's hardboiled Brixton district. The parties are soon brought to a halt by a combination of too many crack dealers and too many police, but Buxton and Ratcliffe are having it. They move into Ratcliffe's home studio where they continue to brew a mix of New York house and London's club culture that will recall the original atmosphere from The Loft and filter it through the two beer slinging lads' grey matter. They cut a few singles which receive more than usual attention with giddy style blends and fabulous hooks, and when the Basement Jaxx debut album "Remedy" is launched in 1999, both the hype- and the buzz machine are running at their maximum. The duo refer to their music as "punk garage" – underground dance music with bits and pieces of latin, ragga, hip hop and vocals spread all over like after a shell in the pit of the stomach of music history. They cross R'n'B songs with swampy house, yelling and screaming with squashing garage beats, bass with trumpets, cut it all up and glue it – apparently – randomly together, and in other ways do what they can to spice up every rule in tactful dance music with a sneering south London attitude. According to New Yorker DJ Armand van Helden's risqué description, the two have "fucked house music up the ass."

The duo also surrounded themselves with flamenco dancers, MCs, singers and

CREATIVE DESTRUCTION:
transformation in the music industry

percussionists when they played live on stage. For their wicked innovation of house music is of course not confined to recordings. When DJ'ing across the world from Japan to Australia, California to New York, like Nietszche – the German philosopher – the pair philosophize with the hammer, with the tongue firmly placed in the cheek and a musical daring, that will take us through all and everything from Beenie Man, Public Enemy and "Love Is In The Air".

Case 2 Bumpkin on Business Class: Kenneth Bager

Guru and enfant terrible, in the late 1980's Kenneth Bager brought both house music and club culture to Scandinavia from Ibiza.

> "When I look around at clubs across Europe," says Kenneth Bager with his mouth full of fried chicken wing from the local joint round the corner, "I see a tendency away from that mix-thing, where it is the same genre running all night long, and a tendency towards an other kind of disc jockey'ing where it is more about the music."

Kenneth Bager has been called all sorts of names: Dance legend; Chill-out maestro; Techno pioneer. And "das enfant terrible der dänischen House, Techno, chillout-Szene." He is Denmark's answer to London's Paul Oakenfold, who brought the sound of Ibiza back with him from The White Island during the 1980's and centrifuged Balearic in the local neighborhood. And just as Oakenfold was instrumental in landing house music on the British Isles, Kenneth Bager was among the driving forces kick-starting it in Scandinavia.

People came from all the Nordic countries to the now legendary COMA parties (Copenhagen Offers More Action), organized by Kenneth Bager together with a little handful of friends at Lorry in Frederiksberg. When asked, Bager himself points to the music and the door policy as the two major factors making the club kick off the way it did.

"We had a door policy about looking great," Kenneth recalls and sticks a potato boat in his mouth. "So we had a good blend of people wearing a tie, and people wearing suits made entirely out of postcards, and people arriving at the club in cellophane and everything. And then we played all sorts of stuff; it was like one big mixture – just like in Ibiza. It was everything from Michael Jackson and George Michael to Prince, to Eric B and Rakim to Nitzer Ebb to… any odd record. But it was this eclectic mix that made you go with it. It just got more and more crazy, really mad; it just couldn't get crazy enough. We took more and more risks. At one time we played all records at 33 rpm and turned up the bass to a maximum, making it one big buzzing mumble. And then people knew that when I played this certain track with an Arab tune, everything went totally mad, all lights were put out while we covered everything with smoke and strobe lights, and people were just yelling and screaming."

A quick glance through the first 40 years of Kenneth Bager's life shows an image of one Dr. Jekyll and Mr. Hyde – a suitcase with a double entendre, at one and the same time holding a fascination for the wildest pop and the most mysterious underground. A cocktail or tandem of acts like Cartoons, Infernal, Whigfield and DJ Alligator, who have all been released on his Flex label, and then Dub Tractor (also released on Flex), chill-out music and those global beats coming out of his newest label, Music For Dreams.

"It is the extremes. That's what cuts the mustard for me. Cartoons are for me extreme, Whigfield's Saturday Night is extreme – at the time it was so differently produced, she sounded like she sang in a gas balloon. And that's what's triggering me: the fact that they're way off normality. All that in the middle, I don't touch that, it doesn't interest me one bit, that's just hits. And when I have been exited by the mystical underground, there has always been melody or things than can last or be timeless at some level or another."

The man has a drive, or an enthusiasm, as he says himself, when it comes to playing new music for other people. An innate and natural energy present in the smooth-running voice and the alert and communicating eyes, which has also made superfluous all those stimulants the scene has been associated with on countless occasions ("I fall asleep just from drinking beer" and "I had no idea people were on drugs when I first came to Ibiza" are pregnant remarks). It was the same energy that cleared the way for him into the Sweet Silence studio in the early 1980's with a tape full of sound effects and a handful of inspirational vinyl under his arm (New Order's "Confusion" amongst the titles) when Danish pop group TV2 started working on the song that broke them in Denmark ("Popmusikerens Vise") – a stunt that earned him credits as re-mixer on the first Danish 12" single.

CREATIVE DESTRUCTION:
transformation in the music industry

"Even at 40, I'm still that nosey kid, spending enormous amounts of time looking for music, and finding and seeking out new stuff, stuff that can grow. I don't know what to call what I have... an enthusiasm for playing new music for other people. I like people to hear something really good. I think, that when I stopped as a disc jockey in 1998 it was because I felt I was just repeating myself, and I just knew that then people would do this and that, whereas now I think that that whole ambient chill-out scene has brought about a lot of tracks which can't really be predicted in terms of arrangement, and then I have begun to feel like it again because the scene has grown."

The interest in surprise and the unexpected has been with Kenneth Bager since he promenaded disco-style down Mainstreet in Hobro as the only disco boy in town; since he tuned in on the new tunes coming out of Radio Luxemburg and ordered everything he heard at import shops Manhattan and Hits Records in the capitol; since he kick-started house in Scandinavia. Always. And that's also the reason the clubs have been so important: Coma, Baby, Flex, The Melon, Socios and what not. Because with a club you can be the resident DJ – or 'disc jockey' as Kenneth insists on calling it – and as the resident DJ you get access to play or work with the crowd's consciousness.

"There is so much different music, and I have had some of my best experiences when I have been moved myself. When I have heard some tracks that I had not anticipated to hear in that particular context. Then usually those have been the tracks I have thought most about afterwards. A journalist wrote of the first Music For Dreams compilation, that the number one thing for a disc jockey to do, is to entertain and educate at the same time, and that has always been my mission when playing. Many times, when I have packed my records I have thought "Well, people did get to hear those records so at least they have left thinking 'hmm, that was kind of strange what he played there... A tribal dance track' or some other weird stuff". Where they have taken home with them something out of the ordinary. When you have been a disc jockey for 23 years, you just know that if a little piece of the dance floor should come off, we'll just drop something else later. When I play, I like to take 2-3-4 records where maybe not so many people enter the dance floor, but where something else is happening, you know, up in people's heads."

ELECTRONIC MUSIC: STYLES AND MAPS

Case 3 From Pop Stars to Being Real: Ninja Tune

Surviving more than a decade as an independent label is an achievement in itself, but to manage to establish an accomplished and leading label, and strengthen its independent position is remarkable.

They were sorted, the producer duo Coldcut, when towards the end of the 1980's they delivered singers Yazz and Lisa Stansfield at or around the UK Top 10, and every remix they touched went through the roof to take hold of equal chart positions. In other words, Matt Black and Jonathan Moore were doing pretty well. In 1990 they were awarded "Producers of the Year" by BPI and that same year went to Japan where they consumed large quantities of sushi and got consumed in their turn by the Japanese media. In Japan, Matt Black and Jonathan Moore discover the Ninja warrior. He pops up during late night television shows when the duo is chilling after another hard day's work, and when they soon after find the Ninja as a cut-out and with a house full of secret passages, it clicks. Both of them are already pretty much fed up with all the major label hassle, the hot air A&R, and really just want to go back to their roots, release whatever they want, when they want, and all of a sudden, pop frustrations have found a constructive way out. "A Ninja could appear unnoticed and disappear again, jump in and out of the shade," explains Jonathan Moore as I hook up with him and Matt Black ten years down the line, only a couple of hours before the big birthday bash. The venue in Brick Lane looks like it's been shell shocked, but using some of those usual Ninja skills, within hours it has transformed itself into a first class, 3 room venue in two floors under my eyes.

Matt Black elaborates: "We thought it was a good symbol for a different way of doing things. An alternative. And for a way to evade the usual music business that we were in the middle of. We started 100 per cent DIY, went to bed with all the normal record companies, found out we didn't really like that, and decided to escape. And Ninja seemed like a good disguise." There was just one thing wrong: they were tied to a contract with a major label. So, when Coldcut got back from Japan, they would appear instead as Bogus Order or DJ Food, to evade the deal's phrasings about exclusivity. They also started releasing their records on their new label: Ninja Tune.

CREATIVE DESTRUCTION:
transformation in the music industry

Recipe for World Dominion

That same year, in the fall, Coldcut release the album Jazz Brakes vol. 1 using the DJ Food moniker without knowing that the album in years to come will be regarded as a foundation stone in a "new" genre: Trip Hop. From the very beginning, the choice blend of funky hip hop and jazz breaks is the Ninja Tune signature, explains Peter Quicke, who since 1992 has been the Ninja Tune label manager. "The strongest string at Ninja Tune is about the development of the break beat," he says. "That can be heard in the early Jazz Brakes records. It is about instrumental hip hop, about taking the funky part of the hip hop and the jazz and funk records, and making hip hop beats out of it, but without having to submit to the verse-chorus-verse-chorus structure." Peter Quicke mentions 1995 as a landmark year for Ninja Tune. "That year we released three very limited 12-inches: The first Herbalizer 12", the first Funki Porcini 12", the first remixes... and then the first compilation [Ninja Cuts: Funkjazztickle Tricknology]. The first compilation – that was the first time we were taken seriously by a large audience," he says, nodding to the echo of his memories. 1995 was also the year when Ninja Tune released the DJ Food album Recipe For Disaster. The launch party which is held at then ultra cool (now defunct) London club Bluenote, is so successful that they decide to make it a recurring event: Stealth. The new club pulls the crowd all the way around the block (in much the same manner as this evening's birthday party is about to do) and brings a string of prominent guests around: Squarepusher, Kruder & Dorfmeister, James Lavelle and Kid Koala who at that time is a DJ at the tender age of 18.

And 1995 is also the year of Journeys by DJ. In spite of it not being a Ninja Tune release, Journeys by DJ is probably the Coldcut release which has done the most to promote their label. Together with the two DJ Food apprentices – PC and Strictly Kev – Coldcut created with this compilation a mix of hip hop, jazz, drum'n'bass, soundtrack music and much more, which in its genre has become a landmark album in the vein of 4 Hero's Parallel Universe, Kraftwerk's It's More Fun To Compute, My Bloody Valentine's Loveless or Beethoven's Ninth.

Corporate Sausage

In little more than a decade, Ninja Tune has grown from a phantasm to an esteemed player in the industry. "I remember when I saw Peter [Quicke] at the first Big Chill, and he was standing there with his 5 CDs," remembers Stuart Warren-Hill of the Hexstatic duo. "It is incredible what they have done. They haven't sold out and it is just the

ELECTRONIC MUSIC: STYLES AND MAPS

coolest label around if you ask me." He looks at me and then adds with a little smile: "They haven't sucked the corporate sausage," and hints at Ninja Tune's ability to both grow and remain completely independent, faithful to what set them off. But what is really wrong with big business? Matt Black grabs the question with delight and even thanks me for putting it, before he plunges into an unobstructed speech articulated in flawless staccato sentences. They convince alone by the strength in his gaze through the eyeglass. "I'll say there is a war going on. Earlier there were wars fought with guns and swords, now there are wars fought over people's consciousness. And the weapons are the media, television, records, advertising, the net. I don't think it is an exaggeration to claim that there is a war going on – a global war – about the control of people's consciousness. And it is the big corporations against the rest of mankind. The limited companies seem to be some new sort of organism whose only concern is profit. They don't care about individuals, they don' t really care about people, they don't care about the environment, and that – I think – is in direct opposition to what the rest of humanity needs, so it is an interesting battlefield."

Hip hop is about breaking down structures, about transforming the world to a collage that can reveal new secrets, and Matt Black and Jonathan More have for years radicalized the technique in sound and image. That's the reason we find little bits of Disney films and Bladerunner in the visual part of their shows, together with snippets of Tony Blair and Bill Clinton ("I did not have sex with that woman!"). "That's 'Culture Jamming', I think that's a good term," continues Matt Black who by now evidently has warmed up, while Jonathan More at his side seems relaxed in his chair. "It's a cliché, but we are all bombarded with information every day. Much of it comes from the big corporations. They want us to buy things, they want to tell our consciousness how it should work so we buy their shit. The hypnosis- and bombardment techniques are there: How do you defend yourself against it? People need to find new defences like we have antibodies against sicknesses. We need mental antibodies to fight those mental sicknesses that are thrown at us from a lot of different organizations. So to take a piece of information, to cut it, to loop it, to slow it down, to put it under a microscope so you actually have a chance to really analyse it and find out what really is going on, that is a technique that could be worth exploring. In fact, Ninja Tune asks itself these days 'What size do we really wanna have?'" he adds. "- Because with the 10 year birthday and everybody telling us how wonderful we are, and we are slowly selling more records... That's good! We release good stuff; we are strong! But people have had good ideas before and have gone crap, have gone down! We don't want that, and I think that one of the factors is, that if you get too big then communication between people disappears, the individual goes down and

CREATIVE DESTRUCTION:
transformation in the music industry

you have lost the vibe that you started with. So we don't wanna be too big," he underscores and warns: "The corporations are the new governments, and we better take care, because if we thought the former governments were doing a lousy job, then this lot has no morality at all – dollars are what their minds are at. We don't want to complain. We just want to ask people to think about it: Who is it that really runs the planet today? And are they doing a good job?"

[BOX 1]
10 things you want to know about Coldcut
- Jonathan used to teach art and design; Matt is a hardcore programmer and holds a degree in biochemistry
- Their 1987-single "Say Kids, What Time Is It?" is the first UK release containing a sample
- Journeys by DJ topped the 1999 "Best Compilation Ever" list in the music magazine Jockey Slut
- Coldcut's debut album What's That Noize went silver
- With the single "Beats And Pieces" Coldcut heralded Big Beat as early as 1987
- The first DJ Food compilations in the Jazz Brakes series are the roots of Trip Hop
- They sampled all material for the computer game Top Banana from television
- The game was elected "Worst Game Of All Times" by German magazines – much to Matt's pride
- They got crummy 750 $ for their classic remix of Eric B and Rakim's "Paid In Full"
- Their website is at www.ninjatune.net

[BOX 2]
Coldcut's results as remixers and producers include...
Yazz: "The Only Way Is Up" - no. 1 in the UK for 6 weeks running and the best selling 12" that year!
Yazz: "Doctorin' The House" - no. 6 in the UK.
Lisa Stansfield: "People Hold On" - no. 11 in the UK.
Lisa Stansfield: "This Is The Right Time" - no. 11 in the UK.
Eric B and Rakim: "Paid In Full" - a Top 10 hit in the UK that landed Coldcut the DMC "Best Remix" prize in 1988.
James Brown: "The Payback Mix" - no. 11 in the UK.
... not to mention The Fall, Queen Latifah, The Orb, Eurythmics, INXS, Blondie and many more.

ELECTRONIC MUSIC: STYLES AND MAPS

Summary

The diversification of electronic dance music culture in the early 1980s – between the harder hitting techno and the softer, disco oriented house did not signal the end of this music's global influence. As the music transformed like fractal geometry through a plethora of genres - electro, Chicago house, acid house, Detroit techno, Euro techno, jungle/drum 'n' bass, it ultimately returned with a vengeance at the close of the twentieth century in the form of trance- a computer sampled hybrid.

To Prendegast (2000), trance witnessed the emergence of a "truly ambient sound" for the twenty-first century, a kind of veritable sound democracy; as if the music experience itself, rather than the music maker (although still important), was the most important thing together with the scene, the mix, the club and the audience. More than that through its evolution electronic music has torn down many of the barriers that were erected by the music industry between classical, jazz, rock and pop. One only has to point to the Chemical Brothers who have sold millions of records through their fusions of hip hop, acid house, techno, 1960s psychedelia and folk music.

ELECTRONIC MUSIC: STYLES AND MAPS

BRAND AND BRAND BUILDING IN THE MUSIC INDUSTRY

Introduction

When Mitsubishi Motors launched its 2003 Eclipse in the USA, it hit the American homes with a TV commercial showing a group of people cruising a night lit downtown area in the car. All in good spirit and with the girl in the passenger seat throwing some happy dance moves in a pop-locking style to the irresistible groove of the music accompanying the spot. The track was "Days Go By", produced by UK three-piece Dirty Vegas. The year before "Days Go By" had been pushed into number twenty-seven on the UK singles chart by DJs like Pete Tong who played it on his Radio One show for 12 weeks running. But in America, Dirty Vegas were virtually unknown when a marketing man from Mitsubishi spotted the original video for "Days Go By" in rotation at MTV in Holland.

The video showed an older businessman transformed into his younger self by break-dancing outside a retro diner in what gathering pedestrians tell us is an annual dance performed in honor of his lost love. A single shot of the man (then and now) makes up most of the video, with occasional footage of the band inside the diner.

The car commercial that followed was a smash and had people calling into radio stations to request "that song from the Mitsubishi ad." The lush commercial struck a chord, in other words. It created a buzz, or – as phrased by Rolling Stone magazine – it had "the cumulative power of vibe" (Berger, 2002).

In fact, this vibe was exactly what Dirty Vegas themselves liked most about the video when they saw the final result. Vocalist Steve Smith told Yahoo!'s Launch that the video "didn't seem to be about a car, it was about a vibe, you know. There's the gang of people in the car and they're popping, you know, and it's inspired from our video, you know, which we see as a compliment. And we just thought, 'It's cool,' you know?" (Minogue, 2003).

Vegas's Paul Harris seconds that with his remark that adverts are "not as dull as they used to be, and what they're trying to sell isn't the most important thing. In the

CREATIVE DESTRUCTION:
transformation in the music industry

Mitsubishi ad, you don't even know what it is until the very last second" (Minogue, 2003).

Vinny Picardi, Vice President and associate creative director of Deutsch LA, the agency responsible for developing the advertising concept for Mitsubishi, remembers when they began thinking of ideas that would take Mitsubishi's marketing in a new direction. He knew they didn't want to make just another car commercial. Instead, Deutsch came up with a simple concept: show people, especially young people, doing things that drivers and passengers actually do in their cars – such as singing along with songs on the radio (Scott, 2003).

> "People hate commercials," he explains. "We wanted to make little pieces of entertainment."

Mitsubishi Motors have used a string of tracks for the various manifestations of the concept since its inception in 1998. Besides Dirty Vegas, the roster includes artists such as Propellerheads, Gus Gus, Groove Armada, and The Wiseguys. Mitsubishi have also used tracks from bigger artists, such as Iggy Pop, Ozzy Ozborne, and Curtis Mayfield, but – in Picardi's words – "the idea is to have a tune relatively unknown to American audiences become associated with Mitsubishi, rather than have Mitsubishi become associated with an established hit" (Minogue, 2003).

This is in direct opposition to the strategies recently deployed by e.g. Jaguar and the Chrysler Group, featuring mega stars Sting and Celine Dion respectively appearing in person in commercials for their products. By advertising standards, the Mitsubishi campaign is relatively innocent. The 2003 Eclipse looks more like a music video than a traditional ad. The cutting and editing is extremely tight, there's no product commentary, and the song itself is used to set the scene more than to pitch the product (Minogue, 2003).

Strategies for credibility

Such corporate lock-in with credibility is by no means a new phenomenon. In the eighties, a version of the Beach Boys' "Good Vibrations" made up the track for a Sunkist commercial, and in 1967 Jefferson Airplane agreed to sing a Levi's radio spot for Stretch Levi's. But the real landmark in the partnership between music and advertising was shaped when the UK agency Bartle Bogle Hegarty began creating innovative television commercials in Europe for Levi's 501.

At the end of the 1970s and in the early 1980s, the jeans market had become saturated. Levi's were losing market share, and the advertising brief handed over to BBH was strategic; to reposition Levi's against its competitors by foregrounding the authentic value of the product (Mott, 1996).

Levi's brand values are – and have most appropriately always been – "the real deal" – to be authentic, original, and dependable. BBH wanted to achieve a general sense of a mythical America with the advertising, but an America open for contemporary associations. John Hegarty of BBH explains: "I thought it would be more interesting to do the ad with a period look. The 1950s idea wasn't in the brief. It just happened, and out of that we established a mythical period for Levi's. Grapevine, the music that backed the ad, was a 60s not a 50s song – it came to me simultaneously and there was no real logic to it. The aim was to portray the US without the US being boring – a US no-one could object to" (Myers, 1999).

When the ad was aired on Boxing Day 1985, it had model Nick Kamen stepping out of his 501s in a 1950ish set, to treat them to a stone wash in a small launderette, while Marvin Gaye's soulful 1968 Motown hit "I Heard It Through the Grapevine" made up the sound frame, enhancing the atmosphere of authenticity (Mott, 1988).

A lot has been said and written about this ad. For advertising, it has been argued that it marked a turn in how it displayed a fracturing and sexualization of the male body, through the product (Mott, 1988). For Levi-Strauss, sales of its 501s shot up by 800 per cent in the wake of the ad. And by 1987 sales of Levi's jeans were reported to be 20 times what they had been three years earlier (Robinson, 2000). The ad also meant a re-entry into the charts for Marvin Gaye's song. In fact, "I Heard It Through the Grapevine" was the first of four Levi's-related songs to all make the Top Ten. And for the Clash who provided the song "Should I Stay or Should I Go" to the Levi's 501 campaign in the early nineties, it was the band's first number one hit – six years after they split up.

Hence, the launderette ad was also instrumental in developing the integrated marketing package: a commercial on the television, a single in the chart, as well as the '501' logo alongside the artist's name on the record in all the record shops. This may be defined as the turning point for music and advertising; the point that made advertisers realize the importance of selecting the right music. Music, on the other hand, has taken a long time to realize the importance of being chosen.

As that "great divide", as Andreas Huyssen (1986) calls the incongruence and opposition between high modernism and mass culture, closed itself permanently and thus also in the academic sense brought highbrow and mass culture into the same formula, it became legitimate for artists to associate themselves with mass culture. Before that, artists were wary of being associated with mass consumption, possibly seeing the niche as the sign of true art as opposed to pop, and fearing accusations of selling-out. But post-modernity changed that.

Post-modern times have served as a unifying factor in bringing fine arts together with pop culture, a development spearheaded by the likes of Andy Warhol's silk screens and the electronic folk of Düsseldorf four piece Kraftwerk. As the 1990s came to an end, it had become increasingly difficult for artists – musicians and producers – to sell out. In fact, when producer of electronic music Richard Melville Hall, aka Moby, actually did, media reported in awe about how he had managed to license every single track of his album "Play".

When it first came out in the summer of 1999, the album's compelling mixture of electronic beats and visceral blues and gospel samples drew great reviews, but catered little for radio and MTV. So, instead Moby decided to license his tracks to commercials, movies and television shows, and before long, his music was everywhere: on sitcoms and movie trailers, and on ads for Bailey's Irish Cream, Nordstrom and American Express.

V2, Moby's label, signed a license for every track on the album, and allegedly more than 100 licenses in North America alone, for which Moby's cut reached an estimated USD 1 million (Leland, 2001). But more important, the exposure opened doors at radio and MTV, who now helped to promote the album, pushing sales of the album up to a total of around 10 million copies worldwide, or around 50 times as many as the 200,000 copies Moby initially had thought "Play" might sell (Ethan Smith, 2002).

BRANDS AND BRAND BUILDING IN THE MUSIC INDUSTRY

Authenticity

Music is operative at an emotional level, and as consumer purchase decisions in recent years have tipped towards emotional attributes rather than functional benefits, music accordingly has become an integrated part of the marketing plan that focuses on communicating these emotional values of brands. As we have just seen, music has become a vital element in shaping brand messages. The French anthropologist Claude Lévi-Strauss made the following connection between music and mythology: "Just as music makes the individual conscious of his physiological rooted-ness, mythology makes him aware of his roots in society. The former hits us in the guts; the latter, we might say, appeals to our group instinct" (Levi Strauss, 1969).

Ruth Simmons, managing director of London based SongSeekers – one of many new "music consultancies" popping up in recent years, pairing brands and music and developing music strategies – sums it up: "The true marketing potential of music is that without any other stimulus, it can access a mood, emotion, and deeply move specific demographics within a target market in just a few seconds. In addition, the heritage of music, through the artist, genre, etc., can reflect a culture, a time period and lifestyle without even playing a note!" (Simmons, 2003). Music, in other words, bears the blueprint of authenticity.

The authentic has become of vital importance for consumers in today's media saturated world. A recent study by Cap Gemini Ernst & Young finds that consumers today are looking for more from their commercial transactions than the features and functions of the product or service itself. Instead, they are looking for human values such as honesty, respect and trust to be reflected in the context surrounding their transactions (Ernst and Young, 2002).

Abraham Maslow's hierarchy of needs postulates that an individual's needs are satisfied in order of importance, with physiological needs being the most basic – e.g. the need to satisfy hunger and thirst. Once these basic needs are taken care of, an individual seeks to satisfy other needs further up the pyramid. These are safety, social needs, esteem and finally self-actualization (Doyle, 2002). It is at this final stage, when all other needs – needs of e.g. security, love and recognition – are satisfied, that our basic human striving to become our ideal self can be fulfilled. For companies to tap into this fulfillment process, the key is to develop a marketing mix and a communication strategy that are consistent with the social, cultural, psychological and individual forces shaping the expectations of their consumers.

CREATIVE DESTRUCTION:
transformation in the music industry

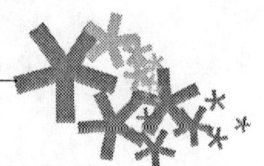

Values and benefits discordant with the consumers' beliefs and aspirations are not going to be effective (Doyle, 2002, p. 47).

The authentic, as David Lewis, head of international consumer research firm David Lewis Consultancy, points out, helps consumers to bridge the gap between their real and ideal selves (Lewis, 2003, p. 29); just as the authentic – at the other end of the supply chain – helps companies develop a compelling brand 'personality' that will appeal to us through the stories weaved around it (Lewis, 2003, p. 33). Music has become instrumental in creating and shaping these stories to a degree that has led Ruth Simmons to introduce the term music equity, as: "the net commercial value of the Brand's relationship to music taking into account its assets and liabilities that can be commercially leveraged and measured in other areas of its marketing activities" (Simmons, 2003, p. 5). In other words, picking the right – or the wrong – track for the commercial is going to have significant impact on brand equity, which is built largely on image and perceived worth.

In her study of club cultures, Sarah Thornton notes that music is inextricably tied to authenticity, that authenticity arguably is "the most important value ascribed to popular music." Music, she says, "is perceived as authentic when it rings true or feels real, when it has credibility and comes across as genuine." (Thornton, 1995, p. 26).

Unilever is amongst those seeking to leverage music's credibility and authenticity for the revitalizing of its Wall's ice cream brand. As part of its GBP 25 million marketing investment in the ice cream range, Wall's has sponsored an MTV dance competition across Europe. The event took the form of a beach party road show that traveled

BRANDS AND BRAND BUILDING IN THE MUSIC INDUSTRY

complete with sand, deckchairs, palm trees and a dance floor, touring summer music festivals. According to industry analyst Datamonitor.com, event marketing is increasingly being used as a marketing tool for consumer packaged goods. From 1998-2003, spend on sponsorship has risen at a compound annual growth rate of 9.5% in Europe, or more than twice the growth rate for advertising, which has risen 4.7% over the same period. Datamonitor.com sees event marketing as more than a mere promotional tool. It is foreseen that marketers in the future will use events to "develop loyal customers, encourage feedback and dialogue of products and needs, and to recruit consumers to promote and sell their brands for them" (Datamonitor.com, 2003).

In Denmark, deployment of the Unilever strategy to pair up with music is carried out by a joint venture between Frisko (the local Wall's, Unilever's top ice cream brand), the web portal Sol.dk and the band Smashing I-Screams, dreamed up for the occasion. Through concerts around the country, the band's own website and hoax news stories, the aim is to reinvigorate the brand among a younger consumer base, using affiliation with music to achieve this. Teaming up with the Smashing I-Screams is only one part of it. Using DJ- and club-imagery on Unilever's Frisko street signs is another.

In the UK, the Carling beer brand is taking a slightly different approach. Carling recently switched the focus of its marketing strategy from football to music, staging a series of "Carling Homecoming" gigs for music artists to play at their town of origin. The gigs are very intimate, limited to about 300 people who all benefit from free entry and free beer. Like Unilever, the Carling brand, owned by Coors Brewers, are using event marketing to squelch out the clutter and reach their target group of like-minded individuals. However, simple sponsorship often fails to provide brands with significant results and does not always guarantee increased brand awareness. Ownership of the event, rather than buying into one, enables brands to build stronger emotional bonds with consumers by being the source of the entertainment and benefit provided to the consumer, just as it enables brands to select the customer profile the event should attract. For Carling however, the real coup could very well turn out to be the deal it managed to secure with Channel 4, who agreed to screen the gigs as documentaries. This will not only spread the brand association to a mass audience, but also enhance this brand association with further authenticity reflected by a TV documentary (Datamonitor.com, 2003).

According to Sarah Thornton, the experience of musical authenticity in our age of "endless representation and global mediation" is perceived as "a cure both for alienation (because it offers feelings of community) and dissimulation (because it extends a sense of the really 'real'). As such, it is valued as a balm for media fatigue and as an antidote to commercial hype" (Thornton, 1995, p. 26). In other words, music has the power to come across as an authentic phenomenon with the ability to offer people a strong sense of belonging. Something that is not media hype, but rather the opposite: genuinely authentic. For David Lewis the opposite to hype is buzz. Buzz is "the natural, authentic version of hype," he explains. It is the gossiping exchange of information about things of genuine interest between consumers. "Buzz is created and spread among consumers at street level. In contrast hype, generated at the corporate level, is targeted at consumers" (Lewis, 2003, p. 104).

When the Lee apparel company in 2000 needed to make their jeans cool again to younger buyers, the London branch of the Fallon ad agency created three cheesy characters – Curry, Roy and the DJ Super Greg. During the campaign, this trio of "villains" would challenge Buddy Lee, the plucky doll who has been Lee's long-time mascot, in a series of competitions. But before the campaign was aired, Fallon set up spoof websites for the three characters. The homepages carried no direct link to the Lee brand or official website, but was modeled over the case of Mahir, a Turkish would-be stud whose shameless self promoting "I kiss you!" homepage grew so popular through word of mouth that he was taken on a heavily publicized tour across the USA (www.turboads.com, 2003). When people stumbled upon the fake websites – at rubberburner.com the long haired Curry wearing a jumpsuit unzipped to the waist described himself as "a slim and handsome race car driver"; SuperGreg.com was the homepage of a Latino DJ in his brother's red tracksuit; and Roy, the

BRANDS AND BRAND BUILDING IN THE MUSIC INDUSTRY

proprietor of borntodestroy.com was a self-taught martial arts expert – either by mistake or through a forwarded link, they thought the sites were real home pages and passed the link on to their peers. Within a few days the spoof websites received visitors in the tens of thousands, all looking for a laugh.

Lee tapped into the impulse to share your cool findings on the Internet with your friends. They did – more or less by chance – what viral marketing guru Seth Godin urges brands to do, namely help consumers talk to each other instead of talking directly to them. The 17- to 22-year-olds that make up Lee's target audience not only severely distrust advertising, they also like to think they've discovered something for themselves (Godin, 2000, p. 18). This tendency towards media- and advertising fatigue has been noted to an extreme especially in Asia, where a paradoxical mix of expert brand knowledge coupled with an institutionalized cynicism towards brand marketing seems to be the order of the day for the young generation. Young Asians routinely avoid conventional advertising messages. They watch very few TV ads, with most of those they actually do see being screened out, and the same goes for outdoor and Internet advertising. While young Asian people notoriously seek to avoid advertising, they are also the most dedicated brand advocates one can think of. And in order to track this group's sources and exchange of information, agencies are putting together "shadow teams" who follow selected members of various target groups day and night for a period in order to uncover their media consumption, relation to technology, places they hang out, dress code, daily routines, fast- and slow food habits etc (Grundtvig, 2003).

The Lee campaign staged the three offbeat characters as authentic through the creation of 'personal' information with a personal touch on their dedicated homepages, and this play with identity is continued in Lee's 2003 campaign: "Behind the scenes since 1889", created by Stockholm based Storåkers McCann, Lee's main European agency since 2002. With the new campaign, targeted at audiences in Europe, The Middle East, Africa and parts of the Asian market, Lee is moving one step closer in on authenticity, presenting what is allegedly Robbie Williams' fan-mail coordinator and Kylie Minogue's pet care director as the new Lee models. The creative plays with the concept of celebrity, but instead of actual endorsement from celebrities the campaign focuses on the people who support and work for them, people "behind the scenes."

Celebrity branding

When it comes to endorsement, famous people enjoy a high degree of attention and recall which can be used to increase awareness of a company's advertising (Schlect, 2003). In the case of Lee's "Behind the scenes" campaign, we are not seeing a direct endorsement by a celebrity, but instead a more subtle attachment between the Lee brand and two of the most celebrated stars of popular music. The campaign plays upon the aspirations of many people to become famous today (and the possibility for them to become just that). However, neither Robbie Williams fan-mail coordinator nor Kylie Minogue's pet care director are in fact quite ordinary people. They are swept in the aura of genuine pop stars, they are "behind the scenes", founding their authenticity in two worlds: that of the pop star, and that of the 'real' world.

This makes an interesting slide in the concept of celebrity endorsement, which has been on the rise for at least the past decade. In recent years we have seen people like Moby, Macy Gray, Kim Gordon and Shirley Manson endorse Calvin Klein, Madonna taking BMW for a ride, doing apparel company GAP with Missy Elliot. Daft Punk have also done GAP — and Moby too, while Sting and Celine Dion have endorsed Jaguar and Chrysler respectively. David Bowie has decided to support French mineral water brand Vittel, and with his wife Iman agreed to front the launch advertising campaign of Hilfiger's Spring 2004 collection. The company declared at that occasion, that the two are cultural icons that represent Tommy Hilfiger's "long time love of fashion and music" (www.just-style.com, 2003). This is just the people in the music business — and just the top of the iceberg! As the year 2001 was coming to an end, USA TODAY reported that one of the few taboos left in Hollywood was about to come to an end, namely that of stars appearing in ads: "Top actors and musicians, who balked at appearing in ads for years, now are giving star power to TV commercials, magazine ads and billboards. The trend ranges from veteran megastars to the hippest members of young Hollywood" (McCarthy, 2003).

The Lee campaign and the way it pulls leverage from celebrities in the music business is essentially different from the way for instance the Vittel brand uses David Bowie. Both Lee and Vittel communicate the value added by (music-) celebrity through product to consumer, but in the Lee case the link between celebrity and product, and between consumer and celebrity, is much more subtle and indirect.

Sarah Thornton speaks of two different kinds of authenticity: one that involves issues of originality and aura, and one that is about being natural to the community or organic to subculture (Thornton, 1995, p. 30). This is also pointing to the main difference between e.g. the Mitsubishi ad, and advertising for Jaguar and Chrysler involving the personal appearance of Sting and Celine Dion respectively.

Where Sting and Celine Dion's explicit personal endorsement circles around the artist as originator, the Mitsubishi ad is — as we have seen — far more about a vibe. About being true to the community or subculture. The main difference between the Mitsubishi ad and the Jaguar / Chrysler ads is therefore, that while the latter lean on the status and personality of celebrities Sting and Celine Dion, the former creates an integrated narrative, using a virtually unknown tune rather than an established hit to build on what is already at play, namely the break dancing from the original Dirty Vegas video. Thus, Mitsubishi creates 'a little piece of entertainment' which 'doesn't seem to be about a car, but about a vibe'.

Actually, the Chrysler ads with Celine Dion have been accused of not being about a car either. Instead, the ads are said to be more about Celine Dion than about Chrysler — a fact emphasized by figures showing that while sales of Chrysler rock-bottomed (dealers sold only 4,828 Pacificas in the first three months on the market after projecting selling 60,000 in the first year), Dion's new album, "One Heart", went through the roof selling more than 2 million copies (Stein, 2003). On the other hand, the Jaguar ad with Sting turned out a smash for both car and artist.

The question is whether the match between product and artist is right, whether it appeals to the target audience. In the case of Dion and Chrysler it obviously did not. In fact, when Chrysler's advertising agency — BBDO in Detroit — embarked on the job, focus groups showed them that Celine Dion appealed to consumers with an average age of 52. BBDO warned Chrysler about this, but Chrysler decided to go ahead anyway, inked a 3-year and USD 14 million deal with Dion and went on to spend another USD 2-3 million a spot.

In contrast to this, the Mitsubishi TV commercials not only pay substantially smaller fees (Dirty Vegas allegedly received USD 3,500 for the rights to use the track), they have also been quite successful in increasing sales and customer recognition. From 1998 to 2001, Mitsubishi says its brand awareness rose 36 percent while sales increased 69 percent. And the average age for Mitsubishi owners is 38 years with 38 percent of the company's customers younger than 35 (Scott, 2002).

Maybe the difference is essentially that of age: the difference between communicating with a mature and a younger audience. A lot of attention has been given to issues of 'new' vs. 'old' types of consumers and marketing. The difference between younger and older also signifies two different ways of thinking marketing. Where the old marketing style, as marketing guru John Grant puts it, "was to steal a creative film clip or character", new marketing needs "to have its own intrinsic authenticity" (Grant, 1999, p. 98).

Cool marketing

Authenticity in music basically gets circulated in two different discourses: that of the 'black' tradition and that of the 'white'. For the black dance music tradition the use of vocals and funky instrumentation is of key interest, whereas the white dance music tradition is more preoccupied with futurism and the revelations of technology (Thornton, 1995, p. 72). In fact, when Juan Atkins – one of the founding fathers of techno music – heard European synth-pop from the likes of Kraftwerk, Telex and Devo played on the radio in Detroit around 1980, he thought they were good, but that they weren't "funky" (Eshun, 1998, p. 165). Tracing the word "funk" back to the African state Congo in the 17th Century, we find that it originally was used as an expression for the scent of the body, and it would seem appropriate, as Sarah Thornton maintains, that black authenticity is bound to a rhetoric of body and soul, while the white dance music tradition seeks to minimize the body and the human (Thornton, 1995, pp. 72 – 75).

Maybe this is part of the explanation why companies have increasingly turned to black culture in their search for authentic cool factors to integrate into the building of their brands. One of the best examples of this is how German shoe manufacturer Adidas bought into the credibility of American rappers Run-DMC, whose signature style of black-and-white Adidas tracksuits and sneakers worn without laces was hugely copied amongst their huge fan base. In 1986, after the release of the Run-DMC hit single "My Adidas", a homage to the brand they had always worn, Russell Simmons, president of Run-DMC's label Def Jam, approached Adidas to probe into the possibility of a sponsorship for the act's 1987 Together Forever tour. Adidas was skeptical about being associated with rap music, but when invited to a Run-DMC show where thousands of animated fans waved their Adidas sneakers over their heads during the "My Adidas" song, Adidas not surprisingly decided in favor of the deal and subsequently backed the tour with USD 1,5 million. And not long after the show, a new line of Run-DMC shoes was presented: the Super Star and the Ultra Star – designed to be worn without laces.

This brought new meaning to the notion of product placement – the integration of a product into the entertainment medium itself, blurring the distinction between the two. Product placement was quite a big thing in the years following the Second World War, when large companies like Proctor & Gamble financed soap operas in return for having their products worked into the scripts. The practice faded in the 1960's as producers believed consumers preferred a clearer boundary between entertainment and advertising, but returned strongly in the 1980's with confectionary maker Hershey's decision to feature Reese's Pieces in the E.T. movie (www.productplacement.awards.com, 2003).

Product placement can be divided into three different types: 1. visual placement, when a product, service or logo can be observed; 2. usage placement, when a product, service or corporation is actively handled; and 3. spoken placement, when a product, service or corporation is integrated into dialogue, voice-over or – in the case of rap music – the lyrics.

For apparel company Tommy Hilfiger, the break came in the early 1990s when Hilfiger's nephew managed to successfully place Hilfiger products on some major Def Jam artists. Revenues went from USD 138.6 million in 1993 to USD 227.2 million the year after when rapper icon Snoop Doggy Dogg stepped onto the Saturday Night Live show with the Hilfiger logo on his jersey (www.headstoreentertainment.com, 2003).

CREATIVE DESTRUCTION:
transformation in the music industry

The American rapper Busta Rhymes' hit "Pass the Courvoisier" from 2002 is often mentioned as yet another landmark in the deal between brands and bands. Like Run-DMC with "My Adidas", Busta Rhymes made an artistic choice to include the Courvoisier cognac in his song – in fact both in the title line, in the lyrics and in the video – but solely because the Courvoisier name fitted. At least, this is the official story. Informed sources speculate that Russell Simmons' marketing agency dRush, hired two years before to reinvigorate the Courvoisier image, could easily have brokered a deal (Parker, 2003). As trivial as this may seem, it is a question of vital interest for the street credibility of the artist. And though Busta Rhymes apparently did not receive any means of payment to use the brand in his song, his management company, Violater, later reached a promotional agreement with Allied Domecq, who owns the cognac brand. According to Allied Domecq, "Pass the Courviosier" helped increase the sales of the cognac by 4.5 percent in the first quarter of 2002 and brought growth into double digits later in the year (www.allaboutgeorge.com).

Countless rap artists are now name checking corporate products in their lyrics, and high-profile rappers like Jay-Z has increased the urban profile for products like Nike, Motorola, Belvedere, Versace, Chloe, Range Rover, Filthmart, Rolex, and Mercedes-Benz (Parker, 2003). Almost half of these brands appear on the American Brandstand (www.americanbrandstand.com), a chart based on the brands that appear in the lyrics of songs in the top 20 songs of the Billboard Hot 100.

Quite a few celebrities in the hip hop community now also have their own product lines to flash in their songs, videos and public appearances. Snoop Dogg, Busta Rhymes, Nelly, P. Diddy, Jay-Z, Ice-T and Eminem are among those with their own clothing lines, and Russell Simmons' spin-off to his Def Jam label, Phat Farm, is a rap-inspired fashion label dealing with everything from women's wear, perfume and sneakers to cell phones, and with an energy drink in the pipeline. The rap phenomenon 50 cent has teamed up with Reebok to develop his personal shoe line, just as Jay-Z did before him, and Ludacris has made a deal with Sole City Inc. for his own shoeline. The list is never ending and is now broadening in perspective to also include "regular" pop music jumping the bandwagon with the launch of Kylie Minogue's lingerie collection, LoveKylie.

BRANDS AND BRAND BUILDING IN THE MUSIC INDUSTRY

Summary

It would seem that we have reached a level in popular culture in which we – paraphrasing the words of Marshall McLuhan – have begun to program the planet itself (McLuhan, 1966). Evidence of this cyberspace-made-flesh can be found in the increasing use of celebrity endorsement, in the interplay between music video and TV commercial, rendering the two virtually indistinguishable, and especially in the product placement marketers use to buy into street credibility and authenticity for their products.

An Australian study from 2002 has shown that the super model is now in demise as a means of promotion in favor of other types of celebrities such as athletes and entertainers, who can provide far more interesting models with "real" lives and "the blemishes and flaws that consumers can relate to their own experiences" (Morrison, 2003).

Advertising is tapping into the interest in "real" lives, in real people, with real stories, just as television at another level has done with a string of reality TV shows like Big Brother, Pop Idol, and Survivor. And players in the music business have accordingly upgraded their attention towards new sources of authenticity for their products to be associated with.

The creation of a street level buzz has proved much more effective than traditional, old school marketing. As David Lewis has shown, buzz is created when cool hunters pick up on things and spread the interest to early adopters, who again influence an early majority to follow and spread the buzz even more. Next step is the late majority, from where the trend finally reaches laggards – by which time the following trend has largely become the latest buzz (Lewis, 2003, p. 107). To a large extent, cool hunters and mavens define themselves against the mass-produced and mass consumed, just as they are extremely skeptical of advertising. That means, that in order to reach this audience advertising needs to create an authentic vibe. This is the added value in the brand equation. And music seems to be instrumental in shaping this vibe. Vibe is about youth culture, and youth culture is about vibe. It is tempting to quote Quincy Jones when he summed up Vibe Magazine with these words: "Vibe is the voice and soul of urban music and culture."

CREATIVE DESTRUCTION:
transformation in the music industry

BRANDS AND BRAND BUILDING IN THE MUSIC INDUSTRY

THE INTERNET AND ARTISTS

Introduction

Artists who get a contract, license their copyrights to the record label or publisher. The latter promote the artists to the mass media, event organizers and retailers who then try to create a demand among consumers by employing push-marketing strategies (Gerlach and Minda, 2000). Consequently, those artists who do not get a contract remain outside the club. They do not get the chance to introduce their music to a broader public. Niche music genres are frequently marginalised, especially on a global basis (BPW, 2002). Even with copyright law, which is supposed to guarantee benefits to all artists, these independent artists mostly do not earn a living with their music. On the other hand, superstars who are generally promoted by one of the five large record companies which dominate the industry (2), mainly profit from the copyright institution. In the industry it is said, that only 10% of all artists receive 90% of all royalties (Deters, 2001). The hit-driven selection of labels further leads to a limited variety of music and to an overrepresented music mainstream offer of CDs and in the mass media, especially on radio (BPW, 2002).

However, MP3 technology now gives artists a means to upload samples of their own music to their websites or on the sites of well-known Internet portals such as mp3.com to make them familiar to a broader - even global - public. Thus artists can get directly in contact with and sell their music to the final consumer.

Therefore, the focus of this chapter will be to analyze the changing nature of the music industry from the independent artist's perspective. The aim is to try and answer two fundamental questions:

1. How do changes in the environment of the music industry influence independent German artists and their business?

2. Which strategies can these artists pursue in order to produce and sell their creative work?

CREATIVE DESTRUCTION:
transformation in the music industry

Technology and the Artist

Altinkemer and Bandyopadhyay (2000) identified local bands, or artists of obscure, less mainstream music as one category benefiting from the reach of the Internet. These artists are no longer limited by geographical boundaries; instead they have fans across the globe. 95% of independent artists responding to the RelaxOnline (2002) survey declared providing MP3 downloads on their websites. For this reason the following hypothesis is put forth.

In the digital music business, the tendency can be observed in which artists, especially local ones, join networks in the form of online portals such as bandforum.de. This step facilitates the creation of communities of consumers in order to profit from network effects and reach critical mass, for instance in a specific genre or region. Furthermore, artists can exchange information with each other in networks. New connections to managers or concert organizers can be established and communities built. The co-operation of lesser-known artists in building communities was also seen as one possible scenario by Kretschmer et al. (2000), based on their qualitative research in the music industry.

In the music business, it takes a lot of time and work for an artist to develop lyrics and melodies but even more time to finalize songs and make them ready for the final recording. The recording as well as the promotion of the CD requires a high financial investment. But to obtain a good reproduction one just needs a CD-R, a CD writer and a few minutes, which explains why many consumers make use of this.

Moreover, the Internet provides the possibility to lower production and distribution costs of music. Independent musicians, who are not able to obtain a recording contract and are running on a low budget, can record their music in MP3 format at modest cost by employing new recording software (Fisher, 2000). Afterwards, they can either sell the digital files directly without a physical carrier as downloads or by burning them on CDs and distributing them via the Internet. The respondents to a songwriter survey conducted in the US (Freemann and de Fontenay, 2001) support the pursuit of this strategy. More than half viewed the uploading of songs to their websites as adequate or satisfying. It was further reported that 15% of songwriters (more than 50% are also artists) use the Internet to distribute and sell their songs to the public.

This procedure reduces the costs of production and distribution significantly and consequently makes artists less dependent on the financial help of third parties.

However, lower start-up capital costs can be regarded as diminishing barriers of entry for all artists. This has the effect of increasing competition, making it more difficult to stand out from the crowd (Smudo, 2000; May and Singer, 2001; Altinkemer and Bandyopadhyay, 2000). This suggests that musicians will have to search for ways of attracting consumers, which again calls for the promotional support of established third parties (Kretschmer et al., 1999).

New technological solutions allow more artists to compete for consumers' attention and spending. The unequal distribution of information between market participants calls for a high level of coordination in order for transactions to be carried out to exchange this information (Zerdick et al., 2000). Most transactions in traditional markets did not take place directly between supplier and customer, but rather through intermediaries arranging and controlling the exchange of products and services. These coordinating activities lead to information and communication costs (i.e. transactions costs) (Zerdick et al., 2000, p. 148). In the music industry, record companies and retailers are placed between artists and consumers.

With the Internet, it is possible to execute these intermediary transactions by means of electronic information and communication systems, thus enforcing disintermediation. Furthermore, consumers increasingly have the opportunity to carry out activities them-selves, which consequently lowers transaction costs. It also leads to an erosion of traditional value chains because the performance of realization activities shifts from intermediaries to consumers. This can be observed in the music industry where consumers increasingly can download/buy MP3 files directly from artists and burn them onto a CD.

On the other side, musicians can offer tour dates, lyrics and music (in form of MP3 files or CDs) directly to consumers on their websites. This reduces transaction costs such as search time, printing or shipping tremendously. Nevertheless, Zerdick et al. (2000, p. 149) state that new or old intermediaries may succeed their re-intermediation by adding high perceivable value to end consumers.

As consensually stated by Grant (1998) and Zerdick et al. (2000), in order to obtain profits in the traditional or network economy one needs to provide value to customers. By writing and performing music pieces artists create this necessary value which than passes through record companies, media and retailers to reach the final consumer. In return, artists as well as intermediaries receive an income from sales revenues.

CREATIVE DESTRUCTION:
transformation in the music industry

To guarantee this value creation copyright law is supposed to preserve the economic incentive for people to come up with brilliant ideas and inventions and grants authors the control of their work (RIAA, 2001). Furthermore, it prohibits the unauthorized duplication, performance or distribution of a piece of creative work. As the production and promotion of music requires a certain financial investment, artists assign their IPRs to record labels and the like who provide these resources. In return, these creative artists receive royalty fees which aim to provide a financial incentive by ensuring that they earn an income for products which they have created to the benefit of society (Dolfsma, 2000).

International and German copyright law have constantly been adapted and supplemented to respond adequately to economic realities and to the changing technological environment. In spite of this, it seems that income is unequally distributed in the music industry. Meisel and Sullivan (2002) stressed the fact that even though the typical recording contract includes a payment to the performer, it also ensures that this money is directed first to reimburse the record company for marketing and distribution costs. This leads these authors to the assumption that unless artists control the IPRs of their songs, few of them will earn significant money from sales of recordings.

In an online survey conducted by RelaxOnline (2002) among independent artists, a majority stated that the essential services provided by traditional record labels for a successful CD project are promotion, distribution and the recording budget. 34% would give up 50% of their income from CD sales for these services, 35% even more than that. However, 77% would not be willing to give away a percentage of their income and all their IPRs in order to obtain a recording contract. If possible to earn the same income otherwise, 70% of responding artists would release their own product instead of signing a record deal. This supports the predictions of Parikh (1999) who believes "More and more artists will choose to remain independent."

Many authors have examined the costs or earnings of a music CD in a traditional music business (e.g. Gerlach and Minda, 2000, Lechner, 2001). They showed that each of the several intermediaries inflates the cost of recorded music to the final consumer by extracting profits from the price of a typical CD (LeComte et al., 2000). Revenues from CD sales for artists were calculated between five and ten percent (May and Singer, 2001) A large proportion of the total revenue generated from sales of recordings is captured by retailers and those record companies that control distribution channels.

THE INTERNET AND ARTISTS

Figure 5.1 shows only the main revenue portions, which are estimated for 100,000 CDs.

| Artist 8% | ⇨ | Major Record Company 5% | ⇨ | Retailer 25% | ⇨ | Consumer-Price 15€ |

Distribution 23 %   Promotion 11 %

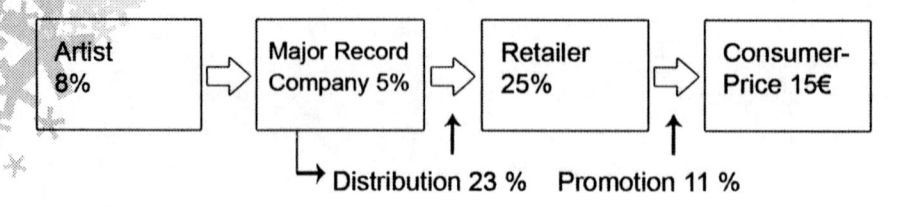

figure 5.1 CD revenue distribution
    Source: Merck, 2000.

Many authors are predicting a fundamental restructuring of the way music is delivered from the artist to consumers (e.g. LeComte et al., 2000; Kretschmer et al., 2001, Parikh, 1999), and this means that income distribution within the value creation system will change as well. New intermediaries who perform promotion and distribution activities, which were previously executed by traditional record companies or retailers, offer higher proportions of revenue to artists (as indicated on their official websites). Mp3.com, which was integrated into Vivendi Universal, is a subscription-based service offering downloads and music streaming. It promotes the music of 250,000 musicians and produces CDs on demand. The artist sets the price and receives 50% of the revenue but still keeps his/her IPRs (mp3.com, Hummel and Lechner, 2001). Vitaminic.com offers independent artists the possibility to promote their MP3 files without licensing away their IPRs. In an online songwriter survey (including 50% solo performers or band members), nearly half of respondents believe digital licensing will represent an important part of their earnings in the next five years (Freeman and de Fontenay, 2001).

However, traditional revenue streams of record labels, which can be considered as suppliers of financial resources and marketing competence for artists, are partially undermined by these new online models. These companies get less return for their investment in musicians due to decreasing CD sales (Lett, 2000). For this reason, the president of the German Phonographic Federation worries they may reinvest less in new talents in the future (IFPI, 2002). On the other hand, many authors argue that in an oversupplied market, artists need record companies for marketing power and promotional activities (Kretschmer et al., 2000).

Parikh (1999) stressed that artists have different sources of income. In the future, he predicts, artists will rely less on the sale of records and the associated copyright payments for income and more on live appearances, corporate sponsorships, and licenses of merchandise. Parikh (1999) also sees this as a possible scenario for the future.

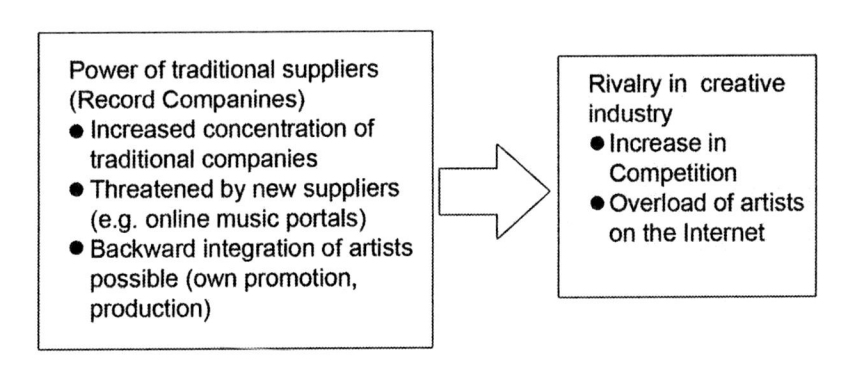

Power of traditional suppliers (Record Companines)
- Increased concentration of traditional companies
- Threatened by new suppliers (e.g. online music portals)
- Backward integration of artists possible (own promotion, production)

⇨

Rivalry in creative industry
- Increase in Competition
- Overload of artists on the Internet

Figure 5.2 Porter's Five Forces adapted to the creative business
Source: author, based on Porter (1998)

Many artists (stars or independent bands) seem to have recognized this need of consumers. They offer listening samples of their songs on their private websites to provide fans with a chance to try the music before they consider purchasing the album. In response to the RelaxOnline (2002) survey, 95% of aspiring artists declared offering MP3 downloads on their websites.

LeComte et al. (2000) believe that the access to and introduction of music of lesser-known artists could drive incremental sales. They argue consumers would expand their loyalties and try new, previously unheard music that may enhance their overall music collection. With regard to these results, the following key areas of importance were identified.

Willingness to Pay for Online Music Offers

Another important question with regard to artists' future earnings is if consumers will be willing to pay for MP3s. "Some consumers may wait for less expensive but legal options to become available because they want to avoid illegal activity, the transaction costs of 'free' MP3's, and because they want their favourite artists to earn some revenues" (Gallaway and Kinnear, 2001). This opinion is supported in their survey by over 60% of respondents who "[...] showed their willingness to wait to acquire downloads in order to avoid breaking the law" (Gallaway and Kinnear, 2001). Among all respondents, the maximum willingness to pay ranges from $0.27 for songs that are eighteen months old to $1.42 for new songs. In response to a 2001 Gallup survey in the US, 76% of teens said they think artists and musicians have the right to be paid for their work which is shared online (Crabtree, 2002).

In contrast to this, Haug and Weber (2002) doubt that students will be willing to spend money for online music offers due to students' non-commercial motivation to use these services. According to the most recent data presented by Jupiter Research (2002), 41% (-6%) of European Internet users are reluctant to pay for online content. Despite that, it seems that broadband connection will be the key driver to the gradual change of this attitude. 25% of broadband users and 18% of narrowband users admitted they would be prepared to purchase music.

Even if a large number of consumers seem reluctant to pay for music online, it is important to artists that many people believe they deserve to be paid for their creative work. However, as most of these studies were online-based their results are valid for Internet-users but do not reflect the attitude of non-users.

Relationship Between Consumers and the Creators of Content

In an MP3 survey (De Fontenay et al., 1999) respondents involved in the music business see independent artists (37%) and consumers (42%) as the beneficiaries of new technology. Overall, Meisel and Sullivan (2002) predict a closer relationship between artists and consumers at the expense of record companies. Gerlach and Minda (2000) writes: consumers "[...] will increasingly coalesce in fragmented communities with closer relationships to the creator of content."

The Artists Perspective

A total of sixteen bands were interviewed in person between the 24th of February 2003 and the 20th of March 2003 including the test interview. In ten cases only one

CREATIVE DESTRUCTION:
transformation in the music industry

bandmember was interviewed, whereas six bands participated with two or three members. Thus, a total of 23 participants answered the questions. In most cases interviewees were the informal managers of the band. Two of the sixteen bands were interviewed together due to their limited availability. However, responses could be clearly assigned to each band allowing separate analysis. This interview lasted approximately 2 hours 30 minutes. In general the duration ranged from 45 minutes to 90 minutes with the majority lasting about 75 minutes. All interviews were undertaken in Germany.

Table 5.1 below presents some key characteristics of participating bands.

Foundation	N=16	Genre	N = 16
1993 or earlier	4	Rock (various kinds)	8
1994 – 1997	1	Pop (various kinds)	4
1998 – 2000	8	Country	1
Later than 2000	3	Psychedelic	1
		Gothic	1
		Reggae-Ska	1
Label contract (in Germany)		Album/CD	
No	7	1 album	6
Yes	4	2 albums	2
Own label	3	3 and more	3
In negotiation	2	Only EP	2
		Maxi-CD	1
		Only Demo	2
Intermediaries		International activities	
Distributor	7	No	11
Booking Agency	5	Yes	3
Management	4	Rarely (Europe)	2

Table 5.1 Key characteristics of research sample

Note: It should be noted that all artists/bands have their own homepage; however one does not employ it. Nevertheless, utilization in the near future is planned.

To guarantee confidentiality, all bands were given names of European soccer teams, which are used when quotations are included in the text.

No.	Pseudonym	No.	Pseudonym
1	Arsenal London	9	Inter Milan
2	Bayern Munich	10	Juventus Turino
3	Celtic Glasgow	11	Lazio Rome
4	Dynamo Moscow	12	Manchester United
5	Espanol Barcelona	13	Newcastle United
6	Feyenord Rotterdam	14	Olympic Marseilles
7	Girondins Bordeaux	15	Paris SG
8	Hansa Rostock	16	Real Madrid

Table 5.2 Pseudonym names of interviewees

Reach of the Internet Versus Other Channels

In this section the data collected during interviews are presented. The first part analyzes the impact of economic aspects on the situation of independent artists. The second part is concerned with their perception of consumer attitudes and behavior.

> "Actually, it is more than a hobby, but less than a job.
> Considering time, it's a job."
> ~ Olympic about his band (author's translation) ~

To determine whether independent artists prefer the Internet to other channels to reach fans, it seems appropriate to take a look at the media and channels used by them to promote and distribute their music. These are illustrated in Table 5.3. Secondly, independent artists' opinions on the importance of the Internet compared to other channels are summarized..

With regard to distribution channels, 15 out of the 16 bands interviewed sell their CDs at concerts and also use this occasion to reach their audience. Of these 15 bands, four use concerts as the only way to distribute their music. Furthermore, a majority (11) additionally offer CDs for sale on their homepage. Moreover, in six cases CDs are also sold on other websites such as on-line retailers and in nine cases they can be purchased in stores. One band even offers the paid download of both their album and its cover on their homepage as a cheaper option compared to the real CD.

Distribution of CDs	N	Promotion	N
Concerts	15	Concerts	11
Homepage	11		
Internet (other sites)	6	Newspapers/magazines (adverts, reviews, interviews)	11
Stores	8	Radio	6
Second-hand-stores	1	TV	1
Mail order	2		
Friends	2	Internet sites (and portals)	7
None	1	Homepage	5
Music files on the band's website	**N**	Internet Magazines	2
Samples	10	Newsletter	1
Complete songs	3		
Cross-section of songs	1	Word-of-mouth	4
None	2	Posters	4
		Flyers	2
Music files on other Internet sites	**N**	On-the-place-promotion	1
Tracks for download on mp3.com	2		
Tracks for listening on other sites	1	Demo-CD	2
Online single tracks sale	1	Presentation kit	1

Table 5.3 Channels of distribution and means of promotion

Of those using several distribution channels, eight bands gave their preference to concerts declaring that they sold most of their CDs at live-performances and only a small number on their website. Manchester is convinced a CD purchase is initiated as follows:

"There are actually only two ways to make you buy a CD. Either you see the band at a concert and you say 'That's great, I want to have this CD' or you go to the store and listen to a CD. In this case, your attention had to be drawn to it before. That could have happened through the Internet, but generally it is a newspaper or lately even TV, at least in our scene."

This statement summarizes the opinions of some other bands declaring that many consumers still purchase CDs through traditional channels and that people do not search the Internet to find a band. If they do purchase something on the Internet, respondents believe it is because their attention was caught during concerts or through another real stimulus. And Girondins pointed out:

"Most of them come through concerts or the CD. Through what comes real. Through what comes from outside, after that they go on the Internet and not the other way around. For instance, after an article in the newspaper, someone will buy a CD, only after this article. Only by an Internet click, nobody will buy a CD."

This leads to the common conception that the Internet presentation of a band occupies its rank behind the live-performance and the album. With these two means a band must convince consumers. The Internet serves only as an informative tool for those who have already heard of the band. Paris SG explained:

"I don't think, that the Internet is at first instance, that someone gets to know a band through the Internet and automatically visits a concert or buys a CD. I think — I don't know with which percentage - that in any case it works the other way around. You have seen the band at a concert or listened to the album and after that you ask for the Internet address to obtain further information. I think this is how it works."

Concerning the promotion of their music, independent bands rely on several means and media. Concerts and newspaper advertisements rank first with eleven votes each. The Internet is also highly employed as means of promotion. Bands make use of their website, apply for reviews in Internet magazines and utilize other Internet sites such as band portals, for instance. Independent bands also try to get an airplay on radio, especially on free stations. Posters and flyers are also distributed, mainly with regard to an upcoming concert. In this context, some respondents also mentioned word-of-mouth.

Most respondents share the opinion that the Internet is just another presentation or advertising platform. Juventus explained:

> "The Internet is a medium, which came in addition to the others. It spreads out. In the past you only had newspapers, then you had radio, you had both. Then TV joined the group and the usage redistributed. And now you have the Internet. It has split in quarters now."

The usage of the Internet by consumers, however, depends on other promotional means and media, as stated by eleven bands. Interviewees recognized a mutual interdependency between the Internet and other channels in reaching and keeping fans. Nine interviewees agreed that people visit their website before and especially after concerts to get more information, sign the guestbook, order the newsletter or even buy a CD. But if on the other hand the band has not released an album lately or has not given any concerts the homepages are rarely visited. In five of these cases, bands definitely declared that the live-performance is a more important way to reach fans and that especially after their concerts they achieved a higher number of visitors on their websites. Espanol stated that:

> "There you realize that the Internet is just another platform; it really depends on how present you are on stage."

Five bands believe homepage clicks are induced by newspaper articles, TV or radio promotion or word-of-mouth. Girondins stressed this fact:

> "Actually, the more people you reach through concerts, advertise-ment or anything else, the more people come to your website. Well, you know, with radio and Internet that works really well."

Some see this as source of information before concerts as potential visitors can listen to music samples. Feyenord said:

> "And if there they are interested in it or they like the music, chances are much higher they'll come to a concert, than if you didn't have that."

This statement partially explains, why a total of 14 independent bands declared that they provided audio samples on their website. In four cases the respondents stated that the main promotion business is still in newspapers, on the radio, with posters and so forth, even if the priority was given to a different medium in each case. The major drawback on the Internet mentioned by eight independent band members is its overload with bands and the resulting disorder. Some called it "a chaotic, complex platform", where you can "disappear in the masses" (e.g. Dynamo, Lazio, Juventus). Olympic said:

> "Of course you should serve all these Internet stories. But in the end it is just a bottomless pit."

Those bands that are really in favor of the Internet pointed out advantages such as the cheapest or easiest means to call for attention to which millions of people have access. Inter uses the Internet for promotional activities and hardly relies on any other means. Newcastle even acknowledged:

> "Our Internet presence is what brought us the most at a large scale because the Internet is huge - a huge platform. This is what has actually contributed to our success."

Lazio also relies heavily on the Internet because:

> "Today, people who want to listen to music other than the usual mainstream, have to get informed somehow. And this is where the Internet comes into play."

Nevertheless, the traditional media also have their drawbacks. Two bands believe it is easier to get an album review in Internet-zines or magazines than in actually

CREATIVE DESTRUCTION:
transformation in the music industry

published magazines. Two other bands experienced the same with Internet radio and broadcast radio.

In general it can be said that independent bands make use of the Internet as additional means of distribution and promotion. The majority sees a mutual interdependency between traditional channels (concerts, album and real media) and the Internet. Yet, the latter occupies a subordinate rank. It serves as a means to provide information for those who have already heard of the band. Interviewees doubt they can reach new fans only by this medium.

Networks

Ten of the sixteen bands interviewed participate in band portals, which is one kind of network. Out of this group six are involved in more than one band portal. The portals joined are partly regional with focus on Saxony and partly Germany-wide. Furthermore, some of these ten bands use other forms of networking like link exchanges with other bands, file-sharing platforms and Internet magazines. Of the six bands who do not take part in band portals, two are involved in other network-like Internet activities, which provide a broad reach as well as a link to their homepage.

According to the bands, reasons for network participation are:

- The possibility to draw the attention of new people to their website/increase their popularity (7)
- To get in contact with other bands, organize concerts together (4)
- The attempt to convince labels and event organizers (3)
- To have another linkage (3)
- The opportunity to have another form of advertisement (2)
- It is little effort to join in (1)

As can be seen above, the main motivation for independent bands is the chance that people visiting these portals or the pages of other bands can be drawn to their own homepage. Thus, they can get to know the band, obtain detailed information and may well order the album, if they like what they have seen on the website. Espanol expects:

THE INTERNET AND ARTISTS

> "A greater popularity in many ways. Less in business matters, but absolutely with regard to fans. I think, this will increase, as people get informed on the Internet about bands or that they listen to such a Web radio. These aren't any commercial things, not yet, so there is still a chance to get in."

Feyenord explained:

> "This networking is in any case good to generate the interest of people who are actually on this page because of another band."

Indeed, three bands consider joining networks in the future either by exchanging links with other bands, participating in portals of a specific genre or joining some larger portals.

Yet, on the other hand some respondents talked about their negative experiences especially with band portals. The major aspects they mentioned are as follows:

- Overload of bands in portals (3)
- Business people do not visit these portals (3)
- No offers for concerts from organizers (2)

Real stressed that:

> "All these forums are full of bands and this oversupply can't be overlooked anymore. All these bands that are penned up in bits and bytes believe they somehow get the great deal. It's just another possible form to present yourself, nothing else. But sometimes a concert with one of the other bands can be organized."

And two interviewees who participate in band portals are just not sure if this pays off in any way.

Finally, the case of Lazio should be mentioned in which the respondent pointed out the negative aspects of band portals but put great emphasis on having established its own network of distributors, bookers and friendly bands. This provides consumers with many possibilities to buy their music and reach their website through links. Furthermore, Lazio believes:

> "That happens in the music industry as well, that music islands form like for instance Wave and Gothic, where they network worldwide. In this case, the people are just faster than the corporate groups."

Overall, it can be concluded, that twelve bands participate somehow in networks, to either draw the attention of fans and event organizers to their homepage and to the band itself or to get in contact with other bands.

Competition

This section analyses whether independent bands believe that new technologies lead to increased competition because they facilitate entry into the music market. Being asked about the number of bands they are competing with, an interesting attitude came to light. Eight bands stated that they have to compete with all bands or many bands. However, three of these eight bands agreed with seven others that there is no competition, at least not between small bands. They stressed the fact that they should help each other instead of competing.

Concerning the role of new technologies, four respondents stated that Internet and MP3 hardly have an influence on competition. They said that nothing has changed. Alternatively, six bands have the impression that competition for attention has increased, because the Internet offers a presentation platform for all artists. Even unknown bands can create a website, which can be accessed by a broad audience. Therefore, they also see a quantitative augmentation.
Feyenord gave an example:

> "Through the Internet, competition has endlessly expanded. If someone looks in an online sales portal and finds the CD of Feyenord for instance, and another of a Russian band and one listens to both and likes them, then it doesn't matter where the band is coming from if one can order them for the same price. One listens to both of them and buys the CD one likes best. From that point of view competition got infinite."

And Paris SG exemplified:

> "Without the Internet, out of one million bands in Germany, you would only know of one third."

In spite of this, three of these bands emphasized that if bands make an effort to produce and present good quality (album, cover, performance, and website) they do not have to worry about this development. Dynamo and Espanol also share this opinion. The latter explained:

> "It is a platform for us and for others, too. But you don't have to be afraid of it, because in the end quality succeeds."

Nevertheless, this also means facing the risk of disappearing in the masses or as Girondins put it:

> "If you mess up with that, you are just one in a million."

Dynamo and Espanol also belong to a group (4) who stressed the fact that all bands have equal chances to present themselves on the Internet. They do not have the impression that the actual number of bands increases just because of the possibility to have a Web presence.

The other two respondents of this group though believe that it is not the Internet but computer technology that allows those persons, who do not play an instrument, to enter the market by programming music with their PC. Bayern explained:

> "Because of the existence of computers more people are making music. Many people who don't know how to play a guitar or anything else but know how to program some rhythms."

And Lazio pointed out:

> "You can actually produce your music on the computer, place it on the Internet and you're present as an artist. You have completely new possibilities."

Furthermore, two respondents reported that it is more difficult to compete. On one hand, the interviewee stated the number of artists grew in general, which he attributed to television (Newcastle). On the other hand, Manchester believes major labels have financial resources at their disposal to better employ the Internet as a means of communication and promotion. Thus it gets even more difficult for independent bands.

Looking at these statements it seems difficult to come to some conclusions as half of the respondents did not perceive an increase in the number of competing bands or at least did not attribute this to the Internet. On the other hand, when approaching the subject by aggregating the bands that recognized a higher level of competition due to either computer or Internet technology, the number adds up to nine. Thus overall rivalry appears to intensify.

Intermediaries and Income

There are different intermediaries artists can rely on: managers, booking agencies, record companies, distributors and so forth. The focus is first on record labels, as they often group the tasks of several intermediaries. The survey reveals that four of the interviewed bands have a record contract. Three founded their own label. Of these three, two had a record contract before, but were disappointed; the third does rely on independent labels in other countries but not in Germany. Of the four bands that have a record contract, one respondent expressed his wish to found a sub-label for the next record release, mainly for financial reasons. He (Paris SG) argued:

> "Therefore, it will continue moving in this direction, that with the next album we do it on our own. For example, I'm getting now 1.50 per CD. But if I do it on my own, I can get 4 per CD. That is reason enough to do it yourself."

The remaining nine bands are looking for a record label that supports them, but prefer an independent or medium-sized company. Two of these nine are already in negotiation and one foresees a contract only in the long run. Table 5.4 shows the main reasons specified during interviews on why record companies are needed by independent artists.

As it is clearly visible in this table, independent artists search for financial support from record companies and their access to the mass media. Of the four bands that are bound by contract with an independent label, two obtained advanced financial aid for the production of their album. In the other cases, the label committed itself to purchasing a certain number of albums after production.

Reasons	N
Promotion, access to media, advertising	11
Label barcode is requirment to get reviews	2
Financial support (costs for pressing, costs of media like TV and radio)	10
High-quality production, pressing, better conditions e.g. studio	5
Organization, management	3
Distribution	3
Connections	3
Artists can concentrate on music	3
Better album sales, more people at concerts	2
Have this team	2
More time in studio	2
Experience of record companies	1

Table 5.4 Reasons for contracts with record companies

Feyenord, belonging to the first group, illustrated the advantages of a sizable label:

> "Bigger labels have a larger network of media, for instance. They even dispose of more money for each production. They can provide more advertising and due to that more people come to concerts and because of that more albums will be sold. And you can make a better live-performance; they also can work together with booking agencies or can get concerts on their own at huge festivals, these well-known labels. You can play everywhere, reach a huge audience. One can play into the other. You have numerous advantages."

On the other hand, two bands named advantages of small labels compared to majors. These are a lower degree of interference and having the opportunity to talk to a contact person. However, independent bands also put an emphasis on keeping their rights and their independence within a contract. Five bands declared that they are not willing to sign permanent contracts or that they will try to get an acceptable deal in pre-negotiations.

When asked whether the Internet renders intermediaries and especially record companies unnecessary, most respondents declared that this is not the case. Furthermore, during twelve interviews respondents said retailers will still be needed in the future, even though two of them think their retail business will slowly shift to the Internet. Of the remaining bands two believe that retailers will hardly be necessary in the future and one band is not sure. Additionally, four bands are glad to have a manager taking care of their affairs and five bands explicitly said they need management. Three respondents wish for booking agencies whereas five declared they already rely on a booking agency.

With regard to new online intermediaries, only one respondent already relied on an Internet record company. However, he belongs to the group striving for a record contract with a traditional label. Three interviewees mentioned their albums are also sold through online retailers like Amazon for instance. Moreover, eleven interviewees doubt that it is possible for independent bands to promote and sell their music only on the Internet without relying on the help of intermediaries. Arsenal underlined:

> "More is needed for a good promotion than that your name is written some place. All media belong to it, TV, radio and all that has to be financed by a record company and with a recording contract. There, the Internet is not enough."

Further points were stressed by Feyenord:

> „In any case, it doesn't make labels redundant, because the Internet cannot take over the organisation and neither press and print CDs."

THE INTERNET AND ARTISTS

Rather it was stated that the Internet will be stronger employed by the existing intermediaries (record companies, retailers). Paris SG assumes:

"The structure will remain. The most that could happen is that the existing structures integrate the Internet a little more, that they strengthen the third leg a bit."

The preceding answers show that traditional intermediaries are still important to independent bands. Most interviewees are striving for a record contract and expressed the need for other intermediaries like managers, distributors or agencies as well.

With regard to the financial investments made by record companies in aspiring bands the following was found out. Seven bands realized that the changes in the music industry in general (3) and especially the dwindling CD sales of record companies (4) also affect the funding of newcomers. They believe that it is more difficult for independent bands to get a contract because of record companies' financial limits and their fear to invest in long-term projects. The latter reason however was not associated with the Internet. Girondins asserts:

"They are just really afraid of investing in newcomers who want to work long-term. None of them does that. They only get on board once everything is set up."

When asked if their income and costs have changed, eight bands explained they save postal charges because event organizers and agencies can obtain information and song samples on their homepage. Furthermore, bands can send MP3 files and information via e-mail.

Newcastle illustrated:

"As a band you have the advantage that you can send MP3s to record companies or event organizer, for instance. They can then, of course, visit your website; can download your pictures and the band biography as well. That means, you don't have to send 5000 letters costing 1.50 each."

Four saw a benefit in their ability to burn the CDs themselves, which they send out or sell. The possibility to produce albums cheaper on their own was noted by two bands. Surprisingly, only one band recognized an increase in income due to the sale of tickets and albums on their website, although eleven bands sell their CDs on their websites. Other bands reported having hardly sold CDs on their homepage. Especially artists whose records are sold in stores or by the label at a much higher price do not understand why the sales on their homepage are so limited. Three bands see neither positive nor negative effects. They estimated that savings in postal charges and lower time-consumption of information search offsets costs of the website. One band recognized negative effects in the form of the greater effort necessary to run the website.

Summarising, independent artists did not experience any changes in their income because of Internet utilization even though costs of transaction and production are lower.

General Usage of Internet

Independent bands employ the Internet as a presentation, information and communication platform for business people, fans and themselves. As already stated, the Internet is also used as a means of distribution and promotion. The following table presents the detailed data from interviews.

Internet usage	N
Music samples, draw attention to music	14
CD sale/order	12
Band presentation on homepage, image (for business people)	11
Business contacts (e-mail, homepage)	10
Direct communication with fans (Chat, forum, guestbook)	10
Information for fans (homepage)	10
Promotion, advertisement, reviews	10
Search information (on cheap production companies, contact data etc.)	6
Newsletter, mailing list	5
Communities	5
Communication between band members (information exchange)	5
Feedback from fans	3
Merchandise sale	2
Software, plug-ins	2

Table 5.5 Internet usage of independent artists

Outlook to the Future

Interviewees were asked to give a short insight on their view of the future in the music industry within the next three years. Interestingly, in four cases no remarkable changes are expected. With regard to music sales and purchases some respondents expect an increased utilization of the Internet by consumers and by the existing structures of the music industry. Furthermore, few bands shared a need for solutions to the file-sharing problem. However, the main concern of these independent artists is that more short-lived superstars or "marketing products" are promoted instead of investing in "real" musicians over a longer period. Yet, artists hope record labels recognize that profits could be earned with enduring bands. No agreement was found regarding the further existence of small and major labels.

Possible scenarios seen by artists include major label concentration resulting in a diminishing perceived variety of music, bankruptcy of independent labels or the proliferation of small labels and the downfall of the majors. Overall, most of them explained that their goals for the future are making good albums and giving concerts. If possible they would like to earn a living with that (7). A minority mentioned signing a record contract as being the main objective.

Networks

Concerning network participation, the findings of the study showed that this course of action can be found in reality. The majority of independent bands are involved in band portals and the like, aiming for higher popularity among consumers and hoping to be discovered by concert organizers or A&R agents. Yet, some respondents complained that these portals are overloaded with artists, limiting the chances of being noticed. These statements call the positive spiral effect mentioned by Zerdick et al. (2000) and other authors into question. Due to the crowd of artists participating, interviewees see the value of these networks shrink for them. Here, the author supposes that it depends on several variables whether a positive network effect occurs. These variables include the popularity and the reach of the network itself. The attractiveness of a network can also be perceived differently from another user's perspective (e.g. organizer or consumer). The fact that half of the bands joined several regionally focused portals supports the predictions of Kretzschmer et al. (2000) that lesser-known artists will co-operate in communities based on location or genre. Given the fact that this kind of portal provided the author with a source of contact data for recruiting interview participants, these results may be distorted and should be considered with caution.

Summary

The objective of this chapter was to find out how changes in the environment of the music industry affect independent artists and their business. This chapter has tried to provide answers to this initial question. The starting point of this research was the assumption that new technologies like the Internet and MP3 altered existing economic principles of the music industry as well as consumer attitudes and music consumption patterns. The major changes reported in recent research or theories build the basis for studying the impact on independent artists' situation in Germany. The following can be concluded:

In general, independent artists employ the Internet as a supportive means of distribution and promotion, in addition to traditional channels and media. They encountered a mutual interdependency between these means and their Web presence. Yet, by providing further information or an additional point of sale, the Internet often occupies a secondary rank. Nevertheless, it offers easier access for independent artists than do conventional media.

With the intention of reaching a broader audience and increasing their recognition among fans and intermediaries in the industry, independent artists join network structures in the form of band portal sites or online music providers. They want to draw attention to their website, allowing them to inform and convince interested persons of their music. Additionally, contacts to other bands can be established. However, the relevance for establishing business contacts is questioned.

As the Internet offers the above-mentioned possibilities to all artists, one major disadvantage arises for them - the problem of oversupply of musicians. This dilemma was experienced in band portals, but also reported in regard to the Internet in general. The cost-effectiveness and the low effort needed to establish a website allows even unknown bands to be present in the market. In addition to this, the worldwide reach of and access to the Internet even leads to a competition between independent musicians of many countries. Yet, independent artists are convinced that delivering music of a good quality is the key to success.

In order to be able to produce and present good quality, independent artists attempt to sign a contract with traditional record companies, feeling the need for financial support and media access for promotional measures. Yet, obtaining a long-term investment gets more difficult. On the other hand, independent artists also reported a tendency to work independently through the foundation of their own label.

Thus, hardly any alteration of the existing procedures along the value chain was encountered, as alternative providers based on new technologies are rarely used. However, it was predicted that the existing structures will integrate the Internet to a higher extent. Concerning retailers, artists still see them as needed for distribution and sale of CDs. They believe that consumers continue purchasing CDs and prefer doing it in stores. Most artists hardly sell any CDs on their website. Again, increased purchases on the Internet are anticipated.

This is one of the reasons why independent artists do not see a strong need to sell single songs in the near future. In addition, they hardly expect to earn an income with downloads. According to independent artists' convictions, consumers will not start using paid download services as long as music can be obtained free of charge. Besides that, artists regard an album as a complete piece of work. They are reluctant to break it apart completely. However, they do show a willingness to sell only a few songs.

Independent artists already offer free downloads of complete songs or song samples on their website and online music portals. Partly because of that a slightly higher interest in their music was encountered. In general, a more important role in generating interest is attributed to concerts or word-of-mouth. The Internet serves as tool for binding prospects and building fan communities.

Nevertheless, the slight increase in interest was not reflected by a rise in consumer spending on music of independent artists. Rather the contrary is held to be true. Independent artists encountered consumers' reluctance to spend money on "unknown" bands' music. Moreover, the tendency that consumers are generally less willing to pay the demanded prices for CDs was recognized. Artists believe this is caused by extremely high prices for CDs, thus leading consumers to search cheaper or free options to get the music. However, these free but illegal options for obtaining music could not be prevented by copyright law.

This study has given an insight into how independent artists experience changes in their business environment and adapt their strategies. The author recognized that these artists have a very idealistic approach in pursuing their work. They experiment with new techniques, channels, media and so forth, often without knowing whether this is advantageous.

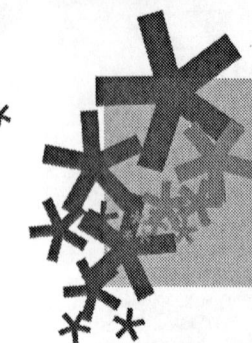

DISRUPTING SUPPLY CHAIN INTERMEDIARIES

Introduction

The structure of the music industry is likely to undergo fundamental changes that will certainly lead to the elimination of some activities and actors as well as to the creation of new roles. But does it mean that the future of the music industry will be taken out of the hands of record companies and put into the hands of other players? Will we find the same players in a new value creation system or will some of them disappear? Who will have a competitive advantage to retain its position and who will have to change its business model?

To answer these questions it is necessary to look at each player in the current music value creation system (VCS). The aim of this chapter is to take a closer look at the record companies and their leading position in today's value chain. They have the most to lose, but also have a chance to set the standards for value creation in the digital age.

Actors in the Music Supply Chain

Historically, there are three levels of intermediaries between the creator of music and the music consumer. Each intermediary adds a layer of costs and profit which leads to a higher final product price. By removing intermediate layers it would be possible to lower this price and to reach the consumer directly (Mouygar, 1997).

| Artist (Creator) | Record Company | Distributor | Retailer | Consumer (Listener) |

Figure 6.1 The actors in the traditional music supply chain

Record companies provide the necessary initial capital as well as the marketing know-how to create, market, and distribute music on a large scale. They have the expertise in creating superior sound quality and packaging, and have key relationships with press, radio stations and music TV channels as well as with retail stores. Record companies add value to the product as they match composers and artists, provide creative input through A&R managers and producers, and capture creative work for reproduction as well as engaging for manufacturing, marketing and distribution activities.

The major record companies have made significant investments in distribution infrastructure. They are now major distributors of physical music products to the retail stores (Poel and Rutten, 2000). The nature of music retailing changed from small, specialised stores to superstores such as Virgin and Tower Records (de Fontenay, 2000). They provide a one-stop-shopping location and make money by selling high quantities of physical musical goods to the end user (Feferman, 2001). Securing retail space is crucial because there are only a limited number of physical retail points in a geographical location with restricted shelf space. Major record companies and their affiliated distribution companies have close relationships with big retail chains. They provide them not only with the pre-packaged product, but also with technical and promotional assistance.

Governing Mechanism

The music industry is a high-risk business. This means that products demand a high, up-front investment that is combined with uncertainty about the return of investments (Poel and Rotten, 2000). The music industry is characterised by high market entry costs and a scarcity in the number of distribution channels. The costs are associated with the market presence necessary to justify the initial sunk costs in artists and repertoire (A&R), recording and manufacturing as well as marketing. Music distribution is very inefficient and accounts for more than 50% of the costs of each CD (Sriber et. al., 2002). Traditionally, the music industry has been very label-centric. Five major record companies are the dominating force controlling about 90% of the of music market (Dolfsma, 2000). Independent labels share the remaining 10%, mainly covering music niches.

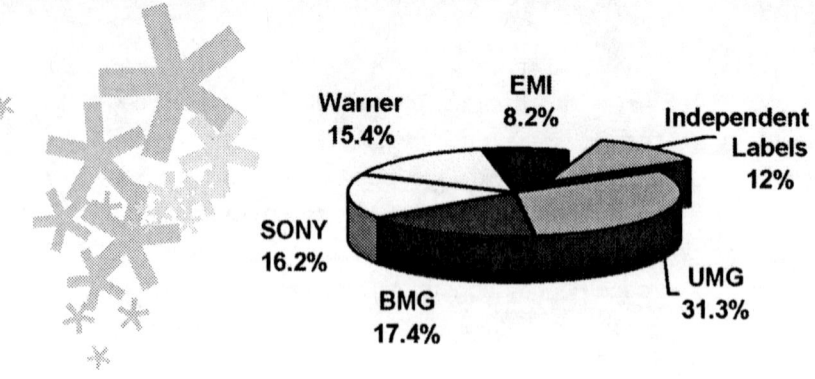

figure 6.2: Market share – the music industry in 2002

The governing position of the major record companies has been built on vertical integration and growth-through-acquisition. They have purchased forwards and backwards in the supply chain, e.g. bought new labels, manufacturing and distribution companies, or hired their own stables of producers and A&R managers (MacQuarrie et. al., 2000). By integrating vertically, record companies achieved economies of scale and were able to lower their average unit costs. They do not need to negotiate a manufacturing or distribution deal each time they sign a new artist, which avoids high contracting costs.

The high costs to establish a distribution system and the control of distribution channels by the major record companies have created high barriers to entry in the music industry. Unsigned artists have almost no chance of competing against these conglomerates. They either remain small in a niche market or end up signing long-term contracts. Thereby, artists give up the intellectual property rights of their work and rarely receive more than 16% of the product retail price. Their only alternative has been to sign with independent labels. However, in order to reach a larger audience, independent labels also rely on the distribution systems controlled by the "Big Five" (Fox, 2002). Thus, these major record companies govern what consumers worldwide get to hear and dictate the price structure for products.

Co-ordination Structure

Co-ordination in the music supply chain occurs through a very hierarchical structure and is primarily dyadic, e.g. the communication of orders for goods between record companies, distributors, and retailers (Hardaker and Graham, 2001). One example of an inter-organisational information and communication system is electronic data interchange (EDI). With EDI, two companies are able to communicate and exchange information between their organizations electronically replacing paper based transfer of information. In addition, point of sales (POS) scanning systems, introduced in the 1990s, allow for more accurate tracking of record store inventory. These technological advances have lowered the distortion effect and increased the efficiency in the traditional music supply chain.

Impact of New Technology upon the Music Industry

The Internet is the key technology that enables and drives the explosive growth of a virtual marketplace. It allows millions of customers simultaneously to interact with companies at any hour, from any place around the world (Rayport and Sviokla, 1995, p. 83). Similar to many other industries, the Internet has impacted on the retail link of the music supply chain. Electronic retailers (e-tailers) have emerged and started to sell CDs over the Internet. They first built up a worldwide presence and offered millions of CDs without spending huge amounts of money on maintaining physical outlets with only limited shelf space. Their electronic catalogues provide goods that are directly delivered from the distributor's or manufacturer's warehouse through a third party logistic company like FedEx. E-tailers like CDnow are able to sell music content at 20% to 30% below the retail price (Parikh, 1999). Consumers can easily find and buy a CD of their favourite artists by using their PCs without leaving the house. Unsigned artists are theoretically able to sell their CDs directly to consumers.

With the first wave of the Internet, the transaction costs in supply chains have been tremendously reduced and music retailing has gained in efficiency. It has altered the retailing environment by providing more options to consumers but, as shown in Figure 6.3, it has only slightly changed the structure of the music VCS.

Creator/Artist › Record Company › Distributor › Off-line Retail Model / On-line Sales Model › Consumer (Listener)

Independent Artist

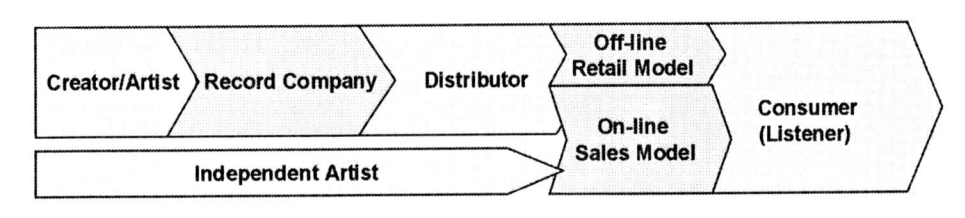

Figure 6.3: The transformation of the music supply chain – the first wave

DISRUPTING SUPPLY CHAIN INTERMEDIARIES

The Second Wave - Virtual Music Creation and Distribution

As electronic networks allow digitised information to travel unbundled from physical mediators, it will be possible to deliver digitised information products with no physical component. The music industry with its information-intensive content is among the first users of this technological development. Digital audio technologies, such as MP3 work to compress music files almost without any quality loss. These files are small enough in size to be transferred over the Internet, downloaded and stored on a computer hard disk. Unlike the first technological wave, music no longer needs to be carried by a physical container like a CD; this will lead to major changes in the way music content is created, marketed, and distributed (Singh, 2001).

Streaming technology is another innovative audio technology. In contrast to MP3 files, streaming audio files cannot be downloaded, stored or copied. Users have to stay online in order to listen to music (Parikh, 1999). Broadband technology enables users to access the Internet at a high speed and provides the crucial infrastructure and bandwidth required to distribute music. Downloading a song is four times faster than with the earlier dial-up access. Small portable audio devices allow consumers to carry the downloaded music with them. CD burning technology enables music consumers to create their own high-quality CDs from home at almost no cost. Furthermore, the equipment required to create a high-quality recording has become less expensive. Theoretically, the entire recording and mixing process can be done cheaply at home using affordable recording equipment in combination with a computer.

Implications for Actors in the Music Supply Chain

Unfortunately for the major labels, new technology has made each of the value adding activities less necessary and less profitable. This makes the venture-capital-like deals that record companies offer less attractive to artists. Theoretically, with destructed entry barriers and the Internet as the new infrastructure for inexpensive music delivery almost anyone could create a music label – contracting directly with the artist, promoting them, and distributing their music electronically over the Web. If downloading becomes the most popular form for purchasing music, the current distribution and retail business models will become extinct.

However, technological innovations should not only be seen as a threat to the business models of the traditional players because they also offer inventive opportunities for value creation. Record companies can no longer resist integrating the Internet into their overall strategy. Their business revenues had stagnated at the end of the 1990s (Singh, 2001). By implementing new technology every aspect of the content life cycle from A&R costs through production, marketing, and distribution could become cheaper and more efficient.

Researching the Retailers

The objective of the research was to gain a deeper understanding of the technological impact on the traditional music supply chain with specific reference to the intermediaries operating in it. Research was conducted to reflect the supply chain dimensions of the future music industry. The personal interview method seems to accomplish the objective of the research most effectively. It allows collecting rich data for a fuller picture of the latest industry developments. Furthermore, it enables you to interact with interviewees and to explore new topics that might arise during the interview (Friedrich, 1990).

A total of 15 interviews were conducted and they took an average length of 45 minutes. Specific details of the interviews are presented in Table 6.1. Germany has been deemed to be representative of music developments in Europe (McBurney, 1994, p. 203) and additionally, as all major record companies either have their headquarters or at least a main subsidiary in New York City, United States, this city has been considered as representative of music developments world-wide. For the purpose of gaining a deeper understanding of the way technology has impacted on the supply chain structure, and especially on the governing mechanism in the music industry, a non-probability sampling technique has been chosen. That means not every group of the population has been taken into consideration.

Contact data for record companies has been found on both Internet registers and company web sites. Data to find suitable artists has been provided by Internet search engines but also by several online music services. [MP3.com, CD-Baby]. Another technique that was used to find suitable interview partners is that of "snowball sampling". This technique identifies one participant, and from him or her other potential participants can be identified and access may be easier. The interviews have been conducted in January 2003. Before the actual interview, participants received a short description of the purpose of the interview and the nature of questions to ensure a certain degree of preparation. A final number of 14 one-on-one interviews ranging from 30 minutes to 2 hours were conducted and tape-recorded. The remainder of this chapter will present the results.

The Impact of the Internet on the Structure of Business Activities

The way record companies carry out their business activities and conduct business has fundamentally changed. All interviewees explain that product data and information are increasingly shared electronically, internally and externally. E-mails have become the main form of communication. Interviewees describe the changing communication behaviour as follows:

- "...it is much easier to get information to my business partners..."

- "...we do not have personal meetings anymore. Instead we have virtual meetings..."

- "...it has made my job much easier to get the artist information out there..."

- "...e-mails have made it easier for me to co-ordinate a recording session, [...] bringing together producers, engineers, studios and working with the A&R people..."

- "...everything is becoming electronic and digital. We have become more flexible, faster and we need fewer people to track things..."

The Internet has not only extended the reach of information but also the richness:

Name		Company	Title	Date	City
David	Weisbrot	Universal Music Group	Senior business analyst B2B Applications-Informaton Technology	09.01.03	New York
Ray	Roldan	Universal Music Group/ The Island Def Jam Music Group	National Director Media & Artist Relations	09.01.03	New York
Jonathan	Hull	Universal Music Group/ The Island Def Jam Music Group	New Media Co-ordinator	09.01.03	New York
Hilda Y.	Williams	EMI Record Music/ Virgin Records America INc	Senior National Director Urban Promotion	17.01.03	New York
Michelle	Ryang	EMI Record Music/ Virgin Records	Senior Director A & R Administration	17.01.03	New York
Frank	Corso	Bertelsmann BMG	Director Information Systems	27.01.03	New York
Dana	Renert	Bertelsmann BMG	Senior Director Production & Creative Service, Special Products	02.02.03	New York
Kevin	Lopartin	Bertelsmann BMG	Senior Director Information Systems & Technology	31.01.03	New York
Caroline	Evans	Bertelsmann BMG	Sales Representative Special Markets, Special Products	22.01.03	New York
Nina M	Collins	Bertelsmann BMG	Senior Director National Sales, Special Products	31.01.03	New York
A.G.	Gillis	Bertelsmann BMG	Associate Director National Sales, Special Products	30.01.03	New York
Maria	Ferrante	Bertelsmann BMG	Sales Representative Special Markets, Special Products	30.01.03	New York
Sherika	Laung	Bertelsmann BMG	Manager Contract Administration, Special Products	31.01.03	New York
Kevin M	Clement	Bertelsmann BMG	Senior Director New Technology	18.01.03	New York

Table 6.1 Details of interviews carried out with record company executives (1)

DISRUPTING SUPPLY CHAIN INTERMEDIARIES

> "I think it [new technology] has made our jobs much easier. A couple of years ago it wasn't really possible when you talked to people on the phone to give them a visual idea what you were talking about, it wasn't really good for imaging. You could not really describe the look and the voice of an artist. Now with the Internet we can e-mail a picture and even a song snippet. It helps imaging the artist a lot more."
> Ray Roldan, 2003[24].

Most interviewees from record companies also agree that since they have been using the Internet they more often seek help from external companies to perform activities:

> "Instead of hiring experts we will increasingly establish relationships with independently working business partners."
> Frank Corso, 2003[25].

The completed answers have been categorised as indicated in Table 6.2 below:

Area	Description
Online Sales/ Distribution	• Online Retailer [Amazon, CDnow] • Online Subscription Services
Online Marketing/ Promotion	• Online Platforms • Online Subscription Services
Technology	• Hardware and Software development • Copyright Protection Technology
Web-based Technology	• Hosting • Server Technology

Table 6.2: Record companies and external help

The following exemplary statements are related to online sales/ distribution:

- "…we started out thinking we should control the pipe [supply chain], the hosting and service area, the retail. But we are a content company. We don't want to get involved anymore in the encoding, hosting or the serving. We develop content and we want to work together with companies like Pressplay, MusicNet, or Liquidaudio to make our content available…."

- "…we want to focus on music content, not on the distribution or the technical infrastructure…"

- "…we have no intention of being retailers. It is not what we do well…"

- "…we need strategic partners like Yahoo, Pressplay, Microsoft, and AOL…."

- "…we could not generate the type of traffic that had been obtained by Amazon.com or CDnow…"

Initially, record companies tried to establish online sales services on their own, but none has been successful. Their strategy has changed over the past years towards partnerships. Partnerships are now seen as way to deal with the operational work of online sales and distribution. Record companies are engaged in even competing music services, e.g. UMG has relationships with Pressplay as well as with MP3.com. This also shows that record companies increasingly work with external partners.

Choice of Actors

The majority of interviewees agree that the Internet facilitates the establishment of business relationships. They state that it has become much easier to find and also to interact with business partners. The types of business relationships range from very close partnerships to loose collaborations, e.g. with hardware companies. The majority of relationships are based on formal long-term agreements. None of the interviewees believes that the nature of their business relationships will become more short-term just because the Internet facilitates establishing ad-hoc relationships. Record companies seem not to be interested in contracts that only last for the length of one business opportunity. Long-term relationships are seen as important to profits.

Most interviewees refer to media partners as an example of a long-term relationship. The following statement is typical of the majority of answers:

"I don't believe that our business relationships will change from long to short term. The creative side will always need studios, engineers and producers. [...] As far as advertising and radio go - these relationships will always be necessary. They may need to be tweaked slightly from time to time, but I don't think they will change drastically or become more short-term."
(Ryang, 2003[26]).

Further evidence for the preference for long-term relationships can be found by taking a closer look at the current online distribution strategy of major record companies. Even though all of them license content to different music subscription services, a majority of the interviewees agrees that record companies do not want to give up control over content completely. Thus, all major record companies have bought equity stakes in two major music services they deliver content to, Pressplay and Musicnet.

Record companies work together with a variety of technological partners on solutions for digital distribution and copyright protection as well as on the hardware side. These relationships have been described as loose partnerships. This could hamper the development of new music devices and technologies. Strategic alliances seem to be essential for coping with fast technological development. New technology has clearly changed the way business is conducted and how relationships are maintained. The majority of all interviewees have agreed that flexibility in choice of a suitable partner has improved with the Internet. However, looking at record companies, it does not seem that new technology has really changed the long-term nature of their relationships.

Governing Mechanism

The majority of the interviewees believe that an increasing number of artists will create and distribute music on their own. The record companies were in general agreement that artists will become more self-sufficient. They stated for example:

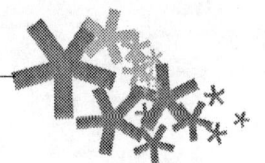

- "...artists will become savvier in turns of what the agreements are..."
- "...deals will have to become much more artist-friendly..."

However, the interviewees also believed that artists would continue to sign with record companies to profit from their marketing know-how.

A firm's competence refers to its fitness to perform in a particular field. A company has a competence if it has the necessary knowledge (know-how, know-what) and the capabilities (skills to perform a specific activity) (De Witt and Meyer, 1999, p. 199). As record companies see their strength in the area of promotion, marketing and A&R they should build their new business model around these competencies. To perform these activities resources are needed. Resources can be both tangible and intangible. For the music industry intangible resources are critical. Human capital becomes a key asset as success increasingly relies on the ability of talented and creative individuals (Gomez and Kung, 2001, p. 100). Thus, employees and artists must be central to the new strategy of record companies.

In addition, relationships with traditional broadcast and print media have been assessed by artists and record companies as another important asset. They agree that it remains crucial that consumers hear a product before they look for it, whether in a record store or online:

> "Record companies have not successfully been able to show a direct connection between an Internet or e-mail campaign and the purchasing of an album. Whereas they have made a lot of studies that show a direct link between the sales figures of a music product and either a radio airplay, music video or an article in a newspaper or magazine. Thus, traditional ways of marketing a music product are still seen as the more successful ways."

Kevin Lopatin[27] (2003).

Other interviewees stated:

- "...when you look at what has been searched for at file sharing services then you see that it is all these major acts that they see on MTV..."

- "...kids will buy what they see and hear on the radio..."

DISRUPTING SUPPLY CHAIN INTERMEDIARIES

The findings suggest that music videos remain important promotional instruments for becoming a highly successful artist. Although new technology has significantly lowered the costs of music production it has not affected the costs relating to the creation of music videos. As costs for video production remain high the financial power of record companies becomes another considerable reason for artists to sign with a record company.

Many interviewees from record companies have stated that the complexity of their organizations makes it hard to react quickly to market requirements. Different executives reported that it has been difficult for them to put new strategies into action which were meant to deal with the latest industry changes. They explained that this problem is mainly due to the multiple layers of their organization. Record companies will have to address this complexity in order to increase their flexibility and responsiveness.

Another aspect that will alter their organizational structure and the governing mechanism is the pressure to outsource activities. This pressure is a result of dis-intermediation and the decreased cost for production as well as co-ordination. It is no longer necessary to average costs through vertical integration in order to have a competitive advantage. Instead, it will be necessary to have cost advantages at every step in the value creation process (Evans, 1998). The findings regarding the diminishing vertical integration of record companies have been summarised in Table 6.3 as follows.

Area	Changes
Recording studios	Perform independently and are no longer integrated in major record companies
Manufacturing plants	increasingly being outsourced
A&R departments	• Producer operate increasingly independently (but have close relationships to record companies)
Digital Distribution	Establishing a digital distribution infrastructure has not been successful. It has been too expensive and also requires technical know-how and resources that record companies do not have. • e.g. BMG has outsourced getmusic.com

Table 6.3 Outsourcing areas

CREATIVE DESTRUCTION:
transformation in the music industry

This clearly shows that record companies have indeed started to outsource activities that have traditionally been integrated in their value chain. Thus, they will not own the actors in the supply chain any longer. Therefore, it can be surmised that they will lose their dominant position in the music industry.

The dominant role of the major record companies is fading because of the emergence of new technology. Entry barriers to the music industry have been eliminated with decreasing transaction and production costs. Artists no longer depend on record companies in terms of product creation, marketing or delivery. This suggests that record companies will lose their imperial position in the music industry. However, record companies still seem to offer unique capabilities related to their marketing and promotion know-how. Although there are a few opposing examples, artists still perceive contracts with record companies as necessary to reach an advanced artist level. Record companies see their competitive advantage in marketing, promotion and A&R activities.

Record companies have started to outsource different areas that traditionally have been integrated in their value chain to become more profitable, e.g. in the field of content (re)-production and distribution. Thus, it can be confirmed that they focus less on integrating activities in their organisation. This trend has been generalized by (Evans and Wurster, 1997, p. 69) as a result of supply chain deconstruction. They state that supply chains will fragment into multiple businesses, each of which will have its own source of competitive advantage.

The results of the interviews do not allow for a final judgement about the governing mechanism in the future music VCS. However, it can be confirmed that record companies have lost power and control over traditional distribution channels, as those channels are no longer necessary. As stated before, the new VCS will consist of many different players that can easily enter the music market. Because of new technology, artists and consumers have gained bargaining power. Although record companies are likely to remain a strong player they will certainly lose their dominant position that was due to the high entry barriers and the hierarchical structure in the music industry. These findings are confirmed by the work of Porter (2001, p. 66) who says; "The Internet eliminates powerful channels and shifts bargaining power to consumers.

DISRUPTING SUPPLY CHAIN INTERMEDIARIES

Coordination Structure

It has been found that all record companies have started to interact with consumers directly. They have established new media departments that focus on deploying new technologies to directly interact with music consumers, e.g. through company's websites as well as websites of signed artists. Thereby, the focus is not on sales but on online promotion activities. Interviewees explain that this gives them the opportunity to learn about consumer needs.

However, many interviewees feel overwhelmed by the reach of the Internet. For instance, one of the interviewees, Raldan at Universal explains:

> "The Internet has made my job so much easier, but at the same time it has also made it a lot more difficult, just because there are so many [web] sites. A few years ago we just talked to journalists, editors, and magazines. Now my contact database has over 7,000 people in it because everybody has some type of publication on the web or has a little web scene."

The access to Internet portals has been described as really important by most of the interviewees. Record companies look for central focal points on the Internet to sell and promote their products. Amazon and CDnow are the most common e-tailers that record companies use. They have used different online platforms to distribute products virtually. BMG for example has signed deals with many different service providers, e.g. with Terra Lycos, an Internet service provider and portal. An issue that has come up during the interviews is related to the coordination structure. It has been found that both the traditional structure and systems will need to be altered substantially to support the information necessary to manage the sales of digital music. The questions that record companies need to address are:

- How to deliver the music content to virtual partners;

- How to process the sales information that is received back;

- How to pay royalty from the given sales information.

When asked for reasons why they would avoid signing to an online platform the following was stated:

CREATIVE DESTRUCTION:
transformation in the music industry

Group	Arguments (grouped)
Cannibalization of Physical Products	• physical formats will remain important • improvement of physical products as essential for their existence • so far there is no significant income from virtual music distribution • will have to find ways to add value to their physical product in order to make them more attractive for music buyers
Afraid of Copyright Infringement	• it will not be possible to protect music content • The development of new technologies that protect music from illegal distribution is conditional

Table 6.4 Reasons for avoiding online platforms

Most interviewees believe that the popularity of downloading music will increase. However, the majority also believes that physical formats will remain important. Most of them see the improvement of physical products as more essential for their existence than virtual product development. Some interviewees mentioned that so far there is no significant income from virtual music distribution and they see illegal file-sharing systems as the main reason. By taking a closer look at their current strategy other reasons have come up for discussion; for example, that the two affiliated subscription services MusicNet and Pressplay are competing and do not offer products from rival music labels. As main reasons for this battle interviewees state the disagreement about:

• How to price the product.

• How much freedom the consumer should have to use the content.

• What kind of additional services/offers should be included?

Copyright infringement still seems to hinder record companies from integrating virtual music distribution in their strategy. Only a minority of all interviewees believes that it will be possible to fully protect music content. The majority, especially people from new media departments, think that there will always be ways to distribute music without

DISRUPTING SUPPLY CHAIN INTERMEDIARIES

authorization. They state that it will hardly be possible to stop people that conduct music piracy professionally. Traditionally, the music VCS has been very static and the choice of actors extremely limited. Nowadays, as shown in the interview analysis, artists and record companies increasingly work together with external partners in order to carry out business activities and to create value. These relationships vary in their nature.

Record companies are mainly interested in co-operative long-term relationships. They have established alliances, partnerships, and distribution licences, as well as outsourcing agreements. Artists have primarily established short-term relationships that are often informal and sometimes only based on verbal agreements. They use the possibility of nonexclusive contracts with on-and offline services. The results of this research confirm that with the emergence of new technology the flexibility in the choice of actors has increased. By using the Internet it has become much easier for everybody in the music industry to establish business relationships.

However, it cannot be confirmed that because of the possibility of establishing business relationships ad-hoc through the Internet all relationships are likely to be short-term and last only for one business opportunity. Relationships become important assets because they allow for utilizing resources and the knowledge of partners.

The Emerging New Music VCS

Although it is not clear if physical products will completely disappear it can be verified that virtual marketplaces have become widely accepted for music sales and distribution. Thus, the role of traditional intermediaries, e.g. physical retailers, is likely to diminish. The evidence from our research is that the Internet has become the dominant infrastructure in the music industry for conducting business electronically. Thus, communication and co-ordination in the music industry will not be hierarchical and dyadic any more as everybody can communicate with everybody. Artists as well as record companies have started to interact with consumers directly through the Internet.

However, they are confronted with the problem related to the infinite choice offered by the Internet. Reaching a critical mass becomes crucial. The Internet is subject to strong network effects. Network effects occur when the value of products to consumers rises with the number of consumers. Artists and record companies solve this challenge by using online navigators, e.g. portals, and subscription services. Both groups however are looking for central points to reach a wider range of consumers, especially for promotion, communication and music sales. These findings are replicated in a study of the music industry by Bhatia et. al., 2001), which drew the conclusion that online platforms will own the consumer relationship and therefore play a dominant role in the digital music industry.

In the future, music VCS's will no longer contain a few highly integrated companies that will be responsible for activities necessary to create value. Instead, the system will consist of a variety of players that directly interact with each other and share in the creation of value. Each player will focus on core competencies. They can either work together just for the length of one business opportunity or by establishing closely co-ordinated relationships. Music consumers will also become value creators as they participate in value creating activities. The structure of the new VCS of the music industry will look significantly different. As stated before, the configuration will rather be depicted by a network structure than by supply chain structure.

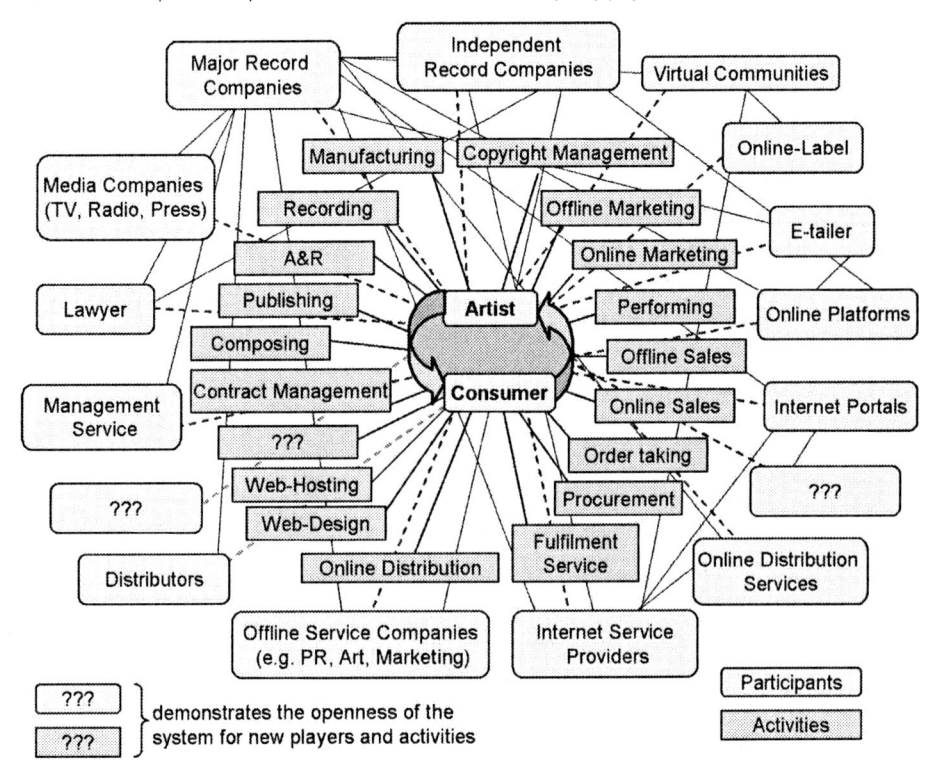

Figure 6.4: The new music value creation system

DISRUPTING SUPPLY CHAIN INTERMEDIARIES

The Internet and new technology have led to the transformation of the music industry's structure. However, the dimensions that have been determining the music supply chain are likely to be found in the new music VCS. But, as illustrated in 6.4, the characteristics of the dimensions will be significantly different.

Towards a New Business Model for the Music Industry

The major record companies have to realize that they cannot stop the latest developments in the music industry, but instead must react and redesign their business models. The new business model of record companies must be able to satisfy the needs of all consumer groups. This includes the changing behaviour towards digital content consumption. Enhancing technology will even increase the popularity of downloading. In addition, as children get older it is very likely that they will stick to their download habits.

Although in the short term it is recommended that record companies perform in both markets, online and offline, in the long-term they should focus on online activities. Nobody can predict the future. However, there is much evidence that the music industry will shift towards the Internet. Thus, record companies have to strategically prepare themselves. Naturally, it will be very difficult to enforce the cannibalisation of their current revenue sources. But they must realize that this will allow them not only to cut down operation costs but also to find innovative ways to perform activities as well as to generate higher revenue. Record companies should enforce the shift towards an online music industry because it supplies them with the following advantages:

- Providing a wider range of music becomes possible (serving niches easily).

- Decreasing costs (production, distribution, marketing, and A&R).

- Digital delivery simplifies utilisation of back catalogues and makes catalogue titles even more profitable.

- Lowering product prices becomes possible (physical products are seen as overpriced by consumers).

- Internet allows customisation through personalised marketing activities and interaction with consumers

Dimension	Supply Chain	Network
Structure of Activities	Serial interdependent Sequential logic of activities in a linear value creation process High vertical integration of activities/ resources Physical goods/ marketplaces (physical value activities)	Networked (Complex constellations) Simultaneous, parallel activities belonging to different value creation processes Focus on core competencies Partnerships/ collaborations allow sharing resources and capabilities Increasingly digital goods/ marketplaces (virtual value activities)
Choice of Actors	Static Limited choice of actors (high vertical integration of record companies) Relationships mainly long-term	Dynamic High flexibility in the choice of actors Relationships vary from: • long-term to short-term • formal to informal relationships ad-hoc with an arising business opportunity
Governing Mechanism	Dominant position of major record companies because: • Entry barriers due to high transaction and production costs • Economies of scale and scope (competitive advantage due to high vertical integration) • Control all distribution and marketing channels Artists depend on record companies Consumers are restricted (in terms of choice of music)	Elimination of the dominant position of record companies • Low entry barriers due to decreased transaction and production costs • Economies of scale and scope do not apply (vertical integration means no longer competitive advantage) • Loss gatekeeper position Artists gain more control (over their music and activities) Consumers gain bargaining power
Co-ordination Structure	Dyadic (hierarchic structure) Communication through proprietary information systems (EDI) • Sequential communication flow • Bullwhip effect (over-and underproduction) Physical intermediaries co-ordinate information and product flow	Myriad (complex constellations) Communication through the universal and open information systems (Internet) • Real-time interaction with multiple suppliers/ customers • Diminished Bullwhip effect Virtual intermediaries become important for co-ordination structure (central points)

Table 6.5 Emerging dimension in the new music VCS.

DISRUPTING SUPPLY CHAIN INTERMEDIARIES

As explained before, the new industry structure allows record companies to focus on core competencies and to outsource activities that are not profitable. Considering the analysis results it is recommended that they focus on content creation. That is where they can provide unique capabilities that no other player can easily create or copy. Thereby, the following activities presented in Table 6.6 should be the core.

Artist Development:	Creating a consistent image - the artist brand, developing the artist skills.
Artist Management:	Matching talent, taking care of legal needs, copyright and publishing concerns, arranging recording sessions.
Marketing/Promotion:	Cross-media promotion activities including online and offline campaigns (Radio, TV, Internet, Internet-Airplay,
Publicity:	Online & offline press campaigns
Performance:	Planning and organizing live shows and tours; Internet as additional live performance platform;

Table 6.6 Core activities to be supplied by the record company

A&R costs have been exorbitant. Therefore, it is highly recommended that record companies integrate the Internet into their A&R functions. The Internet can be used as a vehicle to test the new recordings and to receive an immediate feedback from consumers before a broad marketing campaign is put into action. This will also reduce the currently high flop rate tremendously. In addition, by searching through the Internet it will become much easier to find new artists.

CREATIVE DESTRUCTION:
transformation in the music industry

For the success of record companies, artist development will be essential. During the last decade, record companies have neglected this competence while the focus has been on creating the next "one-hit-wonder". Artist development helps to guarantee a longer life span for artists. This will provide record companies with more consistent sales, which will justify the high up-front investments necessary to achieve it. Record companies should continue to outsource activities that are not profitable or where they cannot offer unique know-how. The new music VCS structure will allow for entering inexpensively into relationships. This way resources and capabilities that belong to other B-web partners can easily be utilised. Thus, outsourcing must be subject to further research to improve profitability.

The new organizational structure of record companies should be characterised by a very limited number of hierarchical levels. They must reduce layers whose economic costs have become unsustainable. As people are connected electronically, middle management layers that were needed to distribute information become less necessary. In addition, functions such as A&R and marketing should be organised in a modular form. These units can work as independent profit centres that can be plugged in to different value creation processes, internal and external. This also increases the flexibility to react rapidly to market changes and arising business opportunities.

Record Companies should perceive themselves as service companies. Thereby, artists must be seen as an important customer group. As stated before, the success of a record company highly depends on artists that they can market. As noted in the analysis, not all artists necessarily want to work independently. A majority would like to receive support especially in the field of marketing and promotion. But current record deals are not perceived as very artist-friendly. Artists are afraid of losing creative space, the rights to their music and of getting unacceptable profit shares.

Thus, artist relationship must become a high priority in the new business model. Record companies have to find ways to attract artists. They must get back to the point where artists felt honoured to be chosen by a record company for a carrier on one of their labels. The author highly recommends the development and integration of an Artist Relationship Management (ARM) tool in their overall strategy.

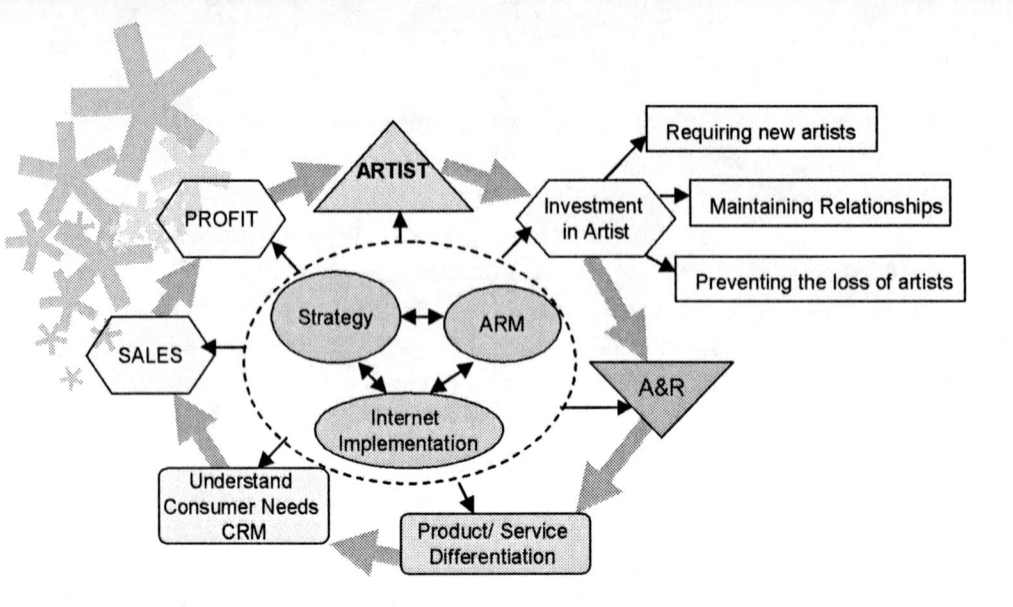

Figure 6.5: Combining product strategy and ARM and Internet implementation

A similar service tool that can be found in management literature is customer relationship management (CRM). The advantage of CRM has been acknowledged by many companies. The issues that should be addressed by ARM are arise in the interview results:

- Alteration of the current recording contracts (including recouping advances, the duration of contracts, 7 album rule28).

- Artist and record companies should work together as more equal partners (including decision making rights and profit sharing).

- Constant care for artists (listen to what the artist wants "in good and in bad times", treat them as people not as working capital).

- Make artists feel part of the company (the artist as stakeholder).

Alteration of Profit Sharing and Royalty Systems

The royalty system must become much more elastic and transparent to the artist. Artists increasingly complain about the profit shares they receive. One approach to improve the current royalty payment system could be that record companies pay larger advances and offer higher profit sharing in return for tour, merchandise and publishing rights. Another approach to improve the royalty system could be that record companies subdivide their support into different modules, ranging from one-off service offers to long-term contracts. The price for one-off services should be fixed and naturally higher. Thereby, record companies receive a small profit margin and can use the artist brand name and the content only for a short period of time. On the other hand, record companies should offer long-term packages that include services such as artist management and development. Here the contract conditions have to be elastic in terms of splitting risk and profit with the artist. A more equal revenue share seems inevitable to establish successful artist relationships. The highest priority must be that both contract partners profit from a long-term relationship.

Online Distribution

Record companies have different ways to sell their content. One option would be to only concentrate on content creation. Thereby, they would license their products to different business partner such as online platforms (portals, subscription services), radio broadcaster (on- and offline), TV stations, e-tailer, re-tailer, and mobile phone services. This would minimize the risk of failing with an owned subscription model and allow them to only concentrate on content creation.

Another option would be to develop an affiliated subscription service. What could be more convincing than a music expert, navigating through the jungle of music? The main advantage could be to develop direct relationships with music consumers to understand their needs. Real-time consumption data will provide an instant feedback on how consumers respond to a label's campaign. It will allow record companies to instantly adjust their marketing mix. However, in this case the alliance with a partner that provides the technical know-how is highly recommended. As said before, record companies are music experts and should focus on this competence. Thus, they must look for strong partners that have the technical know-how to provide the infrastructure and services, e.g. hosting or network maintenance. The highest priority must be to develop a service that is absolutely convenient, hassle free and easy to handle, by all users.

In terms of pricing strategy, the research results have indicated that a high percentage of music consumers that download music would be willing to pay to keep this privilege. So far, they have not had a legal alternative to the illegal file swapping services. It has been shown that current subscription services that major record companies license music to, have significant disadvantages that hamper their success. Therefore the price system must be simplified. Unlike current services, there should not be any compulsory membership fee or monthly payment because it would just raise the barriers to joining a platform. Only if customers want to use additional services, which are not accessible anywhere else, should they have to pay a monthly fee to become special members. They could gain for example, the right to join a recording session of their favourite band live via the Internet and have the ability to suggest improvements. The price for music should be as low as possible and not exceed US$1 for a single and US$10 for an album for end-consumers.

The age of the music consumers is a critical factor that hampers the implementation of a service where consumers have to pay for music content. As shown by the research analysis, a large consumer group that downloads music are teenagers who are unlikely to have credit cards at their disposal. This issue needs to be addressed. Related to this issue, another approach for a new business model could be a service platform where music will be offered for free. Under this model, revenue would be generated from associated products, merchandising, added-value services and advertising. However, for the success of both models building a critical mass will be crucial.

Achieving the Critical Mass

One fact that will be essential, for the success of an online music service is that all major record companies offer their music at the same online platform. This has not happened yet and this may be one of the major reasons for the failure of current subscription models. Searching for music costs the consumers their most valuable commodity – leisure time. They are looking for something which provides the widest range of music and artists from one location. This indicates that the new music platforms should not only offer music that is mainstream but also that is on the margins (niches). In addition, it would be only logical to give independent musicians the possibility to provide their music at the same online platform. This would not only make the platform more attractive to consumers, but also allow record companies to find new talents.

Adding Social Benefits

Consumers and artists have to be central to any kind of subscription service. Personalisation and customisation, resulting in a higher customer engagement and satisfaction, could justify the price charged for services and content, e.g. the ability to readily customize their music collections, integrated Internet broadcaster to play music by demand (in pre-set order). An important factor for success will be the integration of virtual communities in the platform that allow the establishing of social links with like-minded people. Consumers, artists, music experts and any other B-web participant should be able to interact on the platform. Consumers can find new music through recommendations and get in touch with their favourite musicians. Music fans in Hong Kong can chat with fans in South America about the latest release of an artist. Musicians can interact with their fans, distribute music, chat with other musicians, and get professional help from music experts of any kind.

Copyright Protection

Another reason for the lack of success of current subscription services is certainly that record companies hesitate to distribute their major artists online because of the fear of piracy. However, if they want to be successful they have to overcome this fear. The writers believe that if consumers get to try hassle free, legal downloading services many of them will be willing to use them instead of unreliable illegal file sharing systems. Thereby, consumers should be able to burn files onto CDs or to upload onto portable devices. But copyright protection will make it more complicated for the average consumer to pirate music and should be subject to further research. Therefore, the alliance with technological partners that provide the necessary know-how will be essential. Digital Rights Management (DRM) is only one promising effort to protect copyrights. Another field for further research could be the verification of the possibility of integrating a copyright security mechanism into the next generation of operating systems of personal computers.

Summary

New technology has certainly started to impact on the music industry and to deconstruct the traditional supply chain. After the re-construction, the music VCS is more likely to be a network than a supply chain structure, and will consist of a larger number of participants. New intermediaries, e.g. online platforms, will evolve and co-ordinate the network. Although some disintermediation effects can already be observed on the Internet there has also been a level of re-intermediation. E-tailers are increasingly taking over the function of traditional retailers and selling music in virtual marketplaces. In addition, music is more and more distributed online without being stored on physical carriers. Thus, traditional distributors and retailers are likely to become marginal. But it is too early to predict that physical products will completely disappear. Nonetheless, all traditional players need to react to the changes that are starting to transform the music industry.

Thanks to new technology music consumers have received bargaining power and they are the obvious winners in the age of new technology. Tomorrow's consumers will be better served at lower costs than ever before. They will be able to choose from a broad range of music, artists, and genres without being restricted to the limited product range in record stores. In addition, their demand for digital music that can be downloaded is clearly increasing. Music consumers will participate in value creation processes. Online platforms will gain importance in an oversupplied market. They will not only offer central points for virtual music distribution, but also added-value services for consumers, musicians, and other participants. These platforms are subject to network effects, which means that the more customers use their offers, the more attractive it becomes for others to join. Thus, attractive offers and broad marketing campaigns are essential for success. Theoretically, everybody can set up such platforms. In reality, financial resources, know-how and also a brand name will be crucial to attract potential users. For example, almost 97% of music consumers know the brand "Napster", whereby only 12% are familiar with "Pressplay".

To create a worldwide brand name and awareness for music, marketing expertise is demanded, which musicians do not often have. Although the Internet provides an additional platform for worldwide marketing campaigns, traditional marketing channels will remain important. With some exceptions, only established artists with a worldwide brand name will be able to continue their success story online - without the backing of a record company. Thus, their bargaining position will become much stronger, although thanks to new technology many artists will be able to make a living from their music. They will not have to deal with burdens such as recouping advanced money or losing the rights to music by signing a record deal. Record companies will have to face the deconstruction of their traditional business model and the loss of their competitive advantage, built up on vertical integration, large-scale production, and the control of distribution channels. However, competitive advantage will stem from other sources. Record companies are able to provide unique marketing and promotion know-how and have important relationships with traditional marketing and promotion platforms, e.g. TV, radio, press. They also have the financial power to support expensive marketing and promotion campaigns that include video production and touring. Thus, record companies should start to transform their traditional business model on their own.

The new supply structure should be able to support their core competencies in a way that will leave them much more profitable than ever before. Record companies should see new technology as a chance to fundamentally redefine their business and to boost sales. Thus, they should start to translate their core competencies into the new medium. Record companies must learn to create exclusive added-value services, which are difficult if not impossible for a third-party supplier to copy. It becomes essential that they find ways to operate successfully in both the online and offline market. They have the financial power and important relationships with traditional media companies to take advantage of cross-promotional opportunities. Copyright protection remains an issue as content becomes more widely available in digital form. As long as illegal file sharing services are the most convenient ways to acquire digital music they will be the method most favoured by consumers. So far, technology that fully secures music does not exist. It is also not very likely that it will ever be possible to completely stop music piracy. Preventing illegal file sharing through law enforcement is not very promising either. In fact, the development of convenient alternatives to illegal services has to be the primary goal of all players in the music industry. http://news.com.com/2009-1023-255148.html?legacy=cnet

DISRUPTING SUPPLY CHAIN CONSUMERS

Introduction

The earlier chapters in this book have shown that electronic music has evolved from a musical genre to become a way of life – a perfect match for the Internet generation: the generation that has – allegedly – been causing quite a few headaches at executives' offices in the record business around the globe for the past decade. First it was home copying that threatened to kill the music business. Then it was Internet downloads. However, recent research from Forrester indicates that home copying and downloads should not be blamed for plummeting CD sales. The general economical weakening and competition from other types of media are more crucial factors, according to Forrester (Elmrose, 2001).

But the Internet does without question hold a great potential for the distribution of music, as various so-called peer-to-peer (P2P) services have shown, Napster being the obvious example. In Denmark, more than two thirds of the population have access to the Internet, and 6.5 per cent have access to broadband. According to the United Nations, International Telecommunications Union, Denmark has the world's second best potential for exploiting mobile technologies, measured on twenty-six different factors, surpassed only by the Chinese province Hong Kong.

The music audio market is currently dominated by the CD format, which accounts for nearly 90 per cent of gross dollar volume sales. The so-called "Big Five" record labels (EMI, Sony, Universal-Vivendi, AOL Time-Warner, and Bertelsmann BMG) control the market in terms of both production and distribution.

The industry faced its worst loss of confidence and income for more than twenty years in 2003 (Milmo, 2003, p. 15). The value of music sales in 2003 slumped by 4 per cent to £1.18bn. This came after five years of buoyant performance in which it had bucked the trend of falling sales of other markets such as America and Germany. But now that era seems to be over. Sales of singles fell by 12 per cent compared to 2001, continuing a process that has seen the sector – once the most lucrative in the industry – shrink by a third in the past five years. The recording industry say the

CREATIVE DESTRUCTION:
transformation in the music industry

cause may be the estimated 2.5 million computer users – some 15 per cent of them British – who download more than 730 million music files from the Internet last year.

Numerous websites are offering peer-to-peer (P2P) technology-based services for music sharing over the Internet, often free of charge and sometimes infringing on traditional copyright laws, to consumers around the world (Kwog, Lang and Tam, 2002). Online services like Napster, Gnutella, Freenet, Mp3.com, iMesh and more recently post-Napster29 services such as Audio Galaxy, Groxster, KaZaa, Morpheus or Lime Wire have allowed users to swap and download music with such an ease and convenience that millions of music users have begun to switch to the new digital music format.

Milmo (2003) writes that the global piracy industry is now estimated to be worth about £2.7bn, which is about 4.5 million counterfeit CDs worth £20.5m sold each year in Britain. In May 2003 the Recording Industry Association of America (RIAA) reported that 100 million songs were available illegally on the Internet from file swapping sites such as Gnuitella and Kazaa. In two minutes four albums can be burnt on to a CD at 25p.

In response the record companies have set up their own rival download sites such as Pressplay and Musicnet and launched an aggressive lobbying campaign for tougher enforcement of copyright rules by national governments. The International Federation of the Phonographic Industry, which with Universal Music is now pioneering copy-proof CD's, has also considered suing the Internet service providers that provide access to the pirate sites.

DISRUPTING SUPPLY CHAIN CONSUMERS

Background Information on the Global Music Market

Table 7.1 gives the top ten music markets worldwide for 2002 and, clearly shows that Germany is an important market for the global music industry.

Pos	Sales turnover	US$m	Sales turnover	US$ per capita	Sales volume	millions of units	Sales volume	units per capita
1	USA	13,193	Norway	62.8	USA	1,037	UK	4.1
2	Japan	6,521	Iceland	57.0	India	420	USA	3.8
3	Germany	3,012	Japan	51.8	Japan	350	Norway	3.6
4	UK	2,856	Denmark	49.5	UK	237	Switzerland	3.5
5	France	2,135	UK	49.0	Germany	236	Denmark	3.3
6	Brazil	1,056	USA	48.2	France	137	Canada	2.9
7	Canada	969	Switzerland	45.0	Brazil	105	Sweden	2.9
8	Spain	681	Sweden	44.2	Canada	89	Germany	2.9
9	Australia	607	Austria	42.3	Russia	86	Japan	2.8
10	Italy	598	Germany	36.6	China	78	Iceland	2.7

Table 7.1 Top-10 music markets wordwide in 2002
Source: Institut Mediacult, 2002.

In 1995, the five largest companies, i.e. Sony, AOL Time Warner, Vivendi, Bertelsmann Music Group (BMG) and EMI, controlled about 80 per cent of the global music market (in 1986 it was 68 per cent). Table 7.2 gives the worldwide market shares of these record companies from 1997 to 2001.

Until the end of the 1980s, the number of vinyl records (LPs) sold exceeded that of CDs. However, since the introduction of the compact disc (CD) in 1981, it has increasingly become the standard format for transferring and distributing music, which in turn has had a huge impact on the sales of vinyl recordings. Nowadays, LPs and music cassette (MCs) tapes have all but disappeared from the sound carrier market. Only in developing countries are tapes still playing a predominant role as a

CREATIVE DESTRUCTION:
transformation in the music industry

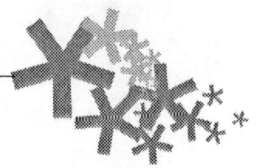

music format.

Year	1998	1999	2000	2001	2002
Market Size (bn) Market share (%)	na	38.7	38.5	27.1	31.0
BMG	13.9	Na	12.5	13.0	12.0
EMI	14.9	Na	13.2	13.0	14.0
Sony	16.9	Na	17.7	18.0	17.0
Universal	23.2	Na	21.2	21.0	24.0
Warner	14.7	Na	11.1	11.0	13.0
Others	6.4	Na	24.3	24.0	20.0

Table 7.2 Market shares of the major music corporations (1998–2002)
Source: Der Spiegel, No.50 10.12.2001, p199.

Chapter 3 is very much UK and US centric in terms of its coverage of electronic music, so in order to readdress this, it is appropriate to provide background information on the electronic music scene in Denmark, Germany and Finland, the countries which have provided the basis for our international comparison on the impact of the Internet on the consumer, with specific reference to electronic music.

Electronic Music in Denmark

Electronic music in Denmark dates back in recent times to the legendary COMA parties (Copenhagen Offers More Action) held in Copenhagen in 1989. Organizer Kenneth Bager imported the concept from the UK where Balearic was the style and the Danish capital went into COMA practically overnight. Following the COMA adventure, Bager went into production (as Dr. Baker) and founded the record label Flex, later to become part of the EMI empire. Recently Kenneth Bager has founded Music For Dreams, a label specializing in chill out music.

Denmark (Copenhagen) had experienced a fair amount of rave culture, and small clubs and nights began to pop up here and there. Early movers were the club Mantra and one-offs like the Orb playing Trekroner (a former fortress situated on a small island of the Copenhagen coast).

In 1993, Copenhagen saw the birth of no less than two new record shops. Baden Baden and Loud opened and started to inject electronic music into the veins of the city, at that time predominantly served by indie rock stores and of course the major chains. Big trance parties were held in places like Christiania, and Pakhus 11 at the deserted docklands became a regular place for trance and techno events (the entire area is now renovated, very clean, extremely posh and mighty expensive).

Towards the end of the twentieth century printed music media plunged and almost the entire market was wiped out. Fanzines like Jam (indie/electronic), F100 (hip hop) and NN (a Danish MixMag wannabe) were the first to sink, but glossy magazines like Blender, Zoo Magazine, and Mix all suffered closure as we crossed the threshold to the 21st Century. One of the few remaining players, Gaffa, went bankrupt but surfaced immediately with a complete re-design and a new financial construction. Solid youth magazines Tjeck and Chili kept on going as they always had, while magazines targeted towards young women exploded. This market, previously dominated by the two main competitors, Alt For Damerne and Eurowoman, suddenly saw three new players with the arrival of first Woman and then Bazaar and Sirene simultaneously the year after. These new magazines all target a more "girlie" audience (14-19 years), whereas the two older magazines are targeted towards a more mature audience.

At the turn of the century the "Clubbing" phenomena also reached Copenhagen. Following the success of Club Lust (established at the beginning of 1998), the indie stronghold RUST was turned into a clubbing paradise with a huge 1 million EURO re-building and in 1999 became an umbrella that had a new club for (almost) every day of the week. At the other end of town, VEGA had found its feet after a couple of turbulent years and was rapidly developing a successful concept for both live and club music. Today VEGA Nightclub is amongst the top clubs in Europe with a solid name all over the world, and the city has grown steadily into housing some 20-30 regular clubs and club nights with new ones appearing every week.

The key Danish labels in electronic music are April Records, Brother Brown Records, Disco:Wax, Flex, Music for Dreams, Hobby Industries, Homebrew, Hypnotic, Iboga, Morena, Welt, plus the majors. To a certain extent, these labels also operate in different areas or genres of electronic music.

CREATIVE DESTRUCTION:
transformation in the music industry

Electronic Music in Germany

To understand the German market for electronic music, it is perhaps necessary to understand its history, which gave rise to the current scene and emerging styles and genres.

Not surprisingly the German market for electronic music is a mixture of different scenes and genres. In contrast to rock music, electronic music has developed over a much shorter time. Around 1985 the first producers found out that synthesisers are not only helpful devices to play some background sounds, but can also be instruments to record whole pieces of music. The term 'trackmusic' describes the fact that most music produced electronically is based on tracks of different sounds, drums, bass, hi-hats and many others. Because in the beginning most producers resigned from using vocals, the word song was not adequate to specify this music.

In Germany, a club culture soon developed. Frankfurt and Berlin have been the first two centres, both with a unique sound. The slogan "Sound of Frankfurt" became a famous address for Trance, which is a fast, psychedelic music that transfers dancers into a trance-like mental state often supported by taking drugs. In the Eastern part of Germany, other factors were responsible for the success of clubs. With reunification in 1989 Berlin offered many old houses, basements, stores and other buildings, which were perfect for half-legal parties without being controlled by national authorities. One of Germany's best clubs was the 'Tresor', which started inside an old bank security container.

In the mid 1990s, Cologne, Munich and to some extent Hamburg also became centres for electronic music. The music was played in basements and old warehouses and even in forests on plain ground. The parties were easy and cheap to organise since only a few devices are needed: two record players, 'turntables', a mixer, a loud system, a DJ. The visitors were informed by word-of-mouth recommendation and with so-called 'flyers', i.e. little pieces of paper with information about date, time, location and the performing DJ's or live acts. Large numbers of consumers discovered Techno, and money came into the scene. This development strongly influenced the music industry. Trend scouts checked the scene and especially the popular DJ's.

Electronic Music in Finland

The electronic music sub-genre is rapidly gaining popularity in Finland (Nurmela and Parjo, 2002). The most popular types of electronic music such as trance and house are beginning to influence the more popular styles of music and are beginning to draw the attention of larger audiences and the major record labels. The techno-cultural environment surrounding electronic music seems quite promising. Internet penetration of the Finnish population is amongst the highest in Europe, and increasing. The use of the Internet is very common, especially in large cities, where the electronic music scene is most active, and among young people, who supposedly account for the greatest share of electronic music consumers. Online shopping for music, generally is becoming much more popular. Moreover, music is among the most popular products purchased online.

The Finnish rave scene came into being in 1988 with the first acid house nights of the Berlin club in Helsinki. They were followed by illegal techno parties organized by the Hyperdelic housers in Turku, and the first rave party at the old cable factory in Helsinki, organized by the MetalBassOrganization of DJs Mr. Kirk and H2. Since the late 1980's, the electronic music scene has been growing slowly in numbers of events, artists and record sales value, and gaining popularity. The year 1999 saw the most massive increase that could be described as an explosion.

The Finnish market for music generally, and electronic music specifically is very small. As part of the 127 million euro market, the electronic music market is probably worth some million euros (get a figure for this). There has been a growing electronic music scene in Finland since the late 1980's, and electronic music has been gaining popularity quickly especially since the late-1990s. Currently, electronic music is being fused with more popular styles of music, and it is becoming more and more popular among a larger audience while even drawing the attention of the major record labels in Finland and in other European countries, most notably in Germany. There is an active electronic music scene with numerous events in the largest cities.

Despite the fact that Finland may not be the most attractive sound recordings market, there are several record stores dedicated to electronic music in Finland. Although the Internet has brought the offering of foreign record stores much closer to music consumers, in Finland the Finnish online electronic music stores have remained very popular compared to their foreign competitors.

The business environment of electronic music seems promising in Finland. Internet penetration is among the highest in Europe and increasing. The use of the Internet is very common, especially in the larger cities where the electronic music scene is most active, and among young people who supposedly constitute a large proportion of electronic music consumers. Online shopping is becoming more and more popular. Moreover, music is among the most popular products purchased online and therefore obviously very suitable for electronic commerce. But to date one can only find three Finnish online digital music stores (Emma.fm, Soneraplaza Kaista, Streetbeat).

Legal private digital copying is a problem facing the music recording industry. Nevertheless, the small size of the Finnish sound recordings market and the so far rather poor success of Finnish artists abroad work to the advantage of the industry regarding illegal distribution of music on the Internet. In a nutshell, it is more difficult to find Finnish music illegally distributed on the Internet.

Drawing Some Comparisons Between the Four Countries

In order to draw some meaning from the results it was deemed necessary to try and make some comparisons between the four participating countries involved in the Leonardo project. Given that we have explored a wide-ranging and diverse number of issues in our study we have selected here the more pertinent issues, those deemed to be potentially interesting for further exploration by the researchers.

Figure 7.1 shows that the most popular method (across the four countries participating in the Leonardo project) for accessing the Internet was for the individual to use their own computer. Most notably this was the most popular method in Germany (191) and the least popular in Denmark (57). The second most popular method was that of university access. Again this method was the most popular in Germany (44) and the least in Denmark (21). Friends and family proved the third most popular method and here the UK (47) had the highest usage with the least popularity for this method being split between Germany (30) and Denmark (26). Of the other hand it was the Internet café which proved most popular in the UK (70), and the least popular in Denmark (14), then the Internet HUB which was very popular in Finland (76) but with no usage in Germany. The least popular method was the WAP phone. A fairly equal split was found between the UK, Germany and Finland, but there was little use of this means in Denmark.

DISRUPTING SUPPLY CHAIN CONSUMERS

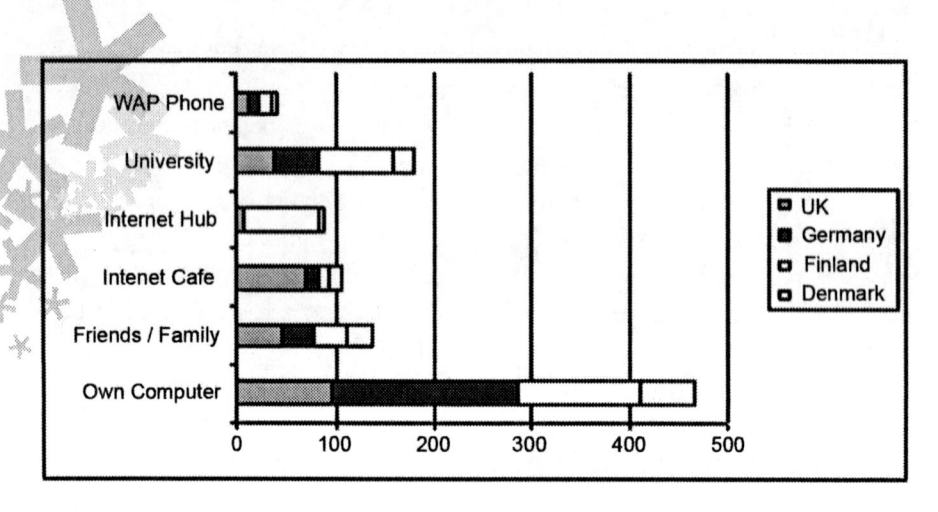

Figure 7.1 International comparisons of how people access the Internet

One area that the Leonardo project team really felt that it would be interesting to look at was that relating to the different music sub-genres coming under the umbrella of electronic music. The categories were derived from consultation with the professional partners participating in the project.

As shown in Figure 7.2, the levels of knowledge in respect to trance and house tend to be higher than the remaining music sub-genres. If we start to explore things on a genre basis then some quite interesting patterns begin to emerge. Let us begin with trance. The highest level of knowledge of trance is in Finland (3.03) where 4 is the highest level of knowledge and 1 is the lowest, which is slightly higher than in the UK. Denmark has the least knowledge of trance (1.81). There are fairly equal levels of knowledge demonstrated for house between Finland (2.64), Germany (2.62) and Denmark (2.51). Overall, it is Germany that appears to have a more consistently higher average of knowledge of electronic music. The UK seems to have a relatively low level of music knowledge in comparison.

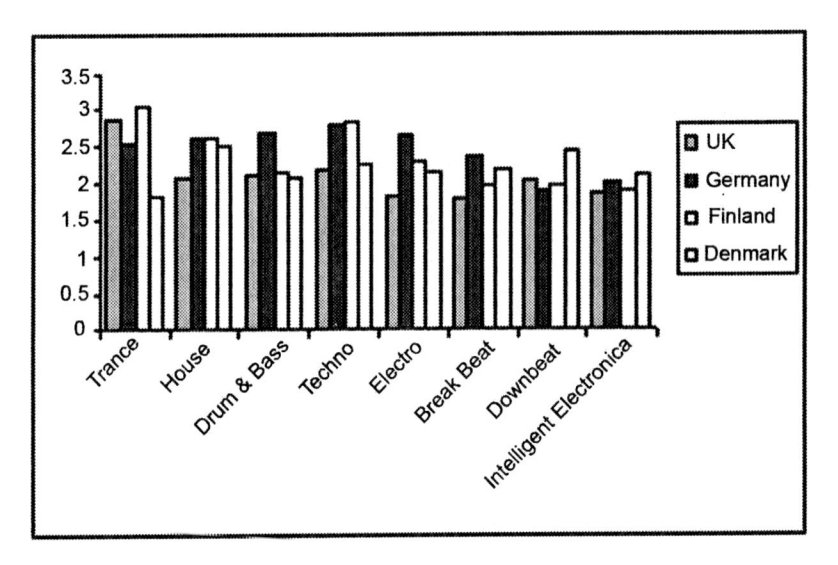

Figure 7.2 International comparisons of knowledge of different music types

Preference levels for music seem to vary considerably across countries, as shown in Figure 7.3. The main preference for trance is in the UK (3.31) and the least in Denmark (1.67), where 1 is the lowest preference level and 4 is the highest level of preference.

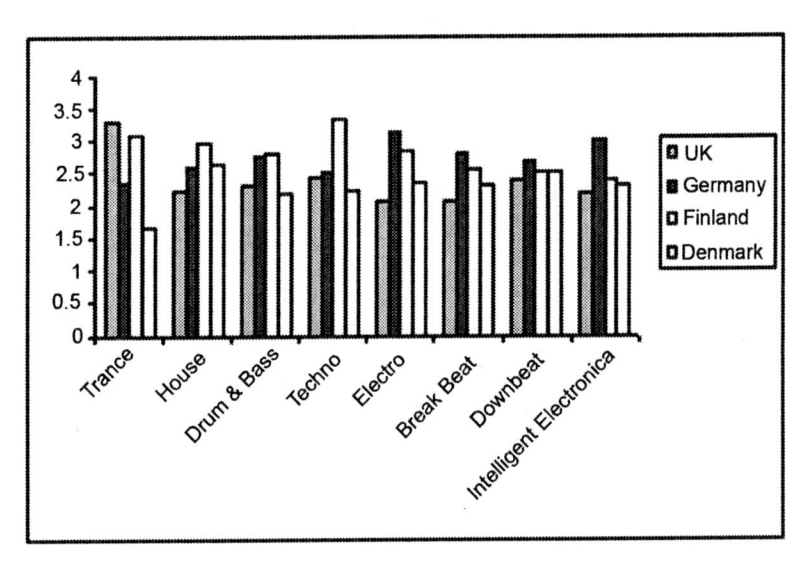

Figure 7.3 International comparisons of preference levels for music

DISRUPTING SUPPLY CHAIN CONSUMERS

With respect to House music one sees that Finland has the highest preference (2.98) for this genre while the UK seems to have the lowest preference (2.22). Drum& Bass appears to have fairly even levels of popularity with a slightly higher score for Finland (2.80) and slightly lower for Denmark (2.19). Looking at Techno the popularity of the genre in Finland (3.34) far outstrips the other countries. Electro is more evenly distributed with a slightly greater popularity given to it in Germany (2.67) and a slightly lower popularity in the UK (2.05). This pattern of popularity repeats itself for the remaining genres Break Beat, Downbeat and Intelligent Electronica.

With regard to preferred formats of music, figure 7.4 shows that CD seems to be by far the most popular format, followed by vinyl. It is interesting to note that vinyl is far more popular in Finland than elsewhere and minidisk is much more popular in the UK than elsewhere.

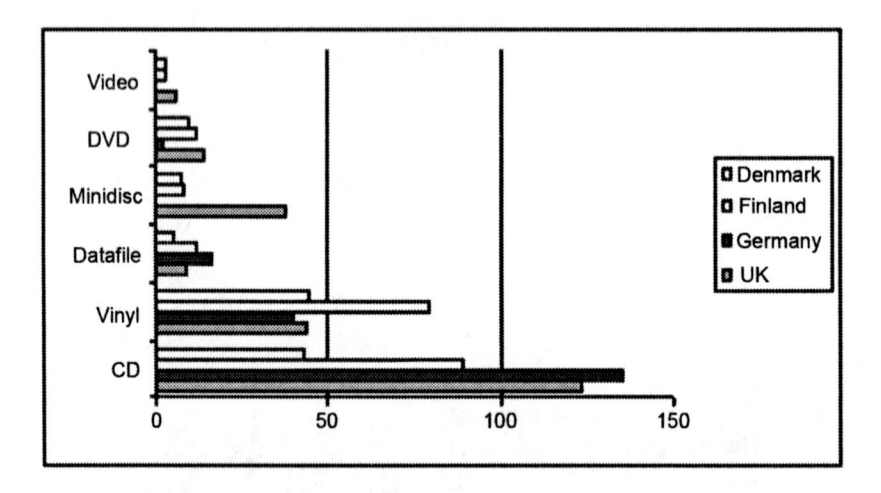

figure 7.4   International comparisons of preferred formats of music

Figure 7.5 shows that spending on music is fairly equal from country to country, with the exception of the large amount spent in the UK on trance music.

CREATIVE DESTRUCTION:
transformation in the music industry

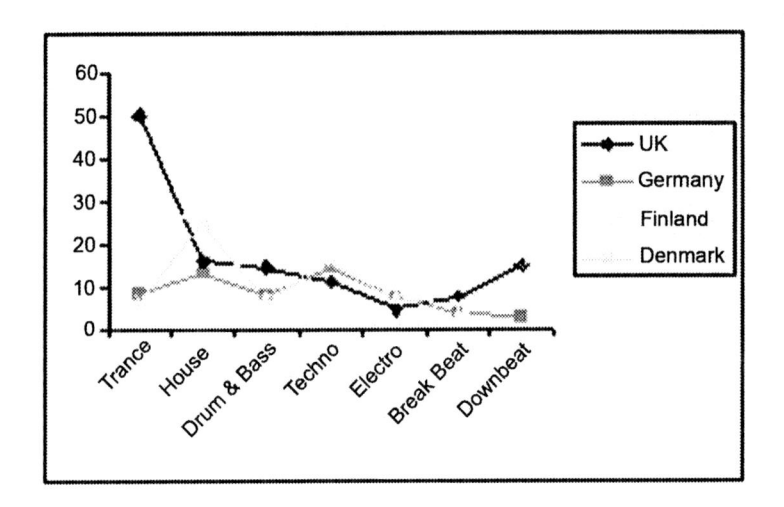

Figure 7.5 International comparisons of spending by music type

With regard to comparisons of preferred purchasing locations, Finland is clearly different from the other countries, with a high number of people preferring to purchase music from the supermarket and by mail order. Germany, UK and Denmark on the other hand all have strong preferences for purchasing from independent retailers, followed closely by major high street retailers, as can be seen in Figure 7.6.

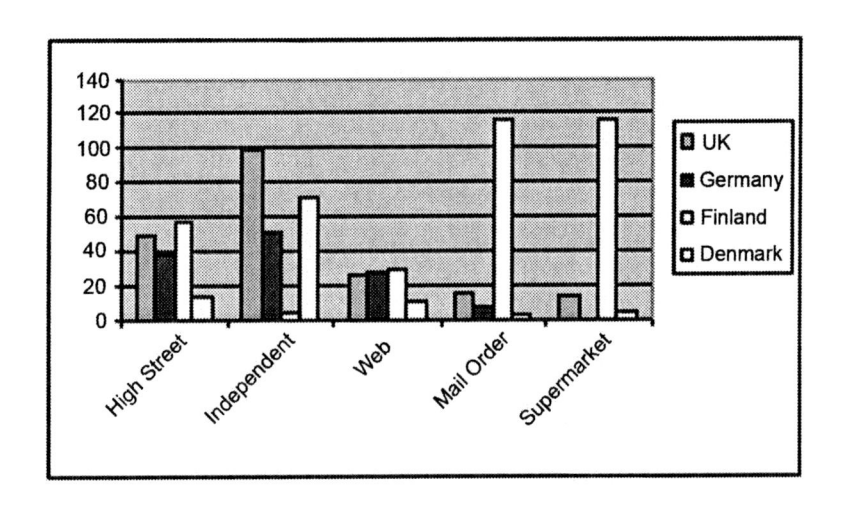

Figure 7.6 International comparisons of preferred music purchasing locations

DISRUPTING SUPPLY CHAIN CONSUMERS

To some extent this may be a reflection of the fact that in the other countries there is much tighter control by the record companies in the supply chain in what music is getting distributed at the retail level. Electronic music tends to be perceived very much as a specialist, niche music and that restricts it to the independents unless the music should make the popular music charts or make national radio

This research aims to reflect Internet-based phenomena on a European level. The advent of online retailing has really being superceded by underground trading in music, more appropriately on the Internet termed P2P (peer-to-peer) trading. Although it is an illegal activity there are no recorded levels of tracks being downloaded in Europe. So it was very fascinating for us to actually get some concrete evidence for the extent of this activity, and, more importantly to present the first recorded evidence on a county by country comparison. Figure 7.7 shows the wide variance between countries regarding the number of mp3 tracks downloaded per month. As can be seen, UK and Finnish respondents claimed to download over twice as many tracks as German and Danish respondents.

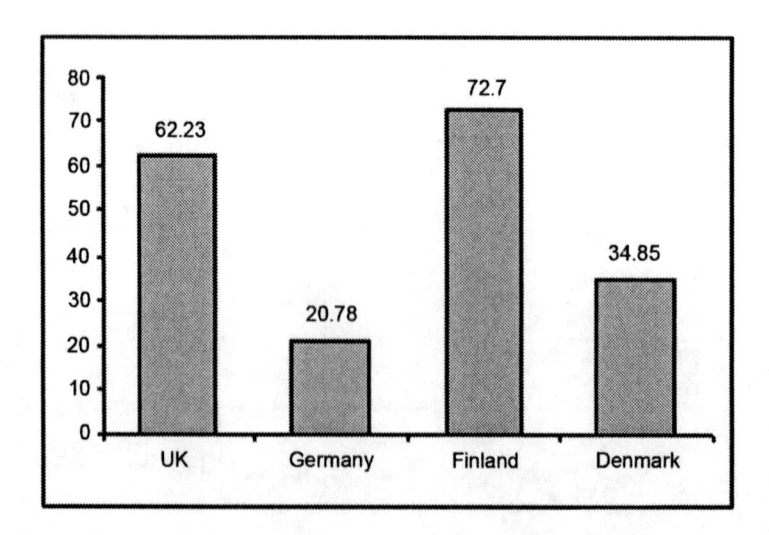

Figure 7.7 International comparisons of average number of mp3 tracks downloaded per month

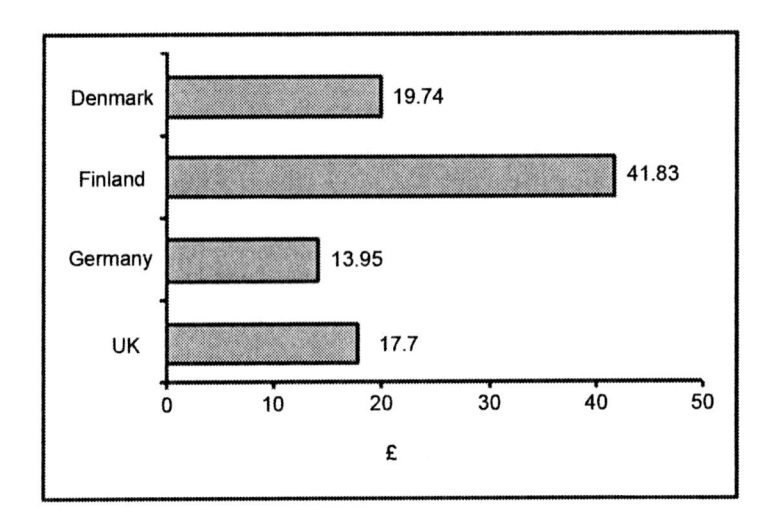

Figure 7.8 International comparisons of mean amounts consumers would pay for subscription services

With regard to how much consumers would pay for a music subscription service, it seems that Finnish consumers would pay considerably more than other countries at £41.83, with Germans willing to pay the least at £13.95 (Figure 7.8).

One interesting issue that was uncovered in the literature was the extent to which the Internet was impacting on consumer behaviour. It was felt important to explore the reasons for consumers buying things from high street retailers. Figure 7.9 shows German respondents having different priorities to those of the other three countries, giving delivery speed as their most important factor, whereas accessibility was more important in the other 3 countries. Interestingly, a long-term relationship and the physical environment in which the retailer was located were deemed to be on the whole the least important factors generally among the four countries.

DISRUPTING SUPPLY CHAIN CONSUMERS

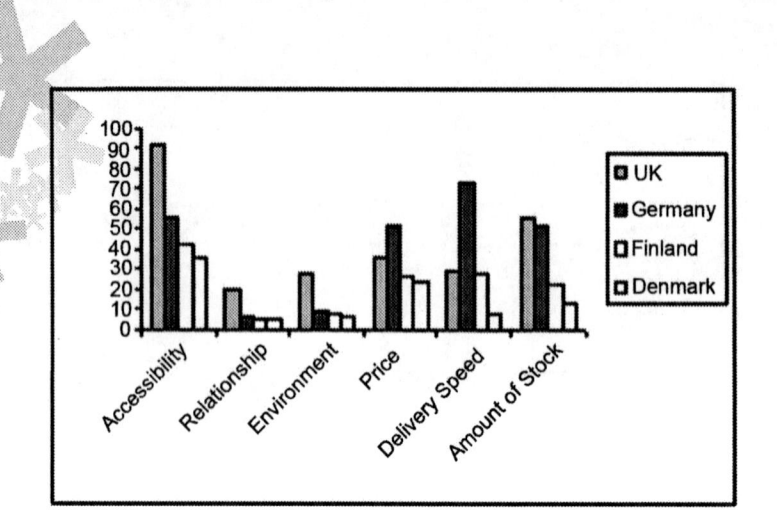

Figure 7.9 International comparisons of why consumers shop at a major high street store

With regard to why consumers shop at independent retailers, rice appeared to be the least important factor across all countries. Relationship was most important in UK, Germany and Denmark, whereas amount of stock was more important in Finland.

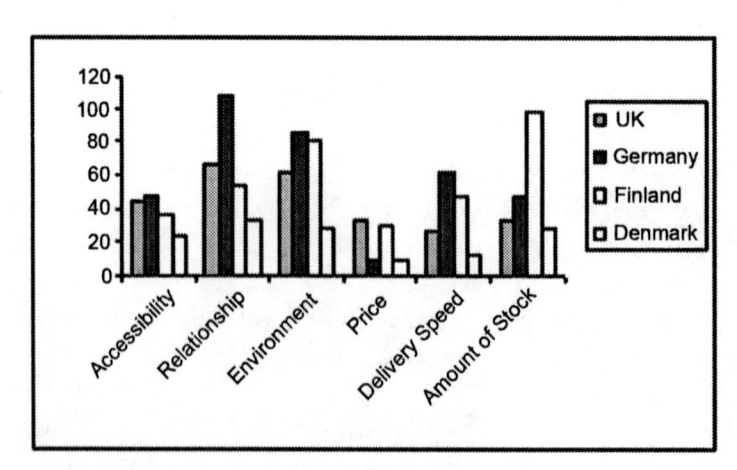

Figure 7.10 International comparisons of why consumers shop at independent retailers

CREATIVE DESTRUCTION:
transformation in the music industry

The independent retailers who participated in our survey had spent much time and effort in building close and long term relationships with their customers (Figure 7.10). This is a very fast moving genre and the independents are continually striving to keep their knowledge up to date and update their stock on a weekly basis.

The amount of stock was the most important factor as to why German and Finnish respondents shopped on the web, whereas accessibility was more important for UK and Danish respondents. Not surprisingly, relationship and environment were relatively unimportant across all countries.

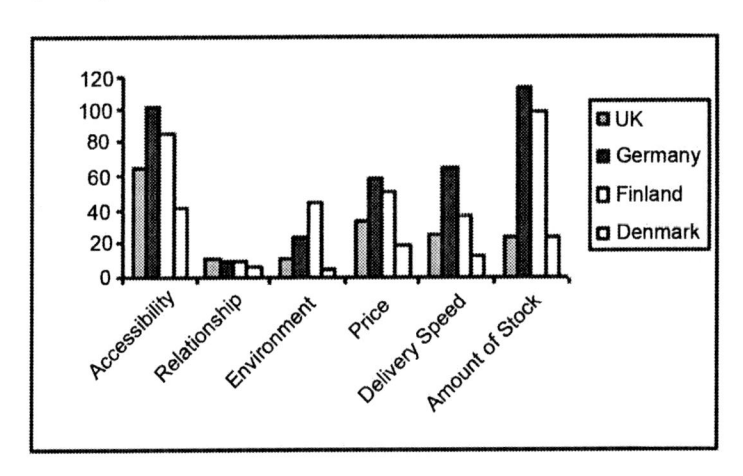

Figure 7.11 International comparisons of why consumers shop on the web

A key driver for the consumer using the web (Figure 7.11) does appear to be the greater choice of music than they could ever achieve in a physical setting. To some extent the web facilitates more opportunities for suppliers to distribute their music. But equally important is that the consumers must have the knowledge and information to know what they are searching for. That is why this is a very dedicated community built around specific genres and music creators.

Remarkably, the majority of respondents from all countries expected they would be shopping in independent retailers in twelve months time. Interestingly, all countries seemed to expect an increase in web purchases in the future, as indicates in Figure 7.12.

DISRUPTING SUPPLY CHAIN CONSUMERS

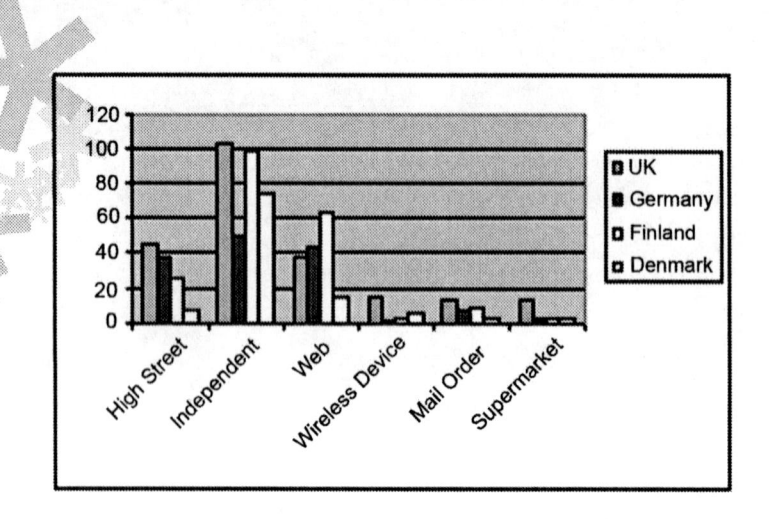

Figure 7.12 International comparisons of where consumers expect to be shopping in next 12 months

A high degree of variance can be seen with regard to the value consumers place on s single track of music, as shown in Figure 7.13. Danish respondents recorded an average three times higher than the second highest average (Germany) and more than seven times higher than the lowest average (Finland).

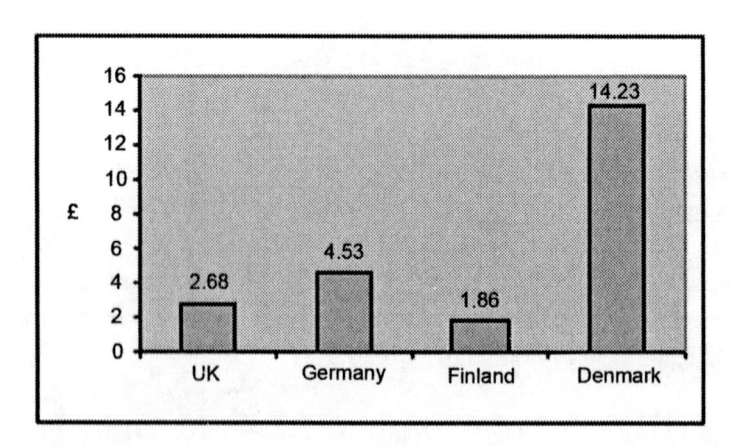

Figure 7.13 International comparisons of mean values placed on a single track of music

CREATIVE DESTRUCTION:
transformation in the music industry

Cash was by far the most preferred method of payment across all countries, as seen in Figure 7.14. Surprisingly, cheques were the least favoured form of payment.

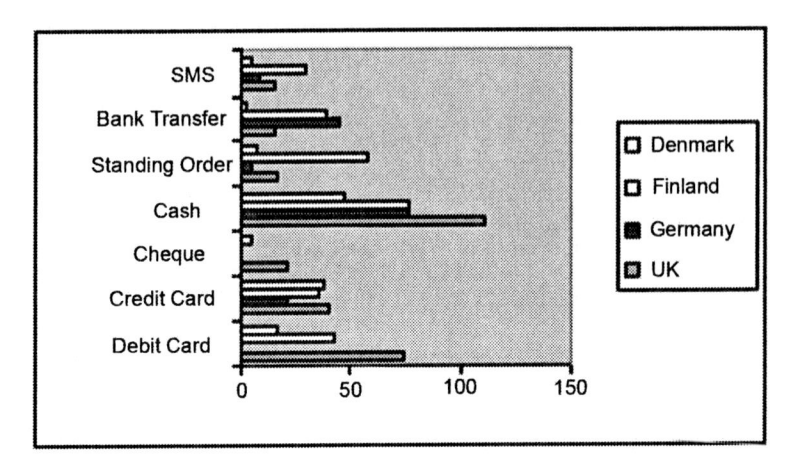

Figure 7.14 International comparisons of preferred payment methods for music

Figure 7.15 shows that when searching in a retail branch, the majority of consumer from the UK, Finland and Denmark preferred to search by style/genre, whereas in Germany, the majority preferred to search by artist. Searching by record label was least popular in all countries.

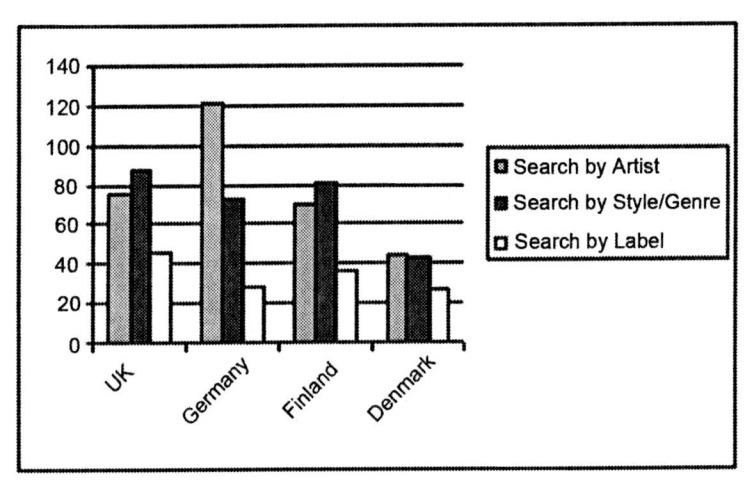

Figure 7.15 International comparisons of how consumers search for music in a retail branch

DISRUPTING SUPPLY CHAIN CONSUMERS

Similarly when searching for music on a website, the majority in the UK, Finland and Denmark preferred to search by style/genre, whereas in Germany the majority preferred to search by artist. Again, searching by record label was least popular across all countries (see Figure 7.16).

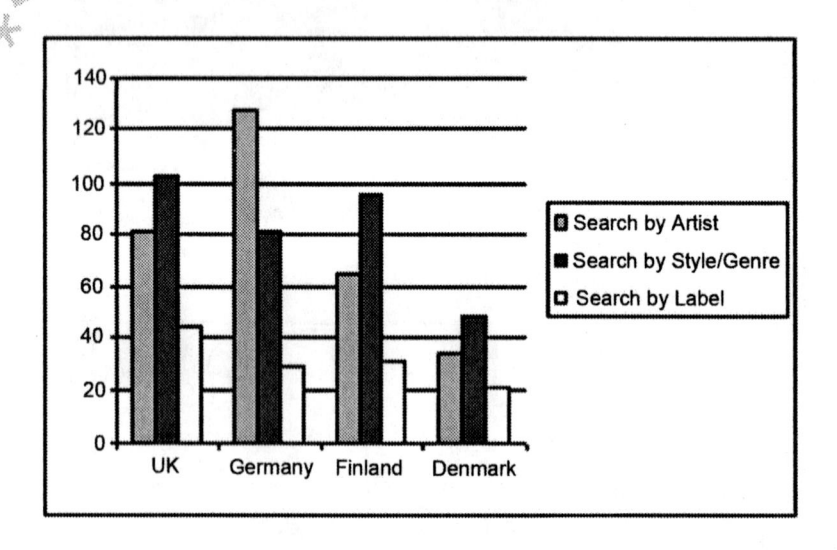

Figure 7.16 International comparisons of how consumers search for music on a website

Summary

This chapter has explored the different factors affecting electronically sold and distributed electronic music – e-music – in Denmark, Finland, Germany and the UK. It has presented a range of results from our Leonardo funded research undertaken in the independent music sector, in each country, respectively.

One of the themes of the book is to reflect Internet-based phenomena on a European level. It does appear that throughout the European countries appearing here, the advent of online retailing has really being superceded by underground trading in music, more specifically on the Internet termed P2P (peer-to-peer) trading. Although it is an illegal activity there has not been to date much evidence of the levels of tracks being downloaded in Europe. So it was very fascinating for us to actually get

CREATIVE DESTRUCTION:
transformation in the music industry

some concrete evidence on the extent of this activity, and, more importantly to offer possibly the first documented evidence from a county by country comparison.

In relation to the types of electronic music sub genres, this study has presented valuable evidence on the popularity and the levels of knowledge among consumers across Europe. Preference levels for music seem to vary considerably across countries, as shown in figure 7.6. The main preference for trance is in the UK and the least preference was for House. Drum & Bass appears to have fairly even levels of popularity across the partner countries. Techno has by far the greatest the popularity in Finland.

It is apparent from the research that electronic music is a rapidly evolving and exciting music genre evidenced by its growing popularity across Europe and the high levels of knowledge recorded on the different sub-genres. It is really the first pan-European music type in which technology has facilitated a universality of production, supply and consumption on an unprecedented scale, such that no one country is dominant. Our received notions of music's margins and its centre have ceased to apply. The Internet is creating a much more informed consumer who is European in outlook with a much wider choice of music available to them, who is able to access electronic music networks that transcend nationalities and geographical boundaries. On the other hand its destructive power is very evident from the work presented in this chapter. The Internet is allowing illegal downloading to such an extent that it is becoming cyclical in nature and any attempt to set up a working business is bound to be beset by problems stemming from whole groups of consumers cultured on free music.

DISRUPTING SUPPLY CHAIN CONSUMERS

WINDOWS INTO THE FUTURE

It is evident from the findings of Creative Destruction that the history of popular music runs in parallel with the technology that helped to create it. Record companies still form the foundation of the music industry, even as the apparently solid rocks of production and distribution begin to crumble in the face of post-web technologies. For example, as we have seen, downloadable music offers new ways for consumers to purchase, use and even remake music. In addition, music is becoming even more ubiquitous than ever before owing to newly emerging innovations in delivery technologies. For example, music can now be downloaded digitally on an array of gadgets including mobile phones, iPods and PDAs (Webactive, 2004, pp. 14 – 20). Meanwhile, major record companies are attempting to survive out of a commitment to shareholders and synergies associated with high profitability in a general media market, while they search for business models that can compete with the availability of low-cost and free music, often illegally distributed over the Internet.

P2P technologies help to open the market to the user. Although the downloading of MP3 files does not help users overcome the problem of many vertically differentiated products, it does go a long way to helping them to deal with the vast quantity of horizontally differentiated products. It opens the market for the consumer, allowing them more choice in their future purchasing and/or listening. That the consumer does not have to pay for listening to their music increases the chances of them downloading something new and original, as they do not lose out if they do not enjoy the music.

There has been much public interest and debate about the impact that the Internet is having on the music sector, though the focus has been largely on the implications of the Internet for the large record companies. Creative Destruction set about redressing this by looking at the independent electronic dance music sector. This work ultimately sought to provide insights into the impact of the Internet and the response of regulatory agencies such as the RIAA and the British Phonographic Industry (BPI) to it, on the supply of music. It has also fulfilled the need for work exploring the consumption of digital music.

CREATIVE DESTRUCTION:
transformation in the music industry

There is a real need for some future work, which will look into the changing meaning of music in the digital age - from an aesthetic commodity to information-intensive gift. Some clarification is then needed on the potential impact on the roles to be played - by both consumer and producer.

Finally, it would be beneficial to undertake research that explored in more detail than that covered by Creative Destruction, some of the implications for power relations – between, say independent artists and the record label intermediary - in the supply of music.

The path followed in this project was to explore the extent to which the Internet and post-web technologies have led to changes in the supply and consumption of music, with a focus on electronic dance music. This sub-genre was deemed by various commentators and the EU to be one of the most innovative and creative in its nature. But history has shown us, with shellac, vinyl and the CD, that often the destruction of one format leads to creation of a superior one, though in the past these improvements were restricted to either music storage or composition. With the Internet we are seeing radical changes for both producer and consumer. Ironically rather than end our path of inquiry with answers, we are ending it with a series of questions, which we feel warrant further exploration:

1. How is the aesthetic meaning of music being transformed as it moves along the digitalised supply system from artistic creation to streamed consumption?

2. In what ways is the independent, electronic music supply chain being shaped by the different regulatory bodies and the Internet?

3. How are the changing practices of consumption allowing for new forms of power relations, lived experiences and engagement in the independent, music sector?

The resulting synthesis of the literature and primary research presented in Creative Destruction enabled the development of an initial theoretical framework for the modelling of the digital supply of music, which can be empirically tested with future research. Suffice to say at this stage it conceptualises the state of affairs currently existing in the music sector. In the future, the supply of music will no longer involve a few highly integrated companies, controlling actors in a linear sequence of stages, each independently responsible for different activities, for adding value to the music composition(s). Instead, the system will consist of a variety of players that will directly interact with each other and share in the creation of value.

Each player will focus on their own peculiar, core competencies. They can work together either just for the duration of one business opportunity or by establishing closely co-ordinated relationships. Music consumers will also become value creators as they participate in the value creating activities. The preliminary structure of this platform for supplying music on the Internet will look significantly different to the pre-web model. Figure 8.1 below shows that the new supply configuration will be depicted as a business web rather than by a supply chain structure.

The main difference between the digital platform and the physical supply chain mechanisms is that consumers and artists will be much more central to supplying music on the Internet. Personalisation and customisation, resulting in higher customer engagement and satisfaction, will justify the price charged by the platform for services and content (e.g. the ability to readily customise their music collections), integrated Internet broadcaster playing music by-demand (in pre-set order). An important factor for success will be the integration of virtual communities, in the platform that allows the establishment of social links with like-minded people. Consumers, artists, music experts and any other B-web participant should be able to interact on the platform. Consumers can find new music through recommendations and get in touch with their favourite musicians. For instance, the music fan in Hong Kong could chat with the fan in South America about the latest release of an artist. Musicians can interact with their fans, distribute music, chat with other musicians, and get professional help from music experts - of any kind.

The proposed model for supplying music on the Internet implies a royalty system which is much more elastic and transparent to the artist. In the pre-web model one often finds that artists increasingly complain about the royalties they receive. One approach to improve the current royalty payment system could be that record companies pay larger advances and offer higher profit sharing, in return for full merchandise and publishing rights. Another approach to improve the royalty system could be for the record companies to subdivide their support into different modules, ranging from one-off service offers to long-term contracts. The price for one-off service should be fixed and naturally higher. Thereby, record companies receive a small profit margin and can use the artist brand name and the content only for a short period of time.

On the other hand, record companies should offer long-term packages that include services such as artist management and development. Thereby, the contract conditions would be elastic - in terms of splitting risk and profit with the artist. A more equal revenue share seems imperative in order to establish successful artist relationships. The highest priority must be that both contract partners visibly profit from a long-term relationship.

For the record companies the model suggests that they have a number of different ways to market and sell the music composition. One option would be to concentrate only on content creation. Thereby, they would license their products to different business partners such as online platforms (portals, subscription services), radio broadcaster (on- and offline), TV stations, e-tailer, re-tailer, and mobile phone services. This would minimize the risk of failing with an owned subscription model and allow them to only concentrate on content creation.

Record companies may also seek to develop an affiliated subscription service. What could be more convincing than a music expert, navigating through the jungle of music? The main advantage could be to develop direct relationships with music consumers to understand their needs. Real-time consumption data will provide an instant feedback on how consumers respond to a label's campaign. It will allow record companies to instantly adjust their marketing mix. However, in this case the alliance with a partner that provides the technical know-how is highly recommended.

WINDOWS INTO THE FUTURE

As stated before, record companies are music experts and should focus on this competence. They must look for strong partners that have the technical know-how to provide the infrastructure and services, e.g. hosting or network maintenance. Their highest priority must be to develop a service that is absolutely convenient, hassle free and easy to handle, by all users.

In terms of pricing strategy, the research results have indicated that a high percentage of music consumers that download music would be willing to pay to keep this privilege. So far, they have not had a legal alternative to illegal file swapping services. It has been shown that for the current subscription services that major record companies license music to, there have been significant disadvantages that hamper their success. In essence, the price system must be simplified. Contrary to current practice, there should not be any compulsory membership fee or monthly payment because it would just raise the barriers to join a platform. Only if customers want to use additional services, which are not accessible anywhere else, should they have to pay a monthly fee to become special members. For example, they could gain the right to join a recording session of their favourite band live via the Internet and have the ability to suggest improvements.

Essential for the success of an online music service is that all major record companies offer their music at the same online platform. This has not happened yet and this may be one of the major reasons for the failure of current subscription models[30]. Searching for music costs the consumers their most valuable commodity – leisure time. They are looking for something which provides the widest range of music and artists, quickly from one location. This indicates that the new music platforms should not only offer music that is mainstream, for example rock and pop music, but also genres that are on the margins (niches), such as electronic dance music. It is logical to give independent musicians the possibility to provide their music at the same online platform. This would not only make the platform more attractive to consumers, but also allow record companies to find new talents.

The record companies have been very hesitant to distribute the content of their major artists online, because of the fear of piracy. But, if they want to be successful they have to overcome this fear. This research indicates that if consumers get to try hassle free, legal downloading services many of them will be willing to use them instead of unreliable illegal file sharing systems. Therefore, consumers should be able to burn paid for files, onto CDs or to upload onto portable devices. One could point here to the success of Apple's Ipod[31], in the US. Therefore, alliances with technological partners that provide the necessary know-how will be essential, although more important still will be the success of technology designed to protect copyright, such as Digital Rights Management (DRM).

The power of negotiation has traditionally been with the record labels, who designed the contracts to assure their own survival and profitability. Since most acts are not profitable, the companies' contracts were designed so that the royalties paid to their best-selling acts were low enough to assure that the profits from these acts were sufficient to pay for their full operating costs plus profit (Clemons and Lang, 2003, p. 273). Equally important, profitable acts will no longer rely as much on the added value of their less famous label brands. They have established their own brand names and are more easily recognisable without promotional support from the labels. That is, they could negotiate far better contracts or simply bypass the existing distribution systems.

Kretschmer points out (2001, p. 431) that Bowie is a landmark in the development of 'disintermediation' – where you have the phenomena of a major-creator-to-consumer market. This occurs because when long-term contracts come up for renewal between the record company and the artist, 'superstars' are in an extremely strong position to recover and retain their intellectual property rights. Such artists are branded products in themselves; they increasingly have access to alternative methods of finance; and they are using digital networks to repackage and distribute globally.

This is evidenced by Kretschmer et al (2001) who point to the trend for third parties to act as brokers for copyright to media. The so-called "Bowie Bonds" issued in 1997, are an example of the possible access of established artists to the financial markets. An institutional investor, the Prudential Insurance Company of America bought the rights to David Bowie's master tapes and publishing catalogue that had been transferred into a vehicle company by the underwriter – Pullman Group. A higher advance than was possible from a new distribution deal with the record company from the underwriter enabled Bowie to buy back publishing rights in some songs owned by a former manager. Other market deals have involved Rod Stewart, Iron maiden, the Rolling Stones and Elton John. Issuing banks include Nomura, Merrill Lynch, Citibank and Morgan Stanley. It is a method available only for very established artists with a clear projected royalty stream. A big challenge for widening securitisation is that co-ownership of rights is typical in the entertainment field, and all owners must be willing to participate in the issue (Fairfax, 1999).

WINDOWS INTO THE FUTURE

Future of the Underground

The term "underground" is often associated with subversion and the counter culture. Dance music is cited to be the biggest sub-cultural movement since punk rock (Hesmondalgh, 1998). It espouses a music and style system that is highly relative; it is all about position, context and timing (Thornton, 1995). Its built-in obsolescence means that it is not only the prerogative of the young, but the "hip". Creative Destruction shows that in terms of music consumption, there is a subversive digital generation growing up, who are not rebelling against the body politic or mainstream culture, like the punks, hippies and 'Beat' generation, but are more into subverting the power and control of multi national media conglomerates, that have largely acted to commoditise culture and securitise the aesthetic.

Today, the Internet has facilitated the development and mobilisation of movements which are not physically clustered together, say like the "beats", "punks" and "ravers" of the past, but who can now be virtually brought together to share music, philosophy and style. They are used to music as a "gift" (Mauss, 1969), not a commodity to be purchased. And the major record companies have at last got the message that for all mainstream music there will always be an underground offering an alternative — legally or illegally.

Summary

The music business as we know it today was built around the twelve-inch long-playing record which then developed into the usually longer CD. Singles were released to act as trailers for this high-value, extended artefact that arrives once every couple of years. Downloading puts the choice back in the hands of the consumer. Digital distribution is new for the music industry. The music industry is going to have to offer music fans a range of appealing options for listening and buying digital music. Listeners will need to be offered packages geared to their hunger for new catalogue selections to overcome the subversive digital wave of illegal downloading. That's the aspiration. We will all find out soon, when the industry opens the window into its future.

ENDNOTES

1 Quoted in Damian Reece's article entitled:- "An industry pole-axed by the power of the Net", The Independent, Wednesday, 31st of March, 2004, p. 40.

2 Quoted in Reece.

3 Ibid.

4 The most successful online legal service has been Apple Computers iTunes which downloads music tracks onto its iPod personal music player. A week after its launch in May 2003, one million songs had been purchased. The number has now soared to 30 million (ibid.).

5 Microsoft recently announced plans to offer portable gadgets in response to Apple. The would be "iPod Killers" will be released in the second half of this year and are able to play music and movies (Arthur, 2004, p. 39).

6 The history of electronic music, though, can be traced further back, to people like Karlheinz Stockhausen and Pierre Schaeffer, Edgard Varèse, John Cage, and before that, the futurist and Thaddeus Cahil's Telharmonium apparatus for "Generating and Distributing Music Electronically", patented in 1897.

7 Quoted in The Independent, Wednesday, 31st of March, 2004, p. 40.

8	The word "funk" plays an important role. Techno founding father Juan Atkins has explained how he took inspiration from groups like Kraftwerk, but wanted to add a funky element (Trask, 1988, p. 44). The word "funk" can be traced to the 17th Century Congo as an expression for the body's odour. The word has developed an ambiguous semantics containing both the beautiful and the dreadful. Funk has come to signify a black authenticity (Poschardt, 1998, p. 417).

9	From Mark Lewis (2000), unpublished MSc dissertation entitled: - "Technospace" , University of Copenhagen 2000.

10	This entire paragraph is based on Mark Lewis's article:- Clubbing for folket, Berlingske Tidende, Metro, pp. 14-17, August 24, 2001.

11	A synthesiser is an electronic sound generating device, which can be triggered by devices such as a special keyboard or by a programmed sequencer.

12	In the early 1980s it was also possible to buy a sampling box which contained one chip which could record one sound; this device was especially popular with drummers of small bands.

13	The sound texture and pitch of the recorded sound bites can be changed. It is also possible to reverse the recorded soundbite. They contain a 'time stretch' device which one can manipulate the length of the recorded sound as well.

14	As is the case with the writing procedure on a word processor, the programmer does not need to be fluent in performance skills, since mistakes can be corrected, sequences can be restructured and rhythms can be 'quantised'. However, this does not mean that the programmer does not know anything about music, or indeed is unmusical, as some would put forward in the discussion of digital musical technology. This is to confuse the notion of technical musical skill with the notion of musical knowledge. As will be explained later in this book, electronic technology invites a different type of performance skill.

ENDNOTES

15   SMPTE is 'the standard originally developed by the Society of Motion Picture and Television Engineers', pronounced SIMP-ty (Braut, 1994, p. 105).

16   To overdub is to record a new track along an existing recording, so that it becomes part of the recording.

17   my.mp3.com, from early to mid-2000, established itself as the major MP3 portal.

18   However between 1992 and 1994 the British MCPS (mechanical copyright collectors) took the dance label Shut Up and Dance to court over sampling infringements and won the case. The label went bankrupt due to resulting costs but still no precedent was set (Rietveld, 1998, p. 152).

19   His article is entitled "Beat Generator," and it was quoted in Andrew Goodwin, "Sample and Hold, Pop Music in the Age of Digital Reproduction", 1988, Chapter 17, p. 271 in S. Frith and A. Goodwin, On Record, Routledge.

20   This is a self definition which seems to have connections with German ideas on the machine as was defined during the epoch of the neue Sachlicheit in the 1920s and 1930s.

21   In the age of mass production, the increasing use of digital technologies gives enormous credence to Benjamin's (quoted in Goodwin, 1990, p.259) celebration of the end of the "aura" where the audience is no longer concerned with an original textual moment because digital technology ensures that there is no discernible difference between the sound recorded in the studio and that reproduced on the consumers CD system. This is something new: the mass production of the aura.

22   Here the focus will be on drum 'n' bass, trance and electro which with techno and house are a central focus of our survey research on consumers presented in Chapter 7.

23 Bogdanov (2000) notes that techno is the dance music choice throughout most of continental Europe with corporate sponsored raves in Germany and Belgium commonplace.

24 Interview conducted at the Universal Media Group on the 9th of January, 2003, New York City (NYC).

25 Interview conducted at Bertlesmann on the 2nd of February, 2003, NYC.

26 Interview conducted at EMI on the 27th of January, 2003 in NYC.

27 Interview conducted at Bertelsman on the 23rd of January, 2003 in NYC.

28 Commonly, record companies bind the artist in a contract for 7" albums

29 Napster 2.0 was recently launched as a subscription-based music trading site.

30 In the UK the most successful to date has been Peter Gabriel's company, On Demand Distribution (OD2, www.od2.com). But it only supplies tracks from the big 'five' record companies and it is not compatible with Apple iPod the UKs best selling portable MP3 player (Webactive, 2004, p. 18)

31 Apple's iTunes site (www.apple.com/itunes) has proved hugely popular in the US, notching up a million downloads in its first week (Webactive, 2004, p. 17).

ENDNOTES

REFERENCES

Alderman, J (2001) Sonic Boom: Napster, P2P and the Battle for the Future of Music. Fourth Estate, London.

Altinkemer, K. and Bandyopadhyay, S (2000). "Bundling and distribution of digitized music over the Internet". Journal of Organizational Computing & Electronic Commerce, 10(3), pp. 209-225

Apple.Computers (2004) http://www.apple.com/itunes. Read: January 9, 2004.

Armor, J (2002) "Dirty Vegas Single Powered By Car Commercial", http://launch.yahoo.com/read/news.asp?contentID=208909. Read: October 26, 2003.

Arthur, C (2004) "Microsoft plans 'iPod killer'". The Independent, Friday 19th of March, p. 39.

Barr, T (2000) Techno: the Rough Guide. Rough Guides/Penguin, London.

Barthes, R (1973) The Grain of Voice. Hill and Wang, NY, USA.

Bathia, K.., Gay, R and R. Honey (2001) Windows into the Future: How Lessons from Hollywood Will Shape the Music Industry, Columbia University, New York.

Baudrillard, J (1983) Simulations. Semiotext[e], New York 1983.

Beadle, J (1993) Will Pop Eat Itself? Pop Music in the Soundbite Era. Faber and Faber, London.

Berger, A (2002) "Dirty Vegas", http://www.rollingstone.com/reviews/cd/review.asp?aid=2044115, Read: July 2, 2002.

Bidder, S (1999) Rough Guide to House. Rough Guides/Penguin, London.

REFERENCES

Billboard (1975) "New on the Charts" in: Billboard, March 22, 1975, p. 33.

Blesser, P and J. Pilkington (2000) "Global Paradigm shifts in the audio industry, part one". Journal of the Audio Engineering Society, Vol 48, No 9 pp 861-872

Bogdanov, V, Woodstra, C, Erewine, S and J. Bush (2001) Electronica: the Definitive Guide. AMG/Backbeat Books, San Francisco, CA, USA.

Bogdanov, V, Woodstra, C, Erlewine, S and J. Bush (2001) Electronica: The Definitive Guide to Electronic Music. AMG/Backbeat Books, San Francisco, CA, USA.

BPW, (2002) Phonographische Wirtschaft. Josef Keller, Verlag, Germany.

Braut, C (1994) The Musicians Guide to MIDI, Sybex/Macintosh Library, Alameda, CA, USA.

Bussy, P (1993) Kraftwerk: Man, Machine and Music, SAF Publishing Ltd., Wembley, Middx..

Cage, J (1970) "The Future of Music; Credo" in: Kostelanetz, R (ed.), John Cage, pp. 54-57, Praeger Publishers, New York – Washington.

Cap Gemini/Ernst & Young (2002) "Searching for the Global Consumer: A European Study of Changing Lifestyles and Shopping Behaviour", Cap Gemini Ernst & Young, Copenhagen, Denmark.

Carvalho, H (1992) "De harteklop van de duivel: gabbermuziek is uitgroeid tot jeugdcultur", in NRC – Handelsbad, 5th January, Rotterdam.

Chadabe, J (1997) Electric Sound: The Past and Promises of Electronic Music, Prentice-Hall, New Jersey.

Clemons, E and Lang, K (2003) "The Decoupling of Value Creation from Revenue: A Strategic Analysis of the Markets for Pure Information Goods". Information Technology and Management, 4 pp. 259-287.

Crabtree, S. (2002). "A new spin on music distribution". Gallup Tuesday Briefing, July, pp. 1-5.

Dallach, C and Wellershoff, M ((2001) "Das Mitpfeifen", Der Speigel, No. 50, December 10, 2001, pp. 198-201

Datamonitor.com (2003) "Carling: Using Music to Break Away from 'Lad' Culture", Datamonitor.com. Read: September 12, 2003.

Datamonitor.com (2003) "Unilever: Marketing on the Beach", Datamonitor.com. Read: July 18, 2003.

De Fontenay, E (2000) "The Digital Economy: How Digital Goods are reshaping the Rules of Commerce, http://www.musicdish.com/acsel/DigitalEconomy.pdf. Read: February 02, 2003.

De Fontenay, E., de Fontenay, S., Kibbee, R. and Shulman, S (1999) "MP3: Digital Music for the Millenium?". White Paper on the: Impact of Downloadable Music Distribution for the Music Industry Based on a MusiDish/MP3.com. Co-Branded Survey, Tag it, June

De Wit, B and Meyer R (1999) Strategy Synthesis, International Thomson Business Press, London.

Deters, M (2001) "Musikindustrie, 'geistiges Eigentum' und Internet. MP3, Napster und die Folgen", Inprekorr, 361, November, http://inprekorr.de/361-nap.htm, Read: December 20, 2002.

Dolfsma, W. (2000) "How will the Music Industry Weather the Globalisation Storm?", http://www.firstmonday.dk/issues/issue5-5/dolfsma/index.html. Read: March 06, 2003.

Dolfsma, W (2000) "How Will the Music Industry Weather the Globalization Storm?". www.firstmonday.com . Read: November 5, 2002.

Doyle, P (2002) Marketing Management and Strategy, Prentice Hall, London.

Elmose, K (2001) "CD-salget falder", Computerworld.dk, May 21.

Elmose, K (2002): "Pladeselskaber anklager net for cd-tab". Computerworld.dk, August 28, p. 20.

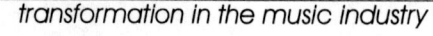

Eshun, K (1998) More Brilliant Than The Sun, Quartet Books, London.

Evans, P.B (1998) "How Deconstruction Drives De-averaging", http://www.bcg.com/publications/publication_view.jsp?pubID=241. Read: 15 April, 2003.

Evans, P.B and Wurster, T.S (1997) "!Strategy and the New Economics of Information", in Harvard Business Review, September - October, pp. 69 – 82.

Fairfax, L. M (1999) "When You Wish upon a Star: Explaining the Cautious Growth of Royalty Backed Securitisation". Columbia Business Law Review, pp. 441-88

Feferman, M (2001) "Evaluating the Diebold Report: What does the Market Need?", http://musicdish.com/mag/index.php3?id=3139. Read: April 05, 2003.

Fisher, W (2000) "Digital Music: Problems and Possibilities". www.law.harvard.edu/Academic_Affairs/coursepages/tfisher/Music.html. Read: October 4 2002.

Fleming, J (1995) What kind of House Party is this? History of a Music Revolution?" MIY Publishing, London.

Fortune (2000), vol. 142, no. 12., Time Warner Publishing, p. 118.

Fox, M (2002) "Technological and Social Drivers of Change in the Online Music Industry", http://firstmonday.org/issues/issue7_2/fox/index.html Read: February 10, 2003.

Freeman, A. and de Fontenay, E (2001) "Songwriters in the new millennium, Changing expectations & realities". MusicDish Songwriter Survey e-Report Series, Tag it, August.

Friedrich, J (1990) Methoden Empirischer Sozialforschung, 14. Auflage, Westdeutscher Verlag, Opladen.

Frith, S and A. Goodwin (1990) On Record: Rock, Pop and the Written Word. Routledge, London.

REFERENCES

Frith, S. (1987). "The making of the British record industry 1920 – 64" in J. Curran, A. Smith and P. Wingate (Eds) Impacts and Influences. pp. 278-290. Metheun, London.

Gallaway, T. and Kinnear, D (2001) "Unchained Melody: A price discrimination-Based Policy Proposal for Addressing the MP3 Revolution". Journal of Economic Issues, 35(2), June.

Gerlach, C. and Minda, K. (2000) "The Endgame for Old Media? Path to Profotability", www.mainspring.com. Read: November 5, 2002.

Gibson, W (1986) Neuromancer, HarperCollins Publishers, London.

Godin, S (2000) Unleashing the Ideavirus, Do You Zoom Inc, Copenhagen, Denmark.

Goldberg, J (1995) "Recalling Totalities: The Mirrored Stages of Arnold Schwarzenegger" in: Gray, C et.al., (eds.), The Cyborg Handbook, pp. 233-254, Routledge, London.

Gomez, P and Küng, L. (2001) Creating Value in the New Economy. Do Old Economy Management Concepts Have a Future? Die Unternehmung, Volume 55, 2001, Number 2, pp. 97 – 109.

Grant, J (1999) "The New Marketing Manifesto," Texere, p. 98.

Grant, R.M (1998) Contemporary Strategy Analysis: Concepts, techniques, applications, Malden, MA: Blackwell Publishers, 3rd ed.

Gray, C et.al., (eds.), The Cyborg Handbook, pp. 233-254, Routledge, London..

Grundtvig, R (2003) "Verdens bedste brand-advokater undgår reklame", Mediaedgecia.dk. Read: October 25, 2003.

Hamilton, A (1997) "We Can Be Heroes" in: Mojo, 41, pp. 54-80, London.

Hardaker, G and G. Graham (2001) Wired Marketing: Energising Business for eCommerce. Wiley, New York, US.

Hardaker, G and Graham, G (2001). Wired Marketing: Energizing Business for e-Commerce, John Wiley & Sons, West Sussex.

Harvey, J (1975) The Music of Stockhausen, Los Angeles.

Haug, S. and Weber, K. (2002) "Kopierst du mir, kopier ich dir...Musik aus dem Internet: Ergebnisse einer Online-Umfrage", NMZ, February, p.7

Hayles, N. K (1996) "Boundary Disputes: Homeostasis, Reflexivity, and the Foundations of Cybernetics" in: Markley, R (ed.), Virtual Realites and Their Discontents, pp. 11-37, The John Hopkins University Press, Baltimore – London.

Hesmondalgh, D (1998) "The British Dance Music Industry: a Case Study of Independent Cultural Production. British Journal of Sociology, Vol 49 no 2, June, pp. 234 – 250.

Hodgkinson, T (1987) "Pierre Schaeffer Interview" in: Recommended Records Quarterly, vol. 2, no. 1, online text: http://www.civc.fr/association/shaeffer_interview.html.

http://www.aber.ac.uk/media/Modules/MC30820/launderette.html. Read: October 23, 2003.

http://www.allaboutgeorge.com/retro/000177.php. Read: October 24, 2003.

http://www.headstoneentertainment.com/company.html. Read: November 30, 2003.

http://www.turboads.com/richmedia_news/2000rmn/rmn20000822.shtml. Read: Nov. 21, 2003.

http://www.villagevoice.com/issues/0237/parker.php. Read: Nov. 29, 2003.

Hummel, J. and Lechner, U (2001) "The community model of content management. A case study of the music industry", JMM, 3(1) www.mediajournal.org, Read: November 6, 2002.

REFERENCES

Huyssen, A (1986) After the great Divide, Indiana University Press, Bloomington–Indianapolis, USA.

IFPI (2002) "Massenhaftes Musikkopieren und Musikpiraterie im Internet gefährden Musikmärkte", www.ifpi.de/news/. Read: November 5, 2002.

Institut Mediacult, (2000) "Musik und Globalisierung". Wien, Germany.

Jameson, F (1995) "Progress Versus Utopia: or, Can We Imagine the Future?" in: Wallis, Brian (ed.), Art After Modernism: Rethinking Representation, pp. 239-252. New York.

Jupiter Research Report (2002) "European Paid Content and Services Consumer Survey". London.

Just-style.com (2003) "David Bowie, Iman To Appear In Hilfiger Adverts". Read: October 28, 2003.

Kempster, C (1986) "The Artists: USA. Introduction" in: Kempster, Chris (ed.), History of House, pp. 11-20. Sanctuary Publishing Ltd., London.

Kempster, C (1996) History of House. Sanctury, New York, NY, USA.

Krauss, R (1985) "The Originality of the Avant-Garde" in: Wallis, Brian (ed.), Art After Modernism: Rethinking Representation, pp. 12-29. The Museum of Contemporary Art, New York.

Kretschmer, M, Klimis, M and R. Wallis (2001). "Music in electronic markets: an empirical study ". New Media & Society Vol 3 No 4, pp 417-441

Kretschmer, M, Klimis, G and R. Wallis (2001) "Music in Electronic Markets". New Media & Society, Vol 3(4), pp. 417 – 441.

Kretschmer, M. and Klimis, G.M. and Wallis, R. (2000) "The Global Music Industry in the Digital Environment: a Study of Strategies Intent and Policy Responses (1996-99)". February.

Kwok, J, Lang, R and Tam, K (2002) "Peer-to-peer Technology Business and Service Models: Risks and Opportunities". Electronic Markets 12 (3), pp. 1 – 9.

Larkin, C (1998) The Virgin Encyclopedia of Dance Music. Virgin, London.

Lechner, W (2002) http://dimsa.informatik.uni-remen.de/vorlesungen/einf_wiinf_ws0203/v/wi1_medienindustrie_bis27.pdf. Read: November 6, 2002.

LeComte, P. and Sherman S. and Vialle B (2000) The Revolution Will Not Be Downloaded. The Dawn of Music Hyper-Availability. Kellog Tech Venture Anthology, pp. 521-548.

Leland, J (2001) "For Rock Bands, Selling Out Isn't What It Used To Be", The New York Times, http://www.elephant6.com/press/NYtimes.html. Read: March 11, 2003.

Lett, R (2000) "The Music Industry: Globalised and Spinning". Music Forum 7/1 October.

Lévi-Strauss, C (1969) The Raw and The Cooked, Harper and Row, New York, USA.

Lewis, D (2003) The Soul of The New Consumer, Nicholas Brealey Publishing, London.

Lewis, M (2000) Technospace. Unpublished MSc dissertation, Copenhagen Business School, Copenhagen, Denmark.

Lewis, M (2001) "Clubbing for folket", Berlingske Tidende, Metro, August 24, pp. 14–17.

MacQuarrie, R., Gu, Y., Guerra, E., Corredor, N and Hill, W (2000). "Music CD Industry", http://www.soc.duke.edu/~s142tm1/main.html. Read: December 15, 2002.

Mauss, M 1969 (1933) The Gift. Routledge: London.

May, B. and Singer, M. (2001) "Unchained Melody". McKinsey Quarterly, Issue 1, pp. 128-138.

REFERENCES

McBurney, D. H. (1994). Research Methods, Brooks/ Cole Publishing Company, Pacific Grove, USA.

McCarthy, M (2003) "Stars come out for trendy Gap ads", http://www.usatoday.com/money/advertising/2001-11-12-ad-gap.htm. Read: October 26, 2003.

McLuhan, M (1966) "The Emperor's old Clothes", in Gyorgy K (ed.), The Man-Made Object, Studio Vista, New York, USA.

Meisel, J.B. and Sullivan, T.S (2002) "The Impact of the Internet on the Law and Economics of the Music Industry". Info 4(2) pp. 16-22.

Millard, A.. (2001) America on the Road; a History of Recorded Music, Bloomsbury, New York, US.

Milmo, C (2003) "Analysis of Pop Music Report". The Independent Thursday 20 February, p. 15.

Minogue, S (2002) "Selling the Sizzle", http://www.exclaim.ca/index.asp?layid=22&csid1=1058. Read: October. 26, 2003.

Morrison, M (2003) "Super models' no longer super sellers", http://www.bandt.com.au/articles/d2/0c00abd2.asp Read: October 25, 2003.

Mort, F (1988) "Boy's Own? Masculinity, Style and Popular Culture", in R. Chapman & J. Rutherford (eds), Male Order: Unwrapping Masculinity, pp. 193-224. Lawrence & Wishart, London.

Mort, F (1996) "Cultures of Consumption: Masculinities and Social Space in Late Twentieth-Century Britain", Routledge, pp. 108-112, quoted in http://www.aber.ac.uk/media/Modules/MC30820/launderette.html. Read: October 26, 2003.

Mougayar, W (1997). Opening Digital Markets: Battle Plans and Business Strategies for Internet Commerce, McGraw-Hill Companiesm, New York, USA.

Myers, G (2002) "Ad Worlds: Brands, Media, Audiences", Arnold,, pp. 23-28, quoted in http://www.aber.ac.uk/media/Modules/MC30820/launderette.html. Read: 26 October, 2003.

Nurmela, J. and Parjo, L. (2002) "Verkkokaupan käyttäjien määrä kasvaa tasaisesti". Tietoaika. Vol 8, pp. 10–13. Statistics Finland, Helsink, Finland.

O'Shaughernessy, C (1992) "You've got the music in you now's the time to get it out," in: 'Spring Student Special', The Independent, London.

OD2 (2004). www.Od2.com. Read: January 7, 2004.

Parikh, M (1999). "The Music Industry in the Digital World: Waves of Changes". Institute for Technology & Enterprise, August.

Parikh, M. (1999) "The music industry in the digital world: waves of changes" http://ite.poly.edu/htmls/musicwave.pdf. Read: March 25, 2003.

Parikh, M. (1999) "The music industry in the digital world: waves of changes" www.document: http://www.ite.poly.edu/htmls/musicwave01.htm. Read: 21st of May, 2002.

Parker, E (2002) "Hip-Hop Goes Commercial", September 11 - 17, quoted in http://www.productplacementawards.com/history.html. Read: November 29, 2003.

Peyser, J (1971) The New Music: The Sense Behind The Sound, Delacorte Press, New York.

Platt, C (1995) "Superhumanism" in: Wired 3.10, October 1995, pp. 144-149, San Francisco, USA.

Poel, M. and Rutten, P (2000). "Impact and Perspectives of Electronic Commerce: The Music Industry in the Netherlands". http://www.oecd.org/pdf/M00027000/M00027095.pdf. Read: March 09, 2003.

Porter, M (2001). "Strategy and the Internet". Harvard Business Review. March, pp. 63 – 78.

Porter, M.E. (1998) Competitive Advantage, The Free Press, NY, USA.

Poschardt, U (1998) DJ Culture, Quartet Books, London 1998.

REFERENCES

Prendegast, M (2000) The Ambient Century: From Mahler to Trance – the Evolution of Sound in the Electronic Age. Bloomsbury, London.

Rayport, F. J and Sviokla, J. J (1995). "Exploiting the Virtual Value Chain". Harvard Business Review, November – December, pp. 75 – 85.

Reece, D (2004) "An industry poleaxed by power of the Net". The Independent, Wednesday 31st of March, p. 40.

RelaxOnline (2002) www.relaxonline.com/indieguide/iras.html. Read: January 10, 2003.

RIAA (2001) www.riaa.com. Read December 5, 2002.

Rietveld H (1998) This is Our House. House!. Ashgate, London.

Rietveld, H (1995) "House Music: the Politics of a Musical Aesthetic". Unpublished PhD thesis, Manchester Metropolitan University, Manchester.

Rietveld, H (1998) This is Our House. House Music, Cultural Spaces and Technologies. Ashgate, Aldershot, Hants.

Robinson, M (2000) "100 Greatest TV Ads", Harper Collins, pp. 119-121, quoted in http://www.aber.ac.uk/media/Modules/MC30820/launderette.html.

Russcol, H (1972) The Liberation of Sound, Prentice-Hall, Englewood Cliffs, N.J, USA..

Savage, J (1996) "Machine Soul: a History of Techno", in Time Travel, Chatto and Windus, London.

Schaeffer, P (1967) La Musique Concrète, Presses Universitaires de France, Paris.

Schlect, C (2003) Celebrities' Impact on Branding, Columbia Business School, New York, USA.

Scott, T (2002) "Music Highlights Mitsubishi TV Ads", quoted in http://pub114.ezboard.com/fthecableboxfrm32.showMessage?topicID=21.topic, June 9, Read: October 26, 2003.

Scott, T (2003) "Music Highlights Mitsubishi TV ads", June 9, quoted in http://pub114.ezboard.com/fthecableboxfrm32.showMessage?topicID=21.topic. Read: October 26, 2003.

Shapiro, P (2000) Modulations: A History of Electronic Music Throbbing Words on Sound. Caipirinha, New York, US.

Simmons, R (2002) "MusicEquity: The Power of Music in Branding", quoted in http://www.buildingbrands.com/interactive/ga_013.pdf, p. 3, SongSeekers. Read: October 27, 2003.

Singh, A (2001). "Cutting through the Digital Fog". http://www.bain.com/bainweb/about/insight/ pract_insights.asp. Read: April 10, 2003

Sinker, M (1996) "Electro Kinetik" in: Kempster, C (ed.), History of House, pp. 93-102, Sanctuary Publishing, London.

Smaizys, S (1975) "Kraftwerk Interview" in: Triad Magazine, June 1975, online text: http://pages.ripco.com:8080/~saxmania/kraft.html.

Smith, E (2002) "Organization Moby", Wired Magazine, issue 10.05, May, quoted in http://www.wired.com/wired/archive/10.05/moby_pr.html. Read: October 26, 2003.

Smudo (2000) "Smudo: Musiker sollten mit Musik auch Geld verdienen können, on: Heise Online", www.heise.de/newsticker/data/chr-29.11.00-002.. Read: October 4, 2002.

Sribar, V and Burris, P and Zachmann W (2002). "Online Music Post Napster", http://news.com.com/2009-1023-255148.html?legacy=cnet. Read: May 15, 2003

Stein, J (2003) "Inside Chrysler's Celine Dion Advertisings Disaster: Selling the Celebrity Instead of the Product", http://www.adage.com/news.cms?newsId=39262, November 24, Read: November 29, 2003.

REFERENCES

Strickland, E (1993) Minimalism: Origins, Indiana University Press, Bloomington – Indianapolis, USA..

Struthers, S (1987) Technology in the art of recording in A White (ed) Lost in Music Culture, Style and Musical Event, pp. 241-258, Routledge, London.

Thau, C (1993) "Menneske-automaten" in: Kritik nr. 105, pp. 46-59, Nordisk Forlag, København.

Thornton, S (1995) Club Cultures. Polity Press, Cambridge.

Thornton, S (1995) Club Cultures: Music, Media and Subcultural Capital, Polity Press, London.

Tomas, D (1995) "Feedback and Cybernetics: Reimaging the Body in the Age of Cybernetics" in: Featherstone, M & Burrows, R (eds.), Cyberspace / Cyberbodies / Cyberpunk, pp. 21-43, SAGE Publications Ltd., London.

Toop, D (1992) "The robbery with intent". The Wire, No 98, April, London.

Toop, D (1995) Ocean of Sound: Aether Talk, Ambient Sound and Imaginary Worlds, Serpent's Tail, London.

Toop, D (1999) Tommy Boy's Greatest Beats, CD booklet, Tommy Boy Music Ltd., New York, USA.

Trask, S (1988) Future shock in C Kempster (ed) History of House, pp. 41-40, Sanctury Books, London.

Trask, S (1996) "Future Shock" in: Kempster, C (ed.), History of House, pp. 41-48, Sanctuary Publishing, London.

Wiener, N (1954) The Human use of Human Beings: Cybernetics and Society, second edition revised, Doubleday & Company, Inc., Garden City, New York, USA.

Webactive (2004) "Let's Face the Music. Special feature on music downloads". Webactive, December/ January. pp.16 – 21.

Zerdick, A (200) European Communication Council Report. E-conomics: Strategies for the Digital Marketplace. Springer, Berlin, Germany.

REFERENCES

Printed in the United Kingdom
by Lightning Source UK Ltd.
101976UKS00001B/106-168